Isobelle's Journey

*For Pat
with best wishes

Elsa Joubert*

March 2003.

For my grandchildren

Isobelle's Journey

ELSA JOUBERT

Translated by
CATHERINE KNOX

JONATHAN BALL PUBLISHERS
JOHANNESBURG & CAPE TOWN

TAFELBERG
CAPE TOWN

All rights reserved.
No part of this publication may be reproduced or transmitted,
in any form or by any means, without prior permission from the
publisher or copyright holder.

© Afrikaans original version – Elsa Steytler 1995
© English translation – Elsa Steytler 2002

Originally published in Afrikaans in hard cover under the title
Die reise van Isobelle by Tafelberg-Uitgewers Bpk in 1995.

This edition published in English in paperback under the title
Isobelle's Journey in 2002 by

JONATHAN BALL PUBLISHERS (PTY) LTD
P O Box 33977
Jeppestown
2043

in conjunction with

TAFELBERG-UITGEWERS BPK
28 Wale Street
Cape Town
8001

ISBN 1 86842 133 3

Front cover photograph from *The Face of the Country* by Karel Schoeman,
published by Human & Rousseau, Cape Town
Design by Michael Barnett, Johannesburg
Typesetting and reproduction of cover by
TripleM Design & Advertising, Johannesburg
Typesetting and reproduction of text by Alinea Studio, Cape Town
Printed and bound by CTP Book Printers, Caxton Street, Parow, Cape

Contents

PART ONE
In the Beginning
1

PART TWO
Agnes
113

PART THREE
Belle
251

PART FOUR
Leo
445

Hennie
(brother)
Josias van Velde
x
Emma Anderson
Issy
(sister)
Stuart
x
Agnes
Greylinck
Frikkie
x
Kowie
Victoria
Leonora
Philip
x
Maude
Hendrik
x
Rina
Robert
x
Estie
Ozzie
Belle
x
Holtzhausen
Arnold
x
Lulu
Miemie
x
Stoffel
Barry
2 daughters
3 daughters
Benjamin
2 sons
Leo
Fred
Koba
Josias
Phil
Emma

Valeria Greylinck
Piet
x
Naomi
Daniel
x
Irma
Jannie
x
Lettie
Agnes Valeria
Piet
Jan
Daniel

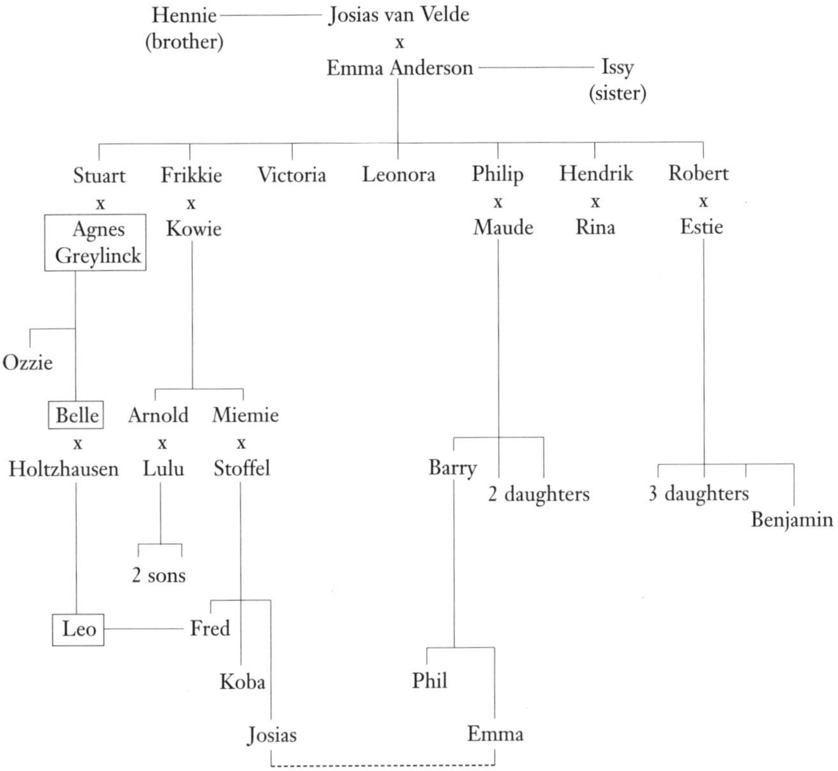

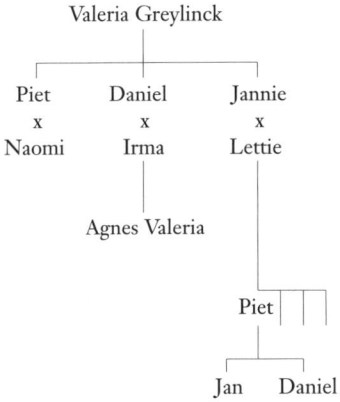

PART ONE
In the Beginning

1

Later, Issy was to say to Grandma, 'Emma was too young to be allowed away for the weekend on her own. And too impressionable.'

Miss Golightly, a stocky, permanently anxious woman with a generous bosom, slim ankles and nervous movements, was to be her chaperone for the half-day train journey from Worcester to Stellenbosch.

Much to the chagrin of the young Emma Anderson.

They parted ways on the platform at Stellenbosch station: Emma to go to her Cousin Charles and his daughters at the pastorie; Miss Golightly bound for less-elevated company. After Sunday dinner, Cousin Charles carefully dabbed his splendid silver-grey moustache before rolling up his table-napkin and slipping it into the silver ring. An oil painting of his father hung on the wall opposite him. The painting was a source of daily inspiration for Cousin Charles.

Just as the presence at the table of his wife, his sons and daughters and, today, his pretty little second cousin as well, was a source of gratitude. The Lord was good to him.

'I have a small task for you,' he told the girls. 'In honour of our Heavenly Father on His holy day.'

Before saying grace, he pushed his napkin in its ring an arm's-length away, paused to get their full attention, then added, 'This afternoon at half past two a student candidate for the ministry is to deliver his trial sermon. My colleagues and I will be present – in the back pews. It is difficult to give of your best in an empty church. The presence of the pastorie family will be a heartening sight to the young man.'

And that is how Emma Anderson came to be sitting in the second row that quiet, stiflingly hot Sunday afternoon, her head thrown back, her gaze fixed devoutly on the pulpit. Wilful beads of perspiration collected on her upper lip and she dabbed at them as unobtrusively as possible, trying to move her hand imperceptibly, keeping her head still and her gaze upward as she tucked her handkerchief back into the small black silk reticule that lay on the pew beside her.

And when the young Josias van Velde mounted the pulpit to send his words heavenwards, his eyes closed and his face pale with devotion and patent nervousness, she felt powerfully drawn to him: there rose in her an urge to protect the young candidate, a feeling of commitment such as she had never experienced in her life before.

The dimness of mid-afternoon in the church and the motes of dust dancing on a ray of sunshine that had thrust in through a window were, for her, suddenly inseparably associated with this new feeling. Could it be related to that unmentionable word: love?

She had read about it in her books – in Tennyson, in Lord Byron's poems. She had fantasised about it in her daydreams, and now, here, it took possession of her. She stopped breathing; her heart seemed to have stopped beating. Until her body could no longer bear the strain. Then her breath forced its way out in three small gasps; her chest gave three little heaves. As though in three little sighs it acknowledged the inevitability of a new existence. She was amazed at how emotion invaded her body.

Her cousin cast a concerned look her way, but she was oblivious to it.

The candidate had noticed her too. In the second row from the front, along with his promoter's haughty daughters. The dark curls had come loose from under her straw hat, as though they wanted to be free of the restraining limits of chignon or hat. The sweet face that she turned up to him wore a worried expression, pulling her eyebrows together in a slight frown, as though, in her concern for him, she lived through every word that he spoke. Across the chasm between the pulpit and the second row from the front, he saw her in a halo of radiance and he felt himself bonded for ever in a voluntary, unbelievably joyous enslavement.

He was invited back to the dominee's house after the sermon.

Standing beside Emma, he held her cake plate while she sipped the weak black tea with its sliver of lemon. The fine line of her nose, the luxuriant mass of brown hair – released now that the hatpin had been removed and the hat set aside – but specially the large dark eyes that looked up at him as intently and as filled with concern as they had in the church, the slightly bowed upper lip – they all melted his heart.

The mundanity of eating and drinking was unthinkable.

'No tea for me, thank you. I am not thirsty.'

He claimed her as his own that afternoon. They were married a year later, in November 1894. Emma was nineteen and Josias in his late twenties.

'Nothing good will come of it,' predicted Issy, ten years older than her sister and already set in the stubbornly opinionated ways of a spinster.

Miss Golightly made the wedding dress. Cousin Charles married them in Worcester. Emma's mother, a pastorie widow herself, was only reconciled to the marriage when Josias was called to Worcester, her late husband's parish. Perhaps Cousin Charles used his influence; perhaps he was relieved, what with the growing demands of his own family, that the privilege/duty/burden of temporarily caring for the widowed cousin and her daughters could be transferred to the willing shoulders of Josias van Velde.

Heavens! So young! Cousin Charles felt his years. How much time was left to him? His estimable progenitor in the wooden frame on the dining room sideboard had been scarcely 60 when he died. As Cousin Charles joined the young couple's hands before the altar, their youth was suddenly unbearable to him. He felt mortality approaching like the stroke of a dark wing.

What Issy could not reconcile herself to was the fact that Josias's family were business people.

'In trade.'

'Fresh blood, Issy,' Cousin Charles consoled her. 'And he is a pious young man.'

He knew that the congregation was relieved that the minister's widow and her daughter were to move in with the young pastorie couple, thus relieving them of the burden/duty/privilege of paying the rental for their small house, and with that, of the guilty sense that the monthly allowance to their beloved late minister's family was so meagre. It was actually a blessing that the pulpit had fallen vacant.

'God's mercy is too wonderful for us to comprehend. Be at peace, little Issy.'

'Little' was a patent inversion of reality because Issy was tall and bony, her hair scraped back and twisted into a bun. Her features might have been attractive had her eyes not glared out onto the world with perpetual mistrust and displeasure.

'What makes your Aunt Issy such a sour old lemon?' a friend of Leonora, one of Emma's daughters, was to ask her at one stage.

And she and Leonora, their heads full of the poetry they were so fond of reading, diagnosed a romantic disappointment. But the idea of Aunt Issy with an admirer set them to such uncontrollable giggling, they ended up rolling on the pastorie lawn.

Unaware that Aunt Issy was at the sitting room window, watching them from behind the lace curtains, asking herself: Where did my youth vanish to? And, feeling the panic rise in her: Is it all over?

Cousin Charles's 'little' was really more applicable to the mother who had been called 'Grandma' since the birth of Emma's first child, a son, a year or so after the marriage. Even her old parishioners began to notice: she was getting smaller. As old people have a way of doing. But the head was still held as high on her narrowing shoulders. Her hair was scraped back like her older daughter's, and now and then, when she wanted to emphasise a point, she'd smooth a strand back. Her quick footsteps still struck determined echoes from the long wooden floors of the pastorie passages. And her voice remained just as emphatic.

Her opinions too.

To preserve the peace, Josias agreed to have his firstborn baptised Stuart, after the baby's grandfather on his mother's side. Josias respected the Anderson line. Godfearing people, which was more than he could honestly say of his own ancestors. His father had been a good solid citizen, but always that derogatory label: 'in trade'. Agent and auctioneer in nearby Wellington. With interests in wagon-making, an industry that declined frighteningly as the century drew to a close.

Scarcely a year after Stuart's birth, Emma suffered a miscarriage.

Grandma and Issy cast reproachful glances at Josias, something they were to do frequently in the years to come – a pained expression round mouth and eyes.

That heart-stopping moment of indrawn breath when she first caught sight of Josias in the pulpit had boded well for an untroubled and fulfilling physical union in their marriage, but the promise did not come to fruition. In their large double bed, when Josias lay with his head on her breast, completely given over to her, she closed her eyes and tried with all her might to summon up the golden dust motes that danced in the ray of sunshine slanting in through the church window. While she could lie still, stroking his head, even smoothing his eyebrows with a loving touch, it was good, and even the weight of his head on her breasts was pleasurable and released surprising new awareness in her body. But when he grew more fiery, when that strange expression – was it lust? – came over his face, then the dancing golden motes slipped from her mind. Then she heard again her mother's words spoken during their 'little talk' the night before her wedding.

'It will be hard, my dear. Submit with dignity.'

Tenderness for Josias she never lacked – right to the end. But no one had warned her of the dire consequences to her body of 'submitting with dignity', time after time – pregnancy after pregnancy. And the irrevocable process of pregnancy – the nausea, the dizziness, the weakness as strength drained from her in perspiration – made her wander through the house with hair all awry, her body swollen to an unsightly mountain by an alien invader who kicked and writhed inside her.

At birth, the first baby was handed over to Issy for care.

She recovered from the miscarriage remarkably easily. It was not long before her dear Josias could nestle against her again and, while the dust motes danced on their sunbeam, summoned with a fiery concentration, she 'submitted with dignity', at times even eagerness. An eagerness that took her by surprise.

Early in her third pregnancy, four years into her marriage, they were visited by Hennie, Josias's younger and only brother. He brought his betrothed with him: Jessie, daughter of a Wellington wine farmer. She was chaperoned by her tante.

These young Bolanders of the nineteenth century come back to us insistently through the haze of old family photographs, from old letters and relics and family stories that have been passed down. Protected young Bolanders. The young women with narrow corseted waists, high-necked gowns and the ubiquitous chaperones, the men with high-buttoned waistcoats and fly-away collars, stare at us earnestly from the photographs.

The demure apparel, the strict formality and the code of manners that governed their daily lives can be taken as proof of how precious they were to their earthly parents. They obviously felt precious. And that sweet feeling of being precious was easy to extend to one's relationship with the Father in Heaven. Who had actually shed His blood on their precious behalf. Born and brought up during the last half of the last decade of the nineteenth century, the time of the Boland's great religious revival, these young people burned pure as flames for the Lord.

In a letter from Emma to Josias shortly before their marriage:

My dearest one, our Lord has made our hearts beat as one. May our lives be spent in His service.

And the lost sheep that strayed from the heavenly fold? There were surely some of those too. A father who drank, an adulterous mother, an uncontrollable urge to tread the 'primrose path', or unmarried motherhood? A veil of silence was drawn over these, as if by unspoken agreement in the community. And transgressors were simply cast out of community life. Euphemisms proliferated in this late-Victorian society. Bodily urges had to be sublimated. Men who could not control themselves and consorted with women in the lower town, even sometimes having children by brown women, were condemned behind closed doors and drawn curtains. It was something one never referred to. Yet everyone in this baking hot Boland town knew in which backyard the brown woman, with the redheaded or blonde child, dug in her heels and refused to leave until maintenance was paid. And the knowledge was stored deep in the communal memory.

The church? Disciplinary action? Confidential parish council meetings?

Sometimes. Sometimes a weeping woman confessing her sins after the service while children, sent outside beforehand, tried to listen at the keyhole. Only to be betrayed by sisters at the Sunday dinner table: *you did, you did* ...

With Emma being pregnant so often, Josias began to suspect his mother and sister-in-law had lumped him in with the men 'who could not control themselves'. Already 'the sublimation of the flesh in God's service' had been proposed to him obliquely. But, oh!, he did love her so much. When he saw the dark brown hair loosened and fanned out on the snow-white pillows, those dear, wide brown eyes, the white arms reaching up to him, the upper lip pouting slightly, the teeth so white and moist, he could not suppress with any will on earth, or even in heaven, the powerful surge of blood through his young veins.

Hennie, Jessie and the tante-chaperone stayed a weekend longer than planned in order to hear a sermon from a visiting cleric, a celebrated hero in Christ, the coming Sunday evening. They all sat together in the pastorie pew. First Grandma, then Issy, then Jessie's tante, then Emma with Jessie and Hennie beside her.

The oil lamps on the walls flickered every time a member of the congregation entered, and they burned unevenly, even erratically. People streamed into the church. The wind gusted strongly outside. The organ filled the space with deep sonorous notes pumped out with some difficulty by the organist. There was something wrong with the instrument.

Emma closed her eyes. When she looked again, two figures in black stood at the pulpit steps, one hand on the wooden rail, Bible clasped under the arm, head bent. How young and slight her Josias looked, two steps lower than the larger and much older figure of the visiting preacher. She felt the familiar protectiveness rise up in her.

He made the announcements and then introduced the preacher. He sounded agitated. Had the prayers in the vestry moved him so?

'Dear congregation, thanks to the mercy of the Lord, we have the honour and the privilege to have in our midst a remarkable servant of the faith: the reverend gentleman Dr Karl Kumm, missionary in God's service in the Sudan and Nigeria. Even though he works there amongst the benighted heathen, he has a message for our congregation.'

He moved to his seat and the older man took up his position behind the lectern. Minutes stretched out as the large figure stood motionless, his arms straight, elbows locked, fists gripping the polished rim of the lectern.

He said nothing. The congregation stopped fidgeting. Even the sporadic coughing died down. Still he said nothing. The oil lamps now burned more steadily, the church doors were locked, the wind whistled outside. Still grasping the lectern, he shifted slightly. The shadow of his body flowed grotesquely with the movement. He turned to the right-hand wing of the church and called in a loud voice: ''Allo!'

The congregation sat perplexed.

He turned back to the nave of the church. He waited. He called: ''Allo!'

Then he turned to the left wing. ''Allo!'

He waited a while. 'Can you hear me? Are my words reaching you?'

For the emotionally receptive congregation it seemed that the preacher's form defied the force of gravity, as though he came closer and then receded again. Even the lamplight seemed to be affected by the voice, and started to flicker in response.

I will find refuge in the shadow of the Almighty, mused Emma, starting to feel nauseous.

'The lamps hear me. Do you hear me?'

The white bib on his black toga, the generous thatch of white hair came closer and receded as he swayed forward out of the gloom of the pulpit only to sink back again. He raised his arms. The two polished jet buttons reflected rays like the light from a star. The sleeve flaps of the robe cast dark shadows that flowed against the walls. Slowly he turned again in all three directions in succession.

''Allo! 'Allo! 'Allo! Do you hear me?'

The congregation sat as though turned to stone. At last he spoke. The tension and attention did not diminish.

'It came to pass on the West Coast of Africa. Five souls adrift in a rowing boat. Enshrouded in mist that stretched from horizon to horizon. They had no idea where they were. Even when the mist lifted they had no idea where they found themselves. Five lost souls. Their suffering was great: they had no drinking water. Racked by thirst. They saw another rowing boat approach across the waters. The oars rose and fell soundlessly, as though driven by one hand. They could not see the oarsmen. They shouted: "'Allo! 'Allo! 'Allo! Can you hear us?"

'"We hear you," came the answer.

'"Then please help us. We are dying of thirst."

'"Fill your buckets from the water on which you float."

'"But the water is salty. We will die!"

'"You have entered the river mouth. The water is sweet. Fill your buckets and drink. You are surrounded by water."'

Quietly, without any gestures or emphasis, as though he was talking to himself, or was suddenly weary, the preacher repeated: 'With the death of our Saviour, we entered the river mouth. Fill your buckets and drink. The water is all around you.'

After the last hymn and the blessing, it was a subdued congregation that began shuffling out of the pews, waiting in turn to be taken up in the flow of people in the aisle.

Issy, Grandma and Jessie's tante were already on the way out. They didn't notice Emma sit down again, holding on to Jessie. She felt dizzy and nauseous. Miss Golightly noticed – the traffic in the aisle was thinning – and moved into the pew with her short steps. She was now working as a dressmaker somewhere, and her experienced hands knew just how to loosen a corset discreetly. She dabbed eau de cologne on a handkerchief and held it to Emma's nose. The three of them remained seated with heads bowed as though in prayer. Miss Golightly's form shielded Emma.

In the study later that evening, the quiet, earnest young Hennie told Josias: 'Doctor Kumm has inspired me. Jessie and I are at one on this. We are going to offer our services to the mission.'

Josias pressed his brother's shoulder. 'I would go with you, brother. But, as you can see, that is not possible.'

In their bedroom, a weeping Emma had told him she was expecting again.

'I already have my teacher's diploma,' said Hennie. 'Perhaps another year at the Missionary Institute. Then I would be, physically speaking, ready.'

Fill your bucket. There is water all around you.

I don't really understand, Emma complained. What water?

The love of God, Emma, the love that surrounds us.

Let the field I till be my congregation, thought Josias.

The second living child to whom Emma gave birth was a boy as well. Josias insisted he be named Frederik after his father. Which Grandma and Issy promptly shortened to Fred. But, supported by Emma, Josias stood firm and the boy was known as Frikkie, his grandfather's nickname. This stuck in Grandma and Issy's throats, but they had no choice but to accept it.

The two women in their black cotton or taffeta were a dominant presence in the house – Grandma with her velvet choker and, pinned to her jabot, the mourning brooch bearing a lock of her late husband's hair mounted in gold, Issy with a cameo on her stiffly pleated black collar. (A gift from whom? When?)

From their tones of voice and their instructions to the nursemaid it was clear that Stuart was the favourite. But Frikkie was an easy child who gave no trouble.

The arrangements for Hennie's and Jessie's departure for the mission field lagged. They'd been married a year and were still waiting. The threatened war in the north between the British Empire and the two Boer republics affected missionary activities as well as polarising group allegiances even in the remote Boland. Old leanings, pro-Boer or pro-Brit, came increasingly to the fore.

The war had already been waged for a couple of months when Hennie finally heard that arrangements for their departure were in place. They would travel to Beira in a Portuguese ship, then go up the Zambesi to Tete, traveling overland from there to Nyasaland. The journey could take months.

It was the end of December 1899.

They came to Worcester to bid farewell to Josias and Emma, staying over to see the century out with the pastorie family. The New Year's Eve service had been held in the afternoon so the district's farmers could be home before dark. The townsfolk as well. News reports told of Boer commandos scourging Natal, slaughtering unprepared Tommies in the Free State, and pushing as far south as Colesberg and the Stormberg. There was talk that military law was imminent.

The evening's celebration was subdued. While the women awaited the new century in the sitting room, Josias said to his brother: 'Come out on to the veranda. Let's get some fresh air. I've never had a sweet tooth.'

The women were taking tea, served with cakes and sweets. The cakes and dainties, passed round in their silver dishes, repelled him tonight. The confectioneries – fruit cake, heavy and dark with currants, preserved figs and nuts, topped with hard white icing; the pink and white meringues, the sponge cake, the butter sandwich cake – were excessive. The sitting room reeked of lavender. It was a family dominated by women: he'd realised that for some time. Even the decanter of dessert wine that stood ready on a side table – the wine a serene red jewel, his contribution – set his nerves on edge.

The camphor creeper had shot up since the spring rains, and long fronds hung from the trellis on the veranda. Even the plant smelled sickly. He took out his pocket knife and started cutting it back, tossing the fronds to one side. He was short of stature, so he could not reach all of them. He snapped his knife shut testily.

'I'll bring a stepladder tomorrow,' he said.

'How can you take out your ill temper on a plant?' asked Hennie. He sucked at his pipe peaceably. Too peaceable, thought Josias. Could he not feel the divisions in the house? In the country?

'Put that pipe away and have a cigar with me.'

Even the case from which, now and then, he thriftily took a cigar, was a gift from Cousin Charles, he thought ruefully. But it was appropriate tonight, New Year's Eve, new century's eve: this small indulgence – in spite of the donor being English. He took out two cigars but Hennie shook his head.

'Very well, then.' Josias tipped the cigar with his pocket knife, licked first the cut end and then the length of the cigar. He spat. The lucifer flared. He puffed quickly and repeatedly until the small spark began to smoulder. 'Ah, that's better. The Lord pardon my indulging in this weakness, but the cigar does help.'

Hennie sucked at his pipe, one foot up on the low veranda rail. The sitting room windows were directly behind them and, beyond the front door, the study windows. The casements were open, the shutters folded back. An oil lamp burned brightly in each opening.

'We must light in the new century,' Grandma had said, lighting the lamps herself. So that the community could see that the pastorie welcomed the new era decorously.

'Enough gloom around us. Let us shine a light where we can.'

Josias was silent awhile, eventually saying to his brother: 'I find no fault with her sentiment, but I cannot identify myself with the specific light that she favours.'

The oil lamps burned steadily. The flames only disturbed by a light breeze now and then. They seemed to tremble momentarily. Then burned on steadily. Wall lamps bathed the sitting room in a rosy glow, festive compared to the muted hues of the women's gowns. Taffeta folds caught the light when someone stood up to replace a cup or Emma's sleeve moved as she leaned forward to pour tea.

'Sit down, Emma. Everyone has had sufficient. If the men insist on remaining outside …' Issy took the teapot from her and swept icing sugar crumbs into a heap on a cake plate. 'Well, if they insist, they can go without their tea.'

The subject of Jessie and Hennie's journey and the disturbance caused by the war was resumed for the umpteenth time.

On the veranda, the men smoked in silence. It was a dark, moonless night and little noise came from the town. They watched the searchlight – brought to the station in anticipation of military law – with its regular beam that cut a swathe through the darkness. The streets were illuminated for a moment and then plunged into darkness again. Unconsciously, the two men allowed their conversation to be punctuated by the movement of the beam, falling silent and giving their attention to the light.

'The young men at Mrs Blair's boarding house are fond of taunting the soldiers. I hope they stay in tonight.'

'Ah, youth!'

'The town is divided. Probably your town too. Pro-Boer and pro-Brit. Grandma and Issy make no bones about their loyalties. Sometimes I fear the pastorie has come under suspicion from Boer folk.'

Holding out his cigar hand, he pressed the pulses of his wrists together.

'Handcuffed. That's how I feel.'

Grandma's shrill voice sounded sharply in the sitting room behind them. The conversation had moved from the war and its iniquities to the British forces and the old queen. Her voice rose to a pitch almost of hysteria, they noted.

'Listen,' Josias nodded to his brother.

'Like her Gracious Majesty, Queen Victoria, I am not interested in the possibility of defeat.'

'Colenso, Magersfontein, Stormberg. Those losses took her completely by surprise. I almost pity her. You wouldn't believe how many portraits of the wretched old woman she has on her bedroom walls.'

A small flame lit the glowing tip of his cigar as he drew on it.

'God forgive me, but I finally put my foot down. I refused to allow the portraits to invade the sitting room or even the dining room. It was not easy. She never lets me forget that, in her time, she was the lady of this household.'

Hennie just shook his head. 'Ma also favours the British. But Pa keeps her in check.' His tone was bitter too.

'Not that Pa is not making good money from the war. Horses, fodder, even donkeys. You can't imagine what our backyard looks like at home.'

'What is the war doing to us, brother? Even us, the people of God. I am ashamed. But people can't exist without loyalties. It must be a relief for you to be going.'

Hennie heard the longing in Josias's voice. 'This war must pass. Look beyond the present, Josias. This is a temporary disturbance in your house. Maintain the peace.'

But his brother shook his head. 'Our own people are dying at English hands.'

'We must not allow ourselves to grow bitter,' Hennie warned. 'We are answerable beyond eternity for every uncharitable thought.'

Josias pondered that for a moment. Hennie was the only person to whom he could speak frankly. 'I am constantly aware of the division. I ask myself if my feeling for my people must be in conflict with my Christian charity. Is it my duty to remain silent in my own home for the sake of peace?'

They strolled slowly up the veranda and stopped at the study window where the lamp had started to smoke. Josias adjusted the wick. When he straightened up again, he said: 'You know my nature. I like to … No, more than that: I have a need to commit myself heart and soul to a cause that I feel for. Heart and soul, yes: passionately.'

'You have the freedom to do that, in your work for God.'

'My mother-in-law irks me. Oh, brother, how she provokes me!'

The grandfather clock in the passage beyond the open front door started to chime away the quarter hours. Four times. Then the hour chimes began. They counted. Nine, ten, eleven, twelve. A shot was fired somewhere in the town. The sound came from the direction of the military barracks. And then, perhaps from the English church, a tentative peal of bells. It died away again. The dominee had not required the warden to come out and ring the bells. He embraced his brother.

'A blessed new year to you, brother. Happy new century. May God's blessing fall upon your work.'

'You must keep heart, brother. These things will pass. God bless you, too.'

They stood like that awhile, moved by the momentousness of the time. Then they went inside.

Emma's dark gaze was directed up at him questioningly. Fleetingly, there was a dissatisfied glint in her eyes, normally so soft. She had watched the veranda from the time the clock started chiming.

'What kept you so long? Grandma thought you might lead us in prayer.'

'Let me do so now.'

He glanced around, indicating that they should all bow their heads. He took both Emma's hands in his. Then he bowed his head too. 'Heavenly Father, grant us Thy blessing in this new year and in this new century. May the young couple about to depart for darkest Africa always be aware of Thy Presence. Grant Thy Peace to this divided land. May Thy Justice prevail. Grant us Thy Peace.'

'Happy new year, Josias,' whispered Emma. Raising her arms, she clasped her hands behind his neck, allowing her head to rest for a moment against his chest. 'Grandma wanted you to pray for the Queen, but it doesn't matter. It's all right. But you must wish her well, for my sake …'

His mother-in-law permitted him a peck on either cheek, saying meaningfully, 'May God guide you.'

Issy too, offered him her cheek.

Only Jessie embraced him properly – Jessie, that spontaneous young country girl with her blue eyes and the golden lights in her hair. Then she held his eyes steadily with her gaze, saying quietly, so no one else could hear: 'I helped to bathe your two sons tonight. Stuart insisted that Uncle Hennie should shoot a lion for each of them. It seems we all have our lions, don't we?'

What would the new year hold for these two young people? Where earlier he had fleetingly envied his brother, he now felt heavy with concern.

'We will not hear from you for a long time.'

'And neither will we from you. We won't even know how the war goes. It troubles me.' Her eyes were sad. He knew her parents were pro-Boer.

'Sometimes I doubt that I will be able to bear leaving all the people I love. Sometimes I am filled with fear, and I imagine that we will walk into the long grass and bush and that the grass and bush will close over us. And we will be completely lost.'

'Not lost, Jessie. Never lost.'

'No, I don't really think that. Not lost, but trapped.'

Then Emma called him to the serving table. The small long-stemmed glasses had been brought out of the cabinet. He took the decanter from her and poured the ruby-red syrup to within a half-finger width of the rim of the glasses. It was pretty: each glass a small red sparkle.

'Happy new year. Happy new century.'

Emma looked at him. The dissatisfaction was gone from her eyes, and he shared with her their special intimate smile. 'To you, my darling Emma.'

Yet he was glad to finish his wine and pick up his cigar and re-light it. He stood at the open door so the smoke would not trouble his mother-in-law. The bulge of the second cigar in his inner pocket was oddly comforting.

2

The celebration of New Year's Eve, 1899, was more sophisticated in the widow Valeria Greylinck's home in Sunnyside, Pretoria.

Scores of candles were lit in the chandelier over the long dinner table. The gentle glow was reflected as small rubies in the elegant wine glasses. The candlelight lent a tender gleam to the young women's wine-moist lips and to their dark eyes.

The widow Greylinck, mother of three sons in combat, had exceeded her self-imposed limit tonight. She raised the umpteenth glass to her lips.

'Oh, how we miss our young men – our sons, our betrothed, our husbands,' she sighed. Then she inclined her head graciously to the older men, seated between every third or fourth woman: men were a scarce commodity in wartime. These were the fathers of friends, members of the diplomatic missions still based in the city, an elderly doctor, a businessman.

'Our little party tonight would have been so dull without your presence.' Her pout was inappropriately coy at her age but it could still arouse sympathy. She enjoyed a special rapport with men, that had always been her pride. She raised her glass again, licking the rim with the tip of her tongue. 'Without our gallant gentlemen!'

The men bowed their heads slightly in acknowledgement, first to her at the head of the table and then a smaller gesture to the women on either side. We share the feeling, said the smiles, said the careful dabbings of wine moisture from moustaches. Mindful of their official and, hitherto, strictly observed neutrality in the war, the diplomats would refrain from joining in a toast to the combatants, or to the victories which had so elated the citizens of Pretoria in the past few months.

And, so as to avoid embarrassing her guests, the widow Greylinck did not propose these toasts. Instead, she stretched out her hands to include the guests on either side of the table, her plump arms gleaming in their black satin sleeves. Arms as extravagant as her dinner, arms that embraced everything, just as her warm heart did, included everyone (even her daughter-in-law, for the moment). Lavish in the certainty of glorious victory for the Transvaal Republic's dearly loved four-colour flag. Generous in the certainty of the gentlemen's heart-warming gallantry. In her prime, she'd been irresistible.

'Here's to our loved ones – and everyone can drink to this – who could not be with us tonight …'

She raised her glass high, and slightly awry, the red liquid threatening to splash over the rim. One little sigh and then she continued robustly: 'And may the Lord keep them and heap blessings on the task that has fallen to them.'

The glasses clinked. Even Irma, the daughter-in-law, clinked and drank wholeheartedly. Apart from the diplomats, she was the only one who knew that it was wishful thinking, futile hope that underwrote this celebration. Through her connection (in the fullest possible sense) with one of the younger members of the French Diplomatic Mission, she knew that 'the glorious victory of the past months, the seizing of armoured trains, the blowing up of bridges, the threatening of towns' to which her mother-in-law had referred earlier in the evening, and which had been generally adopted as proof and solace, was just a temporary show of strength.

Likewise, many gentlemen of the corps at the widow Greylinck's table tonight, were deeply troubled in their hearts about what the future held for the two brave little republics. The Italian consul, the second-in-command of the Netherlands consulate, and the German consul were increasingly uneasy, even anxious. These people have no idea, they thought, that the British lion has yet scarcely stirred in its sleep. Once it awakes and flexes its muscles, they are all in for trouble, this vulnerable little capital, these big generous women, these impressionable young girls with dreams still dark as smoke in their eyes, this wretched country which they obviously value so highly.

Uncertainty also dogged them in their diplomatic missions. The Boers could not offer resistance for long. Would Pretoria be defended, evacuated or laid waste?

'Let us drink to the friendship between our nations.'

The gentlemen from the Netherlands, Italy and Germany raised their glasses.

There was genuine emotion in their voices, which ranged from gloomy and old to bass and tenor as they repeated, each one in his turn: 'To the friendship between our nations.'

The hostess gave the cue: the meal was over. Chairs were pushed back, and the company adjourned to the reception room where one of the ladies was to lead a quartet in song. She was sorting her sheets of music in preparation. Irma, the daughter-in-law, touched her mother-in-law's arm and gestured with thumb and middle finger to her temples. Headache, she indicated. She would like to go and rest.

Later, thought the widow Greylinck, I'll give this problem some attention. Later.

She received no co-operation from Irma. As had happened before, the younger woman's bedroom door would be firmly closed, if she wanted to go in there after the guests had left. Hitherto, she had refrained from turning the knob, to test whether the door was locked or not. But one of these fine days … The thoughts churned in her white-powdered, slightly perspiring forehead under the smooth dark coiffure, as she exchanged a word with one of her guests, shared a smile with another as she led them into the parlour. One of these fine days, she would open the door and demand that her daughter-in-law account for herself.

She opened the piano with her own beringed fingers. Only to give way graciously to a gentleman who had hurried forward to assist her. She sat on an upright chair with padded arms and a brocade upholstered seat. The gold thread in the fabric had started to tarnish here and there. The black silk gown fell gracefully around her still-slim ankles. Silently, the right foot began to keep time to the rhythm of the introductory passage that was being played, and this regular movement set a languid feeling of relaxation flowing through her body. It could also, perhaps, have been the wine.

She closed her eyes, and her head and plump jaw moved in time to her foot. But she did not doze off. She took full and intense pleasure in the women's trilling voices that wove in and out of one another like a flight of light-headed swallows.

After the ladies, a soloist performed. Then, by request, the Italian gentleman who had an attractive tenor voice. The rich, tender tremolo and the hand even more tenderly pressed to the heart moved the ladies. While some unobtrusively dabbed a tear with a lace-edged handkerchief, the widow Greylinck suddenly raised her head. She looked round the room. Irma, to whom she had given her beloved son Daniel, whom she had welcomed into her home as a daughter when her own mother died and she had no relatives in the country and the mother's boarding-house, which she had helped to run, fell under the hammer … Irma had not yet returned.

The clock in the passage started to chime. First the light tone of the four quarters, then a tiny silence. Then the deep hard strokes started to count off the hours.

The guests fell silent at the first chime, the music forgotten. Those who were there together sought each other's hands. Some of the guests counted silently, their lips moving. After all the jollity, all at once the portentousness of the year, of the century that was being chimed in seemed unbearable.

Eight … nine … ten … eleven … twelve.

A young girl who had been allowed up late in adult company for the first time, started to weep. Her mother comforted her. The girl's father and brothers were all in the veld. Her mother wept too.

'To a speedy reunion with our loved ones,' said the Netherlands consul, diplomatic discretion forgotten.

'To a speedy reunion,' repeated the others, and it seemed to provide some comfort.

The widow Greylinck was overcome. She wanted to press Irma to her heart. When all was taken into account, they shared the same torment and they had only each other for support. But she was not here. Alone in her room, the moment would be even bleaker for her. She looked around her. It was not possible to leave her guests or she would have hurried to Irma.

Just as well, for Irma was not alone. Nor was she in her bedroom. In the garden of the Greylinck residence, veiled by the shadow of the grapevine, she stood clasped to the chest of the young French vice-consul. She stroked his cheeks, his eyes, his forehead. She stroked his lips until they pushed her fingers aside and greedily sought her mouth as a more satisfying conversation partner. And finally devoured the still more precious nourishment of her body, recklessly offered and taken with an equally reckless appetite.

It must be acknowledged that this scene may be imaginary. What is a fact, because it was recorded, is that, in the first half of 1901, when the war was at its most critical, the concentration camps at their cruellest, and Pretoria had been under British occupation for nearly a year, the French vice-consul acquired a travel permit from the authorities for a woman and her four-week-old baby, and that the woman, who was 'of Dutch/Boer extraction', travelled with her baby to the Cape Colony.

Also that, because it was similarly recorded, the retreating Boer commandos, more or less ten months earlier, in May 1900, fell back exhausted and despondent to Pretoria for a day or so of respite with their loved ones, then, refreshed by the comforting arms of their wives, went back to the fray – some to die, some to finally put their hands up, Mausers thrown down, giving themselves up, others to fight on to the bitter end.

For Irma, the woman who had completely abandoned herself to the vice-consul, the sudden return of her husband Daniel with the Boer commandos, fleeing the advancing British forces, was not only unexpected but also highly perturbing.

She was in the kitchen helping her mother-in-law prepare meat – with the kind of diligence and focus with which women often seek to conceal a clandestine escapade – when the word came: the Boer commandos were limping back to Pretoria. They'd been shot to ribbons; they were retreating; the English troops were advancing.

The widow Greylinck wiped her plump efficient hands with the nearest cloth and rolled down her sleeves, carefully fastening the jet buttons on her cuffs.

'Thank goodness we baked yesterday.'

She couldn't understand her daughter-in-law's lack of enthusiasm. Was it shock? She took her shoulder: 'My dear, do you realise what you've heard? Our soldiers are coming home. May the Lord grant that my sons are still alive. Don't you understand? Your husband is on his way home.'

Reports exist from the eye-witnesses who crowded four and five deep along the streets of Pretoria to welcome the procession of tired horses, the dead-tired, dishevelled riders. Who noted a strong contrast with the marching vanguard of the British troops a few days later, and said: Witnessing this contrast, despair overwhelmed us for the first time.

Yet there were also stories about young girls taunting the Tommies where they lay relaxing on Church Square beside their firearms and rucksacks. The girls said: The war isn't over yet. The war has only just begun.

The daughter-in-law didn't get much chance to contemplate the military implications of this unexpected return. Compelled by necessity, she had to give her attention to another more personal problem – while her hands, even more swiftly than her mother-in-law's, made up beds, took clothes from wardrobes and sent them down to the back garden to be hung up and aired, opened rooms and had them swept and dusted, carried fresh water for the wash-stand ewers.

'I'm in an absolute state,' said her mother-in-law, a hand to her forehead as she suddenly sank down onto a chair, sipping from the glass of water that Irma brought her. Then she straightened up again. 'We must leave off getting the house ready and think about food. We must mince meat and fill sausages.' Her face crumpled as though she were about to weep. 'We could have had so much biltong ready if we'd only known.'

'We can bake rusks and let them dry out tonight,' said Irma, hitting on a solution to her own problem. I'll work right through the night, you can sleep, Mother. I won't wink an eye, she thought as she made her plans: How could she get a message to the vice-consul to let him know that their meeting under the pergola that night, and goodness knows how many more nights after that, was out of the question?

The mother-in-law looked at her gratefully, but with some calculation too.

'I'll ask old Mieta to come in and keep an eye on the drying process.' As she gave the glass back to her daughter-in-law, the other hand stroked the young waistline, still so flat. 'My poor child,' she said, all the aggravation of the past months gone from her voice, 'the separation has not been easy for you.' Then she rose from her chair with renewed energy.

'Probably we should just leave everything and go out to look for news of them.' She unbuttoned her voluminous apron, folded it and put it away. 'We must get ready. You too, dear. Our soldiers will be strengthened by the sight of a well-turned-out woman. They must be able to believe they are fighting for something of value.'

But when the buggy was finally brought up to the front door and the two women were about to climb up for the journey to the centre of town, the older woman gripped the younger by the shoulder, holding her back.

'Listen.'

They heard the sound of horses' hooves coming slowly down the road. The horses weren't trippling or prancing as they had the morning, almost a year earlier, when they'd left. Even horses' hooves can speak of defeat.

'Listen.'

The older woman, till holding fast to the daughter-in-law's arm, shut her eyes and turned her head so that her face was almost against Irma. She was afraid of what she might see. Which of her sons?

But the younger woman's eyes were sharp and she was less emotionally involved. She pushed her mother-in-law away gently, her eyes fixed on the street.

'I can make out Piet,' she said. 'And Daniel a bit behind him. And there are others coming round the corner, Jan might be among them. Mother, don't be so frightened, have a look.'

She unclasped her mother-in-law's hand from her arm and indicated that the groom should take the buggy back and return the horses to the stable.

Then she picked up her skirts and dashed to the gate, pulling it open, and nearly staggered under the hooves of her husband Daniel's horse.

She barely recognised the large burly man with the red-brown face and the long, dusty rusty-brown beard as he slipped from his horse and flung his arms round her. She was pressed against his body, she smelt dust and sweat; she was embraced so tightly that the bandoleer hurt her, and she freed herself, but then his hand lifted her chin and he gazed at her as though he were measuring his memories against what he saw before him now. Were those tears that glistened in his eyes? He took her head in both his hands and pressed it against his chest. She almost suffocated in the smell of his body. The baths, she thought, we forgot to put the cans of water on the stove to warm. They'll want to … they must bath. Then he held her away from him, the better to see her. His eyes were still the same pale blue, almost childlike in the ruination of his face, the roughness that scars had left on his skin. The repeated sunburn and peeling had made the skin leathery and wrinkled. His red-brown hair had bleached, hanging unkempt in his neck and partially matted from filth. She only realised now that the embrace had caused him physical pain. He released her and cradled his left elbow in his right hand.

'I must greet Mother. And then we can go in.'

Piet had already reached his mother. How ridiculous to think we should pretty ourselves up for the men. Their vision reaches so much further, their perception is on a completely different plane to ours. For a moment something had attracted her to this strange man with his childish but wise eyes, in which tears welled up when he looked at her, as though in the power of his emotion he owned something that she would never reach, saw something that was concealed from her. For a moment she had a sense of the depth to which feeling could reach; feeling for another person, bigger, wider, more eternal than anything she had ever experienced. For a moment she stood on the threshold of breaking through to him, of understanding that faraway look in his eye, of loving him. But when he broke the contact, stopped embracing her, the moment passed.

She laughed nervously.

'It seems to me that you have all grown larger, or we have shrunk.' Now, in her turn, she wanted to touch him, but he was still protecting his left elbow with his right hand. She wanted to say: Just look how big Piet is, and your mother looks like a child in his arms, but instead of that her words were concerned: 'Oh, please don't say you have been wounded.'

'Luckily my left arm. And it's an old wound.' He held his left arm away a bit when his mother turned from Piet to press him close against her. He bent over to kiss her forehead. She raised her head to ask: 'And Jan?' When they didn't answer, she looked from brother to brother. Her youngest son. Her mouth puckered as though she was going to cry, but she restrained herself.

'But how could you have news? You didn't even leave at the same time. Come, let's go inside.'

'Don't go imagining the worst, Ma. Jan is a good fighter. He will have looked after himself.'

She didn't answer as she went into the house ahead of them. She busied herself with getting the table set and dishes brought through from the kitchen. Her daughter-in-law helped, Daniel's eyes following her every movement. If she passed close to him he touched her arm, her waist, her hair, her neck under the hair. She could not bring herself to return his caresses, even by so much a squeeze of the fingers. She mourned the feeling that had glimmered briefly, but she could not recall it.

The doctor who had been called to house after house since early morning, only got round to looking at Daniel's wound after dark. His mother brought buckets of water and stood by the doctor; she had buried her own husband and, in spite of her coquettish ways, she was a seasoned old trouper. She watched as the doctor removed layers of torn rag from the wound and dropped them on the floor, filthy, blood-stained, and here and there yellow with pus; she saw the dark blue swollen wound on his upper arm. It was only then that she allowed the tears to roll down her cheeks. Without wiping them away, she tore up a sheet for clean bandages and brought whatever else the doctor required. She didn't look away when the wound was reopened so the pus could run out, or when the disinfectant flowed into the wound and her child shrank from the pain. She thought about her youngest, Jan. Until Irma, who had kept herself busy in the kitchen for an unnecessarily long time, came in with more hot water and clean towels and said: 'Mother, why don't you sit down now? I will help.'

Daniel's eyes were shut, his lips pressed together.

'He is in a good deal of pain,' said the doctor. 'But it is clean now, and I will dress it again.'

Then the doctor had to leave. There were numbers of sick and wounded waiting for him. He left a sleeping powder to ensure the wounded man a good night's rest. But the patient preferred to find forgetfulness in the arms of his suddenly shy wife.

Irma was pregnant. The war dragged on. As those girls on the city square had predicted: the retreat to Pretoria was only the beginning. The Boers operated in small mobile groups, attacking military targets, stinging like horse flies, ripping like hyenas, exacting a toll in lives and property, but suffering losses themselves.

The mother-in-law sent letter after letter with the numerous Boer spies who came to the city for supplies, specially medicine and ammunition, sometimes weapons too, to take back to the fighters in the veld. Her son must know: his wife was expecting a child.

One of the letters did reach him. In the veld. He closed his eyes against the cries of death and suffering. He bowed his head under the broad starry sky and thanked God that amid death and destruction, new life could also be created. There were tears in his eyes. The stars made long rays and touched each other in the black cosmos, as though with fingers. He spent the rest of the night beside his comrades. He helped the wounded, bringing water to the thirsty, he prayed for the dying. There was a glowing ember in his heart, a sense of satisfaction and fulfilment that he had never experienced before. That night a strength shone out of him that reached his fellow combatants.

In later years he would not want to think back to that night.

He managed to borrow some writing paper and wrote to his wife, tenderly and concerned. Unfortunately she never received the letter. The messenger was shot through the temple as he tried to creep under the barbed wire with which the invaders had encircled Pretoria.

The letter was confiscated with his other documents. Once the reports had been read and the facts extracted, the personal letters were placed in a box where they lay until the end of the war, whereupon they were stored in a cellar with other papers where they probably still rest.

Irma could not keep her pregnancy a secret for long.

After hearing the sounds of retching three mornings in succession as she walked past Irma's room, her mother-in-law turned the door knob and walked in. Irma sat on the edge of her bed holding the slops bucket.

A few dribbles of saliva still hung from the corners of her mouth; her hair hung in rats' tails. She smiled weakly when she saw her mother-in-law, put the bucket down, and wiped her wet forehead with the back of her hand.

'So it's that time, is it, darling?' The endearment came as a surprise, it was the first time she had addressed her daughter-in-law in such a way. Irma nodded.

The widow Greylinck sat down beside her and place a stout arm round the shoulders that drooped so wearily from the strain of vomiting. She squeezed the shoulders so the young woman was pressed up against her. 'You should have told me. If you only knew what joy …'

But Irma had leaned over to grasp the bucket again. She gasped and the contraction jerked through her body. But nothing came out. The mother-in-law released her shoulders, smoothed the pillows and said with concern: 'Lie back a minute, there you are. I'll bring you something that will make you feel better.'

When her mother-in-law had made an appointment for her to see the doctor, Irma insisted so determinedly that she would go alone that the older woman had to concede to her wish. The doctor reported that she could expect the child in the second month of the new year, 1901. On the way home she told the gardener, who was also the groom for the buggy, 'Let me get down here in town. The doctor said I must have exercise. I'll find my own way home.'

The vice-consul was surprised to find her on the doorstep of his office. She held on to the door jamb and it seemed she was about to stumble.

Getting up from behind his desk, he hurried to help her to a seat. He brought her a glass of water.

'I am expecting a child,' she told him.

In spite of her obvious distress, she observed him closely. He realised that she was watching him. He threw up his well-manicured hands in a gesture of disbelief, then joyful amazement. The slight, carefully controlled movement of his fingers was the only indication of the whirlwind of emotions sweeping through him. He looked almost regretfully round the small office. He would have to leave.

'I will ask to be transferred,' he said then. 'You will come with me. Europe, or perhaps another continent.'

Not much time had passed between her words, his incredulous hand movement and his decision. She was relieved and grateful. She was genuinely in love with him.

But he was practical. 'Your mother-in-law?' he asked.

'She knows. She thinks it is her grandchild.' Now she looked down at her hands, which lay on her lap. She realised the implication of her words, but whether or how it struck him too, she preferred not to see. He would not be able to keep his feelings about this from her. Better not to see.

'But it is your child, I know that.'

He picked up a pencil and fidgeted with it. 'I wouldn't be able to get a transfer so soon. It can take months. You would no longer be able to travel.'

'I will stay here for the confinement. They will take good care of me.'

Am I formulating this too melodramatically? Emma's daughter Leonora asked herself, two decades later when the story of the war romance and confinement in Pretoria was told in the Worcester pastorie; when she listened, all ears; when, with the streak of contrariness which was to become so marked in her later, she capriciously sympathised with the adulterous Irma.

But how else can I imagine something that happened in a time before I existed? she thought. And the frightening thought struck her: How else can we imagine anything? Even things that have happened to ourselves. Can we ever plumb the hearts of those nearest to us? Here in the pastorie with me: Aunt Issy, Stuart, Father … We can only imagine. And believe in our imaginings.

And then, like a solution, the thought: we do believe what others suggest to our imagination. And what the magic lantern shows us. When we sit in the darkened school hall on a Friday evening and the beam of light hits the cloth and the shadowy figures begin to tremble, like reflections in water. And the little midget woman up front at the piano bends over the keys, pounding out the notes, and along with her music the figures on the cloth start to live. With a hand pressed to her bosom, the woman in the long old-fashioned dress pours out her love, plucks a rose from her bosom, throwing it at the feet of the man who no longer desires her.

A melodramatic silent film: Forbidden love. This is what Herr Winterbach used to draw the young people in, enraptured, when he visited the town in his brightly painted caravan with his two horses, Whisky and Champagne, and his midget wife Emily in her shiny black dress on the seat beside him. An unbelievably miraculous beam of light that told stories of love and hate and grief and happiness, so that one's own was forgotten for a little while. Reality could be replaced by this beam of light.

The heroine, eyes closed, rose on the ground, hand to her breast, utters the dreaded words: 'I am expecting your child!'

But that was the magic lantern. Nearly two decades later.

Perhaps we are missing the simplicity, thought Leonora. Perhaps it was murmured softly one night under the pergola, while she leaned against her lover. 'I am pregnant. Do you still want me to go away with you?'

And he answered: 'Yes. And I want the child too.'

And, with a twinge of guilt about the caring mother-in-law under whose wing she sheltered, she told her lover: 'If it is a girl, we will give her your mother's name, Agnes, and my mother-in-law's Valeria as her second name. That's lovely. If it is a boy, you can choose.'

An increasing sense that she received, but would give nothing in return, and that she would have to deceive her mother-in-law for many months, reduced her to tears at times. Also that she perhaps misled her lover, because in late-night honesty she had to acknowledge to herself: I myself do not know whose child it is.

Surely she was not really devoid of feeling?

She believed she genuinely loved her lover.

Yet a person could speculate that she deceived herself. Love or desire? Desire for the physical bewitchment in which Daniel, the ordinary fighting man, could not equal the French lover. Desire that gradually tarnished?

Would she lie waiting on a sofa in a Paris hotel room, day after day in the gloom midday hour, the child blessedly pushed out into the park with the servant girl he had hired, while she waited for his rapid tread on the stair?

Would she watch the stirrings of the muslin curtain? The French doors onto the small balcony had been thrown open. From the noises that rose up from the street she could tell how far the afternoon had advanced: the clip-clop of horses' hooves, the call of a hawker. But he would always come, she would hear his key in the door, and he would hurry across the room to take her tenderly in his arms where she sat with her embroidery or just sat waiting, trying to make it seem as though she was not waiting. But he would always prevaricate … not yet, the time was not yet right to go south to Bordeaux where his parents lived. And later, when she didn't fall pregnant again, he would wonder if little Agnes (his mother's name was an embarrassment, he preferred Valeria) was indeed his! If she was not, then his obligation would be so much lighter.

Three, four, five years went by. He was transferred to Canada. A wife and child would be a nuisance, a millstone round his neck. Understand, my darling, understand. She understood. He would pay the child's school fees in advance, until the payments became more and more irregular before ceasing altogether.

But the brave woman who had taken the train in war time to the Cape Colony with a limp baby in her arms, who braved the boat trip stoically, would not take it lying down. To while away the long mornings, she began helping at the reception desk of a small Paris hotel. And when the owner's wife died, she closed her eyes and kept vigil by her. It was she who comforted the bereaved man, called the son, controlled the comings and goings at the hotel. She had some deep reserve of knowledge of the business from her mother's boarding house in Pretoria, and the fact that she was fluent in English made the small hotel sought out by 'les Anglais'.

And one evening – little Valeria was at boarding school – she would comfort the old owner in his room. Her intention merely to bring him his customary 'tisane de camomille' before bed time: a deed of love and care for the distressed, bereft, lonely man. A small ritual that confirmed her place in the hotel.

His hand reaching out to her from the bed seemed to her to be nothing more than a pleading gesture for understanding and friendship, and relief from the dark loneliness that preceded his own death. She would have taken his hand, and once she had placed the 'tisane de camomille' on the beside table, sat down on the edge of the bed, and gently and slowly raised his hand, to press it against her cheek.

He sat propped up on his pillows. His short wispy grey hair that was pushed up by the pillows into a halo round his forehead – such brave grey hair – moved her suddenly in a way that she did not recognise. She leaned forward to place her cheek against his cheek. He closed his eyes and drew her body nearer with both arms. Old hands, she knew, with freckles and grey hair on the knuckles that were beginning to become gnarled. But even the thought of those old hands moved her. She felt the desire rising up in her to reaffirm life to this old man who had only done good to her. Of her own free will, she inclined herself to him. Lay with her full body on the bed beside him. She stayed with him all through the night; allowed him to caress her, stroking his body in her turn. She felt his heartbeat, fast and then slow; she wiped the perspiration from his forehead. She saw the desire in his eyes, then felt it in his body. Wildly, almost desperately, she threw her clothes off. She felt no desire for him but a fierce urge to comfort him. Perhaps it would be the first time that she knew genuine affection – could it be called love?

The fact remains that in 1901, when the war was at its fiercest, and the British had occupied Pretoria for almost a year, it was recorded: on behalf of the vice-consul of France an application was made for a travel permit for a woman 'of Dutch/Boer extraction' and a baby to travel to the Colony. The application was approved. The vice-consul himself had been transferred back to Europe a few months earlier.

There was no doubt that the widow Greylinck was a woman of considerable influence. She received the news that her daughter-in-law was going to leave the country with her baby calmly and with dignity. She didn't plead, she didn't weep. She managed to get a letter through to her son, who was still in the veld, telling him of the planned departure of his wife and the child. Her doubts about the fathering she kept to herself. 'She is running away like a bad dog,' were her words. She also managed to get an answer from him: 'Let her go then, but I want to keep my child.' Whereupon she made arrangements with connections in Cape Town.

The journey was horrific and long, the child sick and fretful, the mother feared croup sometimes in the chill of the small hours – she was clumsy, unhappy, uncertain. The bailiff was waiting for the train on Cape Town station. He took her to lodgings in Kloof Street, saying formally: 'My instructions are to take the baby away from you and return it to the father.'

'We are tired, can't you see how we look? I can't give you the baby now.' She begged, 'Let us rest first.' She started to weep. 'I can't give you my baby like this. In any case, you must first find someone to care for her on the return journey.'

She pulled herself together and began to think, looked round the lodging room. 'Anyway, I can't run away from here. Where could I go to? I have to wait here for a passage.'

'The widow Greylinck, whom I gather is the child's grandmother, has family in the Cape. They are making the arrangements on her behalf, the baby will stay with them until the return journey is possible,' said the bailiff.

But the young mother's plea: 'Please let us rest first, first get a trustworthy person to look after the baby on the return journey!' softened his heart. She had a point, he thought, where could she run to?

3

Even the southernmost reaches of the Colony – including the mountain fastnesses of the Boland inland from Cape Town – were not left unscathed by the difficult war years. The sharpening of pro-Boer and pro-Brit polarities caused friction between children and parents, between brothers and between friends. It led to a split that would live on in the communal memory.

Boer commandos attacked the border towns of the Colony – Colesberg, Burgersdorp, Aliwal North. In the north-western Cape, Jannie Smuts pressed through as far as Clanwilliam. Colonials in their hundreds joined up with the Boers. The scenes that played themselves out on many a market square were the same as had been seen months earlier in the northerly republics: the mounting of horses, the clipping on of bandoleers, Mausers thrown over shoulders and leave taken of families as new recruits rode after the commandos. After all, these beleaguered people are our kin.

Of the nearly four thousand rebels, a couple of hundred of those who were captured were found guilty of high treason. Under civil law, traitors to her majesty, the Queen. In the hearts of the people, national heroes.

Military tribunals condemned them to death.

The cabinet was divided on the question of punishment. Merriman, who had pleaded amnesty for all but a few ringleaders, resigned. Acrimony divided Schreiner, Solomon and other ministers. In the House of Assembly it was asserted: You are cleaving the country irreparably in two.

Finally Lord Kitchener, the British high commander, deemed it politic to act upon only 33 of these sentences. Some of the rebels were executed by firing squad, some were hanged.

Public enforcement of the sentences raised opposition nation-wide. And 33 was still 33.

One of the 33 was a young man from Dominee Josias van Velde's parish at Worcester. With deep self-recrimination, the young dominee held himself responsible for the young man's departure and subsequent death.

It had been a few months after his brother Hennie and his sister-in-law had finally departed for Nyasaland. The early Boer victories were a thing of the past. Sporadic surprise forays into the Colony from the north, with the possible collusion of the inhabitants, had the officials on their toes. Even in their sleepy little town military law was strictly enforced. Blockhouses were erected along the railway line. Soldiers were to be seen everywhere, even openly entertained in some houses. There was talk that young men who failed to enlist with the British army would be locked up.

The first Boer prisoners from the north came through the town in rail convoys. The stationmaster was pro-Boer, and he organised that the engine driver would sound the train whistle three times when there were Boer prisoners aboard. People hurried to the station with food and clothing, fresh fruit, bread and milk. The dominee too sent provisions from his garden and larder – fresh vegetables, fruit, dried fruit, newly baked bread.

Grandma, as the little boys had been taught to call her, made her mouth thin and white with disapproval. She looked on, holding a grandson's hand in either of hers. 'The parsonage and the holy office should not be used for this!' Her head was thrown back in eloquent displeasure. If she could have taken hold of the stirrup to keep old Booi and the horse cart back, she would have done it. Josias restrained himself as he had had to do so often recently. 'I am sending it in the name of charity. In Christian love.' Her black dress swished as she swung round and stalked off. She did not deign to answer. Her whole bearing spoke of disdain.

It was at that moment that he was called to his study.

He washed his hands at the garden tap and dried them on a cloth hanging on the washline. He had wielded a fork himself to assist with the gathering of vegetables. There was a sense of fulfilment for him in the physical labour of digging and pulling and shaking soil from roots. The radishes and potatoes – where on earth were the wretched people going to cook them? He helped Booi pack the stuff, adding a few quinces and a couple of late figs. Let these afford the weary burgers a few moments of pleasure, perhaps memories of their own farms. There was soil under his fingernails, which he carefully removed with the tip of his pocketknife.

Before he went inside, he wiped his forehead with his handkerchief.

The work or the exasperation had caused sweat to bead on his forehead. His mother-in-law had withdrawn to her room, and neither Issy nor Emma was anywhere to be seen. The wall clock started chiming as he went down the passage. Twelve strokes. Booi must get a move on, he thought. If only he could have gone along himself, to squeeze a despairing hand, offer a word of comfort.

But a man and wife from his congregation waited in the study for him. They were farmers from the district, the man a committed member of the church. He rose to his feet as the dominee entered. Before he sat down again, his hat held in both hands, the inner ribbon sweaty, he asked: 'Dominee, can we close the passage door before we speak?'

The dominee's first impulse was to take umbrage at the request, but he obliged just the same. He pushed the door shut with such force it made the church almanac which hung behind it sway. But he ignored the man's gesture towards the window that said he wanted that closed too. 'There is no one outside on the veranda,' he said. 'We are completely private here.'

The man's actions had merely confirmed what he knew already: his household was suspect. The almost militant attitude of his mother-in-law and sister-in-law were known in the congregation. It found approval with the British-leaning parishioners. But not with this man. Nor his wife. They were clearly very tense. The woman was dressed in dead black. A month earlier he had buried her new-born baby. She had been too weak to attend the funeral herself. And now here she was in his study.

'Braampie wants to join the Boers,' said the farmer. 'This has struck us very hard, dominee.'

The child who died, a late lamb, had been a boy. They had three daughters, and then the first-born, Braampie, their only surviving son.

The woman looked at the closed door. The veil on her straw hat was thrown back. Then she looked at him, her eyes a faded blue. She looked at him as though everything was sliding out from under her and she wanted to cling to him. 'It's because my brother and his sons are in the veld. He wants to go to his cousins.'

'And she is taking the guilt upon herself, dominee,' said the man. 'But it is different for them, her brother farms in the Free State. It is a duty for him and his sons to fight. It isn't Braampie's duty.'

Josias had confirmed Braampie. He was an intelligent boy. In spite of his own pro-Boer sympathies, he could not accept the boy's departure without further ado. His feelings were divided. He could not sit so he got up and paced up and down in the study. The almanac on the closed door stared him in the face every time before he turned. The movement of time, from last year to now, came to him with spine-chilling clarity. And what still lay ahead?

'He knows what happens to Colonials who go away to fight?'

'He knows.'

'Being a rebel is very different to being a patriot.'

'He is a devout child,' said the mother. She raised her hand in a weak gesture. Then the hand sank again and her words were scarcely audible. 'He might listen if you speak to him, Dominee.'

The dominee bent over her chair and took her hand in both of his. 'I will have a word with him. And I shall pray about it. God knows, these times are not easy.'

But even when the farmer knelt and he prayed with them, he knew with an icy premonition that more travail awaited these people. Would that he found the right words if Braampie did come to talk to him. He and Braampie empathised with each other. He would be able to share his own doubts with Braampie. They could allay them together. If only he would come. Then he would leave it to the Lord to put the right words in his mouth.

But he was right in the premonition that Braampie, his trusted confirmand, would not come to talk to him. He waited in vain. Then, by chance, he heard that the boy had already left. He had to fight hard against a bitterness for the two British sympathisers in his house whose presence had probably kept the boy away from him.

Sometimes he was tempted to harden his heart against the suffering in the north for the sake of peace in the home. It could have been so different. So harmonious, so loving. Like the afternoon when he permitted himself to linger awhile in the garden with Emma. A beautiful garden: on one side, the rose beds, then the more rampant, less formal area with the climbers, wisteria, alyssum, rambling roses over an archway, and a place to sit under the oak.

Emma had had two cane chairs carried out there; they were only removed to the veranda during wet weather. She was fond of sitting out here with her back to the house. This afternoon she had the two little boys with her, they leaned close, wanting to climb over her. She leafed through a book, simplifying the story as she read. *The Wide, Wide World.*

He drew the second chair closer to hers. 'May I listen in?'

Things are still very good between her and me, he thought. Near him stood a stray zinnia with a small scarlet flower. He opened his pocketknife, cut the stem, and laid the flower on her lap beside the book. Wherever he was, he always wanted to give her a flower. She held it in her left hand as she leafed on through the pages.

Even when Issy called from the front veranda: 'Bath time. Come on!' her sharp tone brooking no opposition, it didn't disturb his sense of peace. Even when he noticed Grandma keeping an eye on them from the veranda where she sat crocheting, he was unperturbed. Yes, he did experience such moments too. If he could only keep the war out of his thoughts.

Queen Victoria died in January. The newspapers carried full accounts. British supporters tied mourning crepe on their doorknobs, tacked it to door jambs and wound it round veranda posts as a sign of grief. Girls were sent to school with black ribbon chokers and boys with black bands on their sleeves, whereupon they were waylaid by the Boer children who tore off the black bands and punched until noses bled. Then, singing the national songs of the two republics at the tops of their voices, the Boer boys dragged their coat-tails past the Tommies who were at work in front of their tents on the commonage. The Tommies, of course, didn't even recognise the songs.

The dominee's best horses had been commandeered under military law, which made his district visiting extremely difficult. He came home hot and tired from the office of the commandant.

He needed a permit to stay overnight beyond the boundaries of the town. He had waited the whole morning to see the commandant. At noon he was still waiting. Just after twelve the orderly came to say to him: 'No bloody use waiting, parson, the commandant has gone to lunch. You might try to come at two, or make it half past. Or even three.'

Annoyed, he got to his feet. The whole morning wasted.

When he went through the street door, he saw the commandant crossing the dusty street en route to the hotel canteen. He knew what the commandant was like after his extended midday eating and drinking. Red in the face, bombastic, nit-picking. He would battle to control his temper. Right then, what could he do? He took his hat and walked home. Though he tried to ignore the mourning crepe on the verandas he walked past, he knew with self-reproach that in the back of his mind he would store precise information about who had put crepe on their houses. Many people of whom he would not have expected it.

It was hot. The shops were preparing to close shutters and lock doors for the midday hour. A couple of parishioners greeted him at the post office. Even amongst them were those of whose feelings he was unsure. The suspiciousness grieved him.

He was glad to approach his own home, with the prospect of cool spaces, a rest after the meal in the darkened bedroom, the fragrance of Emma. Perhaps the gentle unfastening of her buttons, one by one, so the soft, sweet flesh was slowly exposed, swelling out to him; her brown hair loosened and fanned out over the pillow, her head pushing this way and that way against the pillow until at last, with a soft sigh, she was at peace. The Lord forgive him, out here in the street …

He passed quickly through the garden gate. The rose garden had been irrigated early that morning, but the moisture had dried up again leaving only a darker harder mud between the furrow ridges. The roses, specially the fully opened ones, hung limp, but a strong fragrance wafted towards him. He took particular note of the new buds. Tonight at dusk he would pick a bunch for Emma. On Mondays he permitted himself to work in the rose garden. He loved his rose garden. The vexation and injustice he had to endure during the morning fell away from him.

He walked slowly up the garden path to his house, climbing up the steps past the climbing plants. For a few moments he could not believe what he saw there. Not on his house. Black and purple crepe fastened round the doorknob and tacked to the doorjamb. His eyes must be deceiving him. This could not be the handwork of Grandma and Issy. Not after Grandma's repeated assertions that the pastorie must be above suspicion and could not take political sides. Someone who had slipped in from the town? Someone in his own community maligning him?

His breath came faster. Then he tore at the crepe. Frayed shreds hung from the nails; he ripped it all off. He walked into the house with the cloth in his hand. All three women sat round the dining table, Grandma, Issy and Emma. They were waiting for him. He held out the crumpled black and purple cloth. The women stared at him in deathly silence, Emma's large brown eyes gazed into his.

'How dare you?' said Grandma. Her eyes were narrowed to slits, her lips thin. Then suddenly something gave in, her shoulders sank forward and she started to weep.

'Do you realise what you've done?' Issy stood up and placed a thin black-clad arm round her mother's shoulders. Her eyes flashed at him. She's starting to look more and more like Grandma, he thought, she's made of the same fabric. Thank heaven Emma is different.

'And you dare to speak of Christian charity!'

His Emma had also risen to her feet, how clearly he saw everything today – there were black rings under her eyes which seemed larger and darker, her hair seemed to be too heavy for her neck, she looked confused. She came to him, removed the black and purple cloth from his hand, took him by the arm: 'Grandma is upset about the queen's death. I told her you would not be pleased if she tied on the crepe, but she wouldn't give in. "Why would my grief about the old queen's death upset him?" she asked. She doesn't understand.'

She understands all too well, he thought.

'I am taking Grandma to her room,' said Issy. 'But don't let that spoil your appetite.'

That afternoon in their bedroom he spoke to Emma.

'I brought you over the threshold of this pastorie as my wife, not as the daughter of your mother or sister of Issy. You are my wife. You must stand up to them.' Her eyes were serious, as though she had already thought about this.

'I wanted to, Josias. I have tried. I can't. I think that the admonition: honour your father and your mother is woven so deeply into my being that it would tear me apart if I did not obey it. I tried to stand up to her only once. She turned her back on me. I spent the whole afternoon on my bed crying. And I asked forgiveness on my knees the following morning. It was when you were away on a district visit.'

'We'll leave it there,' he said, moved by what she'd said. My darling Emma, your wellbeing is my only wish. I will always shield you. He repeated: 'Then we'll leave it there.'

The war dragged on. More and more people streamed to the station when they heard the engine driver sound the whistle three times in the distance. They didn't just take food, they also asked the prisoners of war for news of family members and friends. They heard about the women's concentration camps and the suffering in the camps and the thousands of deaths. They heard that farms were burnt and the old people, the women and the children carted to the camps in open trucks. After a long debate, the Cape Synod announced: Where a parish council is willing to let a dominee have a few months off, he may with the necessary permission of the British command go as temporary dominee to the camps to support the women and children and the elderly.

When he heard this news Josias knew that he had no choice. By the grace of God, he had been granted the opportunity to support his countrymen within the limitations of his calling.

That afternoon he went to sit with Emma in the garden again. The two little boys were riding on their hobby-horses. Whoa! Whoa! They shouted as they galloped through the long grass, burst through the shrubs, rushed to Emma with scratched faces for a touch of comfort.

'You know that I have no choice.'

Her fingers busied themselves with a scrap of white needlework on her lap. She nodded. She had told him the previous night that she was expecting again. She is not making it easy for me, thought the dominee.

'If it were not for your condition, it would be easier for me to go.'

'I am in good hands.'

In fact she thought, as she bit through a thread, if he must go, he may as well just go.

As soon as he was gone, she could leave the care of Stuart and Frikkie, now five and two, completely to Issy. She would be able to spend long spells in her bedroom, on her bed with the shutters closed, luxuriating in the smell of cologne. Without the perpetual friction between Josias and Grandma and Issy the tension would be eased. She would have time and leisure to grow accustomed to her body as it took over once more, or she could put it out of her mind for a little while, just read and read, or lie and stare at the ceiling … She would revel in the sublime aloneness, the aloneness that her days so lacked, without any feelings of guilt or responsibility to anyone else. She would be able to submerge herself in the seclusion like a pool of water. And long before her time had come he would be back.

'Go,' she said. 'I know how close this matter is to your heart.'

Once the table was cleared, just before the grace, he smoothed his moustache flat, first both sides and then the left-hand side again, in a gesture that warned Issy something was coming, and he said to the women at the table, in calm and measured tones: 'Shortly, once the arrangements have been made, probably not longer than a fortnight or so, I am leaving for the north.'

Grandma held her head slightly at an angle, her expression questioning, almost incredulous. The old queen's death had set her back, her eyes were permanently moist and vague, and she had to really concentrate if anything called for her full attention. Her wrinkled neck was adorned with a black velvet choker, with the mourning brooch fastened to it.

But the power of the hand that gripped Emma's forearm restrainingly, the power of her will was unimpaired. She stared at her son-in-law. She cleared her throat. Her voice sounded shrill.

'To the north? Would you do me the ultimate injury to take up arms against England?'

Even the suggestion that this might be possible grieved him.

'If I was younger and had no responsibilities, I would certainly have considered it.' He was sorry after he'd said that. He'd wanted to remain polite and calm.

'And poor Emma,' Issy added. 'Have you considered her condition?'

'I did take it into consideration. She believes she will be able to come through her pregnancy in your care.'

He forced himself to speak in a calmer, more conciliatory tone. 'I will be back long before the confinement. I want to stress this: I am not going to fight, I am going to offer spiritual care to those suffering in the camp. I am going to bury dead children. Let us give thanks.'

Josias van Velde was one of the first Cape dominees to visit the camps. Travel opportunities were scarce. It took him a fortnight to get to Springfontein where he was allocated. There were plenty of troop trains. They steamed through the stations. The trains where he finally got a place were pushed onto sidings to make way for the supply trains that roared past. The Karoo stations were hot. Nelspoort, Hutchinson, Richmond Road. He had to get out at every station: papers, permits, passes and more passes. Sometimes it seemed to him that there were khakis wherever he looked: they stood up from the ridges, poured out of the station buildings – singing, foul-mouthed khakis, sent to exterminate his nation.

In some of the trains travelling southwards he came upon Boer families. At De Aar a woman grabbed his arm from the train and begged: 'Dominee, you must pray for us, my husband sent us away, he signed up with the English. Dominee, it would have been better if he'd perished.'

'Where are you going to?'

'To my brother's farm in the Stellenbosch district. How am I and my children going to survive the disgrace?'

He held her hands in both of his and comforted her: 'These hard times will also pass.'

That night he travelled far off his course. The conductor came to fetch him from the waiting room, bundled him into a train, and he woke up at Hopetown. There he had to wait again for a southbound train. 'Dominee, you can come and sit in the caboose.' He had only one travel bag with him and his food basket. The doctor had given him remedies, as many as he could pack into the basket.

'I know it's only a drop in the ocean,' the doctor had said, 'but maybe it will help someone somewhere.'

His food only lasted a few days. Sometimes, when the train was shunted from the main line to a railway village and he could get out, he would walk into the town to buy bread and milk. Often the town was deserted, and he bought a few carrots, or turnips or a piece of fruit from the black people who tried to cultivate the devastated vegetable patches. But these were scarce. He washed the carrots at the station tap and began to eat. At Nauwpoort where he could climb off again at last, he was issued with rations along with the soldiers. He ate these with more difficulty than the raw food. Nauwpoort, Colesberg, Norvalspont. The country was grey and dry, the Orange River no more than a series of mud puddles.

He was a fastidious man, and the lack of wash facilities (or even water) was a trial. His black broadcloth suit was red with dust, his shirt collar and his white bib grimy. He could dust his black hat off with his white handkerchief until the handkerchief too was brown with dust. His moustache and beard felt hot and scratchy. He itched. The carriages he rode in were crawling with lice.

When he took his Bible out and tried to read it, it prompted so much mockery and loud blaspheming from the soldiers, he preferred to leave off. He could try to pray with his chin on his chest and his eyes closed as though in sleep, his hands concealed under the hat which he held on his lap. But he felt that what he prayed was no more than words. God, give me the strength to do Your work, I am too weak alone.

At long last he reached Springfontein station where he was to disembark. He was surprised to see the field of tents so close by, right near the town. There were no arrangements for anyone to meet him. He began to walk slowly, but after a short way he was picked up by an old black man with a donkey cart. He sat up front with him on the wooden bench.

It was April, and a dry dusty wind blew. With his filthy handkerchief, he tried to mop the sweat that ran from his forehead. They crossed dry river beds. There were no animals to be seen, finally a group of white children collecting wood. They trotted past a deserted farmyard. The two gum trees in the yard were tattered. 'I tore those leaves off with my whip, oh Lord, the old lady in the camp begged me so politely. They boil the leaves for the children with croup. Yes.'

The guards must have known the old black man because they let him through. The camp commander was red and sweaty behind his table;

the heat inside the tent was worse than outside. The dominee was billeted with two junior officers. When asked and offered a reward, the orderly brought him half a jug of water to wash with. He also brought and erected a camp bed.

Apart from those children gathering wood, the dominee was still unaware of the inhabitants of the camp. Wherever he looked, the tents stretched motionlessly in their white rows, the pathways between them empty. The midday heat was intense. The air hung heavily.

He must have dozed off on the camp bed because when he awoke he heard people singing. His shirt was wet with perspiration but it was slightly cooler. Going by the shadows in the tent, the sun was setting. He got up and washed his face and hands again hastily in the used water and smoothed his hair flat. The singing came closer. When he stepped out of the tent, he saw a crowd of women and children, some children in arms, others clinging to skirts. Some of the older ones ran ahead, others stumbled behind wearily. Some old men accompanied them.

Other refuge have I none;
Hangs my helpless soul on Thee;
Leave, ah! Leave me not alone,
Still support and comfort me.
All my trust on Thee is stay'd,
All my help from Thee I bring;
Cover my defenceless head
With the shadow of Thy wing.

When they saw the dominee coming out, the group stopped moving. But they kept on singing. They are welcoming me, he thought. These were not women like those he knew from his Boland towns. They were dishevelled, their soiled dresses dragged in the red soil. The large bonnets on their heads were unstarched and hung so limply that he couldn't always see the faces. Where a bonnet brim was folded back and he could see the woman's face, he was struck by the despair in the eyes and round the mouth. The children were thin and ragged. People from the wrong side of the tracks, he thought, and was instantly ashamed of the thought.

A few of the guards had come closer, alerted by the unusual gathering. The sight of the soldiers incensed him so much that he felt something tearing inside him. He stepped up closer to the group and started singing with them, his voice low and strong among the women's reedy voices. He added the next verse:

Thou, oh Christ, art all I want;
More than all in Thee I find;
Raise the fallen, cheer the faint,
Heal the sick, and lead the blind –
Just as holy is Thy name;
I am all unrighteousness;
False and full of sin I am,
Thou art full of truth and grace.

When he raised his hands, they stopped singing.

The dominee bowed his head. 'Let us pray.'

The old men in the group said, 'Amen, amen' when he finished praying. A few of the women wept openly. He himself felt deeply moved.

The next few days he went from tent to tent. He got acquainted, wrote down names, gave advice, raised spirits. There was a sick person in virtually every tent. An old person, a child, a baby, an expectant mother. On Sundays he conducted an open-air service. Sick babies were brought for christening.

The hot weather changed unexpectedly. Untimely thunderstorms broke. It rained throughout the night, water streaming into the tent, until some of his possessions floated. The two orderlies were put to digging ditches round the tents. He dressed and hurried outside. A grey dawn was breaking. Women and young girls with blankets round their shoulders knelt in the mud, trying to make furrows with their hands to redirect the water. He commandeered a spade from one of the orderlies and set about helping round the tents. He raised ridges, dug the furrows deeper. As soon as things were improved at one tent, he moved on to the next, feeling powerless before the scores of tents. One young child who was digging started to cry when she saw him. She held her hands up to him. 'Uncle,' she cried, 'my hands have got so stupid.' She wiped the tears from her face with her wet forearms, her hands were grimed with mud. 'They won't do what I want them to, they won't move.' She looked at the fingers which she had splayed out.

'You go inside,' he said. 'I'll finished the digging. Ask your mother to rub your hands until the life comes back into them.'

At eleven, the rain stopped and the sun came out again. The sick ones lay on sodden mattresses, for there were no beds. Where they could, women dragged mattresses and bedding out into the sun. Here and there someone started to heat water to make coffee, but the wood was wet and the rations in the tents soaked through.

'Run around,' he told the children, 'run, keep moving so you warm up and your clothes dry out.'

Sickness increased. He was called from tent to tent. After the rain came colds, fever, measles, lung complaints – sometimes it seemed to him that the camp was coughing itself into shreds. The gasping grating cough of old men that continued all night; the dark cough of women who were trying to suppress the sound, pressing blankets and clothing to the mouth so that just the dull jerk of the breath could be heard. And then the pathetic monotonous cough of the children.

He wanted to block his ears at night.

Often during his morning rounds he found more than one little corpse in a tent, then he prayed and said the bodies must be taken out. The fierce possessiveness over the body of a first child who died made way for a dead acceptance among the women. 'Just take him then, Dominee.' It comforted them visibly if he carried the child himself to the mortuary tent.

One mother lost all her four children. Only then to fall sick herself. She glowed from the fever. The women who shared the tent kept vigil all night by her side. She died after two days. There was no timber for coffins. The sheet in which a sick one died served as shroud and as coffin. On one day eight women were buried, wrapped only in the sheets under which they had died.

'She was such a proud woman, Dominee, thought she was better than the next. If she only knew …' He did not admonish. Who is without sin?

He spoke to the commanding officer, asked for more blankets, medicines, doctors, better food, more latrines. Did the commander realise that the latrines that were meant for 500 people were now being used by more than 2000 people?

His polite requests brought no results. He grew angry, accused the British regime of large-scale murder. The commander in his turn flew into a rage. 'Who gave you the right to address me in this fashion? I am the representative of his majesty the King!'

'And I, sir, however weak and unworthy, am the representative of God.'

And in a strange sense, Josias van Velde felt this was true. These suffering women and children, he felt, had brought him closer to God than he had ever been. It was as though the narrow divide between life and death which he experienced here brought him to the edge of the Invisible. He got little sleep; every night he held a wake. He was particularly moved by the old men who died with a verse from the Bible on their lips, and the soft despairing singing of the women.

Periodically more people were brought in and the tents were overcrowded: 14, 20 in a tent.

Each day he tried to neaten himself up, took his Bible and hymn book and led the group of people to the piece of fenced ground that served as a graveyard. When the graves were dug, the boys or the women or whoever had strength to do so, dragged the little wagon with the body. Sometimes he just remained standing there because the one grave had scarcely been closed over when the next group started the procession with its little cart. One day he buried 16 corpses.

That night he was called to Tant Hester Prinsloo's tent. Eight sick ones lay in the tent. 'Ag, Dominee, we don't know who to help first when we get here. Four are so serious that we can't leave them on their own. There's scarcely room for us in the tent.'

Tant Hester was dying. She was unaware of those around her, her sick children, or her daughter who sat on the ground beside her bed. 'She was our pillar of strength, Dominee. She always talked courage into us. We give her up unwillingly.'

He could smell death in the tent. He sat on a little trunk and opened his Bible. He leafed through the Bible, uncertain what he should read. Lord, where to, where to? He pleaded wordlessly.

And then all of a sudden the smell of death was gone, and something like the lovely smell of tuberoses filled the tent.

The dying children on their mattresses were still and their eyes opened, suddenly clear. The dying woman also opened her eyes. She said softly but in her old sweet voice: 'How heavenly it is and look at the crowds of angels gathered round us.' And then she closed her eyes and died.

No one said a word. Tears streamed from Dominee van Velde's eyes, but he did not want to move his hands to wipe them away.

The others who had kept vigil were also silent, as if they too felt the presence of the angels. Later no one could say how long this silence lasted. But slowly, as the soul takes its leave of the body, the smell of tuberoses and that presence of the Invisible gradually receded.

Those who kept vigil and those who lay sick became aware once more of the chill in the tent, of the darkness of the night outside. But still they remained motionless.

They began to sing softly but with great love.

Abide with me; fast falls the eventide;
The darkness deepens, Lord, with me abide!
When other helpers fail, and comforts flee,
Help of the helpless, Oh, Abide with me.

At last the dominee took his handkerchief from his pocket and dried his eyes. Was suffering the price of an awareness of God? he wondered as he walked back to his tent. Was it really true that suffering was the tool that God used to bring his children to Him?

The months went by. October was the worst month. A hundred and fourteen new graves in the graveyard. November offered no respite: 104 new graves.

And then one day the postbag from the Cape Colony brought him a letter from Issy. He started at the sight of her name on the back of the envelope, almost illegible under the jumble of official stamps. He tore it open and read. 'A daughter has been born prematurely, but the mother and child are doing well.' Under Issy's precise, upright, compressed script, Emma had added a few words. 'All's well, no need to come. As always, my love.'

The sight of Emma's familiar loose broad handwriting, the round letters that lay like full-blown roses on the page, only three or four words per line, jerked him, more than the news about the baby, back into the reality of his own existence far away from the camp. He pressed the letter to his face, but it was Issy's granny lavender that he smelt rather than Emma's perfume.

At the end of November the deaths began to reduce. The leave of absence which his parish council had granted had also run out. He must go home.

The dominee took leave of the women in the camp painfully. He felt bound to them with invisible threads. These few months could never be erased from his memory. As the day of departure approached, one by one the women took up their lives again. The war could not in all conscience last much longer. Some would take a surviving child or two and return to the ruins on the farm, waiting there for a spouse who might or might not return. Some, helpless, would be dependent on others for a roof over their heads. But whatever their circumstances, the small events of the resumed life would begin to rule their attention.

There were times when he was deeply depressed. As he walked through the tents, he heard yet again the women quarrelling, shouting at the children, bickering over rations. He felt that those of them who had been together here should never be at odds, but support one another in the name of the suffering they had experienced.

He kneeled in his tent and prayed: We cannot cope with Your gift. As the people could not bear Your Son in His radiance, so we could not maintain those moments in Your shining Love.

The experience in the camp, even the laying to rest of children, the carrying away of the stiffened corpses, his steps crunching over the frost, his arms numb from the cold precious weight, were for him more beautiful, holier than anything he had experienced up until now. We are one in the body of Christ, the suffering people for whom he had such a deep sympathy.

The evening before his departure a few of the women, on behalf of all of them, brought him a gift. What could they possibly have to give? They had torn pieces of canvas from a tent that had blown into shreds. Their action had unleashed the fury of a guard and as loudly as he yelled at the women tearing the canvas, just as loudly and unrestrainedly they shouted back. He remembered the event well.

And who was he to judge their rage? Because from the pieces of canvas, washed clean and bleached with their precious soap, the women had made him a little tent, about two feet high. 'To take for your child who was born while you were with us, Dominee. To remind her that you were here.'

It was beautifully made, careful stitches, nicely finished off, with a tent pole that one of the old men had fashioned, with a door flap, side flaps just like a proper tent.

He took the three women's hands and pressed them, one after another.

'I don't need anything to remember you by,' he said. 'I will never ever forget you.'

He knew he would not see any of them again.

There was no one to meet him on Worcester station. No one knew of his return. He climbed out of the train and looked around him with dazed eyes. A group of people at the ticket office, the crack of a whip and a horse cart that pulled away, the call of a brown woman to her child. He picked up his bag. Did these people have any idea of what was happening in the north?

The stationmaster recognised him and came up to him with outstretched hand. 'Dominee! Back at last! Tired too, I can see.' He called a cab driver. 'Take the dominee to the pastorie.'

As the horse's hooves clopped over the familiar road, the driver calling out the familiar words, the dominee could not shake off the feeling that he had returned to a world where he was a stranger.

The driver carried his bag, wanted to press the bell at the front door, but Josias opened the door and went in. He stood in the half-dark passage. He wanted to call out: Emma! But it was not necessary. He heard the swish of her dress and the indrawn breath, smelt the exotic toilet water. She was strange to him, untouchable.

'Josias!' It sounded more like a sob than his name. His arms were round her and she pressed her body against him. 'Josias.'

But when he heard the quick steps of his mother-in-law and the louder tread of Issy approaching, he stood back from her. He took of his hat, brushed the dust off, and hung it on the hall stand. Then he greeted them.

'Thank the Lord you are safely home,' said his mother-in-law.

'My safety is not of prime importance.'

'But our little girl …' said Emma who would not let go of his hand.

'Yes, our little daughter …' His voice was tender. Had he forgotten her?

In the nursery, it was Issy who placed the little bundle wrapped in fine wool and silk in his arms. Hesitantly? Because he was begrimed with dust? No, not that.

Emma spoke. 'She was born prematurely … I didn't want to let you know … she was weak and Grandma said we must christen her before she perhaps died. Cousin Charles came from Stellenbosch to christen her. She was named Victoria. Grandma wanted it that way. I begged …'

Then she began to cry. So uncontrollably that he had to give the baby back to Issy and take her in his arms. He pressed her head, as of old, against his shoulder; his hand stroked her thick dark hair. He had to force himself to do it. It was not her fault. Although the thought was inevitable: Emma was still the mother, Emma could have refused. Was there something intentional in her submission? Perhaps pique at his long absence? It was painful for him to have to criticise his beloved Emma, but naming his daughter after the old queen, in whose name horrific deeds had been perpetrated against his people! He tried to talk calmly but his words were cold and hard.

'You, my mother-in-law and my sister-in-law, have seen fit to do me this great injustice. Knowingly and deliberately. Knowing my feelings. May the Lord forgive you. I do not know if I am capable of that. Just do not speak to me again about Christian love.'

'Well!' said Grandma and she turned on her heel and stalked off.

Issy gave the baby back to Emma. 'If you call that gratitude ...' she said and followed her mother.

'Josias, I was weak, I gave in ...'

It was only now that he noticed how pale she was.

'Hush, Emma, hush now. Show me the baby. Our first daughter. Whatever her name, she is still my child.'

Later he unpacked his few clothes – most of them he had given away to camp dwellers – but he left the package with the little tent in the bag. He would not unpack it. Not even in front of Emma. Perhaps he felt that the rage which he could not control when he heard the baby's name was unworthy of the tent. How weak the flesh was! But dear God in heaven! Me with my godly education and all, not much better than the bickering women in the camp, he thought wryly. I am just as unworthy of His gifts. He yearned with a terrible longing for the camp.

At the table that night no one in the family spoke much. He was not asked and he did not tell much of his experiences during the past seven months.

'When he was already very old, in his late seventies, Father told me a story that stuck with me,' said Emma's second daughter, Leonora, to her niece Leo more than half a century later. 'I told you my father and I were like this' and she bent her middle finger over her index finger. 'Strange that he never told me about it sooner. Or opened the parcel and showed me what was in it. He told me after he had read a book about the Second World War. And heavens, where are the politicians dragging us to now ... a third or a cold or a hot war ... or annihilation.' In spite of her own age, or perhaps because of it, Leonora was a fierce environmentalist.

They were on the beach at Camps Bay; Leo, lying on her back so she could suntan evenly, wanted to know about the 'old days'.

'I think he was afraid he would not be able to stand a mocking expression round Aunt Issy's mouth or a contemptuous back thrust of Grandma's head. And he was tired of conflict.

'Maybe he told Mother before her death. I don't know. But that day he pulled the book closer and said: "Look. At Mons in Flanders in the 1914 war after the great slaughter, they told that thousands of dying and wounded soldiers saw a host of angels in the sky. Journalists put it down to imagination. But it isn't impossible."

'Then he said very quietly: "I have experienced something like that myself. I know that the presence of angels can be felt. After times of deep suffering. And the death of many."

'Then he stood up and stooped near the study chest and took out a package which he had stored there for all those years. But he did not open it.

'He said, 'The women who gave me this gift experienced it with me.'

'My old father's faded blue eyes welled full of tears. "The Godly still touches people. But we are too weak to receive the gift and hold it."'

Leonora let streams of sand run through her fingers, to form heaps which she then flattened.

'There was also a story about a camp in Natal where a huge number of children died. Weeping mothers told that, after the funeral, on their way back to the camp they saw a host of angels in the sky before them. Father heard about that but he couldn't get corroboration anywhere. But the thought remained with him, even in the time of suffering that awaited him.

'I helped him upright again and back to his chair. He was bald by then, and I had had a black velvet skull cap made for him in the Cape. He wore it indoors because he felt the cold. He was proud of his little velvet skull cap. A tuft of silver hair stuck out on either side. His skin had got soft and fine with the years, the red and blue veins shone through.'

'You are the only one who tells us about the old days,' Leo said quietly.

Shortly after his return from the camp, the dominee was summoned by the commandant. The commandant was angry. Sitting behind his desk, he exhaled forcefully a couple of times. He was a heavily built man, hot in his uniform, red in the face perhaps from the whisky consumed every midday in the bar over the road and probably also in the mess of an evening. He ran his forefinger in under his collar as though he was trying to get more breathing space.

'It is not a pleasure for me to see you today,' he said. 'Not for me and even less of a pleasure for you.'

The dominee had no idea what he was referring to. Then he noticed a package wrapped in brown tarpaulin on the desk. There was something final and irrevocable about the package. Something sombre and threatening. The commandant pushed it over towards him.

'The things in there belonged to the Nel boy. We got word that he was captured, then convicted of high treason. I regret to say that the sentence was carried out a few weeks ago.'

His voice rose. 'My God, Dominee, he was hanged. In the public square at Burgersdorp. And the people of the town were forced to watch. These public hangings have been banned in Britain for half a century. There'll be a public outcry. What in heaven's name possessed them?'

He shook out a khaki handkerchief and wiped his face. 'This is a terrible war, Reverend. Neither you nor I like what is happening. If only the bloody boy had stayed on the farm. I think it suitable that you as their pastor should go to the farm to inform the parents, and to take them that ...' He couldn't go on. He took a sheet of paper and began to make out the permit necessary for the dominee to leave town and to stay overnight at the farm.

'I have a boy of my own,' the commandant said. 'You can tell the parents – now what in hell can you tell them? Oh, get going, can't you?'

'It is too far for my two old mares. You'd better give me a permit for the train up to the Osplaas halt. From there I shall no doubt get assistance.'

So he found himself sitting waiting on Worcester station once more. In his travel bag that had already journeyed so many roads with him that the leather had started to crack, lay the tarpaulin-wrapped package. Tied with string and sealed. The sealing wax like a gob of blood on the knotted string. A blotch of blood on the chest. Not blood. The boy had been hanged.

Uncle, is it awful to be hanged? asked the boy, not yet 20, of the man with him in the cell.

It is just the walk onto the gallows, my boy, just those three steps that are awful, the rest is quick.

The package in his travel bag grew large and heavy.

In Cradock the congregation gathered together in the church a little before nine and sat with bowed heads, praying for those who were to be executed by firing squad. Not a word was spoken, simply silent prayer. That was all, that was enough. People went their ways after the bell had rung nine hours. Never had people attended a more devout service ...

It seemed to him that he could scarcely lift the bag from the bench on which he sat waiting. The stationmaster had come to tell him a train was on its way.

'You can get on, Dominee. I'll tell the guard you are coming along with them.'

It almost seemed as though he too was aware of the weight that lay in the travel bag. Why else would he have said: 'I would help you in myself and carry your bag for you, but I'll be busy up front with the engine. I'll call a boy to carry it.'

The dominee didn't object. He heard the approaching train, felt the shudder as it drew to a halt, heard the steam hissing out from under the carriages. He scarcely saw the Tommies who leaned from the windows, wisecracking, swinging their arms, or jumping out to buy something. He had no feeling of antipathy for them. He saw them as in a dream, walking over the plains, row upon row, as they stumbled forward to be mown down.

The conductor wasn't very talkative. He jumped in just as the train pulled out of the station, he had paperwork to go over. He had folded down the little chair in the guard's van for his passenger. The journey took a little more than half an hour. At the Osplaas halt the train was pulled over on to a siding and a train from the north rushed by. The conductor held him by the elbow as he climbed down the steep steps. The he passed his travel bag down to him. Just as he reached the ground, the other train came hurtling past. The earth shuddered. The train was almost empty; coupled in among the goods wagons there was one passenger coach, and at a window he saw the face of a young woman staring out with huge bleak eyes. Then she was gone, and the goods wagons lurched away into the distance like a clumsy animal.

'Will you be all right, Dominee?' called the conductor.

'Something will turn up,' he answered.

And not long after the train had departed, a donkey cart appeared driven by a farm worker he vaguely remembered from a previous visit. He was bringing pumpkins for the signalman. The two donkeys trotted along briskly. He approached as the pumpkins were being off-loaded.

'Of course you can ride with us, master.' But no matter how energetically the donkeys stepped out, it seemed to the dominee that they made no progress. The veld stretched out on all sides to the distant ridges. It was as though they were trapped in this vast space.

The old farm worker did not talk. He sat stooped forward in his jacket with its frayed elbows. His trousers were worn through at the knees, and his shoes had given in at the toes. Everything threadbare, frayed, worn through, his skin wrinkled, wizened. His hands on the reins were gnarled from work, his skin dry and cracked, chapped. How did he see him so clearly, as though for the first time, in this frozen moment? He had no teeth and his sunken mouth worked over a piece of tobacco, and periodically he spat down onto the soil.

Finally the dominee asked: 'What is your name?'

'Kiewiet, master.'

That was all they said. The farmhouse they were bound for materialised in a fold in the hills. Suddenly, too soon, they'd arrived. The farmer who was accustomed to scanning great distances had already seen the passenger from a long way off. He came walking towards them over the yard. Recognition and fear flashed through his eyes. He whistled for Kiewiet to pull up and helped the dominee down.

'Before we go inside, dominee, tell me your news.' He swallowed hard, his Adam's apple bobbing up and down more than once. The grip on the dominee's arm tightened and then went slack. 'Is it Braampie?'

The dominee said nothing and the very fact that he did not answer confirmed the man's fears.

'God,' he said, 'not Braampie.'

Now the dominee could talk. 'I do not bring you good news, brother.'

'Has he been killed?'

The dominee did not answer.

'In God's name, what then?'

The words came with difficulty; they were spoken quietly, as though they should not be heard by the cart, the donkeys, the yard, the trees, the cattle kraal, the barn and especially not the house.

'Your son was taken prisoner, tried and found guilty.'

The farmer did not understand. 'Tried? For what? By whom?'

'As a rebel – he was tried for high treason by a military tribunal. You knew that this was a risk he ran.'

'We knew, yes. He knew too, but it did not stop him. I'll go to the Cape, I'll appeal. Dear Father, the boy is not yet 19.'

Now the dominee took the farmer by the arm and said in a slightly louder voice: 'Peace, brother, the time for that has passed. They hanged your son on the square at Burgersdorp.'

The dominee picked up his travel bag. 'We must go inside. I must tell your wife.'

Later that evening, after the daughters had gone crying to bed, frightened by their parents' grief, still not grasping what had happened, that they would never see their brother again, the dominee opened the travel bag and put the package wrapped in tarpaulin on the table.

'These are his things. They asked me to bring them to you.'

The farmer cut the string with his pocketknife; the woman in black pulled the package near and plucked it open almost eagerly. Not much. A Bible, a letter, some clothing, a second letter. Before she opened her letter, the woman read the name on the second one. It brought on a fresh flood of tears.

'It's to his sweetheart, Dominee. You must take it, but the people have moved. They were from Touwsriver, but I don't know their new address.'

He put the letter into his bag. He knew nothing of these people. 'I will try to see to the letter,' he said.

Then she opened her letter and read it aloud between her sobs.

Dearest Mother and Father,
I take this opportunity to send you a few lines to let you know that I am going away to the fatherland. I have stood trial and have been condemned to death. But, my dearest Mother and Father, you must not grieve for me. I am safe with our dear Lord. So you have faith. Oh, dearest Father and Mother, I have longed for you so, but I will endure my lot with patience. I will never meet you again on earth. I go alone to meet God. I close with warmest greetings to all of you. I remain your son.
Abraham Nel

The dominee gave mental thanks to God that the boy had died in faith. And then he too wept for Braampie.

He had to wait a long time for a train the following afternoon. The farmer had taken him to the station personally. Two half-empty trains rumbled by, the signalman signalled through to the next station: In God's name, let the next train stop here. They hadn't said anything to him, but he could feel the despair that hung about the two men.

'It's the dominee, man, you must stop for him.'

The dominee held the farmer's hand for a long time in his when they saw the snout of the train appearing in the distance. It shuddered to a stop.

'My thoughts will be with you, brother.'

The bag they passed up to him once he'd climbed into the train seemed light. The dominee set it down on the seat beside him. His hand rested on it. The train picked up speed, and the dominee's body swayed slightly from side to side with the movement of the coach. Perhaps he dozed, he could not say. The conductor suddenly shouted 'Worcester!' and jerked the door open, urging on the couple of passengers who wanted to get in. He was in a hurry to make up for the time they'd wasted stopping at the halt.

It was late afternoon, almost dusk, when the dominee reached the pastorie. The family sat at table. Issy cut the bread and served out the soup. He washed his hands, kissed his wife, and took his place without a word. No one spoke. He did not eat much, pushing his soup aside after a few spoonfuls, toying with his bread.

Once the others were finished, Issy got up to bring the Bible for evening worship. It was their custom to read from the Dutch Bible in the morning and the English Bible in the evening. It was placed before him. He opened it. The English words began to blur before his eyes. He couldn't read. He shut the Bible and pushed it away.

'Please bring me the Dutch Bible, Emma,' he said.

Neither Grandma nor Emma said a word as Emma took the English Bible away and placed the Dutch one before Josias.

'I read from Psalm 43. I have been told that men condemned to death draw great strength from this.'

He leafed through the pages with fingers that had regained their strength, and he read in a strong voice:

> *Judge me, Oh God, and plead my cause against an ungodly nation: Oh deliver me from the deceitful and unjust man.*
> *For thou art the God of my strength: why dost thou cast me off? Why go I mourning because of the oppression of the enemy?*
> *Oh send out thy light and thy truth: let them lead me; let them bring me unto thy holy hill, and to thy tabernacles.*
> *Then will I go unto the altar of God, unto God my exceeding joy: yea, upon the harp will I praise thee, Oh God my God.*
> *Why art thou cast down, Oh my soul? And why art thou disquieted within me? Hope in God: for I shall yet praise him, who is the health of my countenance and my God.*

After the meal, when Josias went to his study, Emma took the English Bible to their bedroom and placed it in her bedside locker. She knew that from then on they would read the Dutch Bible during both their morning and their evening devotions.

Issy said nothing, but that night as she helped her mother get ready for bed, when the wispy hair was brushed and tucked in under the sleeping cap, the tablet swallowed and the doily straightened to her satisfaction over the glass of water at the bedside, and the paper-thin eyelids had started to droop, she could no longer keep it in:

'I told you years ago that no good would come of this marriage.'

The old woman's misty blue eyes opened. She gazed up at Issy thoughtfully. 'Perhaps our dear Lord knows best. These trials are sent to test us. Good night, my dear.'

4

But eventually even the war that so rent the land was over and past.

In the spring, life sprouted again from even the most desiccated of old pear stumps.

The burnt ruins of farmhouses were built up again; children were born.

New young life came to the pastorie in the Boland. The two little boys grew, squabbled, went to school, had their noses bloodied, made peace again. On rainy days the long passages of the pastorie echoed with their play; their roller skating, banging and pushing against the walls, until Aunt Issy was obliged to intervene. Victoria grew into a fragile, pretty brunette. Another four children were born. First a daughter, Leonora; and, seven years later, after two miscarriages, three boys in close succession: Philip, then Hendrik, named after his uncle Hennie, and Robert – a concession to Issy who had to take over the entire job of caring for him with the help of Nellie, a white nursegirl. Robert Moffat had been Issy's hero from her girlhood.

Grandma died, just like that, one night in her sleep. Emma took her death very badly. Weakened by her pregnancies, she turned increasingly inward.

Josias van Velde pondered over the things that had passed. The death of Braampie Nel still gnawed away at him.

Opposing injustice, specially if you are not directly affected, and standing up for the rights of others: was that not the highest offering – giving your life for your dear ones – that Christ called us to? he asked himself. Braampie's death was thus not a meaningless waste, but an honourable end. The outcome of the kind of deed without which a people could not survive. The sort of action that was like a new shoot, providing a growing point for the people's spiritual life. But if the opposition included rebellion against the legal authorities? He heard once again the voice thundering in parliament: You are tearing our people asunder. Where is God's instruction of peace?

Is such an act of opposition then, alas, not a node of spiritual growth, but, considered objectively and viewed in the light of the Word, really the seed of noxious division? Directly against God's commandment? As he had experienced in his own home.

Again the dichotomy, that eternal conflict. God or nation? Insoluble. War or peace? Loyalty to the regime or to justice? Verses in the Bible could be applied to arguments on either side.

Was it perhaps God's will that the stubborn little Afrikaner nation should be obliterated? He could not accept that. Lord, the people over the Groot River were his own flesh and blood. The question plagued him: what was he actually himself? Married into an English family; his children brought up half English. He was emotionally bound to his people. But who were his people? Not his father and mother, who, for the sake of personal profit, had grown ever more English since the war. So what made him, heart and soul, so much a part of the Boer people? What glued him to his people? Was it, above all, their Bible? No, not simply their Bible. Issy and Grandma were Bible-lovers. Their belief in the God of the covenant? This belief that they were the people of the covenant that stirred him so. His chosen people. Where did it come from? Where would it lead them?

He longed for Hennie. He could talk his heart out with Hennie.

But the news from Nyasaland was not good. At first the letters told of the excitement of a new country and the new work. The great joy when Jessie fell pregnant. But the lovely, spontaneous Jessie died in childbirth. And the child died two days later. Hennie was inconsolable.

In Pretoria, after long delays, a baby girl was given back to the widow Greylinck for care. The grandmother herself waited on the station for the train that brought the child and its nurse. She kissed the baby's forehead, two months older than she had been when she parted with her. In the buggy she insisted on carrying the baby on her own lap; she pressed her to her breast and felt the tears prick behind her eyelids as she smelled the old familiar baby smell in the fat little neck.

Although Daniel was still out on commando, she asked the dominee to come and christen the child in her Sunnyside house, using the names

Irma had given her: Agnes Valeria Greylinck. Her old friend and lawyer was the witness. After the departure of the nurse she cared for the child herself, engaging a nanny when the task became too much for her.

Her three sons survived the war. Piet's health was permanently damaged and his moods dark. Jannie avoided Pretoria, because, as the story went, he had laid down his arms to swear an oath of loyalty to the king long before peace was declared.

She placed the baby with pride in her dearest son Daniel's arms. He was deeply embittered by the fickleness of his wife and the defeat of the two republics.

'I can't envisage myself living under the British flag. I am making plans to pack up and leave, Ma.'

It was with a heavy heart that she took leave of her son and his baby daughter. She had done her best to put him off going, telling him of the dangers the journey and the rough new world held for the child, of infant deaths on trek and in the concentration camps. But he was determined.

With three other families he left by train for Lourenço Marques to wait there for a boat to British East Africa. A girl from the De Wet family who were fellow travellers cared for the baby. He recompensed her, and the money helped her family. They travelled by boat to Mombasa, and then again by train through a rough dusty region. They covered the last stretch to the highlands of Uasin Gishu by ox wagon. Land was being given there to Boer people. For further payment, the De Wet girl remained with Daniel as nursegirl until the little Agnes could walk properly and was able to manage alone with her Pa in the thatched mud hut.

5

Agnes and her father and a couple of Kikuyu workers lived on his holding on the Uasin Gishu plateau. In a four-roomed thatched house with a smooth-trodden yard, a hen house and pit privy a little way off. Two horses and a cow under the lean-to. Thin dogs with long waggy tails. Short stubbly grass round the yard, a few large thorn trees. Succulent shrubs that had survived the years of drought. When it rained the earth sprang to life, and the greenness stood waist-high.

At sundown when the work was done and the Kikuyus had gone back to their huts, she and her father would take the kitchen chairs and sit outside watching the sunset. They listened to the dusk, the night insects first, then, later, the far-off roar of lion and, later still, the eerie laughter of hyena. Only once it was completely dark, and the glow of his pipe the only visible light, did they go inside. He pulled the screen door to and lit the lamp. She brought the food from the outside kitchen area where the coals still glowed under the cooking pots.

They didn't talk much. But every night, once she had cleared the table, she had to bring the Bible and read some verses to him. They had nearly completed the second reading of the whole Bible.

He sat upright, his head slightly forward; as though he was looking under his eyelids at the Bible while she read. Her finger moved from word to word, the shadow of her finger moving along with it.

Agnes didn't know that he was looking at her, not at the Bible.

Then, one night after she had put the Bible back on the shelf, he said: 'Sit down a moment, my child.' Now she realised that the change neighbours had speculated about for so long was going to happen.

He knocked his pipe out, searching for words.

'It is not good alone here with me in the wilderness.'

'But you have educated me, Papa.'

She tried again. 'And Tante Let is teaching children on 64. You can take me there, Papa. You could have taken me there a long time ago.' She did not climb onto his lap but stood pressed up against him, between his knees, gazing at the candle flame on the table before them. He held her tight with his good arm and kissed her cheek. She pressed her head against him so that he could not move his face away. She felt his thick beard against her neck; it smelt of pipe oil. His arm pressed against her chest and a strange feeling stirred in her. There was also a strange tone in her father's voice.

'It's because I didn't want to let you go.'

'It isn't you, Papa. It's me. I don't want to go away.'

She said it as though she knew she was going to stay with him. She stood dead still, staring at the candle flame, feeling his arm round her. She was happy; she drew a deep breath, because when she released her breath, her chest rubbed against his arm and it made her even happier. She got a fright when he suddenly pushed her away. Was he angry with her?

But he was not angry. Moving his arm away from her chest, he placed both his large, calloused, sunburnt hands on her shoulders. Gently, but she still felt the weight on her. He pressed against her, just slightly, so she had to turn round and look him full in the face. What he saw in her eyes made him close his own eyes, made him shake his great head – a couple of times, back and forth. It was as though he could not well believe or understand something.

Then he looked at her again. 'Now listen to me carefully. Tante Let's lessons are not good enough. And there are many other things you must learn. You are nearly twelve. You must go back to the Transvaal.'

She said nothing.

'You can go with the Portuguese a little way into Tanganyika. Then Ojal will take you into Northern Rhodesia. You can catch the train in Kitwe.'

The Portuguese had finished bartering with them, their camp had already been in the yard for a week, and she knew it would not be long before they left. The fact that her father had already spoken to them forced her to believe him.

She started to cry. 'What will become of you, Papa?'

'I'll manage.' He took his hands from her shoulders, fiddled with his pipe. Through her tears, she wanted to cup her hands round his pipe as she had often done, but he pushed her hands away.

'I am sending my best boys with Ojal to look after you. It's a good thing that you can shoot. You'll go to your Uncle Piet in Middelburg. He and Naomi are childless, so they'll be pleased to have you.'

'You must come too, Papa.'

'They'll rob me blind if I stay away from here for any time. I don't care for the Transvaal in any case. Ojal will take care of you.'

She said nothing. She had stopped crying. What did it help? Ojal was his best worker. If he wanted to send Ojal, nothing she could say would make him change his plans.

'You must get to some women. You can't stay here alone with me.'

She kept aloof from the two Portuguese traders. They rode on donkeys, but both of them were overweight and the donkeys had a hard time of it. Their progress was slow, the rests were frequent. The four bearers that her father had sent along kept up easily. Two carried the litter in which she lay, two trotted behind, and then they changed over, in midstride. Another two carried her little tent and a couple of cooking pots, a sack of maize meal, a supply of coffee and sugar, and the few clothes which her father had sent with her.

She lay uncomfortably. She'd begged her father to let her ride on a donkey too, but he wouldn't allow it. The bearers were fit and as nimble as the donkeys, jumping from rock to rock so quickly on the steep parts that sometimes she feared she would be tossed out of the litter. Sometimes, when they were moving across a plain and the bearers jogged steadily, she would doze off.

On one occasion she slept so soundly that she looked around her, frightened and confused, when she awoke. It was dusk: her father would be sitting outside now, drinking coffee and smoking his pipe. He would gaze into the gathering dusk, listening for the hyenas. She wept silently. She could see the food on his plate, the meat he cut up with his pocket knife, the stiff maize porridge he rolled between his fingers before biting into it; she could smell the coffee in his mug. She sobbed out loud then, not caring whether they heard her or not.

The Portuguese in front yelled: '*Chegamos!*'

She heard the donkeys stumbling on the rocky slope as they were pulled sideways; someone was cursing the pack donkeys. Then they were unloaded.

The front bearer let the litter poles slide off his shoulders and placed them on the ground on either side of his feet. She slipped out. Her legs were numb, and she felt nauseous as she stood upright. Her head spun and her stomach did too.

The two Portuguese – as her father had said, more to convince himself than for her benefit – were middle-aged and had daughters of their own. They would not be impatient with her. In fact, they tried to be friendly towards her. She was sweating and grimy, and she knew they could see the tracks her tears had left on her cheeks.

'*Agua*,' said the one to his servant.

He and his partner had come seeking ivory tusks from the farmers. They travelled about wherever there were farmer's dwellings on the Uasin Gishu plateau, making overnight camps as they went.

'Come, come: *agua*.' The servant was afraid to go into the darkness of the bush so close to the ruins where the spring was to be found. The Portuguese took his gun and went with him, thrusting the branches to one side. The other one scolded the bearers who should have been collecting firewood. The cook knelt on the ground, laying a fire with twigs and leaves, then bigger branches and then stumps of wood. She made out from what her bearers said to one another that they were afraid of this place. She had a limited knowledge of their language.

'*Vem ca*, come here, child,' the Portuguese beckoned to her, and she came a little closer. The snapping flames that leapt ever higher made her feel less forlorn. Ojal and one of the other bearers had erected her tent a little to one side. He swept the ground inside her tent with a leafy branch, removed a few rocks, and brought in her baggage. The older Portuguese returned with a tarpaulin bulging with water. He had a jug brought out of his pack and poured washing water into it for her. He tried to put her mind at rest: '*Bom, muiyo bom lavar,*' and he mimed washing his face. She carried the jug of water to her tent. She felt better once she had washed.

It was now pitch dark. In the flickering of the great fire, she saw the ruins clearly one minute and then, the next, they would melt into the gloom again. If a piece of wood caught alight and the flames flared up, she could see every single packed stone, even the grain in the bark of the camel thorn tree close by, and the shadows the leaves cast on the tree trunk as the wind stirred them. Then they were gone again. She looked carefully at the ruins. The walls were built in a strange way, like a hive: round. She could swear there was something lurking there. She sat with her coffee mug in her hand, drinking slowly to make it last.

The cook scraped the coals to one side. He stirred meal into the saucepan of water to make pot bread. A buck had been shot along the way, and he began to slice strips of the meat.

'*Um pingo de vinho.*' The Portuguese offered her a sip of wine. He rubbed over his stomach. '*Muito bom.*' But she shook her head. The way the one Portuguese was sitting on his log, bent forward, his dark beard reddish in the firelight, reminded her of her father. She didn't want to think about her father now, otherwise next thing she'd be crying again. She thought: he sent me away from him.

The Portuguese threw the great wicker-covered demijohn of wine over his shoulder and filled his mug.

The baggage had been unloaded from the donkeys, including the elephant tusks and the rhino horns which they had bartered for. The donkeys were tethered close to the fire.

The two Portuguese talked to the bearers animatedly with much hand gesturing.

'*Nada, nada,*' they said. The one explained to Agnes: 'Lion no like this part. Spooks. Lion feel it. Kaffirs scare, no need.'

Then he laughed out loud, took another great gulp of wine, and wiped his mouth on his sleeve.

She had already heard about haunted ruins in the bush and seen signs of the strange round walls, also the slave pits where slaves were packed at night during their marches down to the coast. But here? The locals didn't build this way, and a trek boer wouldn't either.

It was her last night with the two Portuguese and their party. From here they were travelling south-east to the sea, and she and her carriers were going south, inland.

As her father had instructed, two of her bearers slept at the entrance to her tent every night, taking turns to do so.

She dreamed.

She dreamed of the mother who had died shortly after her birth. She saw her with a long white dress and wings, like the angels at the sepulchre of the Lord. Her mother flapped her wings gently backwards and forwards as though she was trying to cool herself.

The night was hot and she awoke. The mosquito net was pulled awry around her. She jerked it off the stand and threw it in a heap on the ground. Then she couldn't help it: she thought of her father and the tears flowed again. She needed to pee so she just did it right there in the tent in a little hole that she dug. When the wet soil started to cave in, she pushed at it with her shoe. She peed and she wept. Then she raised the tent flap a tiny bit.

The two Kikuyus were fast asleep in front of the tent. Everything was very quiet now. The Portuguese and their servants slept a little way off. No, there was Ojal, still stirring at the fire; he threw on more wood. The camp was lit up and once again she could see the strange packed stones of the old ruined wall. She listened to the night sounds: the hooting of an owl, veld noises, but no lions or hyena. Perhaps the lions were indeed afraid of the ruin.

The stars were bright. She thought of her mother who was up there somewhere beyond the stars; and she missed her even though she had never known her. She longed for her father. Sniffing back her last sobs, she lay down again. But she could not sleep. Papa! Papa! she called, her face pressed into her pillow.

They packed very early. The Portuguese were anxious to be on their way. They instructed the Kikuyus to look after the girl carefully. They shook hands with her; if there had been anything suitable, they would have given it to her as a present. They just gestured to the laden donkeys and shrugged.

She and the six Kikuyu travelled on. They traversed savannah. Sometimes the grass stood as tall as a man, then the one resting bearer had to go ahead with a panga to make a path, a path so narrow that the grass brushed against her litter. For something to do, she grabbed at it but the blades of grass were so sharp that they left bloody stripes. The cuts got dirt in them and began to fester. At night she tried to clean the wounds with boiled water, and for a few days she felt sick, but then it passed over.

She was accustomed to being on her own and without conversation, so that did not bother her. Sometimes one of the resting bearers would trot beside the litter pointing out game in the distance to her. Once they even saw a herd of elephant. Ojal, the most trustworthy according to her father, carried a gun over his shoulder. He shot for the pot. She could shoot too, but there was only one gun.

The fire burned all night in the little camps they set up.

She had grown accustomed to the litter, but it was boring. She wasn't crying so much any more either. Some days they made little progress. The thorn scrub was rank, and sometimes the footpath was overgrown. The bearers set her litter down and all hands had to help hack the path open again, the bearers arguing amongst themselves, squabbling.

She sat waiting under a thorn tree or a mopani on a small rise amongst the rocks. She was glad of the chance to sit and look about. She could watch the small animals and insects that she couldn't see from the litter. She sat like that for a long time, her knees pulled up under her chin. A field mouse crept out from the scrub and then scurried away, but she thought the mouse knew about her. She watched a dung beetle up on his back legs, pushing against his load, then he landed on his back when a stone got in the way and upset his balance. She picked up a stick to help him, but before she could do that a large black shadow started circling over the grass in wide silent circles. She looked up to see an eagle coming closer in the white-hot sky. Creep away, my little mouse, creep away; hide, my rock rabbit, my lizards, everything that shelters in the long grass and the bushes. If you put out so much as a snout, it'll all be over for you. She felt something bite her, then she slapped the ants swarming on her legs and stamped her feet. Tears rolled down her cheeks as she slapped and scratched and then ran to where the bearers were waiting.

Other days she walked a little way. In spite of the bonnet she wore she could feel the sun getting to her, and at night her face would burn. She knew her skin was fair; if she'd had a mirror, she'd have seen how the freckles she hated almost overlapped, there were so many of them. Her hair was filthy, and she no longer loosened her braid every night.

The rainy season was on the way; that was why her father had been in such a hurry, she now realised. The first rain broke over them. She stayed in her tent for a whole day listening to the bearers arguing about whether they should push on or not. They set off again, sometimes foundering up to their knees in the mud that filled every hollow. She and the litter were wet through, and she felt as though she was being dragged through brown sludge. There were no animals to be seen – it was weeks since they'd eaten meat. Just slivers of biltong and the pot-bread that was cooked over wet steaming logs.

Her father had taught her: in the rainy season you must boil the water before you drink it. She drank cold bitter coffee. We must keep the sugar for barter, said Ojal. She didn't mind drinking bitter coffee. In the evening she did not sit beside the fire, but went to her tent when it got dark and waited for her food under the mosquito net. She knew about mosquito bites.

The first rains passed and the earth dried out again. The bearers talked of a Nyanza with settlements beside a lake, they wanted to get to some people to barter for food, cassava, manioc, salt, oil. It's on our way, said one bearer, there are no people on the path we're taking now, we will die here.

The bushveld gave way to ranker vegetation growing closer together. The plants had great fat leaves, the trees grew taller. Sometimes during the day it seemed to her that they were walking in darkness because the trees closed over them like a roof. But they covered ground faster because the road had already been hacked open. Sometimes, where the foliage hung low and the bearers had to bow their heads to push through them, the collected moisture splattered onto her. It was so hot that her clothes were dry again in no time. Now they encountered more black people on small paths that led into the forest. The bearers chatted excitedly.

What were they to do with her?

She must come with us, said Ojal.

They had her climb out of the litter. More and more huts, more and more bare-breasted women coming from the bush with babies on their hips, staring at them, trying to make conversation with the bearers.

They came to a clearing where a market was being held, but she was more interested in the stretch of water she could make out through the trees. Look, she said to the bearers. They just nodded. So they didn't know the name of the lake.

The bustle of the market made her nervous after the weeks of solitude. Everyone was talking or calling out, children darted about and a pig was squealing. There was a parrot and other birds in cages.

Fowls with their legs tied together struggled until they wore themselves out, their combs no longer thrashing around in the sand. The women who were selling the goods sat with their legs stretched out in front of them, their hands continuously arranging and rearranging the goods they had displayed in front of them on woven mats. Piles of what looked like sweet potatoes, mounds of chillies, dried fish, clay pots with beer or what looked to her like sour milk, stacks of cassava tied into bundles with plaited cords. Her bearers bartered for these. Ojal told her in sign language: we grind the cassava fine to make bread.

The people at the market didn't pay her much attention until one woman got to her feet and took her by the hand. At first she was reluctant to go with her, but Ojal urged her on. She was led by the hand to a group of women and children beyond the circle of traders. There, the woman gestured and the other women pushed forward a child who was just as white as Agnes, even whiter because his eyebrows and lashes were white and the tight curls on his head were white, and his skin almost transparent, with large brown marks like her freckles. But his lips were full and covered with blisters which were breaking so blood trickled from them. His eyes were also different from ordinary eyes, but she knew from his curly hair and his lips that he was a local. She had never seen anyone like this before and she was startled. But the women couldn't stop looking at him and then at her. They were not unfriendly. The one woman pressed a red fruit into her hand, another a little bundle of dried fish.

They pushed her back to Ojal.

They talked loudly and excitedly among themselves.

We must be on our way, Ojal said to the other bearers.

They loaded her in the litter, and the bearers swung the baggage up onto their heads and set off at a trot. She bit into the red fruit, but it was almost all pip with a rank flavour. She tore a piece off one of the dried fish with her teeth, but it was so salty that she spat it out again. She was thirsty all the time.

At last they reached a farm, but the farmer was out hunting and his wife was dead, according to the workers. They took a break there and bartered for mealies and a pumpkin. There was also an increasing number of local villages. The women were better dressed, and most of them wore copper ankle-rings. She remembered her pa referring to the Copper Belt. In the distance she saw a couple of brick houses.

Even before they saw the little town of Kitwe they heard the racket of shunting and the blast of steam from an engine. The bearers put her litter down. 'Is this the place?' Ojal asked her. She didn't know. He tried to talk to the other black people but their language was completely different; they pointed to the road that led to the station.

The bearers wanted to pick her up again, but she shook her head.

There were white people walking in the streets. She climbed the steps to the station building; she had money for a ticket to Middelburg in the Transvaal where she was to stay with her Oom Piet so she could go to school. She had to speak English to the man in the black jacket who stood behind the copper railing. It was difficult for her. He leaned forward to assess her age; only her head showed above the counter. Eventually she realised that it made a difference to the cost of a ticket if she was older than twelve. She shook her head. No, eleven.

'Now what the hell do I do with you? The train only leaves tomorrow. It's best you go to the waiting-room. Have a wash.'

'You please give me paper and pencil?' she stammered. She'd promised her father she'd send a letter back with Ojal.

He gave it to her. She wrote in careful capital letters. A group of black people had gathered round her bearers, and they looked at her inquisitively as though she was something strange. She gave the letter to Ojal. Not only Ojal, but the other Kikuyus too looked as though they were sorry to leave her behind. She was also sorry, she'd known them almost all her life.

In the waiting room she sat bolt upright with her few possessions beside her. After a long time she heard horses' hooves. A buggy pulled up at the station. It was the stationmaster's wife, who had come to fetch her to take her home so she could spend the night with them. She bathed and tried to rinse her clothes out and put on clean clothes. She loosened her hair and washed it and braided it again, still damp. The stationmaster's wife spoke English to her, and that made her shy. But she was grateful for the food she received for the journey. The woman accompanied her to the station the next morning. The coaches for Europeans were empty. The carriages the black people climbed into were crowded.

'Only one Boer waif. And the Lord alone knows how she got here,' the stationmaster told the conductor.

The whole day, she sat at the window in the compartment staring out. Other passengers came and went, trying a little conversation, and then letting it pass. Some offered her food, which she took and ate. They bundled up the leftover bread crusts and chicken bones, and threw them out to the black children who ran along beside the railway line. They showed her where to find the lavatory in the turn of the corridor.

At first she was afraid to walk down the swaying passage, but eventually she grew accustomed to that too.

After three days on the train she was accustomed to the jerk on the rails, the gentle sideways rocking when she lay on the bunk under her own blanket. She kept her folded hands under her head because the thick dark green roll that passed for a pillow on the bunk was too hard and high.

She had to get off at Mafeking. She lay awake most of the night, afraid that she would miss the stop. She had a letter from her pa to the stationmaster; he would put her on the correct train for Middelburg. She sat dozing in the waiting room until he came to call her.

Back on the train she fell into an exhausted sleep. She woke once when the train jerked and then slowed down, and she saw a signboard that said Pretoria in the dim lamplight. Then they came to a halt. She heard people walking and talking, and doors opening and banging shut again, but before the train moved on, she had fallen asleep once more.

The conductor woke her at Middelburg. It was morning. There was no one else in the compartments, they had all disembarked at other stations.

She gave the stationmaster the last of her letters. Her father had written to her uncle via seamail to let him know she was on the way, but he had warned her that it would probably take longer to reach him than she would. 'So take this letter to the stationmaster. He can let Oom Piet know.'

The stationmaster sent a messenger with a note that he wrote himself. She waited until she heard a woman talking to the stationmaster and then accompanying him to the waiting room. She didn't know the woman, but she came up to her and put her hand behind her head where the braid began and pressed her head against her body. 'Oh, my poor child. Still so small and you've travelled so far.' She was suffocating and wriggled free.

It seemed to her that the woman was talking for the benefit of the stationmaster. She was large, with a swarthy complexion and large dark eyes. Her small hat had a scarf round it with dots embroidered on it. Agnes had never seen anything like that in her life. The woman carried a handbag under her arm, and her dress went down to the floor. The one arm gripped the handbag, the other arm was still fiddling behind Agnes's neck. The grip of the hand was strong, and she couldn't free herself. 'Just like that: out of the blue. A short note: your brother Daniel's daughter is at the station.' She looked up at the stationmaster. 'You can imagine how we felt. Taken completely by surprise.'

The train had left again a long while back, the station was deserted. The woman talked on. 'I said to Piet: I dreamt that dream again last night. I knew something was coming today, and it has come in with the train.'

She and the stationmaster laughed together. He showed the woman the letter from her pa. He read out the date. 'My word,' he said. 'The child has been on the road for nearly three months.'

'She must be dead tired. Come, dear,' said the woman. 'It isn't far to walk.'

'I'll get my boy to carry her bag,' said the stationmaster.

Oom Piet, her father's own brother, hadn't come to meet her.

'Where is Oom Piet?' she asked.

'Oh, so you do have a tongue. He's at home, the war destroyed his health,' said the woman. 'He's miserable.' She whispered as though she was afraid that the black youth with the suitcase and blanket who walked ahead would hear.

'The kidneys ... he has stones, but the doctor in Pretoria says he will pass them, just like that, in the chamber pot. Now he can't even go outside to the privy, he has to do everything in the chamber pot.'

Oom Piet was waiting at the front gate. When he saw them coming, he opened it and stepped out, putting his arms round her. It was just like being with her own father, but he smelled of medicine, and he coughed, and he walked crookedly with his hands on his back over his kidneys. He was not her own father. She tried not to cry, but because he wasn't her own father, she couldn't help it.

'Weep, my child,' he said, stroking her head. 'Weep as much as you will. We live in a time of despair in the land of misery.'

'Oh, come on now, Piet,' said the woman. 'Open up and let's go inside. The girl has put the porridge on and I'll fry some eggs. You can see the child is perishing from hunger.'

Later she explained to Agnes: 'It's since the war that he's been so depressed.' They had eaten and the woman – 'my name is Tante Naomi, dear' – made up a bed for her. 'It's lucky that we have this room. There, tuck that sheet in, didn't your pa teach you anything?' She spread the blanket on top, plumped up the pillows. 'He's also in a lot of pain. I don't always know whether he still knows what pain is. If the pain keeps up the whole time, eventually you don't really even know it. If he could only pass the stones. It could happen any day.'

She threw a crocheted blanket over the bed. Then she unpacked the suitcase and looked at the contents. 'I will get my niece in to do some needlework for us. A couple of dresses for school. Meantime we'll hang these old things in the wardrobe, and put those in the chest of drawers. Shame. It's a good thing that you have come to stay with us. I think you take after your pa, yes, the eyes and the nose, but that fair hair, where does that come from? You will be company for us, dear. We have not been blessed with issue. Have a rest now, sleep until lunch time.'

She took off her shoes and lay on the bed under the crocheted blanket with its pretty patterns. But before she closed her eyes, while Tante Naomi was still busy at the wardrobe, she asked:

'Tante Naomi, what does waif mean?'

Tante Naomi's English was not up to explaining. She called Oom Piet.

Oom Piet thought it over, cleared his throat and said: 'It just means a small child, sweetheart.'

'And a Boer waif, Uncle Piet?'

'I might have guessed,' Tante Naomi cut in. 'It's those English who have such a low opinion of us. It's a Boer throwaway child, and that's where she heard it: among the English.'

'You're too harsh, my dear,' said Oom Piet.

He drew Agnes close. 'A waif is just a child who ended up on the wrong track. Who was a bit lost, but is now safe again. Does that explain it, sweetheart?'

'Yes, Oom Piet.'

She woke at intervals through the night, and every time she heard a movement in the room next door, she pressed her ear to the wall to see if she could hear the clank of kidney-stones in the chamber pot. But all she could make out in the small hours was a trickling sound in the pot and that embarrassed her, so she went back to bed.

Her grandmother's house in Pretoria was a wonderful place for Agnes. She clung to Oom Piet's hand – he'd come to visit the doctor. The iron gate was heavy with lots of curly patterns, and it scraped over the cement, making a white mark in it. They walked under two tall palms and between shrubs to the long shallow steps up to the veranda, with a little pillar on either side and a fish on each pillar. And the red and white tiles on the veranda and the ferns in the niches beside the huge front door and the coloured glass windows! And the dark passage that was so cool and where her shoes made such a racket that Tante Naomi told her to shush! And the sitting room where Ouma Greylinck sat in the bay window enjoying the afternoon sun with the colours of the panes of glass falling on her: red patches over her nose and a strip of green light over her eyes and purple on the fingers that laid her crochet work aside as she said: 'Oh, my darling child, my heart is overflowing.'

She was thrust forward by Tante Naomi; the old woman's arms were round her and she was pressed against her. She smelt powder and lavender and started in fright when a parrot beside the chair said something in English. She looked at the parrot, but her grandmother said: 'No, look at me, child, let me see you.' The ouma wiped her eyes with her lace-edged handkerchief. 'So this is Irma's child. These hands brought her into the world.' She showed Tante Naomi and Oom Piet the hands as though they had never seen them before. 'These hands ... these hands ... and now I can embrace her once more.' She kissed Agnes's face all over, so her cheeks and her forehead and even her eyes were wet, but she couldn't wipe the wetness of the kisses away because the ouma held her arms tight to her sides. Then she sneezed and the old woman said: shame. Just as Tante Naomi had said: shame. Her grandmother gave Agnes her own handkerchief to wipe away what she'd sneezed out.

Papa, Agnes thought. I want to go back to Papa. But she grew accustomed to the house and the ferns and pot plants and the bird and the cakes she could eat as much as she liked, and the bell which the ouma just rang and a servant girl came in a dress just like hers but in dark blue floral with a long apron, to bring cakes or glasses of fruit juice or teacups on a tray.

Her grandmother wasn't much bothered about Tante Naomi; she felt sorry for Oom Piet; but she only loved, really loved, Papa. Daniel, she kept on saying, my wonderful son.

Agnes lived with Oom Piet and Tante Naomi, but she felt more at home with her grandmother.

Later, when she was older, she went to visit her grandmother on her own, or she spent the school holidays there, and stayed there while Oom Piet had the operation that left him so weak.

She liked the cool house and shady garden, and even began to know what to say and how to behave in order to get her grandmother to do what she herself wanted to. She pinned the lace fichu round her grandmother's shoulders: 'This is the new fashion, Ouma, come, let's fasten it a little higher.' She brushed the ouma's hair and teased it up over the places where it was thinning. She emptied out the old woman's drawers and tidied everything away again, and she was always rewarded with a little something that had taken her fancy. 'How did I get by all these years without you, my darling?' said her grandmother. She confessed guiltily: 'I seldom see your Oom Jan's children and I don't have much time for them.' She added plaintively: 'There are so many of them I can't possibly remember all their birthdays. And Lettie never writes. My poor Jan. Not that I have anything against Lettie. It's just her family: they all hang round her neck. Jan too, had to start again from scratch after the war.'

Agnes was glad that the old woman didn't like the other grandchildren very much, that she was the favourite grandchild.

Agnes often heard the stories of how the farms were burnt to the ground in the war, how Piet, the ouma's first-born, was left with kidney problems, and Jan with his nerves shattered. She encouraged her grandmother to tell the stories because her father had spoken so little about it all. Not even about why he had moved to British East Africa. Her grandmother never referred to Agnes's angel mother. Agnes tried to question her, but she stopped when she saw she was distressing the old woman.

'You were born in this house, my dearest,' said the stout old creature time after time. 'These old hands drew you from your mother's womb in that back room. This is your home. At any hour of day or night you must always feel: I can step over the threshold, this is my home.'

Then her grandmother sighed and the plump arms sank down wearily – they had been stretched wide to include the house and the passage and the drawing room and the back rooms and the veranda and the garden. The stiffening body shifted a few times in the chair; the kindly face on that pile of chins which moved as she spoke, gazed with deep satisfaction at her possessions.

She was a meticulous old soul. No matter whether it was morning or afternoon, she always dressed as though she expected visitors, even though no one knocked at the heavy front door.

'One dresses for oneself, darling, not for others,' she told her granddaughter.

Agnes thought her clothes were exquisite: dresses with frills that stood up round the neck; gowns with necklines cut down to the waist in a deep V that was filled in with row upon row of fine lace – a jabot as she called it – that lay flat on the breastbone, with a long string of pink-sheened pearls. Pinned high above her left breast was a tiny silver container that looked like a vase, and if you removed the stopper, the fragrance of 'something from the Holy land' tickled your nose. Agnes touched it so many times that eventually her grandmother had to give in: 'Very well, unpin it and fasten it to your dress, just for a minute.' She kept an eye on Agnes while the girl checked in the mirror to see how it looked on her dress, then she said firmly: 'That's enough, take it off now.'

'Where did you get it, Ouma?' asked Agnes, stroking the bottle.

'Oh, just a friend.' Even at her age she could smile very coyly. 'From an old, old friend. Your ouma had many admirers in her time. And they brought me lots of gifts from all over the world.'

'Tell me about them, Ouma. Tell me about them.'

But she never spoke about Agnes's deceased mother.

She spoke of the days before the war, of the musical soirees she held in her drawing room. Agnes, a high school girl now, conjured up alluring visions of ladies on the arms of gentlemen, a woman bending like a lily over her cello, her ouma's beringed fingers flying over the keyboard.

'Ouma, we can hold the soirees again, can't we?'

The grand piano still stood in the drawing room, a shawl thrown over it, the fringed corners hanging almost to the floor. She was not allowed to touch the porcelain vase on top. She stroked the shiny black surface of the piano with her fingertips.

'Ouma, can I also take music lessons when I am at College?'

She talked less and less about Uasin Gishu and her father.

He only came once to see her and his brothers and mother. He travelled by boat to Lourenço Marques, and from there by train to the Transvaal. He got off the train at Middelburg early one morning. She stood on the platform waiting with Tante Naomi and Oom Piet. She was cold and her mouth trembled. And when he climbed down and looked around him, before the train steamed off again, he didn't see her at first. He didn't recognise her in the different style of dress, she thought. But neither could she run to him and fling her arms round him as she had so often imagined, or press her head against his chest. Her face felt stiff; her mouth no longer trembled but also felt stiff and pulled into a crease; her throat was thick as though she was going to choke. She didn't think she would be able to talk.

He greeted Tante Naomi and Oom Piet first, and then he said: 'So this is Agnes.' Who else did he think it was? For a moment she hated him. Why did you send me away? her eyes asked him. But he did not look at her for long.

It wasn't only her. He was different too. His clothes were different, he smelt different. When he took her shoulders and bent to kiss her there was a sharp smell on his breath which she didn't recognise. Not the smell of his pipe, something different.

'The stink of coolie,' Naomi told Piet that night. 'So there's some truth in the rumour that he's living with a coolie slut in British-East.'

They didn't think she could hear them, but she heard. She brought in the food, watching him all the time. His face was darker, more sun-tanned than before. But that wasn't what was different, it was his bearing. It was as though his head sat uneasily on his shoulders, and moved uncomfortably backwards and forwards as he ate, like a bird's head. That wasn't the way she remembered him. He was nervous, and his eyes seemed to avoid hers.

'Yes, I like school, Papa. Yes, I am doing my best. Oom Piet and Tante Naomi are kind to me,' she answered the few questions he asked her.

He sent me away from him, she thought, it isn't my fault that we feel like strangers to each other now. He was just as awkward with her as she with him. He didn't insist that she go back with him. He didn't even ask her to come on holiday with him. Just the two of them. As it used to be.

He had come by boat and then by train. Why hadn't he allowed her to travel that way back then? Had he wanted her to perish, alone with the black people in Africa?

He went to visit his mother in Pretoria and his brother Jan. Agnes and her uncle and aunt went to Pretoria to be with him for the last few days. He never ever said the two of them should go for a little walk together. He never ever put his arms round her and held her close as he'd done before she left. Papa, Papa, she longed to cry, why don't you like me any more?

She was glad the evening he left by train. But when she saw that sunburnt hand with the red-brown hair lying so close to her on the compartment windowsill, just before the train pulled out of Pretoria station, she suddenly thought: he is leaving, and she couldn't bear it any longer and she started to cry and stuttered: 'Papa!' and darted forward to snatch his hand and press it to her cheek. Tante Naomi tried to pull her back, because clouds of steam were gushing out from under the train and the carriage was beginning to jerk forward. The whistle blew and the steam burnt her, but she hung onto his hand and was dragged along with the carriage. Then she had to let go. Her eyes were wet with tears and her arm almost dislocated as Tante Naomi dragged her back.

'There, there, child. You're only making it harder for your pa. Come, he left a present for you. Dry your eyes. There, there, come on now.' She opened the parcel on their way home in the cab. It was a brooch with green stones.

Tante Naomi put her arm round Agnes's shoulders. 'And do you know what he said? He said I must tell you the stones are as green as your eyes.'

Agnes was in her seventeenth year. A pretty girl, pale-complexioned with a tendency to develop freckles in the sun; silvery-blonde hair, slim as a willow wand. Sometimes the green eyes looked mistrustful, with something like the expression in her pa's eyes during his first and only visit. But she was affectionate to her grandmother because she was sure of her love and had no reason to suspect that the old woman would ever feel any differently towards her.

It was the middle of 1918. She was in the first year of her teacher training at the Normal College at Heidelberg. During weekends, short breaks and even longer holidays, she went to her grandmother. Not only because it was closer than Middelburg, and members of staff chaperoned groups of girls on the train journey as far as Pretoria, but also because she enjoyed the status that her grandmother's household gave her.

At Middelburg she was poor old sickly Piet's niece. In Pretoria she was the widow Greylinck's favourite granddaughter. A considerable difference.

This weekend she was eager to get to the Sunnyside house as early as possible. It was her grandmother's eightieth birthday. The house guests were to include not only Oom Piet and Tante Naomi, but also Oom Jan and Tant Lettie and a few of their children – heaven only knew how many. She and her grandmother had planned every detail of the weekend meticulously. She felt as though she were the co-hostess. Specially when her grandmother squeezed her fingers with that dear wrinkled old hand and said: 'You'd better come and sleep in my room, dear. That will leave your room for Piet and his family, and the guest room for Jan's family.'

She'd never ever spent the night in her grandmother's room before. She wouldn't be able to sleep a wink, for staring at the walls and ceiling, breathing in the strange feeling of far-off lands and old romances. There were two huge framed pictures: one showed a girl torn from her mother's arms and dragged down into a dark hole in the earth by a monstrous man, and the girl in the second one sat on the globe mournfully clasping a cross. There were fringed silk panels against the walls, and an oil lamp with a shade made of what looked like gilt-edged flower petals.

And she, Agnes, was going to sleep there with her grandmother!

Tant Lettie was immediately put out. 'If my daughters hadn't gone down with the measles and had come with us, where would they have slept? Kleinjan and Fanie have to go to the outside room which stinks of horse fodder. But only the best is good enough for the little princess.'

Tant Lettie's rancour afforded Agnes enormous pleasure.

Oom Jan bore a grudge against his mother. Jan's Boer fighting spirit had been rekindled at General de la Rey's meeting at Treurfontein, the farm only a few miles from his own where the Rebellion was hatched. In response to the general's call to arms he waved his hat and shouted: 'I'm your man!' It was August 1914, the wind blew chill and the veld was dry and desolate, but he was fired up. And when the general was so treacherously shot, Jan became De Wet's man. He would have gone to German South West with Maritz if his mother had only parted with the cash. He thought bitterly that he would be a hero of the Rebellion if his mother had only put her miserly hand in her pocket. And conveniently, he forgot about Lettie's impoverished people who'd lost their land after the pathetic rebellion and now hung about on his farm, not much better than squatters. One had principles, proclaimed the pounding of his Boer heart. Even if the Germans were suffering such appalling losses at the moment. And even though the English seemed once again to have got the Lord over onto their side.

He made sure there was brandy in the house. At his mother's expense.

'Ouboet,' he said to Piet, 'it's tragic to see you in such bad shape.'

'It's the Lord's will,' said Piet whose Sunday suit hung on his wasted frame as though on a skeleton – in spite of the fact that Naomi had tried to take it in. Lettie's complaints are absurd, thought Piet, her sons aren't accommodated any better at home on their farm.

The celebration was on Saturday afternoon. Neighbours, friends, family members packed the veranda, the hallway and the dining room where plates of milktart, Jan Smuts/Hertzog cakes, apple pie, sandwich cakes, queen cakes, jam tarts, apricot flans and koeksisters were crowded round an enormous iced fruit cake on which the words *Geluk met Uw Verjaarsdag* had been worked in pink sugar, with generous flourishes from which little green leaves and yellow blossoms sprouted. And below the words a giant figure eight and a zero. Two neighbours' wives poured tea at a serving table. Behind his mother's back, Jan poured brandy for the men on the veranda.

Agnes held her slim body still slimmer as she moved through the guests, greeting one here, offering something there. Her colour was high and she was very evidently concerned for her grandmother in the armchair in the bay window. Even Agnes felt slightly claustrophobic in the crowded sitting room. It seemed to her that the birds and the small furry creatures on the women's hats wanted to come to life.

The feathers were fluffed up, the fur bristled and the beaks and snouts opened, ready to peck and nip and gnaw. As the monumental women under the great hats bent over the cakes and tarts, side plates in one hand and knives in the other, to pierce and cut so the pastry crumbled and the filling poured out, to be scooped onto plates, the beaks and the snouts were ready to take a bite of the confectionery. Only to be pushed back upright again, snapping at the air. Or snapping at her, she felt. On the hats without animals, feathers nodded; the fully pleated organza or silk of the toques that were coming into fashion were repulsively, effusively sensual.

Agnes suddenly felt threatened in these familiar rooms on this festive afternoon. She had no idea why.

Why were the rooms, the furnishing, suddenly dangerous? Why did she want to flee, the Agnes-waif who had found such a comfortable haven here?

The neighbour's wife had hold of the carving knife; the sinews on her arms knotted as she forced the tip into the hard white icing. She took her right wrist in her left hand and thrust the blade downwards until the icing gave way and the blade cut down into the soft, dark fruit cake. The yellow almond paste lay like a thin protection between the moist cake and the crumbled icing on the plate.

'There,' said the neighbour's wife to Agnes, for whom she didn't care much. 'The first piece of birthday cake for your grandmother. There, take it.'

And it was as Agnes bent solicitously over the old woman to take the cup from her lap and put the plate of cake in its place, that she heard the piercing voice: 'It is such a privilege to be here this afternoon, madam. You don't know me. I'm from the Cape Colony – visiting an old friend of yours up here. And when I heard your name I knew I had to come along, because there's something I must tell you.'

Agnes didn't straighten up. Her back was turned towards the voice.

The guests encircling the old lady listened, cake forks halfway to their mouths; birds with beaks ready to peck, listened; feathers swaying on a slightly turned head, listened.

The voice continued: 'Thanks to the good Lord, I escaped from Europe just before the war. I was so nearly trapped on the Continent! But it is another extraordinary coincidence that I want to tell you about. In Paris I put up at a marvellous little hotel – the name had been given to me in London – and, guess what? The woman at reception – I think she was the manageress, if not the owner – anyway, she told me her name was Irma Greylinck. It might not mean anything, I know: there could be many Irma Greylincks …' She drew a circle in the air, still holding her little fork, but fortunately there was no cake on it. 'But what really caught my attention, was hearing your granddaughter's name this afternoon: Agnes Valeria Greylinck. Exactly the same name as the attractive little brunette who assisted her mother in the Paris hotel. Isn't that fascinating? Thank you,' she said to the woman who took her teacup to refill.

'Fancy that? Out of the blue!'

'My word, we are hearing things here this afternoon …'

'Imagine!'

The words spun round Agnes's head. It was as though the animals and the birds and the feathers on the women's hats around her grandmother had come to life again, to peck, to nip, to gnaw. She straightened up and pushed her way through to the kitchen, where she asked one of the servants for a glass of water. She leaned against the table, holding her temples. 'My head is spinning,' she told the servant. 'It's the crowd of people.'

'I don't know how the madam can bear it,' said the servant. She helped Agnes to a chair. Agnes gulped the water. But she knew she had to return, back into the fray. The story was not all told yet, warned a completely new instinct that had arisen in her. She edged her way through the guests and down the passage. The woman from the Colony had come to deposit her empty tea cup in the dining room. Agnes wanted to keep an eye on her but she also wanted to go to her grandmother. But the people were still packed around the old woman. She nodded to this one, to that one, pressed a hand, received yet another gift on a lap already piled with packages. Later, she would talk to her grandmother. Later.

The old friend – was she really a friend? – who brought the guest from the Colony had already taken her leave. She and her companion moved down the passage to the veranda, making their way to the street. On the veranda the friend was waylaid by an old acquaintance, leaving the Colonial lady alone briefly.

'Would you like me to show you my grandmother's winter garden?' Agnes offered.

The woman was surprised but nevertheless she followed Agnes down the steps, along the garden path and round the veranda where they stood in a sheltered little corner, almost like a small glass-roofed conservatory.

'I'm interested in what you said about the woman in Paris,' Agnes said.

The woman took off her glove and touched the ferns and the exotic plants with little cries of pleasure, although she was probably quite familiar with them.

'There may be a number of Irma Greylincks, but the girl with my name: that must be rare.'

The woman looked at her, calculatingly. 'One can make mistakes with European girls but I would say she is more or less your age. Perhaps give or take a month or so. But completely different in appearance. Not that you aren't just as charming with that fair hair and slim figure. Could she be a cousin?'

She put out her hand to Agnes, but Agnes pulled back. She still had to find out the most important thing.

'The name of the hotel and the address. Do you remember that?'

'Of course. It's really very simple: Hotel Josephine, Rue Bonaparte. Sixth *arrondissement*. That means district, as you know. But how could you possibly know? Such a huge city, they have to have districts otherwise they'd never get their mail … One simply writes Paris 6. Yes, yes, I am coming,' she called to her friend who was walking down the garden path.

The gate remained open after they'd passed through. It had to be pushed open and shut with a squeak and a groan over the cement path and there was no point in doing that with the comings and goings all afternoon.

'Goodbye, dear child,' the Colonial personage waved to Agnes with her parasol.

It was only later that night after supper that she and her grandmother could talk – when the guests had gone to their rooms and the old woman had changed into her nightclothes with her hair in a short braid over her right shoulder and Agnes had brought her a glass of milk with a splash of brandy in it.

The widow Greylinck lay back against the pillows. How papery thin her skin was! How wispy her hair! The hands holding the glass of milk shook ever so slightly.

'Ouma, do you know anything about the Irma Greylinck in Paris?' Agnes asked. 'Can she be a cousin with the same name? Surely not, because Greylinck was my mother's married name.'

Her grandmother shook her head. 'I don't know anything about her.'

'And the girl who has my name?'

Her grandmother shook her head.

Agnes was determined. 'It just can't be. Ouma, you said that mine was a special name chosen by my mother. Agnes and then your name.'

The widow Greylinck no longer felt like drinking her milk. She pushed the glass away so Agnes had to take it again. Tears trickled from the faded blue eyes that were heavy with weariness. Agnes felt sorry for her, but not sorry enough to say they could talk about it some other time when her grandmother felt better.

Something forced her to find out now. 'Can the Irma Greylinck in Paris be the same Irma Greylinck as my mother?'

She'd never been taken to visit a grave. No one had even spoken to her about a death bed. Her father had never spoken his wife's name. So she pressed on: 'Is my mother still alive?'

The widow Greylinck's lips scarcely moved. 'It could be so.'

'Do Oom Piet and Oom Jan know she is still alive?'

'We don't know that she is still alive. She may quite possibly have died during the years of war in Europe.'

Agnes paced up and down; she wore her nightgown and her hair hung loose.

The old woman reached her arms out to the girl. 'My angel ...'

That brought the tears to Agnes's eyes. 'Please leave angels out of this, Ouma.' She knelt beside her grandmother's bed, clasping the trembling old hands in hers. 'Why was I led to believe she was dead? Why did I have to be deceived? Why, why? What are you still hiding from me, Ouma? Please tell me, for the love of God. Please tell me now!' She dropped the old woman's hands and clenched her fists, the knuckles white. When she opened her hands again there were red marks where the fingernails had dug into the flesh. Then she spoke more gently. Perhaps the betrayal was her father's, perhaps her grandmother wasn't the guilty one.

'Shouldn't you tell me everything, Ouma?'

'Your father was out in the veld, fighting. She wanted to go away to Europe. Your father forced her to leave you behind here, to give you to him.'

Agnes raised her head. Through her tears she said: 'No proper mother, no mother with any heart, would have let her baby go. You have no idea of all I have gone through, Ouma.'

'The woman was confused, the man had talked her out of her senses. And then didn't ever marry her, if her name is still Greylinck.'

Agnes looked up at her grandmother and the look of mistrust was back. 'What man?'

'The Frenchman she left here with.'

Agnes rested her head on her grandmother's breast. Her grandmother stroked her hair with a shaky hand. 'She must have loved you very much and longed for you desperately to have given the other child your name.'

But Agnes knew her grandmother was improvising. When she had returned to the sitting room from the garden and bent over her grandmother, she had looked through the coloured glass windows onto the veranda. She realised then that she and the Colonial had been directly in her grandmother's line of vision. She would have been able to see their faces, striped with the blue and red and gold; she would have been able to watch them talk. Why hadn't she asked her what the woman had said? Was she afraid to hear what else the woman had said? Was she still concealing something?

But she was also keeping something from her grandmother. She repeated it over and over again in her mind. Hotel Josephine, Rue Bonaparte, Paris 6.

Her mother might still be alive. She couldn't cope with the magnitude of it.

As she lay on her grandmother's breast, she sobbed so bitterly that her grandmother finally said: 'There, there, child. We acted with good intention. And we never stinted you our love. How could a young child have understood … and how could we choose a time to suddenly come out in the open and say to you: your mother is not dead?

'There were so many orphans after the Boer War, you can be grateful that you still had a father.

'I am very tired now, dear. Get into bed and try to sleep.'

But Agnes's heart was hardened afresh against her father.

That Sunday no one referred to the Colonial visitor and what she had spoken of. Perhaps the widow Greylinck had forbidden her sons and their families to refer to it. And Naomi, who was very fond of the girl in her own off-hand manner, had no wish to cause her any pain, even though the girl had neglected her grievously. As for Lettie, she certainly wasn't fond of Agnes, but Jannie forbade her to talk: Keep your mouth, wife. If you go against the old woman in this, she is quite capable of bequeathing everything to the waif.

The widow Greylinck didn't want to expose Agnes to further speculation and gossip, so she broke off all contact with the person who had brought the Colonial lady to her birthday tea. Perhaps she felt that if you ignore something it will go away.

But Agnes did not forget.

She wrote a letter to the address in Paris. For months she waited but never received a reply. She blamed the World War for the delay. As soon as the war was over, she consoled herself – and according to all reports, it couldn't drag on much longer – she would get her letter. Then her mother would invite her to come to Paris. And the Colonial gossip had just fabricated the fact that the other girl was the same age as her. They could come to some arrangement about the name – call her Valeria or something like that.

But, in truth, the mother in Paris was just as unsubstantial as the mother with wings.

And the grandmother did not leave all her possessions to Agnes, as Jannie had feared. On the contrary, after the death of her benefactor, the waif left the house in Sunnyside with less than nothing.

And she travelled, not to Europe as she longed to do, but to the Cape Colony.

6

The certainty that the war over the water – a war waged far away but still leaving its scars – could not last much longer, brought new life to the heart. All over the country.

October 1918, and it was spring in the Boland.

Karel du Plessis sent old Jan to collect the young people in the red and green wagon with the four lively black horses. Saturday was picnic day. The pastorie children were the first to be picked up.

Leonora, the youngest of the four to be invited, skipped down the steps, hat with its long ribbons in one hand, skirts bundled up in the other hand; head thrown back with its dancing curls.

In a good mood this morning, observed Aunt Issy, who didn't have much time for Emma's second daughter – that 'wayward, violent child'.

The sky was a hazy blue, the world fresh; the sunshine sparkled on the frangipani, the jasmine, and the roses as a gentle breeze stirred them. Some of the roses were full-blown, while others still cupped the short tender stamens with unfurling, dew-drenched petals.

'Walk like a lady,' said Aunt Issy who was watching Leonora from the front room window with the lace curtain raised to one side. 'If you can't behave, you stay at home.' The child must have heard it: a thin rasping noise that died away in the speaking of the words. Will Aunt Issy's eye be on me all through my whole life, she wondered, even when she's buried, even when she's been eaten up by worms? And she wished her aunt was already dead and buried and eaten up by worms.

But she forgot about Aunt Issy when she heard Victoria coming down the steps in the passage. She took her older sister by the hand, pulling her down the veranda steps. 'Come,' she said. 'Sniff, sniff, sniff!'

Victoria's hair was as dark as her mother's, done up in a chignon today, fastened with one of her mother's tortoiseshell combs and covered by her straw hat. She was 17 and her ankle-length frock with its narrow flounces belled out as she walked. She was regarded as nearly grown-up but her eyes were more childish than Leonora's.

'Smell the gardenias! Smell the air! To me, it smells like … roses and eau de cologne … and Mother!' She squeezed Victoria's hand as hard as she could. 'Promise me we will never stop sniffing the flowers, Vicky.'

The abbreviation of her sister's name was always defiant. 'Vicky, Vicky, Vicky …' she carolled. And hoped Aunt Issy could hear her. One of the black horses raised his tail and great soft blobs of dung tumbled down. The girls pinched their noses and giggled. Leonora twirled around. I love you Vicky, and I love the horses and the gardenias and the roses and the orchard and the water furrow and the mountains and the sky, and the heap of horse dung that smells of the stable.

Stuart was going to the picnic with the 'children' very much as an older brother. He was already up on the wagon with old Jan and he was getting impatient. 'Put your cases and things on the wagon and help the silly girls up so we can be away,' he ordered Frikkie, the second-oldest brother. The 'cases and things' were Frikkie's camera and tripod and case with plates and heavy cloth. He loaded them carefully.

'Get on with it,' said Stuart who dusted off the seat with his handkerchief before sitting down. He was proud of his new white trousers and he didn't want to get them soiled on this ridiculous outing. With them, he sported a striped blazer and his new straw boater. Before too long, just as soon as the wagon was full of young people, he would say to old Jan: 'Move over, I'll take the reins.' And as they pulled away, as he felt his power over their movements, those four gleaming black horses with their great neck muscles and tossing heads and combed tails and swaying rumps, the white clothes and boater would be forgotten. Once the town girls' eyes were on him and he heard their squeals when the wagon bumped over a rocky patch or swayed round a bend, and they had to hang on to each other and cry: 'Stuart! Stuart!' in shrill frightened voices, and his whip cut ever sharper through the air, his clothes would be forgotten, Leonora thought with a smile. She was glad he was coming with them. Even if it was only to get him out of the house, away from Father. She didn't mind that he had a reputation as a lady-killer.

But she could swear Aunt Issy was still watching them from behind the lace curtains. Aunt Issie was obsessed with Stuart.

Leonora sprang nimbly up into the wagon but Victoria struggled. 'You're tickling me,' she cried to Frikkie, who had grasped her under the arms to pick her up. He climbed in the back and sat as far as possible from his sisters, legs stretched out, his arms protectively round the camera, the tripod and the cloth.

'Whoa! Whoa!' called old Jan as the horses grew restless at the narrow entrance to the pastorie garden and he had to pull their heads now to one side, now to the other.

The wagon filled up as they collected young people from house to house. They swung away from the town, took the bumpy road to the farm. Stuart had the reins and whip. The wagon creaked with the motion and with the happiness aboard. Leonora sat right at the back, her legs dangling. She felt the air hissing between her knees; she was bumped so high that if she had not been able to catch hold of her friend Amy, seated beside her, she would have landed on the ground. She screamed with laughter.

'I think she was engaged to a man who died in the war ...' gasped Leonora. They were shout-talking to each other about Aunt Issy.

'This war?'

'No, the Boer War.'

'Was it an Englishman then?'

'I can't imagine her marrying a Boer.'

'I would rather be shot in the war than be engaged to your Aunt Issy.' The wagon started to jog steadily and their bodies took up the rythmn.

'Oh, it's so romantic to have a fiancé who dies in the war, you could put flowers near his portrait,' said Amy. 'And then you don't have to marry and do all those other things with him.'

Leonora didn't want to discuss 'all those other things' with Amy. 'I'd rather have a fiancé who was torn to shreds by a lion in the mission field. In darkest Africa.' Like Oom Hennie. She loved Oom Hennie, she loved him so very much. If he was her fiancé she would have taken care of him even though his one eye had been torn out and his left arm missing, and he stumbled along with the aid of a walking-stick. He lived on charity. 'Never-ending alms,' said Aunt Issy. 'Why Emma and the children should be deprived ...'

Victoria was sitting deeper into the wagon, pressed up against her boyfriend, Adrian. 'He isn't my boyfriend, he isn't!' she had protested the night before as she and Leonora brushed out their hair. 'He just wants to get fresh with me and start all his tricks and claim me as partner for every game.' She leaned forward, her neck exposed as the dark hair cascaded down. The short new hairs growing in her nape stood up like feelers as she brushed, her arms long and pale in the candlelight. Leaning over like that, her neck looked like Anne Boleyn's just before she was beheaded in the Tower of London, thought Leonora.

'Nonsense. Look how you're blushing.' She dragged Vicky over to the mirror, but her cheeks were not flushed in the small, oval, dimly reflective piece of glass. They were pale, oh, so pale!

The young people sang *You'll take the high road and I'll take the low road*. The girls started on too high a note. The boys stopped them and started over again. Adrian's deep bass harmonised so beautifully. Leonora did not sing. She looked down at the earth road that unrolled below, faster on the down slopes, more slowly as they trundled uphill. She watched the gravel spray up behind the wagon wheels. She had thrust her dress under her knees and thighs. Now it seemed to her that the wagon was motionless and the road rolled out under her, like ribbon from a great bobbin. She hadn't realised before that red, ochre and silver soil particles could hurt deep down in your heart with their beauty.

'Ay! Hoeka!' shouted Stuart who was trying to imitate old Jan. He reined in the horses and old Jan shambled off to open the farm gates. 'Take it very slowly, master, very slowly ...'

The wagon barrelled over the narrow rough farm track, swaying perilously, throwing the young people's bodies against one another. Frikkie took his cases with the camera and the glass plates up on to his knee, hanging on to them with both hands. He paid no heed to the girls pressed up against him; just became part of the movement of the boys' and girls' bodies as the wagon swayed, and the nervous laughter as the one gripped the other and the high spirits increased.

The picnic place was in a grove of poplars. Delicate green marks made a lacework on the wet tree trunks. Moss covered the stones beside the stream; spiders had spun webs over the decaying leaves washed up against the rocks. Leonora stooped to trail her fingers in the icy water. She carefully removed a piece of moss and held it in the palm of her hand.

Snow still gleamed on a far peak in the blue mountains that encircled the valley bowl. Spring was late that year. Oom Karel had had a rustic table knocked together in a clearing among the trees. The picnic baskets his wife had filled stood ready waiting for them. But no one was hungry yet, the exhilaration of the wagon ride still coursed in the blood. And when one set off to the marshy clearing splashed with white by arum lilies, the others all streamed after. The boys stepped onto the wet ground and their shoes sank into the mud. The girls picked their way from stone to stone to the flowers and then stood wide-legged to bend and take hold of the lilies with both hands and pull. While they balanced precariously on the stones, the boys sloshed through the mud and grabbed them from behind. Hands slid over the slippery stems and the girls leaned backwards against the young boyish bodies. The stems were pulled out bulb and all and thrown aside.

'Ugh, my hands are all slimy,' said Amy. No boy had come to grab her by the waist.

Frikkie set up his tripod, screwed his camera onto it, and busied himself with his case of glass plates. Two girls watching him snatched up the black cloth and threw it over his head. But he freed himself. 'You're such a silly billy,' they cried. Leonora watched Stuart with old Jan and the horses. Two of the older girls were tagging along with him. 'Where are the saddles?' he demanded. 'But these horses are too wild, otherwise I would have let you ride ...' Or ridden himself. So the girls could admire his style in the saddle. That was all he had brought back from the war, he thought bitterly. The townsfolk had been uneasy about his going to German South West with Louis Botha to apprehend Manie Maritz and his rebels and to seize the territory for the Crown. They'd been uneasy because of Father, whose attitude everyone knew; they were uneasy when stories circulated about rebels who had been captured and executed. Only Aunt Issy was on his side. Later, Leonora told him that the day he returned, Father forbade anyone in the household from going to the station to meet him. Only Aunt Issy had defied him. She went alone in the trap, taking the reins herself. When they got home, he threw his baggage down in the back passage and said: 'Am I then a villain returning? Perhaps I should have perished in German South West.'

Mother was pregnant again and she had walked slowly up to him and put her hands on his shoulders. And then rested her head against his chest.

'You mustn't speak like that, Stuart. You'll anger God. You knew how your father felt. It will pass. I pray every day that the feeling will pass.'

Leonora was crying. 'I wanted to come to the station but Father said I couldn't. He said it was a bitter blow for him that his son should have taken up arms against his own people. And Mother said I must obey Father.'

Leonora saw Stuart take first one girl round the waist and swing her round in the air and then the other one, as though they were playing their own game, and she thought: Only Aunt Issy went to fetch him. I hate Aunt Issy but if it hadn't been for her, Stuart would have arrived at the station with no one to meet him. And then he had to go and spend another two years in the barracks in Cape Town.

She trotted behind Stuart and the girls. Old Jan had outspanned and led the horses away behind his little house at the edge of the poplars. The mat of fallen leaves deadened the sound of her footsteps. Old Jan's children crowded in the door of his house, hands in their mouths, shy of her. Children ran out of other houses too.

'Go back to your friends,' Stuart told her.

He had taken off his jacket and it hung from his forefinger over his shoulder; the boater was pushed back on his head. He and the girls were returning; the girls picked sorrel flowers and sucked at them. They held up their long skirts to keep them from getting dirty, and hung on his every word. With their pretty summer hats and the light muslin dresses they seemed to Leonora like flowers on long swaying stems.

The younger crowd was romping. From far off she could hear the singing and shouting; she recognised the tunes of *The Jolly Miller*, then *Ellie Rose*. Excited, she started to run towards them. Amy came to meet her, taking her by the hand: 'Come, we'll be partners.' They joined in but the boys separated them, each taking a girl, and they played, chased and caught one another, swung each other round. Finally she dropped out, leaning against a poplar to catch her breath, her back to the trunk, her head thrown back. She wanted to say: dear tree, beloved tree. But she couldn't. A hollow, dark frightened feeling invaded her body; and in her mind churned the verses Mother had read to them the night before. Every Friday evening they sat at the dining room table and Mother read to them, and now the verses she knew so well droned through her head, more insistent than the singing of the players, clearer than the sunshine, the green of the flower stems in her hand:

> *She left the web, she left the loom,*
> *She made three paces thro' the room,*
> *She saw the water-lily bloom,*
> *She saw the helmet and the plume,*
>   *She look'd down to Camelot.*
> *Out flew the web and floated wide;*
> *The mirror crack'd from side to side;*
> *'The curse is come upon me,' cried*
>   *The Lady of Shalott.*

The arums lay drooping where they had been thrown down, the slimy stems drying; the sorrel lay forgotten in the straw, the tender yellow petals bruised; the stems of flowers on the footpath were trampled in the spongy marshiness.

> *Who is this? And what is here?*
> *And in the lighted palace near*
> *Died the sound of royal cheer;*
> *And they cross'd themselves for fear,*
>   *All the knights at Camelot;*
> *But Lancelot mused a little space;*
> *He said, 'She has a lovely face;*
> *God in His mercy lend her grace,*
>   *The Lady of Shalott.'*

They sat at table; the lamplight fell on the book before her, on Mother's beautiful white hands, stretched out over the pages, and when she picked them up to turn a page, her wedding ring gleamed. But she could not see Mother's face. Neither her dark eyes with the long lashes, her nose and her lips, nor even her hair swept up high. Only her white hands and the white, white fingers. Mother was away from them, far away. Please don't read that, she wanted to beg her mother, but she couldn't. I don't like Lancelot. Mother, please stop reading. But this is your favourite poem, came the voice of Mother.

She started. Stuart took her hand. 'Stop dreaming, Norie. Look, I am leaving the other girls, I'll be your partner. Come, wear my boater. Now you're the prettiest.' And he dragged her along with him. But she flung off the hat.

In the pastorie, Issy was supervising the preparation of the midday meal. Although the cook pared the vegetables and put them on the stove, kept the fire going, and would wash the pots after the meal, only Nellie, the white nanny, was allowed to prepare the meat and serve it. Miss Issy was punctilious about the serving. Nellie knew Miss Issy was watching her, and it made her hands clumsy; she dropped the crockery. She broke more things than the maids, said Miss Issy. But it was those eyes on her that made her so clumsy.

Without the three older children and with only three places set, the dining room table seemed empty. The three younger children, all boys, who had followed close on one another's heels seven years after Leonora's birth, took their meals in the nursery with their nanny. Nellie filled their plates in the kitchen. When she had finished serving, the housemaid put the food dishes on the dining room table and rang the bell, then Nellie went to the nursery with the meals for her and the children.

'Emma is not at all well today.' Only Issy and the dominee were at table. Accusation radiated from her entire being. It radiated from the way she served a small portion on the third plate, rang the bell, sent the maid to fetch a tray and then set the plate, a knife, a fork and a serviette on it and said: 'Take that to the bedroom for the madam, please.' It radiated from the way in which, with her skinny neck bent forward and her eyes closed, she waited for grace to be said. It radiated to him that she blamed him, the husband, that Emma did not feel well.

The good Lord only knew that he probably deserved it, thought the dominee, but if it wasn't Emma's pregnancy – and she fell pregnant if he so much as looked at her – it was something else. This woman at the table with him was pious. But she was hardly loving. Except towards Stuart. He had learned to bite his tongue for Emma's sake. How many hours had he spent on his knees trying to still the conflict in his heart, raining self-accusation down on his own shoulders like whip lashes, chastising himself like one trying to tame a headstrong animal? What had become of love and kindness?

Yet he remained the head of the household. Even though his mother-in-law had remained in the house up until her death. Issy was a chip off the old block, right down to the small mannerisms: the self-righteous way she pulled her head up, the small sideways nod of the head, the narrowing of her lips.

At night, alone in their room, he consoled Emma: 'Don't distress yourself so, dry your tears. We wouldn't really manage without her. Just don't let us ever take it out on one another.'

But she was no longer his Emma. She had withdrawn somewhere deep inside herself. Every approach from his side seemed to push her further away.

He waited for Issy to lay down her knife and fork, said the closing grace and stood up. 'I will look in on Emma; I have a meeting in about an hour. The children will probably only be back in the late afternoon.' He tried to lighten the atmosphere. 'Isn't the weather superb? A real October day.'

'Wipe your moustache, there's food on it,' was all Issy said.

He drew the serviette out of the silver ring once again, one of the two on which his and Emma's names were engraved, along with the date of their marriage. He wiped his moustache and left the serviette on the table.

She heard the door of Emma's bedroom open and then close again, and she heard him come out again after a little while. It was only then that she took up his serviette, folding it and thrusting it into the ring.

'Now poor Emma can have some peace,' she said out loud.

Emma lay on her bed in the darkened room. The shutters were closed, the curtains drawn. Her eyes were closed and a lavender-soaked cloth rested on her forehead. She did not open her eyes when she heard Josias enter. She kept her eyes closed when he stooped to raise her hand from the covers and kiss it. She was deeply weary in body and soul. Only here in the shadowy room could she turn in on herself, into silence and darkness, to find peace, and allow her body to sink away into a kind of non-being, the exhausted body that was such a burden to her. Sometimes it seemed to her that she was floating, that the room and the furniture, even the bed, disappeared below her so she was nothing more than a small awareness of herself, reduced to a small speck behind her closed eyes. Then her weariness evaporated and there was no stress in the painless, wafting weightlessness. Then she did not want to be disturbed, didn't want to hear the firm tread on the wooden floor.

The food was untouched on the small bedside table.

She knew Josias was standing there, gazing at her; she knew that if she stirred so much as a finger he would fall on his knees at her bedside, stroking her arm, gradually higher and higher under the sleeve of her dressing-gown, right up to her armpit. She kept her eyes closed, her body motionless. Who had said that weariness was also a form of pain? Was it Grandma? Was it the relentless little foetus inside her that so exhausted her? Dear Lord, what evil spirit has taken hold of me? Dear Lord Jesus, You know I long for the good, but the flesh is weak. Is it Your will that the flesh should be so violated, dear God? I did love Josias.

Josias did not speak to her. He tiptoed out of the room. He went to sit in his study with his eyes closed, trying to regain calmness and distance, love in his heart and compassion for his wife. Suddenly he longed for his brother Hennie. Was he helping Hennie enough? Could he do more? Seven surviving children and another on the way. Five sons, perhaps another son. Hennie's wife had died out in the mission field during her first confinement. He thought with mournful tenderness of dear, lively, uncomplicated Jessie, whom he had known for such a short time. Hennie would still not talk about her death or his accident a few months later.

Later, decades after his death, Leonora would say to Leo: 'As a girl I often clashed with Father. He was the authority in the house. Possibly to assert himself against Aunt Issy. And God help us on the rare occasions when they did agree, like the time I was to play a male role in the school play and had to wear men's clothes and she joined forces with Father to forbid me to do so. His disapproval was just as strong as hers.

'But I think at the time we had absolutely no conception of Father's inner turmoil. I think he had a battle to keep his faith alive. Faith in the love of the heavenly Father. Particularly after Hennie's misfortunes. Mother withdrew increasingly from him and from us. The war with the English was still waged in our house. The afternoon after Stuart went off to German South West Africa with General Botha, he paced up and down in the garden, one hand behind his back, the other holding his cigar. It made an impression on me because it was an unusual time of the day for him to be smoking. I lay in the grass with a book; I don't think he knew I was there, or he didn't care whether I heard him or not.

He said aloud: Lord, I have drawn your drinking water, but it is brine in my mouth.

'It must have distressed him – all the strife. And then, Sunday after Sunday, he had to step up into the pulpit and reach his arms out to his congregation, watching them stare at the words embroidered in silver thread on the lectern cloth: *Vrede zij U lieden. Peace be with you.*

'Maybe Father was too emotional to be a dominee. Perhaps he was the one who should have gone out as a missionary, the aggressive adventurer; not Oom Hennie, the quiet one ... leaving Father with his Englishy in-laws.

'And yet, right up until his death, his children called him Father without his ever objecting to it. And all her life we called our ma Mother. After his death, when I was going through his papers, I found a note Frikkie had written to him at one or other of the synod meetings. It touched me that he had kept it. I remember the words:

Dear Father,
I am sorry I have not written before, but I forgot. The black hen is brooding 13 eggs ...

'In spite of our clashes, perhaps because of them, Father and I were very close. I could give him a warmth that the others couldn't. I sometimes felt sorry for Vicky: it wasn't her fault that her name was so repulsive to him. Do you know that father only spoke her name once in his whole life, and that was when he buried her?'

A large tarpaulin was spread on the ground, still damp from the late winter rains. The girls sat in groups, their knees pressed together, their long skirts tucked under their thighs, as they made way for the boys who brought ginger beer and lemon syrup. The boys gripped the bottles of ginger beer between their knees, worked the corks loose, shook the bottles until the corks shot through the air. The beer fizzed out over the bottlenecks and into the mugs which the girls held out; they licked the edges of the mugs where the beer had overflowed and cried: 'Careful! My dress!' or 'Careful! You did that on purpose!'

The food was brought on large trays: rissoles, cold chicken – thighs and wings and breasts and pope's noses which some of the boys took up and made lewd gestures with, so the girls covered their eyes. Labourers carried bushel baskets on their shoulders filled with late-winter saffron pears. Oh, those small, sweet, juicy pears with the wrinkled skin and the little stalk you take hold of to bring the tastiness to your mouth and to bite so the juice runs down your fingers. Bite and suck until the palate is sweetly sated and the baskets empty.

Stuart sat to one side with a group of the older girls. The prettiest wore his straw boater; she flirted with him. And then he lay back and they fed him: strips of chicken, chunks of sweet potato, and finishing up with bits of pear which they bit off and dropped into his open mouth.

Frikkie was busy with his tripod and camera. The girls near him teased, calling him: Come and sit with us! and when he paid no heed, they crawled up to the tripod and pulled faces as though they were being photographed. Or they tried to get behind him and tug the black cloth off his head. But he didn't let them put him off.

Then, suddenly, a girl looked into the camera, a girl whose face he had never seen before but he saw her now, as he adjusted the lens, like a face appearing in water that suddenly became calm: the shape of a cheek, an eye socket, a mouth. Gentle sunlight fell through the trees and caressed the soft line of this cheek, stroking the dark lashes and filling the wide eyes with an expression of unutterable tenderness. The full moist lips were yearningly directed to him through the distance of glass. A plate lay ready in its slot in the camera, and, without a second thought, he pressed the shutter release button. He took the plate out carefully and stored it. Then the moment was gone; he drew the black cloth off his head, leaving it to dangle from the tripod. He looked for that face among the girls before him on the tarpaulin.

'Take a picture of us too, take one of us too,' nagged the others. But he said: 'Later, later, I'll take pictures of everyone later.' He took a sandwich from the basket and bit into it, his eyes still searching. There was a girl with her back half-turned to him and when she turned fully he saw it was Kowie. Her face looked different in shade, the chin thinner and more pointed, the mouth moved as she chewed, the eyes were hidden. But he recognised the curve of the cheek, the line of her eyebrow. It's her, it's her, he jubilated. With my lens I have captured an image of her that no one has ever seen before. It is mine; she is mine. And because he knew that, he made no effort to get closer to her or to talk to her. But he knew it with a deep certainty.

The young people pressed around the camera: Take one of me. Take one of us together – a courting couple. He clicked and clicked. 'What about you?' he asked the host and hostess. They looked slightly nervously down the lens. Leonora thought: I've never seen Frikkie so relaxed.

'Let's have a group now,' he said and the young people drew closer. He let them sit against each other, some in the front, others kneeling, some standing. The men posed nonchalantly; the one swung his hat in a salute to the camera, another put his arm round the hostess's waist. He took several group shots. 'You too, come on: you too,' called Leonora and he set up the camera, emerged from under the cloth to sit beside the girl in the front row. It was not her, but he didn't mind. He owned the image. And he knew with certainty that she was his too.

The camera clicked and the group broke up.

The young people started gathering their possessions. A few helped the hostess to pack the remaining food into the baskets. The labourers' children crept closer through the trees, little dark heads bobbing up and down, here and there a scrap of ribbon tied round a lock of hair, a frayed shirt untucked from the shorts, or a pair of pants pulled up under the armpits and secured with a piece of string. The one spied a chicken drumstick, half eaten and then tossed over a shoulder, snatched it up and began to eat. Now the others searched in the grass; everything they found went straight to their mouths. The hostess shooed them away but they couldn't get enough.

A small group stood a little way from the picnic spot, staring at Frikkie's equipment.

Frikkie unscrewed the camera and folded up the tripod. The used plates were carefully returned to the case; the case with it precious contents was wrapped in the black cloth. This was one of the first big cameras to reach their town.

Father, he had begged, please come with us just once to the magic lantern show. And Father had come and stood at the back, watching row upon row of children, including his own, completely entranced by the shadowy mysterious figures which old Herr Winterbach conjured up on the old sheet hung at the front of the hall.

'An edifying story, I can't find fault with that,' he said as they walked home, a little way back from the others. 'But ...'

'It's an amazing thing, Father. The light comes from the lantern and inside it are the reflectors and the slots where you slide in the plate. Herr Winterbach is teaching me ... there's the limelight, but it's actually the condenser lens that collects the rays of light together and causes the image, and then there are the mirrors that catch the rays and direct them out to the screen. Can you imagine it, Father? All that happening in that big beam of light that is projected from the back of the hall onto that cloth screen.'

Then he rushed on: 'Herr Winterbach has brought a camera and tripod for me. I have saved up nearly enough pocket money and if you could make up the difference, Father, I could afford it.'

He would never forget the stretch of street they walked down as he asked. A water furrow, narrow enough to jump over, ran beside the street, and even now, so late, nearly night, with the street's gas lamps already alight, there were reflections here and there on the rapidly-flowing water. In places, it seemed to him, the water arched its back to catch the gaslight, holding still for a moment, shining like quicksilver. Quite still so that new water had to flow in under the reflection. And the winter trees, the shapes of the bare oak branches in the moonlight – the patterns, all around him he saw patterns. He had to close his eyes to blot them out. He couldn't cope with them.

But Father said nothing. When they reached home, he took him to the study and asked him to sit down.

'You don't often ask for anything, Frikkie. And when you do ask, I know you are serious.'

It was as though Father had sensed what this meant to him. He knew he was going to get a sermon and was constrained to listen to it.

Father took a book from the shelf, leafed through it and began to read.

'Photography: from the Greek: to enscribe with light. Herr Winterbach's beam of light writes a powerful language, my boy, more powerful than the pen. On condition that you remember: enscribe with light.'

And then he gave him the money.

Enscribing with light. The words bewitched him. He took the book from his father and traced the Greek letters with his finger. Writing with light.

But next day at the dining table, when everyone was talking about Herr Winterbach's wonderful show, Father said, 'Don't forget the contribution of Emily, the little dwarf woman.'

Emily travelled from town to town with Herr Winterbach. She wore a black dress with sequins and sat on the stool at the piano, and she looked up at the images as they began to tremble on the white sheet, her stubby fingers ready on the keys, and then she leaned forward and played. Softy and mournfully if the heroine was sad, hard and brutally if the villain made an appearance. Caressing, exciting; the emotions flowed through the stubby fingers.

'Oh, she just plays honky-tonk,' said Leonora, but Father corrected her. 'I watched her, Norie. Did you notice? She waits until just after the image has appeared, a few seconds, as though she wants to feel the mood of the audience, fear or anticipation or sadness, and then those fat little hands go down and she hits the notes.'

'Do you think …?'

'I think, Norie, that there was something alive between us and her, something that didn't happen between us and the pictures, and it would be different with every different audience, she would play slightly differently. That is real creation. You give her and she gives back. You create something new. Every evening. Only the pictures are dead.'

The children round the table listened; Mother and Aunt Issy did too. Father didn't often talk this way.

Leonora, who always disagreed, said. 'So would you say books are also just dead letters on paper, Father? They don't change every time we read them.'

Father wanted to end the conversation and say grace but the children wouldn't allow him to do so.

'Every time you read, you experience something different. That's what I am trying to bring home: you make your own pictures as you read.'

'That's not so, Father. We read in the same way, and Mother tells us the same stories over and over again, or she reads them to us again.'

'And why do you want to hear them over and over again?'

'Because we like them.'

'Because you make up your own pictures in your imagination. Because you and the books change and grow together.'

'And if we go to see the Magic Lantern again?'

Father didn't answer. He asked Victoria, 'And you, my girl?' They'd all noticed how she had sat and watched completely entranced.

'I think the Magic Lantern is beautiful, Father. But Mother's stories are also beautiful.'

Even Mother said she was going to go along next time to Herr Winterbach's wonderful pictures. Frikkie promised her he'd show her everything, and, because he was so happy, he said Aunt Issy could come too.

But next time Herr Winterbach came, Mother was dead and so was Victoria, and Aunt Issy simply didn't have the heart for it. Neither did Leonora. Herr Winterbach was sick, and Frikkie helped him when he saw how he struggled to carry the heavy equipment. But even he didn't see it out. Without the little dwarf woman who had also died of the 'flu – with another man at the piano who played any old thing with a cigarette dangling from his lips – it simply wasn't the same.

Inscribe with light, Leonora thought later about Father's words.
Transfixed by the light.
Frik had got himself well and truly involved with Kowie.
Or had he?

'I really don't like Adriaan at all,' Victoria told Leonora in their room the evening after the picnic on Karel du Plessis's farm.

'And that little stroll with him? So we eventually had to go in search of you because the wagon was already being loaded? The two of you, off somewhere together the whole afternoon?'

Victoria's colour was high again. She leaned forward; brushing out her long brown hair, thankful that Leonora could not see her face. Still brushing, she talked through the thick tresses.

'It's entirely his fault. He said he wanted me to come and see something, but there was nothing there.'

'Just a kiss and a squeeze?'
'You're horrid!'

Victoria threw herself on to her bed, buried her head in her arms and started to weep. Leonora took her by the shoulders. 'Whatever is there to cry about? There, there, tell me. Nothing. It is right that he should hug and kiss you. Aunt Issy can forbid us as much as she chooses. It's right, right, right. Vicky, listen: it's right. It's nonsense that we are like gardenia blossoms that are spoilt once they've been touched.'

Victoria wiped away the tears with the back of her hand.

'Norie,' she said softly, looking up at her sister, tears still glistening in her great brown eyes. 'He put his hand out and touched my bosom. Just softly, Norie. And then he said we must sit down, so we did, just like that on the wet grass. We sat close to each other. It made me feel very odd ... his hands were trembling. Even if it was a sin, I will never ever in my whole life forget it, even if I live to be a hundred.'

She looked past Leonora through the window. The curtains had not been drawn; the oil lamp threw a pool of golden light over the table where it stood. The moon was full and a strange white haze hung over the garden, over the street, over the town, over the darkened houses.

'Blow out the lamp,' said Victoria. And she leaned against her sister as the cold white light of the moon filled the room, so they could make out the carpet, the dressing table and the wardrobe in the dead white light, lifeless patches of darkness in the dead moonlight.

'Hold me close, Norie,' said Victoria. 'I'm afraid.' She trembled, even though the night was unusually sultry and the heavy fragrance of frangipani hung in the air. She pressed her head against her sister's breast. 'Close the window, Norie. I'm cold.'

The whole night through she shivered with cold. Leonora took the blankets from her own bed and threw them over her. The fear rose in her until eventually she took up the candle to go and call Nellie, but Aunt Issy heard her in the passage and came out of her room, a shawl thrown over her nightdress.

'Victoria is not well, Aunt Issy.'

That's what happens when you sit on wet grass, Aunt Issy would say later, but when the fever didn't abate, when sweating it out made no difference, when Victoria tossed her head from side to side tugging at her hair from the pain, when the hair was cropped short on doctor's orders but it brought no relief, and Victoria started coughing horribly and her face grew thin and hollow in three short days, Aunt Issy had to concede: this was more than the consequence of simply sitting on damp grass. There were other cases of illness in the town. More and more. From tens the figure climbed to hundreds.

Victoria was the first in her town to die of the Great Influenza of 1918.

It was a small funeral. Too many were nursing their own sick or else they paid heed to the warning that gatherings were to be avoided. Only the dominee – Mother was already sick – Aunt Issy, the children, a few friends. Adriaan stood a little way away until Leonora called him closer.

And Father's voice.

'Almighty God, the Lord of life and death has called the soul of our sister, Victoria, my dearly beloved daughter, home to God: dust are we and to dust shall return.'

Everyone thought Mother would survive. After she lost the child, she was weak for days, lying with closed eyes, never responding to what they asked of her so urgently: 'Talk to us! Please say one word!' They could not discern any movement of her chest under the covers. Had she stopped breathing? There was talk of a coma.

Then, little by little, she began to recover. Eventually she was able to sit up on a chair in her room with a crocheted rug over her knees. Aunt Issy kept the children away from her. They tiptoed down the passage past her room. She sat there quietly until darkness fell and someone came in to light the lamps.

'She feels Victoria's death,' Aunt Issy whispered, 'but her grief is unnaturally controlled. If she would only mourn.'

'She was so near death herself and had to give up the unborn baby too, so perhaps she no longer fears death.'

Josias realised with surprise that he wanted to comfort Issy.

And then one day, as Leonora knelt beside her chair, and Mother was smoothing back her hair with a gentle hand – the wilful hair over her forehead was still a vexation to Mother – she whispered: 'I had a vision. It was unmerited ... given His unworthy servant by God's grace ... I was close to the Hereafter, my fears left me. I would not wish my darling Victoria back. Do not mourn her so, child.'

Leonora went crying to her father: 'Mother has changed, she is going to die too.'

'Hush, dear,' said Father. 'We must have faith.'

When she got up for half an hour, first in the afternoons, later in the mornings too, to sit in her chair at the window – Aunt Issy still didn't allow them free access to go in and lean over her and tire her out – they noticed as they crept past that she was continually writing. Until her weary head dropped into her hands and she rang the little silver bell at her side. Then Issy or Nellie or Leonora helped her to make her way back to bed, step by faltering step.

When she fell ill again, she died within two days.

Had one of her few visitors carried the infection back to her? Where had Vicky contracted the illness? What use was there in asking? And why Vicky? Why Mother?

The evening after the funeral – the 'flu epidemic was subsiding and a great many people had gathered in the cemetery, standing a little way back from the grave – only the three older children, Aunt Issy and the dominee sat down to dinner. Nellie and the little boys took their meal in the nursery. The dominee read from the Bible and prayed. He was very pale. After his wife's death he had remained in his study for the entire day without eating or drinking, without even allowing Leonora to come in. Aunt Issy busied herself about the house. The sadness and confusion and a strange feeling of guilt made the children, even Leonora, helpful and loving towards her. With Father behind the closed door, Aunt Issy was in an odd way still their bulwark.

Once he completed the grace, Father said in English, to conciliate her: 'These past years we have transgressed the laws of God. We have been loveless.' He looked up at Aunt Issy. 'We ask you to remain in this house with us. We ask God's Grace to put the past behind us. May our beloved departed wife and our dear departed daughter forgive us.'

Aunt Issy used her serviette to dab the corners of her eyes. She didn't say a word, simply bowed her head in acquiescence.

'I think that for her part she also tried, I can't recall that she ever insisted on speaking to Father in English again,' Leonora recounted later. 'But Father had more to tell us. On the table before him lay the writing pad with which Mother had busied herself so diligently during her last days.'

'I think it is only fair to you,' said Father, 'that I read her last message to us.'

He cleared his throat and turned back the cover sheet.

'A Vision,' he read. And all at once it seemed as though Mother sat with them at the table, as though her voice sounded in the soft lamplight.

> *I had been laid low on a bed of sickness in my chamber. Could do nought but think the thoughts as they came to my mind. My thoughts had been occupied greatly with my beloved departed daughter. And as I thus thought, a strange weariness crept over me and I felt as if I went into a stupor or half-conscious state. And as I thus lay, methought I heard a voice say: 'Come and I will show thee the realms of the blest.' In an instant of time, I know not how, I found myself in a place for which the grandeur and glory and brilliancy of its light so dazzled me that I was well nigh bewildered, nor can pen ever describe the vastness and the wonderful glories of those mansions fair. I thought of all the beautiful scenes I had beheld on earth, sunrise and sunset and rainbow, it was all this and much more – floods and floods of golden light, tinted with the most exquisite colouring.*

'Now she describes flowers and plants and beautiful scenery, which you can read later yourselves,' said Father. 'And then she saw someone whom she knew long ago on earth.'

> *In my gladness I would have called out to her, but my voice sounded so harsh and discordant, that I feared and kept still and I hid me behind a cloud, which hovered round me, for I felt no sight of earth must intrude on the saints here, to mar their perfection of bliss. Just then someone*

came along the way, with halting step, and she also wore the white robe, but there was a look of bewilderment on her face akin almost to fear. So that I knew she had but just reached the heavenly shores. Then she on whom I had been gazing glided forward and, placing her arm round the stranger and in her sweet winning way, said: 'Welcome home, dear friend. Come with me to our garden and rest awhile and soon you too shall see our King in His beauty for erelong He passes this way.' Thus she conversed most sweetly, and, smoothing her robe with her hands, said with a low laugh: 'There are no threads of earth in our Heaven-made garments. We have no cares. Does not our King send His guardian angels, to watch and guard our loved ones and guide them safely here?' And as she thus talked, I noticed the strangeness and bewilderment on the face of the newly welcomed one had entirely passed away. Just then methought I heard the sound of music like the singing of a great multitude in the distance and, at the sound, all in that garden rose and, with a look of glad expectancy in their eyes, they stepped forward into the golden street. Even the little children who were there left their play and their flowers and, joining hands, skipped along for very gladness.

By this time emotion had almost got the better of him.

'I think she is telling us not to grieve. Not to fear death. With her childlike faith she is already at home with our Father.'

'She wrote in the idiom of the time,' said Leonora years later when she and Frikkie found the 'Vision' amongst the old papers and read it in full. And she asked Frikkie: 'Must a time first be splintered before we can master its idiom?'

'How I wish I could remember her more clearly,' said Leonora. 'Just the image of Mother reading stories and poems in the lamplight: Lord Byron, Tennyson, Longfellow. Who smoothed the hair back from my forehead and gently admonished me: 'Not such a tomboy, Norie, be my sweet, gentle girl.' Gentleness, gentleness. For me it is a dreadful word, Frikkie, but how could Mother say a dreadful word?'

Worcester, on the direct railway line from Cape Town, the harbour city, was more severely hit than the other Boland towns. More than 12 000 fell ill, 700 died. The dead were buried in blankets as coffins were impossible to come by. One whole family was wiped out.

Looking back later, Dominee Van Velde was to think, almost incredulously: The Great Influenza did less lingering emotional damage to our town than the death of a single Boer rebel fighter 17 years earlier. So is a catastrophe at the Hand of God more acceptable than the damage man inflicts on man? Is self-interest and self-justification the stumbling block to healing? And is blame the breeding ground of these emotions, even blame for that wretched old woman, Queen Victoria? It seemed to be harder to forgive her than to accept the hundreds of deaths at the Hand of God.

The human heart remains a mystery, he thought, in his turmoil of grief and remorse.

Life went back to normal again.

Stuart secured a post at the bank and continued to live at the pastorie. The dominee tried to develop a closer relationship with him but they had little in common. Even Aunt Issy thought at times: My darling, Stuart, if only you could be more reliable. Especially when she wandered through the house with her lamp in the small hours, and reluctantly opened his bedroom door and found the sash window pushed up and his bed empty. Had she been too lenient when he was small? Then she must not repeat the leniency with Emma's three little orphans, the three young ones who were now in her sole care.

7

In the Transvaal the story went that the infection had come ashore in the Durban harbour with soldiers and seamen from the *SA Salamis*. The fever spread in a swathe up the railway line. In Johannesburg, Krugersdorp, Boksburg and Pretoria thousands of people died – the death toll for the Transvaal was 10 000. Very nearly 200 000 people fell ill.

When one of the instructors died suddenly at the end of October 1918, the Normal College at Heidelberg where Agnes was studying was closed until further notice.

Hostels were converted to hospitals within days. In the ward of the girls' hostel the sick lay in rows on narrow stretchers that had been hastily brought in. A sheet soaked in Jeyes Fluid hung over the doorway. The heat was unbearable. The girls, feverish and drenched in sweat, tossed restlessly. Some coughed their lungs out, others moaned incoherently, and called for a mother or a sister. Numbers of them lay terribly still with their complexions turning grey before your eyes. Some of the nursing helpers thought the windows should be opened, others decided they should be kept closed. The green blinds were lowered, increasing the impression of a toxic incubator.

The doctor came every day but there was nothing he could do. Girls who were still up and about were given leave to go home. 'As soon as the slightest sign of 'flu appears, those who remain must go to bed,' the doctor told the principal. 'They must stay in bed. Administer the medication that encourages perspiration and as much water as they can drink.' The medication for perspiration was not necessary; the girls lay in a steaming haze of fever. Yet he prescribed cinnamon or aspirin, or the new remedy from the Cape Colony: ysterbosch leaves picked in the Oudtshoorn district, which you simmered in boiling water.

'If the fever breaks, they will lie weak and helpless, weak nigh unto death. If the fever doesn't break, then they will die.'

The doctor, who was also the district surgeon, discussed the arrangements with the principal. Loitering in the passage, Agnes overheard their conversation. 'Volunteers will come with stretchers for the corpses. Remove them from the ward as quickly as possible, as soon as death is confirmed.' He took the terrified principal by the arm. 'There, there, it isn't so bad. Just keep your spirits up.'

Frightened, Agnes made her escape as he came out. If there were no volunteers, or not enough stretchers, or if no one had the strength to carry them out, what would become of them then? Her imagination ran riot ... the bodies will simply be left in the back garden, sheets over their heads, pushed to one side, forgotten, until they start to stink and we all die.

Agnes was still well when they were given leave to return home. She could have stayed on as a volunteer, but she chose not to do so. Not only the sick ward but the whole hostel building filled her with panic. The smell of the disinfectants used to wash the floors and walls, and which was added to the washing-up water in the scullery, turned her stomach. Day in, day out and all night through, she could never escape the smell. The girl she shared a room with fell ill and died after three days. There was no one to come and fetch her, her parents had also fallen ill. Student volunteers carried her away.

Agnes knew: If I get sick here, if I die here, I will also be carried out by strangers because who else will come and fetch me? Oom Piet is an invalid, Tant Naomi has to take care of him. Perhaps they are also already dead and I have no one.

She didn't want to die before reaching her mother. If she could just get to her mother, everything would be all right. Surrounded by death, she yearned with all her heart for her mother in the Paris hotel as she had never yearned for the angel mother. The answer to her letter had not arrived but she waited.

She packed her things – just one small case, because how could she carry more? – and told the matron she was going home. The newspaper posters screamed in huge letters: *Avoid crowds ... BEWARE!* With her suitcase in her hand, she walked to the station. A station, yet again. All the old childhood fears came flooding back.

The train was virtually empty. No one came to ask for her ticket. The train was shunted onto a siding at Germiston. Another train steamed in and stopped alongside; she saw with a shudder that it was a hearse train. They had called for volunteers for the hearse train, but she didn't want to be one. The volunteers went out in the morning in the empty train, which stopped at stations to collect the dead bodies from houses. To show that there was a body to be collected, people tied something red to the gate – a red rag or an item of red underwear, a red tie, a red hot water bottle cover.

As though compelled, she gazed at the corpses in canvas bags or wrapped in blankets and piled up in the compartment opposite her window. The windows were closed and she saw the long grey forms through the glass as though they lay in another world or under the sea. Name cards were fastened with string round the ankles. It seemed to her that she lay there with them and she could feel the scream rising in her throat. She was the only human on the train, which was never going to jerk into life and pull forward again.

Something moved, but it was the train of death; the body bags shifted as the engine came to life. Finally the carriage in which she sat also jerked and her train steamed to life.

There was scarcely a soul to be seen on Pretoria station. She waited a long time for a tram. I am so tired, I will also get sick now, she thought. The newspaper had said: avoid fatigue. It is because they are so tired that so many of the nurses are infected. She walked slower and slower to avoid feeling so tired; she felt sick with fear, her suitcase grew heavier and heavier. She put it down and walked on, but then went back to fetch it.

Her grandmother was happy to see her, but also not quite as happy as she'd expected. The Widow Greylinck was tired. The housemaid and the gardener lay sick and she had to take food and drink to them. The old woman had grown thinner and smaller; she had also started to cough. I ran away from the sickness and I find it here, Agnes thought. But the grandmother cheered her up, saying, 'Child, get some rest, they're taken care of for today. You can assume duty tomorrow.'

She stayed with her grandmother. Many people lay sick in Middelburg, they heard. But there was no news of Piet and Naomi.

Her grandmother didn't fall ill. Neither did Agnes. The gardener died and so did the housemaid. They sent word to family members who came to fetch the bodies from the mortuary for burial. Amongst her grandmother's friends nearly every single family had lost someone. Piet and Naomi recovered, Jannie lost a daughter. After a few weeks the epidemic had burnt itself out. Too many people had lost loved ones to want to take part in the joyous celebrations when world peace became a reality on 11 November.

The losses of the Boer War less than two decades earlier – 7 000 men-at-arms perished, 27 000 women and children in the camps, 14 000 black people in their own concentration camps, 22 000 thousand British (without including the imperial or colonial numbers), in a period of three years – seemed paltry set against the 140 000 lives claimed by the 'flu all over the country in less than six weeks. So pondered the retired Dominee van Velde in his study at Worcester years later, when he opened up his collection of newspaper clippings and started to tear them up. Who still thought about the influenza these days while stories of the Boer War could still wring hearts, and leaders still called out for reparation?

And again he asked himself: Is self-righteous emotion the stumbling block to healing?

In the new year the college reopened and Agnes, still living with her grandmother, returned for her second and final year.

One cold winter morning near the end of the second term, she was called by the head. A telegram lay on his table. Her grandmother lay sick with pneumonia, she was failing rapidly and they feared the worst. If Agnes packed her things quickly, the head would give her a lift to the station in his recently acquired Sunbeam motor car.

'Take a long scarf, if you have such a thing, to wrap over your hat so you don't lose it,' said the instructress who helped her collect her things together.

She couldn't dwell on her grandmother's illness during the short ride to the station; the whistle of the wind made conversation impossible and she had to battle to keep the scarf in place. They travelled so fast she had to hang on for dear life.

Once she was alone in the compartment, she folded the scarf and put it in her suitcase. The folding of the scarf and the closing of the suitcase held something final for her, and she knew: her grandmother was dead. She sat in the corner at the window, crying quietly. Whether she wept over the letter which she had not yet received or over her grandmother, she could not tell. She still had so many questions about her mother and now it was too late. Her grandmother had always avoided talking about her mother. Why, Ouma, why?

Suddenly calculating, she thought: Perhaps Ouma left me the money to go to my mother. Perhaps she wrote a letter telling me to go immediately. Perhaps it was hard for her to talk so she tells me more about my mother in the letter.

There was a black frost the morning after her arrival in Sunnyside. The poinsettia at her bedroom window had died overnight. The leaves hung like mourning crepe, the previous day's challenging red flowers were black and shrivelled. The sun shone unnaturally hard and yellow, but a deathly grey haze in the distance, like a mirage, warned of inclement weather to come.

Agnes shivered under her blankets. She could not get the thought out of her mind of her grandmother waiting for her, cold and still in the dim, well-known but still mysterious bedroom, hands crossed over her breast, head on a flat white pillow devoid of lace or decoration. Two copper ha'pennies had been placed on her eyelids to keep them closed.

Had she lain the whole night with the weight of the two copper ha'pennies on her eyes?

What would happen if the pennies were removed? Would the eyes open, and her grandmother look at her?

In spite of the haste with which Agnes left the college, she was too late even to take her grandmother's hand and squeeze it for one last time. With the nurse's steel grip on her upper arm, she bent over and kissed the thin paper-dry skin on the forehead; the pennies looked up at her like a monster's eyes.

She could not weep. The nurse was inquisitive and fiddled about in the room, continually smoothing the coverlet, and when it was smoothed to her satisfaction, she took out her handkerchief and buffed the knobs on the bedstead to a shine.

What was Agnes expected to do? She did not know how to cope with death. Should she throw herself onto her grandmother, embracing her, trying to shake her awake? Not even when her father had sent her away had she felt as alone as she did that morning after her grandmother's death. And so exposed to scrutiny. At last they went to bed.

Piet and Naomi arrived after breakfast on the train from Middelburg. They took a cab from the station. Piet pressed Agnes to him and she smelt medicine. He was very sallow – 'His liver has also failed,' whispered Tant Naomi when Agnes took her to her room. There were two beds. Jan and his family were to arrive later and then Agnes would have to give up her room. Where would she go? To her grandmother's room?

'We'll put a camp bed in our room for you,' said Tant Naomi who'd noticed the fear in Agnes's eyes as they stepped over the threshold. 'That you should have been the first …' she said.

Agnes swallowed. 'It doesn't matter.' She thought it would be appropriate to weep, but she couldn't manage it.

Naomi's eyes were red but that may have been from a sleepless night on the train.

'Now I want to see the body.' Naomi was quite at home with sickness and death.

Agnes opened her grandmother's bedroom door but she didn't go in. She just looked quickly: the pennies had been removed and the eyes were peacefully closed. So it was all a lie. Once the people had left, she and her grandmother would sit together in the bay window looking through the red and yellow and blue panes of glass and talk about the guests.

Jannie and Lettie and two of their children arrived that afternoon; the older sons worked on the Rand and would come over for the funeral. Lettie sobbed beside the corpse but didn't touch her mother-in-law with either lip or fingertip. Jannie, who had grown portly of late and red in the face, croaked in a broken voice: Mamma!

He poured himself a brandy at the sideboard in the dining room. 'What about you, brother? If you could see what you look like. What have they been doing to you?'

'It's the Lord's will, I must endure it.'

'Is Naomi looking after you, or is she too busy getting your shroud ready?'

He laughed, a short bitter little laugh, drained his glass and refilled it.

'If you regret not having heirs, don't. If you only knew the worries my children have caused me …!'

Neighbours came over and offered to accommodate Agnes and Jannie's daughters. Supper would be provided as well. Agnes wasn't happy about this; she felt she was being pushed out of the house. The first night she hadn't been able to sleep for the thought of her grandmother so dead and quiet in her room, but now she didn't want to be far from her. It was humiliating to have to share a room with the two gossipy girls. She thought bitterly: For them this isn't about Ouma, it's no more than an outing to Pretoria.

There was a heavy frost again that night. A large bed of cannas was burnt black, the flower heads and the leaves hung limp. The wind blew chill.

The funeral was held the following afternoon. Dead grass and blue sky and the cold wind. The new grave a dark red scar. There were not many mourners, for the widow Greylinck had outlived her contemporaries. The singing was slow and thin. Agnes's voice rasped out as though she didn't want to acknowledge the reality of her grandmother's death by singing the funeral hymn. That morning, Naomi had called her into the backyard to help make two wreaths on a table – one from her and Piet, one from Agnes and Daniel. She'd brought two old wreath forms in a big shallow dress box from Middelburg. 'I knew I'd find a use for them, so I told my neighbour the day she was clearing up her husband's grave: Give them to me.' She bound sprigs of cypress foliage, bent them and attached them to the form with a practised hand. Agnes picked loquat leaves and washed them as Naomi instructed, dried them off and then stuck them into the cypress foliage. They lay on top of one another like fish scales, and were also fastened in place. The leaves shone attractively. When Piet arrived with the statice that he'd fetched from friends, they were ready for it. 'The ribbon,' lamented Naomi, 'we forgot the ribbon.' She took the purple and Agnes the white statice and they fastened sprigs of it amongst the loquat leaves. Still not satisfied, Naomi rubbed the loquat leaves to a shine with a dab of cooking oil on her cloth.

'You know the house,' she said to Agnes. 'Aren't there any old ribbons stored in one of your grandmother's drawers?'

Even though the coffin with the body had been carried through to the dining room, Agnes shook her head. She wasn't going to scratch about in the bedroom.

Jannie's family had bought a memorial arrangement. A black-edged card with *In memory of our beloved Mother* written on it in gold script, nestled under the thick glass dome amid a wreath of white wax lilies. There were few wreaths; a huge palm leaf with red and yellow red-hot pokers fastened to it stood like a poisonous golden sun at the foot of the grave. Flowers were scarce.

'Ours is the grandest,' Lettie whispered to Jannie, 'it's a pity she can't know how much you paid.'

Back at the house, after the tea had been sipped and the funeral cake nibbled, and friends and neighbours had taken their leave, a stranger in a dark suit went from one group of family members to another. Agnes had seen him at the graveside, standing next to a very old man; he had taken off his hat and held it over the old man's head to shade him.

'I'm not aware of how long the family who have travelled a distance will be in town,' he said. 'My father deemed it in order to discuss the will this afternoon. Then it is taken care of.'

First he spoke to Piet and Naomi, then to Jannie and Lettie, and then he came to Agnes who was stacking cups on a tray before taking them to the kitchen. 'You too, Miss.'

When Jannie objected to her being singled out, he said, 'Very well, let your children be present too.' And when the front door closed behind the last departing guest: 'I think the sitting room? And kindly close the door into the passage.'

The old man is sitting in Ouma's place, thought Agnes, Ouma will never sit there again. The thought thrust through her with a physical pain. The young man pulled up a chair beside his older colleague and opened a briefcase on his knee. And then came the thought which made her immediately ashamed: They – she'd finally recognised the old man as Mr Reyneke, the attorney – had singled her out to come; Jannie's daughters were simply allowed in. There must be something particular to do with her. An inheritance?

The old man spoke so quietly she had to strain to hear. Or was it that her heart was beating so loudly in her ears?

'I attended to the late widow Greylinck's affairs from the time she moved into this house. I wish to finalise matters personally. Certain complications have occurred which require delicate handling.'

He took the papers his son handed to him and read them peremptorily, as though he was already familiar with the contents. 'The will itself is straightforward. The residue is to be divided evenly between her three children or their descendants. There will not be a great deal. You may not be aware of the fact that, in order to live in the style to which she was accustomed, the late widow Greylinck took out several large bonds on the house, the only real asset in the estate. The bonds will have to be repaid from the proceeds of the sale of the house.'

The old man laid the paper aside and took up another that had rested on his knee. He seemed to pick it up unwillingly, as though handing it was distasteful to him. It was a sheet of pale blue paper filled with large script, clearly written by a woman.

'I have had this letter in my hands for several months. You will understand why I did not deem it necessary to enlighten you as to the contents any earlier. It is from Mrs Irma Greylinck, currently resident in Paris, France.'

The letter she had waited for so desperately! Agnes sat bolt upright, she had to force herself not to get up and rush over to the old man. But why had the letter been addressed to him?

The old attorney put his pince nez on his nose and held the letter at arm's length. His bearing said: I distance myself from this letter, but duty compels me. Then he changed his mind, removed the pince nez and laid the letter down with the other papers.

'In summary, she writes that on the grounds that she was never divorced from her husband Daniel Greylinck, she lays claim to a portion of his inheritance. She is aware of the widow's imminent demise. She had apparently received a letter telling her of the old lady's failing strength ... (I told her in my letter, thought Agnes. Was this prompted by my letter?) ... a portion of the inheritance is for the 'dot', that is the dowry customary in France, for her daughter Agnes Valeria Greylinck, a young woman of 18 years old who intends to marry a young functionary who is evidently not very well off. She enclosed with the letter,' and the old man picked up another sheet of paper, which he read with the same distaste, without looking directly at anyone, '... she enclosed a baptism certificate for one Agnes Valeria Greylinck who was christened on the ship *HMS Promotor* at sea between Cape Town and London by one MS Bentley, an Anglican priest. Needless to say, I verified both the name of the ship and the presence of the priest. The date, 27 April 1901, appeared to be correct. Now you will ask me,' he spoke rapidly to get the business over and done with, 'how there can be two Agnes Valeria Greylincks. She explains that too.'

He replaced the pince nez, took up the letter and read out loud:

If my deed will be laid on me as a sin, bear in mind the inhuman sacrifice that was asked of me: to give up my child. Bear in mind too that the baby who was taken in her place to my mother-in-law was assured of a better life than the fate that would have befallen her as an orphan.

'I can summarise the remainder: Daniel Greylinck's wife waited in a boarding house in Cape Town for a passage to Europe where she was to be reunited with her lover in Paris. The baby was sickly and she hired a helper, or "meme" as they were known in the Cape, to assist her. The "meme" was concerned about her employer's grief and incessant floods of tears. She came up with a plan. Shortly before, she'd assisted at the confinement of an unmarried mother, and she knew the infant was available for adoption. The new baby was duly brought to the boarding house and handed over to the nurse, a few hours before the adulterous Mrs Greylinck and her baby were to embark for Europe.'

And now, at last, he looked at Agnes, who stared at him in disbelief. Then he read the last paragraph:

You understand why I could not answer the letter from the orphan child. What was I to say to her? Ask her if she would have had it any other way. Ask for her understanding. I can't give her much assistance in tracing her real mother, should she wish to do so. I stayed at the Bloemendal boarding house. If I recall correctly, it was in Kloof Street. I have no idea whether the meme *is still alive or not.*

'I always said the child was too light-skinned,' said Jannie. 'Now we must drink a toast. This is great news. And Ma made such a fuss of her. It just goes to show.'

'Come here, Agnes, dear,' said Naomi, 'Come and sit here with me, it doesn't make any difference.'

But Agnes couldn't move.

Jannie couldn't contain himself. 'Didn't Ma ever smell a rat? Or are you hiding something from us, Mr Reyneke?'

'She never doubted that the child was her daughter-in-law's …' The young attorney took over, sensing his father's discomfort and fatigue.

'But …?'

The old man set the truth above all else. 'Initially she wondered whether Daniel was the father or whether the lover was. But she pushed the doubt aside. She believed the mother herself probably didn't know who the father was. She genuinely loved Miss Agnes.'

Because Agnes remained frozen in her seat, Naomi got up and came over to her. She put a hand protectively on her head, but Agnes dodged the hand. She asked: 'Did my mother-in-law make any provision for her?'

'Our firm was instructed to pay her tuition fees and board and lodging annually. That was already taken care of earlier in the year. Nothing further.'

'She got an education out of the old woman, which is more than my children got,' said Lettie.

Piet's bladder was troubling him and he wanted to bring things to a conclusion, so he said, 'My child, our door is always open to you. Nothing has changed for us. You were sent to us.' How often the words, *Oom Piet, what is a waif?* came back to him! 'And we welcomed you with love.'

Jannie's daughters were giggling: she'd always been so high and mighty: my ouma this and my ouma that. That infuriated Agnes. She still didn't grasp everything. The young attorney was talking, but she didn't listen. Only when he said: 'Is that in order, Miss Agnes?' she had to ask: 'Is what in order?'

'That you remain in the house once your uncles have departed – how convenient that it is the college vacation – and help us with sorting things out and holding the sale. You will be remunerated, of course.'

'I will stay,' she said angrily, 'but I will not take any remuneration, and you'll have to watch me like a hawk, after all, you never know, with my background …'

'Come, come, Miss Agnes, we know you well. There is no point in bitterness …'

'Dear Lord, help me,' said Agnes who'd finally realised: The dream of being my Ouma's dearest child, the dream of my angel-mother reaching tender arms out to me, was all fabrication, deception. The mother waiting for me in France was the greatest illusion of all.

She didn't weep, she hadn't yet shed a single tear, not even for her grandmother. She is cold, thought her aunts. Even Naomi, against her will. As though she hadn't already known that for years. And learned to accept it.

Strange that Agnes didn't immediately seek a reckoning with her father, her pretend-pa.

She only thought of him months later, after the news finally reached him, and he could get a message back: Give Agnes my share, the daughter in France is nothing to me. But Agnes was not his daughter; now she could go back to him.

Except that he was already taken care of.

Except that he didn't write asking her to come back to him.

She waited to see whether a letter might not possibly still come. Until she wearied of waiting. Until she thought: The only thing left for me to do is go to the boarding house in Kloof Street. I must finish my studies and then try to get a post somewhere in the Cape Colony, as near as possible to Cape Town.

I can't just simply be nobody.

PART TWO
Agnes

1

Did fate decree that it should be Stuart, irritated by the tentative and then persistent ringing of the doorbell, who finally went to see who was there? And who found the girl standing at the door in a ray of sunshine? The girl he came to know as Agnes Valeria Greylinck?

She stepped over the threshold. And then she did something extremely odd. She pushed passed him and, with a barely audible sigh, knelt beside the lion skin that served as a rug in the passage. Taking one of the paws in both her hands, she pressed it to her cheek.

As though she were completely unaware of his presence.

A shaft of sunlight slanted into the passage, lighting the whiskers, the claws, and the ripple that spread through the skin like a nervous impulse when the paw was lifted. It also shone on her hands, her slender fingers with their tiny golden freckles.

When she eventually rose to her feet again, his face was shadowed but hers was illuminated. He saw strong emotion wash over her features, he watched the lips try to regain control of themselves, the eyelids try to conceal the gleam of tears. Her bobbed flaxen hair caught the sunlight under her small pale-green cloche hat. The hair was slightly windblown, not curly, nor quite straight either, with a soft movement of its own. The little green hat and the short green frock deepened the colour of her eyes to emerald green when she opened them again and looked at him. His face was still in the shadow, but she was aware of his physical presence and of something in his bearing that was dark and tense, and directed at her.

'I'm the new teacher and I'd like to see Dominee van Velde,' she said.

Later Leonora insisted: I was the one who first saw her standing at the door in a ray of sunshine. She always wanted to claim everything for herself: 'It was me, miss. I put my hand up first! It was me ...' The girl asked to see Father, that's why I invited her in. She was taken down the cool dim length of the passage to the study where the shutters were open and small spikes of sunlight made the colours in the room shimmer like a luminous web.

Then, said Leonora, the girl did something very odd.

She knelt on the floor beside that lion skin that the missionaries had sent to Oom Hennie – the skin of the lion that wounded him – but he couldn't bear to keep it. He'd said to his brother Josias, 'Take it if you want it. That lion cost me much more than my arm and face.' The girl knelt in the study beside the lion skin, she took one paw in her hand and raised it so the skin quivered into movement, and she pressed the paw to her cheek.

Her skin was fine and there were small red scratch marks on her cheek when she laid the paw down again.

Pressing on the floor with one hand, she stood up again, so, as he came into the room, the dominee saw only the rising movement and the smoothing down of a skirt that seemed to him to be far too short. With her small green hat and green frock, the green of her eyes struck him too. And the tiny golden freckles on the back of the hand she held out to him.

Stuart and Leonora both claimed the first acquaintance. Later they couldn't even remember whether the lion skin lay in the passage or in the study.

Perhaps there were even two lion skins.

The dominee introduced himself.

'I am Agnes Valeria Greylinck,' she said, and he recognised the name. The name she pronounced so emphatically. The name, the old attorney had assured her, is yours. That was what you were christened. I was there myself at your christening, and that is how you are named in the baptismal register. You can keep the name legally, even though you must give up everything else.

'Agnes Valeria Greylinck,' repeated the dominee. 'Our new school-teacher. I'm so glad you came to call on us.'

The sitting room shutters were closed against the heat. In cool half-light, she watched the figures that served tea: Miss Issy filling the cups, Leonora passing round, Stuart moving a small table closer to her so she could put her cup on it. She drew her breath in sharply: the table was an elephant's foot with a round top of polished wood. The rough, wrinkled dark-grey hide – almost black – the curved nails and the thick flat sole so close to her brought memories welling up. For a few moments she could neither talk nor sip her tea.

Leonora offered her a small cake.

She heard children's voices and someone scolding them in another room.

Miss Issy went to the door and called out, 'Frikkie, your tea!' The figure of another young man was introduced; he took his cup and disappeared down the passage again. But Stuart stayed. Stuart and Leonora accompanied her back to the hostel.

And the next time the shutters were open and she could see into every dark corner of the sitting room. It was furnished differently from her ouma's in Pretoria; strange and familiar at the same time. Arranged among the knick-knacks and ornaments, on side tables with cloths that hung to the floor, were curios from Africa. Carvings of animals and long-legged birds, woven mats and baskets, clay pots the red-brown and black colours of the earth with delicate patterns scratched round the rim.

She noticed the thick, heavy, copper ankle rings that were used as doorstops.

'They all come from the mission field,' said Miss Issy, who had sharp eyes. 'We made the contributions. Our congregation works hard for the mission. All these peculiar things are brought to us by missionaries who stay over here on their way back to the mission field.'

She showed Agnes the round lidded basket where she kept her darning. 'It was once my poor dear sister's, now it's mine.' She pointed out the pastorie's own mission collection box, shook it once and then replaced it on the shelf.

Agnes began – hesitantly at first, then more openly — to talk about her sojourn in Africa and her journey southwards in the litter. Miss Issy was overwhelmed with pleasure. 'Dear child, so you know the land of the heathen!'

The pastorie family all insisted on hearing more stories. The new world that was opened up for them provided a shared interest that strengthened their still tenuous unity and helped to ease their grief at losing mother and sister.

As a teacher, Agnes sat in the church gallery every Sunday morning with the seminary girls. They were early. She waited. Sunday after Sunday she watched the pastorie family come down the aisle and shuffle into the pastorie pew. They filled the front row. Stuart on the aisle, Aunt Issy beside him, then Frikkie and Leonora. Next came Nellie with the three restless boys: Philip, whose head already topped the back of the pew when he stood up; then the little plump one, Hendrik; and the youngest, Robert. And if Robbie was too full of beans, he was scolded and then eventually climbed onto Nellie's lap and fell asleep against her. Then Philip, too, snuggled in under Nellie's arm. And she saw how Aunt Issy's bony head nodded with an air that would have been pride had she not been so staunch in her humility.

As the head was bowed for the personal little pre-communion prayer, Agnes could see the one strand of grey hair that had come loose from the bun and strayed from under the black hat – a sight almost too intimate. Agnes watched them all, but she looked at Stuart the longest. Even when he stood up for the long prayer, she looked at him.

She was invited over to the pastorie regularly.

Later she would take off the cloche, toss it on the sofa and run her fingers through her hair so the fine wavy flaxen locks fluffed out like an aureole. Then the green of her eyes would shine as though they contained unshed tears, or was it just the radiance of youth and love? In love for the very first time?

Had she made use of darkest Africa to insinuate herself with the people of the pastorie? Especially Stuart?

If that was so, it was not without cost. The regular sight, the feel and the smell that still clung to the pots and skins and mats and baskets, opened a flood of memories in her. Her almost forgotten childhood welled up and hurt her where she was most vulnerable.

At night she tossed and turned on the narrow bed in the hostel where she had to live as a young teacher. Her body longed unbearably for her pa, for the smell of her sweaty pa striding into the house and pressing her against him with his good arm. For the soft touch of his damaged arm, protectively; the intimacy of the sweat-soaked shirt against her cheek; the smell of his armpits; his beard which he rubbed back and forth against her head, like an animal demonstrating his pleasure at being back with her; and the stiff, red-brown, dusty prickliness of it when she raised her head to look at him while she waited for the words: 'Right, my girl, where's the coffee then?'

And the pain of: You must go.

When she was younger and alone, with Oom Piet or Ouma, she had not longed for him with this intensity. In this new environment, her time in the Transvaal faded into the background as though it was no more than an episode in between: Pappa, then, and now here. The experience of a father who was the centre of a family, loving and caring, sharpened her longing. Or was it Stuart? And the new awareness of her body?

In the afternoons she might stroke the elephant's foot, exploring the ridges with her fingertips – her fingers were long and dainty but the nails were bitten to the quick – but at night those feet trampled her. She heard the elephants crashing through the bush and the long grass, the splintering of branches and stems; she could smell the heaps of dung.

'The droppings are fresh, girl, we're close to them,' said her pa.

She didn't realise she remembered these things, she didn't know whether she'd even experienced them, but her visits to the pastorie, with the fragments of embalmed Africa in the cluttered Victorian rooms, aroused the memories so vividly that, along with Stuart's physical propinquity, caused image after troubled image to possess her at night.

'Almost identical to this basket, but bigger and shallower – Stuart said he'd seen it on the pier at Cape Town. And the Indian played a flute and a snake rose up out of it,' said Leonora as she placed Aunt Issy's work basket on Agnes's lap. 'Have you ever been to Cape Town?'

That night the snake came, the tent, the camp beds, the scream, the swaying head as her father chopped and chopped and chopped at the body. She struggled and awoke to find her top sheet tangled up on the floor beside her bed. Thrown off, as she had sometimes pulled the mosquito net off her camp bed in a nightmare and stumbled over to her pa's bed to find her rest against his hard body.

She got up and went over to the washstand for a drink of water. Her room in the girls' hostel fronted onto the balcony with a door and a narrow window. She pushed the door open and went out. A full moon hung motionless in the sky. Suddenly it came back to her: the night the Portuguese pitched camp beside the ruins, the desolation, the black dreams, waking at dead of night, calling out: Pappa … Pappa … She rushed from the tent, the Portuguese were there, she was halted by the armed bearer who slept at the opening to her tent. She thrust the weapon out of her way, ran to the Portuguese, threw herself against him and clung, until he managed to tear himself away from her. The tent canvas flapped, flapped in the moonlight, and moaning, she took the pillow and pressed it to her body, to her stomach, rubbing her face against the gravel. 'Pappa, Pappa …'

'Have you ever been to Cape Town?' Leonora asked her.

Why? wondered Agnes. Why did she want to know? Did she suspect something?

'No, not yet, but I'm going with a friend for the short holiday.'

'Then you'll have to kiss the old woman's toe on the station,' sang Leonora, dancing round the room. 'Then you'll have to kiss the old woman's toe on the station …' until she was quite out of breath. And Aunt Issy hushed her up irritably.

2

The train journey from Worcester to Cape Town took four endless hours. She stood in the corridor, then sat down again, tried to read, put the book down, tried looking through the window, but the glass was misted over, with small trickles of rain seeping down in the frame.

'Settle down,' said her companion, who'd also been appointed to the seminary recently. 'There's nothing to see outside.'

The world was shrouded in mist. The station platform was black with rain; when the carriage doors slammed shut the water dripping from the roof splashed out in a shining shower; the conductor was invisible in the mist, and his whistle sounded as though it came from far away.

It wasn't cold. Just clammy and dark.

'It'll clear up once we get closer to Wolseley,' said her friend. 'But it'll be pouring down again at Wellington and Paarl. Mark my words.'

'And in Cape Town?'

'Who knows?'

Glimpses of vineyards and fields through the mist, people under umbrellas on the station platforms, voices and shouts, and then the slamming of doors again and the distant whistle. There wasn't even a glimpse of the sun. Water was now running in rivulets down the window panes.

Agnes couldn't control her restlessness. It wasn't only what lay ahead, but also what lay behind her: the associations called up in her by the jerk of the coupling between the carriages, the swaying this way and that and the conductor's whistle. What was she travelling towards this time? For the very first time, she suddenly longed for Tant Naomi. To be pressed against her as she had been that morning on Middelburg station, so tightly that she could hardly breathe.

They stayed at the YWCA. Aunt Issy had given them the address. They took a cab, sharing the cost. The horse's hooves clip-clopped over the wet streets; the coachman sat hunched up in his raincoat, he flicked his whip at the stubborn horse. It was still overcast and growing darker. They saw little of the city through the transparent but misted-over window blinds.

The YWCA offered a simple supper of soup and bread. Agnes hung about in the entrance hall. She waited until her friend had gone up to bed before going to the manager's office. She asked the way to Bloemenhof in Kloof Street. Yes, the place still existed. She got directions. It was close enough to walk. Now that the place she had thought about for so long was suddenly real and within reach, she could barely conceal her emotions from the manager. She pressed her hand to her mouth, as though trying to suppress a groan.

'Would you like to sit down?' said the manager.

'No thank you. It's nothing.'

But she stepped outside into the street and stood in the drizzle. Folding her arms, she grasped her elbows and hugged herself to still the trembling of her body. It was only when she became aware of the moisture on her face that she was calm enough to go in to her bed. Her hair hung in rats' tails.

It was dull and wet the next day too. Her friend wanted to go shopping, but Agnes pleaded fatigue, saying she'd rather go later.

'Very well,' said the friend, hurrying out, pausing only for a second at the door to say, 'I hope you aren't sickening for something. You look awfully pale.'

She'd hardly gone when Agnes dressed, put on her hat and took up her handbag. Then the fear overcame her. She put her bag down and started straightening the beds again, rearranged the few things they'd laid out on the dressing table the night before. Finally ventured downstairs.

In spite of the weather, the streets were busy: the water was splashed against her ankles by the vegetable barrows that trundled past. Malay urchins sang tunes and words that were strange to her ear. Now and then, as the clouds cleared briefly, she made out the wet bastion of a mountain close by. At the top of Long Street she had to cross the road and continue up Kloof Street. She began to watch the numbers on the small buildings that were packed more tightly together than she could have imagined possible. In Kloof Street there were dwellings, cafés, small shops. Her heart beat faster; in spite of the cool weather, she was wet with perspiration.

She pushed open the gate of a boarding house under the signboard Bloemenhof. She'd been brought here as an infant. Either by her real mother, or as an orphan by a coloured *meme*. She'd been carried up this garden path by who knows whom. That was her only certainty. But could the story of the orphan be true? Wasn't it just a fabrication by the adulterous woman in France?

She put her finger on the doorbell, pressed and heard it ringing down the passage. A brown woman in an apron came to the door.

'May I see the manager, please?' Her voice sounded strange.

She was taken to an office where a middle-aged woman with spectacles and upswept hair worked on her cash books. She removed her spectacles and looked up at Agnes.

'If you're looking for accommodation, I'm afraid we have no vacancies.'

'I'm not looking for accommodation.'

'How else may I help you?' She gestured to a chair.

Agnes sat down, but seemed to have lost her tongue. Her fingers snapped her bag open and shut and she looked down at her lap.

'I wanted to enquire about a woman who stayed here a long time ago.' Then the words tumbled out. 'I can't tell you exactly when. It was in April, or possibly a week or so into March.'

The manageress's tone was not friendly. 'Which April, which March? We're in April now.'

Agnes swallowed. The whole quest seemed futile now. She could scarcely answer but she had to, the woman was waiting. 'In 1901 ... I know it's a long time ago ... but you have records, perhaps something was written down ... I had thought, if you were older, you might possibly have remembered something yourself ...'

The woman rang her bell and ordered a tray of tea.

As well as she could, Agnes began to tell her about the woman she'd thought was her mother, and the second baby who was brought and sent away. 'I think it's all fiction, but I have to be certain. The people who took me in believe the story; but I still have my doubts. I don't know whether I'll ever be able to believe it. But if I don't believe it, it will always bother me. Who am I? Did my real mother lie about me?'

The woman sipped her tea. Her interest seemed to be quickening.

'It was 19 years ago. I've only been here for ten years. Our records don't go back that far. But I'm only the manageress. The proprietor is old and she might recall something.'

She drained her cup and straightened her papers. 'Have you finished? I'll take you to her. She is deaf and crotchety. Let me do the talking.'

They went down the passage. A servant was polishing the floor. She looked up when they knocked at the last door in the passage.

'The old missus has a headache and she won't let me come into her room.'

The manageress opened the door and they entered. The curtains were drawn and because it was an overcast morning the room was dark. Agnes heard a voice before she'd made out the shape of the old woman under the bedding.

'I told you they mustn't come bothering me,' said the voice.

The old woman lay flat, without a pillow. Her hair was plaited in a long stringy braid over her shoulder. The hair was grey and unkempt. A wet cloth covered her forehead and eyes. Her arthritic fingers plucked at the cloth. Then she raised one corner and a watery eye glared out at them.

'I told the maid no one was to come and bother me.'

'Just listen first,' said the manageress. 'Miss Greylinck here wants to ask a question about the old days.' Then she whispered to Agnes, 'She enjoys talking about the past.'

'I know nothing, please leave now.'

'Just listen for a minute. She wants to know if you remember a woman with a baby staying here in March or April of the second year of the Boer War.'

'What does she want to know about that? There were many people here during the war.'

'She wants to know about the baby and whether the woman sent the child back to the north with a nursemaid.'

'And what of it?'

'She wants to know if there was a second baby, brought by the *meme*. She wants to know whether the woman exchanged the babies.'

The fingers had now completely removed the cloth from the forehead and both eyes watched them suspiciously. She turned on her side with considerable difficulty and tried to prop herself up on an elbow. When she was erect she threw the blankets back and allowed her legs to hang over the side of the bed. She wore a white night-gown with a ruffle round the hem. Her toes were a dingy grey-white and it had been some time since her toenails were last clipped. She smelt unwashed.

She looked first at Agnes and then at the manageress.

'Have you come to put words in my mouth?' she demanded shrilly. 'I know nothing of babies being exchanged. Go and ask Katie. Why do you come and ask me?'

'Katie was the *meme*,' the manager told Agnes. She said to the old woman, 'You know very well that Katie died during the Great 'Flu.'

The old woman lay back again, pulling the bedclothes up; her fingers sought the facecloth. They got a whiff of lavender as she refolded the cloth and placed the cool side over her eyes again.

'I know nothing. I told Katie I deal in food and accommodation, I don't sell children. How would I know which child went to the docks with her mother in the cab and which child went to the station with the nurse?' She waved her hand in their direction. 'Now be off, leave me, I told the maid no one should come and bother me.'

'We'd better go, she won't say any more now.' Agnes left the room with the manageress.

Behind them they heard the old woman muttering, 'I told Katie if she makes anything out of it she can have it. Katie gave a lot of babies away for people.'

The manageress had done her bit. At the door of her office she shrugged and said, 'I am afraid that is the only help I can offer you.'

'Katie?'

'It would be impossible to trace her children for you, if she ever had any children. I never even knew her surname.'

'The woman would have taken her own child with her on the ship,' Agnes said. 'She wouldn't have taken the other baby.'

The manageress looked her up and down, gauging her appearance. 'Things don't seem to have gone too badly for you. What's past is past. Your life lies ahead of you. You should put all this behind you.'

'It isn't so easy to do that. You want to know where you come from, who you are.'

'I'm afraid I have work to do now. I would have liked to help, but I can't.'

I've made no progress at all, Agnes though when she was back in the street. Just that I know there were two babies. Or there could have been. So that was that. And perhaps the woman was right: my life lies ahead of me. And it's for me to make of it whatever I choose. But she couldn't stop trembling.

And she couldn't dispel the forlorn feeling in her heart. The address of the boarding house in Cape Town had been her only clue. And it had come to nothing.

Her companion was waiting for her at the YWCA. That afternoon, they took a tram over Kloofnek to Camps Bay. It was the first time she'd ever seen the sea, but the beach looked so wet and treacherous and the waves rolled up onto the sand so grey and sluggishly that she felt no desire, even the following day when the weather cleared, to go and look again. But she went to the pier at the harbour, and there she saw the snake in the Indian's basket, and she heard the tune he played on his flute and saw the snake move slowly upwards to sway like a reed in the wind.

As they were leaving she saw the old brown woman at the station, huge and fat with dark, dirty skirts spread about her. She sat like the stump of a great tree, a thick brown root among the bunches of herbs and dried pods.

She shuddered at Leonora's story about having to kiss the old woman's toe.

The sun shone throughout their homeward journey. The Boland landscape unfolded on either side of the tracks in all its green glory with the autumn colours starting to show.

'You don't look as though you've had a holiday,' said her friend who tried to keep a conversation going. 'You look miserable.'

'Oh, it's nothing serious,' said Agnes. She pleaded a headache. Does what I discovered, or didn't discover, make a significant difference to my life? she asked herself. She resolved: I won't allow it to make a significant difference. My life in the Transvaal and Oom Piet and Tant Naomi and Oom Jannie and Tant Lettie are all behind me.

I feel nothing for them. I'm going to try to be happy now. I am going to start a new life in this new world.

'I'm not miserable,' she told her friend.

She was even excited to see the seminary again when she climbed out of the cab. She took her suitcases and parcels up to her room, unpacked, and arranged the things she'd bought.

That night she stood on the balcony and looked out over the dark town. Perhaps Stuart was also standing outside tonight, perhaps he was looking in the direction of the hostel and thinking of her. The girl from the mysterious north. She played with the idea. She wasn't nobody, she was the girl from the far north. That wasn't nothing.

After five the following afternoon, Stuart's visiting card was brought up to her. His name was written on the one side, hers on the other.

'The young master is waiting downstairs,' the servant girl told her.

It was the first time he'd called on her. On his own. Coming to her alone. She turned the card over and over in her fingers – his name, her name.

'Tell him I'm coming, please,' she said to the servant girl before she went to the mirror to pretty herself up for his visit.

3

It was inevitable that Agnes and Stuart should fall in love. She was so different from them, so blonde, while the pastorie children were as dark as their mother. Except Robbie with his fair cockscomb.

For Stuart she had the allure of the exotic; and, anyway, the local girls didn't seem so keen on him anymore. It could be that they no longer trusted him. They also knew too much about his father's objections to his expedition to German South West with Louis Botha's people, his extended stay there, the talk that he'd shot one of the Boer rebels, which was untrue. He was aware of the gossip.

The politics hadn't yet been sorted out.

And there were Agnes's eyes. Such unusual green, with golden flecks round the pupil; eyes that seemed to change with every colour she wore. Whatever the years were to bring, he would never forget that first afternoon when she knelt near the lion skin, in the green dress with the green cloche on her blonde head. When she wasn't wearing the close-fitting hat, she would fasten a band round her head, fitting closely over her forehead and ears. She'd sometimes wear a long string of beads. Even her dresses were different from his sisters'; she brought big-city sophistication to the Boland town.

Little did he know of the meagre resources she'd had to stretch in order to buy the outfits, how courageously she'd splashed the bulk of Daniel's inheritance on a wardrobe for her new life.

And then naturally: Aunt Issy approved of her. Evidently something to do with the connection with the missionaries. Aunt Issy's grasp of African geography was shaky.

Agnes was quickly accepted as part of the pastorie family.

Leonora lay on the lawn playing with her cat. Agnes sat on the swing, using a foot on the ground to keep the seat swaying gently to and fro. She wore white stockings and flesh-coloured high-heeled shoes with straps. Leonora was getting to know Agnes. She missed Vicky. Missed her badly. She counted the cat's toes; the sharp little nails scratched the palm of her hand. She counted slowly out loud. It was a quiet, sultry afternoon; Stuart would be back later from the bank where he worked.

Stuart was different these days, they all sensed a kind of excitement in him. He walked differently, he was lighter on his feet and took longer strides. He would catch Leonora's braid and swing her round playfully to look at him: 'Well, well, well! Are the fellows already writing notes to you, Norie?' And he had started taking Frikkie's photography seriously, always asking Frikkie to take pictures of them, specially when Agnes was there. Say you want to take pictures of her on her own, that's all he really wants, Leonora said to Frikkie. He must ask first, said Frikkie. Let him ask, let him beg.

Try to be a friend to Agnes, Aunt Issy asked of Leonora.

Agnes wasn't very talkative; Leonora had to make all the effort.

'I like words,' Leonora said, 'Words tell stories. Numbers too. Numbers are better: you can make up stories about numbers. I have stories for every single one. I like number six the best, I want five and six to be married and then they must make 12. When I was younger, it made me cry to think that they could never make 12, only 11. What is 11? Just two skinny legs … and, no matter what the Bible might say, I don't trust seven.'

'You do think up odd things,' said Agnes from the swing.

'Shall I go on?'

Agnes nodded.

'I was secretly in love with six. That was my big secret. I wrote six on a slip of paper and folded it up and placed it in a box, wrapped in silver paper, and then I buried it in the garden. Even Vicky didn't know about it.'

She counted the cat's toes over and over again, from one to five. Even now she wouldn't say six lightly. Six was written down and buried.

Agnes leaned back on the swing. She said nothing. She wondered, half regretfully, why she never thought of things like that. Leonora was the only friend she had ever had. Leonora didn't have a mother either. She was half glad that there wasn't a mother in the pastorie. A mother would surely have questioned her already.

'What sort of person was your mother?' she asked. 'Was she like Aunt Issy?'

The 'aunt' didn't escape Leonora.

She shook her head. 'No. She was very different.' She didn't want to discuss Mother. Not with Agnes. She let the cat jump from her lap and it disappeared into the shrubbery. She didn't want to discuss Aunt Issy and Grandma either. She had already said too much.

But Agnes continued, 'I like your father.'

She was happy to talk about Father. The people from up country don't know what we're like, she thought.

'Father was pro-Boer during the war. That caused problems in town, and after the war he said it was not right that Boer children from the two old republics – the children of Boer generals, the daughters of General de Wet – should have to sing English songs with us in the school hostel. Imagine it: "When the mists have rolled in splendour," or the sentimental "Tell Mother I'll be there." He went of his own accord to conduct the morning service for them in Dutch. Father and I are close …' She crossed her forefinger and middle finger. 'If it weren't for me, I don't think Father could have coped with life after Mother and Vicky died.

'I think …' – she was actually thinking it now for the first time and felt slightly disloyal as she said it – 'in a way I was Father's ally against Aunt Issy. No, that's actually not the case, it was more so before Mother died. I remember once we played such a trick on Aunt Issy! I am very good at recitation. I memorise things very easily.'

She sat upright, threw her head back and began to recite a verse in High Dutch about old Father Bach sitting at his hearth surrounded by his children.

'Sometimes I teased Father and called him Father Bach. He liked that. Specially the bit about the hearth. Mother was still alive then. I wanted him to grow a beard but Mother said the moustache was all she could cope with.'

Then she recited a Dutch verse about Kleine Jantjie stealing from the sugar pot and getting 'bedot'. She laughed: 'Even now I don't know what "bedot" means …'

Agnes kicked against the hardened hollow that had been trodden out under the swing. 'I had to learn that one too. Bedot means caught out or fooled. But I can't recite it now.'

Agnes schemed: Aunt Issy doesn't like Leonora very much, she likes me, and I'm going to be her soulmate.

'Father egged me on,' said Leonora. 'I had to speak in the debate on "Is the pen mightier than the sword?" And Father told me: "Speak in Afrikaans tonight. Why all this High Dutch?" I was scared, but Father was in the audience and I couldn't let him down. So I took a deep breath and switched from Dutch into the Afrikaans we speak at home. It was the first time Afrikaans was spoken in our school. Father was so proud, he had lemon syrup biscuits brought from the pantry for us all when we got home. Aunt Issy was furious. She said: "My beloved seminary! It's a disgrace." I think she wanted to have only English spoken at our school.'

It's speaking English that I'm worried about, thought Agnes. Out of loving kindness, Ouma Greylinck had tried to speak English to her. But she still spoke awkwardly, and Aunt Issy sometimes took her tactfully to one side to correct a word or to give her the correct pronunciation. This made her feel worried and humiliated.

What really made Aunt Issy angry, Leonora remembered, was the way I reddened my cheeks with cochineal and geranium petals for the debate.

And, when the lights went out, a boy in the row behind her had thrust his hand through the rungs of the chair and started fondling her breast. She got such a fright she went ice cold, and then nearly died of shame when she felt the nipple suddenly harden and press against her bodice. When the lights went on again, she cast a surreptitious glance behind her. This kind of thing had never happened to her before. It must have been talking Afrikaans, or the red geranium petals and the cochineal from the pantry.

Then she discovered it was Vicky's Adriaan behind her.

'We had to speak High Dutch at school,' said Agnes who wasn't particularly impressed by the bit about talking Afrikaans. 'But no one spoke it very well, so it was a hotchpotch. Even the teachers weren't fluent.'

The following Saturday Leonora had crushed red geranium petals again and smeared them on her cheeks with cochineal and then sat waiting tensed up on her chair, for there was a row of boys behind her again. And though she felt ashamed and guilty that it was Vicky's Adriaan, she hoped it would happen again. But it was a debate in English and nothing happened. Then she knew it was not the geranium petals or red cochineal, but the talking of Afrikaans that had caused it.

They heard the garden gate squeak and then Stuart's tread on the path. Agnes left the swing, ran her fingers through her hair and went across the lawn to meet him. He opened his arms wide to receive her.

Leonora had taken Agnes's place on the swing. She shut her eyes. She kicked with both legs, swinging high up in the sky, swaying her body, swinging so high that the chains strained against the iron hooks. She swung down, leaning back, her arms stretched out straight against her grip on the chains; she swung until her arms ached from the pressure of the chains, and perspiration beaded her forehead. A black-and-yellow butterfly fluttered close, hovering over the fingers gripping the chain. She felt the fluttering against her clenched hand, her eyes were wide, the wings vibrated out a delicate, scarcely audible note. It's the worst kind of butterfly, said Agnes, as she walked away with Stuart's arm round her waist. The eggs hatch into those caterpillars that eat the lemon tree leaves and the small ornamental kumquats in the veranda pots.

The swing was almost motionless now and the butterfly still fluttered round her. Slowly, she released her fingers from the chain, studying the pollen that had fallen from the butterfly's legs onto the tiny hairs on the back of her fingers. She blew the pollen but the fine powder was sticky.

She longed for Vicky. Agnes would never be a real friend to her, she knew that. She longed for Vicky and her mother. Her eyes filled with tears and her nose started to run. She sniffed and wiped her eyes on her forearm, working with her legs and her body weight until she was swinging high, high up in the air again.

Now Stuart must just go and break Agnes's heart as well, she thought, and then felt ashamed of the spite in her heart.

Stuart was a regular visitor to the girls' hostel. He would lean against the veranda post, waiting for Agnes, waving to the girls, whistling happily as she strolled up and as he waited. He devoted his time to

Agnes every afternoon after work; for the time being he'd forgotten all about his golf. He cut a dashing figure in his boater, white slacks and striped blazer.

The schoolgirls clustered on the balcony as the two of them walked off together. They sighed, they fantasised about the couple. They regarded Stuart as the most handsome creature on earth. They envied Miss Agnes. Sometimes they were catty about her and then they identified with her again.

In their white Sunday dresses, they would line the garden path when the dominee walked from the pastorie to the church with Agnes on his arm, a bride in clouds of white – she wouldn't look her best in white, they gossiped, she had no natural colour, she was too pale. They would strew the path with rose petals for her to walk on, dreaming of their own weddings one day.

On the arm of her bridegroom's father ...

Agnes's family or lack of family came up for discussion early in the betrothal.

The night after Stuart's first passionate embrace, his lips forcing hers apart, his body thrusting against hers with increasing urgency, his hands pulling her thighs insistently against him – he must have missed her, it was the first evening after her return from Cape Town – she tossed and turned restlessly on her narrow single bed and already the bleak dilemma gnawed in her mind: What am I going to tell them about who I am?

But the feverish memory of Stuart's embrace and her response relegated the question to the back of her mind again. And she decided: I'm going to lie to them. I'm going to tell them all about my father in East Africa – they already know about him by inference. And I'm going to hang on to the story that my mother died giving birth to me. Ouma Greylinck is dead, Oom Piet is virtually bedridden, and I've no idea where Oom Jan finally ended up.

But the doubts returned after more evenings in the garden with Stuart, when his obvious efforts to restrain himself moved her to tenderness. He had the inexplicable desire to wait until after their marriage before possessing his golden girl – to wait until then before 'going the whole hog', as his friends thought he'd already done. 'Damn my reputation,' he said once, smashing a geranium with his stick. He'd never known anything like this tender, protective feeling before. He wanted to preserve her blonde untouchability. Preserve it for himself. He was surprised by the deep satisfaction he experienced from reigning in his desires. He would push Agnes away from him after a passionate embrace, careful to prevent her from letting her emotions run away with her – 'Just a little longer to wait, my sweetheart, my go-go girl, my darling!' – and then hold her close again, his cheek against her hair, until their heartbeats steadied.

This behaviour moved her so deeply that later, lying sleepless on her narrow little bed, she resolved: I'm going to tell them the truth tomorrow.

She tried to build up her resolve. I did try to find out, I got a post in the Cape, I went to Cape Town to see what I could discover, I did my best. I came to the pastorie that Sunday afternoon to ask the dominee to help me find my parents, but when I saw him and when a new life, a new family, was offered to me so wholeheartedly, so warmly, how could I help but give in to the temptation? Can they hold that against me?

Will my background make a difference to Stuart's love for me?

And Aunt Issy who is such a stickler? And the dominee – Stuart is his firstborn ... For the first time she feared that bad blood might run in her veins.

So her resolve shifted from night to night. But once they could no longer conceal their feeling (and no longer wished to) from the rest of the household, and Leonora, in her forward way, began to speak out of turn about a wedding date and a bridesmaid's frock, it was the dominee who asked her carefully, but hesitantly – for what did he actually know about the girl? and, oh, how he missed Emma's fine-tuned intuition! – 'Will your father travel down here for the wedding?' He fidgeted with his fork, looked down at his plate. 'And are there other family members to whom we should break the news?'

Stuart had spoken to his father the previous evening. 'Agnes and I wish to be married. I have proposed to her and she has accepted.' And his father wasn't opposed to the proposal either. Stuart must settle down, marriage would give him a sense of responsibility.

Now they were at table, she joined them for meals more and more frequently.

Aunt Issy, who was seated beside her, took her hand, placed it on her lap and pressed it in encouragement. The others at the table were all ears. Even Stuart looked at her questioningly. Heavens, he thought all at once, I actually don't know anything about her, we simply never made the time to talk about her family. He smiled at her as if to say: I know, we had better things to do than talk about families ... But the older generation always wants to know ...

She wiped her mouth with her serviette. She didn't return his smile.

Something is bothering her, thought Stuart. Whenever she was troubled, the green eyes would darken and the golden flecks round the pupils would become more visible. It stimulated him to see her this way. Father mustn't cause trouble now.

Something is worrying her, thought the dominee, who noticed the colour rise in her cheeks and then spread down to her neck. The awareness of her unease stirred him to action.

He folded his serviette and, once he'd said grace, he asked Agnes, 'Perhaps you'd like to come and have a chat?' He pushed back his chair. 'Shall we go to my study? Stuart, will you join us in a little while, please?' He stood aside so she could enter first and then closed the door behind him.

She'd never been in the study with the door closed before. It cut them off from everything else and this increased her agitation. An old almanac hung behind the door. It was yellowed and hopelessly out of date: August 1900. As though time had stood still. Bookshelves rose up as high as the picture rail against two of the walls. Book after book, row after row. The third wall held the window through which the sun had streamed on her first afternoon in this room. But there was no sunshine now. She looked at the family portraits that hung on either side of the window. His late wife, Aunt Issy's sister. And beside her, hanging slightly lower, a young girl with the same features as the mother, the same luxuriant dark hair, the same dark eyes. This was Victoria, she knew.

Realising she was studying the portrait, the dominee said, 'I lost her young, far too young.' Thoughts of Victoria and the course of her short life brought realisation: I must be careful with this girl and put my objections, if there are any, aside. I must make it easier for her to talk freely. Once again the old regrets over how he had treated his late daughter. Might the Lord grant him the mercy of understanding, specially if it was – Dear Lord! Please do not let it be so – understanding the sins of another. If it was indeed some sin that bothered the child so. The child from nowhere.

At his warmest and friendliest, he took her elbow and guided her to a chair.

'And now I'm getting another daughter in her place. There, there, don't be nervous! Tell me everything. Nothing is so awful that it can't be talked through. Tell me about your father in British East Africa.'

Was it the sight of the lion skin on the floor, the movement of her shoe against the hairy paw, the familiarity, the longing, the love and hate which it summoned up, which enabled her to say at last, very quietly, 'He isn't my father.'

The dominee waited.

'I don't know who my father is.' She still spoke quietly but a note of bitterness had crept into her voice.

The dominee regretted bitterness in one so young.

He regretted too, that she'd led them to believe an untruth all the months she'd been here. But he said nothing. He didn't want to staunch the emotion he saw flooding her face. He didn't want a single word from him to make her clam up again.

'I don't know who my mother is, either.' He could scarcely make out the words.

'Your grandmother, the late Mrs Greylinck?' he prompted.

'She wasn't my grandmother. My name is all I have. The lawyer said no one could take that from me.'

'Then you have no one.'

'No.' Was there a challenge in her tone, in the way she raised her chin? Submissiveness discarded? Accept me or reject me.

The dominee took up a pen from the inkstand and balanced it on the index and middle fingers of his right hand. 'I used the wrong words. Nobody has no one. Let us go back to the beginning. Where were you born?'

The answer came quickly. 'I don't know.'

'Very well, then: where were you baptised?'

Slowly and reluctantly, but also with some relief, she told him of the mother who was not dead after all, but living with her child in France; of the foundling she'd sent back to her husband in place of their natural child, a foundling baptised in Pretoria with the same name as her own child.

She started to weep. 'I don't know whether my father was also taken in, or whether he knew I wasn't his child and that's why he sent me away from him. Tant Naomi said I was young, my life lay ahead of me and I had my education – as though they begrudged me that as well.'

She took out a handkerchief and blew her nose. Then she raised those strange green eyes to meet his. He had to say something.

'Let's approach this logically,' he said in a deliberately calm voice. 'Old Mrs Greylinck and the lawyer both said your name was yours, which means they both must have been present at your baptism. And they both believed you were the real Agnes Valeria. Correct?' She nodded. 'But you were not the real Agnes Valeria.' She nodded again. 'Now who did Mrs Greylinck's daughter-in-law say you were?'

She realised the dominee wanted to say more, but she shook her head.

'The lawyer said she didn't know. She'd have said if she'd known. Only that a baby born to a Cape Town woman was brought to the boarding house. That is why I wanted to get a post in the Cape.'

The dominee was filled with compassion. He touched her arm.

'To try and find your real mother and father?'

She nodded.

'My dear child! How on earth did you think you were going to do that?'

'During the April holiday I went to Cape Town and called at the boarding house, but they couldn't tell me anything. The old *meme* who brought the baby died during the Great 'Flu.'

Could he believe her? the dominee wondered. Dared he not believe her? A foundling. Almost certainly born out of wedlock. During war-time. Would there be records? Certainly baptism registers. But the baptism was not the problem. She had the lawyer's word for that. Was there a woman somewhere today consumed with longing for an illegitimate baby she'd had to give away? Or a father who didn't realise he had a daughter? Was the father dead? Was the mother dead? Were they both dead and the girl a genuine orphan? Then he couldn't reject her. Neither as a man nor as a cleric. The sins that may have been committed were not hers.

He replaced the pen on the inkstand and came round the desk to her.

'Stand up,' he said. He kissed her on the forehead. 'As I told you: you were sent to me as a new daughter. You must never ever say again that you have no one.'

And to still his own doubts – a foundling, and his own bloodline at stake! – he resolved: During the coming synod in Cape Town, I'll try all possible sources to trace her origins. After all, 20 years is not so long. There must still be someone who knows. But which sources? It had been during war-time.

It was hardly surprising that the girl's striking blondeness, the idea of war-time, and the old church almanac behind the door should raise the memory of the Nels's Braampie in the dominee's mind.

Braampie who'd been hanged as a rebel: he, too, had been very fair. Was it a coincidence that the parents of the girl to whom he had delivered the second letter in Braampie's pathetic little bundle of belongings – a Miss Marais – had unexpectedly moved from the neighbourhood to

Cape Town shortly after Braampie's departure? And that the girl had been heavily pregnant when he finally managed to track her down in a small cottage in New Church Street?

Wishful thinking? What was the fraction of a percentage of a chance that she could be Agnes's mother?

The possibility, however remote, was not to be denied. Yet he never could confirm with certainty that Agnes was Braampie's daughter. He didn't tell Agnes of his surmise. Nor of his meeting with the woman. It was, after all, guesswork. He'd been free the morning after the synod ended. He was to take the afternoon train to the Strand to visit his brother Hennie.

Where should he begin searching? Why not at the Marais'? Twenty years was not such a long time. The people still occupied the small house against the slopes of Tamboerskloof. Just this side of the Buitengracht.

When he walked up the garden path, he heard the sound of scales being played; monotonous notes repeatedly climbing up the scale and then down again. The mother opened the door to his knock. She did not recognise him at first. The door opened towards the light and all she could see was a dark silhouette standing there. But then she made out the white bib and the frock coat. Hesitantly, she invited him in. Only once he was in the room with her did she realise who he was. Can she read on my face as clearly as I do on hers the toll the years have taken? he wondered.

'Please take a seat, I'll call my husband,' she said.

'Kerneels, the dominee from Worcester is here.'

But when he indicated he wanted to discuss the baby her daughter had carried, she shook her head: 'Don't stir that up again. It's all behind us now. Thank the Lord. It's past.'

The man was slovenly: braces over his collarless shirt, slippers on his feet. Unshaven. His eyes narrowed.

'What is it that you wish to know, dominee?'

'I'd prefer to speak to your daughter personally.'

'Why dig up that old business now?' asked the woman. She took off her apron and dropped it onto a chair. 'Our daughter cares for us, she supports us by her talent.' The scales ceased, the piano was closed, footsteps sounded in the passage, the front door banged, and then the daughter came into the room where they sat.

How old would she be? wondered Dominee Josias. Thirty-eight?

Forty? Still in her prime. On the thin side with an angular face and figure, and with a certain mistrust in her eyes. He was hesitant about speaking of the baby. So long ago. The mother was right, it was past. But the scars remained.

And he thought of Agnes again.

'The dominee wants to talk about that old business,' said the mother.

'Is that necessary?'

'Indeed, I think it is,' said the dominee.

'I had the baby taken away for adoption.'

'Do you know by whom?'

'It was better not to know.'

'Who took her away?'

'The midwife. It was certainly not the only baby she had ever given to new parents.'

'Can you tell me her name?'

'Katie, but I don't know whether she's still alive. Why do you want to know?'

'A girl the age your daughter would be now is looking for her mother.'

The younger woman pulled a chair clumsily closer. She collapsed on to it as though her knees could suddenly no longer bear her weight. Then she looked up at the dominee with the emptiness of old age in her faded blue eyes.

'What good would that do? Do you think I'd recognise her? Or that she'd be able to sense I'm her mother?' She dropped her gaze and then looked up again.

'I must assure you, dominee, I would not acknowledge her as my daughter.' Her voice grew bitter. 'People still talk of Braampie as a hero. I reckon it is my duty to consider his reputation.'

'And do you think about the child?'

She gestured to the room where they sat, the sparse, cheap furnishings, the state her father was in. 'I barely manage to keep things going here. What could I do for her?'

If it wouldn't have been banal, he would say: to give her love and certainty. But he said it all the same.

'There'd never be certainty,' said the woman. 'I don't have any love to give her.'

She looked him full in the eye and he was struck once again by the emptiness and the resignation in the pale blue eyes.

'Perhaps she has something to give you.'

The woman clasped her arms against her chest as though she was suddenly cold. So it had been a shock. Her hair was scraped back and he saw a streak of grey in it. More scars. The eyes. The slight hollows under the cheekbones. The shoulders that were stooped in spite of her youth. From bending over the piano, eyes fixed on the notes which the pupil could not play correctly; perhaps too hard-up for a pair of spectacles?

'She was assured of being well cared for. Better than here.' She rocked back and forth on her chair, her arms still clasped around her.

To the dominee, the movement was like a soundless wailing. He said gently, 'Can I tell her to come and call on you? Just once?'

She didn't look up. The rocking continued.

'She can come, but I will not acknowledge her. So rather spare both of us that.'

And the older woman said, 'You can't prove anything, dominee.'

The old man interjected, 'She may have inherited money.'

The dominee shook his head. 'No, she isn't a heiress. It was for love's sake that I came. But in vain, I realise now. No thank you, no coffee for me.'

He saw that, amongst the grey hairs, the old man's eyebrows were very light, almost flaxen, and there were pale freckles on the backs of his hands. If only one could be certain. The cottage felt to him like a prison. A young woman who had transgressed, the prisoner. Condemned to serve a life sentence?

He made his way slowly back to the city.

The previous evening, dining at home with a colleague whose wife was known for her welfare work, he had asked, 'How can one trace the records of an illegitimate birth 20 years ago?'

'Were they church-goers? No? That sort of birth was kept so secret that even close family members didn't know about it. Sometimes the baby was brought up by the grandmother, passed off as her "autumn lamb". It was regarded as a great scandal.'

'And if the baby was put up for adoption?'

'Also a secret transaction. It would be difficult to trace either the parents or the child.'

'Would the midwife organise the adoption?'

'Yes, and probably for a fee. Remember that it was war-time. Many a girl was seduced by a soldier.'

He tried to trace the 1901 birth registers in the appropriate office but was told: The registers were all sent to Pretoria in 1918. You can write to them.

But what certainty would he gain from a list of illegitimate baby girls born in 1901? Yet, someday, he could ...

He hurried to the station where he caught the train to the Strand where his brother lived. He needed Hennie now.

It was the last fitting of the wedding dress at Miss Golightly's. Agnes had invited Aunt Issy to accompany them: Agnes came to the pastorie so they could all walk together. Leonora pushed her books away. 'Oh, clothes, always clothes.' As though she hadn't simply taken it for granted she'd be the bridesmaid without ever consulting Agnes.

'No, brother Stuart, you cannot stand before the altar without your sister.' Your only sister. But she didn't say the word 'only'.

As he did more often these days, Stuart took hold of her braid and swung her round. She was out of breath, but, in sheer exuberance, he carried on until she was dizzy and fell against him.

'I agree completely, Norie.' And he said the words: 'The only sister I have.' She hated him for saying the words.

The pavements were too narrow for the three of them to walk side by side.

Agnes and Aunt Issy went ahead, with her following half in the furrow, which was dry this afternoon. She didn't like walking behind them. Every now and then she skipped on one foot. Sixteen and still so childish, thought Aunt Issy. Agnes carried the flat dress box containing the train – she'd stitched the pearls to it herself. Miss Golightly was to fasten it to the headdress. She walked carefully, supporting the flat box on her outstretched arms.

Miss Golightly lived three blocks away in a house where she rented two rooms – the veranda room was her workroom, the other a bedroom. She shared the owners' bathroom and kitchen. She had lived there for as long as the townsfolk could remember.

The room was half-dark for coolness, but a shaft of light came in through a side window. The sewing machine stood in the light. The space was cluttered with boxes and fabric, there was a tailor's dummy and a long oval mirror in which clients could admire themselves in their new outfits.

Miss Golightly was all of a twitter about the dresses for the bride and bridesmaid for the pastorie wedding. When Aunt Issy knocked, she threw the door open wide and said, all nervous excitement: 'Oh, my goodness! Today's the day!' She welcomed them in with outstretched arms. She wore her working dress and the pincushion lay against her high bosom. It hung round her neck on a ribbon but it looked as though it was supported by the up-thrust bosom, right in the middle, between the two breasts, like a barricade.

Against molesting hands, thought Leonora, who sat to one side on a pink corded-velvet ottoman. The sharp ends should point outwards so they could pierce the molester. Miss Golightly breathed agitatedly as she helped Agnes to change, and the pincushion heaved up and down on the bosom. A stuffed red heart studded with silver pinheads. Leonora couldn't take her eyes off it. Then she thought: Who would want to touch Miss Golightly?

The gleaming white wedding dress, nearly complete, was flung over Agnes's head.

Miss Golightly's plump, nimble fingers plucked a few pins from the cushion on her bosom, and tucked them between her lips, to be used one by one as she trotted round the bride. Here easing a seam a tiny bit with the tips of the scissors that she held at the ready, not through the loops but on the shaft, while she made little clicking noises with her tongue against her palate.

Out came another pin from between the lips, to fasten a folded-over seam, to pin a small adjustment. The wedding gown was ankle length with a voluminous gathered skirt, and two pleated net frills on either side of the bodice, almost like a generous fichu. The long transparent sleeves had wide ruffles at the wrist. The bouquet, which Miss Golightly was to create, would nestle among the ruffles.

'I do think it's beautiful,' Miss Golightly said humbly. 'But of course, the bride carries it off.'

'Your handiwork, Miss Golightly,' said Aunt Issy graciously. 'How proud our dear Emma would have been.'

And Agnes studied herself in the mirror, with a little tug here, and slight jerk of the head to make the train fall over the left shoulder, an approving stroke over her hips.

'It is beautiful,' she said at last. 'I'm sorry to have to take it off.' She stared at her hazy reflection in the mirror, shiny-eyed, completely absorbed in the moment.

When she stepped out of it, the dress was gathered up like a precious treasure by Miss Golightly, lovingly stroked and draped over the tailor's dummy on its wooden stand.

'Now for Leonora. Come, child, slip off your dress.'

Leonora's frock was pastel pink and of the same fabric and design as the bride's. She stood before the mirror while Miss Golightly deftly fastened the hooks and eyes at the back. At first the bodice edges wouldn't meet, but the plump hands tugged determinedly. 'Pull in your stomach, dear.' The shiny pink fabric strained tight as the hooks were fastened, the pink frills of the fichu stood up like wings. Facing her reflection in the mirror, Leonora stamped her foot. 'I hate it! It's an ugly dress! It makes me look like a puffed-up frog.'

'Come, come! We'll just loosen one seam and it'll fit perfectly.'

'I don't care about the fit, the dress is ugly.' She flapped her arms with the flounces at the wrists. 'I can't wear something like this.'

'But you were happy when you first tried it on.'

'These hideous flounces weren't there then.'

'This is absolute nonsense,' said Aunt Issy. 'Control yourself, Leonora. We'll decide what you'll wear. I see nothing wrong with the dress. You yourself thought Agnes looked beautiful.'

'I am not Agnes.'

Miss Golightly saw her dream of the group in pink and white at the altar start to crumble.

'Tell us, Leonora, what worries you?' she asked courteously.

'The whole thing.' She was on the point of tears. 'The colour and the fabric and frills and all the puffiness.'

Snip-snip-snip went the tips of the scissors, and first the one flounce and then the other fell from the bodice. More snip-snip-snip, and the flounces fell from the sleeves.

'A plainer style. Is that what you want?'

'Oh, Leonora,' said Agnes, 'I so badly wanted us to look alike at the altar.'

'But we aren't alike.' She rubbed her eyes with her balled fists. 'We aren't alike and we'll never be the same and leave Mother out of this whole affair.' She tried to scramble out of the dress and Miss Golightly only just managed to prevent her from ripping it.

'Something quite simple? I'll redo it. In two days' time you may come for a fitting. Will that please you?'

Leonora nodded.

As they left, Aunt Issy said, 'Miss Golightly, I do esteem you. I might even say I envy you.'

But on the way home when Leonora asked why Miss Golightly should be 'esteemed' – after all, she was being paid – she was told bluntly: Because she is a woman on her own, keeping body and soul together with the labour of her own hands She is beholden to nobody. 'Now put that on your plate and eat it.'

But there were other things on Leonora's mind as she walked in the dry furrow, kicking up the loose soil, hanging back a little way from Aunt Issy and Agnes. Out of the blue, the thought had suddenly come to her when she saw the dress on the tailor's dummy and Agnes, shy, even tremulous, stood there in her petticoat with her arms bare, her hands folded over her stomach, as though she – she, she dare not think it, but she thought it all the same – as though she wanted to protect something unnameable. There were two Agneses. Not just the one in Miss Golightly's dim workroom. Somewhere there existed another one. Agnes had told her about the other one, but no one had ever said anything about her again. It would be her secret – the other Agnes Valeria. The girl in France – a brunette like Vicky was, as pretty as Vicky. If only she could have had her as a friend instead of the white-faced Agnes. But how could she ever get to know her?

The dominee didn't tell Agnes about his visit to Cape Town.

On her wedding day, he escorted her up the aisle on his arm and gave her to his son Stuart, before climbing up into the pulpit where he bowed his head and prayed in silence and then joined the two of them in holy matrimony in the presence of the congregation.

Fortunately, he thought wryly, this time I'm not acting contrary to Issy's wishes.

Frikkie set up his tripod beside the path that led from the pastorie to the church. He started taking pictures as the newly-weds emerged from the church. Agnes narrowed her eyes against the sudden bright light and the first pictures were a failure. Even in the others she looked slightly startled.

But the white tulle on the band on her forehead suited her, and the dress made by Miss Golightly, in the newly fashionable ankle length, strewn with small pearls which the bride had stitched on herself, reflected the sunlight, and this, along with the slightly startled expression on her face, made it look as though she was floating.

Father, Aunt Issy and the pastorie children walked solemnly behind her and Stuart; they were missing Mother. Leonora in her pink dress, remade to her taste, walked beside Father.

Stuart's hair gleamed with oil and his swarthy skin with sweat, his morning suit and starch-fronted shirt were a trifle too small for him. He realised that a new life was beginning for him.

The camera clicked and clicked until everyone had disappeared into the house.

4

Herr Winterbach had told him: Photography comes from the Greek words that mean 'inscribe in light'.

Or had Father told him? Frikkie wondered.

The wedding pictures he'd taken and developed hung drying on the line. Fastened with clothes pegs. From the time he'd seen Kowie's cheek take shape in the developing tray, the gentle curve coming nearer, and the eye, so tender, so close, so exposed, he knew she was his. More and more of the prints he made of her image hung from the line he'd strung over his bed: cropped out of group photos, reduced, enlarged, lighter, darker, cropped this way, cropped that way. Father, he asked silently: Have I not inscribed in light? In beautiful radiant light that makes my heart soar and fly with the swallows, drift among the clouds? And she is mine. Because I alone possess her, here in my room, day and night.

Father was disappointed that his second son, Frikkie, who was more intelligent than the older one, did not want to study beyond his first year at university.

There had already been talk of this during the July vacation. He came home at the end of the year with good marks: distinctions in Greek and Latin; satisfactory pass marks in Dutch and Mathematics, a good pass in English, passing all his 11 subjects, but he showed no sign of becoming a scholar.

'Use my library,' Father offered eagerly that first day over lunch. Aunt Issy had laid on a special meal; the table groaned with Frikkie's favourite dishes. 'There must be some tasks you have to complete during the vacation. I'm so proud of you, my boy – Greek and Latin were my special delight. We can read together. What a pleasure! An hour or so, of an evening!'

Father had to dab his moustache and beard, because the chicken dish was dripping with gravy. In his excitement over the return of his son he hadn't eaten as carefully as usual; faster too, because expressing his pleasure was uppermost in his mind.

I haven't seen Father so animated since Mother and Vicky died, thought Leonora. Frikkie meant everything to him ... Frikkie, Frikkie, I love Father too, my dear brother. Don't hurt him now, Frikkie. Not now.

In July Frikkie had confided in her: I loathe studying; those dead languages, Norie ...

Not now, not on the first day, she begged with her eyes.

He didn't notice. But he too was aware of his father's joy, and he spoke carefully, as one would to a child: 'Later on, perhaps. I'm going to have a bit of a holiday first, Father.'

'Of course! Of course! Forgive me. It's just that I'm so proud of you. Later, yes, later.'

'Let's say grace.'

The dominee waited in vain after the evening meal. Night after night. It was summer and darkness fell late. He strolled in his rose garden. I'm neglecting my duties, he thought, waiting for him. I took the books down from the shelves, they lie ready on the table. The words ran through his mind. Virgil:

Arma virumque cano, Troiae qui primus ab oris
Italiam fato profugus Laviniaque venit
litora, multum ille et terris iactatus et alto
multa quoque et bello passus ...
vi superum, saevae memorem Iunonis ob iram.

'I sing of arms and a man – the exiled hero ... the first to step on Trojan shores ...'

I'm seeking joy and nourishment in my books again, he thought. I dare not open them alone. My son must be my excuse. When I read Virgil, I think of Emma. Our initials are interwoven on the flyleaf. Everything I read makes me think of her: the E in Evangelism, the E in Esther.

My gentle Emma, our young love was so sweet. E twined so tenderly around the upright J. I see it everywhere in the margins and the white spaces of my books. Now I wait for my son, your son, to bring you back to me.

But his son was wrestling with matters of the heart. His love lay unfulfilled ahead of him, his love had yet to be won. I simply cannot spend another year in a town far from where Kowie lives, Frikkie decided. Seeing Kowie four times a year wasn't enough. He could no longer endure the uncertainty. He, too, was reminded of her by everything he read.

Sumer is icumenin;
Lhude sing cuccu!
Groweth sed, and bloweth med,
And springeth the wude nu.
Sing cuccu!

That hurt. God, it hurt. The picnic, the tripod, the communion in the lens. Of which she was unaware. But he'd make her aware of it, she had no idea of what he felt.

After lunch, he changed into his white flannels, blazer and straw boater. If that was what she wanted. Fine, he'd do it.

'Kowie is cheating you, Kowie is cheating you,' Leonora sang from her bedroom window, the net curtain pushed aside as she watched him walk away. His gait was full of expectation, his whole lean body spoke of it, his head, his shoulders. He wasn't as handsome as Stuart, neither in face nor build, his hair not dark and curly but straight and mousy, but his eyes were tender, more vulnerable than Stuart's, she thought, immediately regretting her spitefulness. Do I always have to be so awful? she thought and prayed out loud, 'Dear Lord, please let Kowie be good to him.'

Kowie's people lived in a poorer suburb, her father was a carpenter who did odd jobs round town. Kowie wasn't interested in further study.

Frikkie knocked at the small semi-detached house.

'Is that you, Kareltjie? Just come right in, I'm out here at the back.'

He turned the doorknob and stepped over the threshhold. This dark narrow passage with the linoleum and the coat rack where everyone's jackets and raincoats hung with the smell of the people caught up in them, the cat rubbing up against the frame of the passage door ... he sighed deeply: this threshold marked the entrance to the unknown, the mysterious, the inevitable. How long he'd yearned for it!

He came into the dining room. The door to the back veranda stood open. Blinding light shone in from outside.

He saw Kowie stand up and come forward with her head bent over forwards. A waterfall of shining red-brown hair hung over her face, then she tossed her hair back and it fell like brown mountain water over her shoulders. Her thin, pert little face was revealed.

'Oh, it's you.' She pulled her blouse closed over her breasts: to get the blouse out of the way while she washed her hair, she'd undone the top buttons and tucked the collar in all round.

'I thought you were only coming tonight. My, but you do look smart.'

He held his boater in one hand and his other hand reached out for her arm, but she evaded him, and as she swung away he saw once again that which had wounded him so mortally: the tender line of the cheek, the slight rounding of the chin where it met the neck, the dear, dear nostril.

He was weak at the knees.

He was dumbstruck.

'You can help me dry my hair if you like.'

'Did you wash your hair for me?' He almost whispered the words.

'Maybe. Maybe not.'

She handed him the damp towel and bent her head over so the hair fell forward again. He took it reverently, and began to rub her head gently.

'Harder, take it and rub it like you rub washing.'

He couldn't manage the rubbing, he just touched the hair; pressing gently like one would dab cottonwool carefully on a wound.

'Give me the towel.' She rubbed her hair dry vigorously.

'Is your mother home?' Frikkie asked. Aunt Issy had taught him: you greet the lady of the house. You don't visit young eligible girls alone in intimate circumstances. He felt confused. But excited too. The hair dry enough for her liking, she began to brush it out, then she twisted it into a chignon, which she fastened with hairpins taken from a box on the veranda table and held between her lips as she worked. With her hair up, her face looked smaller, almost childish.

As the sun sank behind the veranda, the red lights dimmed in her hair.

He put out a hand to touch her cheek. But she dodged him again. 'Come into the kitchen. I'll make coffee.'

He could smell the fresh lemon fragrance of her hair. He saw the warm damp cleft between her breasts as she pulled out her collar and fastened the buttons again.

They drank coffee. A racket at the door, the stamping of feet and in came Kareltjie, an old school friend, Kowie's one-time school boyfriend. He was very much at home and took a chair before he was invited to do so. He was powerfully built, broader in the shoulder than he'd been at school. His eyes were small and close-set, his face was rugged and burnt red. He dug a friendly elbow into Frikkie's chest.

'Our learned gentleman is back. About time. You chaps actually do bugger all. My pa could do with another hand.'

His father was a building contractor. Father and son were both strong men.

'Pa and I will soon get some muscle onto you ...'

'Oh, stop it,' said Kowie. 'Just leave him be. Frikkie's muscles are here ...' and she tapped her head.

'Ah, but I know of some better places ...'

Kareltjie slurped his coffee, winked conspiratorially at Frikkie and then laughed so much he slopped coffee into his saucer. At first Frikkie was offended by the wink, but then decided that, in a sense, it included him in a new league. A league that called on girls alone at home and dried their hair ...

'So what are the plans for tonight?' asked Kareltjie.

'I thought ...' said Frikkie, but didn't get any further. Kareltjie interrupted him.

'Guess what? I also thought ...' and he guffawed again, until Kowie threw a dishcloth at him.

'It's Frikkie's first night back. I also thought ...'

'Okay, calm down. There's bioscope tonight. We're all going. Frikkie's pockets are bulging with money.'

Oh dear Lord, thought Frikkie. The word 'bioscope' had dispelled the pleasant sensation of conspiracy and bonding. Kowie and the ray of light that took me into a wonderland. Must I share them with Kareltjie? Must I hear his comments; keep an eye on his hand to make sure it doesn't creep onto Kowie's knee; put up with his complete disrespect for my two miracles: Kowie and the light?

But he couldn't let them go on their own.

'I'll pick you up at half past seven, Kowie,' he said. 'Shall I ask your parents if you can come?'

'They'll probably also go and they'll be only too pleased that they don't have to pay for me as well.'

She went with him to the door. In the passage she whispered, 'I did wash my hair for you.' Then the door was closed again and she went back to Kareltjie.

Frikkie heard them laughing behind the closed door.

She's playing with you, my boy, thought Leonora who'd seen him return to his room and knew he was lying on his bed gazing at the photos that encircled him. But you don't want to face up to it.

Leonora was lonely. Misery sat heavy on her heart. She'd lost Stuart and Frikkie. There was strife between her and Father. Even Aunt Issy was against her – the older woman was completely wrapped up in Stuart and Agnes.

She yearned for Mother and Vicky. Every night she gazed up to heaven. Mother and Vicky – were they up there somewhere, up with the stars? Was there a heaven somewhere like the one Mother had described? She lay on her back on the lawn and gazed up into the sky. It felt as though a pale blue lid was pressing the life out of her, and she had to stay under this lid until the day she died.

But everything was not dead under the lid. At night she leaned on her bedroom windowsill counting the stars as they came out. You couldn't keep up once they started to shine. She had to turn her head first this way and then that but they always beat her. She decided: one night she was going to stay awake all night, she alone in the whole world, watching the universe fill up and start to shine with stars like jewels. And she would keep watching until day broke and they had to give way, growing dimmer and then disappearing behind the pale blue lid.

Then I will have possessed them, she thought, and they will be mine forever.

She frowned because that was what Frikkie had told her about Kowie: I have possessed her, she is mine.

And Kowie was going to cheat Frikkie, she could swear to that.

Nellie and the three little boys came to the garden. Nellie sat on the lawn with her basket of mending, the boys played with a ball. But they didn't kick it about much, preferring to mill around Nellie. Even Philip who was already at school leaned against her, playing with the strands of hair that had come loose from her bun. As usual, Robbie, the youngest, climbed on her lap and threw an arm round her neck so it was difficult for her to get on with her mending. Only Hendrik, the little plump one, tried to kick the ball, ran after it, caught it clumsily and came running back. He would be going to school the next year.

Leonora sat up, suddenly filled with love for her three motherless brothers. She wanted to hug them so close they'd lose their breath. She still had them.

'Come,' she called out. 'Come and swing, I'll push you as high as the sky!' They scrambled through the fence after her. 'Robbie first because he's the smallest.'

She picked Robbie up and put him on the swing. 'Hold on tight,' she shouted, 'Hold on as tight as you can, I am going to push you up very high!'

Robbie screamed with pleasure. One after another the little boys got a turn. The iron rings which hadn't been oiled for ages screamed along: claiing, clang, claiing, clang, claiing, clang.

Then she had Philip sit tight on the wooden seat and turned the seat round and round, winding the two support chains round each other, tight, then tighter still, one more turn, then she let go, and she staggered back and the suddenly silent boy on the swing spun round and round like a top as the chains unwound.

'Was than fun, Philly?' He nodded, dizzy.

Hendrik tugged at her dress: 'Me too, Norie, me too!' Until she gave in and repeated the game with him.

But Robbie was back on Nellie's lap. Leonora wanted to snatch him up and hug him, but he was frightened of the spinning swing. She kneeled on the grass and ran her fingers through his little crest of hair; he pressed his head against Nellie's breast.

From the veranda, Aunt Issy called Nellie and the children.

'Excuse us please, Miss Leonora,' said Nellie, taking the children and her mending basket inside again.

From his study, the dominee heard the play. Life turned out so differently from what one expected. Was Norie now his mainstay? Yet, when she came to stand behind his chair, her hand on his shoulder and said, 'Father, when I've finished school, I'd like to go to university. I want to study Greek and Latin and I'll be the one who'll read Virgil with you,' he pushed her hand from his shoulder.

'I'd planned to send you to the Normal College in the Gardens in Cape Town.'

'I don't want to go to college. I want to go to university.'

'There are still three boys to be educated.'

'But if Frikkie doesn't return to university?'

'I must think of the boys.'

She started to weep. 'It's not fair, Father. You put them first. It's because I want to read Virgil with you that I want to go to university.'

But he didn't hear her, she was already walking out of his study. Issy must teach her not to mumble so, he thought as he got back to work.

She couldn't sleep that night.

She lay listening to the sounds in the house.

Her father was restless. What was he fidgeting with downstairs? She wondered if he'd ever marry again; members of the congregation had already asked her. What was he doing down there? The shutters on the veranda doors and windows had been closed and fastened long ago. The front door opened, she heard him move a veranda chair, then come inside again, come upstairs. After a while, everything was quiet again. Tonight was the night she'd go outside.

She tiptoed down the passage. There was no strip of light under his door. She crept down the stairs, treading on the outside edges so the boards wouldn't creak. The house looked different at night. She saw the table, the easy chairs, the sideboard; they were like dogs, about to stir and keep her at bay, but she said: There, there, go to sleep. In the kitchen the linoleum seemed to cling to her bare feet, but she said: Hush! Let me go. Slowly, she drew back the bolt on the kitchen door.

It was lighter outside on the back veranda; there wasn't a moon so it must be the stars. Her heart began to thud as she left the veranda and slipped out over the backyard. She was frightened now. What might be lurking in the dark shadows round the outhouses? She heard the horses in the stables. Hush, hush, she whispered, stroking the dog that came staggering out of its kennel and tried to jump up against her. He licked her hands. In the pitch darkness, she felt for the rail on the steps up to the wagon shed loft. The wood was rotten and it was out of bounds for the children. In the pitch dark she felt for the first step. The hem of her nightgown was bundled up in one hand, the other hand slid up the railing.

She had to climb under the railing to get from the small platform in front of the loft door, jumping down onto the tin roof and scrambling between the pumpkins set up to ripen, then stepping on the pumpkins, and still clutching her nightdress, she tried to climb from there up to the high flat roof of the stables. The corrugated iron creaked when she jumped onto it, she clambered over the pumpkins on all fours, but the dogs didn't bark, there was no disturbance in the yard, and she could go on. The sharp edge of the iron cut her hands when she grabbed hold of it to pull herself up, but it didn't hinder her, she'd made it onto the top. She crept along as far as the gable end of the wagonshed, because she felt safer there, and then lay flat on her back.

For a moment she couldn't believe the sight that met her eyes. The stars streamed round her from all sides, like midges circling her head. It was as though the stars were sinking down onto her. She tried to draw back, feeling her spine press against the iron roofing. Then she was drawn up into the cosmos, among the stars. Her heart pounded uncontrollably. Whichever way she turned her head, all she could see was the glitter, the terrible, insistent presence of all the dazzling stars. Her eyes sought out the larger ones which she recognised: the Southern Cross, the evening star, the Hunter with his girdle and dagger, the two dogs following him. She sucked them in, drank them, drew in great gulps of their light. The Milky Way was like a hand on her head.

Dear Lord, she thought, is this where You live? Is this what You look like, so that we can prostrate ourselves at Your feet? Vicky, Mother, is this where you are, in the terrible light of the firmament?

But Vicky and Mother were unreal, remote, and they didn't comfort her. She could not bear it. So much, so much, so huge, so much Light. She began to weep. Her legs were ice cold against the iron roof, she was stiff from lying still, she could feel the cuts on her hands, her hair was damp and heavy and cold like a dead thing on her head. But she couldn't move. As the tears trickled from her eyes, the stars went streaky. She wiped her eyes with the sleeve of her nightdress.

The she turned on her side and lay for a while with her hands on her cheeks.

The iron close to her face also seemed beautiful. She stroked the corrugations gently – the shadow in a hollow, the light on the ridge, the tiny speckles in the iron.

She didn't know whether she had wept for Vicky or Mother or the stars, but she did feel comforted. Beneath her, the milking cow was at the manger. If she had been closer, she would have been able to hear her chewing the cud, and hear the horses snorting ... and perhaps the cat was in there with them in the straw and the dog was outside in his kennel.

Dear Jesus, she thought, You were also born in a stable. Perhaps the universe seemed just as huge to you. She felt comforted by the animals so close by.

When her teeth began chattering from the cold, she crept carefully back over the roof, made her way down the rickety steps, slipped over the yard, in through the kitchen and up to her room by the back stairs. Her nightdress was damp and soiled. She stuffed it into her wardrobe and put a fresh one on. How was she going to explain to Aunt Issy?

But Aunt Issy's attention was completely focused on Stuart and Agnes's small household. They had rented a two-bedroomed house in a street not far from the pastorie, and from the time that a shy and blushing

Agnes had announced what Aunt Issy referred to as her 'holy secret', the older woman had been forever taking things down to her and giving advice.

It was a terrible blow to her when they heard Stuart was to be transferred, with a slight increase in salary, to Wellington, a neighbouring town just over the mountain.

The dominee didn't drive a car, and the only access was by train. The long way round. From now on a visit would involve a major expedition instead of a short walk with a freshly baked loaf of bread or a crocheted baby jacket which Aunt Issy had bought at the church bazaar.

Unlike the way she had been with her sister, Emma, Aunt Issy took the keenest interest in Agnes's pregnancy.

Agnes was five months pregnant when they had to pack up and move house. All their possessions – furnishings, kitchenware, houshold linen and clothing – were transported to the station and loaded in a truck. It was a train with passenger coaches and goods trucks. And when it steamed off and as she watched Agnes's trembling hand wave to her and then disappear, Aunt Issy felt desolate.

Leonora, who was at school, had said goodbye the night before and was not overly concerned about their departure. Whenever she could, after school or on Saturday mornings, she'd go to help Frikkie in the room he'd hired as a studio. The room was on the main street and opened out onto a long veranda. At the back, a staircase led up to living quarters which were also rented out.

Frikkie whitewashed his studio, built a partition, and Leonora, who was good at art, painted pillars and palm trees on the large canvas curtain which served as the backdrop for his photography. She loved being there in an overall, away from Aunt Issy's admonitions; making great sweeping strokes over the canvas and watching the colours create form. Never mind that her sea was lumpy and unnatural and the palm fronds, which were supposed to be swaying in the breeze, looked as though they were leaning forward onto the blue sky. Her Greek pillars were slightly more convincing.

She couldn't spend too much time with him because Kowie seemed to be getting jealous, even possessive of Frikkie. I'm doing you a favour, my boy, thought Leonora who took up her school bag and left for home when Kowie showed up after her day's work at the pharmacy. She's scared that you're too fond of me. She's jealous of me. She wants your undivided attention.

It made her pleased but also sad. She was going to lose Frikkie too.

But, to her own surprise – and to Kareltjie's who was also courting her and earning more than Frikkie – Kowie decided to marry Frikkie.

'She is only marrying you because you are a dominee's son and more high class than Kareltjie,' Leonora said spitefully.

'You're wrong, Norie. She's marrying me because I claimed her as my own,' Frikkie said serenely.

She made a pretty bride in a frock of pastel pink tulle. Frikkie took so many pictures of her that the wedding guests had to wait half an hour before the couple appeared at the reception. Aunt Issy had a headache and didn't attend the wedding. The photos of the bride were so beautiful that more and more couples asked Frikkie to take their wedding pictures. He was able to hire two rooms above the studio and set them up as living quarters. Slowly but surely, he built up his career.

5

Married life in Wellington started off on a less propitious note for Agnes and Stuart. In an uncharacteristically courtly gesture, Stuart lifted Agnes up in his arms and tried to carry her over the threshold. She was five months pregnant with their first baby and he whispered in her ear, 'This is our first real home.' Then he stumbled and, even though she landed on her feet, she threw her arms so anxiously around his neck that his efforts to regain his balance failed and he fell flat on his face. And as he fell, he pulled her down with him.

He stood up and dusted off his trousers before noticing, to his surprise, that she was crying.

He heard her say, 'The baby.'

A bed was hastily off-loaded and carried into the front bedroom. A blanket was thrown over it and a pillow was produced from goodness knows where. Cautiously, she was led to the bed.

And so it happened that Agnes was laid up when the furniture was carried in, and Stuart had to say helplessly: this comes here, that goes there. Her own house felt strange to her for months. It felt to her as if the furniture was placed awry, the living room wasn't hers, the dining room furniture looked bigger and heavier than it had in the rented house in Worcester. She didn't have the energy to get everything moved around again.

And when the baby was born – they named him Josias after his grandfather – he kept her so busy she didn't have time to worry about the furniture.

By the time Frikkie and Kowie's twin boy and girl were born in Worcester, Agnes was pregnant again. This time she carried more easily. This time it was a girl, and to everyone's surprise she wasn't named after Stuart's mother or grandmother, but after Aunt Issy. Her full name: Isobelle. The child was known as Sussie – 'little sister'.

Agnes now had the time and energy to rearrange the house, but she was accustomed to the strangeness. She'd adjusted to it. But she found it more difficult to adjust to the town. The long wet winters, the equally long, oppressively hot summers depressed her: not a breath of wind from morning till noon, the thick, scaled branches and toothed, voluptuous dark leaves of gigantic potted plants pushing out shoots, sucking the energy out of the barren earth in the plant holders. Like the plants in the pots, she often felt confined in her house and in the valley. Between walls, between mountains. The mountains here were closer to town than those in Worcester. In summer, a hazy blue, the sides of a basin; in winter sharp, jagged and gleaming in the rain.

Stuart adjusted himself more easily. House ownership, even though it came with an enormous mortgage, gave him the status he'd lacked in Worcester. He was proud of the son he called Ozzie, even though the lad was too whiny and sickly for his liking. He threw Sussie up in the air and caught her again and again until she shrieked with pleasure. If only it were Ozzie crying with pleasure instead of fear, his cup of joy would overflow.

He was good to Agnes. On a Saturday morning when her hair was washed and rubbed dry, shiny and golden, and she sat in her little green dress on the back stoep shelling peas, basin in her lap, he was as amorous as he'd been before the wedding. It was a little task that she enjoyed: maybe she knew that the green of the pods echoed and emphasised the green of her eyes. Her slender fingers moved quickly as she opened the crisp young pods and sent the peas raining down into the basin. Then he'd say eagerly: 'I'm coming home earlier from golf today. You pack us a picnic basket, and we'll drive up the mountain pass and have supper out there tonight.'

Just once, couldn't she put the basin aside and throw her arms around his neck and say joyfully, 'What a wonderful idea. It's so lovely and cool in the mountains at dusk.'

But usually all he got was: 'Ozzie has earache' or 'I have to finish sewing Sussie's dress' or 'The wind'll be too chilly tonight.' So that nothing came of the outing.

And if only she knew what a sacrifice it would have been for him to give up that time with his fellow players at the nineteenth hole. But he'd have done it, and lovingly.

He wanted to be good to her. He wasn't a bad lover; he knew that. But because Agnes had little confidence in her mothering she worried about everything; she often heard a child cough or toss restlessly at night. He reassured her and he even tried speaking sharply to her, but eventually he had to admit regretfully that their love life was unsatisfactory, even boring. It was hard to believe that he'd had to hold her back in the hostel gardens of an evening, had to cool ardour: 'Later, my love, my go-go girl, later, when we're married.' He brooded over this. Had he lost the secret art of making her go weak in his arms, her body answering his lovemaking? Maybe the fault lay with him? Maybe it was just his nature to tire of one woman? Her apparent coolness, with the fire behind it, had initially titillated him, but all that lay behind the coolness these days was whining. And God knows, a man is, after all, only a man.

He wondered if giving birth to the two children had changed things. Did she find a satisfaction in them, which made him redundant to her? But she wasn't such a dedicated, loving mother either. The anxiety at night was a constant source of irritation to him; he even suspected her of feigning concern. Sometimes she could be so short with them. She remained an enigma to him. And a man is, after all, only a man.

Yet it wasn't until Ozzie was nine and Sussie seven that Agnes was told openly that Stuart was cheating on her.

She didn't have many friends. A neighbour with a collection box made herself comfortable on Agnes's couch – it just happened to be 11 o'clock – and said, 'A cup of tea would be nice; I need to get the weight off my feet.' Agnes offered her some special little cakes with her tea and the woman mistook her uncharacteristic hospitality for intimacy. And took it upon herself to say, 'It's probably my duty – as a friend, dear – to tell you there are stories doing the rounds about Stuart and Viljee's widow.' Complacently, she bit into the crumbly product of Agnes's new recipe and washed it down with a sip of tea. 'They say you can see his car parked at her back door every afternoon after work. In the evenings he goes round there on foot. The bank is doing her estate, so he goes in to give her extra advice. What else extra, one can only guess.'

The expression on Agnes's face told her she had miscalculated her 'duty'; she put her cup down hastily, jumped up, straightened her dress and said, 'My cup isn't even cold yet, but please excuse me. This box has to do the rounds still.'

She hurried down the garden path, and slammed the gate shut in a way that said: how could I have known ...?

When Agnes heard the gate she closed the front door and leaned against it, her fists clenched so tight that her nails cut into her palms. She looked down the hall, but saw nothing. The only thing she was aware of was not being able to swallow; she was choking from the shock. Just as she hadn't been able to swallow that afternoon in her grandmother's living room in Pretoria when the lawyer read out the letter from that woman from France.

The same old panic welled up in her. Will Stuart reject me? If Stuart rejects me, where can I go? What'll become of me? Am I nothing more to him than a foundling, a nobody to reject when he chooses? But I am nobody and I have nobody: that's all I'm sure of, no matter what Father said there in his study.

And then the fear: Aunt Issy must never know about Stuart. She'd blame me, not him. Stuart was her blue-eyed boy. She would turn against me. Father wouldn't take my side against his son either. He must never know. He'll say it's my bad blood. That's what he was afraid of, no matter what he said: bad blood. His eldest son.

This was silly. She shook her head from side to side to try to clear her thoughts. Then she banged her head against the closed door, her fists still clenched. Then she thought: Stuart is in the wrong, not me. I'm not thinking straight. But everybody in town knows. They must or the woman would never have blurted it out like that.

Stuart came home for lunch. The children, thank God, were only due later. They ate in silence. He noticed that Agnes was as white as a sheet, and asked if she was feeling ill. 'I have a headache,' was all she said. She didn't want to say anything while the maid cleared the table; she went to their room. He followed her. She closed the door behind him, lay down on the bed and started to cry. Then she sat up and wiped her tears. Her nose was running.

'I know everything about you and the widow. How could you do this to me? And to the children? The story is the talk of town.'

He sat down beside her and sighed. 'I've been wondering why it's taking the gossipmongers so long to get to you. The good Lord knows, I didn't go looking for it. If I got more sympathy at home, it would never have happened.'

'Now it's my fault?'

He tried to put his arm around her shoulders, but she pushed him away.

'You see?' he said. 'You'd think I had the plague. Anyway, it isn't the end of the world: it happens in the best of families. And you can stop whining, it's over.' He couldn't suppress a nasty little smile. 'Or almost over. The widow doesn't find me repulsive.'

But he was right. When the estate was finalised by the bank, the widow locked up her house and went overseas with her money.

The stories died down.

Then Agnes started to distrust his golf.

'It's indecent, what with the drought and the depression and the country's suffering, to spend money on things like that. We can never go on holiday, thanks to your golf and the Essex.'

The car came in for its share of the blame. The neighbours were still driving horse-drawn buggies when Stuart, despite the '33 depression, pulled his first car, a pearl-grey Essex, into their driveway. Not that he was such a terrific financial success. He'd been promoted to accountant at the bank, but she deplored his habit of buying on credit.

For a while, after the widow's departure, he took Ozzie with him to the golf course – his violation of Father's name also grieved her. He allowed the boy to carry his bag and even hit a ball every now and then. Ozzie was skinny and not at all sporting; it broke Agnes's heart to see how hard he tried to win his father's favour.

'You're taking him away from his friends,' she protested.

'Do you ever see him with that many friends round here?'

It was with Sussie that Ozzie played in the big, unkempt yard; climbed over the gooseberry bush behind the outbuildings, pushing branches aside, to build a play house; tore open the pale papery scales of the gooseberry pod to get at the small, round, golden fruit and then swallowed the sweet-sour juiciness in one gulp. Or climbed the fig tree, each claiming a branch, yelling the English rhyme to each other: *I'm the king of the castle, and you're the dirty rascal.*

The Essex took them over the dreaded Bainskloof Pass on an outing to Worcester every once in a while. Agnes grew increasingly nervy with time. She never slept the night before these trips.

She had good reason to be nervous, she thought. At the pass entrance was a large board with the admonition: *Be prepared to meet thy God.* Whoever had erected the board knew how narrow the road was and how steep the precipice, especially on the Wellington side where one had to keep to the left on the edge of the abyss, with only the odd stunted oak tree as marker. On the other side, going down the mountain, at least you were on the inside and there was a stone wall as safeguard.

Stuart made the children watch the turns in the road ahead to check if there were horse carts or cars or even donkey carts coming in the opposite direction. At each turn their father hooted loudly. In rainy weather, they postponed the trip.

Father, Aunt Issy and Nellie, the white girl who still worked for them, were glad to see them. Aunt Issy was ageing fast and even her beloved Stuart and his children exhausted her. A big meal was served; more food was packed for the drive back. Robbie was the only one of Father's three younger sons still living at home. He was in his final year at school. Philip and Hendrik were at university in Stellenbosch, and Leonora teaching in Cape Town. But Robbie was too preoccupied to spend time with his niece and nephew.

They played on the swings. And at tea time, Frikkie and Kowie arrived with their twins, Arnold and Miemie. Nellie gave the children orange squash and ginger biscuits in the garden. At first they were standoffish, but when Stuart called: 'Come now, time to go!' the play suddenly got going and they didn't want to be parted. Sussie and Miemie promised to write to each other, but never got round to it.

Now and then, for a birthday or some other occasion, Frikkie would hire a car and bring Father and Aunt Issy over to Wellington. The two of them sat on the back seat, with the children on two foldout seats on either side of them.

On these occasions Leonora would take the train from Cape Town to Wellington and spend the day with them. The train left Cape Town at half past eight and Leonora was usually in good time to catch it. One Sunday, though, she'd bought her return ticket and was making her way to the platform when she suddenly felt she didn't want to go anymore. The conductor stood on the bridge and held the low door open for her, but she shook her head. She didn't know where this indecision came from. People walked past and some bumped into her; she stood back on the platform. Today she wasn't going to her people, she knew it as clearly as if somebody had told her. Despite the sweets she'd bought for the little ones, now weighing down her handbag. Sussie was her favourite and she was sorry she wouldn't see her today. The conductor hung out of the train on one arm, looked up and down the platform. He saw her again before he put the whistle into his mouth and blew. She waved at him.

As the train steamed out, she turned back to the big lobby. The train would arrive in Wellington at 10.30 – there was time to ring and let them know she wasn't coming. She didn't want to upset Father by making him wait in vain. On Sundays there were often delays with trunk calls so the sooner she got it over with, the better. She reserved her call at the first of the rows of booths and waited outside until the operator called back. Picking up the receiver at the first sharp ring, she said, 'Sorry, Stuart, the train's gone. I'm still here, yes, in Cape Town. Just tell Father and Frikkie I'm sorry. Give my love to everybody. No, there's nothing wrong. No, the next train is only at one, and that's out of the question.'

She knew Adderley Street so well, but now, at half past eight on this Sunday morning, it was a new experience for her to walk through the empty street. Is this what I was looking for, she asked herself: experience outside my routine existence? The no-longer-so-young teacher who strolled alone down an empty Adderley Street on a Sunday morning was suddenly aware of feeling relieved. A newspaper, flapping in the wind, then falling back onto the pavement; a beggar, sleeping. A coloured family in their Sunday best crossed the street on their way to St Stephen's. She'd lived in this city for seven years. Two years at college, five years teaching.

She walked to the old Company Gardens, one of her favourite places. The flowers were always beautiful, whatever season it was, and little birds chirped in the big aviaries like souls possessed. She knew each tree individually, and each nameplate fired her imagination. The tall palms with the rough, loose fronds and windblown branches came from South America and from Australia. The birch with its silver trunk and fine foliage came from India, the wild date palm and the Judas tree from Southern Asia, the small bunya bunya tree from Australia. From Australia too, the flame tree, the giant wild fig; from the Far East two remainders of fruit trees that the Company was supposed to have cultivated: the black mulberry and the pear. And then the giant rubber tree from India and tropical Asia, with its small pointed fruits strewn over the ground.

Children crouched in the garden walkways and fed the doves; a little boy was luring a squirrel closer. There were a number of Malay families, the women in colourful dresses and gold-embroidered headscarves, the men with their red fezzes and long white coat dresses.

Another universe from the small world of her family, who would sit at the dinner table in Wellington today. She felt lighter, different.

She sat on a bench under a tree for a while, and then sauntered past the bird cages, along the flowerbeds to the fish pond where the sound of water fell softly on her ears. Water spouted from the fish a cherub clasped to his chest. She knew the marble statuette well, and smiled again at the fervour of the boy's embrace. Fish swam beneath the waterlily leaves. Schools of goldfish. Against the fence around the pool, she saw a notice. This coming week goldfish would be sold every morning at a certain time. Children who wanted to buy should bring their own containers.

So you're going to get away, she thought, away from the swimming and swimming and swimming round this cramped fish pond with the dark green water and the water lily leaves growing bigger by the day, shutting off even more sunlight than before.

Strange coincidence, this notice, Leonora thought, because now she knew she'd also get away. Yes, dear goldfish, I'm also taking my chance, just like you. Who knows what bucket we might land up in? Maybe darker, smaller. Now she knew why she couldn't get on that train. First she had to make her decision. Then she could come with an accomplished fact, not asking for advice.

She was in a hurry to get home and fill in the forms she'd requested at school. A stack of forms, in triplicate. An application for a post under the Commonwealth exchange scheme. Her five years of teaching qualified her. A year in London! Her colleagues wouldn't apply. Never! they said, mindful of boyfriends and family that would be left behind. There was nothing to keep her. After filling in the forms, she wrote to Father to tell him about her decision. I will miss you Father, she wrote, but I know you will grant me this.

It was months before the application was accepted and the necessary arrangements complete, but finally everything was in order and her suitcases packed.

Frikkie hired a car and brought Father and Aunt Issy and Nellie to Wellington to sleep over before they travelled in two cars to Cape Town the next day.

They were going to see Leonora off on the mail boat to England.

Father had difficulty shaving; he kept the rest of them waiting. He didn't have an appetite for breakfast. He was plagued by thoughts of his lovely, only daughter who'd be teaching in the back streets of London for a year. One couldn't expect them to give her a post in the best of schools. Applicant from the colonies, he thought bitterly. But if this new experience and everything that went along with it brought her restless soul to rest, then he wouldn't begrudge her. During the holidays she could go across to the Continent. She'd get to know the classical Rome that he knew so well from his own studies and reading, but could never experience personally. He'd given her a little extra money for this.

Leonora waited for them on the passenger deck of the *Edinburgh*

Castle. When she saw them she ran to meet them halfway down the gangway, hugged the children, threw her arms first around Father, then around Stuart and Frikkie. She kissed her sisters-in-law on the cheek. Her hair was cropped short; she was wearing a new three-quarter-length dress in a Kodak blue candy-stripe. She'd slimmed down; her eyes were wide and shining. This afternoon, here under the blue heaven, on the blue water, with the slow rocking of the giant liner, the damp smell of oil and sea, the rolling gait of seamen on deck, she was happier than they'd ever seen her before.

'Father, you'll never guess what's happened! Philip and Hendrik came by train from Stellenbosch. They're waiting on the fore deck, keeping us a place at a table. But how silly, I can't even offer you anything to drink.' She threw her arms wide. 'They only serve once we're on the open sea!'

The open sea! The open sea! The whole wide world awaits me! exclaimed her eyes, her lips, her wide-stretched arms, her shiny hair, her new dress.

She's in her late twenties, nearing 30, thought Father. But she doesn't look it. And still no man had won her heart. If only on this journey ... But then his heart shrank. No, not a foreigner for Norie. She must come back. He felt as though Norie was the only part of Emma that he still held. The dark eyes, the dark curls.

He now regretted that he hadn't let her continue her studies at university. Her brain hadn't been put to full use, he knew. Maybe that was why she was so restless. Forever changing schools, changing her lodgings. Her fickleness – let him rather call it by name: her discontent – was his fault. Due to a misjudgement on his part. He should have tried to borrow the money somewhere and sent her to university. But he'd reckoned, a girl ...

Then the orchestra struck up the first hesitant notes, the word went round: visitors should start leaving the ship.

Pressed against the railing, Leonora threw blue, yellow, pink and green rolls of paper streamers down to her family on the quay. She held on to the ends while her family below let the streamers slowly roll down as the tugboat started to push against the liner. The streamers formed a dancing rainbow between the ship and the quay. First the stern banged; the dark green, dirty, slimy water mulled against the quay; the heavy mooring ropes, soaked with sea water and oil, started to unroll with a moaning, cracking sound; a seaman called out; the rope was thrown into the water with a splash and was sucked into the deep. Sussie couldn't take her eyes from the rope falling away into the water; she unrolled her paper ribbon mechanically. 'Watch out, Sussie!' called Stuart, 'your streamer is going to break off ...'

Then the bow swung out and the strip of dark water between the ship and the quay slowly broadened. The orchestra on deck played with gusto now: *Auld Lang Syne.*

It was all so very beautiful it made Sussie want to cry – the blue of the water and the sky, the smell of the sea, the music wafting over the bay, the strangeness, Leonora going away.

The streamers stretched taut, a few had already snapped, and the friends who came to say their goodbyes, started to move to the furthest quay where the ship would pass, bow to the open sea. A young woman had pushed in next to Stuart; she looked up into his face: 'Help me with this darn streamer,' they heard her say. Stuart leaned towards her, untangling her streamer from his. Agnes watched, her heart contracting. Was constant jealous watchfulness to be her life now? He broke his streamer so the woman's could flutter free. She laughed with him, and he put his arm around her; pressed her against him; taking advantage of the moment's camaraderie ...

At last Sussie's ribbon tightened until it tore. Now there were really tears in her eyes. Good-bye, Tannie Leonora, my dearest Tannie Leonora.

Philip who stood next to Frikkie, half a head taller than him, said, 'Just another year or so, then I'll be on my way. My professor says I can count on a bursary.'

Frikkie shook his hand. 'Congratulations, Boetie.'

The tug, still with its nose against the mail boat's belly, sounded its horn a couple of times. The sound echoed across the harbour, bounced against the mountain and came back to Leonora. She'd already taken leave of her family in spirit – the broken paper streamers trailed in the water behind the ship; she threw down her ends even before they broke. She held on to the railing, because as the boat neared the open sea it started to roll. There was a strange disturbance in her insides. She shuffled to the front of the bow, clinging to the metal railing. The wind caught her short hair, the ship rolled, a boisterous spirit invaded her: she would cross the horizon, the world was wide, boundless. The salt in the sea breeze against her face made her eyes smart.

Maybe Stuart was more discreet in his amorous escapades; maybe the townspeople grew accustomed to his flirtations because self-appointed friends didn't tell tales to Agnes anymore.

There were other ways in which she found out when Stuart was straying again. He whistled while he shaved in the morning. He took more care in choosing his clothes – she saw him choose a tie, drape it across his hand, consider it, then settle on another. When he got up from the table, he waited until Sussie's mouth was full so she couldn't object, and then playfully pulled her hair; he asked Ozzie about his schoolwork.

When he announced one morning: 'It's too hot to walk home for lunch, and it's extravagant to take the Essex out every day. I'll take sandwiches if you save a plate of dinner for me to eat at suppertime ...' she knew what he was up to. The past week or so, he had gone in the course of duty to examine the books of a bankrupt client who owed the bank money. The books were at a factory on the other side of town. A female bank clerk had to go along to help. Then she knew: he had his floozy on a plate. No prizes for guessing what went on behind those closed factory office doors during so-called lunch hours: who could avoid noticing how rosy the clerk's cheeks were, how shiny her eyes and how impudent her hands when the guard opened the doors again at two o'clock and let the other workers in?

What could she do? She couldn't pack her bags and apply for a teaching post in the Boland, as she had done when she heard the news from the lawyer in her grandmother's living room. She couldn't leave her house and her housemaid and her garden just like that. She couldn't take her children and walk out. Where would she go?

Sometimes at midday, when Stuart was absent again, she'd lie on her bed crying. Sussie came in and sat with her on the bed, even though she was already late for school.

'Don't worry, Mamma, the headache will be gone soon.'

If only she could love the child more. Couldn't she love anyone? Was her heart a stone?

'Don't worry, Mamma, don't cry so much, crying only makes the headache worse.'

'Run along now, you're already late.'

There was something she could do. Something she should have done ages ago, and it came up again when she thought about what the lawyer had said in her grandmother's living room in Pretoria.

When Sussie had gone off to school again, she rose and got out her writing material and a pen. She wrote a letter to the Department of Home Affairs, to the division of Birth Registration. She sucked on her pen for a long time, wrote and crossed out, crumpled up, started again. Her month of birth was February 1901. The exact date she didn't know, but her christening date was somewhere in May. She was about four months old when she was christened in Pretoria. She wrote:

It is with hesitation that I am asking if it is possible to obtain the names of baby girls born in the month of February 1901 in Cape Town and registered on your lists. I am trying to find out who my parents were. I would especially like to get information about those cases where only the name of the mother was noted and the father as unknown, or where the surnames of the mother and the father are different. I ask this, and these words are difficult to write, because I suspect I was born outside wedlock.

Her head and her hand were wet with sweat by the time she finished writing. She folded the letter, put it in an envelope, got her hat and set off for the post office. In the Cape telephone directory she looked for and found the address to which she had to send the letter.

This action imbued her with a greater purposefulness. She felt stronger – as if it was the first positive thing she had done for a long time. She waited a good while for an answer. And when the letter finally came, it only stated that all files of birth registrations were sent to the archives in Pretoria after Unionisation, and her letter had also been forwarded there. There would no doubt be a delay before she received an answer because of the legal protocols of confidentiality.

When she finally received the letter from Cape Town, her hands were shaking so much that she could hardly tear it open. She kept the letter in the drawer with her underwear.

At night, when she lay awake, she thought: That letter I wrote to the woman in France caused a whole lot of trouble. It was that letter that made the woman write to the lawyer. Was this letter not going to cause even more trouble? But I had to do something. And what else was there for me to do?

Whatever Stuart does, she thought resolutely, I won't let it get me down.

She'd always been interested in needlework and crafts. The south veranda was glassed in, and the shelves left by previous tenants had dark, mouldy stains on them that spoke of potted plants. She bought plants and earthenware pots and got cuttings from Aunt Issy who had created a stoep garden now that she had time on her hands what with Robert off to Stellenbosch. Her plants were another chain in the link with Aunt Issy, a bond that she wanted to make even stronger. She had to keep Aunt Issy on her side. With care and skill she created a green hideout for herself on the side stoep, cool with wet potted plants, redolent of mouldering earth, damp black humus, and sometimes the delicate flavour of a single lily.

She had her sewing machine brought out and organised a cupboard for her fabrics, threads and patterns. She spent long summer afternoons here. During the holidays, Sussie sat with her and threaded and pinned and hemmed.

Sussie enjoyed sitting with her mother while she worked. Sometimes, very seldom, her mother told her about the dense bush country through which she'd been carried in a *masjila* as a child; about the thick swathes of leaves that thrashed over her face and showered the rainwater over her. Sussie put the atlas on the floor and paged through it until she found the region through which her mother had been carried. She looked for woods and savannah over the whole world; she started to dream about dripping trees that were so dense that the sun didn't shine through them, even at midday. But her mother didn't want to talk about it very much.

'I can't remember,' she'd say. 'I was barely older than you are.'
'And Oupa?'
'He stayed behind.'
'But where did you go and live then?'
'With your late Oom Piet. His wife, Aunt Naomi, taught me how to sew all these different stitches. Watch: you loop the thread like this round the tip of the needle, and then catch it down ... that's lazy-daisy. And this is satin stitch – keep it nice and even so it feels like satin under your finger, and chain stitch, come on, try the flowers on this cloth. This one is a French knot for the pistil of the flower, and that's crewel stitch, and herringbone.'

There were also thicker pieces of cloth on which her mother pinned pieces of cardboard, cut out like petals, and then she had to work sideways and over them with wool; a small stitch on both sides, and then you pulled the wool on the cardboard so that it bunched up until it looked like swollen fingers. Then, when she was finished, her mother would take a razor blade and cut the fingers through lengthwise and take out the cardboard and shake the work loose so it looked like thick, puffy flowers.

The only work that was sent out was the buttonholes for the tailored dresses that her mother was so fond of. And belts. The dress fabric stitched onto buckram with the buckle covered to match and holes punched.

For that Agnes sent Sussie to Koster Street. Shortly after lunch (her father hadn't been there) in the early afternoon, Sussie set off along the four blocks to Koster Street with the measurements for the belt written down, with the cloth and the marks for the eyelet holes carefully pencilled in, and the whole parcel wrapped in brown paper. It was the summer school holidays. The four blocks down the hill to Koster Street were an adventure to Sussie.

Her bare feet burned on the gravel, but on the sidewalk she could jump from one tuft of grass to the next and then grab the wire fence to steady herself when she lost her balance trying to walk on the sides of her feet. She held on until the fence threatened to fall over to the street side and a dog came charging out of its kennel like a lion, his snout wet and slimy against the fence, his teeth and his tongue too close to her. She stood frozen like a pillar of salt against the fence, until he stopped barking and slunk back to his kennel. If I stand as still as a pillar of salt, how would he know I'm a child? she thought. And it worked time and again.

She walked cautiously past the house that was set deep back on its erf. She didn't want the woman to see her and come out: she'd had nine miscarriages, and Grieta said she was looking for a child to steal. The woman was pale and skinny and always wore a black dress. Actually she was more sorry for her than afraid, but she didn't want the woman to rub up and down her arm again, as she once did when her mother wasn't around. She rubbed up and down along her bare arm, and then, half regretfully, dropped her arm. Since then she'd been afraid of her.

She hung onto the parcels and jumped from tuft to tuft. The grass grew wild here. The long, light-green blades which you could pull and pull and then more pale pieces came through the fence, also scared her. She knew that the blades of grass would coil around her ankles and run up along her legs, and cling to her if she dared to stand still, which is why she jumped along just as soon as her feet had taken a rest on the tuft.

She enjoyed crossing the street. There weren't a lot of cars, and only now and again a donkey cart with vegetables or a Scotch-cart with pine cones – the driver would hit the horse to go forward and then back up again when a maid came out to buy cones for the geyser. And the postman was there on his bicycle; she ran to him, but he wouldn't tell her if there were letters for them. Jus' check in the box, he said and pressed on. She saw coloured men with hessian bags on their heads carrying blocks of ice on their shoulders to the few rich people who needed them for their iceboxes. The rest of the ice went to the cafés.

The people who had jobs had gone back to work after lunch, so the streets were empty. Some of the maids who worked only half day walked with their carry bags – full of stolen food, her mother always said – back to the township. The township was next to the river, and white children lived there too. She would have liked to go and play there, all along the river path, but her mother didn't allow her to.

She could hear the sound of the steamroller in the distance; they were tarring the main road. It was a kind of half-chopped-off train that pulled the roller and flattened the wet black tar thrown out by the drumful. A black cat once ran in front of the roller, and he was squashed in the tar, dead as a doornail. A cat still mewed there when you walked by at night.

She'd passed her four blocks, and now she had to turn off downhill into a dead-end road with two semi-detached houses. She was to drop something off at both these houses today.

In the one lived the little dwarf who picked up ladders in stockings. And because the dwarf couldn't climb off her high chair every time someone dropped something off, there was a secret sign that her clients knew about. Sussie also knew it. She slammed the lid of the letterbox down three times, and then she carefully pulled on the string hanging on the inside and slowly pulled up the big front door key. The string was long enough so she could unlock the front door, and lock it again when she left and drop the key back into the box.

She stood in a dark hallway. A door was open to the left and it was lighter there.

'Girly, come here!' called the dwarf's squeaky voice. Her hands were sweaty from the parcels. A sharp electric light shone over the dwarf. She sat on a high chair, with a high backboard and arm rests. The little stumps that were supposed to be her feet, and were always strapped up in high black lace-up shoes, rested on a shelf nailed to the chair. Her arms were short and she had little stumps instead of hands, but at least the fingers had started to grow, up to the first digits. And because the first digits of the fingers were swollen and puffy, she could only clasp the steel hook between the index and middle finger of her right hand to pick up the ladders in stockings. The stump that was supposed to be her left hand pushed the wooden darning egg against her breast, and pulled the ladder in the stocking tight over the wooden furrow. Because she couldn't see that well, and was always pushing up the thick spectacles that slid down her nose when she bent over the stocking, the sharp electric light shone straight onto the darning egg and the ladder.

'Your mother's stuff is finished,' said the dwarf in her shrill voice. In front of her on a high table lay the rows of small brown paper bags, folded closed and with the client's initial written in pencil on top. 'Take ma'.' Sussie put the new parcel she'd brought onto the little heap that wasn't finished yet.

'Laddered again,' said the dwarf. Her chest was also deformed, because when she spoke, she heaved a little and her ribcage pulled up almost to her chin. Then the black dress would shine here and there in the bright light.

She pointed to a calendar lying behind the parcels. Black circles were drawn around all the dates when she was booked up. Sussie looked for the first day without a circle, nodded and said: 'I'll come on the fifth.' Who drew the circles? she wondered. Who lifted the dwarf off the high chair in the evening, and put her back again in the morning? How did she eat, how did she wash? The hair looked like a wig to her; it was thin and tucked under a little net, and where the net pulled tight, the skin was pinkish. The dwarf herself was sallow and had big dark eyes and her thick black eyebrows met in the middle, which was scary when she looked up at you from under the heavy glasses.

The dwarf's head was bowed low over the steel hook that climbed all along the fine ladder in the stocking into the sharp light; she tripped up the ladder as she climbed up the steps with the stitch that had slipped. That comforted Sussie, the fine, shiny fairy ladders that the little dwarf could climb all day long: she pushed the crochet hook in, then she caught the stitch, then she slipped it out under the spar, then the stitch was on top again.

'It's pretty,' said Sussie to the dwarf. The dwarf smiled ever so slightly, but her head stayed down on her breast, her eyes glued to the steel hook. Sussie took her parcel and slipped down the hallway, pulled the door closed behind her, locked it and pushed the key through the groove.

In the other semi-detached house lived the woman who made button-holes on the tailored dresses. Here Sussie knocked and the woman's mother opened the door and took her inside. Sussie swallowed and wanted to give the second parcel to the mother, but she said: 'Oh no, dearie, come and tell Betta yourself.'

Betta was pretty with red cheeks and a yellow bun. She had beautiful hands that could touch the sewing machine softly and beautifully to stop it, or to make it go a little slower, or to control a few difficult stitches herself. Her one hand touched the wheel lovingly; the other beautiful pink hand pushed the cloth through under the sewing foot, or unpicked, or kept it in place as if that hand was in love with the cloth once more.

Betta was a lovely person: she had a bag of sweets on the sewing machine and she gave Sussie a couple. Then she popped one into her mouth as well, even though her mother said: 'You'll get too fat, sweetheart, you know you have to watch out.' But Betta sucked and then wiped her mouth and fingers with her handkerchief, and started to stitch again.

Sussie didn't want to look at the floor, because Betta pedalled with the wrong leg. Her other one was a wooden leg and even though it had a sock and shoe on, and even if it swayed just like a real leg when the tannie walked about the house on crutches, it couldn't pedal the machine. She had been engaged to be married, then the train chopped her leg off. And then her boyfriend left her, even though it was his fault, because he was driving the car when it stalled over the railway tracks.

Betta laughed with Sussie and waved to her when she left, but the old mother walked with her to the door and said, as she said every time, 'You don't see the tears, my girl.' Then she jerked a shoulder towards the house next door, and whispered to Sussie: '"Tis better to have loved and lost, than never to have loved at all." I'd rather be Betta than the dwarf any day.'

And what about me? wondered Sussie as she walked home along the road that didn't have woods or lions or ghosts of cats or things like that anymore, just became a normal road. Would she rather be a dwarf, with golden ladders that she could climb day after day, or the woman with the wooden leg that swayed under the sewing machine?

No, she thought, she'd rather the golden ladders. Much rather.

She threw the paper bag with the mended stocking from the one hand to the other. She skipped on the sidewalk. The parcel was so light it could easily float away in the wind. It was a magic ball, it could float away and she would drift after it, high up in the sky, high up over the mountain, up with the golden ladders.

She tried to run airily, because her name wasn't Isobelle anymore, it was Tinkerbell. As she had read in the book that Tannie Leonora sent her. And she liked to feel sad like Tinkerbell who was always sad because Peter Pan liked Wendy better than her. But Tinkerbell drank the poison that the pirates meant for Peter Pan, even though she knew it would kill her. Because she loved Peter Pan so much. Wendy wouldn't have done that; Sussie hated Wendy. She danced from one tussock of grass to the next and her feet didn't burn anymore. She'd also drink poison for somebody she loved that much.

She was glad to get home because Ozzie would be back and he was allowed to wind up the gramophone and screw in the needle and turn the record and carefully put the needle in the groove. And just because, she started singing the song that Ozzie liked playing so much:

Old King Cole was a merry old soul and a merry old soul was he ...

'Can't you children wait until I've rested? My head's splitting. Can't you ever spare me?'

He called for his pipe and he called for his bowl ... the gramophone started to whine as Agnes tried to stop the record with her hand.

... and he called for his fiddlers three.

'Not like that, Ma! You're damaging it, and Pa will punish me ...'

'Don't worry, I'll say it was me, Ozzie, he wouldn't hit me, he wouldn't hit me,' said Sussie.

'Can we play *Coming for to carry me home*, Mamma?'

Sussie knew her mother liked that: *Swing high, swing low, sweet chariot ...* That time when Oupa and Aunt Issy were here, she played it all the time. Aunt Issy wiped the tears from her eyes with her handkerchief. 'The dear, dear heathen,' she said over and over. 'Their sweet souls ...'

6

On warm windless days they would drive in the Essex to the Strand. It wasn't too far. Stuart would drop Agnes at the missionary house on the beach front where Father's brother, Hennie, lived. Agnes couldn't bear lying on the sand; even sand blowing against her legs or crunching between her teeth in a sandwich irritated her.

But Agnes had a good deal to talk about with Hennie. In addition to their own picnic basket, she always packed another basket with treats for him. From the first time Stuart had taken her to meet Hennie, she had felt empathy for him. He was the only one of the Worcester family who knew Africa, in spite of their missionary fervour. Africa had called him, just as it had called her father. He knew the smell of the soil, the bush, the grass seeds; he knew the heavenly blue against which the white clouds grazed like white lambs. He knew the wide-open spaces, not only the cooped-in life here between the mountains.

He opened the door to her knock and then followed her with heavy steps down the passage to the sitting room. She knew the tap-tap of his walking stick. Before sitting down, she kissed him on the lips.

'I've missed you. How've things been here?'

'So-so. Hester Visagie's husband collapsed again. She isn't strong enough to get him up again so we lent her a hand.'

There were several houses: allocated along with a stipend to retired missionaries, or people whose health had been so broken in the mission field that they could no longer work. Hennie, who had lived here since before he turned 30, was the oldest resident.

'I offered my life to the Lord, but He had no use for it,' he had said to Agnes many times. To others as well. It gave him a kind of martyr status.

Agnes made tea and opened her cake tin. 'It's a new recipe. In fact, the same little cakes I offered the woman who came to tell me about Stuart, that first time.' Hennie was the only person she spoke to about Stuart.

He was distressed by the tone that came into her voice. 'Don't allow yourself to get bitter, dear.' He knew bitterness.

Then the words poured out. 'I don't know where I stand, Oom Hennie. I never know when or whom he's involved with. If a pretty young woman walking down the street seems to give me a funny look, I wonder whether this isn't perhaps another of his floozies.' She took out a handkerchief and blew her nose.

'Perhaps you're being too sensitive.' He battled to balance his teacup in one hand. She had over-filled it, he had to slurp up the first sip. That irritated her. Oh, no! She couldn't be irritated with Hennie too! Her nerves were eating her up.

'I told you about the girl who helped him over the lunch hours at that factory. The work is finished now but I could swear he's seeing her at night. It's nothing but overtime and more overtime and then the month-end work.'

She collected the tea things. 'Let's leave it. Let's change the subject. I'll get the photos out.' She was the only one with whom he ever shared the photographs he had brought back from the mission field.

'Perhaps looking at the photos will ease the pain in my heart.'

He seldom took the album from the bottom drawer of the sideboard because he had difficulty in bending and was too weak to lift anything heavy. She knelt to get it out. 'It's jolly heavy. You have so many, I have none. Sometimes I think the things I'm trying to remember only exist in my imagination. Or I am making them up.' She dabbed her nose again. 'If only I had just one photo.'

She opened the heavy album and began leafing through it.

Sussie was numb when she came out of the sea. She shook out her towel and wrapped it round her shoulders. Her teeth chattered, and, even with the towel round her, she shivered. She couldn't lie in the sun because her skin was too sensitive. Her father wanted to pull her down beside him, but she dodged his grasp. There, catch it! He aimed the beach ball at her but she missed it and Ozzie had to jump up and retrieve it from near the water. Ozzie wanted to play ball with him, but her father looked away from Ozzie down towards Melkbaaistrand. He had rubbed suntan oil all over himself: he tanned beautifully. His new bathing costume had large armholes bound in white. The children said he was the best-looking father; she wished he wasn't. She watched him as he jumped up and started running along in the shallow water. Every now and then he would scoop up a handful of seawater and splash it over his chest, making sure the women on the beach were watching. Ozzie stood holding the ball, not sure who he should throw it to. He had to be careful of the sun, his skin was already red.

Sussie took the clothes she'd left in a tightly rolled bundle beside her father. She looped a finger through the straps of her sandals and hugged the ends of the towel against her chest. Then she sprinted over the road to Hennie's house. Her hair had been plastered flat by the breakers that had knocked her down and rolled her over. Trickles of water ran down her neck. She went in through the garden gate and round to the tap in the small backyard, hopping from one foot to the other on the hot cement.

'I wish you'd known my father,' she heard her mother's voice in the sitting room. 'Oh, Oom Hennie ...' her mother carried on with the familiar old complaints that usually made Sussie stick her fingers into her ears. But now she listened intently. 'I can't even say "my father". If only I had just one photo. What can I do? Who can I turn to?'

'If you're so unhappy with Stuart, why don't you go away? Back to British East Africa? Even though he isn't your father, he did love you.'

'How can I? You know yourself ... all that gossip about the Coolie woman ...'

Sussie pushed the back door open further and went inside, wet as she was. Her mother was pulling her handkerchief out of her pocket again. Her eyes were red and swollen. She knew her father would have something to say about that. She climbed onto her mother's lap.

'I can't, Oom Hennie.' Her mother shoved her away. 'Oh no, now I'm soaking wet. Go and get dressed, Sussie, you're shivering.' She said to Hennie: 'Little ears pick it all up.'

The bathroom door didn't have a catch. She wanted to pee. She'd go and get dressed in the outside toilet. It was oppressively hot and it stank in the little tin privy. There wasn't much space. Gingerly, she slipped the straps off her shoulders, already stinging from sunburn, and then pulled the bathing costume off. It caught on her legs and she trod onto it to pull it down. She sat naked on the wooden seat, with her hands pressing on either side so she wouldn't fall through into the deep pit below. It was actually quite pleasant sitting there naked on the wooden seat; your pee felt warm when it came out while you were still cold from swimming. She took her knickers and vest from the roll of clothes and pulled them on. Then her dress. It was a floral print but it chafed her on the shoulders and round the armholes because it was too skimpy for her. Then she returned to the sitting room.

'Greet your oom properly,' her mother said.

His beard prickled her cheek and his mouth was wet in the beard. He stroked her wet hair and pressed her against his shoulder with his good arm. She didn't mind, but she didn't like the saliva in his mouth when he kissed her. Her mother had made tea, but she got lemon syrup and some of the little cakes her mother had brought.

'The child is getting more like you every day,' said Hennie.

'If only she'd inherited Stuart's skin ... she burns so easily.'

Sussie tried not to look at his eye that had been torn out and grown over again in such an ugly way; she tried not to look at the dark purplish-red scars on his cheek that had puckered up like river tributaries on a map. But in between sipping and chewing, she did look. His left sleeve was pinned against his jacket. His walking stick leaned against his chair. The many items of furniture in the room were placed to give him handholds as he walked. He walked heavily. The skin of the lion that had wounded him in the mission field lay in her grandpa's study in the pastorie at Worcester. Or was it in the passage? She couldn't remember. Her mother had brought him some salve for his rheumatism. His one shoulder bent forward, even when he was sitting. He was actually her great uncle, but she called him Oom Hennie. And she loved him. In Sunday school, when they sang: '*Hear the pennies dropping, watch them as they fall, for Jesus and the Mission, heathen children all...*' she always thought of him.

Her mother chivvied her from the room. 'Run along, now. Your glass is empty. Take your ball – this child goes nowhere without it, Oom Hennie – there, it was in my pocket. Go and play in the backyard. You look frozen, your mouth is blue, play until you get warm again. I don't like children lolling around the house.'

'I want to see the photos, Mamma.'

'Not today, Sussie, do as you're told.'

The album, which Hennie so seldom took out, lay on the table in front of her mother, but her mother's tone brooked no defiance.

When the child had left the room, Agnes drew the album closer, using the full width of her hand to turn the pages. The transparent sheets that interleaved them fluttered and then lay still again. She let the thin sheets rest on her hand as she turned the pages. Where a photograph had come loose, she smoothed the yellow cracked corners and then replaced it.

'The houses at Uasin Gishu didn't look like that.' She pointed to the faded image of a mission house of undressed stone with its wide veranda, low thatched roof, and wooden supports. 'They were simpler, of reeds and clay, as I remember them. They didn't have verandas either, just the unprotected back door and the cooking shelter outside.'

She looked closely at another photograph. 'These are the very same mopane trees and the same bushveld. How I long for them!' She didn't pay much attention to the picture of a missionary hunter who posed with rifle in hand and one foot on a dead kudu.

'My pa hunted too.'

'That is me before I looked the way I do now. Your Tant Jessie took the picture.'

He couldn't ever talk to his brother the way he talked to this young woman. 'I sometimes wonder what course our lives would have taken if Jessie had not died in childbirth. I wonder if it was wrong of me to take such a young woman into the wilderness. I feel responsible for her death.'

'I have told you so often already: out there on the Uasin Gishu many women delivered babies without help ... so you shouldn't feel guilty about that. I remember a woman on 42 had twins and her husband had to pull them out. She was torn but she still lived. If the Lord had wanted Tante Jessie to live, He would have kept her alive. Whether it was in the Union or out in the mission field.' Then she dared to voice the thought that had come to her a long while back: 'It is actually the Lord who must take responsibility for her death.'

'We'd better put these pictures away, I think,' said Oom Hennie.

'For my part, Oom Hennie ... it was also very difficult for me to leave the Uasin Gishu, I don't know whether I'll ever get over it. And there are still so many questions. Father told me I should never say I had nobody because I have all of you. You are the only person I have told about Stuart' – she heard the hard bounce of the ball on cement, the child would not be able to overhear her – 'It's so humiliating, Oom Hennie, that everyone in town knows what he's up to.'

Hennie's thoughts still lingered in the past. 'It is not for us to question why. Perhaps everything had to happen this way so that you could be a second daughter for Josias. And for me, the child that I lost.'

'And Stuart?'

'How can we fathom what lies in his heart?'

She raised her head and asked sharply: 'Do you think it's my fault?'

'Hush, child. I do not talk of fault. I just think you have been blessed with the children. Perhaps more understanding …'

She thought: so even Oom Hennie doesn't accept me anymore. I'm being criticised again; even he is rejecting me. Now I'm really on my own. She packed her basket. When Stuart and Ozzie came to collect her, she was ready to leave.

'Don't get me wrong,' said Oom Hennie, while Stuart carried their things out to the car. 'I have your own best interests at heart.'

But her face had set in the severe line that made her seem so hard. She scolded Sussie who couldn't find her sandals; she scolded Ozzie who was red with sunburn. She said nothing to Stuart beside her in the car.

Sussie waved to Hennie through the back flap. He nodded his farewell, his hand on his stick. She hung with both hands on the support where the flap was fastened when it rained. 'You must hold on too, Ozzie,' she told her brother. 'You know what Mamma said.' The wind blew her hair all over her face. Her pa was driving very fast, more than 30 miles an hour. Her mother hung on to her hat but said nothing. The car bounced down the road. Sussie imagined she was riding on a horse, like Ozzie's bioscope hero, Tom Mix. If she only had a black handkerchief to tie over her mouth she'd be Tom Mix.

She pressed her lips together and blocked her ears, refusing to listen to the accusing words that were finally slung back and forth between her mother and father in the front.

Hennie went back into his house. He battled to push the album back into the sideboard with his one hand. A photo that had come loose from the little black corners fell to the floor. He leaned his stick against the sideboard and gingerly knelt to pick up the picture. Had Agnes forgotten to put the album away, or had she left it out deliberately? He pressed the hand holding the snapshot against the chair back for support. At last he was upright again.

He sat down, holding the photo until dusk fell. He had opened up more than usual to Agnes. Even after his brother's loss of wife and daughter during the Great 'Flu, he and Josias had not really spoken entirely openly with each other. Perhaps he wasn't altogether honest with Josias. Josias's self-reproach after the deaths was so much more straightforward than his. Perhaps Josias' trust in forgiveness was also much more childlike.

The old snapshot of Jessie in his hand – in the garden of her parents' house, barely a woman, still a girl, with her beribboned hat, her mouth and eyes smiling at him. How vividly the deaths of Jessie and her unborn baby rose up in his mind after all these years, achingly poignant. His house suddenly seemed claustrophobic. He endured it until dark, then he couldn't any longer; he took his stick and did something he seldom did: risked the beach in the strong wind. He could feel the sand blown against his legs even through his trousers that slapped backwards in the gusts. His lapels flapped against his neck. He lifted his face into the wind to feel the sand against his face, against his cheeks, his chin, his forehead. He kept his eyes screwed up; he felt his way up the beach keeping to the hard sand. The wind was welcome to take what remained of his hair. Sometimes he staggered, specially when his bad foot landed askew.

These rare nights on the beach, dark, moonless, no people, with only the wind, the flying clouds, the hard wet sand under his feet, and the perpetual roar of the breakers in his ears, eased his depression. Far off in the gloom, a fisherman shouted to his mate: Ay-hoo, ay-hoo, then the sound was swept away by the wind. He wanted to hear it too: here, tonight, on the beach he wanted to hear again the eternal 'allo, 'allo, and a third time 'allo. As he had so long ago.

The powerful silence in the packed church, the strong baritone voice, the waiting congregation, the unexpected 'allo, first to the nave, then to the left aisle and then the right aisle, and the silence that had transfixed the people so no one dared draw breath. Take the buckets and fill them with water. Jessie just as moved as he was when after the service they shuffled out in the crowd – her shoulder and arm, her young breast pressed against him as she looked up at him. If only she'd known: now it was all over for her. If only she could have known: he would take her by the hand and lead her to her death in the mission field.

Ay-hoo, shouted the fisherman again through the darkness.

Where now was the bucket he should use to scoop water? He had hauled up nothing but brackish water. And death for her. He was overwhelmed with longing for her – a physical yearning he thought he'd mastered ages ago. There was never any other woman. How could there be? he had already asked himself bitterly. With his crippled body. And since his return, he could no longer talk to his brother.

A letter from Father arrived in the letterbox a few days after the outing to the beach. Agnes, who watched the box like a hawk, found it and tore it open.

As you know, I will be retiring soon. After long reflection, I have decided to spend my last years in your town. As you know, I was born in Wellington. Please keep a look out for a suitable house.

The prospect of having Father and Aunt Issy living in the same town was good news for Agnes. Wonderful news. She didn't make friends easily. Aunt Issy came from a well-known church family; her connections would be respected, and her presence in town would be a support to Agnes, especially when it came to Stuart. She began to plan ways in which she could help with the move. For his part, Stuart was not overjoyed about Father's announcement. He threw the letter aside once he had read it. It was Agnes who kept an eye on the auction notices; it was she who heard one morning that the house called Rozenhof in Villiers Street had come on the market. Not very large, but with enough rooms; the slight slope necessitated veranda steps – not a good thing for the elderly – but there was a pretty garden. Stuart took leave from work to bid for it. It was not long after the depression, and he got the house for a reasonable price.

Father's retirement was marked by a number of solemnities. He received an illuminated address and a gift of 20 pounds.

As winter set in, Father, Aunt Issy and Nellie moved into their new home, only a couple of blocks from Stuart and Agnes. Since Mother's death, Aunt Issy had been much friendlier to Nellie, because was Nellie's presence not indispensable if she wished to continue to live respectably in Father's house? And Heaven knew, where else could she live?

Father was happy to be back in his birthplace.

He was sorry to have to say goodbye to Frikkie, Kowie and the twins in Worcester, but it wasn't so far, and sometimes the problems under the surface of that marriage were simply too much for him. The only friction between him and Issy now occurred after a visit from Frikkie and his family when she would murmur under her breath, but loudly enough for him to hear: 'She is obviously not quite our class.' But he controlled himself and, Heaven help him, he sometimes wanted to agree with her. They seldom called at Frikkie's house on the outskirts of town. He regretted that Frikkie's intellect had never been developed to its full potential. He also regretted his own snobbishness which made him feel slightly embarrassed if he had to say that his second-oldest son, his clever son, was not a professional, only a photographer. Yet he earned enough to support Kowie comfortably – she had been sickly since the twins' birth.

His three youngest sons, Philip, Hendrik and Robert, had turned out well. Philip was studying law in Leiden, Hendrik was about to leave for the University of Columbia where he had a scholarship to study economics, and Robert showed every sign of following in his brothers' footsteps. He was proud of them. Yet he always regretted his dream of reading together from Virgil that had never materialised. The lines still echoed in his mind:

Arma virumque cano, Troiae qui primus ab oris
Italiam fato profugus Laviniaque venit ...

He had only a scanty knowledge of the subjects in which his younger sons excelled: constitutional law, industrial psychology, statistics, market research, economics – subjects which had been developed after his time.

The move, the parting from his congregation and from the graves of Mother and Victoria, wore him out. He felt his years.

Let Issy and Agnes, who was always in the house, just get on with it. Only the back room – allocated as a study – was his. Sometimes he let Sussie join him there, taking down the Bible picture book for her to leaf through. And on days when his hands were shaky, he allowed her to help him light his cigar.

He didn't have much time for Ozzie. When he was in his grandfather's house, his mother referred to the boy as Josias. It confused him. They shouldn't do it, thought the grandfather. No matter how much the name Ozzie irked him, he was even more irked by double standards. Although he never spoke the name Ozzie. So they seldom spoke to each other.

What was Stuart doing to the boy? He wondered sometimes. He could see how the child looked at his father, like a dog asking to be stroked. The child was not stupid; he must have a word with Stuart. But he never got round to it.

Once he felt stronger, he was going to plant roses. There was space in the long narrow side garden, with the black clay soil roses thrive in. He spent hours in his study, sitting at his desk in his old chair with his eyes closed, the cigar smouldering in the ashtray. Sometimes he dozed off. You'll set the house alight one of these days, predicted Issy. Already past the 70 mark. It was hard to believe. He had provision for Nellie written into his will.

Once he was rested and felt stronger, he started to read the religious books and magazines which he subscribed to. Sometimes he was visited by Dominee Louw, the minister of the congregation he now belonged to. When he accompanied the dominee back to the veranda, Issy would come in with a rolled-up copy of *Huisgenoot* to fan the smoke away.

He began work on his rose garden once spring took over from the pouring rain and damp winter, which lasted for months here in the Wellington valley.

Sussie read about the man who wanted to climb up to heaven in one of her grandfather's church books. It was a calendar of the town's church history.

'Look, Oupa,' she said, pressing the book open so he could get a better look at the dull, coarse-grained picture which had faded slightly. It showed a man on a stretcher. His face was half backwards, drawn with pain; the corners of his mouth pulled down; his open eyes stared fearfully into the camera. The terrible despair in the eyes took hold of Sussie and drew her in. She wanted to look away, but she couldn't. From what she could see of him under the blanket the bearers had thrown over him, he seemed to be a thin wasted man.

She read: He broke both his legs and several ribs; a rib had pierced his lung and he eventually bled to death.

Her grandfather wanted to page on, but she prevented him.

'Come, now child.'

'I want to look some more, Oupa.'

'Leave the picture.'

'What happened, Oupa?'

'The unhappy man was obsessed.'

'What is obsessed?'

'It's when you feel very, very strongly about something; unreasonably strongly.'

'What did he feel so very, very strongly about, Oupa?'

'About God, my darling. He was obsessed with God.'

Her grandfather snapped the book shut and replaced it on the shelf. 'Obsession with God is not granted to everyone, my child.'

'It said he tied ladders together and tried to make the ladders stand up from the church roof against the spire, and he climbed up them believing that God would take him the rest of the way up to Heaven.'

He drew her close, stroking her hair. 'I don't think he did the right thing, Sussie, but I can find no fault with the desire behind what he did.'

It was as though after all the years, he could hear the song of the women in the tent again. The little tent was still folded up, still carefully stored away. Shouldn't he give it to this child? Then he thought: It would still hurt to open the package and have to explain. He heard Issy coming down the passage with the tea.

'Perhaps we should all be a bit more obsessed. Obsessed with God. Will you remember that, Sussie? A bit more obsessed with goodness, with God.'

On the way home that afternoon – it was still stormy and the clouds were banked up and low – Sussie went past the church. She walked round and round the church, trying to imagine where the ladder had stood, how many ladders the obsessed man had joined together for God, how he had fallen. That night, just before she fell asleep, she could still see those weak desolate eyes in the picture. Was he with God now? The book said he had worn a long white nightshirt to climb the ladders and at the top he had stretched out his arms as if to say: 'Here I am, Lord Jesus.' And then he had crashed to the ground.

He wanted to be like the angels in his white nightshirt, Sussie thought. She pictured the high church spire, now in darkness with clouds churning round it, wet and slippery in the rain, shining like wet iron; no stars, not even a moon, just the threatening rain clouds and behind them, the dark sky. It happened this month; she'd read in the calendar. She could feel the gooseflesh all over her body. To want to go to God, alone in the night, up the precarious ladders into the dark wet sky. And to feel the ladders start to sway, first to one side and then the other, and when the highest ladder started to tip, to grab at the wet masonry; or to cling with both hands to the tip of the spire or the weathercock in his long white nightshirt. No, he wouldn't cling, he wanted to go up into heaven with a loud cry, free from the earth, feeling the hand of God at his elbow for that moment, like Peter on the water, even if it was only for a second, then falling.

But why the despair in his eyes when they carried him away, frozen but still alive early next morning? Had there not been such a moment? I must ask Oupa, thought Sussie, as she fell asleep.

'You are filling the child's head with nonsense,' said Aunt Issy. 'You know how impressionable she is.'

'There's nothing wrong with her mind.' He took the church calendar down from the shelf to show Issy. 'Look, there it is.'

'Talk about emotional instability! Medieval. Infantile.'

'Without a doubt,' he conceded. 'Should I tear it out?' He held the page between his fingers, ready to tear it out.

This was often the way he called her bluff. It was a kind of communication between them; an indication, oddly enough, not of enmity, but of the closest they could get in understanding, even sympathy.

She shook her head, the hint of a smile playing round her mouth. 'I suppose you have your reasons.'

Sussie was still half asleep when she heard the lorry driving down the road and the roll of drums and the shrill blast of a trumpet. The tune was not very familiar, but it sounded like the English song *Rule Britannia* the English children at school taunted them with.

The rainwater trickled down the gutters and she wanted to go back to sleep because today was a holiday and everyone was lying in, but Grieta who was making up the fire in the kitchen couldn't contain herself and she appeared in the doorway.

'Sussie, you should see, the flags on the lorry, they're holding up a tarpaulin so the music things don't get wet. Oubaas Jon Borchards next door has put a Union Jack up on his pole.'

Mr Borchards loved the English, Oupa had often said that before. Befuddled with sleep as she was, it occurred to her that something was expected of her, because she too had a flag. She wished she didn't have a flag. She pulled her clothes on but no shoes, she could walk barefoot on the wet roof.

Her South African flag wasn't as big as Oom Borchards's but it would be seen from the street.

When she went into the rain at the back of the house she nearly turned back. Her hair was already drenched, she knew her hands would slip. The iron veranda pole was wet and slippery, but her hands knew it from much climbing. She pulled up with her hands and slid her feet up, straightened her body, pulled and slid. She got a grip on the gutter. She was carrying the rolled flag in her mouth like a dog carries a stick. The iron sheeting of the veranda roof made a racket so she walked on the edges of her feet. The hardest part was getting up onto the roof of the house. She tried with the flag in one hand, slid back; then she tried legs astride where the iron sheets were joined, a sort of gutter that gave her a foothold. She was carrying the flag in her mouth again. The water ran into her face and down her neck; her feet were getting colder and colder. She tried to climb the roof corner as she would have climbed up a doorframe, pushing sideways with her hands as she moved her feet up, but it was difficult with the flag in her mouth. She climbed the roof foot by foot, slipping up, until she was high enough to get hold of the ironwork that made a little lattice high on the gable. An iron pole stuck out like a spear on either point of the lattice.

She pulled out the rope that she'd stuck into her shirt and fastened the flag stick to the one spear; winding the rope round and round it. The stick stood upright but the flag wouldn't unfurl. She tugged and shook it, round and round the stick. Finally it opened, but it hung so wet and lifeless that you couldn't even tell it was a South African flag. Then she began to cry, clinging to the latticework with both hands. The rain ran down her face and into her mouth; she couldn't tell which were tears and which were raindrops. The water ran down her neck and in under her clothes; her hands ached with cold.

Then she heard her father's voice. He was in his pyjamas and he was angry. Her mother stood beside him in her dressing gown, holding up an umbrella. Ozzie was still half asleep.

Grieta must have told on her. She hated Grieta.

'Come down!' bellowed her father.

'I can't, Pappa.' She was too terrified even to look down. She thought of the man who had climbed up on the church because he was obsessed with God; he had also been scared, and his hands had slipped on the roof tiles. She was crying loudly now. Her hands were locked; if she let go of the iron spear, she'd fall down. Her feet had gone dead from the cold.

'I'm frightened, Pappa,' she wailed.

'What the hell will the neighbours say if there's a South African flag on our roof on the king's birthday?' Stuart shouted at Agnes. Agnes screamed back: 'I didn't do anything, it's your pa who puts crazy ideas in the child's head.'

'And what about my job? Roof over your heads, food in your bellies.'

'You can be grateful it isn't the old Transvaal Republic flag.'

'How the hell am I expected to get that flag down?'

'We have to get the child down too.'

'Don't just stand there with your mouth open,' he shouted at Grieta.

Then his eye fell on Ozzie. 'Were you involved in this?' But Ozzie retreated to his room.

'I suppose I'll have to damn well climb up there. If I fall and get killed, you'll all be sorry.'

Grieta fetched a ladder and he climbed up to the veranda roof. He was already soaked through when he tried to climb up the angle where the kitchen and house roofs met. But he was too heavy to manage it. It was raining harder now. The iron pole from the latticework on the gable wouldn't be strong enough for a rope that could bear his weight. He threw his slippers down and Agnes picked them up. Barefoot and through sheer willpower, he battled his way up to the top. He couldn't unclasp the child's frozen hands; he had to rub them, finger by finger, almost cracking the knuckles. Then he sank back a little and pulled at her. She came loose in a rush, crashing onto him, and they both tumbled down the wet iron onto the veranda roof.

'God save us!' screamed Grieta. 'Oh, dear Lord,' cried Agnes. Then they realised that Stuart had straightened up and was forcing the howling Sussie onto the ladder. It was only when he was safely back on the ground that Stuart realised he'd forgotten to remove the flag.

Fortunately it was raining so hard that no one on the street would ever take the drooping scrap of cloth on the roof for a flag.

'Change out of those wet clothes and go straight to bed. I'll bring you a hot drink,' said Agnes. The child was white and on the point of collapse.

But Stuart was in no mood to let her off that lightly. He took up a wet slipper and grabbed her hand. 'I'll teach you to make fools of us!' He began to beat her, but she tugged at his grasp, lurching forwards and he had to swing round and round to get at her backside with the slipper. She screamed more from the fear and wetness than from the punishment.

When he finally released her, he said, 'Next time I'll beat you so hard you won't be able to sit down for a week.'

'You're the one who's going to catch your death of cold,' Agnes told him from the back veranda. 'Come and drink your coffee.'

That afternoon, Sussie took refuge with her grandfather.

'Oupa, you said a person should be obsessed, and I know it was mad, but something told me to do it. I couldn't bear the English flag in our street.'

Father stroked her head. 'Obsession, my child, but with God.'

'I felt like the man on the church roof, Oupa.'

Something else seemed to be concerning Father. 'And your brother, Sussie? Wouldn't he have helped you?'

'I didn't want to wake him up. I knew Pa would be angry and he hits Ozzie very hard. He only hit me with a slipper.'

Her grandfather hugged her close. With her head against his waistcoat, she felt so safe she could confess. 'It was very funny, Oupa, the slipper was wet and it went swish-swash as he hit me. Then he stopped because it wasn't sore at all.'

'And the flag?'

'The gardener had to get it down once the rain stopped.'

'There, you see: that's what comes of your stories,' was all Issy said. 'How can you expect a child of her age to keep it all in perspective?'

One pleasure of retiring to Wellington was that Hennie was more accessible.

One warm summer day, Josias took the train to Eersterivier, where he connected with a train from Cape Town to the Strand. He needed to talk to his brother; he would stay the night.

Hennie stood waiting a little to one side of the platform at the Strand. Always holding back, still sensitive about the gaze of strangers, wearing a white jacket – dating back to his missionary days? – and a Panama hat, pulled well down, his walking stick hooked over his elbow.

It was another one of countless hot, windy days. The black suit was warm, but he would only permit himself to loosen the white tie and remove the black jacket once he was in the sitting room of his brother's mission cottage. The wind howled, but they were sheltered in the back streets of the small town. It was baking hot. As they came round the corner, along the sea front the wind blew with a force that made them stagger as they came round the corner.

'At least the wind cools things down,' Hennie said as the door finally banged shut behind them. 'Take a seat, Josias.'

He prepared coffee laboriously with his one hand.

'How have you been, Boet? I worry about you.'

'Nothing particular to complain about. And with you?'

'Fine. Just too many women in the house.'

Once they'd drunk the coffee, Josias made himself comfortable. He sat back on the sofa, arms behind his head. 'I thought so much about you on the train. Since I read that report in *Die Kerkbode* you've been on my mind continuously.' Hennie showed no sign of interest, but he continued nonetheless. 'It was about a black missionary on his way to a kraal some distance from the mission station where you were based. Obviously it's much bigger, with more people, these days. He was overtaken by nightfall. Then he saw a lion ahead of him on the footpath. A large male. He was terrified but he prayed: "I am out on your work, Lord. If You wish me to do the work, please rescue me from this fix."'

Hennie remained silent, apparently not even listening, but Josias saw a muscle twitch in his scarred cheek. With age, the scars had pulled the cheek tighter and more askew; the corner of the mouth was also dragged up slightly. His heart contracted at the sight of his brother's face and the expression that showed no sign of inner peace. Just a haggard, twisted question mark.

He continued. 'They say that just as he finished praying, a lioness appeared out of the long grass, rubbed against the male and the pair of them turned and simply walked off. Then I thought of you, my boet. And it bothered me. My faith faltered. The black evangelist did not have greater faith than you. No one had.'

'Allo, 'allo, 'allo. Do you hear me, are my words entering your ears, are they going through to your heart? Dip your bucket in the water and scoop. Bring the bucket to your lips and drink. The light from the gas lamps flickered on the church walls, the large man in the pulpit came closer and then receded, like a reflection on moving water. Just the white of his bib and his hair, snow white, and his shining cuff links moved like plasma apparitions in the darkness of the pulpit.

Drink of it.

God is with you, drink of Him.

With the first leap, the lion had him down. The paws tore his shirt, his chest; the teeth were on his forearm. There was no pain yet, just amazement; staring into the yellow, brown-streaked eye. Was this God? That gaze, eye to eye, at the moment of death? The saliva dripping from the jaws before he ripped the flesh from your bones; the powerful smell of him, the surge of muscle and life under the brown hide, pent up like lava about to erupt, the inner fire the earth spews out to give form to the universe? Was this the power that is God – the mass of muscles under the hide, the seething energy, the heartbeat, the claws tearing my skin?

I shudder, I tremble, I am a minuscule atom, I cannot look upon your power. Remembering, I cannot summon up your violence, or I would surely die.

Hennie sat with closed eyes. The tumultous emotions, the flood of memories released by his brother's words, shot through him like a physical pain. His hand locked on to the walking stick which was always close by. The thin, knotted hand; his lifeline. Josias's voice came to him from a long way off.

'That black evangelist was walking from your station to the village. In the knowledge of what had happened to you: he was one of the lads who carried you back. Because the lion had released you. It was extraordinary, they said. Just as though the lion no longer took pleasure in you, and left you, so they could approach – none of them was armed – and carry you back. Think about it, brother. What happened to you gave the black evangelist a faith as solid as rock, so that not only he, but others too, could walk upon it. It was not in vain, in spite of what you say. Never in vain.'

'So? What are you trying to tell me? God certainly has the free will to decide whose prayers He will heed. Whom He chooses.'

'Very well. I'm sorry I spoke, if it has only added to your bitterness.'

'Let's take a walk,' said Hennie. The conversation had disturbed him. He busied himself with the washing up. Clumsy, slow, tremulous, he washed the cups, pressing them one by one against his chest as he tried to dry them. He replaced the sugar bowl on the shelf; he covered the milk jug with a doily and it went back into a basin of water to keep cool.

The wind dropped just before sunset. The beach was deserted under a cloudless sky and all was quiet. Shallow waves pushed up and then drew back, leaving small ripples like shells in the wet sand. A gold rim circled the horizon, a pale pink shimmer rested on the distant blue of the open sea.

What an exquisite, peaceful evening, thought Josias. They had only to cross the road and they were on the beach. A low wall kept sand from the pavement and he sat on it to remove his shoes and socks and roll his trousers up to the knee. He helped Hennie to loosen the knots in his shoelaces, and pulled the socks off the reluctant, bony white feet. He was suddenly impatient to get his own feet into the sea water. They made their way with some difficulty through the heavy dry sand. Hennie with the aid of his stick.

The lapping waves were a balm on the ankles. They strolled through the shallow water in the direction of Melkbaai.

'It's memorable: such a lovely evening.' He felt like a boy with his brother again as toes curled in the wet sand when he bent to pick up a scrap of seaweed, twist it and throw it back, then stopped again to watch the tiny snails tumbling in the receding water, their trails erased when the waves flowed back.

They carried their shoes by the joined laces, socks stuffed inside. The lines on Hennie's face had relaxed too, Josias observed. Did his burden seem lighter out here in the open?

After supper that night, once Josias, as the elder, had read from the Bible and said a prayer, Hennie said, 'To go back to our conversation ... You are wrong, Ouboet. The evangelist's faith was the purer. He was purer in God's work.'

'And you?'

'I challenged God. I was wilful, I took chances. After I lost Jessie, I wanted to die. I threw myself off the proverbial cliff saying: If You are God, catch me and save me from destruction. That is something different.'

He wiped his eyes with his sleeve, speaking almost reluctantly. His eyes still had a tendency to water, after all these years ...

'He didn't catch me, but He didn't let me fall to my death either. That is what I cannot forgive Him. To this day I ask myself: For what purpose ... what use is my life ... all these years? Do you know how the time drags?'

'I can imagine.'

Josias took a sheet of paper from his inside pocket. 'I wrote down this thought for you. You know, Boet, after the Great 'Flu epidemic I too had to wrestle with doubt. How often I asked: God, why? Why my saintly Emma, and my daughter? And I was filled with the bitterest self-reproach. But read this passage yourself: it's by De Caussade, a French Jesuit. Very well, I'll read it aloud.' He looked up. Hennie kept his eyes shut. He read: *'Do as you are doing now, suffer as you are suffering now. To do it with holiness nothing is needed but to change your heart.'*

The reading light was dim, he made a mental note to bring Hennie a better light, perhaps a standard lamp. He read on calmly: *'Holiness is desiring in your heart that which befalls you through the will of God.*

'It struck me as the most difficult challenge set before me in all my years of service.'

'Desire in your heart?' Hennie was looking at him now; Josias noticed that the one eye was slightly bleary. Was he developing a cataract? And that nervy twitch of the corner of his mouth? My brother! My brother!

But Hennie sat upright. He had been listening, after all. And he was ready for an argument. 'Oh, no, Boet. Up until now, you have said: resign yourself. Submit to the authority and will of God – I know my catechism too – accept. I had no choice, defiance was hopeless. How would I have survived if I hadn't made my peace with this …' He looked round the small room and then down at his crippled body. 'Submit …' and now his voice was bitter, 'accept that my life limps through the mission cottages at the Strand and not over the plains of Africa ... accept that it's useless to comfort myself with the endless repetition of "Let My blessing on you, for what you are, suffice ..." And now you are asking even more: that I "desire with my heart those things that befall me through God's will".'

'I don't ask, God asks. He asked it of me too. I find it extremely difficult. A rough road. Not allotted to everyone. Because now I ask myself too: Is your lot, Boetie Hennie, that is so much harder, not ultimately the more blessed? Your challenge so much greater? The final Communion with God so much purer? Haven't we read that the saints were jealous of suffering? Better the lion that springs than the lion that passes you by?'

The final Communion? Hennie shook his head mutely.

'Desire with your heart. The Lord knows, Josias, those are difficult words.'

And he thought: Being crippled as the price for one moment of divine vision?

Josias's voice again: '... to drink with joy the water that Dr Kumm spoke of. For the water is God.'

7

At long last, after weeks of waiting, after days of organising her routine around the arrival of the postman; days of despondency and eventually indifference, Agnes's letter arrived from Pretoria. There was no stamp on the long buff envelope, just the large blue letters IDVSM and OHMS. In Diens Van Sy Majesteit. On His Majesty's Service. Together with the Pretoria stamp. Thank goodness Stuart wasn't home when the mail arrived. The children were busy with sport; otherwise they'd have snatched it up. Sussie, especially, was a nosy child.

Agnes put the other letters on the hall table and went to her room with the buff envelope. She put off opening it. First she went over to her dressing table. Her pots of cream and flasks of perfume and lotion and the hand mirror and hairbrush looked accusing. Of what? Of secretiveness? Did she have to come clean to everybody? Was that what marriage meant? Always reporting everything to everyone? After a while she started to breath more evenly, but she could still feel her heart beating too fast.

She opened the envelope.

Only a few sentences. Her request had been noted. Certain names and addresses had been found which might have a bearing on her problem. She was required to: a) draw up a letter with her full name and address; b) make it clear that her intentions were only to meet her potential parent(s); c) the Department of Birth Registration would send a certified copy of her letter to her potential parent(s); d) it was the parent(s) prerogative to contact her or not. This procedure would preclude any violation of the laws about confidentiality.

She crumpled the letter and threw it on the floor. Then kneeled and carefully ironed it out with her hand on her bed. Didn't anybody ever think of her? Would she always be like that albino child who was fetched from the back of a hut and shown to her at the market – a freak of nature, like her? What put this image into her head? Had it been there, suppressed all these years because the hurt was too deep?

Laws of confidentiality! It was the parent's prerogative to contact her! And what about her rights? Didn't she also have two legs and two arms and a head and two eyes and a nose? If they could, they'd have hidden her at the back of a hut as well.

But she'd shown them. She'd made a life for herself. For the moment, Stuart's straying was forgotten. She could get him back, she knew it. She had a house and a garden, and Grieta the housemaid, and somebody to help in the garden, and two healthy children. She wasn't hideable. The grandfather clock in the hall started to chime. Three o'clock. She was to meet Aunt Issy. They were going to a Women's Missionary meeting together. She was a respected member of a reputable family. Since Father retired here, and particularly since Miss Issy seemed to be fond of her, stories about Stuart no longer found their way to Agnes.

She put on her hat, took her handbag and then went back to the bedroom to double-check that the buff envelope was locked in a drawer. She had to run down the garden path so as not to keep Aunt Issy waiting.

Aunt Issy was standing on the veranda, hat on, handbag under her arm. She was well into her seventies, but her posture was still as upright as ever, the head was still held up with dignity. The hair, now white as snow, was combed up strictly against the small head; there were hardly any wrinkles on the thin face.

'She hasn't enough skin to make wrinkles,' Stuart bantered one day.

'Pappa, did Great-Aunt Issy ever have boyfriends, or other friends besides Oupa and Ouma's children?' Sussie asked.

'Never, never, Sussie,' teased her father, 'and you mustn't follow in her footsteps just because you've got her name!'

'I don't really have her name, I'm not Issy!'

But Ozzie mocked her: 'Sussie isn't Issy!' Until their mother shut him up.

'I've felt for some time now that she's too grown-up for Sussie. Let's call you Belle,' said Agnes.

'Isobelle, Belle...' Sussie savoured the names. 'I like Belle.'

Aunt Issy was secretly pleased, but didn't know how to express her satisfaction and her affection for the child.

'Thank you, Agnes, it's most gratifying. But you should insist that Grieta call her Miss Belle, my dear. She's a young lady.'

Admonition was the first recourse for Aunt Issy. But Grieta stumbled over MissieBelle, which became SussieBelle, and the name stuck.

Agnes held Aunt Issy lightly by the elbow as they started down the veranda steps. Then Aunt Issy stopped abruptly. She held Agnes back. 'Don't forget the letter, dear.'

The letter? Was Aunt Issy a mind reader? How could she know about the letter that had only been delivered that afternoon and was now locked in her drawer? The colour surged up into Agnes' fair neck, spread over her face. 'The letter?'

Aunt Issy didn't notice anything, her eyes on the steps as she was afraid of losing her footing. 'Our dear Leonora's letter. She's arrived back in London. Such an interesting letter. She loves London so.' Leonora was on her second year-long exchange visit.

They were now at street level. Aunt Issy kept up with Agnes easily – she walked briskly considering her age. They often went to the Afrikaans Women's Institute – the ACVV – and Women's Mission League meetings together. Although Agnes felt less vulnerable now she had Aunt Issy and Father as allies, she knew Stuart was up to something. She could tell from his manner, the way he whistled in the morning, the new tie, and the new shirt. He was after all, only a man, she thought bitterly, and it had been quite a while since he'd slept with her. He must be going somewhere else. But she accepted it; they'd learnt how to avoid bickering. What did words help? she often thought. This afternoon she couldn't focus on the meeting. Her thoughts kept returning to the letter from Pretoria.

After much deliberation and many attempts, she wrote the answer that Pretoria had requested, the letter that would be sent to any unknown potential parent(s) who might be traceable. The wait for an answer would be unbearable, she thought as she slipped the letter through the post-box slot. The self-exposure and her need 'to just know' were too deep an intrusion.

On an August afternoon in 1938, Agnes was part of a group of eight ACVV members raising funds by serving tea and coffee in a tent at the showgrounds just outside town. None of them was very clear about what the occasion involved, but the word from the Cape Town head office was that a number of people were expected and in the rainy weather, coffee and tea and maybe also pancakes would go down very well.

They'd seen pictures in the newspapers these past few days of two ox wagons that had left Cape Town on their way to the north. SussieBelle was told to come to school in her Voortrekker guides uniform because they were going to get off early to see the ox wagons. Ozzie wasn't going because being a Voortrekker scout didn't appeal to him. He didn't want to be a Boy Scout either, in spite of his father's encouragement. No one in his class was a Boy Scout.

The newspaper photographs showed strikingly large groups of people gathered round the ox wagons – they came from far and wide and there were even men on horseback representing old-fashioned horse commandos. The group of women riding on the wagon wore old-fashioned dresses and bonnets, and the men wore broad-rimmed hats and red handkerchiefs tied round their necks. They were commemorating the trek northwards of 100 years ago, and this re-enactment would culminate in the laying of the foundation stone of the Voortrekker Monument in Pretoria.

The women behind the trestle tables in the tent pulled up their coat collars against the cold. Kettles hissed on the Primus stoves, cups and saucers stood in line, the coffee pots kept warm on the blue-flame stove. They'd mixed the pancake batter half-heartedly. They had no idea of how many takers to expect. The ACVV head office said on the telephone that morning: more and more people were coming to see the wagons, they could expect crowds. Now they looked dubiously at their preparations. And around the tent. What if it started to rain?

'Let's start with the pancakes,' said the convenor. 'We won't be able to keep up once they start coming.'

Four of them manned the pans at another trestle table at the back of the tent. Each one at two stoves, with two pans. One even had three pans. They were the dab hands. Agnes would pour coffee.

They checked their watches. Time was running out. The Primus stoves roared; a sharp smell of paraffin rose from the blue-flame stoves.

'Turn that down a little.'

Then they heard the children singing from afar. One of the women stood at the tent opening. 'It's the little Voortrekkers. They've lined up at the gate.' The singing that started so valiantly died out.

'Is it raining?' asked Agnes.

'Not yet, thank goodness.'

But the air was dark; the clouds hung low, and puddles from last night's rain still lay about on the showgrounds. Townspeople started gathering. The children who weren't wearing Voortrekker uniforms walked in crooked lines into the grounds under their teachers' supervision. Somebody struck up *Die Lied van Jong Suid-Afrika – The song of Young South Africa* – but people were too far apart and it died out.

The horses brought the excitement. The women abandoned their stoves and stood at the tent flap. The first rider was mounted on a dapple-grey horse and he had a pole with a fluttering Vierkleur – the flag of the old Transvaal Republic – stuck into his saddle. He galloped onto the hill and into the showgrounds. Then there were horses wherever you looked and wide-rimmed plumed hats, and scarves and flags and more flags. The Free State, Transvaal and the Union flag. The horsemen made their horses tripple past the waiting crowd, bowing a greeting here, calling out a word of reassurance there: 'It won't be too long now, Oom, the wagon will be here soon.' And teased the women: 'Hey, tannies, where are the long dresses? Why aren't you joining in?'

Then out of nowhere, somebody started singing: *Kent gij dat volk vol heldenmoed* – the national anthem of the old Transvaal Republic – and the crowds started singing along; slow and almost bemused. A small boy in corduroy pants and waistcoat, with a brown shirt and red necktie and a broad-rimmed hat, appeared at the entrance to the showgrounds, leading the oxen forward between the rows of inquisitive Voortrekkers who'd never seen anything like it. He led the span of 14 oxen by a thong. They followed slowly, pulling the creaking, swaying wagon with its white canopy and the group of people in old-fashioned dress. People sang, almost overcome, as if they hadn't realised they remembered the words or the tunes. After *Kent gij dat volk vol heldenmoed* came the national anthem of the former Orange Free State Republic: *Heft, burgers, 't lied der vrijheid aan* and then the wagon came to a standstill, but before the group of people in old-fashioned clothing climbed off, they started to sing, as if it was a prayer: *Prys den Heer met blijde galmen – Praise the Lord, the King of Heaven* ...

The pancake makers wiped their eyes. The convenor said quietly, 'If only the weather holds,' but everybody knew she said it just to say something. They weren't here to listen to the mayor's speech: Goodness gracious, was ou Beneke here too today, that old blood-Sap! Or to the head of the Voortrekkers, or the dominee who was asked to deliver a short prayer. It was back to the kettles and cups and the pancake batter, poured in a thin layer and then spread on the pans with a slight flick of the wrist, and nursed until little bubbles started pushing up and talking back. Then the pancakes were sprinkled with sugar and cinnamon and rolled up.

'Please give us a hand with the wrapping, Agnes: there're too few of us here. I'm going to round up a few reliable helpers from outside. Thank God we have enough coffee and tea. We're mixing more batter. Let's get going.'

The group from the wagon – the ones in old-fashioned clothing – was brought into the tent first.

'The people are cold, tannies, what do you have to offer this afternoon? Coffee, pancakes?'

If only we'd known beforehand, thought the convenor, imagining the stacks of sandwiches, the biscuits, the fudge they could have sold. But it was too late now. The travelling group needed looking after. And what about all this 'tannie' business? She wasn't accustomed to that.

More and more people came into the tent while the speeches were being made – the man who led the expedition in a corduroy suit also made a speech. No townspeople had come in yet, but the horsemen who'd unsaddled at the showground stables started filling the tent.

'We want coffee, we aren't tea drinkers. Did you take us for Englishmen? Ag no, tannie, how could you do that?' The convenor was seized around the waist and swung about behind the trestle table. Flustered, she tried to push her hair back into place. The corduroy-clad riders smelled of man and horse and sweat. When a hat was pushed back, it left a line of sweat around the head.

Agnes first saw the hat, because the man stood with his back to her. And she got the smell of horse and sweat. She went ice-cold inside when she saw the narrow kudu-hide hatband. The black and white pattern made her close her eyes and bite her lip. Her heart pounded. From a great distance away she heard her voice say: 'Here's the coffee,' and saw her hand handing over the cup and saucer.

The man turned to take it from her. He had a farmer's suntanned face, his complexion was fair, and his short beard was rusty brown, the same colour as the damp hair pushed back from his forehead. The hand that took the cup and saucer was big and strong, with light rusty-brown hairs between the knuckles. She had to forcibly prevent herself from dropping everything and grabbing his hand, bringing it to her mouth and kissing it. A strange passion took hold of her. Her hands shook so much that the coffee slopped into the saucer. The man steadied it with both hands and their hands met around the saucer, supported the cup. 'Take it easy, girl. Slow down.' He must be about her age: she noticed a grey streak in his beard. His eyes were blue and clear and friendly. And warm as he looked at her.

'I have to take another cup outside. Here's one that's been poured already; I'll take it along. Then I'll come back.' He laughed. 'And make sure there's a pancake waiting for me!'

First she wanted to tell the others she felt sick: she had to go home immediately. She was afraid he'd come back. But God knew she didn't want to miss a second meeting. She needed it. Like food. Her heart cried out to him where he had gone to take the coffee to someone else. To his wife? The thought paralysed her. No, not his wife. To his comrade at the horses. What was she going to do when he came back? She heard her voice say calmly to one of the pancake makers, 'Let me have the next one over here. It's been reserved.' She sprinkled the sugar and cinnamon and wrapped the pancake herself. The knowledge that he was going to eat it, that it was going to be chewed between his lips and swallowed, was almost too much for her. It's the smell, she thought, the smell from her childhood, the smell of her father, that washed over her. No, it's not the smell; it's the tenderness, the smile. Or is it the hat, the strip of hide around the hat? Oh, she couldn't think straight. What was she going to do when he came back? How was she going to control her hands, her voice?

But he came back in a group. He pushed through people to get to her and asked, 'My pancake?' She held out the parcel to him. His hand touched hers only slightly, but the feeling went straight through her body. His eyes were intimate, as if he'd known her for years.

'See you in Pretoria, green-eyes.'

Did he really say that? How many times wouldn't she ask herself; how many days and nights? 'See you in Pretoria, green-eyes.' *Your eyes are as green as the stones* – in the brooch that she still kept, that she had never worn.

Will he come back to the tent?

She waited until it was almost dark, when the other women wanted to leave because they'd put away their kettles and pans and dishes, the cups and saucers were washed and packed.

'Come and have a look,' cried the convenor, 'they've outspanned the oxen and led them away. And the Voortrekkers are pulling the wagon. Ag, it makes you feel so strange.'

People started to sing again. Spontaneously, and mostly hymns and psalms. They didn't even mind that it was drizzling. 'Hey, the children are going to get wet, enough is enough.'

She stayed in the tent until everybody was gone, but he didn't come back. He couldn't, she told herself; he was one of the horsemen. They were saddled up; they were riding around the showgrounds for the last time. Which one was he? Was he looking this way? Was he waving?

She only gathered her things together when SussieBelle came looking for her at the tent, saying that Ozzie had gone home long ago. The child helped with the carrying; almost silenced by emotion. 'I helped to pull the ox wagon, Ma. The wagon will stay here tonight and then they'll trek early tomorrow morning. People are bringing all sorts of stuff for the wagon – food and wine and honey, and the farmers are bringing fodder. The tannies and oom on the wagon are sleeping over at the pastorie.'

'The ooms on the horses?'

'They aren't staying over, Mamma, they're going back to the farms.'

The women only realised later that they hadn't asked for payment for the coffee, tea and the pancakes. The convenor, always down to earth, tried to make excuses. 'I don't know how it was, one was so taken, you felt almost odd, you couldn't think about money.' Then she added hastily – she'd never been apologetic, 'I'm just sorry that we didn't have more to give.'

But what astonished the town most, was that old Aunt Dora van der Spuy wrapped an old shawl and a piece of tarpaulin round her great-great-grandfather's wooden cradle that dated back to the Great Trek and gave it to the people on the wagon.

'They made me feel good about myself,' she said, 'in a way I never felt before … Now the cradle is going along, all the way to Pretoria.'

'It's madness,' said Aunt Issy as the weeks passed and reports told of increasingly enthusiastic responses to the ox wagons as they journeyed north. From all parts of the country wagons were trekking up to Pretoria to be there on 16 December, the Day of the Covenant. *See you in Pretoria, green-eyes.*

'Oupa said one can be mad, it's necessary sometimes to be possessed by madness,' said SussieBelle precociously. She cut out all the pictures of the wagons in the newspapers and stuck them in a book.

Her grandfather stroked her head. 'Madness for God, I said, madness for God.'

'But it's very, very religious this, Oupa. People are singing almost nothing but psalms and hymns, and they give Bibles and things to the wagons, even their oldest family Bibles, and they always read the Bible and pray.'

'Madness for God, my child, just remember that: madness for God.'

There was dissension at home because SussieBelle wanted to take part in the torch relay. Members of the Voortrekker movement carried burning torches from all over the country to light the bonfire at the laying of the cornerstone near Pretoria.

'My whole team is carrying, why can't I?' She waited until supper, when her father would be there as well.

'Father is putting ideas in her head,' said Stuart. 'With all his stories about passion for the nation. It's his stories that made me go to German South West Africa that time, in revolt. And now he's working on the child.'

'Oupa isn't putting anything into my head. I'm 13. I can think for myself.'

She wished Ozzie could help fight for a change. But Ozzie wasn't worth anything; he wouldn't go against his father. He didn't even want to become a Voortrekker because Pa said they were too narrow-minded. She wasn't afraid of her father. It was only Ozzie who was always sucking up to him.

'I will go and carry the torch. You can't stop me, Pappa, no matter what you say.'

She knew her mother wanted her to carry it, even though she said nothing. She just didn't fight with pa openly. Her ma was different these days; it almost felt as if she was closer to her. She'd always spoken up for Ozzie, but now she seemed to be on SussieBelle's side too. This was something new and it made her feel warm inside. Her pa was making a fuss about carrying the torch at night. But they had to carry in relays through the night; the flame had to be kept burning and moving. The thought of the flame being carried through the dark night, over plains and ridges, gave her goosebumps.

'If you think I'm going to drive out in the middle of the night to drop you off in the veld in the middle of nowhere, you can think again,' said her father.

'You don't have to. Oom Japie is going and Aunt Sally said I could come with them, and Mamma can also get a lift. Oom Japie likes the torches, he says it's something very beautiful.'

'You're all completely crazy. In the middle of the night. In the veld. And how do you know where and who and how? You'll set yourselves alight, that's what'll happen.'

He unfolded the English paper, which was delivered every evening, and started to read. But his thoughts were still on the torches.

'Is it responsible to have organised this? Do you know how much paraffin weighs? Do you know what can happen if the wind gets hold of the flame, or if the paraffin spills?'

'Japie van Lingen is a responsible man,' said Agnes. Her cheeks were still flushed, she couldn't help it. The colour spread to her cheeks when she started to talk about people's commitment. 'He, his son-in-law and Oom Pallie from the Voortrekkers figured it all out. They even went to Cape Town after the meeting.'

'Such a carry-on in the middle of the night, the whole house in turmoil ...'

'I'm going in any case, Stuart. I'm driving with Japie, and I can look after the child. If it were so dangerous, they wouldn't have...'

'How you can work yourselves up like this? I can't understand it. Ozzie and I will enjoy a good night's sleep anyway. Won't we, Oz?'

Something else Agnes could do in secret was make herself a long dress and a bonnet. She'd been singing in the choir for a few years now, and the choir members were going to wear long dresses for the evening service on the second Sunday in December. She could copy from the magazine and newspaper pictures of the old dresses. The whole choir was going to be in white. Her dress had to be really pretty. Miss Nancy was known round town for making the neatest frogged loops for the buttons. The dresses buttoned in front from the high neckline to the waist which sloped down in a point and was trimmed with piping. SussieBelle had to take the parcel to Miss Nancy.

'Is it only one dress, Mamma? It's such a huge parcel.'

Again her mother got that colour in her cheeks. 'Run along now. I made an extra dress for myself.'

'And for me, Mamma? A long dress and a bonnet?'

'Yes, yes, I thought of that, but yours won't button up in front. I'll put the hooks and eyes onto the sideslip myself.'

SussieBelle hugged her mother and kissed her. 'Thank you, thank you, thank you, Mamma. The teacher said we can come to Sunday school in long dresses on the day you wear yours to sing in the choir.'

When the child was gone with the parcel, she walked back to the closed-in veranda with the pot plants. Nobody knew, but she was one of the members of their choir who'd volunteered to go and practise with the bigger choir in Cape Town, and maybe, maybe, just a small maybe, be chosen to go to Pretoria.

She paced up and down in front of the windows. *See you in Pretoria, green-eyes.* She was completely thrown off balance by the strange feelings surging up in her – feelings she'd last experienced as a child when Aunt Naomi gave her the brooch from her father. Oh, the longing for her father! Her love for him was eating her away! The only emotion she still had that was her very own ... and yet it wasn't her own. But who could tear love out of their heart like a piece of rotten flesh? The second dress in the parcel was made of green taffeta, the green of the stones in the brooch. In case she could go. Just in case.

She said nothing to Aunt Issy. She could have spoken to Father. She could have at least told him about the choir. But she kept it all a complete secret.

SussieBelle couldn't fall asleep that night. She heard the clock in the hall get ready for the chime, then she counted down the strokes. Ten o'clock. Her parents were not ready to go to bed; the light in the hall was still burning. The buckle of her uniform belt glowed where the light was shining in. Her black shoes had been polished, the black stockings lay ready to put on, the uniform was spread out on the other bed, and the hat was waiting. She had loosened the rope and twisted it again and attached it to the belt. The end was still neatly edged; she didn't have to bother with that. Her Voortrekker knife hung on the other loop.

She was wide awake. Then her parents went to their room, switched off the light. The clock in the hall struck 11 o'clock. But she was so excited, she still lay stiff as a ramrod. Her mother would come and wake her up at half past two. Half past two was a time she couldn't imagine. Then she would dress quickly, and at a quarter to Oom Japie would pick them up at the garden gate. What did the garden gate look like at half past two in the morning? What did the flowers look like? Was it half past two when that man fell off his ladder? Were there stars at half past two?

Half past two, half past two, it chimed in her head when she felt her mother shake her arm. 'Come on, wake up, get dressed. Come to the kitchen, I'm going to make us some coffee. But very quietly. Shush now. Keep your door closed, the light mustn't wake Pappa. And switch it off when you come.'

'Am I ready, Mamma?' She was half asleep. She allowed her mother to straighten out her uniform in the kitchen, pull up her stockings that were sagging. Her mother folded the stocking once at the top and then hooked on the suspender. She couldn't swallow all the coffee. Her mother poured some of it in a flask and put a few rusks in a paper bag. 'Come on,' she said.

They went out the back door and down to the garden gate, where they waited for Oom Japie. The cold woke her up a bit more. 'Buck up,' said her mother. 'You can't carry the torch if you're half asleep, you'll spill paraffin and set everyone alight.'

They were told to keep the torch upright, with both hands. Hold it tightly, upright, with your arms in front of you. And then run. Don't race, run.

Oom Japie's car came out of the dark; his headlights bright on the road. Oom Japie's daughter Dorothea sat on the back seat in one corner. She looked half asleep.

SussieBelle shook her arm. 'Dorothea, are you awake?'

Dorothea immediately sat up. 'What do you think, silly-billy?'

'Quiet now, children,' said Oom Japie. 'You'll always remember what happens tonight. You're links in the chain of light.'

SussieBelle swallowed, she wanted to cry. She tugged her mother's arm. 'Ma, Ozzie should have come too. You should have told him to come.'

She and Dorothea were both wide awake now. They'd left town and were getting closer and closer to the main road to the north. In the distance they saw dots of light that they couldn't decipher.

'It's the torches, Pa,' yelled Dorothea.

But it wasn't the torches. They drove past group after group, each time a few grown-ups and a child in uniform. The grown-ups had lit campfires, and shone their torches to look at maps or their watches. Oom Japie stopped at one of the waiting groups. 'Here, I've brought your bearer.'

There wasn't a child here. I'm the child, thought SussieBelle.

Mamma wasn't supposed to be here, I should've been alone. If Mamma says something or touches my arm or anything, I'll die.

'Hey, Oom, you must get a move on,' said a young man who was driving from group to group. He was leaning out of the window. 'The torch is about ten groups away. Everything should be lined up here by now.'

She and her mother stood in the veld next to the road. She didn't know the men at the fire. She shivered from the cold, or was it excitement?

'Chin up, girlie, this isn't the time for the shakes.' He put his arm around her shoulder and pulled her to the fire. Then he spoke to her ma. 'You can relax. I'll run with her. When they're this young, one of us always runs with them. I can carry the diary that goes along as well.' She looked at her ma, whose cheeks were that strange red colour again. She'd pulled the scarf off her head in spite of the cold, she'd combed her fingers through her hair; she looked different, she spoke differently.

The young man who was going to run with her also wore a uniform, with shorts and rolled-up sleeves. He had many badges on his arm and over his top pocket; his arms were strong and gleamed in the firelight, his hair was curly under the hat which he'd pushed back. He squeezed her shoulder encouragingly, but his attention was on her mother. He was flirting with her, thought SussieBelle. He couldn't! Not now. Then his hand lifted from her shoulder and his body stiffened. He was just as tense as she was.

'Here it comes. Dear Lord, here it comes.' She couldn't see, the only thing she could make out was a row of motorcar lights as if there was a procession coming. She heard the breaths heaving, bodies pushed around her; out of the dark came a child in uniform who was stumbling along with a heavy, upright thing with a flame burning on top. People surged around her, the man in the uniform had taken hold of her shoulder again; then, suddenly, he pushed her forward to start running. He was behind her, clamping her hands around the wooden handle close to the flame at the top. It was so heavy, she would have dropped it if his hands weren't above and below hers; she would have let it flop sideways if he hadn't kept it upright. When she got going, he dropped first his one hand, then the other. 'That's right, my girl,' she heard next to her, behind her. Somewhere people started clapping. Using all her strength and willpower, she got it upright, but it was so heavy ... so heavy that it kept on forcing itself forward, and the flame leaned back. A woman put out her hand and burned a handkerchief in the flame. That put her off, but the big hands were around hers again. 'Well done, girl,' said the voice.

Another child and a grown-up started to run next to them. The child stuck her hands out to take the torch from her, but then fell back, afraid. The man with her took it and egged her on.

'That's your relay done, my girl,' said the man who'd helped her. 'You can stop running now, it's over. Stay here, they'll come and pick you up.' But she wanted to go after the flame. The man pulled her against him. 'Don't cry,' he said, 'you did very well.' He wiped her face with his handkerchief. Then he spoke to his friend. 'That woman with the handkerchief in the flame put the child off her stride.'

Her mother appeared out of the dark, she'd walked in the veld next to the road; the road was packed with cars.

'We'll wait here for Oom Japie. Dorothea had her turn further down the line. They're probably stuck in the procession of cars. Isn't it wonderful that all these people at dead of night …'

She didn't say anything to her mother, or to Dorothea in the car. She had a huge lump in her throat, she didn't think she'd ever be able to speak again.

It was two weeks later only, when her mother had already gone to Pretoria to sing with the choir at the laying of the Monument foundation stone, that she spoke to her grandfather about it. They were alone in his study.

'Oupa, you know, when I carried that torch, I felt so strange. I think I felt like that man on the ladder felt – I wasn't me anymore, but someone else.'

'Different than you felt on the roof with the flag?'

'Completely different, Oupa. I only felt scared then.'

Her grandfather looked at her for a long moment. 'I have also felt like you felt with the flame, my darling. One doesn't normally talk about it, but it stays in your heart. You have to be very, very careful with a feeling like that. It's like walking on the edge of a razor blade. You can so easily go over onto the wrong side.'

He looked at her lovingly. 'Even as a man of God, or someone who strove to be a man of God, I let such a feeling lead me to extremes. I'll tell you all about it one day.'

Then he got up from behind his desk, went over to the little built-in cupboard under the bookshelf. 'Shall I?' he wondered out loud. 'Yes, why not?'

He looked over his shoulder at her. 'I'm going to give you a little present, which may not look like much, but it's very valuable. I never gave it to the one it was meant for.'

The parcel he took out of the cupboard was old and discoloured. The old man cut through the twine around it with his penknife. He unfolded the yellowing wrapping. On top lay a paper, also yellowed, on which was written with big, skew, clumsy letters:

Given with love and gratitute
by
the camp women and children
1901
To Ds. Josias van Velde, beloved dominee
Hallelujah, King eternal, His the victory alone!

Under the paper lay something that looked to SussieBelle like a piece of folded, almost drab discoloured sailcloth. Her grandfather unfolded it carefully. It was triangular in shape, and as he opened it up, she saw it was a little tent. With a tent pole which supported it on his desk, flaps that opened and closed, and a little door. The pieces crackled as he opened them, it was almost completely threadbare.

'It's beautiful,' said the child. 'It's so pretty. I'll keep it forever.'

Her grandfather stroked her head, as he was so fond of doing. 'I know you will.'

Aunt Issy conceded that the white dress Agnes would wear on the special Sunday looked good. It was simple and modest, with buttons and loops fastening the front of the bodice and the wrists of the long sleeves. But it fitted a little too closely.

'One doesn't show off one's figure like that.'

But Stuart, who also came to the room to have a look, found this slender figure, with the narrow waist; face concealed under the broad brim of the bonnet, suddenly youthful, mysterious, provocative. He took her around the waist, pulled her against him, and wanted to push the bonnet back and rub his cheek against her soft, fine skin. But she pulled away.

'You're messing up the bonnet,' she said. 'It's difficult to starch and iron it like this.'

But she couldn't break away completely; he held her tight with one hand, while with the other he lifted the flap at the back of the bonnet, and nuzzled his lips into her neck below the hairline. This brought memories back to both of them, the colour rushed to her cheeks.

'Come on, Stuart,' came Aunt Issy's sharp voice. 'Stop playing the fool. I thought you said this whole dressing-up business was religious and sacred.' His behaviour upset her. 'You'll force me to say what I've been thinking all along. Pure pantomime.'

'You see there, Stuart: you're spoiling everything. Leave me alone now, I want to take off the dress.'

SussieBelle was dancing around the front room in her long, blue floral cotton dress. Her school shoes and black stockings looked odd with it. The bonnet hung behind over her back, with the bow fastened under her chin. She stepped around clumsily. Her father didn't give her the attention she wanted. Aunt Issy was also sharp. 'You'll tread on it, it'll tear.'

Her mother came out of the room; her youthfulness, her strange attractiveness left behind with the dress. She was wearing an old skirt and blouse in a colour that didn't suit her. She looked drab again. And tired.

Father, who'd come along, sat in the comfortable chair that was always reserved for him. He'd been the first to be shown the dress; he had said it was pretty. He also said SussieBelle looked pretty. Now he rested with his eyes closed, his hands on his walking stick. It was quite a long walk to their house for him, he was short of breath. After tea, he and Aunt Issy walked slowly home. 'Pure pantomime,' she repeated as they sat down to lunch.

She didn't go to the special service that next Sunday, he didn't either. Because he didn't feel well, not for reasons of conscience. But when he heard in all the subsequent reports of children being christened at the wagons and of the couples who were married there, doubts crept into his mind. And once he read about the dominee who'd worn a corduroy suit under his robe in the pulpit, he thought about the sharp edge of the razor blade and the fine balance he'd mentioned to SussieBelle.

It upset him a great deal when Philip sent word from Pretoria of plans for a Bible with a representation of the completed Voortrekker Monument engraved on the cover in gold. That isn't appropriate, he thought.

But he kept quiet about it.

Despite his general reservations, Father wasn't against Agnes going to Pretoria for the big Day of the Covenant festivities – she'd attended all the choir practices so faithfully, first in their church, then in the surrounding towns' consolidated choir, then in the regional choir, and finally the provincial choir.

'It's good you're getting away for a while. You haven't been away since your wedding. Maybe you could go and see that lawyer in Pretoria again. He might have some information about an exact date of birth, or other details that could help you.'

She was surprised that he touched on the subject again after all these years.

'It's still bothering you, my child.'

She felt guilty that she hadn't told him about the letter to the Birth Registration offices and the answer from Pretoria. It was too late to come clean.

It was decided that SussieBelle would stay with her grandfather and great aunt, and that Ozzie would stay with his father. Nobody but SussieBelle knew about the green dress.

'It's our secret, dear. One can't get by with only one dress in this heat. I can keep the white one for the singing. But Pappa will think I wasted money …'

'I won't say anything, Mamma. I promise.'

8

Leonora dragged her deck chair behind the glass partition to shelter from the sharp wind. The mist condensed into a fine drizzle on the passenger's faces. But they were cozy behind the glass, travelling rugs pulled up to their chins, caps on their heads, scarves round their necks. Leonora was en route to Holland and then on to meet Robert in Germany. She couldn't shake off the depression that had settled on her once she began to make plans for this short holiday.

She could have gone to Paris. Paris healed the spirit, she knew that. But in the dead of winter? Alone? There was someone she could have looked up if things had been different. Even before she'd first left for overseas, she'd asked Agnes: If I ever go over to Paris, should I try to stay at Irma Greylinck's – that small hotel you told us about? Should I look up the other Agnes Valeria? The frightened expression on Agnes's face took her completely by surprise. I won't if you don't want me to, she'd said. But Agnes insisted: I've forgotten the name of the hotel.

She might, on a previous visit, have walked past her, in a park, on the street, or perhaps sat at a table near her in a bistro. Even as a girl, she'd identified with the unhappy Irma. Unhappy? Such a passion for her lover that she travelled with a young baby in wartime half across the world, not even sure if the baby was her lover's! Such passion that she left everything behind just to be with him. I envy her, thought Leonora, I'm jealous of her passion.

Why was she so downhearted? Why couldn't she shake it off? Was it because of the letter from SussieBelle telling of the strange things afoot in their country? Agnes in a long Voortrekker dress and bonnet in the choir up in the organ gallery, and Father and Aunt Issy not going to the service? SussieBelle with her new zeal, almost a stranger to her now?

The ferry's horn bellowed. Lights were beginning to flicker in the distance. A passing ship? The coast of Flanders? Of Holland? As always, sight of the unknown caused a great hungry excitement to well up in Leonora. Perhaps she would find what she was looking for on these dark shores; something she couldn't express in words, even to herself.

9

It was the second week of December and very hot. Agnes got a lift to Cape Town with a fellow chorister, Lettie Scholtz.

Choirs from different regions met at the Cape Town station, and then travelled to Pretoria by train. Second-class carriages that were block-booked for choirs and other groups headed for the laying of the Monument's foundation stone. Six bunk beds and six passengers in each compartment. Four suitcases pushed in under the bottom bunks, two cases and six rolls of bedding and pillows stowed on the luggage racks. Your own bedding saved money on the train fare, and you needed it for the camp at Monument Hill. Not to overlook six boxes of food for the trip. No food baskets, they'd been instructed, only cardboard boxes that could be thrown out of the window once they were empty.

One overweight woman made a compartment uncomfortable; two made it unbearable

There were two in Agnes and Lettie's compartment. Coloratura sopranos who would thrust out their bosoms under the shiny yellow and white satin to send the music up into the dusty wide blue sky above Monument Hill

'Such a strong voice,' murmured a fellow chorister. 'When she sings *Rest in peace, noble heroes* it's so thrilling you feel as if a mouse is running up and down your spine.'

'And the other one?'

'Just as good. Cecilia Wessels is going to meet her match.'

'Is Cecilia coming?'
'Possibly.'
'She isn't.'
'I heard ...'

The afternoon crept on. Some women, bored with sitting, stood out in the corridor; swayed their way off to the water bottles; waited for the latrines to be vacated.

Now that she was actually on the train, Agnes felt tired. She sat in a corner, her head against the window and tried to doze.

The day began to fade. The plains of the Karoo so endlessly wide; the ridges on the horizon etched against the fading light. Telephone poles raced by, throwing shadows that rippled over shrubs and thorn trees. Then suddenly everything was grey.

At the stations where they stopped, there were crowds of people to see friends off, some in long old-fashioned dresses and wearing their bonnets, even though dusk had fallen. The boarding passengers brought the festival clothes in their cases. Was everyone saving her dress up for something special? wondered Agnes. Was there a secret behind each of these excited faces?

Because she had a secret herself, she knew about the primeval currents under the surface of people's lives.

She observed the faces around her. It seemed to her that this was the first time she'd ever looked at people properly. That she had broken bonds of self; that cold self that had made her feel so poor and restricted her whole life. Was she going to break out of the shell that enclosed her, freed by her secret love, her wicked secret love, which the rain raced towards through the darkness?

One of the crowd, one with the crowd ... not lonely anymore, finally one of the crowd?

Doors slammed shut, the guard hung off the train, his arm stretched out to wave the green flag, the carriages started to move, slowly and smoothly at first, then began the rumbling, the jerking – a steady sway to one side and then the other. Her body swayed in unison.

The people on the stations waved to the departing train. The passengers who'd just boarded started shoving their suitcases and bedding rolls down the passages into the constricted spaces of the compartments.

When it was almost dark and she could see her face reflected in the window above the washbasin, when the outside world had faded away and the dim compartment lights suddenly came on of their own accord, one of the plump women began to get the food boxes down from the rack. Agnes stood up.

'I'll go out for a while. There'll be more space.'

She stood on the open platform where the carriages were coupled together. She listened to the rush of wind over the train, to the rubbing of the two metal plates in the coupling, over each other, back, over each other, back. The last time she'd slept on a train was on the way to Worcester and her first post. Eighteen years ago. How long ago it seemed now! How young she'd been! A young couple came and stood on the open platform of the opposite carriage. They leaned against each other; the woman rested her head against the man's shoulder, trying to smooth her windblown hair with one hand.

Are they in love? Agnes wondered. She didn't want to invade their privacy, she felt responsible for their love. She hurried back to her compartment. It was jolly in there. The table had been folded down and the food boxes unpacked. The one woman had brought a bottle of wine, which she gripped between her knees while she tried to uncork it. Pop! 'There she goes!' Amid the swaying of the train the mugs came out and the wine was poured – two fingers each. After they'd eaten they stood in the passage while each woman had a turn to change into her nightclothes and unroll her bedding in the compartment. The passageways were full. Men and women packed in together.

Before long someone started to sing and they all joined in, singing every song they knew. *Down by the old mill stream, Bolandse nooientjie, Ask not, my love, Beautiful dreamer* and others full of sentiment and nostalgia. They avoided the songs they were to sing at Monument Hill. There was something earnest, even melancholy and very tender about the songs they sang on this train as it raced through the darkness. She felt that they were fellow travellers on a sacred quest.

Agnes slept on a middle bunk. As she'd done as a girl, at night on the school train from Middelburg to Pretoria, she lay on her stomach with her chin propped on her folded arms gazing out at the expanse of the world. Later, when the moon came up, one of the others said, 'Oh, please let that blind down now, we can't sleep.' She did so without protest.

They steamed into Pretoria station at two the following afternoon. Buses were waiting and they joined the queue. The cases and bedding were fastened to the roof rack. A bus company had laid on the transport, young men had volunteered to act as drivers and conductors. The year was at an end, and schools and colleges had closed for the holidays.

The station platforms were crowded; one train after another steamed in, bringing its load of people. Flags fluttered along the streets, children in long dresses played on the pavements. They shouldn't, thought Agnes, they ought to wait – what for, she couldn't say. She didn't recognise the city, they turned due west. Out of the city.

When the bus pulled up on the slope of a hill and they clambered out, row upon row of tents met their eyes. A white swathe of tents spreading up the ridge. Here and there an open space where huge four-sided bell tents had been pitched.

Their luggage was off-loaded into a big heap. The women stood round, at a loss. The sun baked down, a swirling wind whipped up red dust and deposited it on them.

'My lips already feel dried out,' said Lettie Scholtz. 'I'm going to burn to a frazzle here. We don't get this kind of sun at home.'

'Get moving, everyone must carry her own luggage,' said an organiser dressed in Voortrekker uniform. 'I'll show you your tents.'

'How many…?' asked one woman.

'We're expecting more than 100 000.'

Eight women per tent, small bedsteads with thin mattresses. Thank the Lord for your own bedding. The ablution blocks were a bit further on, and women queued at the latrines.

Lettie looked at Agnes and shrugged. 'It just goes to show,' she said. What it showed, she didn't explain.

'At least we've got a bed,' said Agnes. She thought of the pretty frocks in her suitcase. Where on earth could one iron? And the bonnets? A few nails had been knocked into the tent pole. She'd brought two hangers. 'Quickly,' she said to Lettie, 'While the others are queuing, let's hang up our dresses.' She shook them out. She had packed carefully, with tissue paper; the creases weren't too bad. Lettie's looked worse.

Lettie untied her long dark hair. 'I'll die if I can't wash my hair.' She bent over forwards and shook a cloud of dust from her hair.

Agnes's hair was short, and she could easily wash it under the shower. Oh dear, she looked after it so carefully at home; seven rinses, with lemon into the last rinse; it shone like gold. Now it was dull and limp.

The large woman came back from the latrines. 'Primitive,' she said. 'But I suppose they couldn't do any better. Have you looked outside? What a sight! There are thousands, millions of tents, up and down the hills. Where is everyone going to get food? God help us if it rains.' She made a few coughing noises as if there was something stuck in her throat. 'Maybe it would be better if it did rain. How I'm expected to sing with all this dust in my throat, I just don't know.'

It rained during the night. Agnes woke up. She heard men's voices outside; they'd come to dig trenches around the tents and to secure the guy ropes. There'd been very few men in the provision tent that evening, the choirs consisted predominantly of women. But the word had gone round: 3 000 men on horseback were expected. Six hundred of them were from the Cape. Their camp was against the next hill.

Agnes wondered if it was the Cape riders who had come in the rain to dig the trenches. She wondered if he'd remember his words: *See you in Pretoria, green-eyes.* In the darkness she could feel her heart pounding. But she liked the soft talk of the rain on the canvas, and the quiet wump-wump of the spades digging into mud – now and then an 'Over here' or 'It's flooding this side' – made her feel safe and cared for. She drifted back to sleep.

With the cruel old question raising its ugly head again in spite of everything: Would he come with the horsemen from Kenya?

A blaring loudspeaker woke her. The sounds were repeated through dozens of loudspeakers up and down all the hills; the echoes and re-echoes gave every word a weird after-echo so the eight women in the tent looked at each other questioningly: Did you understand that? Eventually they'd grow accustomed to the sound of the voices over the loudspeakers, recognising immediately: 'Come to the provision tents for breakfast', or 'Massed choirs must prepare for the procession', or 'Voortrekker Commandos fall in', or 'Will the parents of so-and-so please fetch your child from the first aid tent on the choir hill?'

Children, thousands of them, all dressed in period clothing, bloomed like flower carpets against the slopes.

The women's choirs practised together that morning in the large festival tent. The canvas roof deadened the sound; outside in the open it would fade away under the wide pale blue sky, only soprano voices soaring upwards. After the practice the women walked in a line four abreast to the festival area. They battled to keep their long white dresses out of the mud puddles, bunching up their skirts, picking their way through the mud in their black shoes as splashes soiled their white stockings. What kind of rain did they get here? This was a marsh they had to cross! But after the rain it was blessedly cool. There were still white clouds in the sky and everything was washed clean. The tents looked like white toadstools as far as the eye could see, up hill and down dale. Right in the centre, on a slight rise, silhouetted against the sky, the wooden structure where the foundation stone would be laid on the day of the Covenant.

The loudspeaker announced: 'The wagons have come into sight.' The man's voice was hoarse with excitement: 'Here they come, round the corner! Cheer them, people! Cheer them on!' Car hooters sounded and were silenced. People in their thousands lined the dirt road along which the wagons would approach, and Agnes pressed forward with the other singers to get a view. The man leading the front oxen took off his hat and waved it so the plume dipped and fluttered like a swallow. The people yelled and church bells could be heard ringing in the distance.

Agnes didn't see all the wagons, nor did she count them. For beside her, Lettie had said, 'Look there at the back, behind the wagons, there come the mounted commandos!'

She pushed forward to stand just behind a line of Voortrekker scouts who'd linked hands to keep the people back. Her breath raced and her heart beat wildly. She had a right to stand here in front. Which of these people had grown up like her – on horseback in front of her father, with the dust and the smell of cow dung and sweat dripping from under her bonnet down her temples?

She saw the magnificent horses' flanks ripple, brown and bay, grey and black, the graceful trotting legs, the snorting and neighing, the flexing of arm muscles as a rider reined his horse in, the neck muscles tense as the horse's head jerked back; the corduroy breeches, sun-baked brown hands, red sunburnt faces all but concealed under beards and sideburns. Her breath came faster. Hundreds and hundreds of them passed her until one noticed her, put his hand up to the band of his broad-brimmed hat, upturned at one side, and took a carnation out of it. 'This is for you, sweetheart,' he called as he threw it to her. She caught it and pressed it to her breast. With her other hand she waved; he waved back and moved along past her.

Hundreds more riders followed. Even Lettie got a flower, but an ugly, half-dead hibiscus. 'Your fellow is nicer,' she said.

Agnes knew it was the same man to whom she'd given the pancake. She kept the carnation as she pushed her way back to their tent to collect their plates and cups and then made her way to the provision tent before they prepared themselves for the festival tent and the singing. They filed in and stood in rows. She sang mechanically, her hands, folded in front of her waist, still holding the carnation. But the riders didn't come to listen to the choirs. They had to see to their horses; they were camped on another hill, said the women.

She hardly slept that night. She felt cheated. All the planning, scheming even; and now there were so many people she'd never get to him.

The flower didn't seem so special any more either; some of the other women had also been given carnations. She was weary, so weary. If only her father had come down from the north for the celebration – why couldn't he have come? He must have been able to, it had been said that riders from Kenya would come. It churned round and round in her mind until she eventually fell asleep.

10

Robert was waiting on the platform when Leonora's train pulled into Frankfurt.

'You look German,' she teased as he picked up her suitcase. 'A wintery German with your khaki jacket and woollen hat over your blonde fringe! I almost didn't recognise you!'

He didn't laugh but pushed her roughly forward through the mass of people, his hand on her elbow. 'Don't you hear me? I say you look like an Aryan, Aryan, Aryan!'

'Be quiet, won't you?'

'Why, it's highly fashionable to be Aryan.'

'I'll explain when we get home.'

He pushed her trunk into the back of the tram and paid for their tickets. He'd booked her a room in his pension, on the floor just above his own. The air in the tram was muggy with the breath of passengers, and she didn't see much of the city. They had to get out at one point to wait for a connection. She kept close to him, her breath a plume from her mouth. The plumes protruded like plasma wraiths from the mouths of people who waited with them.

'Colder than London?'

'Oh yes, much colder.'

She felt the cold right into her bones. She felt it in the aloofness of the people, the air of mistrust; in the bearing of a couple who stood to one side, away from the others.

She had a good look at these two.

'It's the infamous yellow star ... I thought it was a fabrication, propaganda against the Germans, and now I'm seeing it with my own eyes.'

On the man's left sleeve – prominent even in the gloom – the yellow Star of David. The girl was pressed up against him and Leonora couldn't see her sleeve.

'Aren't they ashamed of themselves, Robbie?'

He looked around. 'Who should be ashamed of themselves?'
'The Nazis.'

The tram arrived and the rattle of wheels and the buzz of the electric cable dulled the full impact of the word Nazis, which made the people nearest turn their heads to her momentarily. In disbelief? In hate?

'All right, Robbie. I understand: I must keep my mouth shut.'

They rolled on without speaking. At the stop nearest his pension they climbed off. The cold slammed against them.

'The cold is clean, Robbie, it purifies one.'

She tried to ignore the red flag with a black swastika hanging from a window in the building next to the pension. Robert had his own outside key, and they walked up the stairs. On the second floor he pressed the bell and the landlady opened up. She gave him the key to Leonora's room. Also a latchkey for the door on the next landing. The pension took in two floors.

'Your brother will get you settled. A competent, pleasant young man.'

But even with the complimentary words she didn't smile.

'What's going on here?' asked Leonora upstairs as they put her suitcase down in her room. 'Did you hear someone crying in her sitting room?'

'Unfortunate coincidence that it should happen immediately before your visit.'

'What happened?'

Robert removed his jacket, pulled off his hat and scarf and threw them onto her bed. She did the same. His blonde hair was tousled, and the upright cockscomb invited her to run her hands through it as she'd done when he was a little boy. She controlled the urge. Robert had lost weight and this emphasised the fine bone structure of his face. With his blonde hair, fair skin pink with cold and the graceful co-ordination of his body she thought involuntarily: Siegfried. That gave her a fright. Why Siegfried? Later she noted a new fastidiousness in his manner, how he straightened the books and papers on his desk. *Politische Wissenschaft* she read on the spine of a file. The way he split a match, and then inspected his hands – white and flaking from wearing gloves – digging at the clean deadness under his nails with the sharp point of the matchstick. And kept digging. Until he drew blood.

'Should I have come? Are you pleased to see me?'

'Of course, Norie. But people are tense, war is imminent. You have to be careful what you say. There are ears everywhere. My study permit could even be withdrawn. I'd be very sorry about that. Only one more semester in the new year.'

'My clever Robbie. Then you can come and teach us.'

'Sarcasm doesn't become you, Norie.'

'Come and show me your room. I suppose we're going to eat here in the *pension*: I'm hungry.'

They went downstairs past the sitting room again. The crying had stopped but they could hear voices raised in argument, accusing words flying back and forth. Leonora bit her tongue.

There was a letter on Robert's desk. It had just arrived. He tore open the envelope and took out the contents. Newspaper clippings fluttered to the floor.

'SussieBelle?' asked Leonora who'd recognised the handwriting and the cuttings. Robert nodded.

'The child is completely overwrought. I get weekly bulletins on the mass hysteria that's gripped the country. Can you imagine it? Even our cool, introverted sister-in-law Agnes has gone to Pretoria in a long dress to sing.'

She bent to pick up a cutting and read out:

The Afrikaner will never be the same after 1938 as he was before 1938. This was not the work of princes or kings, but of two humble, mute wagons. They couldn't speak but they aroused unprecedented emotions.

'You'd never believe it, but that was written after the wagons had passed through cosmopolitan Johannesburg. Did you hear about the flaming torch SussieBelle carried so dramatically through the night? The impresario who staged the whole show should be congratulated.'

Robert read SussieBelle's letter and laid it aside. He took hold of Leonora's upper arms and squeezed them gently. She lent forward until her head was on his chest. Now he seemed to be the older one, comforting his distressed sister.

'Why are you so cynical now, Norie? What's bothering you? Why do you begrudge SussieBelle her fervour? Didn't Father always say: The tepid is spat out, you have to be ardent, even an obsessed …'

'Obsession, but what for? Father said for God, but all that carrying on isn't for God. Anymore than the things going on here in Germany are for God. I'm afraid, Robbie.'

She moved away from her brother. 'You aren't really condoning the incitement of children, are you? Let me tell you about a cutting she sent to me: A front ox in the span pulling one of the wagons went out of control. The child who was leading them dropped the rope and ran away. A black man ran forward and managed to get hold of the leading rope, at considerable risk, what with the oxen hooves and horns, but he managed to get the span under control again. Then a woman in a long chintz dress and bonnet leaped out of the dumbstruck crowd and snatched the rope out of the black hand, snarling at him: 'How dare you?' And what was the newspaper headline? *The Voortrekker spirit reborn*. And my darling SussieBelle had added an exclamation mark in black ink.'

'I didn't think there was anything overwrought or hysterical in her letter,' said Robert. 'In a sense it moved me. I don't begrudge my people that. Just as I grant the poor downtrodden Germans their wonderful movement. They can hold their heads up high again. Our people must also be able to hold their heads up again after the annihilation of the Boer War.'

'Let's change the subject, Robbie. I came to visit you, not to argue with you. Oh, do you hear that? There's that crying again. It sounds closer, in the room next door.'

'She's leaving tomorrow, then it'll stop.'

'So you know …'

'We all know. You may as well know too. She's the ex-fiancée of the landlady's son. They discovered her grandmother was Jewish. In time, fortunately. The son is a member of the SS. You can imagine what …'

'Who discovered it?'

'How should I know? Maybe a tip-off from a girl who wanted to pinch the fellow from her. Don't be so naïve, Norie, I'm only joking.'

11

Now that their part of the programme had been sung, tension eased in the choir tents. Some of the women lay resting on their beds in their dressing gowns, their dresses hanging bundled from the tent pole.

A woman's voice said: 'May I come in?' She had a list with her.

'I'm looking for volunteers for the guard of honour. Voortrekker-descendants from either the grandmother or the grandfather's side, it doesn't matter which. It's for the ox wagon that will carry the old women who are to lay the Monument's cornerstone tomorrow. She looked round the tent. 'Are there any Transvaal- or Free State-born among you who aren't on the list yet?'

Lettie pointed at Agnes. 'She comes from the Transvaal.'

Agnes sat up. 'My surname was Greylinck,' she said. 'My grandfather was actually German.'

'Your grandmother? Come on, why are you so reticent?'

'Prinsloo,' said Agnes.

'And her mother?'

'I think she was also Prinsloo: she married a cousin.'

'Cape people?'

'I don't think so.'

'Right then, on the list you go.'

When the woman moved on, Agnes got dressed. First the white dress, but then she pulled it off over her head again. She put on the green dress for the first time. The taffeta fell heavy and luxurious from the close-fitting waistline. It was so pleasant to have something fresh to put on. She pulled on clean stockings. She'd already cleaned her shoes.

'What's up with you?' asked Lettie.

'It's too stuffy in here, I'm going for a walk.'

'If you wait a minute, I'll come with you.'

But she'd already left the tent. She walked briskly. The bonnet was tied firmly under her chin; she felt mysterious under the deep brim. It also kept the sun off her face. She wasn't going to join the guard of honour. She made up her mind as she walked along on her own. Under the bonnet brim she was invisible to everyone, as she'd been all her life. An absolute nobody, in spite of the line she'd spun herself.

She walked past rows and rows of tents and heard someone call out to her. It was an old man on a campstool. 'Girlie,' he said, his voice filled with wonderment, 'look around you.' She followed his gesture to the far-flung hills with the white tents. 'Like the hosts of God,' he said. 'They're our people and they speak our language.'

She nodded to him and walked on past festival tents, Red Cross tents, ablution blocks. She needed to walk and walk; she paid no attention to the indistinct announcements over the loudspeakers. Large groups of people were moving in front of her, it was as though the whole hillside had come to life. But it didn't concern her. A children's choir was singing, but the sound was faint and reedy in the open air, and the microphone was too close to the piano. Still she walked on, and where the tents were packed together most closely, she heard the neighing of horses. She sat down on the ground.

She would not be part of the guard of honour. They couldn't compel her. She would not act under false pretences. She sat with her head down as though she was playing with blades of grass. The tears streamed down her cheeks. It was the sound of the horses, the smell of warm dung in the stables, all the familiar sounds that filled her with longing. With her father she'd known who she was. Her nose started to run and she wiped it on the back of her hand. But she wasn't his daughter. So he'd sent her away. She must have been sitting close to the mounted commandos' camp. She didn't care. He'd never find her, even if he wanted to. And even if he found her, would he – would anyone – ever be able to tell her who she really was? Here under the blue Transvaal sky which felt more like Africa to her than the Boland did, the desolation came welling up again.

Yet she was comforted by the bustle of people and horses, the saddling up, the shouts, the stamp of hooves. When she looked up, she saw movement in the horse camp and the first riders already leaving from the opposite end. Far below she made out the commando, four abreast, riding by. Because they were so far away and couldn't recognise her under the brim of her bonnet anyway, she waved, and a couple of riders returned the wave. That too, comforted her.

That evening she walked with her choir group to the hill to see the flaming torches come in. What a pity: SussieBelle had also carried the flame; she should be here. She'd been so busy with her green taffeta gown, she'd never given her a thought.

From their ridge, earlier in the evening, they'd already watched the endless lines of young Voortrekkers mustering on the slope beyond the braaivleis area in their dull green uniforms and hats turned up at the side. For every 30 or 40 of them there were a couple of leaders who carried the flags of the Commando and the Voortrekker movement – the flagpole thrust into a leather holder slung from a waist belt. Boy and girl. They looked so handsome; they walked so upright.

'The youngsters must have been fed earlier otherwise they wouldn't manage. It's going to be a long session tonight.'

'There must be 3 000 of them, how that host …' Lettie could be so prosaic. Would the children even think about food?

The darkness gathered, the last of the Highveld light – pink-tinged gold and then silver slowly fading into grey – drained away behind the hills and ridges. For a few moments the skyline was so sharply defined it looked as though the earth had been etched onto the sky. The light faded behind the hills so fast the children had to bend and grope around on the ground for the small torches they'd been issued with.

The buzz of conversation died down with the coming of darkness.

From the nearer hills, the women noticed older men moving among the children, slowly opening a path amongst them. The children made way – were they children? The young arms were strong; the bodies were the bodies of men and women. There was no jostling or crowding together; those who'd put down their flags to rest raised them again, slipping poles into belt-holders.

The hooters sounded from far away; silenced again. Even the huge waiting crowd made way and, in the gap below, two tiny moving flames appeared. The two runners on the final relay!

Even Lettie was silent.

'It's the torches,' said a woman quietly. Someone began to sing softly: *Praise the Lord, ye heavens adore Him* … Some joined in, others were so bemused, they forgot to sing.

As though someone had poured out a line of paraffin and lit it, the young Voortrekkers' small torches flared up as the passing runners lit them. The two flames were consumed by the rows and rows of flames that closed in behind them.

'God, the children have caught fire!' cried a woman and then fell silent again.

The line of fire spilled over the ridge. No one sang now. It was as though all other lights in the camp had been put out; there was only the line of children with the torches. The hordes of onlookers followed them; the slopes moved like lava.

The flames had reached the festival area and the light of a bonfire leapt up to heaven. Now people cheered and the hooters sounded again. Rockets were set off; stars and fire rained from the sky. Bonfires were lit on the surrounding hills, there was fire everywhere. Lord, could they control the fires? Agnes, too, was anxious now. All those children, the burning torches! Then she remembered they were to throw their torches onto the great bonfire. Half-bewildered, she looked about her. There was fire everywhere; the heat even reached her here. She felt it on her face; her cheeks were burning; there was a horse coming up behind her. She'd fallen behind, she realised, and she was on the fringes of the crowd. Then the horse was beside her, the rider bent low, his arm around her waist. 'Come, quickly,' came his voice. 'Come, I'll swing you up.' She knew what to do; she'd always ridden in front of her pa like this – foot in the strap above the stirrup, and then swing the body upwards. With a swift movement she was in the saddle against the rider who held her close with one hand while he tugged the reins with the other. The horse stumbled on the ridge as the rider pulled his head round, and then he regained his gait on the track leading off into the veld. The hand holding her moved up over her breast, then left her armpit to cup her chin and turn her head so he could see her face in the fire glow.

'Now it's just you and me, green-eyes,' he said.

From where she lay on the ground, moving her head slowly from side to side, she could see the red glow against the sky through the branches of the thorn tree. Still the fires. She thought of the campfires with her pa, the shadowy apparitions that the flames had conjured up on those dark nights in Africa, the sounds of feeding animals – like the horse, hobbled now, grazing near them.

The neat little loops round the buttons on the green dress had been opened, some torn off; some of the small buttons had been torn off too. She had helped with the tearing. Thrown aside, the beautiful green dress. Her bare arms, her back lay pressed against the grass, the twigs, the pebbles. They were her grasses and twigs and pebbles; she lay on her earth. The rider was heavy on her; his weight pressed her deeper into the ground. His lips were on her breast. This was how it would be when she died, she thought, pressed against the earth and covered by the earth. It was right, she felt at home here.

Her hands left the ground and she took hold of his head, pressing it deeper into her. His sucking on her nipple sent tremors right through her body; when it became too sensitive, she moved his head to her other breast. He had raised himself up to pull off his shirt. Her fingers pressed against his back, pushing the skin up in ridges; kneaded the flesh, clutching feverishly. As intense as he was with her breasts, she explored his back, his neck, and the back of his head. There was no hurry. There was a whole lifetime to make up for. When his mouth eventually moved to her navel, his tongue exploring it like a shell while his hand caressed the triangle of hair, the journey was still long, still long. His hand was thrust in under her buttocks and his lips stroked the inner sides of her thighs. She was a veld creature; she was the receiving earth; she was humus and decaying leaves, soft wet leaves, the soft wet bloody skin of a small antelope waiting to be butchered, lying there, stripped. She pressed her hands against his buttocks, his lips were now blind on hers and she felt him thrusting into her. God! she thought. Dear Lord! His body jerked. Then she felt the sweetness flow into her. He rubbed his forehead against her cheek, his skin warm and sweaty; he nuzzled as a veld creature does against his mate.

Green-eyes, he said quietly, you are mine.

But you sent me away, she said.

She'd tried to wash the mud from her white dress so she could wear it on the last day. It had dried overnight and was wearable, even though it was stained. No one was completely clean any more. She walked in the procession with the guard of honour; it would have taken too much trouble, too many explanations to get out of it. What did it matter, anyway? The laying of the cornerstone by four old women in black dresses and bonnets took place too high up for her to see from where she stood. Her head ached from the loudspeakers' bellowing.

From a distance that afternoon she saw the burger commando and horsemen set off for the old Pretoria church square to lay wreaths on the memorials to Pretorius and Potgieter. The crowd was starting to break up. Emotionally exhausted.

Their choir was only to catch a train on Saturday night, so they were free to spend the morning as they chose. Mindful of the money Father had pressed into her hand, she felt she owed it to him to call on the attorney, even though her enthusiasm for the visit had waned. She lingered as long as possible in the deserted tent, but she had to leave once the Voortrekker scouts arrived to remove the mattresses.

She got a lift on a bus to the city centre where she struck it lucky: the firm of attorneys was still in the building she knew. But the friendly old man who'd taken her side when the will was read, had retired. She was received by the young man who was now the senior partner.

Yes, they still kept a file on the Greylinck estate. There hadn't been any new developments in the 20 years since she had left.

The partner remembered the pale young girl who'd had to listen to the contents of a letter his father had received from the woman in France. He remembered his sympathy stirring. He asked kindly, 'Is there something I can assist you with? There must be something, otherwise you wouldn't have come.'

'You haven't heard from the woman in France again?'

Agnes was more distressed than she'd expected to be. The circumstances ... the lawyer brought it all up again so vividly in her mind. She was very pale; the attorney sent for tea.

'She was responsible for my adoption,' she said eventually in a tremulous, scarcely audible voice. 'I wanted to know whether she could supply any more information.'

The attorney poured the tea himself. Then he leafed slowly through the file. 'Just this declaration – I believe you have a copy of it. Nothing more. Not a single page or sentence, as you can see.'

'And the husband in East Africa?' Agnes spoke the words with considerable difficulty.

'As far as I know, he is still living where he was. You no doubt know that the eldest brother, Piet, and his wife have both passed away. We could get the address of the younger brother, Jan, for you without any difficulty.'

'Just leave it at that, thank you,' said Agnes. 'I knew there was only a slim chance ...'

'But one must always try, not so?'

'Yes, one must try.'

She had finished her tea; she wanted to leave. Yet she hesitated. Finally, she said, 'Do you think it's advisable for me to leave you my current address? In case the husband from East Africa ever wants to get in touch with me?'

'Please do so. We would be glad to be of assistance.'

Slowly, she wrote down her new surname and her Wellington address. He took the page from her and placed it in the file, which he then closed.

'I hope you have a pleasant return journey.'

12

To her surprise, Stuart, SussieBelle, Ozzie as well as Arnold – one of Frikkie's twins – met the train.

'We all wanted to come and fetch you, Mamma, but Pappa said there wasn't room in the car.'

SussieBelle pressed up against her mother – she was in one of her friendly moods, Agnes decided. She pecked her and Ozzie who turned his head away when he felt the little kiss. In the few days she'd been away, Ozzie seemed to her to have grown taller and thinner, his Adam's apple unnaturally large. She pecked Stuart on the cheek, greeted Arnold and looked questioningly at her husband.

'Frikkie and his family are staying with us. Father isn't well. They called the doctor.'

'He's better, Mamma, the doctor just panicked.'

'When did it happen?' She walked on ahead with Stuart; the two boys carried her luggage – the one the bedding, the other the suitcase.

'Wednesday night. His heart. Six weeks' bed rest. Oh well, he's had a good life.'

'Don't talk like that, he isn't dead yet. Oh, I should never have gone away.'

The self-reproach in her tone irritated him. 'Even the efficient Agnes couldn't have prevented a heart attack.'

She didn't take the bait. 'I could have helped.'

She had dreaded coming home. But the activity and upheaval were a distraction – Arnold shared his room with Ozzie, his twin sister, Miemie, shared with SussieBelle, and Frikkie and Kowie occupied the spare room.

The room was strewn with the children's possessions. The men's newspapers and pipes lay about the sitting room, and glasses were left where she'd never have permitted them to be. Kowie, who'd put on a lot of weight since the twins' birth, was clumsy in the unfamiliar kitchen. She stood smoking and gazing helplessly at the accumulated debris of Sunday dinner – all greasy crockery and leftovers.

'Oh, hello. I suppose you ate on the train? Doesn't look so hot round here. I'm not the best of housewives.'

Agnes removed the delicate seashell Kowie was tapping her ash into and gave her an ashtray.

'Sorry. I never think further than my nose.'

Frikkie's car had started giving trouble on the pass – luckily on the Wellington side. They had to wait for spare parts before going home. It was school holidays and Frikkie was his own boss, so they stayed on for a few extra days. Kowie and the children enjoyed the visit, and Agnes was glad of all the activity because there wasn't time for questions.

In addition to that, a letter had arrived for her during her absence and its contents occupied her mind as she cooked and cleaned.

During the day, while Stuart was at work, Frikkie walked along with her to visit Father. To her, Father seemed shrunken and fragile, his head flat on the single pillow, his hair fine and silvery, brushed smooth by the nurse. His colour was good, even under the thin hair his scalp was pink with a brown age spot here and there.

But she could see the exhaustion in his eyes. He held her hand tightly. 'Was it as wonderful as you dreamed?' She nodded; he spoke quietly and slowly. 'SussieBelle read to me from the newspaper. Just keep your sense of proportion.'

She could hardly hear the last words. 'What was that, Father?'

He gave a faint smile. 'She got so excited and I told her: Never lose your sense of proportion, Sussie.'

Her answer was sharper than she'd intended. 'Don't worry, Father. I'll never go to extremes.'

On the way home, she told Frikkie, 'Father has known me for such a long time and he still gets me wrong. He hasn't the faintest idea of what's going on inside me.'

'Do you know yourself what's going on inside you?'

Frikkie wasn't looking at her. His eyes were always searching about for a shape or an unusual angle; he remained the observer. His detachment made it easy for her to talk to him. And she had to talk.

'Gradually, I'm getting an inkling.' She took a letter out of her pocket. 'There, read that. Or I'll tell you what it says. I know it off by heart. A letter from the Pretoria birth registration office. In answer to my pathetic enquiry about who I am, what I am.'

Even the pain in her voice didn't make him look directly at her. He picked up a twig, twisted it in his fingers and then threw it down again.

'And?' he said.

She swallowed and then continued as calmly as she could manage. 'They were able to track down a few incidences of births out of wedlock. Goodness only knows how they get the addresses after all these years. They wrote to the parent or parents to say I was trying to discover my origins. Only one woman answered. How did she put it again?' With mock solemnity Agnes answered: 'The woman must in God's name not try to contact me, I forbid the office to give her my address. If she wants to rake over my past mistake, she will destroy my present life, my husband's career, the happiness of my family.' Her husband's career and the happiness of her family? And what about me? My happiness? You ask if I know what's going on inside me. I am finally obliged to have an inkling. I'm finished with doubting. Now I know where I stand. On my own. Alone.'

Frikkie picked a leaf from one of the shrubs and smoothed it against his hand, studying the network of fine veins, the transparency of the plant tissue. 'I didn't realise the old problem was still bothering you. It doesn't bother anyone else, I can assure you.'

Her voice was even sharper than when she'd snapped at Father. 'From now on it will cease to bother me, too. It's actually a liberation.'

She slipped her handbag strap up to her elbow so both hands were free to tear up the letter. Frikkie stopped her.

'Does Stuart know about this?'

'He must have seen the letter, it was delivered while I was away.'

'Does he know the contents?'

She shook her head.

'A word of advice, my dear sister, and you know I'm not in the habit of giving advice. Tell Stuart, show him the letter. In God's name, don't keep this from him.' He took the letter from her, folded it, replaced it in the envelope and put it back in her bag. 'Go on, do it now. And don't blame Father for misunderstanding you. He does his best. Since Mother died, he has tried to be father and mother.'

Kowie was out so she made tea for herself and Frikkie. They didn't say any more about the letter. They talked about Leonora who was due back from overseas in a few months. About Robert who'd be back in the middle of '39. About Hendrik and Philip who'd been told it wasn't necessary to take leave now that Father was on the mend. But that they should maybe plan to come to the Boland later.

It seemed to her that Frikkie was making a good living. Kowie and the twins were well dressed. He was generous with money – the children were forever running down to the shops for a treat. He treated her two as well.

The twins were a year younger than Ozzie.

When she asked him about his photography, he answered laconically: 'I live off people's vanity. Sometimes it beats me why every soul on earth wants a likeness of himself and of the extensions of himself, his children. But that's my bread and butter. And Kowie's jam.'

She turned to watch him as he spoke. But there was no bitterness in his voice.

'But sometimes I can get down to doing what I really want: serious photography. I like wet weather, the woods after rain, tree-trunks and autumn light – the light of May. Then I find what I'm looking for, but it doesn't bring in any money. Yet I like it. I want to have an exhibition: "The Light of May".'

'You're very well known. People drive over the mountain from here to be photographed by you.'

'That's fine.'

'Kowie isn't well, she says.'

'She doesn't want to have any more children. That's also fine. It's her right.'

His laconic manner irritated her. Yet there was something in him that was at peace; she sensed it. Kowie had lots of clothes, but he didn't: his trousers and jacket were shabby. But it's strange how nobody thinks badly of him, she thought. As though his perpetual snapshots made him someone special. As though people thought he could make them other than who they were. Was that why he had power over them, slovenly and aloof as he was? He wasn't really such a genius, after all.

Frikkie and Stuart didn't have much to talk about of an evening. Stuart visited his father and then he and Frikkie, and usually Kowie, had a drink. Then the visit went more smoothly than Agnes could ever have believed possible. Their presence eased the awkwardness with Stuart which she had dreaded after her homecoming.

After they left, she and Stuart sank back into their old lifestyle.

When they returned from visiting Father one evening, she tried to tell him about the letter from Pretoria. He read it carefully. 'I don't think you should allow it to upset you so much,' he said. 'Try to look at it objectively. It all happened so long ago, I don't think either you or a presumed mother would get much pleasure out of a new relationship. Especially without absolute certainty.'

He pulled her closer so she sat on his knee. 'After all, you've got us. You've got me.'

She was touched by the wistfulness in his voice. She didn't pull away from his embrace; she raised a hand to stroke his thick hair. It touched her to note grey amongst the brown.

His attempt at reconciliation and understanding made her more generous-hearted than she had been recently. 'I can't help it upsetting me,' she said. 'Even if I try. I wonder continually: Where do I come from? Who am I really? Up at the Monument hill … I felt I belonged there and no one could take it away from me. Perhaps because everyone spoke our language. Up there, it didn't seem to matter so much who my parents were.' She began to cry because she knew it wasn't true. The business of the guard of honour had upset her.

But she no longer knew how she really felt. 'Everyone else can look back to someone or something, but I can't. You've no idea how alone it makes you feel.'

She felt his head press against her breast. She wiped away the tears and thought: I must put this out of my mind. He's right. I've got him. And the children. And Father and Aunt Issy. I am, after all, what I am, and what I have become here. She felt a tiny surge of pride that she, in spite of her uncertain background, had bound this man to her, borne his children and won the old people's love. Frikkie had been right to tell her to show Stuart the letter. She felt closer to Stuart; she experienced a sense of self-worth – and that was a novelty to her. Had the Monument Hill given her this?

She sat on his lap until he said, 'Ouch, my leg's gone to sleep, let's go to the bedroom.'

Once Father had done his six weeks in bed, it was no longer necessary to keep a nurse in the house and Agnes took over his care. She and Nellie. Until Leonora came.

Nellie promised the people of the parish: I won't let the old master down. She was mature now and she'd make a good wife for one of the district's widowers. Townsfolk speculated: perhaps this, perhaps that farmer. But not until I've seen the old master to his grave, she said.

Leonora returned on the *Winchester Castle*. At the end of March. Frikkie went to welcome her back. For good, she said. The family never really knew why she had returned to England for a second spell of teaching or what had happened to her there. She'd written long letters to Father, so perhaps he knew?

She was quieter. She'd just missed Philip and Hendrik a number of times overseas. Robbie was the only one she'd seen, but in Germany, not her home base. She didn't have much to say to the two older brothers.

Frikkie asked if she'd allow him to photograph her. 'If it'll make you happy, why not?' She sat on a cane chair with a book on her lap, looking out of the window. He didn't want to subject her to having the study exhibited but later it came to be known as one of his best works. And her opinion was: 'I don't look like that anymore. You photographers are con-men, dealers in mortality, or in death, call it what you will. Always seizing the moment that is over, that's past.'

She started teaching in Cape Town again, coming out to Father, Aunt Issy and Nellie at weekends. Father recovered, but his movements were limited by the hilly position of the town, the many inclines, the steep veranda step. He spent most of his time on the back or front veranda, depending on the weather. Or in the level back garden where he'd had a couple more roses planted. The first roses brought him great joy.

It was among the roses that Issy found him after his second heart attack nearly a year later. She wasn't strong enough to lift him. Nellie had gone to the shops and when Issy rushed down the steps to the garden, she tripped and sprained her ankle. She and Father lay beside each other until her faint cry attracted the attention of a delivery boy.

After this second heart attack, Leonora took leave and stayed with Father. One after another, the three younger brothers took leave from the various jobs they'd been offered after the foreign studies and came to Father's sickbed, which was obviously going to be his deathbed. Philip from Pretoria where he practised law – could you believe it? – married with a son of nearly eight; Hendrik the economist-businessman from Johannesburg; Robert, lecturer in political science at Potchefstroom.

Robert was Leonora's favourite brother, and she hadn't seen him since their little holiday in Germany. Shortly before he had to leave again, she said to him, 'I know it's right that you're going back to your job, Robbie. And I know it's right that we have to let Father go, but it's still so difficult for me. I could never accept Mother's and Vicky's death, and I can't accept Father's.' She smiled wistfully. 'I should be able to, I'm almost middle-aged now, and I've encountered death before. But now that Father has to go, I miss Mother so, and Vicky. You probably don't remember them at all. How could you? It's such a pity that you can't remember them.'

The three younger sons loved Nellie, Aunt Issy and Siena who was still the cook in the house. They brought gifts for all of them from overseas. How proudly Aunt Issy displayed her shawl, her jewellery box, her necklaces. And Nellie put away her tablecloth and her Madeira things – for maybe, one day – and Siena her jersey, her headscarf. The three brothers were very close: the three musketeers they'd called themselves as children. Strange how they drew the nourishment they needed to flourish from the lean, acerbic Issy and the barren Nellie. They were educated, purposeful young men, two with dark hair and moustaches, Robert blonde. With life insurance policies, and bursaries earned through their own efforts, each one could take his own direction and study as far as he wanted.

Young men to be proud of, thought Father, looking up at them from where he lay with his soft, silvery hair brushed back on the pillow. Mother would have been pleased with them. His beloved Emma had grown clearer in his memory, which made him smile as he lay alone. She would have been just as surprised to see them as I was, he thought. She'd be amazed that these were her babies.

Frikkie and Kowie and the twins came over while the three brothers were there. Frikkie brought his tripod and equipment.

'Once Father's gone, we'll probably lose touch. Let me take a last photo of all us children together.'

He took a picture of the five brothers and sister. Kowie had to press the button on the thin extension that came out from behind the black cloth. He took a picture of the extended family with Aunt Issy and Kowie and Agnes and the four grandchildren. This time he showed

Nellie how to press the button. He took a picture of the whole group including Nellie and Siena. He set the camera, pushed the delay button and quickly took up his position in the group.

Leonora started to cry. 'Father is lying alone in the house.' She hurried back to him. But that wasn't what brought the tears to her eyes. She'd remembered the photographs taken at the picnic long ago, the last picture of Vicky, the very last. And the first of Kowie – she couldn't help the spiteful thought: Just look at how things turned out for my clever, gifted brother …

She couldn't reconcile herself to Frikkie's photography, no matter how much money it brought in. And she couldn't accept Kowie. Even Agnes was preferable, with all her faults. Sometimes she still wondered about the other Agnes Valeria and what happened to her and her mother.

Because the war had broken out in Europe – the war that everyone expected, but hoped wouldn't materialise. It was the spring of 1939. In Europe it was autumn, and once the harvest was in, the Germans prepared themselves to invade the neighbouring countries.

'Father's illness brought you all back from Europe just in time,' said Stuart. They were all having dinner at his and Agnes's house. The commotion in the old people's house had became too much for Aunt Issy. He carved the leg of lamb and the overflowing platter was passed round. 'Each time I visit him, he asks me about the war, but I think he's confusing the wars. He keeps on dredging up German South West Africa. Then I say: It's the Germans again, Father, but they left Africa ages ago.'

He didn't mention Father's distress about Smuts joining the war as Britain's ally. He sometimes wondered if he really understood it. Still, the old man often said: I'm a Malan man, it's good that Hertzog and Malan are together again. One wondered how confused Father's thoughts really were, thought Stuart. Sometimes he was so lucid.

Leonora who sat next to her father's bed for hours, held his hand and stroked it, and spoke about Mother, and about Vicky, and comforted him, didn't tell them how his mind wandered; how he pleaded with her: Don't allow Stuart to go to South West Africa, he'll have to fire on his own people. Tell him his own people will point a rifle at him, and he at them.

'Let him be,' she said to Stuart now. 'Just console him. Even if you tell him it's another war, he'll have forgotten by tomorrow, and it distresses him that he forgets.'

Young and middle-aged men joined up at the depot in town. Despite his father's illness Stuart also went to join. Agnes only heard about it that evening when he came back, and poured himself a double brandy furiously.

'Those arseholes turned me down.'

She felt sorry for him and stroked his hair as he sat sipping his drink. 'You're not young anymore, Stuart, you have to accept it.'

Later, once he was calmer, he said: 'At least I have a son to send to war.'

Ozzie was turning 18. He wrote matric two months after the war was declared in September. In January he told his mother he was going to Stellenbosch to sign up for a course. He came back in uniform.

His father patted him on the back and poured him a little brandy. 'That's my son.'

Agnes saw how his cheeks and eyes were glowing. 'That's right, Pa.'

He looked thin and gawky in his khaki uniform and cap, quite different to the strong, robust figure his father cut in his German South West African war photographs. Ozzie left on a course: his grandfather thought he was studying but he returned with a red tab on his shoulder, showing he had volunteered to fight overseas alongside the British. Aunt Issy wanted to push him into the sickroom, but Leonora stopped her, full of the old acrimony. 'Don't you dare,' she hissed. 'You will not break his heart.' She used her youth and strength to physically obstruct the older, thinner woman. 'You've done enough damage in this house. It ends here.' She explained to Ozzie about his grandfather's confusion and she thought that he understood. The child was gentle and had changed into civvies when he came back to greet his grandfather.

Aunt Issy retreated before the fury in Leonora's eyes. 'What an ungrateful child,' she said out loud to the portrait of her sister in her room that evening. 'Really, Emma.'

Agnes didn't know where her place was with this illness. As Father deteriorated, it seemed as though he took comfort from Leonora. She read the Bible to him – making up for her long absence? Agnes thought meanly – and she spoke to him about the years when they were young, told anecdotes about the time when Mother was still with them. That gave him pleasure. They also spoke about the new life he was entering; his trust, his peace and his belief moved her.

Why can't I believe? thought Leonora. Father, she wanted to say, help me. The framed text hung over his bed: *The Lord is my Shepherd*. And beside it, as it had done in the old days, in the old house, Mother's text, decorated with mauve flowers, now bleached: *I will guide thee with mine Eye.* The two texts side by side brought tears to her eyes.

Agnes watched this from a distance and thought: I could only ever really mean anything to Aunt Issy. Nellie got into the habit of finishing her tasks and then joining Aunt Issy in a room that got a bit of sun. They crocheted or just sat companionably. Aunt Issy used a stick and walked with difficulty: her ankle hurt and she tried to avoid putting her weight onto it. Agnes took them tea and biscuits; helped to while away the afternoons. She also helped with the visitors. She wasn't really worried about Ozzie. The war was too far away. Even though he'd signed up to fight outside the borders of the country, it was all unreal still; he was still doing clerical work at the Castle.

Frikkie was staying with them again, this time without Kowie, and Agnes was glad when she was asked to accompany him to fetch Hennie.

'They say you've got a way with him,' said Leonora, 'and I don't want to leave Father for the whole afternoon. I'll get an upstairs room ready for him, so he'll be close to Father. He doesn't manage stairs very well. When he's upstairs, he's upstairs.'

She'd put Hennie in what had been dubbed the 'boys' room' by Aunt Issy when they first bought the house.

Every afternoon, when she heard the postman's bicycle, and the snap of the letterbox cover, she hurried down to check for any letters that may have come from overseas.

Oom Hennie! Oh, Oom Hennie!

What was the bond between Agnes and Hennie: a sadness, a blind love, a wound inflicted by Africa?

This is not my country – the dripping vines, the dark pine lanes, the wet black earth, and the claustrophobic, low-lying clouds. Despite her improved relationship with Stuart, these were Agnes's thoughts as she drove with Frikkie through the rain to the Strand. Frikkie, the photographer, who wanted to capture the light of May and the wet branches of the trees. Suddenly she wanted to erase the whole family she'd married into. You're nothing, you know nothing, you feel nothing, you're all just like the mould under your eternally dripping trees. Africa would reject you, shrug you off. You are, and that was the final word, you are colonial English. Father – Afrikaans? That was laughable. But it wasn't the language; it was their mannerisms, their attitudes.

She and Hennie were from this land. They knew how it felt to burrow out of despair into the dry red earth of Africa, to let their tears drip onto the red dust. Africa tempered you. She was just as scarred as he was; they recognised this in each other.

In his little bedroom she packed his few items of clothing. Also his best suit – so old already – which he would wear to the funeral. She packed the picture of Jessie that stood at his bedside.

He limped up to the door to see what she'd put in. He was a shrunken old man, his face obscure, because the scars crept across his face like spider webs, or fungus, or something that lived off despair. The eye that still had some vision was glassy, grown over by a cataract. His fingers on the stick were knotted, and opened and closed painfully. And his legs also moved painfully, slowly and ponderously.

What for, God, what for? How long must this question still mull through his head? For that one moment when he saw God – face to face in the eye of the mauling lion? God the savage lion, hosanna, hallelujah. How long had he been dragged through life, from moment to moment, day to day, year to year, wandering from room to room, always the pain, always the knowledge that there was a goal which he couldn't see and therefore couldn't attain?

What should I do, Lord? What should I have done, all these years? The lion savaged my brain together with my body. Could you hold it against me if I didn't know what to do? If my understanding of Your Grace – grace? – shrunk like a dried raisin, until the withered, dried-up skin couldn't speak of what the fruit was once before.

Lord, have mercy on my wasted life.

If You wanted to waste it, that I could accept. Was that to be my fulfilment? That I should drink the bitter water day after day? That I should drink You? Was that to be my joy?

Agnes took his arm.

'Sit down, Oom Hennie. Please check through what I've packed. Do you need anything else? We don't know how long Father will linger. You probably won't be back until after the funeral.'

He pointed his walking stick at a drawer in the bedside table. She took out a small stack of papers, a few yellowed pictures with worn edges. They went into the little suitcase with his Bible.

'Now the medicines, Oom Hennie.'

She packed them separately into something that looked like an old picnic basket. The bottles could stand upright in there. Some of the caps were screwed on skew and the contents were smeared around the necks of the bottles.

When I was young I never went on a picnic, thought Agnes. Will my final picnic basket also be packed for my deathbed? She had a premonition that Hennie wouldn't be coming back. She and Nellie – because that she also knew: Leonora will be off – would bury both Aunt Issy and Hennie. And it hit her like a revelation: I love them more than anyone in my whole life. My whole life of now. And they love me. I have no one but them. I have only these two old people.

She swallowed the tears as she collected the salves, most of which she'd brought him herself, the powders, the pills, the cough mixtures, the homeopathic remedies, and folded a newspaper into the basket before she packed it.

Frikkie was busy with his camera outside when she led Hennie slowly out. Clicking and clicking. Now Oom Hennie alone, stand away, Agnes; another one, come on; look to the side, Oom Hennie; hell, what a picture! Now together, Agnes, your arm round him. And you alone, Agnes, look into my eyes, I've never seen you like this ... Medusa, Judith – he was calling names she didn't know – even your hair is standing up like I've never seen it before, the tears streaming down your cheeks, perfect; another one; now the old man again; now that anger again ... The camera clicked, he wound the film on; clicked, he wound it on again. Got it! Good. Now where's that suitcase? Ah! A basket of medicines. We should have had that in the picture. Never mind: too late. No, I must take it: Old man with picnic basket. God's truth: old man with picnic basket. Give me the key, I'll lock up at the back, don't you worry, I'll secure everything and lock the front door.

He put the key in his pocket. The wind was ruffling his fringe and for a moment he almost looked young. Then he climbed in behind the steering wheel, looked around to see if Hennie and Agnes were comfortable on the back seat, nipped back to the house for a blanket which he tucked thoughtfully around Hennie. Finally he started the car and they could go. The camera and its accessories occupied the passenger seat beside him.

Agnes held Hennie's knotted hand tight under the blanket, trying to send some of her own warmth into the cold skin and bone and flesh. Under her breath, she wasn't even sure that he heard it, she said to Frikkie: 'You're a monster.'

The white blanket was smoothed over the bed in the sickroom. The body was hardly discernible – Father had never been a big or sturdy man. And he was most comfortable with only one flat pillow under his head.

His eyes were closed, his colour pale, the brown age spots visible under the thinning silver hair. His hands gave the impression of isolation, of a life that was complete; folded on his breast with the right hand over the left hand, as Leonora had placed them after straightening the bedding.

His eyes were closed most of the time, his mouth slightly open as he breathed. He isn't wrestling with death, thought Leonora. He's sliding softly into the darkness ... darkness or Light? He's already left us. As a leaf stem makes a small protective scale before it falls, so that the fall will be softer, easier, so his spirit was already enveloped by the delicate scale of departure.

How different from the death of Vicky: how she fought against death, how desperately she wanted to live, how she moaned and pleaded. How many times her eyes opened and looked wildly at us, as if she was saying: Help me, I'm floating away, I'm going further and further away; hold my hand, keep me with you.

Mother died peacefully, so said Father at the table in the morning: 'I sat with her through the night, holding her hands in mine, until her eyes stayed closed and I knew: she is gone.'

The nurse washed Father and tended his needs. He preferred it if Leonora left the room when the intimate things were done. She understood that. But she kept the sickroom tidy, she brought a rose in a vase, and sometimes he opened his eyes slowly and it seemed that he recognised the rose. He'd always loved roses so much.

Aunt Issy's ankle hadn't healed and she had to walk with a crutch, but the bang of the crutch bothered Father. So, of her own accord, she stayed away. So the good Lord arranges things, thought Leonora.

Twice a day the brothers helped Hennie into the room and his seat beside the sickbed.

'Father, it's Oom Hennie,' whispered Leonora.

She's monopolising Father, Agnes thought, and her bitterness increased when she acknowledged: he is Leonora's father.

The last afternoon he opened his eyes and there was a weak flickering of recognition, a slight movement of the hand towards his brother. Hennie leaned closer. Father's words were inaudible. Leonora put her ear against his lips, but he just shook his head slightly. They helped Hennie to get closer; it was as if Father's lips were trying to form a word. At last they heard it, very softly: 'Wa-ter.' They brought a glass, wanted to help him drink, but he turned his head away.

Hennie wept at his brother's beside, his head in his hands. 'I understand what you're trying to say to me,' he said.

So Father's thoughts were fixed on Hennie at the end, thought Leonora. My young brother Hennie, Father had told her once, is still fighting with God like Jacob fought with the angel. I could never help. I tell him all the agony is unnecessary. God is, and that's all that counts. If God is pain, that's part of it all. Leonora couldn't understand it then, and she was even more mystified now. She stroked the soft silver hair, smoothing it. Lovingly, as she had done when she was a little girl.

They stayed around his bed until dawn, unwilling to disturb the peace and silence around him. When they finally switched the light on, his eyes were closed, and the alienation of death already lay on his face.

Hennie stayed on in the 'boys' room' and Stuart and Agnes put Frikkie and his family up. The three younger brothers, who were hastily summoned again, shared two rooms at a neighbour's – Philip's Maud didn't come along.

While Agnes had felt excluded from Father's sickroom because Leonora didn't want her there, she felt welcome with Aunt Issy and they spent many an afternoon together. She prepared meals at home and brought them over and she lent Nellie a hand in the kitchen.

'You're a treasure,' said Aunt Issy.

She smiled bitterly when she repeated this to Stuart. 'She also calls Nellie a treasure.'

Kowie kept the children busy, and took them to the bioscope.

'You keep quiet about that, do you hear?' she warned them. 'It can't do any harm, but I know your Tannie Leonora will think it shows disrespect.'

For SussieBelle, her grandfather's death would always be linked with Shirley Temple and her songs. Because when they came out of the bioscope, their father told them: 'Oupa is dying,' and he died that night. She hated herself: she couldn't get the songs unstuck from her mind. '*On the good ship Lollipop ...*'

The three younger uncles came with her father and Frikkie to their house for supper. Her father was sadder than the others. His eyes looked funny, as if he'd been crying. He poured brandy for the men and Kowie, and then went to phone. He tried to get through to Ozzie at the Castle: Ozzie had to come home. There was so much to do, everyone had to be phoned, there was always somebody on the phone. The dominee came over from Aunt Issy's. The undertaker came. Her father had to organise it all, but then he started to cry again. It was strange to see such a big man cry. He didn't even wipe the tears, until her mother brought him a handkerchief. Frikkie also struggled to get going, and

Philip, the next son in line, said, 'Leave the organising to me. I'll let Father's previous congregation know. Father wanted to be buried next to Mother and Vicky in Worcester.' Hendrik nodded and said he would send something to the newspapers.

'You'll see, it's going to be a big funeral,' predicted Kowie. 'We'll have to organise tea and things for afterwards. People will travel a long way. They'll have to let us use the hall next to the church. Philip should ask the Women's Institute to provide scones and sandwiches. Surely they have a pet grocer who'll let them have something from under the counter. You can't bake without flour and sugar. Sifting you can't do either; I really don't like these war recipes. I'm glad it's not my party.'

Her mother reacted sharply: 'Everybody knows, Kowie, we can't do much.'

Hendrik just said: 'It shatters me to see the old man in this state. I can't take it.' He was talking about Hennie: he'd been named after him but since his return from overseas he hadn't paid the old man much attention.

Hennie was too weak to go to the funeral. Siena would stay with him. Nellie was determined: she wanted to help bury the old master. She cried non-stop, her handkerchief was always on her eyes and nose. 'Come now, Nellie,' said Aunt Issy. 'Pull yourself together.'

Even Miemie cried, but SussieBelle couldn't cry. No matter how much she loved her grandfather, Shirley Temple songs kept on spinning through her mind. ' ... *It's a sweet trip to a candy shop.*'

The next day Stuart went to collect Ozzie at the station. He would be one of the pallbearers, making up a six with the five brothers. Stuart as eldest son, and Ozzie as eldest grandson and namesake, would lead the group.

Ozzie wore his uniform with the red tab.

'Philip, he can't,' cried Leonora. 'We can't do that to Father. The congregation in Worcester knows how he felt about the war.'

'Do you think it doesn't grieve me too? But what can we do about it? It's what Stuart wants, and actually he's right: it's Ozzie rightful place.'

'Frikkie's son?'

'Ozzie is still the eldest and the namesake.'

'Can the living revenge themselves on the dead in this way?'

'Those are harsh words, Leonora. You know I'm against the war, and against Smuts's red tabs, but when I see Stuart's grief ... do you really think he has revenge in mind?'

Now she cried harder than she had when Father died. 'Then it's life that takes revenge. Oh Lord, he never did anyone any harm. He was so well loved.'

This was attested by the long procession of cars even though it poured with rain; and by all the handshakes received by the daughter and her old aunt, the five sons and their spouses. Handshakes even from strangers.

Later that evening after everyone except Frikkie and his family had returned to Wellington, the children chattered: We recognised most of the people, at least the faces. But that one woman, the one they say came on the Cape Town train, who squeezed our hands and said: He was a good man ... who could she have been?

'She spoke to you, Agnes. What else did she say?'

Agnes was tired and overstrung, as they all were, in fact.

'Oh, nothing really, she just asked if I was Stuart's wife. So I said yes. But there were so many people, I didn't really notice her.'

Things were steadily falling apart at the old people's house – as the children referred to the house in Villiers Street.

Hennie wasted away in the 'boys' room'. He'd taken a few bad falls, he missed his own familiar furniture which supported him when he was walking. He wanted to go back to his little house in the Strand; there were other pensioners there to keep him company. He didn't get on with Issy and Nellie. His godson, Hendrik, who'd stayed on for a while, took him home in his big new car.

They didn't talk much.

'If you need anything – treatment or something like that – please let me know. It would be a pleasure to be able to help.'

After the visit to the Cape family, Hendrik felt a little ashamed of his big income. But he decided he'd better not offer a cheque: he knew their pride. He wrote his name and address clearly on an envelope and left it on the sideboard. Then he held the two cold hands fondly in his.

'I will write, or come to visit.' But he knew he probably wouldn't.

Oom Hennie seemed happy to be back in his little house. Other old people came out of their houses to greet him, just as lame and half-blind or half-deaf as he was. One brought some biscuits, another fresh milk, a third *Die Kerkbode*. They gathered around him, comforted him; they'd all lived through their own losses, they understood him.

Hendrik handed his uncle over to the courageous old people. 'He's a pillar of strength to us,' they said. 'Our pillar' – those were nice words, thought Hendrik, the economist. In his rapidly expanding import and export business in Johannesburg, his own creation, he was a pillar of strength. But was it the same?

He drove away feeling more deeply moved than he had felt at his father's funeral.

I won't always be young and strong and quick at understanding. I'll be like him one day. He wanted to turn back and press the old man to his heart again, but then he thought about the little group that gathered around Hennie. Let me rather not bother him. I could write. But he knew he wouldn't.

Aunt Issy's ankle deteriorated. Leonora came to Agnes. 'She's asking for you.'

The doctor tried the new sulphur pills, but couldn't stop the inflammation. 'You should have taken x-rays,' he reproached. 'The bones have splintered. She won't stand the fever very long.'

She died with Agnes there beside her. She was also buried in Worcester, next to Grandma. The funeral was small: just a few family members.

Now only Nellie remained at the house in Wellington. It was school holidays and SussieBelle helped Leonora to sort her grandfather's papers. The study was just an empty room with boxes and stacks of old paper. Leonora was upset. 'I have to reduce it all, but how?' She smoothed out papers she'd crumpled and thrown away, and took out others that she'd already put into boxes. Stuart came to help after work. He was better at discarding things; he finished in the hour before supper what Leonora struggled to get through in a day.

SussieBelle didn't talk about the little tent. When her father said: 'It looks as though this is a diary that he kept in the camp,' she asked: 'Could I have it?' The stack of her grandfather's things which she wanted to keep grew and grew.

Leonora smiled, although her expression was unsure and troubled. 'You won't be able to keep it all, Sussie.' She resolved to get the child away from this stifling atmosphere.

The hours with Father's papers brought Leonora and Stuart close again – like they'd been before his marriage. They talked about Mother's death; they found a sheaf of papers with *A Vision* written on it in a fine hand. The date was just before Mother's death.

Leonora was overwhelmed. 'Do you remember, Stuart, she seemed to be dead, and then she came back. Once she got up, and sat for hours writing at her desk. These very papers. Father only read us a bit from them.' She put the papers aside.

From where she sat on the floor, she looked up at Stuart who was packing books into a chest; she held papers in her hands, like offerings. 'Death strips you of all privacy. This room was his sanctuary, now his most intimate life is exposed to us.'

The exposure when Agnes and Leonora had to go through Aunt Issy's things was much more painful. In a small flat box, together with Grandma's funeral letter, was the little welcoming programme for the assistant minister in Grandfather's congregation from way back. The date was September 1887. The young man's face was on the cover, a good-looking young man, of Scottish descent according to his name. And on a second programme three months later, the reception for his bride. The pamphlets had yellowed.

'We've always wondered so much about Aunt Issy,' said Leonora to Agnes. 'We said: she never loved. And now here it is revealed to us. She kept these all that time, her hope of love and her disappointment when the bride came. She could at least have destroyed the evidence.'

'She didn't want to,' said Agnes. 'She wanted us to know. If we know, it isn't over. As long as we remember, that poor hopeless love lives on.' Just like SussieBelle and Leonora, she also had her pile of things. She put the little box on her pile.

Leonora became suspicious. 'Maybe she didn't want to destroy the programmes so she could mislead us, to make us think there was a romance. "Tis better to have loved and lost ..." Oh, Aunt Issy! Only now do I start to love her. Over this last bit of deceit!'

Nellie's widower came to claim her. She got married quietly and Agnes had them to tea at her house after the wedding. The widower was accompanied by his only son, Bertus, a stout young man who worked at a fish factory on the west coast.

Nellie was in tears at the farewell. 'Miss Leonora and Miss Agnes, you are like family to me. I'll never forget you.'

'We won't either, Nellie,' said Leonora. 'After Mother's death you were like a mother to our three young brothers.'

The brothers were generous. Leonora brought a fine tea service from Cape Town that made Nellie clasp her hands together out of disbelief. 'For me, Miss Leonora? Really for me?' And out came her handkerchief again.

Siena went back to her home town.

And finally, there was the auction. The tolling of the auctioneer's bell was sadder than the funeral bell. The furniture was carried out. The place was sold to the school board.

Fortunately Leonora had left by the time the bulldozers started work. The erf was worth more than the house. It bordered on a piece of land that belonged to the school board, and a new girls' hostel was on the drawing board.

Window panes, doors and beams were chopped out of the bricks and cement, and carried off; floor and ceiling boards were salvaged. The wiring hung like spider webs from the plundered walls and the ceilingless spaces. Then the corrugated iron sheets were removed. The sheets rattled as they plunged down, and the workers scattered as sharp edges dug into the ground.

Silently, Stuart and Agnes stood watching the demolition of Father's house. Agnes returned in the mornings, when Stuart was at the bank and SussieBelle at school. She watched the big hammers batter the walls, she saw the plaster crack and then shatter, falling in sheets to the ground. The exposed bricks – bleached, light pinks, greys – offered little resistance. Some remained intact and were sorted onto a heap. Most were carted off and dumped as rubbish.

'We should have taken the rose bushes,' Agnes said to Stuart. 'It's a pity we didn't think about that.'

Now it was too late, the rose bushes were broken and trampled and buried under the rubble.

Nellie took slips of plants to the farm. 'You should have taken the roses too,' said Agnes.

'I was too shy to ask.'

Six months after Father's funeral Ozzie was sent away to British East Africa where South African divisions rallied to forestall the Italians who were moving down from Abyssinia. The war was still unreal to Agnes, she didn't worry too much about it. When the telegram came to say that he'd died in Kenya – not on the battlefield, but from black-water fever – she couldn't believe it.

She phoned Stuart and read the message to him. He rushed home and found her still in disbelief, sitting on the chair next to the telephone table, with the receiver still in her hand. He took it from her and placed it back on the phone. Then he kneeled in front of her, his head in her lap.

'I sent him to his death,' he said. He started to sob. Agnes put her arms around him. He spoke through his sobs. 'What is it in me? Why did I want to get at Father, even through my son? Even though I loved him so much.'

Even through her shock, Agnes knew that he meant Father and not Ozzie. Aunt Issy and the obstinate Grandma of whom she had heard so much flashed through her mind. Their beautiful boy, their pet. Was this the bitter harvest of the damage they'd done to him? Suddenly she was overwhelmed with pity for him.

'Don't blame yourself; we are not responsible for the lives of others.' It didn't occur to her that she had reason to blame him.

'We must get SussieBelle out of school.' She said. It was only when she saw SussieBelle that she realised that he was dead, and her tears came.

In a strange way it was comforting that her son was buried in the earth of British East Africa. It wasn't over yet, she knew with certainty. Her son's body was only a pawn; the bond was not broken yet.

SussieBelle sat on her bed with the stuff that had come her way from her grandfather. She'd also got some of Hennie's pictures when she and her mother helped to clear up after his funeral. I want this; and I'd like that too, please, she'd said. She was greedy for the old pictures. It seemed unreal that the people in those pictures were all dead: so many of them lived so vividly in her mind. So many pictures of people without names; people with animals, buck they'd shot, a rhinoceros, a male lion; thatched houses against a background of cliffs, of rocky valleys, or flat bushveld with thorn trees. The old sepia photos created a strange feeling inside her. Because the people in their old-fashioned clothes had all disappeared from the earth. And because those who could have said who they were, and where that place was, were also dead. Many many dead people were staring out from albums all over the world, as the heavy pages were turned and the transparent interleaves fluttered down with a sigh. Now Ozzie was also dead and he could also only stare out from pictures in albums.

She missed her brother. She didn't look at the photo of him in his uniform very often. Ever since he'd gone away, she'd kept a special picture of him in her Bible. It showed both of them on the back veranda. He was about 12 or 13 in the picture, she was younger. They almost looked alike. He was skinny, and struggled to raise the handles of the wheelbarrow where she sprawled, all long legs. They were both laughing, he shyly. She was sorry that she hadn't loved him better when he was alive. Now she loved him more than anything out there in his faraway grave in the strange world of the sepia photos.

She kept all the old pictures and the little white tent together in her cupboard.

In one way there was no connection between them, but to her they were tightly connected. Everything else in her life was just play, she thought. Only the tent and the sepia pictures and Ozzie's grave in that foreign land were real.

13

In 1944 SussieBelle went to Stellenbosch University. At first she came home every weekend, but as she became more involved in campus life, she was home more seldom.

Agnes was lonely.

Since SussieBelle's departure, the closed door of Ozzie's bedroom confronted her every day with the irrevocability of his death. She had too many empty hours. She missed Aunt Issy. It was now three years since her death, but she missed her more than ever. Aunt Issy, with her texts and her comforting sayings: she too had loved Ozzie. It was a good thing for her that she had gone before him.

After the death of the two old people, she lost the impetus to resume her involvement with the Women's Institute or the Women's Missionary Bond. Ozzie's death had turned her inward again. She thought continuously of the grave out there somewhere in the highlands of Kenya, as British East Africa had been known for the last 25 years. Should she return, even just to visit? Even if she didn't know where to find the grave? No; and, in any case, it was impossible with the war still raging; she was glad not to be confronted with the choice.

Thoughts of Daniel Greylinck, the man who'd reared her, no longer preyed on her mind. Sometimes she wondered if she'd even recognise him after all these years. And would he recognise her? But when she held the little brooch with the green stones, she thought of the child on the station, the clouds of steam surging out from under the carriages, steam burning her hand, the train forever disappearing out of sight.

Ozzie's death gnawed at Stuart. Old ailments dating back to his time in German South West Africa recurred. Kidneys, bladder, liver. The doctor attributed them all to the indestructible bilharzia germ. He stayed at home of an evening, depressed. It will pass, the doctor reassured him.

Agnes was in the habit of drinking her morning tea on the veranda once her housework was done. She lingered there, at peace for a while. She sat staring ... at what? Neighbours returning from the shops, delivery boys pushing their bikes into first this and then that gate, servants strolling past pushing prams.

And that was how she became aware of the strange woman walking past her house for the umpteenth time, on the opposite pavement, surreptitiously turning her head to look. Looking at her house. She'd already noticed her on several occasions. She always wore the same dress, navy blue with a small white pattern, with a jacket of the same fabric. A dark straw hat. From her figure and her gait Agnes could tell she was no longer young. Where was she from? Who was she? This thin woman in dark clothing.

One morning, when Agnes felt her loneliness more keenly than ever, and she saw the woman on the pavement once again, she pushed the tea tray aside, stood up, and went down the veranda steps. Just like that: without hat or handbag. But at least she wasn't wearing her apron. She crossed the road and caught up with the woman without any difficulty. As she drew abreast of the woman, about to walk past her, she paused, to her own surprise, 'Oh! I believe I know you!' Because she had indeed recognised her. She was the stranger who had attended Father's funeral, arousing fleeting curiosity only to be forgotten again. But Agnes hadn't forgotten because the woman had sought her out and asked, 'Are you the wife of his oldest son?'

Now her words disturbed the woman. For a moment it seemed that she'd deny her. Clumsily, she took hold of the clasp on her handbag; her fingers sought something, a handkerchief. She pressed it against the corners of her mouth, as though to wipe away moisture that had gathered there. Agnes regretted her abruptness. 'Do you live round here? No, I know you don't. Would you like a cup of tea? The pot's still warm.'

The woman was older than she'd realised. When she took her arm, she could feel the bone. The breast was flat under the navy blue floral dress. The stomach was also flat, with prominent hipbones. The skirt hung limp. She neglects herself, thought Agnes.

'Are you in a hurry?'

The woman shook her head.

'Then please join me, it isn't far: just over there.'

The woman thought a moment and then made up her mind. Without demurring, she walked with her. Agnes shut the garden gate behind them and led the way up the veranda steps. Momentarily there was a dim recollection of another garden gate closing, but she couldn't place it.

'Let's make ourselves comfortable,' she said. 'Shall we stay outside? No, I think it would be cooler inside.'

When she reappeared from the kitchen with a pot of fresh tea, the woman was standing at the corner shelf looking at the photos of her children and Stuart and Father and Mother.

'Did you know them?' asked Agnes.

'Only the dominee.'

'How do you take your tea?'

'As it comes.'

'Sugar?'

'Thank you.'

She took a seat and looked around calculatingly as she sipped her tea.

'Have you come a long way?'

'From Cape Town.'

'By train?'

The woman nodded. Although her complexion was drab, she had strong features. In her time she would have been a woman to reckon with. Could she have been a victim of circumstance? Circumstances beyond her control? Her eyes were grey-blue and almost expressionless. Drained of emotion, it seemed to Agnes.

'For …?'

'I won't disturb you for long, I'm taking tonight's train back.'

'You aren't disturbing me. I'm alone. Please take off your hat if you'd like to, I'll put it on the bench.'

Her longing for Aunt Issy came up strongly: the grey hair flattened by the crown of the hat, the slight sweatiness where the hair was pressed against the scalp. Even the smell of the older woman, a combination of lavender and talcum powder, brought Aunt Issy back. And the bony angularity of the thin body.

'You can't go back alone tonight. If you knew Father, the dominee, he wouldn't have been pleased …'

Then the thought struck Agnes: Would she want to visit his grave?

Had this woman meant something to Father? He had lived as a widower for so long.

No, that was impossible.

'I'll take you to the dominee's grave if you like. But it's in Worcester.'

'I didn't come to visit his grave.' The woman's voice was stronger now, a pleasant voice and the hand which replaced the teacup was supple, in spite of the liver spots that defaced the skin. The fingers were free of Aunt Issy's nobbly arthritic joints.

'In fact, I came because of you. If you hadn't spoken to me this morning, I would never have come again, I know myself.'

Her chair was lower than the one where Agnes sat. Agnes had to lean towards her as the woman spoke quietly. As she spoke she glanced at Agnes periodically. Sizing her up?

'The dominee, your father-in-law, asked me to meet you many years ago, but my parents were against it. They are both dead now. But don't let me obscure the truth: I was also opposed to meeting you.'

She saw the lack of comprehension on Agnes's face, in her eyes.

'Father?'

'He only visited us once. We weren't very forthcoming. He thought there was a possibility you might be my child.'

The woman reached out and took Agnes's hand, squeezing it hard. Her anxiety was increased by Agnes's confusion. Her voice dropped, 'But it's highly unlikely. Don't let it distress you.'

She straightened Agnes's fingers one by one, measuring them against her own. Was she looking for similarities? Would she be able to recognise her as her daughter through her fingers? Agnes was only to discover later that the woman was a music teacher.

'It's a long story. The old dominee was such a good man.' The woman felt relieved now that she had spoken. 'I sometimes regretted not listening to him, but how could I be certain?'

And the handkerchief was pressed to her lips again.

Agnes swallowed. Completely thrown off balance, she went to make fresh tea. She drank the hot tea. 'Is there no way of telling? As you can imagine, I too would appreciate some certainty.'

The woman shook her head. 'I never even put the baby to my breast. My parents decided it was better not to.'

The idea of 'to the breast' of this woman was hard to imagine.

She was now desperately grateful that Stuart wouldn't be home for lunch; she needed time to gather her wits. She'd wanted to know about her origins, so she must follow this through.

'I don't have any birthmarks, or anything like that.'

'I really want to emphasise that you shouldn't let this distress you, my child.' How strange, suddenly, the world 'child'. 'We weren't to blame ... neither you nor I. Perhaps I am, but not you.'

Suddenly the words got through to Agnes – a counterbalance to Leonora's jibes, to all those years of being a waif, to her loneliness now with Ozzie dead and SussieBelle out of the house and Stuart always sick and irritable.

'No, we were truly not to blame ... and now you've come looking for me.'

Whether she was her mother or not, Agnes decided she would care for this woman. She could at least offer friendship. She let her rest, she offered her a meal, and she took her in a taxi to the station in time to catch her train back to Cape Town.

'This won't be the last time we see each other,' she said as she stood at the compartment window. 'I have your address. What should I call you ... what on earth should I call you? ...' The train was gathering steam; the conductor jumped onto the guard's van, hanging onto the copper pipe, waved his green flag, the whistle between his lips. 'What should I call you ...?'

'Just say Miss Marais, as my pupils did. See? I don't want to force you into anything ... I have to think of my reputation, too.'

Then the tears ran down Agnes's cheeks, there on the platform as she stared after the train. 'I have to think of my reputation.' Was that what it boiled down to, in the end? Her non-existence, the denial of her right to an identity – because her existence threatened a good name?

And yet she went to visit: on a day return train ticket to Cape Town. She got to know the small house in New Church Street. Miss Marais took her into the sitting room where the piano stood. With her hands on the white ivory keys – for she'd thrown back the lid and removed the embroidered felt strip – she said with satisfaction, 'I earned a living for us on these piano keys. Single-handed. I always said to myself: that isn't something to underestimate.'

And Agnes's mind flew back to the afternoon so many years ago when Aunt Issy said to Miss Golightly: 'Miss Golightly, I do esteem you', and then to the inquisitive Leonora: 'Because she was beholden to no one' – as though her own life suddenly displeased Aunt Issy.

There were many times when Agnes wanted to tell Miss Marais: 'I esteem you.' A life of your own though not without adversity.

With a new friendship that became meaningful to both of them.

She played the piano to Agnes for hours on end. While they prepared a meal together in the kitchen, Miss Marais told her – at first with some difficulty, later the words came more easily – how her father had sold his farm and bought this house when he learned she was pregnant. Things hadn't been going well on the farm, and it was a relief to be rid of it. But the remainder of the money had been so poorly invested that they eventually came to depend solely on her income.

'And ... the man you and Father thought might be my pa?'

'A boy, scarcely a man. Braampie Nel from the neighbouring farm. He joined up against everyone's advice. He was taken prisoner at Burgersdorp and executed as a rebel.'

She showed Agnes her photograph album. A boy's face, scarcely distinguishable from the group, two hands holding a slice of watermelon, a cow's lick of fair hair. 'That was him.'

Later, when their friendship had deepened, she took out a bundle of letters in a shoebox from the depths of her wardrobe. They were yellowed and almost worn through with repeated reading. The last one remained in the box.

'It isn't only my reputation,' she said, 'there are people who remember him. They regard his execution as a martyrdom.'

And folk heroes who are still no more than children do not produce babies out of wedlock, thought Agnes. Yet she was not embittered. The woman had integrity and she'd also suffered. Who could tell? It might not even have been this couple's baby who was sent to the Transvaal. And to British East Africa from the Transvaal. And stuck into a *masjila* in British East Africa and carried off, it didn't matter whence, as long as it was taken away.

Miss Marais was keen to hear about her past; she had all the time in the world to listen. With Oom Hennie and Aunt Issy dead, Miss Marais's was the only ear open to Agnes, and a strange bond of trust developed between them, predicated for both of them by the fact that their connection was based on uncertainty.

Agnes was touched that, at her age, Miss Marais should have undertaken the journey to Wellington every day for weeks so soon after the death of her last parent, on the slim chance that the dominee could have been right.

In fact it was better to call her Miss Marais than Mother.

Even in her relationship with SussieBelle, 'Mother' had always been a difficult concept for Agnes to grasp. Because she'd never had a mother herself. And it was apparently just as difficult for Miss Marais. Because she'd never had a child. No, it was better this way, thought Agnes. And as the affection between them grew over the months, she realised: The two of us probably get on better than a mother and daughter would. Because we expect nothing and are not obliged to give each other anything.

And with considerable self-satisfaction – for the family had eventually learned of the new friendship – she thought: Even the high-minded

Leonora couldn't find fault with a Cape rebel and an innocent Boer girl as parents. It was just a pity that SussieBelle wouldn't hear of going along to visit Miss Marais.

14

After Father's death, Leonora got a post at the Mowbray Training College where she taught student teachers. She found it much more fulfilling than schoolteaching. With her small inheritance from Father – a little extra to take care of an unmarried daughter – she bought a semi-detached house in Tamboerskloof. The house was on the slope and faced south. She enjoyed the view from her front veranda, across the blue bulk of Table Mountain. From her back veranda she looked out across the fynbos to the slopes of Vlaeberg. She threw out breadcrumbs for the birds, and once she even spied the anxious eyes of a tiny buck among the shrubs.

It was her self-appointed task to ensure that the family didn't split up, especially along the north-south divide. She drove out to Wellington in her little new car to celebrate the birth of Robbie's first child – he had been married quietly in Potchefstroom. She sent flowers from herself, Stuart and Frikkie to Philip's wife, Maud, who'd had two daughters in quick succession ten years after Barry, her first-born. She organised accommodation for Hendrik who, relatively late in life (he was 35), married a nurse called Rina and brought her to Cape Town on honeymoon.

But Leonora was not happy. Father had been gone for nearly nine years. She still felt dislocated without him.

There were no other meaningful relationships in her life. The affair with her friend in England had come to nothing. It was her fault, she knew; Father had also warned her gently. She couldn't contemplate submitting to another in the long term: he absolutely insisted on sharing her secret life, or at least being part of it. She marked out her own space: no admission. Then she felt safe. He couldn't understand it. It made him feel threatened. Or humiliated.

'A love relationship doesn't exist only to boost a man's self-image,' she said to Father.

She could tell that Father, on his sickbed, was thinking of Mother. 'Marriage is something completely different to what you think, Norie. Once there's love, everything is possible.'

'My inner secret life might seem unimportant to other people, but it's precious to me,' she snapped.

She regretted that. Father's death affected her more deeply than she could ever have imagined. A certainty that was gone. More than that. She had become almost jealously aware of a sweet, almost other-worldliness that he possessed, which she had seen evidenced every day beside his bed. Something more than peace and resignation. Rather the knowledge of a reality that would guide him to wherever it was he had to go. Faith.

'Not just believing, but knowing,' he told her one afternoon.

'Knowing what, Father? What? Please share it with me.'

'You must find it for yourself, Norie.' His voice was weak; she could just feel the slight increase in pressure on her hand. 'You will find it.'

And now it provoked her, challenged her. Perhaps I am beginning a whole new phase of my life, she thought. A restless time. I'm shadow-boxing. I feel disembodied. I go upstairs and then down again. I gulp mugs of coffee. Chain smoke. I do my work, certainly. Yet there is still so much time over, so much time ...

Sometimes she thought something must grow from this disquiet. She ought to be glad of it. It was more fruitful than content. Perhaps the turbulence was Father's most important bequest to her.

She asked herself: What about events in the country? Isn't that what's stirring me up? Dr Malan had won the '48 election by a hair's breadth, and he'd started to turn things upside down almost immediately. She remembered the night in Frankfurt, the desolate sound of a girl's sobs. Obviously developments in the country perturbed her.

Something Father had once said occurred to her: The Supreme Being has legions of angels standing ready to go forth and do what He desires should be done. So He does not need us to do His work. He need no more than sigh and the heavenly hosts will heed Him. People would pay heed as well. Dr Malan was a churchgoer. Why didn't God trumpet in his ear that the things he was doing with the people of his country were wrong?

'Why didn't God send his heavenly hosts to help the Boers?' she'd asked Father as a child. His eyes had filled with tears.

Her meeting with Robbie in Frankfurt was etched on her memory. The yellow stars on people's sleeves to mark them as Jews, the sobbing girl. And the letter from SussieBelle with the cuttings. Now her own country seemed to be on the same path to racial hatred. She must get Belle away to where she could breathe different air. Get another perspective. Let her teach for two years and save something and then she'd help her with the balance. She was intelligent, she should study further.

And then what remains for me? Father, wherever you are, please guide me. She went over to the shelf where she kept Father's books, and drew out a well-read volume, *Het Religieuze Leven*. She read:

> *It is not important what life is, but that life is, and to be fully aware of this life.*

Had Frikkie sought something similar through his lens, with his pictures of light in May? *To be fully aware of this life?* But she couldn't agree fully. What about the quality of life? What about Oom Hennie's life? A huge black question mark still hung over his life as far as she was concerned.

She found a quotation from Eckhart among Father's papers:

> *God is obliged to act, even to pour Himself into you when He finds you prepared.*

That was a new thought: to be prepared. She resolved to try, for Father's sake; no, it was for her own desperate sake.

Father had continually referred her back to the Bible. 'Read St Mark,' he'd say. 'St Mark is the sanest guide, I know you distrust emotion.' She would read it. She would interpret it to the letter and do what it said should be done. And she'd keep a daily record. She would throw down the gauntlet to God. It was now in His hands.

3 October
I read about John the Baptist: *I have baptised you with water, but He shall baptise you with the Holy Spirit*. Right, that's a promise. The Lord will also baptise me with the Holy Ghost. (Where's Aunt Issy now to hear that coming from my lips?)

Evening: Made many mistakes during the day, thought now and then about the words 'baptised with the Holy Ghost'. Often forgot. But once it stopped me from saying something nasty. That's definite progress. I always say something nasty about S. I feel slightly more cheerful.

4 October
Thou art My beloved Son in whom I am well pleased. I must accept that, because since childhood I have prayed, Our Father. That I am a child

and that I can therefore enjoy His goodwill? Once again Oom Hennie is my stumbling block. Was God well disposed to Oom Hennie?

5 October
Something strange has happened. R. has invited me to go to the Karoo for the long weekend – to a desert area south of Calvinia. She rang while I was reading the words: *And immediately the Spirit driveth Him into the desert.* I went cold. I hardly know R. I accepted and my finger started to tremble on the words in the Bible. I am playing with powerful things here.

7 October
Drove a long way, I'm tired tonight. The stars seem dimmer, no doubt because the wind has filled the air with dust. I can't sleep, I wrestle with sleep – the strange bed or the strange emptiness out there? I long shamelessly for a bedfellow.

I read tonight: *And He was with the wild beasts, and the angels ministered unto Him.* Communion with wild beasts? Does it mean he also had to wrestle with the animal side of His nature? After all, He was a human like us. Human form; material; flesh and blood. This disciple doesn't say anything more about temptation. Just about communion with the animals.

8 October
Alone this morning, R. and her husband have gone off to a cattle station. I've moved the table so that when I sit writing I can see through the door of the rondavel over the plains to the horizon. The sun is shining on the stone floor. And on my feet. The yellow succulents bloom on the dry shale of this desert world. The reef of mountains on the horizon is blue. I read that He went back to the people to proclaim the Kingdom of Heaven. What does Kingdom of Heaven mean? Those words we have heard since we were children?

I spent most of the day in the rondavel because it was very hot outside. When I looked out over the plains, I saw how the sun moved slowly but surely across the firmament which is like a huge bowl inverted over me. Kingdom of Heaven? Like a basin over me, over us? But He said: it is in your heart.

I read a good deal. New ideas swarm in my head. X says: To survive, the human desires revenge. If he is injured, he wishes to injure another, it affords him relief. The noble spirit says: no more. 'A brave man will try to make the evil stop with him. He shall keep the blow. No man shall get it from him, and that is a sublime ambition.'

Animals do not know revenge. Again a new meaning for Jesus's communion with the animals in the desert.

Perhaps even an answer to what the Kingdom of Heaven within you means: to keep the blow, to make evil stop with you?

Walked over the grey ridges this morning. So hot and dry, the shale crumbled under my soles. Sweet fragrance from the yellow flowers on the succulents – the only plant that grows round here. Huge swathes of dried everlastings too. Thousands, millions of them, the heads dried so tightly that they cast shadows like tiny black ink dots. Looks too strange, these small ink dots as round as pellets that dance about on the rocky ground before you even feel the movement of air on your cheeks or skin. I broke one open – billions of seeds disintegrate in your fingers and float off on the wind. Everything so profuse, even in this parched region.

If I watch the gravel carefully, I catch a glimpse of the little grey tail of a lizard.

Came upon a patch of dry white flowers, more delicate than everlastings, but also with billions of seeds in each head. So extravagant in this barrenness. Beyond comprehension.

With the tiny downy seeds in my hand, I thought of what I once read somewhere: 'Blow on thistledown and the universe reels.' All at once that connected with 'keep the blow, do not pass on the evil'. Can one live in the midst of wrong-doing? And move the universe by absorbing and transforming just one tiny bit of evil? And leave it to God to send His hosts of angels to pound the world back into shape?

I remember a picture that was taken after Hiroshima. After the explosion. When the bang came, the destruction was instantaneous, but the body of one insignificant person had sheltered the piece of tarmac on which he stood. The shape of his shadow is immortalised on it.

9 October
In the night I stood at the open door of the rondavel looking out at the desert landscape, the moon high in the sky, a peculiar light on the earth. Low strips of cloud hung over the plains, the stars twinkled faintly. *And in the small hours of the morning, before it was light, He arose and withdrew to a secluded place to pray.*

I must go out into the desert tonight, but I cling to the shelter of the walls around me and the roof over my head. I am afraid of the white cold and the chilly breeze and the far ridges where the wind howls, the stars will remain icy and remote, and the great fear of the immeasurable freezes me cold as stone. I will scarcely be able to lift my head, I will put my hands over my ears and wrap my scarf round my head and stumble home over the rocks.

10 October
I have a fever; hot and cold at the same time. I can't bear the dry heat of the day and the dry white cold of the night. My body needs longer to acclimatise. If there was more time I would be able to walk in the desert at night. But I am too old. I would have gone if I were younger; now I fear I am not up to it. I am afraid of what I might find out there in the unfathomable night in the desert. Or am I afraid, my beloved Father, that I will find nothing?

This, I maintain in all piety, is where a mere human being can no longer keep up.

11 October
The car bumped and bounced along the dirt road and I was thrown about on the rear seat. I have large fever blisters on my lips and inside my nostrils. There was a bloodstain on my pillowcase this morning.

I could weep when I think of the billions of flower seeds that drift in vain over the parched earth. Can God not let it rain on us?

PART THREE
Belle

1

They are sending me to my brother's grave in Kenya, I'm going on behalf of all of them, thought Belle as she looked down from the train window at her family on the platform, their faces tilted back, hands shading their eyes, degrees of smiles on their lips.

They've battled to keep the family together since my grandfather's death. The uncles in the Transvaal sent me the money to go to my brother's grave, even though they were opposed to the war in which he fell. I must go for the sake of my mother, even though she too was opposed to the war. They believe that this caused the breach between she and my father who sent my brother to the war. And the breach between my mother and Tannie Leonora who was in favour of the war. They think they are sending me to get rid of the cobwebs entangling them. To reclaim the errant brother and heal the wound inside them.

Have I misled them?

Am I going because of Oom Hennie with his pain and his sepia photographs? Put away deep in my drawer with my oupa's little white tent. These things are real, I thought then, the other things in my life are incidental. Am I going in search of this reality? Or am I going for a reason they don't know about: Me on her lap when I was small, pressing my head against her cheek and asking: Mamma, why don't I have another oupa? Mamma, why are you crying? But she said: Go and play SussieBelle.

Perhaps that, too, is the reason why I'm going?

The train began to steam away from the station. Her ailing father turned away from the sun before her coach moved; he was in pain once more, she could see it. Her mother didn't notice, she stood with her back to him, trying to raise her arm higher to wave above the others. Was that so the others could see her waving, and see that she had to stop waving to wipe away the tears which weren't there?

Belle turned her head away. My mother doesn't love me.

Boetie, my boetie. I'm coming because of you and me, scrabbling away behind the gooseberry bush, digging carrots from the wet, muddy soil to see how the roots absorb water, though we never could work it out. I want to stand on the plot of earth beneath which you lie, I want to stand there and ask you: Are you absorbing the rain now; are the little white roots absorbing you; are you the little white roots? Boetie, my boetie, I'm afraid of your grave.

She saw Oom Frik focus down the railway track, without a camera, yet seeing a picture; he showed her pictures everywhere. Steam, water tap, water tubs, white against the warm blue sky, dry grain of asbestos tubs, shiny stripe of railway track.

The train jerked, the coaches bumped against each other as the steel plates of one moved in under the other, meshing together like rams' horns. She was jerked against the seat and had to sit down, her hand withdrawn from the window. Tannie Kowie was still waving, so was Miemie. Her mother's handkerchief covered her eyes. Tannie Leonora went to buy her fruit for the journey, and nearly missed the train, but her hand was the last holding Belle's.

The train swayed steadily, the passenger coaches swung and rocked, back and forth and from side to side. Belle sat with her back to the engine, watching the people become smaller and smaller. I've left them, she thought, it's over. She piled her luggage on the other seat; she was alone, other passengers would board at the next station. Oom Frik had thrust a camera into her hands – not his best, but a good one – and she took it out of the leather case now. Focused forward through the window. The train line took long wide sweeps along the ridge of the mountain; as they went round a bend she could see the coaches, the coal tender, the engine. Around the next curve they disappeared again; the landscape came racing past – she couldn't focus fast enough – farm roads, farm houses, cars, wagons, donkey carts, people working in vineyards, standing up, wanting to wave, but they were past already, the train's speed swallowed them; other objects flew into sight; swaying, she awaited fresh impressions at each turn.

Women bundled into the compartment, there were six of them now. Belle kept her place at the window, watching the sun sink lower, the fine sifting of gold fall across the distant landscape, the vastness of it – God, the vastness, the space, the haze in the distance. She stretched her hands out and the wind tugged at her arms, drawing them outwards; her arms dragged like stems under water.

The sun was gone. The compartment, bereft of light, was close and bleak, the women's faces expressionless, flat, ugly, as they sat swaying with closed eyes. Three opposite Belle – shoulder to shoulder, fat thigh pressed against fat thigh – and two beside her.

Her luggage was stacked on the top bunk. She would sleep up there tonight. Or, better still, on the middle bunk so that she could lower the shutter and gaze out across the dark landscape. Across the wind blowing in white streaks. She saw the wind, even though there were no trees or branches for it to move. She felt the sun even if it was raining; behind the rain, behind the clouds, she felt the sun. Oh, my boetie, my boetie, how deep down does the warmth of the sun penetrate your grave?

One of the women let down the table and placed shoeboxes with food for the journey on it: cold rissoles and drumsticks unrolled from squares of wax paper, and sandwiches with tomato or jam or anchovy offered round on paper serviettes. They tasted one another's food, ordered tea from the steward who rattled at the door with his skeleton key; it slid open to reveal his slender body, his narrow hips in the tight shiny pants turned sideways, the tray held high against his shoulder.

Sixpence a cup, the women whispered noisily: we each add tuppence, then there's a shilling tip for him. They wrapped the crusts and half-eaten sandwiches, and an orange which the tante sniffed at before adding it to the paper parcel. The wind blew in a flurry of soot when the woman opposite Belle let the window down to throw the food to the brown children crowding together at a siding. They waved and scrambled about; the paper broke open; they grabbed the food and peelings, cramming them into their mouths.

The steward brought early-morning coffee. Belle, lying on the middle bunk, with her head at the door end, wondered whether he had slept a wink. She'd heard the tinkling of glasses over beer bottles as he swayed along the corridor until late at night. His voice was comforting, his hand opened a space for the saucer between her blankets, placing the cup on it. Sleep, he lulled, drink and sleep, I'll fetch the money later. Two of the women snored.

They dressed one by one. One stout woman clutched the bunk and wormed her way into her clothes. Then she sat as the thick leg caterpillared into the stocking and the hand groped under the knickers to find the suspender. She sighed, the pale thighs bulging above the stockings.

Belle slipped down from the middle bunk with her clothes and dressed quickly. She slid the door open and closed it again, and the wind from the open window in the corridor hit her. She grasped the chrome rail, her body jerked back and forth. This side of the track was still in shadow, the thorn trees drew no circles, the poles made no stripes, the ground was pale. The sun shone behind the closed shutters where the five old women were dressing, but even in the shade she felt the sun. The steward shifted past her, his body against hers; his hand touched her upper arm as it had when he'd moved the blankets back against her body. For a passing moment he pressed her against him.

She moved down the corridor to stand on the bridge where the coaches were coupled. She shut her eyes against the light. Holding the gate on the bridge, she felt the chill of the night still in the metal. Beneath her the earth raced past.

3

The family Belle left behind at Wellington stood around rather aimlessly at first, then walked back to the parking area. They'd come in Stuart's and Frikkie's cars. Leonora had driven to the station with Stuart, Agnes and Belle. She could still feel the hot touch of the child's hand on hers as the train pulled away. She felt bereft now that Belle had gone, as though a limb had been amputated. Agnes and Stuart didn't say much in the car. Frikkie and his family were to come for tea before they returned home via Bainskloof. Leonora would stay the night before returning to Cape Town.

Over the teacups Leonora resumed the argument that had made SussieBelle feel overlooked and ignored. Because of it, she'd had to pack her suitcases alone in her room, within hearing of the endless arguments in the dining room between her mother, Tannie Leonora, her father and her uncle. And she'd had to do without Tannie Leonora's supportive advice, which she'd been counting on.

Leonora sat down on the sofa and lit a cigarette.

'Can't you understand? I couldn't turn away the poor woman who'd pitched up there in the rain.'

She was referring to their old stalwart, Nellie, who was now married to the farmer who'd courted her so long.

'Believe me, I got a fright: I thought she must have cancer or something the way she sat and wept. Tears streaming down her face: "You must help me, Miss Leonora."' Leonora blew smoke through the open window behind the sofa. She took the cup of tea Miemie offered her.

'I can't understand why you're so reluctant to help. When you think of how much she meant to the whole family!'

'But it doesn't concern her personally,' Agnes said for the umpteenth time.

'Of course it concerns her personally. How would you feel if it happened to you; if your nearest and dearest were declared non-white? You of all people, Agnes?' The minute she'd spoken she cursed her thoughtlessness, or was it deliberate? Agnes had been opposing her the whole weekend. 'I'm sorry, Agnes, you're right, it isn't her personally, but she feels it for the sake of Oom Bertus.'

Klein Bertus, his son, married Baby, a girl from Lambert's Bay. She was pregnant; they were living on the farm and everyone was quite happy. Then came the blow of the identity cards. Her two sisters were declared non-white on the grounds of the photographs they had submitted.

Stuart said, 'You, and Father, were all for Dr Malan and now you see the mess he's made. The only one opposing him is Jannie Smuts.'

'Send the two sisters to me,' said Frikkie. 'I'll take new photos and if I don't make them look white, I'm not a photographer. But I don't agree with this conniving. We should have nothing to do with it; it's unnatural to classify people. Like cattle.'

'It's wicked, Frikkie,' said Leonora. 'I went to listen to Smuts as often as I could, and I can still hear him saying in that high grating voice of his: "The entire perspective of South Africa has been disrupted and there is a sickness of the soul." But they don't listen to him in Parliament; they keep harping on about immorality and mixed marriages. That seems to be all they think about.'

Stuart had left the room and he returned now with some newspaper cuttings. 'I found it after all, Leonora. Listen to this.' He read from one of Jannie Smuts's many speeches in Parliament: 'In the afternoon and evening I walk to my hotel in Queen Victoria Street and I see young people streaming out of the factories. I do not know whether I would be able to decide who is white and who is non-white. I am confused.

'These things are impossible for sensible people to determine, but now perfectly ordinary census-takers have to decide who is white and who is non-white.

'I cannot do it, even though I am an experienced person. But this poor little official, how the devil is he going to manage it?

'Think of the disgrace and the hatred and the heartache that will be created by this population registration. It all gives rise to hatred.

'I reject with scorn the argument that population registration does not give rise to racial discrimination, but simply acknowledges the situation as it exists.'

Stuart put the cuttings down. 'Just do your best, Frikkie, oppose the wretched business.'

But Leonora said: 'There's more to it than the photos. There're the affidavits too. Appearance is only the first criterion. The second test is the group association. If Baby's sisters want to be reclassified, they must not only send new photos, but also sworn statements from friends who are already classified as white. No, don't call on the Almighty, Frikkie. That's what it says in the newspaper.'

'Well, then their friends can vouch for them,' said Agnes. 'What's the problem? Frikkie takes the photos and the friends vouch for them.'

'The problem, my dear sister-in-law, is that the "friends" are too frightened to vouch for them. As Nellie told me in between the tears and blowing her nose: If they've been registered as white themselves, they're afraid of jeopardising their status by vouching for someone who has been classified as coloured. You won't believe it: the sisters say that when the envelopes with the identity cards came, people drew the curtains before opening the envelopes; that others should not see, that others should not denounce them. Because the law also stipulates that you can object to someone else's classification. Send ten pounds and you can object. Ten pounds a friend – or, rather, an enemy. Now you may call on the Lord, Frikkie!'

Leonora drained her cup. 'No thank you, Agnes, no more for me.' She stubbed out her cigarette. The room with its petty bourgeois furnishings depressed her.

'I have the affidavits here and I think we should sign them. These along with Frikkie's photos and a bit of influence from our brothers in the Transvaal: perhaps we'll be able to ease Nellie's burden. The brothers are especially indebted to her. Good Lord, she virtually brought them up.'

'Baby's sisters live at Lambert's Bay, we live here, so how the devil can we sign?' demanded Stuart.

'That's up to the brothers. With their government contacts, Broederbond, and all the rest, they'll know where to pull strings. If it comes to that, I'll even go and stay in the hotel at Lambert's Bay, if I have to sign there. I feel strongly about this: Nellie has meant enough to our family for us to support her now.'

'But it isn't Baby; it's her two sisters who've been classified coloured,' Agnes countered.

'You aren't listening, Agnes. Baby is upset, she says she wants to be the same as her sisters, and her baby will be the same, and her baby is Oom Bertus's first grandchild and heir, and you, more than anyone else, should know how doubt about one's ancestry can poison your life.'

Agnes had remained dry-eyed at SussieBelle's departure, but now she wept. With a handkerchief covering her eyes and her shoulders hunched, she left the room.

What on earth made me say that? Leonora thought.

Even Kowie looked at Leonora reproachfully: 'She never did you any harm.'

Stuart shrugged as if dissent between the two women didn't concern him; he needed to go to the lavatory.

Frikkie said: 'You'll have to apologise, Sis, that was a bit rough.'

'It's the damn self-centred attitude that gets me down. "It doesn't concern me, I don't have to do anything about it." Even good old Nellie very quickly made it clear that there was nothing wrong with her own ancestry. It's because we are all so self-centred that we don't take a stand against these laws.' Leonora was on the point of tears herself. 'You dirty your hands with this conniving, the whole thing is despicable. But when you think what it would mean to the girls: where they may live, whom they may marry, where they may have a cup of tea or go to a film, or have a swim – think of that: even the dear Lord's blessed sea is divided!'

Leonora poured another cup of tea to calm herself.

'I'll apologise, Frikkie. But I'm going to send the girls to you and I'll sign.'

'I did say I'd also sign,' said Frikkie. 'Kowie too, if you need someone else. Not so, Kowie?' Kowie nodded. Stuart had gone to the lavatory. 'Let's leave him out of it; for God's sake not more discord in this house.'

Since Stuart's illness Agnes had somehow taken control.

Stuart struggled down the veranda steps to take leave of Frikkie and Kowie at the car. 'Thanks for your help, Boetie. I was too weak even to help Sussie with her suitcase.' Frikkie had tightened the two buckles with his knee against the suitcase; then carried it to the car; passed it to her through the carriage window.

It was the first mention of her name since they'd watched the train leave the station.

'I hope it goes well for her,' said Frikkie. He rolled up the car window, for there was a nip in the air. 'Go on in, Stuart, you should be in bed.'

They didn't say goodbye to Agnes because she had a headache and was resting in a darkened room. When they were back indoors again, Leonora asked: 'May I phone the brothers this evening? I'll pay for the calls.'

Stuart took offence. 'Heavens, Leonora, I can still afford that!'

3

The train oiled its way silently into Johannesburg station. Slowing down until the steam started to gush out. Then it came to a standstill with a jolting shudder. Tant Rina pushed her way through the throng. 'Am I late? Oh, I'm so sorry, there's so much building going on I got lost, and to find parking ... Thank goodness, I found your platform after all, and here's a porter ...'

She was nervous, her heavy body made it difficult for her to cope with such situations. And her high heels. She'd not been married all that long. Her matronly appearance is deceptive, thought Belle. Even when they were on honeymoon in the Cape she was already motherly. She had no children. Perhaps Oom Hendrik was her child.

The tante battled to reverse the car out of the parking lot; she wasn't a good driver. But she relaxed on the highway, settling herself more comfortably behind the wheel; her colour was high and her hair was sweaty and dishevelled. She patted it back into place.

'Your Oom Hendrik is trying to come home early tonight. He's very fond of you, Belle. But the work, the work! And all the committees ... And then, on top of it all, your Tannie Leonora's problems, you've no idea how that has upset him.'

'It upset my mother too, Tannie Rina.'

'I don't know why Leonora has become so involved. One would think it was her family.'

'You might not know, but Nellie was like family. Pa says she just about raised the three younger brothers single-handedly ...'

'Yes, motherless boys, what a shame.'

'He says she always talked about "my boytjies".'

'But that still doesn't mean they're indebted to her forever. And that they should act against their conscience.'

'I agree,' said Belle. 'We've voted Malan in now and we should go along with what he says.' She enjoyed the smell of the new car and its suspension that caused her to sway so pleasantly on level stretches of road.

'Pappa said I should invite your cousin Arnold over this evening ... he's the only relative we have here, apart from the brothers.'

'Oom Frikkie gave me the camera,' said Belle. 'And Tannie Kowie sent rusks for Arnold. Oom Frikkie says if I take a photo of Ozzie's grave, it might comfort my Ma.'

'Is she still so … still so …?' The cars were banking up ahead of them at the roadworks. Black workmen leaned on their picks as they drove by, spat on hands, took up the picks again. She heard one give the note and the others take it up. They sang a monotonous, sad, rhythmic tune.

'I've never in my life seen so many natives – at every station from round about Kimberley,' said Belle.

'You don't have the creatures in the Cape. But give me a kaffir any day, I always say: they're not such drunkards as the coloureds.'

'Even our Grieta hits the bottle now and then. Pa makes little marks on his brandy bottle. But he says even though it may keep level to the mark, the colour just gets paler …'

They were still driving slowly along the bumpy deviation.

'It looks so dreadful here, but just wait until the main highway has been completed, they say …'

'You asked whether my mother was still so … still so …'

The tante tried to wave the question away with her hand.

'Oh, I meant nothing really … it can't be easy if one's child …'

'I think she'd have coped better if she'd been in favour of the war, because now she feels his death was pointless.' But it seemed to her that Tant Rina wasn't listening; she was concentrating on the heavy traffic, her breasts rising and falling with each breath. She clutched the steering wheel. At last she turned in at a tree-lined driveway.

Belle had never visited Oom Hendrik's home before. In response to Tant Rina's hooting, a black gardener dropped his spade and ran to open the gates. Two ridgebacks leaped around him, then jumped up against Tant Rina. She fended them off with her handbag. 'Just boisterous, Belle, they won't hurt you,' she said, breathlessly. The hems of the black man's white calico knee-length trousers and top were bound with red; he carried her suitcases in. The dogs gambolled around her, sniffing. The garden was filled with trees and shadows, and a red brick path led to the house.

So much demanding my attention, thought Belle: the wet tongues, the clumsy hindquarters against my thighs, the shrubs touching my head. She pushed aside a supple branch of the thorny shrub, the pollen stuck to her hand, bunches of berries between the thorns hooked in her hair. Hard, small, red berries which she picked and put in her mouth. 'Be careful, Belle, they may be poisonous,' warned Tant Rina. She spat them out; the words made them poisonous. The strange, harsh blue sky, with the leaves and branches biting into it – blue sky, white cloud and the red earth on which she walked. She'd never been on the Highveld before.

'This way, Belle. And here's your room. Even if it's only for one night. Arnold is coming later, and Pappa will be here any minute now.' The stout woman beamed goodwill, Leonora's intransigence forgotten for the moment.

There was more barking, the sound of the gates being opened, and, after a while, proprietory footsteps down the passage. Oom Hendrik's big body pushed everything out of his way: air and furniture and Tant Rina. He pressed Belle against him. His stomach was soft and yielding, she felt smothered. Until he exhaled and she could look up. His eyes were small, but affectionate; his face red with fine veins on his cheeks. He hugged her once again. 'SussieBelle! My Ouboet's little girl!' It was not really hot, but he was sweating. Wiped his forehead. 'Mamma, how about a drop of tea?'

'Isn't it a bit ridiculous,' Belle later said to her cousin Arnold, 'this "Pappa and Mamma" business?'

'They're kind-hearted. It's only in front of us. We're family. It doesn't hurt anyone.'

'Yes, but …'

Tant Rina was busy in the kitchen, assisted by the gardener who'd changed into white longs with a red cummerbund. Oom Hendrik served drinks. He dusted the small table on the patio, brought glasses, a container for the chilled wine-bottle, and produced a beer for Arnold. Arnold felt at home in the house. He sat back comfortably and poured his beer. He had an open face with a sprinkling of freckles across the bridge of his nose. Belle decided his resemblance to Tannie Kowie had increased, but he had a weak mouth. She'd last seen him years ago.

'And you, sweetheart? My very own cocktail?' Belle nodded.

'Belle!' called Tant Rina. 'Phone! Oom Robert from Potchefstroom. Hurry!'

She put the glass down so quickly that the cocktail slopped over the wide, delicate rim. Her blonde Oom Robert, the youngest of Oupa's children; she didn't know him well. She'd last seen him at Oupa's funeral. Or, wait, there'd been a holiday at Gordon's Bay, his wife housebound with a sick baby. Tant Rina came to the phone with her.

When she returned, Oom Hendrik glanced at her questioningly. He'd mopped up her spill. And wiped his forehead.

'Oom Robert just wanted to say goodbye and wish me luck. I'm ashamed to say I can hardly remember him …'

'Your Oom Philip will ring from Pretoria any minute.' Tant Rina came to sit with them. 'I think it's because the three brothers lost their ma so early that they're so attached to their family. It's quite a business the way they gather. Christmas, New Year – he who lives farthest starts packing at the crack of dawn. Last year, let me tell you …'

Oom Hendrik interrupted her. 'Did Robert say anything about this business of Leonora's? Whether she's rung him?'

'Nothing, Oom.'

'I'm very concerned, I must honestly say. I wouldn't want it to spoil your little visit, but last night she …' Oom Hendrik barely managed to utter the words, '… put the phone down while I was still speaking. She just won't understand.'

'Is it about the affidavits, Oom?'

'She's stubborn. She got the things signed, how I don't know. Now I or Philip or Robert, whoever has the best contacts, must see it through. We say: they can go to court, even appeal to a higher court. But she says *we* have to get the paper accepted.'

'They're afraid the court will reject the affidavits because the people who signed them aren't residents of Lambert's Bay,' said Belle. 'Ma didn't want to sign either, she said why should she tell lies?'

'What Leonora can't understand is our positions.' Oom Hendrik was pleased to be able to speak to Belle, she seemed to him to be sensible, perhaps she could have a chat with Leonora. 'If someone high up starts to suspect that we're involved in such conniving, distrust will creep in. No smoke without a fire, they say.'

'I understand, Oom.'

Arnold flipped his second beer open with a thumbnail.

Tant Rina sipped a soft drink. 'There it is: the telephone's ringing, Pappa.'

'It's probably your Oom Philip, Belle. Call me before you ring off.'

Oom Philip was her godfather, the eldest of her father's three younger brothers. He too had sent her money for the journey. She called Oom Hendrik. 'I said they shouldn't come to the airport, Tannie, it's unnecessary. Barry is in Standard Ten, he shouldn't miss a school day.'

From the stoep they heard Oom Hendrik talking to Philip.

'I'm just as perturbed. Told you too? And then put the phone down. No, damn it, Leonora is close to my heart. Nellie too. The nearest we had to a real mother. But damn it! Then you'll see what you can do? But be careful. Don't ask just anyone. Rumours start so easily.' He poured another whisky when he returned to the patio.

At table they spoke about her journey.

'I'll have to write a story: *Sister goes in search of brother's grave in Kenya!*' Arnold, who was a press photographer, teased. 'But it won't work. Politically wrong, old girl, soldiers wearing the red tab were no friends of our newspaper.' He raised his glass to drink to her journey: '*In search of my ancestors*. How's that for a headline? Eldorado. The Boere church. The small outpost spreading the word in darkest Africa ... a long-lost ancestor ...'

Belle was annoyed. All these vague references. Did these Transvaal relatives know about her mother's father who wasn't really her father? Her Oupa knew, but she couldn't imagine how they got to hear about it. She'd only ever heard her mother discuss it at home or with Oom Hennie at the Strand. As she sat on the little bench on the side stoep with all the potplants, she had told how she'd been carried through the bush, drops of moisture falling onto her from the leaves as the bearers brushed the thick stems aside. She saw the dark landscape, felt the hot air, she threw her arms around the trees, pressed against the bark, rubbed her cheek against the slippery, wet foliage, felt the drizzle that was not rain. She was no longer afraid, wished the morning would break. Her mother had said: Now Ozzie is lying where I grew up.

'You're talking rubbish, Arnold, my ancestors lived where yours lived, beyond the Hex River mountains. I'm not going in search of ancestors.'

'But what the hell are you going to do there?'

The wine had probably gone to his head, to hers as well. Oom Hendrik cleared his throat.

'Excuse the language, Oom.'

'I'm going to further my studies in French, in Geneva, seeing you ask. I'm simply going via Kenya.'

'It's a splendid thing she is doing, Arnold.' Tant Rina dished up a second helping on the plate he held out to her. 'We'll all be pleased that someone's visited poor Ozzie's grave.'

'You were surely not in favour of his joining up, were you, Oom Hendrik?'

Oom Hendrik pressed his napkin to his mouth, as if a scrap of food had stuck between his teeth.

'Oom Hendrik paid my air fare ...'

'That's right, child, but it was because of family ties, not because ...' Oom Hendrik started to explain: 'Not because I was in favour of taking part in the war. On the contrary. I belonged to the Ossewabrandwag, if you children can remember anything of that. And I'm proud of it.'

'Ma also supported the OB. Before Ozzie enlisted, she wanted to become a member; she'd already submitted her name, I think. With Ozzie in uniform and the red tab she felt she couldn't go through with it.' Belle felt she'd talked herself into a corner. 'But she's a strong supporter of the National Party, especially now. She just doesn't say anything in front of Pa. I've often wondered: perhaps she holds Pa responsible for his death … perhaps that's what …'

'Let's leave it there,' said Oom Hendrik. 'Those things are over and done with.'

It wasn't over.

Belle thought of Ozzie, how he had glanced up at his father over the coffin as if asking: Am I doing the right thing now, Pa? He with the slender young body, one shoulder dragged down by the coffin he was bearing; could Oupa have been so heavy? Or was it the red tab on his shoulder dragging at him, and pulling the other shoulder heavenward, up, up with the army cap clutched under his arm. His face had grown thin in the army, the cheek bones, the bones around his eye sockets, even the cartilage of his nose exposed. Her only boetie, to die so lonely and so far from home.

She took a generous mouthful of red wine. 'Well then, Arnold, should I bring you the wheel of an ox wagon? One lying there in the desolate bush of Central Africa? So that I can peep at you through the spokes and laugh at you and you can take a photo of me and write a story: *On the tracks of the wagon*?'

She spread her fingers like spokes and grimaced through them.

No one laughed or responded.

Tant Rina's upper arm quivered as she rang the bell quickly and hard. The plates were removed. 'Don't mock, my girl,' She wanted to restore peace. 'I mean about the ox wagon. Arnold's newspaper has a big quiz under way, about wheels and spokes and hoods, so that everyone gets to know the names. They broadcast it on the wireless; it's very popular.'

She kept up a flow of chatter while the black man with the red cummerbund placed the pudding bowl near her with the small bowls next to it, and her hands darted about, trying to create order at table in her domestic world.

'But that was 12 years ago, Tannie. I know all about the ox wagon, I carried the torch in the relay myself.'

'Let's leave it that,' said Oom Hendrik, tucking into his pudding. 'It isn't doing anyone any harm. If the ox wagon gives people pleasure, let it be.'

The sepia photographs of her father in uniform lay beside the little tent in her cupboard. How proudly Great-Aunt Issy gazed up at him as he towered over her. His family had been against his going to South West, just as they'd opposed Ozzie's joining up. Why had Ozzie and her father gone against the family's wishes? Where had it started? With Great-aunt Issy? Was she the instigator?

But now she was dead and Ozzie was dead and her father was a sick old man, and the young uncles, Oom Hendrik, Oom Philip and Oom Robert, were the clever ones and the strong ones ...

In the bedroom, Tant Rina said to her, 'They're fighting for white people, Belle, for the preservation of the Afrikaner nation. You saw for yourself all the natives at the stations, it's frightening ... and Leonora comes with her stories, upsetting her brothers ...'

Tant Rina removed the heavy bedspread and folded it efficiently against her chest. 'But we know you don't have such strong feelings about it all in the Cape ... about mixed blood, and half-breeds ...' The tante then put an extra blanket on the bed.

'You are mistaken, Tant Rina. We do have strong feeling, we know all about it, we know which families are tainted – "a touch of the tar-brush" Great-aunt Issy always said.' There was Great-aunt Issy again! 'We were warned, specially us girls. At university there was a very clever boy we were warned against.'

'We say: "Too much coffee with the milk".' Tant Rina sighed. 'If only you knew ... all the meetings, even here at home.'

'I also feel for the white people, Tant Rina. I am also in favour of the government.'

'All the meetings – so secret even I am not allowed to attend. I can't even take the eats and coffee in to them. I leave everything in the kitchen and once I'm in the bedroom they come out and fetch the refreshments themselves.' She had upset herself by talking about it. 'One would think I was a gossip ... If you only knew who had met in this house ... Who are all members of the Broederbond ... I recognise their cars.'

As she was preparing for bed, Tant Rina brought her a blouse as a gift for the journey. It was emerald green with a slight sheen on the fabric. She kissed Tant Rina gratefully. 'It's beautiful!'

'Pappa is waiting for me. Try it on when you get undressed: I thought the colour would go with your eyes.'

The curtains were drawn but she heard a creak and a sigh outside as the breeze dragged the leaves of the banana tree back and forth against the wall. There was a fanlight open at the top of the window and the curtains moved slightly as though they were breathing. The mirror was wide and tall. Belle removed her upper clothes, even removing her petticoat so only her bra was left. The blouse slipped silkily over her shoulders and breasts. She tucked it into her skirt. The gleaming material caught the light, highlighting the pointed shape of her breasts. She wasn't in the habit of looking at herself in the mirror. Only to comb out her thick blonde hair or to flatten her full eyebrows with a licked finger. She knew she wasn't conventionally pretty. Her hair was as fair as her mother's but as thick as her father's black thatch. But hers didn't curl like his did. Since her school days she had worn it cut in straight 'bangs' as Great-Aunt Issy called it, above her eyes. Great-Aunt Issy always had a say in how she looked because they shared a name: 'The child isn't beautiful, but she has something. There's definitely something there. Don't stride so, walk slowly, gracefully, shoulders back. Try walking with a book on your head …' She wore her hair long at the back; fastened up for school, a long pageboy for going out, casual and loose.

Perhaps the dark eyebrows were a clue to the 'something' Great-aunt Issy discerned. Here, in this strange bedroom with only low uneven light shining from the bedside lamp, she looked unfamiliar, even to herself. She had changed completely from what she'd been at university. She was pleased that she had not been in a steady relationship either at university or while she was teaching. She took a few steps back and watched the reflections move on the fabric. In that room her face looked different too. She licked her lips so they were wet and shining, and her mouth seemed larger and full of expectation. She pulled the blouse over her head, unhooked her bra and slipped the blouse on again. The material was soft and silky against her bare skin. As she fastened the buttons her arms brushed against her breasts, sending a strange thrill through her body. When she finally took the blouse off again, it was with some reluctance.

Arnold had offered to take her to the Palmietfontein airport. 'I may just come across a story out there.' But Oom Hendrik wouldn't hear of it. 'It's my privilege,' he insisted. Although he had to be at his office early, the car would come back for her and then pick him up en route. 'I'm escorting you to the airport, no arguments.'

'Let him,' Tant Rina told Belle. 'He can pay up if you're overweight. Those two suitcases look pretty heavy to me.'

Next morning she felt nervous so she was pleased he was taking her. In the dark parking garage where she waited for Oom Hendrik to come down from his office, she felt a knot in her stomach. It wasn't only the departure, but the flight too. He emerged from the goods lift and slid in behind the wheel: he wanted to drive himself. He kept his seat far forward and his head forward too, almost over the top of the steering wheel. His large hands gripped the wheel firmly so that his elbows jutted out sideways.

'These overseas flights are often delayed.'

'You must promise not to wait, Oom Hendrik.'

'I won't be able to, my dear. I'll just have time to make sure you're looked after properly and ask them to keep an eye on you.'

'It isn't necessary ... Have you ever been in a plane, Oom Hendrik?'

'Not yet. They say I should try it. Start by going to the Cape to get used to it.'

Palmietfontein airport seemed to her to be in the middle of nowhere. Just a stretch of veld and the white windsock nosing out sideways. The plane was parked to one side with ladders leaning against it and people at work.

'Lockheed Constellation,' said Oom Hendrik. 'You're flying to Livingstone and then Nairobi. They told me when I bought your ticket. First two-and-a-half hours and then a long pull of seven hours.'

'Why are you doing this for me, Oom Hendrik? Going to so much trouble to help me locate the grave?'

He looked down at her as he switched the engine off, then one hand left the steering wheel and came to rest heavily on her knee. His smile was slightly embarrassed. 'I suppose we want to feel part of you all down there in the Cape, despite our differences. Time flies by so fast. My old brother Stuart, I could have done more ... Oom Hennie ...'

She suddenly felt the same affection for this uncle as she did for Oom Frikkie, as if she belonged with them more than with her own mother and father.

'I don't want to deceive you, Oom Hendrik. I am not only going for the sake of finding Ozzie's grave. My ma doesn't know this, but I also want to look for my Oupa, not really my Oupa, but ... Oh, I don't know whether you know the story Oom Hendrik.'

'That your mother was adopted? Yes, I know that.'

'Not really adopted, but something like that. That's why I'm so pleased that the family isn't sending me straight to Europe, but that I'm stopping over in Kenya.'

'Just look after yourself, SussieBelle. We all love you very much.'

As her luggage was weighed, Oom Hendrik scrabbled in his wallet and put some notes down with her ticket. He pushed some money into her hand too. 'That's to pay from Nairobi onwards. Your things have been booked through as far as that. Take the receipt now and put it in with your ticket. Keep it safe. With your passport. He took her by the shoulders and pressed her against his stomach. 'Good luck, my dear.' He looked across the runway, checked the weather, assessed the windsock, and then studied the aircraft where work was still in progress. 'There's a delay. They can't tell how long it will be.' He looked down at her again. 'There's something of Father in you: you'll be fine. Don't worry about the flight. As I said, I haven't flown myself yet, but everyone says it's safe. I'm actually more confident about your flight than about all those east coast harbours. If you'd gone round by sea.'

It seemed to be a difficult decision for him to make, but once he'd checked his watch again, he said he'd have to go. She saw him to the car.

It was hot in the small waiting room. Her suitcases had been loaded: she saw them being pushed on a trolley across the veld to the aircraft. Another announcement croaked through the loudspeaker. Further delays; a faulty propeller. There was no sign of Arnold; no planes landed. They'd probably been delayed too. Her cool drink was tepid. After some time she bought two sandwiches and then went out for a walk: the veld was green but looked neglected. A couple of natives were wheeling bicycles along, others lay sleeping beside the road, their hats over their faces. Now and then one of them would call out to a passer-by. She went back to the waiting room, sat on the bench, and at long last she noticed the plane reversing but then it stopped again. The waiting room was filling up but she remained aloof from the other passengers.

It was already late afternoon, the shadows were lengthening. It was a relief when they were summoned at last. Not many people boarded: only about 20. She was the only one travelling on her own. She felt a moment of panic when the door was slammed shut and the plane began to move. Initially the ground rolled slowly past the wings. When they reached the runway the propeller turned with a deafening noise; it roared in her ears, the earth jerked past, the body of the aircraft shuddered. Her stomach muscles contracted as the nose started to lift, the small wheels beneath the plane were retracted with a thud, and the earth receded. Her ears were completely blocked.

'Yawn; hold your nose and swallow,' said the steward who came to sit beside her. The plane bucked and trembled but eventually it started to travel along more steadily.

'I'll come and tell you when we fly over the Vic Falls, but you won't be able to see anything because it'll be dark. But you may be able to hear the thundering,' said the steward.

She did hear the thundering far below as the dark water drilled a breach into the still darker earth, no light, no foam, just sultry gloom; she was part of the dark vortex, she was slung about in the whirlpool like an uprooted tree stump, the dark waves closed over her head and she sank.

She stumbled down the steps, half dazed from the journey, the violence of the rough landing and hard braking. She followed the direction taken by the other passengers; they stood around in the waiting room at Livingstone. They were called again half an hour later. She walked back through heavy warm air, and the sky was pitch black with stars like specks of white fire. The pilot was preoccupied with writing up his records and testing his controls in the cockpit; she was seated close to him and he waved a hand in terse greeting. She ducked and squeezed into her seat. He's taking me into darkness, she thought, and into the unknown.

4

Philip, the eldest of the three younger brothers and the one with most political influence, was the most difficult to persuade.

'Once there is the least sign of deviance, even once a difference of opinion is associated with you, it means the end of your career, you must understand that, Leonora,' he said once again. 'If this concerned Nellie herself …' His voice became more conciliatory as he pronounced her name. Even as the eldest of the three 'boytjies' he had been dependent on her as a child; he had, even when it was no longer quite the done thing, crept into her bed with the other two, nestling under her arm, hungry for her warmth. 'If it were Nellie herself, there'd be no question, but people of mixed birth, related to her only by marriage …'

That was when she said: 'Even if it was Nellie herself you'd probably still have objected. You're only too grateful it isn't Nellie herself.'

'Mother would never have taken her into our home if there'd been any question of her background.'

But Hendrik phoned back, still feeling emotionally moved by Sussie-Belle's departure. 'We mustn't disregard our family ties, or our past. Between the three of us we'll do something about it for you, Leonora.'

And he straightened his shoulders. If my service to the nation, my loyalty to my people does not owe me even that – sworn statements from registered Cape Town and Worcester residents, validating two girls from Lambert's Bay ... well then, what's the use ... pillar of the community ... he heard Oom Hennie's words from afar ... pillar of the community. Were the words mocking him?

Two days after SussieBelle left, Leonora drove from Wellington to Oom Bertus's farm to set Nellie's mind at rest: 'Just sent the girls to Frikkie so that he can take new photos. The affidavits have been signed. Frikkie has them; he'll send everything to Pretoria. Hendrik has promised they'll have new identity cards issued. And, if your sisters ever feel awkward about staying on at Lambert's Bay, I'll find them work and decent lodgings in Cape Town, so they can start a new life from scratch.'

They were sitting in the big farm dining room. Nellie went to fetch coffee, and Baby clasped Leonora's hands and kissed them – such thin, bony little hands. What a contrast with the large belly she was carrying.

'There, there,' said Leonora. 'It'll soon be settled.'

But it wasn't settled. Nellie asked Leonora if she'd take the cup of coffee to Bertus who was sitting in his little office and did not feel inclined to join them in the dining room.

'He's distancing himself from us, Miss Leonora,' said Nellie.

She had to walk around the stoep to enter the small office through the outside door. On the wooden step, on a couple of old sacks, lay a bitch with pups. They pushed at the old dog, shoving and nuzzling to get at the teats. The puppies stood on their hind legs, clawed with the front paws, sniffed with their little snouts, bumped and pushed one another out of the way. The old sacks had started to stink. Leonora knocked at the door, turned the knob and entered. Oom Bertus was sitting with his back to the door, on an easy chair, which had been upholstered in leather many years earlier and had worn thin in places. Two walking sticks leaned against the arms.

'And the walking sticks? Since when have you needed walking sticks?' She placed the coffee on the little bench she'd pulled up.

He gave the semblance of a smile. 'Good day, Miss Leonora. Oh, the legs aren't what they used to be.'

'Not as strong as in the days when you came courting Nellie!' She had known him since then.

The feeble smile reappeared, but his eyes didn't smile. He drank the coffee she passed to him. When he took out the khaki handkerchief to wipe his moustache she noticed with concern that he also wiped his eyes. She said nothing.

Against the wall just above the roll-top desk – now open so that the papers and stationery and accounts, packed neatly in piles, were visible – hung two large oval photos of his mother and father. Pa with his waistcoat buttoned right up. The hair brushed with a middle parting, flat against the head, the beard and moustache neatly combed. Ma with breasts pushed up high by whalebone, a brooch pinned on the upright pleated frill around the neck. Her hair was drawn back flat off the forehead. More family photos hung around them, grandmothers and grandfathers. There was a set of antelope horns on a wooden mount, a gun rack, and a pipe stand. She smelled pipe oil.

'Well now, Oom Bertus, one of these days you'll have a grandson. An heir, if it's a boy. How many Albertuses have there been?'

He didn't reply. As she'd feared, he needed to wipe his eyes again. This time she'd seen the tears overflow. She removed the cup and saucer and sat on the little bench. She leaned over toward him. 'What is bothering you, Oom?'

'You're the only person I am going to tell this to,' he said slowly. 'May God forgive me. At night I struggle as Jacob struggled against the angel. But since my daughter-in-law told me she had "mixed" written on her baptismal certificate and I heard about her sisters' identity cards, my heart has been broken. I can't pretend that I don't feel it.'

'But the cards have been corrected, it's all fine now, Oom.'

'You did it out of the kindness of your heart, but it's still cheating. And the same blood flows in the veins of my grandchild.'

'No, Oom, no. It's the devil tempting you to think like that.'

She got to her feet and started pacing up and down the room. Her voice was angry. 'And it's a dominee who has set the devil loose among us. That someone as God-fearing as you should even think of yielding to it. It's as Smuts says, something has gone awry in our nation, we are sick to the soul. You shouldn't give in to these thoughts.'

'My ancestors look down at me from the walls. I read reproach in their eyes, this little room is no longer a refuge to me.' The old man shook his head in the same way Nellie had shaken her head in Leonora's house that afternoon: victim of something they were defenceless against.

'They are reproaching you for entertaining such feelings in your heart. Good heavens, Baby is still the same dear girl you loved so much. Nothing has changed.' She groped for words to convince him. She tried the old argument. 'Why do you think the people in parliament said that at registration ancestry should not be considered? Why, Oom Bertus, why? Because half of them would have to be reclassified if that had been involved … we all have mixed blood, Oom, all of us. And what does it matter? Mixed blood?'

Now she knelt at his feet. 'You're a good man, with a good wife and son and daughter-in-law and a grandchild on the way. Thank God for them. Baby is one of us. She's the victim of a diabolical law. You must compensate for what has been done to her, Oom. You should invite her sisters to the farm before they go to work in Cape Town.'

He tried to speak, but she stopped him.

'I know you aren't a Smuts man Oom, I shouldn't have mentioned his name, but Malan is also only human. Most important is your own conscience. Otherwise the law will succeed in turning us into people of stone. People with stone hearts. We won't allow that to happen, Oom, that's a vow. Living hearts filled with evil are even worse than stone hearts.'

Because her words to Agnes were still bothering her, Leonora went to see Stuart and Agnes on the way back to Cape Town. She slept in Belle's room.

Stuart told her: 'The test results weren't good,' he was sitting with them in the lounge in his dressing gown. He was smoking more, she noticed, and Agnes let him be.

'It's the prostate as well, sis.'

Then the bravado was back – all the familiar bravado of the old days that still irritated Agnes, in spite of periods of reconciliation. He smiled. 'What's the saying? Never say die. There's life in the old boy yet.'

'You must be positive, Boetie. It's really quite common. Are they going to operate?'

'He's scared of the knife,' said Agnes who was sitting knitting.

5

Shortly before dawn they landed at Nairobi. It was the start of an ordinary, warm, colourless day.

There was no delay at the immigration counter, and the white official gestured to a black guard to bring her suitcases. The taxi into which she and her luggage were eventually loaded had a strange smell. There was another passenger on the front seat, an Indian street vendor. His merchandise was loaded in the boot and her two suitcases upended on the seat beside her. She was accustomed to only white passengers in a taxi with her; she clutched her handbag, her camera.

They drove at speed, she felt as though she should duck away from buses, bicycles, rikshas, pedestrians. At the corners she clutched the door handle. She could see people milling about everywhere: indigenous people, half-naked men, hair plaited up and smeared with mud, barefoot black women with lengths of bright material wrapped round under their arms and above their breasts, their arms up, steadying the flat baskets of fruit or vegetables on their heads. She saw a couple of Indian men in white garments with white turbans – she'd learn later that they were Sikhs, who were not permitted ever to cut their hair, all that hair was twisted up under the turbans. There were also Indians in western garb, in cars or on bicycles; rows of small street shops where Indian women stood in the doorways wearing shabby saris. A strange aroma permeated the air. When they stopped at a traffic light she smelled it.

Even after they stopped at the station, the two men in front were still arguing. Paying scant attention to her, the driver called a pitch-black old man in knee-length khaki pants, with a khaki shirt hanging loose over them, to drag her suitcases out of the taxi one by one. The driver accepted a South African banknote from her. But the porter's wizened claw rejected it. She'd have to change her money.

She could get Kenyan money in exchange for her notes at the ticket office, but when she went to buy her ticket her mind suddenly went blank. The ticket seller waited, but she couldn't recall the name of the siding. The porter wanted payment.

'The junction on the main line to Kitale,' she stammered. Oom Hendrik had managed to find out that the men in Ozzie's battalion who'd died of blackwater fever were buried near the village of Kitale. 'Leseru,' said the ticket seller, and pushed her ticket and money through under the burnished copper rails. She'd planned this all for so long, digging up information in the unlikeliest places, and now she was dithering: Have I got the right ticket? Where am I going?

The strange conglomeration of people and sharp light and colour and aromas buzzed around her. She felt faint; she hadn't slept during the night. Whom was she going to? Where? To the Oupa first, or to the grave? She couldn't believe it: when she opened her old atlas to look up Kitale, and saw the little cross her mother had drawn there when she nagged as child: Where, Mamma? Where did you live? Probably not the same place, but certainly in the same vicinity. Strange: no one ever asked how she was going to locate the grave. They were so concerned with putting her on the train and then the aircraft, they never gave a thought to what would happen once she arrived. The sleepless night made her indecisive. Or was it because she had been torn away through the air, the noise in her ears the whole night long? And then deposited in a strange world? She took a firmer hold on the handbag and the camera hanging from her shoulder.

The porter had carried her suitcases to the waiting room reserved for women. He placed them at the door and she had to push them from there. The suitcases were too heavy, they wore her down: she had to get rid of something. Both summer and winter clothing had been packed because Tannie Leonora had said … Tannie Leonora, who had travelled so much. Why hadn't she advised her to travel light? The two suitcases stood next to her like dead weights. She could scarcely move them.

It was hot.

She half-reclined on the bench; she wanted to try to sleep. She rested her arm heavily across the suitcases. The train wasn't to depart for hours. But then she sat up again; she did not want to oversleep. She was hungry and thirsty, but she couldn't leave the suitcases to go and buy something. Carrying them was not an option. There was a black woman who came to wipe the basins and clean the toilets, but she didn't look like a maid: Belle had never heard of a maid who could speak English so well. She felt intimidated. Then she remembered. Of course: Leseru.

She must have slept after all, for when it was announced over the loudspeaker that the train to Kampala was about to depart, she realised the black woman had shaken her arm to wake her. She was grateful.

The black woman also found the porter to carry the suitcases again. She was still confused by sleep when the train left, vaguely saw city lights, then nothing.

In the dark of the night the conductor came to tell her: 'We've nearly reached Eldoret, then it isn't far to Leseru.'

She sat up straight next to her suitcases. The train was almost empty. She went out into the corridor to speak to the conductor, but he knew nothing of the war graves. He knew Kitale slightly: 'It is easier to get there by car.' She continued to stand there. The swaying of the train was soothingly familiar.

An English soldier came staggering along the swaying corridor. He'd been drinking in the dining car. His cap was tucked under his epaulette, and she couldn't tell whether he was an officer or not. He came to stand next to her and put his arm around her, tried to press her against him. His speech was slurred: 'I'm getting off at Leseru too; the conductor tells me I must help you. We sleep on the st … station tonight, too dark to go home.' He began to sing: 'I'm tired anna wanna go home, hadda little drink inne middle o' the night …' By then he had both his arms around her, holding her tight and pawing her clothes, his face burrowing in against her neck. She pushed him away so violently that his head bumped against the sliding door of the compartment. 'Bitch,' he said. Saliva dripped from his mouth as he rubbed his head. He made for her again, but the conductor came hurrying down the corridor, took him by the arm and pulled him away from her. He took him across the bridge to the next compartment. 'By morning he'll have a hangover and he'll be ashamed about this evening.'

'It doesn't matter,' she said. 'I know that type.'

The train drew up at the small siding of Leseru in pitch darkness. The conductor jumped down. The soldier was there again, clumsy and unsteady, and he handed the two suitcases down from the bridge. With the conductor helping her, she had to jump down because there was no platform. The train jerked away and she watched the small light at the back disappear in the distance. The night air seemed sharp to her nostrils.

A lantern hung in front of a sort of shed. Two black workmen came out of the shed, a white man in black railway uniform yelled at them, 'My God, this way, wake up, this way.'

He pointed at a number of wooden crates, which had been unloaded from the train and were stacked a bit further down.

'Hang on a minute, lady. I'm coming.'

The workmen trudged back and forth, carrying the crates to the shed. The railwayman held up the lantern and she watched the strange moving shadows of the stooped bodies with the heavy crates like growths on their backs. The soldier who'd disembarked from the train tugged at the arm holding up the lantern. He had a cigarette in his mouth.

'Gimme a light.' The railwayman produced a box of matches. With his attention still focused on the porters, he spoke to Belle.

'Now what would a lady like you be doing in this godforsaken spot in the middle of the night?'

'Kitale?' she answered

'It'll be two days before the next train goes to Kitale. Trouble on the line. Didn't they tell you?'

'Don' you worry.' The soldier had evidently forgotten about her rejection and was trying to lay claim to her. 'I'm looking after the lady.'

She ignored him.

'Can the boys take my cases to the shed? May I stay with you in the shed tonight? And could you get this pest off me?'

'Will do, lady. But I have to be careful – these army types. Thrown out of India, now they think they own Africa.'

While the air outside was fresh, almost cold, it was close in the shed. The railwayman pushed crates aside and she saw a camp bed. He took the soldier by the arm. 'Let's give the lady the bed, hey? Gimme a smoke, let's get a breath ...' and to her: 'The niggers won't bother you, lady, they're right at the other side ... now don't you fret about anything ...'

She was so tired that she lay down on the camp bed, placing her handbag under her head. The man had taken the lantern with him, it was pitch dark, but gradually the night light permeated the shed. It was a stranger place than even the aircraft when the lights were dimmed during the night. The strong, unfamiliar smell was part of the strangeness. She couldn't see much, only the slightly lighter area surrounding her and the camp bed. She felt cut off from all that had taken place previously. But she felt no fear, rather excitement as though she was standing on the edge of something immense. In the distance the railwayman chatted to the soldier, now and then she heard laughter.

On the plane, at Nairobi station and on the train she had merely dozed off, she now fell fast asleep. But her fingers never relaxed their grip on the straps of her handbag and camera.

When she awoke, she saw that the camp bed was at an angle next to a table with a burnt-out candle in a candlestick. The shed was stacked with crates and bales. To one side tanned hides were packed in heaps, almost reaching the roof. The stench emanated from the hides. Through an opening between the bales she saw the edges of the hides were dried out and curled up. Here and there appeared what seemed to be clots of dried blood, or was she mistaken? Was the hide and hair the colour of blood? The brand names of candles, matches and food were stamped on some of the crates.

She drew a comb through her hair and smoothed her clothes. She walked out inquisitively. It was early morning; as far as she could see were ridges and sparse vegetation; a few camelthorn trees. The sun was still low in the sky; after the stuffy shed the morning air was fresh. She took a deep breath. Right next to the shed ran a gravel road. The train rails shone, the main line disappeared behind an embankment behind which she could see a water tower.

She heard voices around the corner of the shed. A military jeep was parked there with a soldier behind the steering wheel, his arm outstretched; two more came strolling up with the railwayman. Her presence was obviously diverting.

'Sorry, we've no bacon and eggs, or toast and marmalade, but we'll take you anywhere you like, miss.'

She couldn't possibly wait two days for the train to Kitale. Everything seemed to be going her way, as if it was meant to be; taken out of her hands. But when she asked, the soldiers had never heard of a Greylinck settlement. Neither had the railwayman.

'Haven't been here long, miss, and these blokes neither. Come to fetch provisions and their pal.'

The soldier had slept off the previous night's drinking; he climbed into the back of the jeep. The driver thought awhile.

'Like to help you, miss. Look, I'll tell you what. About 20 miles from here, at our turn-off to the camp, there's a small settlement. Coolie-*dukas*, the lot, been there ever since... well, a bloody long time. The coolies or the kaffirs will know. Hop on.'

The railwayman nodded his approval. 'There's safety in numbers, miss ...' There was no opportunity for arguments, for her cases had already been loaded onto the Jeep. The railwayman noticed her hesitation and encouraged her. 'I'd take the lift if I were you. Can't say when you'll get another chance.'

Reverse gear, turn, dust rising from the corrugated road. Squashed between the two soldiers in the front of the jeep, she shook and she jolted. The soldier next to her laid his hand on her knee to steady her, the driver did the same as he changed gear. The soldiers had to shout when they spoke. She answered few of their questions.

It was a relief when they stopped at a group of corrugated iron buildings, drawing up in the shade of a few thorn trees. The two soldiers took hold of her upper arms and lifted her off the jeep. She stamped her feet on the ground to restore her circulation, her legs were stiff from being held at an angle to avoid gears and soldiers' hands. The five soldiers strolled into the *duka*, and came out carrying bottled cold drinks.

'Not cold, but it's wet. Would you like one?'

She shook her head. She walked into the small shop. It was close under the zinc roof, but the earth floor and the half-light created an impression of coolness. The goods for sale – fabrics and clothing, tinned food and soap, ornaments, a couple of tanned hides – were exhibited on shelves against the walls. On the floor were sacks from which dry goods would be scooped and weighed. There was an old-fashioned black iron scale.

An old Indian man stood behind the counter. He wore a silky waistcoat over a long white garment, a small black brimless cap on his head. He had a short white beard, and gold-framed spectacles with half-lenses. He issued the soldiers with change and entered what he'd sold.

'May I?' Belle asked, and when he nodded, she sat on a high seat next to the counter. After the smell of dust and the soldiers' sweat, the stuffy but exotic aroma in the shop – spice, betel nuts, even massala – enhanced the impression of coolness. Or of different-ness. The old man moved down to where she was sitting. He pushed a bottle of dark-coloured cold drink across to her. She took it. It was tepid and sweet, with a tart, almost bitter, burning taste.

'I have come to look for the old man who brought up my mother. Daniel Greylinck,' she said. ' He farmed somewhere round here. But it was long ago. A half-century ago.'

The other soldiers, bored with looking around in the *duka*, had gone outside. They sipped their drinks and stood around.

They were probably waiting for her.

'You've been here long,' she prompted the old man, 'you must surely have known him.'

The old man completed his entries, and then closed the book.

'Yes, we are friends,' he said. 'He is old like me.'

Strange, she thought, when I crossed the threshold, I already knew I would find what I was searching for here. She stood up and leaned across the counter. 'Where will I find him?'

He tilted his head, as they heard a lorry leaving the gravel road and pulling up in front of the *duka*. The old man had a gold filling in a tooth which caught the light coming in through the open door each time he spoke ... He tapped the backs of her hands outspread on the counter.

'Good luck has come with you. That lorry comes from his farm. Hussein Badir brings goods to barter and fetches provisions.'

'Hussein Badir?'

Before he could reply she heard the door of the lorry slam and a young Indian man came into the *duka*. He was taller that the average Indian and had to stoop at the door. She was aware of a vague impression of movement, of a man in khaki clothes doffing his hat, wiping the back of his hand across his forehead and saying, 'Salaam alaikum, old man. And something to drink, please.' He sat down on the chair she'd just vacated. When he lifted the bottle to his mouth and threw his head back, she saw him more clearly: Slender build, probably early thirties; straight black hair swept back from his high forehead, as if combed back carelessly with his fingers, very smooth and black, as though oiled; thick heavy eyebrows and deep-set eyes. After the red, sunburnt soldiers, the dark colour of his skin, particularly around his eyes, was his most prominent feature. He looked at her, and then at the old man.

'She has come looking for you: Old Greylinck's family. She wants to go out to your place. Can you take her along?'

He shrugged. 'Does he know about her?' The old man looked at her. She shook her head. 'I didn't let him know.'

'Well then. If it is his family ...'

He stood up, went out and called the black youngster who'd come along on the lorry. 'Not started to unload yet? Wait, you can't manage. I'll come and help you.'

The jeep started to idle. The driver called to the soldiers to get in. Then to Belle. 'Coming, Miss? Did the old man give directions? We're in no great hurry, we'll take you there.'

She sensed that they felt possessive of her because she was white, and they wanted to present a united front with her against the Indians. This irritated her. Her two suitcases were still on the jeep. She indicated to the old shopkeeper that she would return. She looked at the Indian who was at the lorry busy taking the loaded goods handed to him by the black boy. He glanced up at her, awaited her reply.

What the hell is wrong with me? she thought, say something ... She pulled herself together, after all, she'd known all along what her decision would be. Deep down inside herself she knew.

She told the soldiers, 'I'm going with him. He'll take down my suitcases.'

'The real colonial miss, hey.' It was the soldier of the previous evening. 'He'll take down my suitcases,' he mocked.

'Ag, all right, I'll do it myself.' She tried to reach the suitcases, but the soldiers taunted her, held on to the suitcases. It was so hot, the exertion made the sweat run down her body.

'Let go,' said the driver. 'It's her life.'

They released the suitcase, she put it down, staggering as she did so. The young Indian man came to help her with the second case. He did it unwillingly, with scant grace. The 'Ag' had betrayed her. One of the soldiers teased her, 'South African, hey? They won't like your going with the coolie.'

'For Christ's sake, it's her life, now shut up,' said the driver. The jeep took off in a cloud of dust which hung suspended in the hot, still air.

She returned to the *duka*, digging clumsily in her handbag for money to pay for the cold drink. She had to force herself to control her trembling. In the *duka* she sensed a new enmity. The old man didn't say a word, the young man continued to unload and pack as if she wasn't there.

I didn't mean anything, she wanted to say, but she didn't dare speak.

When he'd finished he only said, 'We're going now.'

Her cases were already on the back of the lorry. He held the door open and when she climbed in, he said: 'Move up. He also sits in front.' He's doing this on purpose, she thought. He knows very well we don't have black people ride up in front at home. But she moved up. She held her legs at an angle away from the gear leaver. He'd taken off his hat and placed it against the rear window. He combed his hair back with his fingers, just as she'd surmised.

In his khaki long-sleeved shirt and long trousers he looked cooler and more comfortable than the English soldiers in their shorts and short-sleeved shirts, the flesh of their thighs swollen and red from sunburn, the fingers puffed up with reddish-brown hair.

Then the boy also climbed in and she was squashed between them. She tried sitting on one buttock.

'Relax, there's enough room.'

The boy sat pressed tight against the door, his arm and elbow on the windowsill. The jeep's cloud of dust had settled.

'Is the camp near here?' she asked.

'Not far.'

'Why are there so many soldiers here now?'

Once again he shrugged. 'Supernumeries from India. They patrol: theft, game theft, ivory theft. Throwing their weight around.'

The road was bumpy and rough. She was thrown about, against the Indian, then again against the boy. She had nothing to hold on to. She abandoned herself to the motion. She relaxed her body and that improved things. The Indian – she couldn't even recall his name – appeared deeply preoccupied, his attention on the road. Twice he stopped so that the boy could climb out to tighten the rope securing the goods on the back of the lorry.

'Is my Oupa's farm much farther?' She asked once when the lorry was quiet and the boy outside.

'About two hours.'

She sensed she'd be unwelcome. Why else the enmity towards her? They were after all her people, her mother's people. She didn't even know who he was.

At last, when the sun was straight in front, he stopped.

'You can get out, stretch your legs. There it lies – in front of you.'

She walked around to the front of the lorry. He came and stood beside her, pointed out a group of small buildings in a valley between a few low-lying ridges. Through the haze she noticed some activity in the faded landscape. She looked at him questioningly.

'There's the house,' he said, 'the leather factory is in the low buildings next to it. The rondavels, then to one side the shop and the workers' houses.'

They climbed in again. The nearer they approached the farm, the more slowly he drove, stopping a few times to allow black people along the road to get onto the back of the lorry. When they drew up between the buildings, there was activity around them. A woman in sandals and a flapping sari came hurrying to them through the black people.

'Thank the Lord you're back, Hussein. I'm so worried: he isn't well at all this afternoon. Since you've been away from early this morning ... you should have come to tell me you were going, I would ...' She fell silent when she saw Belle.

'She's one of the old man's people. I can't introduce you, I don't know her name.'

'Isobelle van Velde,' she said. 'Agnes is my mother. They call me Belle.'

'You can call me Auntie Latifa. Everyone calls me that.'

The woman wore small gold earrings. Her eyes were outlined with black kohl. She shook Belle's hand. 'Come in out of the sun.' The boy had off-loaded her two suitcases. 'Bring them in,' she told him.

'I should have let you know I was coming, but I didn't have your address. If the old man at the shop hadn't known ...'

'You would have found out. Everyone knows about him.'

Belle followed her into the house. Had there been bitterness or warmth in her voice? She couldn't tell.

'I'll have to prepare him first, he isn't feeling very well today. We hadn't expected a visit.'

I'm not a visitor, Belle felt like saying, I'm family, my mother grew up here, and I am after all a white person, I'll take care of him ... My mother loves him. She has been longing for him all these years.

The woman had taken her across the threshold of a large, dark living room. The ceiling was made of poles and reeds, packed with clay, which made it cool; the floor was smeared with clay. It was so dark she couldn't make out any windows. After a while she was able to see. The furniture was the old-fashioned, cheap kind one finds in poor farmhouses, she thought. Neglected. A sideboard with dishes and glassware heaped on it together as for an auction; a veneer table with a not particularly clean cloth. The armchairs were the old deep-seated kind, with unsightly water rings where glasses had been placed on the wooden arms – they spoke of other people, other contacts. There were cobwebs up against the ceiling in the corners.

They walked through to another room. It was darker still. Against the walls hung hides and a couple of mounted trophy heads. There was a bookcase with books, old books. Dried gourds with a variety of misformed shapes lay heaped up in a corner. It seemed as though they'd been thrown on top of one another to conceal something deep. Deep in the old-fashioned armchair reclined an old man, his head thrown back, eyes closed. His mouth was open, toothless; the moustache, discoloured by cigar smoke, moved slightly as he breathed. In an ashtray on the arm of the chair a half-smoked cigar smouldered.

The Indian woman put it out. 'He'll yet set the whole house on fire. Shame. He's having such a good sleep. And so restless this morning! Hussein, I was so worried.'

'Don't wake him,' said Belle.

She was aware of the presence of the Indian who had brought her. He placed a sheaf of papers on an open roll-top desk. She felt more ill at ease with him than with the woman. Even though the woman had a better reason for disliking her.

'I'm tired,' she said, 'if I could go to a room and unpack, and have a bath.'

'Where can we let her sleep?' said Auntie Latifa. 'The other room in the house is a storeroom, the other rondavel as well. There is only …'

'Only my rondavel,' said the Indian. 'They can take my things out.'

'We can have a tin bath brought in. I'll see to her, Hussein. You go to the factory, they were looking for you.'

'I'm causing you so much trouble.'

'We should have been expecting it by now.'

She was too embarrassed to say she was hungry; couldn't remember when last she'd eaten. Had the Indian man, whatever his name was, eaten before his early-morning trip? She was embarrassed to ask for food. 'Could I have some water to drink?' she asked.

The woman had taken her to the rondavel and left. Now she was standing in the space normally occupied by the strange dark man. She'd never in her entire life been in the room or home of a coloured person or an Indian – come away, stand at the gate and call, don't go in, her mother had always told her.

She wasn't even allowed to go into the little shops in the lower end of town – you'll pick up germs, her mother said. Now here she stood in his space; in a dim, cool, round space with a thatched roof. She saw a gecko scramble away into the thatch, she saw a spider hang swaying on a long, sticky thread; she wanted to scream, but killed the spider by bashing it with loose pages which she grabbed from the table.

She shifted her cases together – her island, her stronghold. The dark air was heavy, loaded with flowery sweetness. A black boy in white shorts and vest brought her threadbare sheets and rough blankets. He stripped the bedding from the iron bedstead and she re-made the bed. Her body would have to fit into the hollows on the worn coir mattress which he had ceded to her, reluctantly. The boy came back to remove clothes from the cupboard, khaki clothes, and she saw a silk shirt, tussore silk. He also took shoes, and then shaving tackle from the wash-stand. Where will the Indian man sleep? wondered Belle. The boy greeted her with a finger to his forehead when he entered, apologetically, for the last time. He took books from the table … books? But it wasn't the last time: he came back yet again, dragging a tin bath up the steps to the rondavel and brought buckets of boiling water which he poured into the bath – the small amount which slopped onto the mud floor soon dried. Belle drew the thin curtains across the narrow window, hung her coat in front of it. Then it was completely dark. She sat on the hard coir mattress with her arms folded across her naked body and waited for the water to cool.

The warm, somewhat brackish water rose up over her body and drawn-up legs; then she sank lower so that her legs were over the side and her shoulders beneath the water.

After her bath, she dressed in clean clothes. She'd washed her hair and rinsed it with water from a jug, and fastened it, still damp, at the back with an elastic band.

Then she lay on the bed, her eyes open, gazing up at the thatched roof. She heard farmyard sounds, the crazy cackle of a chicken chased and then slaughtered. Was that what they were to eat that night? What would they have eaten had I not been here? One doesn't put a chicken into the pot while it's still warm from slaughter, she thought. These aren't my kind of people.

Latifa came to fetch her. 'He's awake now. Come.'

They walked back through the dark living room to where the old man was sitting in the armchair. He was deaf; she was uncertain whether he fully understood who she was. He looked at the Indian woman who'd brought her. The woman placed her hand on his forehead. She stroked him. The brown of her hand echoed the dark age spots on his skin, on his bald head. She tried to pacify him: 'It's nothing, my darling, it's nothing, she's just come to meet you.'

She saw anxiety in the watery blue eyes. The hand reached for the woman's hand on his forehead, he clasped it tightly. She had to bend down so that he could hold her hand on his lap; she shuffled her stout body comfortably onto the seat of the chair she'd drawn up.

'He's not so well today, something is upsetting him,' she said.

I don't have the right to upset him, thought Belle. She suddenly felt sure: He has nothing to do with me. My mother was nothing of his; there's been terrible misunderstanding and unnecessary sadness. How, I don't know, but I think my mother caused him just as much harm as he did her.

She became aware of an ominous feeling of irreparable damage, there, in that room. He'd been right to send her away, she thought. Her regret was useless. She would have liked to come closer and touch his forehead too, but she didn't feel free to do so. She was only aware of an overwhelming, saddening knowledge – she couldn't tell what caused it; she wasn't the kind to get carried away by emotion – that damage had been done here, at this place. And the thought she could not banish: I don't want to cause any more harm here.

The man in front of her was not the brave Boer War hero, or the pioneer-farmer – had either of them ever existed? Just a stricken human being, whom the stout Indian woman, the woman who had once been young, was trying to nurse.

'I shouldn't have come,' said Belle.

The woman, apparently satisfied with the condition of the old man, stood up and took her by the arm. 'We'll eat now. We can talk later. We'll leave him sitting here, I'll bring him something and help him eat.'

'My mother …'

'I know, he sent her back to the Union. I couldn't believe it: such a small child. There was something amiss between them, or he was afraid of it. He sometimes talked during the night. Believe me, it was difficult for him.'

'Also for my mother.'

'But she was only a child. She could get over it.'

'I don't know whether she ever did get over it.'

'Come, let's go and eat.'

The Indian man was already seated at the table. He must have washed somewhere too, his hair looked damp; he was wearing flannel trousers and a grey silk shirt. The lamp on the table lit the planes of his cheek bones, intensified the darkness surrounding his eyes, also lit the knuckles of his long, thin slender fingers playing with a piece of china on the table, turning it over and over between his fingers. He lifted his head and looked at her. His eyes were dark and moist. What was it that attracted her to him involuntarily? Was it because he'd brought her into this strange place? Was it the odd journey? Where every word or movement was so inevitably significant? Or was it because they were excluded from the bond of devotion between the woman and her oupa? He continued to look at her.

Something inside her revolted. It is too intimate, she thought. I sleep in the hollows made by his body. On his bed. I breathe his breath.

She started to feel feverish. The dirty tablecloth had been removed from the table and replaced by a clean white tablecloth. It was still limp, unstarched and warm from ironing. The chicken which had been slaughtered was on the table, cubed and curried. 'Hussein,' said the woman, 'pour us some cold drinks.' The glasses had little red patterns on them.

The sleeves of his grey silk shirt were rolled up. His palms and the underside of his arms were lighter in colour than the backs of his hands and the outer surfaces of his arms. There was a long, brownish-red raised scar on the inside of his right arm.

Next to the dish of chicken was a plate piled high with flat pancakes. She saw no knife or fork next to her plate. Latifa laughed at her. 'I'll show you how we eat.' She took a pancake. 'Now this is the *chapati*,' she said, and put it on her plate, followed by a few spoonfuls of chicken curry. She broke a piece off the *chapati* with her right hand, twisted it into a roll, pressed it over the chicken and sauce, and put it in her mouth.

'Give her a knife and fork, Auntie Latifa,' said Hussein, 'you can see she's hungry.' He was eating in the same manner as Latifa, his fingers swift and deft. She felt clumsy and inept, but he paid no further attention to her. The curry was hot, the moistened rolled *chapati* was tastier than bread. She ate, swallowed cold drink. He pushed his plate aside once he'd finished.

I'm getting sick: One minute I'm feverish, the next I'm shivering.

Latifa took food through to the old man. She remained with him for a long time.

'I'm sorry about what I said near the jeep,' Belle said, against her will.

He answered brusquely, 'What does it matter?'

He poured himself more cold drink, then looked at the closed bedroom door.

'You didn't know about Aunty Latifa? None of you in the Union?'

She shook her head. 'Only gossip.'

'There was gossip here too. There is gossip. But he's too old now. People don't gossip about old men.'

'She's pretty, and still so young.'

'She won't leave him now just because he's old.'

'I wouldn't have left him either, if I'd known,' said Belle, 'I would never leave someone I loved.'

Her words suddenly seemed uncalled for; she was annoyed to feel herself blushing. What was wrong with her? But he didn't seem to have heard her.

They finished eating. Aunty Latifa had not yet returned. They had nothing to say to each other. It was completely dark outside; she wouldn't be able to find the path back to the rondavel. He noticed she was looking towards the door and back again, and he pushed his chair back and lit a lantern on a side table.

'Come,' he said, 'I will show you the way.'

He held the lantern so that the light fell on the pathway. She walked in front, but was aware of him behind her all the time. He turned and said 'Goodnight' before they reached the door. She had to push and tug to get the door open over the cement slab.

She couldn't settle down. She'd slept during the afternoon and wasn't sleepy now. The moon had come up and she could see her way from the rondavel to the outside lavatory. With all the stars and the moon the wilderness was lit with a slightly purple glow, like daylight through a filter. The buildings lay like low, dark humps, shapes out of the ground.

The path back to the rondavel was too short; too soon she was back, had to shut the door and the night behind her. Where was he sleeping? Fast asleep after getting up so early, just on a blanket thrown down somewhere, his hair combed back through his fingers before he lay down?

She felt anxious: how would she get through the night? Second after second. I've never had to push time away before, like a wall, she thought. Seconds that had to be survived. She kept the oil lamp burning, she looked at the books left on the shelf after the boy had carried the others away, but was unable to fix her attention on them. She lay on her back, her head on her hands, and stared at the thatched roof.

In the morning, when she woke, the oil lamp had gone out. The sun was high and shone through the single narrow window. Before she lay down, she'd opened the curtain, and it was the sharp light on her face that had woken her. There was a film of perspiration on her face.

After she had dressed, she walked across to the house. She saw no one outside, only a bit further at the shop a few black women waiting on the stoep. Neither did she find anyone in the room where they'd eaten the previous evening.

'Auntie Latifa?' She called hesitantly.

She walked to the kitchen where the door stood open and the sun streamed in and a black woman was bending down to feed wood into the blackened stove.

'Auntie Latifa?'

The woman straightened up and gestured outside with her hand, in the direction of the shop.

'And inside?' Belle attempted.

The black woman didn't reply.

She didn't want to go to the old man's room on her own. She noticed some rolled-up *chapatis* in a small dish on the back of the stove. She took one. It was still warm. She ate it, then another. She also saw a coffee pot, took a mug from a shelf against the wall and poured herself black coffee.

The black woman gestured once more in the direction of the shop. It wasn't far to walk. She could hear sounds of people working behind the closed doors of the flat mud buildings – the factory. As she passed she became aware of the same stink that had been so strong in the shed at the train siding. But the lorry in which they had come the day before – could it have been the day before? – was nowhere to be seen. Then Hussein was not behind the closed door of the factory.

I don't care if he's gone, she thought, yet the yard seemed empty and desolate to her, the morning without purpose. It is only because I'm relying on him to get me away from here again, there's no other reason for me to feel abandoned.

The black women crowded on the stoep of the shop made way for her to get through.

Latifa was behind the counter, assisted by a half-grown black child.

He carried sacks, used the scoop to pour meal or sugar or whatever into brown paper bags placed on the scale, until the holder with the weights on stopped dipping and swaying and came to rest in balance. Then Latifa lifted the bag up, folded the top so that the ends made little ears, and gave it to the black woman who unknotted the money from her handkerchief. The next client placed her own container on the scale and a new, minute weight was added on the holder. The sugar flowed from the scoop until the holder, which had jumped up, dropped and dropped. Add a little, take a little away, add little by little until the balance came to rest once more.

'If you wait a bit, I'll close up here and walk home with you.' Auntie Latifa's sari of faded blue material had fallen back from her head and hung in folds about her shoulders. Perspiration beaded on her forehead. 'I can't just leave things.'

Shelves ran up to the roof on the wall behind the counter. Rolls of fabric, stacks of boxes with lids, thick glasswear, tin plates and mugs, enamel basins and water jugs, aluminium saucepans, cheap writing paper and pencils fastened in bunches, soap and bottles of medicine and packets with powders and pills were packed on the shelves. Three-legged cast-iron pots, leather shoes and sandals were chained to the poles supporting the roof. Through the dirty glass of the large round containers on the counter she saw children's sweets melted together by the heat. A dark smell of sweat permeated the shop.

'Come,' said Auntie Latifa. She drew the door shut behind her. The assistant told the women to wait. They stood back and sat down, backs to the wall, children and flies about them.

'Where has Hussein gone?'

Latifa, walking hastily looked up at her. 'Hussein? Away with the lorry … business. Did you want to go along?'

'I'd like to see the country,' but it sounded feeble to her. 'The reason I came here … to see my Oupa. But you don't allow me. I've scarcely spoken a word to him.'

'Now, why am I taking you to him?'

'But there is also another reason why I came. My brother died during the war and his grave is at Kitale. I must go there too.'

Across the threshold of the house, with the door closed behind them, it was suddenly dark. Past the dining table and chairs, to the inner room. Her eyes gradually grew accustomed to the half light. She smelled something strong and sweet. Latifa had taken a bottle of scent from a drawer and had wiped some across her temples, also on both her wrists.

She wanted to give Belle some of it. 'I don't want him to smell the shop on me,' she said softly.

The old man was sitting on the chair again but he seemed to be asleep, as on the previous evening. But when Latifa bent over him and lightly touched his forehead, and whispered to him: Salaam alaikum, the words recalled him and his eyes opened. Faded blue eyes with little life left in them. He turned his face to Latifa, and when she encouraged him, he looked at Belle.

'Sit,' said Latifa and pushed a bench towards her. 'You can hold his hand, it comforts him.' Hesitantly Belle reached for the hand lying on his lap smoothing and then crumpling the white bedcover that had been drawn over him. Dear God, it is what Great-Aunt Issy always did, she thought, taking the hand. The skin was strangely white for a hunter, with the dark age spots which she knew. The fingers were thin and the knuckles bent, but when she tried to relax them, there was unexpectedly strong resistance.

'My mother is Agnes Valeria,' she said. She bent nearer and spoke close to his ear, because at first she thought he couldn't hear her. 'She's the little girl who was brought to British East Africa. And sent back to the Transvaal.'

It was so long ago, it seemed he didn't remember. His forehead wrinkled, and she was sorry that she'd disturbed him. What for? she thought. So his restlessness can be transferred to me?

Then he spoke. 'The child left with the Portuguese.' To her dismay she noticed his eyes were filling with moisture, as if he was going to weep. Perhaps the flash of memory that had returned to him from somewhere had passed again; it was better that way, she thought. She felt like getting up and leaving but he prattled on like a child now.

'She wasn't my child after all, I didn't need to send her away, but they only told me later, after my mother had died. I could have kept her with me.'

She persevered with the question that had brought her there. 'Did you ever find out whose child she was, Oupa?' She sat down again, took his hands in hers. She no longer felt strange or nervous of him; he reminded her of her Great-Uncle Hennie. Oom Hennie had also been here in the wilderness, living in a thatched house that she'd known from her little sepia photos – was it after all he whom she had rediscovered here? Oom Hennie who'd also been bereft of wife and child, and then eaten away by doubt. She stroked the bony backs of his hands, pushed the swollen veins and let them fall back again, slowly. It made his fingers relax.

'My wife never told me, my wife didn't know, I never saw her again.'

He became restless, the hands struggled from her grip. She was astonished at the strength in the withered fingers. His voice was also stronger.

'She wasn't my wife's child. When I sent her away, I didn't know she wasn't my child. But with the two of us alone like that …'

He began to drool, the tears trickled from his eyes, his mouth twitched. Latifa, who only half-understood his words, told Belle, 'That's enough.' She removed his hands from Belle's, she began stroking his forehead softly, tenderly; it calmed him. 'It doesn't matter. It was so very long ago.'

He knew Latifa's voice and it comforted him.

'What is this child looking for then?'

'She is *her* child. And she had a brother who is buried near here.'

'Many children are buried here. She should rather also have died. Then there would have been peace for my soul.'

'No, come now. There is nothing for you to worry about.'

Belle stood up and walked out. She sat at the dining room table with the dirty cloth and she wept. Latifa came to sit next to her, but did not touch her. On the sideboard amongst the dishes lay a man's handkerchief, Hussein's khaki handkerchief. Latifa handed it to her and she hid her face in it. It smelt strange. She opened her mouth and pushed a corner of the handkerchief into it. She wanted to swallow the scent. She thought again: I'm getting sick. The handkerchief had caused her to tremble again, she felt cold and then hot as if she was running a temperature.

'Tomorrow you can go with Hussein when he drives to the veld,' said Latifa. 'The day after that he can take you to Kitale, I'll tell him. Then you'll have done what you came here to do.'

Then it will be concluded, thought Belle, then she would be able to leave this place where her mother's anxieties had taken hold of her too.

Latifa went back to the shop and Belle wandered about – to an enclosed piece of land that had once been a garden, she could tell from the collapsed fence and the odd self-sown flower that made a splash of colour. Her mother had been too young, it must have been Latifa's garden, when her Oupa was young and strong. The strange emotion she'd fought off earlier engulfed her again. When she thought of a young Latifa and her Oupa. She threw the flower she had picked on the ground, as if it were poisoned, and walked back to the rondavel.

The previous night when she'd not been able to sleep had been endless. Now it was worse. The whole day lay ahead. She took a book from the shelf again. It was poetry by someone she'd never heard of. Muhammed Iqbal. The words were incoherent; she couldn't make sense of it at first. But the book had been read to tatters; it had to make sense.

Tho' I am but a mote, the radiant sun is mine:
Within my bosom are a hundred dawns.
My dust is brighter that Jamshid's cup,
It knows things that are yet unborn in the world.
My thought hunted down and slung from the saddle a deer.

'That has not yet leaped forth from the covert of non-existence.' She repeated the words over and over again.

Through the window, a window last cleaned a long time ago, covered in cobwebs, dusted with pollen from a wild plant unfamiliar to her, she saw the light of day running out. The sun had long since gone over.

Her book lay on the bed next to her with the khaki handkerchief in it as a page marker. She must have fallen asleep. She remembered weeping when she'd been in the living room with Auntie Latifa. Why had she wept? For her mother who had not known her father or mother? That seemed so distant and unreal. For the old man whose life had never recovered after her mother's departure? In her mind's eye, she saw Auntie Latifa's hand on his forehead, her wrist fragrant with the scent she'd dabbed on it first. Was this substitute not more than the child who had left could ever have been? As an adult woman, her mother seemed angular, cold and insensitively white, while Auntie Latifa was velvety brown and soft, with the flowing garment draped over her head and round her shoulder. The sari she'd worn for working in the shop that morning had been faded and washed out. But tonight?

She dragged her suitcase closer across the floor, then the second one, and leaned her knee on the lid to ease the pressure from inside as she unbuckled the leather strap. She unpacked, digging about until she found Tant Rina's blouse. Tonight she wouldn't wear the serviceable seersucker blouse and slacks she travelled in, tonight that green blouse would gleam over her breasts. She brushed her hair out and left it loose. While she was still brushing it, she heard footsteps on the path and a knock at the door.

'Auntie Latifa says dinner's ready.'

Hussein was still wearing his khaki work clothes. 'And this?' he said.

'I thought English girls never wore anything but navy and grey.' She pouted, for she was nervous. 'I'm not an English girl.'

But the pout and her words made her feel awkward. She regretted wearing the blouse, she'd have liked to go back and take it off.

Darkness had fallen suddenly. Latifa was adjusting the lamp in the dining room. As she bent over it and the light flickered and then glowed evenly, Belle noticed that she too had taken trouble with her appearance; a dark red sari, small ruby earrings and a tiny ruby stud in one nostril. Her dark hair – little grey in it as yet – was combed back, and shiny, perhaps with oil. Once again the sweet waft of soft perfume. A delicate, gold-embroidered border on the sari.

'We can go and say goodnight to him.'

He lay on the big bed, with the armchair at the foot of it. She walked around the chair to him. A silky, embroidered bedcover had been spread over the blankets. His grey hair had been combed back. The lamplight fell across his face so that his cheekbones and the line of his nose looked strong and proud. The hollow cheeks and the trembling lips were in shadow. The lines which caught the lamplight gave Belle a glimpse of the face of the man he'd once been: a fighter-Boer, a pioneer in the wilderness. The man her mother remembered.

He tried to speak and she had to bend down to catch the words: 'I bought you a little brooch that looks like your eyes. The stones are only small. I may not give you more, although I long to do so.' Then his chin began to tremble and she turned away. He was talking about her mother's brooch. She knew it well; it always had a special place in her mother's drawer. He was confused, his eyelids had closed again.

'He's wandering,' she told Latifa. 'He's confusing me with my mother.'

They ate chicken and *chapatis* again; the food was sharper, with red chillies. Her throat burned, her eyes burned, and she suddenly felt cheap in the green blouse. It was clear that the hidden things she had touched upon had caused pain.

'There was a white girl in Nairobi with your colouring: the same hair and eyes,' said Latifa. 'Oh, Hussein was so much in love with her! Just imagine!' She gestured across the table with a dripping *chapati* to emphasise her words. 'He actually hired a taxi to wait outside her house the whole day long, and take her wherever she wanted to go. But she just used him. Imagine what the taxi cost!' She took a bite, then added, 'She probably thought seeing she was white she could mess an Indian around.'

There was bitterness in her voice that had not been there before,

Belle noticed. Did they mess you around when you moved in with Oupa, with their prejudice and their scorn? My mother messed around in her whispered conversations with Oom Hennie, my mother's Ouma messed around when her father came to visit and they spoke of his coolie-breath. The people in this country – how did you put it the first day: everyone knows about him? – did they mess Oupa around too, just as his own wife messed him around? And that's why you're messing me around now, Auntie Latifa. Are you envious of the little emerald brooch, which I am not guilty of?

Hussein wished to blot out her words. He threw up his hands. 'Not guilty,' he said, 'I was 16, I spent all my pocket money on the taxi. The woman was probably over 30, I never spoke a word to her.'

'I'll just have to dye my hair black,' Belle said, immediately horrified at her words. What in God's name did she mean? She didn't dare look at him.

She was different from these people, she didn't belong here, she had to leave and get on with her studies in Switzerland. But studying seemed too distant and unreal now. Once more she became aware of the strange effect Hussein's nearness had on her, once more she thought of fever, once more she dreaded the hours she'd have to spend alone before seeing him again the next day. If she did see him again the next day.

Her thoughts may as well have been written on her face.

'Tomorrow I'm going to a prettier area than where I was today,' he said. 'You can come along if you like.'

She nodded.

'Auntie Latifa told me about your brother's grave. I'm free the day after tomorrow: we can go then. But I have to finish work at the factory tomorrow morning. Can you face driving in the heat of the day?'

'Oh yes.'

'You can come along to the factory. You might find it interesting. You didn't see it today.'

'The door was shut.'

He walked her to the rondavel, carrying the lantern to light the pathway ahead of her. This time it was he who first lifted the rondavel door then pushed it open, so that it didn't scrape against the cement step.

'I had the lamp filled with oil,' he said before turning to leave. 'It will burn for a long time if you want to read till late again.'

She wanted to say: I didn't read last night, it was today. She wanted to tell him: I know Iqbal off by heart – my thoughts hunted a deer and slung it across my saddle before it had even leapt from the covering of its non-existence. But he'd already disappeared into the darkness.

Had he also been awake in the night? Had he seen her light burning?

The next morning she and Hussein breakfasted alone. *Chapatis* and egg, and a type of wild plum unfamiliar to her. He drew her plate nearer and peeled a plum for her. It tasted bitter and semi-sweet, something like a prickly pear.

'Has Auntie Latifa eaten already?'

'She eats early, then sees to the old man before going to the shop.'

'Have you also been out already?'

'I went looking for fruit, you must be tired of *chapatis* by now. Eat up if you want to come across to the factory.'

He held the door of the mud-plastered building open for her. The smell, which had been so strong that night in the shed, was overwhelming in the factory.

'We treat the hides black people bring in. Cattle and game. Your Oupa loved to hunt. He started tanning, then expanded.'

Black workers looked up as they walked past. He adjusted something here, spoke a word of encouragement there.

'Do you know how Auntie Latifa came to be here?' he asked as they walked on. 'She was the young wife of a trader who came to barter. He fell ill and died during the night. It was still pretty wild here at the time; they had to bury him immediately. Auntie Latifa stayed on with your Oupa. She was still very young.'

'They surely didn't suspect my Oupa?'

He shook his head, smiling for the first time. His teeth were very white and gleamed in the half-light of the factory.

The dried, cured, shrunken hides lay piled roof-high at the entrance. There was little space to walk; they had to shuffle past in single file. Hussein stood pressed up against the stack of hides to let her pass. She brushed against him; she couldn't help it. Then he fell into step behind her and when she looked back, he indicated the direction with a movement of his shoulder: 'This way. Here are the vats.'

Square cement vats filled with a dark liquid into which the hides are thrown to soak: this was the source of the worst stink.

A couple of black workers prodded the hides with sticks, pulling them nearer, turning them, pushing them away. A bit further on hides were scoured clean across trestle tables. Still deeper in the factory, which had begun to seem to her like a shed, workers sat stitching at articles made from hide. The hides were dried and finished under a lean-to outside. To her it all seemed like something out of a picture book about life in the olden days. Was it the heavy atmosphere, or the smell or the half-light?

'It's amazing when the light falls in a stripe over the man's hands as he stitches,' she said. 'And this one – look: when he snips the hair stands erect on the bits that fall, just as if it was alive.'

He leaned across the trestle table and drew the skin nearer, folded it, allowed the hair to fall back across the folds in light waves. Then he threw it down on the table again. He'd touched her elbow as she moved towards him; the contact was searing. She wanted to see it again, but he'd walked on.

'It's a bit primitive here,' he said when she'd caught up with him and they listened to the chopping and stitching sounds of the machines, the scraping of the wet hides, and in the background the swishing of the dark liquid to and fro in the vats. 'But I have a lot of plans.'

'Do you live here permanently?'

It was as though she still couldn't imagine him here.

'Does it bother you? Auntie Latifa suspects that his relatives in the Union want to come and take over.'

'Take over?'

'When the old man dies. They aren't married. You're probably the blood relatives.'

'I'm not a blood relative. I don't know about the rest of the family.'

'Surely Latifa is entitled to the place, isn't she? It's a living. I came to help out when he fell ill. I like the place, I also like hunting. Perhaps I'll stay, perhaps I won't.'

'There's no thought of taking over,' said Belle.

He went to sit at a desk, not far from where the people were stitching, and began making entries. He called the workers one by one and gave them instructions in their own language. She stood around, picked up something here, looked at a leather object there.

'My people have shops in Mombasa and Nairobi. They take all I can supply,' he said as he closed the record book and put it away.

When they stepped out into the full sunlight, she once again felt the sticky burning on her skin, the dry stiffness, and the inadequacy of her fair skin. She pressed the backs of her hands to her cheeks. 'I must get a hat,' she said, 'like yours.'

'Your skin is too tender.'

He took a cigarette case out of his back pocket, drew out a cigarette and was about to light it, then thought of her and held it out to her. 'I keep forgetting you aren't an Indian girl.' She shook her head. The first match had burned down; he had to strike another to light the cigarette.

6

The young black boy did not accompany them that afternoon. Up until after they'd passed the huts she'd expected him to stop and call the boy. She was only assured they were to be alone once they'd climbed the steep incline, and the long curves lay behind them, and he turned onto a smaller, even rockier road – really no more than a track. There's more room in the cab now, it's cooler, she thought, knowing these were not the true reasons for her satisfaction.

They didn't speak. There was a newspaper on the backrest behind her and she unfolded it over her knees.

'I thought I'd be cooler in a skirt than slacks, but my legs are going to get sunburnt.'

Before long they turned again and the sun was behind them now. The shaking didn't bother her. At one point he let go of the steering wheel with one hand and put his arm around her to prevent her from bouncing too high. With the other hand he steered the lorry carefully and slowly across the watercourse that had washed away part of the track. She lay against the passenger door as the right wheel sank into the donga, and next thing she was tilted against him.

'Gosh,' she said, 'and I thought our farm roads were bad.'

And later, 'But where are we going?'

'Look around; this is a beautiful part of the world. A lot of bush, cattle country. Perhaps a buck now and then. We're going to pick up hides from one of your oupa's outposts. They sent a message that there's a kudu skin. That was a kudu skin I showed you this morning.'

She didn't notice much of her surroundings.

'You haven't told me anything about yourself. I don't even know whether you're married. How are you related to Auntie Latifa?'

'She's my mother's sister. Would I be driving around with you like this if I were married?'

She was longing to find out more, but didn't dare. She glanced at him sideways. His profile was regular, a handsome nose, and an attractive mouth. He was wearing the hat again. His right elbow rested on the sill of the open window; his shirt sleeves were rolled up. She saw the scar on the inside of his arm more clearly now. It reached from his elbow almost to his wrist, as though his arm had been ripped by a wild animal's claw.

'Doesn't the metal burn your arm?'

When he didn't respond, she said, 'We don't want the property. You must see to it that the old man draws up a will leaving it to Auntie Latifa. When my mother last inquired, his wife was overseas. They doubt whether her child is really his daughter. There might be nephews and nieces, but I'm sure you don't want them to get it.'

The track had petered out and he pulled up under a thorn tree. Around the small ring of shade the sun beat down white-hot. It was as silent as the grave. The opening of his door shattered the silence; he came round to open her door. On the ground, she hopped from one foot to the other. It was strange soil; yielding. Rather like a marsh. She slapped midges away.

'There must be underground water somewhere, it's always wet here. Which is a blessing of course,' he said. 'Our cattle kraal isn't far.'

'Is there drinking water?'

'An old well and a pump.'

They walked through a wild world. At times he held thorn branches aside so she could pass. The branches closed over again behind him. She stooped, her bare arms and legs were scratched, and she felt the sweat slowly trickle down her neck, under her shirt collar on either side.

When they reached the clearing, she noticed a slight rise ahead of them, probably a dam wall. Also a kraal of thorn branches, and not far from there a wattle and daub hut with its door closed. The gate to the kraal was open, and although the ground around the gate had been trampled, there were no cattle.

Hussein sat down against the dam wall. He took off his hat and wiped the sweat from his forehead and face with a handkerchief.

'It was a very long day yesterday,' he said, almost as though he was speaking to himself. 'I couldn't understand myself. I wanted to get away from you, but I had to force myself to stay away so long.'

Then he fell silent.

She sat down beside him. The silence whispered around them. Cicadas, she thought, or the hum of the scorching white-hot light. She'd never felt so keyed up in her life. Or so happy. She tried to focus her mind on something. 'What have we actually come to do here?'

He took the keys out of his pocket, selected one, let the rest drop on the ring and pointed to the hut door.

'This opens that door. I have to keep the hides under lock and key.'

He had picked a blade of grass and sat chewing it. Amusement spread from his lips, around the blade of grass, up past his nostrils to his eyes. As he put his hat back on, a lock of sweat-dampened hair fell across his forehead. It made him look vulnerable. She wasn't bothered by his amusement; she was smiling too.

'And have you nothing to say?' he asked.

'I'm still waiting for my drink of water.'

He heaved himself upright, the small shadow his elbows and bent knees had thrown on the dam wall disappeared. He strode up the slope, his body bent forward. She'd expected him to help her up, but he didn't. When he came down again, he said, 'Completely empty. Dry mud. No wonder he's gone off with the cattle. Just look at the grazing around here, exhausted.'

'The pump?'

'This way.'

Behind the hut was a stone wall around a metal drum sunk into the ground, and a pump with a wooden handle shaped like a sickle. An iron pole with a chain on it had been planted next to the pump; the handle was hooked to this. The soil under the pump was purplish-brown in contrast with the pale ground surrounding it. It looked damp: the moisture had dried up but the colour remained, like dried blood. There was a narrow white line of salt round the ring of darker soil.

Hussein unhooked the handle and started to pump. At first the water came in a trickle, but then he got a stream going almost white as foam. It ran off under their feet. He cupped his hand and bent to drink from it. He'd tossed his hat down and splashed water on his face.

'Come and drink,' he said.

She bent down, but even with both hands cupped, she couldn't manage it. The water splashed off her hands.

'Not like that,' he said.

But even when she knelt, not caring if she got splashed, she couldn't get it right. He pumped the handle again. When it rose he fastened it to the chain, and cupped both his hands. The water streamed through his fingers, overflowed at his wrists, then settled. Still kneeling, she drank from his hands. The water was slightly salty, but cool. Her lips couldn't get enough; she lapped with her tongue, touching his palms through the water. In his hands the water was the colour of a mountain stream. She drank it all.

'More?' he asked.

He pushed the handle down again, and as the water streamed out he hooked it fast and his hands caught the water. When her thirst was quenched he helped her up. He took out his handkerchief, bent down and started to wipe the mud from her knees. First one, then the other. He'd dampened the handkerchief at the pump, had her sit down. But when he'd offered her the handkerchief, she shook her head. So he hunkered down before her and with one hand in the tender hollow behind her knee, he rubbed the mud away. Then he wiped away the little trail of muddy water that had run down her leg, through the nearly invisible little blonde hairs. He rinsed the handkerchief and washed the other knee, his hand finding its place again in the tender hollow behind her other knee.

Then he got up. 'I must unlock and load the hides.'

The shadow of the mud hut had lengthened, and the sweet dove-grey light of early dusk crept nearer, filling this basin amid its protective ridges.

'Wait here.'

He pushed through the thorn bushes and brought the lorry nearer by a detour.

She insisted on helping him carry the hard hides he dragged from the hut. Together they lifted them from the ground and half carried, half dragged them to the lorry, where they lifted them and let them slip onto the back. Even where she was standing at the door, the smell was so strong that she had to turn her head away to catch her breath. The edges of the hides were tightly curled and cut into her soft palms. The red she had noticed in the station shed was dried blood between the hairs.

'Don't worry,' he said, but she kept on dragging and heaving beside him. When everything had been loaded, he went to a wooden board just inside the door. With the piece of chalk hanging there on a string, he wrote the number of hides he'd taken. Then he shut the door and pressed the padlock closed.

'We'd better get a move on,' he said once they were back in the lorry. 'It'll be dark soon. The lights aren't good enough for me to see the road clearly.'

The air was still sultry, but pleasant, and the tension had left her. She felt that the cab encompassed her entire world.

Latifa had already eaten by the time they got home. She had the dishes taken back to table. For the first time Belle saw her wearing spectacles, and her old sari in the evening.

'I'm on my way to the shop,' she said. 'Your oupa isn't asleep yet, if you want to say goodnight.' She took the lantern and went out.

'We'll go and say goodnight before we eat,' said Hussein. She followed him into the bedroom. The old man lay with his eyes closed, the bedspread pulled up over him.

Hussein bent over him. 'Salaam alaikum,' he said softly as he stroked the old man's forehead. He recognised Hussein's voice, the eyes opened and a hand emerged from the covers. 'We've had a good day, everything is going well,' Hussein soothed him, 'there's nothing to worry about.'

Belle felt tears fill her eyes.

'Goodnight,' she said. 'Goodnight Oupa.' Even though he wasn't her oupa.

But his eyes had already closed again.

As they ate, she asked, 'Off to the shop like that at night?'

'It is her night for doing the books, it's not because of us.'

They didn't talk much.

'I'm tired,' said Belle when they had finished eating, 'I think I'd better go to bed.'

'It's an early start tomorrow,' he said. 'I like to get going before sunrise.'

He escorted her to the rondavel with the lantern again. Neither of them spoke. He opened the door, placed the lantern on the table and lit it for her, then left.

When the door had closed behind him, she put her lips to the lantern handle, which was still warm from the palm of his hand; then she rubbed her cheek against it.

She fell asleep easily, her body now familiar with the hollows of his body in the coir mattress.

What new world am I entering? she thought before drifting off.

A knock at her door, a quiet Salaam alaikum, a hand on her forehead. 'Time to get up.' Then the receding footsteps.

She lay quietly for a few minutes, secure in the darkness before dawn. But the light lifted so rapidly in the small rondavel window that she dressed with a sense of urgency. Then she opened the door and breathed the chill morning air. The long, earth-coloured house lay low and still and dark. Behind the mud-plastered walls an old man lay gasping for breath. Turning his head from side to side in search of something – what? Then the gentle touch of a soft brown hand smelling of betel nut would bring a degree of peace. Cool brown skin on a feverish white forehead.

Through the silence she heard the stuttering of an engine unwilling to start. Let it take, she asked the heavens, so that no one wakes, for the solitude of the morning darkness was precious. The factory building was still locked; the workers' houses lay in darkness. She saw him bent over under the raised bonnet of the vehicle. And as she saw him, the body above the engine – why so slender, what was he doing there? – she was overcome with awareness of the inevitable. Wherever this road leads me, she thought, I will go.

The engine took, he dropped the bonnet gently, beckoned her to get in. He lifted a flat basket from her seat. 'I'll put it at your feet,' he said. 'There's more room. I had some food packed.'

She nodded.

He had a scarf around his neck, for the air was still chilly. He removed it and put it around her neck.

'And you?' she asked.

He fastened the top button of his open-necked shirt. 'Now I'll be fine,' he said. He put the lorry into gear and eased it forward slowly. Only once they'd breasted the sharp incline did it roar at full throttle.

It was already lighter.

'We aren't going to link up directly with the main road to Kitale,' he said. 'I want to take a detour, that's why we left so early. I want to park on a special ridge so that you can watch the sun rise from there.'

The darkness was lifting, lifting too quickly, the grey shadows of the bushes next to the road were absorbing the light, shaking off the haze of night, and every leaf and twig was clearly etched. They went through a gate which he had to get out and open and then he drew up beside a clump of thorn trees.

She got out and he took her hand to help her up the steep ridge. She scrambled up beside him, one hand in his, the other grasping at stones or branches as they progressed.

They stood on the crest. He gestured with an arm. In front of them lay the plain: first a dry river bed, then successive lines of ridges, stretching into the distance like wrinkles on an animal's hide.

'Mount Elgon is behind us, to the west, a bit to the north-west,' he said. He turned around, then back to her again. 'It's too hazy now, we'll see it later.'

Around them the day began to break – a fine line of light on the green horizon, a glow, soft, pale pink increasingly glowing with gold. She heard birds in the trees: delicate twittering and warbling like water dripping. But suddenly it stopped; the morning breeze had also dropped, everything waited.

'There he comes.' The huge shining orb dragged itself up over the horizon then suddenly broke free, rising faster. The birds fluted and warbled again, the breeze stirred, leaves stirred on the trees and the grass waved.

She sat down, suddenly drained; he also sat.

Around them the radiance of the new day.

She leaned her head on his shoulder; he lifted her left hand with his right hand, held their hands against each other. The nails of his index and middle fingers were stained yellow with nicotine; the nails of his other fingers were a strange topaz shade, as if the skin beneath was lighter. How cool her palm felt against his. His hand moved up and his fingers closed over hers, her thumb moved hesitantly against the base of his thumb. They both gazed at it raptly, as if the hands were something apart from them. Ivory and nut-brown.

'Do you know what that looks like?' he said after a while. 'Like a big cashew nut. The white nut with the brown skin around it.'

He unfolded his fingers and removed the elastic band which held her hair at the back of her neck. Her hair fell loose to her shoulders.

'Why are you so diffident? Your hair is beautiful, loose like that.'

'What is happening to us?' she asked.

'You and I are one,' he said. 'Do you not feel it? Here,' and he pointed to the space and ridges surrounding them, 'here we are one. I give you the world.'

She was not sure that she had heard him right. They sat very still. A wagtail hopped nearer. Hussein made a small sound with his lips; the wagtail came nearer still. Then suddenly flew away.

'And so quiet all of a sudden?'

She recited quietly:

'Though I am but a mote, the radiant sun is mine:
Within my bosom are a hundred dawns.'

'Muhammed Iqbal?'

'I had never heard of him before I found the book in your rondavel. I read it all the time.'

He took up the verse:

'My thoughts hunted down and slung from the saddle a deer
That has not yet leaped forth from the covert of non-existence.'

'That's how I knew you would come.'
'Slung across the saddle?'
'That is indeed so.'
'I also knew,' she said. 'I thought I was getting a fever or falling ill, I couldn't escape it.'
'And now?'
'Now the fever has broken,' she said, 'but I am still sick.'
He took her hand, folded her fingers open and kissed each finger on the inside and then he kissed the palm of her hand before he released her hand. He also kissed the inside of her wrist.

Fair is my garden ere yet the leaves are green:
Unborn roses are hidden in the skirt of my garment.

She felt a flame shoot through her body. 'Indians are very subtle lovers,' she said, but her voice sounded oddly broken. She regretted saying it; the words had put her on the level of blondes on whose whims taxis must wait at the ready.

'Indian lovers have to be subtle,' he replied. 'Indian girls are watched carefully and brought up strictly.' He did not take her hand again.

'And I, going about with you on my own, does that make me cheap?'

Once more she regretted her words. She had to control her mouth for her lips had started to tremble. She couldn't speak.

'What is bothering you?' he asked softly.

'My emotions are written on my face. I don't know what I'm saying. I just barge ahead blindly, as if I'm intent on causing pain. I don't want to cause pain, or I only want to hurt myself, I don't know why. I can't cope with it.'

'Is it because I'm Indian?'

She shook her head.

'Don't try to analyse,' he said. 'Just accept it.'

They made their way back down the hill.

He got the basket which had stood at her feet, put it on the bonnet and took out the food.

As he reached towards the basket, she hesitantly put out her hand and shifted his sleeve up. She touched the scar.

'You don't have to be careful; it's an old wound. One of my first hunting expeditions. I nearly lost the arm.'

'Hunting accident?'

'Lion. With your oupa. If it hadn't been for him I'd have died. The wound healed very slowly.'

Her fingertips explored the skin. A roughly sutured wound, as if a child had done it with needle and thread.

'I wanted to become a vet. The doctors thought my right arm would not be strong enough for the work. When it finally healed, my years for study were past.'

'I have a great uncle who was mutilated by a lion in Nyasaland. He was horribly maimed – face and arm and leg. He never recovered: he was permanently embittered.'

'I thank Allah that he didn't decree such mutilation for me.'

'I know so little about you,' she said.

He began to talk as they leaned against the bonnet eating. 'You asked if I was married. No, I was engaged when I was twelve, to the new-born daughter of a friend of my father's in his home town in India.'

'A childhood engagement?'

'It's an old custom. I saw her once. She'd just turned 13.'

'In India?'

'I had gone to Lucknow with my sister. She's independent, like you; she wants to become a doctor. She went to university there. I didn't want to stay there, this is my country. Shortly after I'd left, the little girl I was engaged to died of fever.'

She was about to speak, but he silenced her. 'It was the will of Allah. It is past. What has been, has been. Let's get going.'

After an hour or so they saw the houses and buildings of the Kitale village in the distance. He swung off the secondary road onto the main road, and pulled in at an Indian *duka*. He parked in the shade and she stayed put. The people knew him. The trader came out with his wife in her sari, visibly pregnant. They chatted and gestured. A little boy of about four took Hussein by the hand and led him to an outside tap. She watched him bend and catch the streaming water in his hands and bathe his face in it. Then he drank from his hands. He came back to her side of the lorry.

'Come,' he said, 'you're thirsty too.'

She held his hand as she got out, but she was clumsy again and shy of the trader and his wife, couldn't get enough water to her mouth to drink. He bent next to her and cupped his hands under the tap. She put her mouth to the water in his hands. She drank. God, she thought, each time I pledge myself to him by doing this.

The little Indian boy brought a serviette for her to dry her hands.

Hussein took the cloth from him and dabbed her mouth and face. Before he got in he gestured with his hand to his forehead and said, 'Salaam alaikum.' He ruffled the child's hair, hair black and smooth as his own. The child clung to his hand, the mother had to drag him away. These are his people, she thought.

'They don't know about the graves,' he said. 'We'll have to ask in the village.'

They drove slowly up the main street. It was a small village; he was looking for somewhere to make enquiries.

'It'll have to be the police station,' he said at last reluctantly, and drew up next to the pavement. A policeman came out of the building with him. He indicated right, then again left. He turned to go back inside, but three soldiers had come up to them. 'War graves? You don't say …'

They were idle and inquisitive, but when they saw Belle sitting in the lorry, they became aggressive.

'If it isn't the little miss from Leseru station!'

'We heard all about you, Ma'am.'

'Tell your driver to buzz off, we'll take you.'

'Come on, get out, you.'

One soldier tried to jerk open the door Hussein had slammed shut. A second one had walked around to her side, indicated that she should move over.

'We'll be better company for you, won't we?'

'Drive,' she said to Hussein. 'They're scum and they're looking for trouble.' She hung onto her door handle.

The engine fired and she looked at him, but could discern no emotion in his face. His hands seemed to be relaxed on the steering wheel, or was that only by an effort of will? For her sake?

Again she experienced the feeling of the early morning haze; again she thought: Then this is what people suffer willingly for; this is what people die for. This devotion to another, the one-ness, for which everything else is sacrificed. The morning's superficial, unimportant misunderstandings vanished into thin air.

The soldiers shouted obscenities after them. He drove carefully and accurately, right at the first turning, then left. For a moment, as he changed gear, his hand rested on her knee. She covered his hand with hers, felt the connection stream through them; she leaned back and closed her eyes. Later he took his hand from beneath hers and placed it on the steering wheel again. The road was little more than a track. She opened her eyes, he turned his head and looked at her, 'Forget them,' he said.

She rested her head on his shoulder. This feeling is too much for me, she thought, I cannot contain it.

'It was so unnecessary for my brother to die,' she said to Hussein. They had searched for a long time in the grass and bushes to find the marker with 47 on it. The number which Oom Hendrik had managed to ascertain with such difficulty. Without it they would have had to crawl around, tearing at creeping plants, wiping grime away, searching up one row and down the next, deciphering all the faint names to find his. But 47 was in the row of 40s. Once they had worked out the layout of the graves between the ridges enclosed only with a simple wire fence, they knew where to look.

Josias van Velde, she touched the creeper they'd removed from the marker and pulled more of it away. It was a hardy specimen, with deep roots. 'Oh, my Boetie,' she said softly, 'is it you lying here? Out here in the veld, among the weeds? When they buried you, there was no one present who loved you; when the grave was filled, we didn't even know you were dead.'

'Should we tidy up a bit?' asked Hussein.

She shook her head. 'It'll get overgrown again.'

'Perhaps it's better that way, overgrown like the others. Perhaps even the numbers will disappear one day.'

'My father went against the wishes of my grandfather to go to German South West ... but you wouldn't know about that. My boetie didn't really want to go to war, he just wanted to please my father. My father was always so critical of him, and he loved my father so much. That's why he came and died here.'

She sat next to the grave, playing with the pebbles she'd picked up in the grass. He came to sit beside her, lifted her head, saw tears in her eyes. He stroked her hair, cupping his hand comfortingly around the contour of her head. His fingers continued the small, soothing stroking motions over her hair.

'You loved your brother. But you don't love your father?'

She shook her head. 'I don't know him.'

'And your mother?'

Again she shook her head. 'I'm not like them. That's why I came here. I don't know who my real grandfather is, I don't actually know who I am myself. I wanted to come to ask this grandfather. I loved my other grandfather, but that's not enough. That's only half of me. I have only known half of myself fully.' She smiled ruefully. 'Here with you I am getting to know myself fully.'

From the distance came the sound of a pickaxe on rock.

He pulled her up. He pressed her closely to him, his hand spread against her back.

She lifted her hand and touched his eyebrow, his cheeks, then the high bridge of his nose and his lips. She brought the fingers with the dull topaz-coloured nails to her mouth. In turn he explored her eyebrows, her cheeks, her nose, her mouth; he pushed her blonde hair aside so that his palm could fit over her ear. He closed her eyelids with his thumb. Then his head lowered very close to her and he kissed her, briefly but intently on the corners of her mouth, first one corner, then the other, so that she opened her eyes in surprise and saw his face so close to hers. The skin around his eyes was so dark brown it astonished her. The emotion flowing from his eyes bound her to him.

'What is it that overwhelms me when I'm with you?' she asked quietly. 'Or away from you? Something like this ... so powerful ... It's strange to me.'

'To me as well. It must be,' and he smiled, 'what the story-tellers call love.'

'No, much more,' Belle said, she laughed softly. 'It's earth-shattering ...'

He laughed too. 'A landslide,' he said. 'But you mustn't be afraid.' He moved his cheek gently against hers, up and down. She closed her eyes again. 'That which exists between us can never end,' he said. 'It has been preordained. For all eternity.'

Ozzie, she said to her dead brother, how I would have liked you to know him. I am pleased to be at your grave with him.

Once more they heard the sound of a pickaxe, and when she opened her eyes, she saw light reflected from wire as it was unrolled. The sun has broken through, she thought, surprised. The trees behind the graves and even the gravestones cast shadows. The sultry hot day had cleared.

'Look,' said Hussein and turned her in his embrace. 'Mount Elgon. I promised you this morning.'

She saw the massive crest dark blue in the distance, white snow on the peaks.

'Snow,' she said, amazed.

'You can tell your folks your brother lies at the foot of Mount Elgon.'

She remembered the photo Oom Frikkie wanted for her mother.

The camera was in the lorry. He fetched it and photographed the grave and its surroundings. He took a picture of her at the graveside. She took a photo herself.

'The mountain looks deceptively close,' he said. 'It'll just be a dot in the photo.'

Her mother would be upset by the neglected graves.

'We can leave now,' she told Hussein.

They didn't drive through the village, but turned down an outer road stopping at a group of Indian shops. He got out to buy cool drinks. As they drove they ate some of the left-over samoosas: they weren't really hungry.

'Rest now,' he said, and she lay with her head on his shoulder. When he turned off into a road, nothing more than two tracks, he drove very slowly, so that he could keep one arm round her and he could steer the lorry with one hand. Only now and then she had to move so that he could change gears. Then his arm slipped round her again and she could lean against him. They drove in silence as the afternoon shadows lengthened into early evening and the sun sank lower.

It was twilight when they drew up in the open space in front of the factory and the grandfather's house and the rondavel where she stayed. It seemed to her that she had been very far away for a long long time.

At table that night the tension between Latifa and Hussein was palpable. She was cool to Belle as well, serving the food but asking no questions.

Then, just before they left the table, she said, 'There were two jeeps full of soldiers here this afternoon. Looking for illegal ivory.' She threw her hands up. 'On top of everything else. A sick, dying man is not enough. Now this nonsense as well.'

Hussein tried to silence her, but she continued. 'I heard the one tell the other, "See where the white girl is sleeping?" and then, "My God, in the Indian's room!"' There were red patches of indignation on her high cheekbones. 'Tonight you sleep in the house. I think the search was just an excuse to find out where you sleep.'

So crude, thought Belle, so hideously crude. So insensitive towards me and so tender to the old man. Is she jealous of his past, does she see me as a threat? But he doesn't even recognise me. Scarcely remembers my mother. But then what do I know about his wandering at night? Who does he call out to? To that young child my mother was?

She looked at Hussein. Rescue me from this mess, help me.

He told Latifa, 'Should I let them frighten me? We came across them in Kitale today. They're scum.'

'They have authority on their side.'

'What authority? Booted out of India, now they want to lord it over us here.'

His father, he had told Belle, was first generation out of India; a vet, just as he, Hussein, wanted to be. He and his sister had been born in Africa. She would return when she had completed her studies in Lucknow: they'd both sworn loyalty to this country.

'You should go and see what a mess they've made in the factory,' said Latifa.

Again the word 'mess', thought Belle. Do people mess each other around? The British with the Indians here, the Boers with the Indians, the English with the Boers who live with Indians? Then she realised with sudden insight: We mess around at home with the other people in our country. With Nellie's people. This thought was suddenly unbearable. She thought: The English messed around with us. All those years right up to his death Oupa couldn't forget it. Is that a justification for us to mess around with others? She saw in her mind's eye the woman in the Voortrekker bonnet grabbing the oxen's lead from the black and snapping at him: How dare you? She thought of how she would never be able to chat to someone like Hussein at home, let alone drive around with him. Was she behaving differently away from her country to the way she would behave there? Was she also messing around with Hussein and Auntie Latifa?

'Come,' he said suddenly and she walked out with him. Outside he took her hand, for the ground was uneven and it was dark. She followed him to the factory building. He had to let go of her hand to take down the lantern which hung just inside the door. He lifted the glass mantle, turned up the wick and lit it. But as soon as it was lit, he took her hand again.

'Where do you sleep?' She had taken over his rondavel so presumptuously, so thoughtlessly.

'Tonight, in front of your door,' he said.

The light of the lantern caused strange shapes, shadows and forms to rear up round them, and climb the low mud walls of the little factory building. The roof-high stack of hides had been pitched over. The hides lay spread in untidy heaps on the floor. The searchers had used a stick and even scratched around behind the heap; the stick had been tossed aside. Hussein picked it up, held her hand higher, pressing it between his elbow and his body, into his damp armpit, while he felt the stick with his fingertips, sniffed it. 'They even poked around in the vat,' he said. 'Dear heaven, do they think I would hide tusks in the vats?'

With the lantern at shoulder height he walked on, again with her hand in his. They walked past the cutting tables. He lifted a scissors and the giant shadow of the two blades staggered up against the wall. As they walked, as the lantern swayed, shapes emerged: the sewing machines, the wooden shelves; then he bent and picked up a fairly large object.

'Ah! He managed to finish it. This is for you.' It was a silky kudu hide bag, with brass buckles. 'It's for you,' he said again. 'Before we left I said: Make me the most beautiful bag that's ever been made here.'

'A travel bag. So you think I'll leave.'

'One day,' he said. 'With me.'

He took a pair of sandals from the shelf. 'And these.' He took down another pair. And a strap for her bag. 'And this.' He looked down at her, the strain left his eyes for a moment. His eyes did not leave hers. Is it possible for eyes to be like that? She looked at him and the contact between his eyes and hers, and returning from hers to his, was so strong she felt as though she must be dying. She pressed his eyes closed with her fingers and shut her own eyes. He kissed her for the first time full on her mouth, his tongue in her mouth, hers in his, and her body melted. Slowly she moved her lips away. With her eyes closed she leaned against his shoulder. The lantern had been put down at their feet; he supported her head against his shoulder. Once again his finger followed the contour of her ear, gently and carefully, then his hand cupped her breast. He bent and kissed her breast through her clothes. She pressed against him more urgently, wanting him to tear her shirt open, tried by her movements to direct his hand to her buttons, but he resisted. 'Later,' he said.

He lifted the lantern again, still holding her hand as he walked further into the factory building. She thought she heard something and looked back. Their shadows stretched far behind them, askew against the wall – one shadow, not two. She pressed closer to him. He bent at a wall cupboard, and her hand slipped back up between his body and his upper arm. She felt the warm damp armpit. Her hand had become part of him, it seemed to her, but she was not yet. But he had said: later. She felt a slight shiver run through her body. He must have been aware of it, for he said softly: 'My darling, my beloved.'

Again a noise behind, where they had entered, but he didn't seem to notice it, his attention was on the cupboard. Again he put down the lantern, again the shadows were thrown against the wall. The stench of the hides rose off the pile of rotting off-cuts and hit her in the face. He'd unlocked the cupboard and taken out a gun – a big, heavy gun; his hands stroked over it.

'At least they didn't take this, he said. 'It's my elephant gun.'

She looked up at him: 'Then you do hunt elephant after all?'

'That's how I earn my living,' he replied.

'Then they were right to come looking for ivory here,' she said.

'Why? I hunt with a licence. Look here, listen here.' He stood with his knee on a box, the gun rested on his knee, his hands caressed the breech. She heard the small click sound of the hammer. 'Hear? So smooth, so delicate, I look after my guns, I take care of them. When I hunt, they are my companions, I must be able to rely on them.' He took her fingers and led them to glide along the gun. 'Can you feel? Soft as a woman's skin. It's not loaded, there's no need to be afraid. I want to know that your fingers have been on it, I will never be alone in the veld again.' She felt the smooth wood and metal, then she also stroked it, until with his hand over hers, he slipped back the breech, pressed her shoulder slightly so that she knelt and, as he showed her, held her head level with the stock to look down the barrel into the dark, her hand on the stock again, caressing. 'Do you see?' he said, 'do you see the elephant, the buck, the rhino, the antelope, the lion, the beautiful, beautiful animals? Oh, I want to take you with me, I want to be in the veld with you, to walk with you to the horizon when it is early and the day not yet born, for you carry the dawning in your breast ...'

These were the last words he ever spoke to her, for a strong searchlight, connected to a generator that roared to life, tore open the darkness surrounding them, pinioned them in the bright light. She jerked her head up, blinked. He drew her finger away from the hammer, and involuntarily, without knowing who or what threatened him, pushed the breech back, steadied the elephant gun. She heard a shot. At first she didn't know why he'd fallen forward across the gun. She grabbed him by the shoulders, sank to her knees beside him. His head flopped against her, she felt warm blood. 'Hussein! Hussein!' she screamed, 'lift up your head, speak to me.' She screamed and screamed. Soldiers with pistols in their hands surrounded her out of the darkness.

'My God,' she heard, 'it was the elephant gun, I told you he was a dangerous man. Not just a thief. Come on miss, we'll get you out of here. You were misguided, I'm sure you meant no harm.'

Then she heard another, familiar voice – the soldier on the train, the one at Kitale? – saying: 'Don't be so sure. What better way to get the tusks to the traders? We'll have to search her baggage.'

'He could have shot us all to kingdom come,' the first voice continued. 'You know what an elephant gun can do?'

An older man, probably an officer, twisted the gun out of Hussein's hands. 'It wasn't loaded,' he said.

'How the fuck was I to know that? Fucking the girl, as if that's not bad enough.'

'Shut up.'

She fought off the hands trying to drag her away from him, clinging to him until the soldiers shoved Latifa through the door. She didn't speak, she just loosened the fingers still clinging to Hussein. Belle couldn't fight against her. Latifa had her own workmen come and they carried him to his rondavel, laid him down upon the bed Belle had slept on. Her nightclothes were still under the pillow; they threw them on the floor. 'You see,' said one of the soldiers, 'there was no mistake about it. Good Lord, what white girls can come to.'

'Mind your words,' the officer told him.

She sat in a corner of the room, on the floor, her knees drawn up against her chin. She did not weep. The blood had been washed from her face.

Latifa didn't weep either. She sat on a chair and her upper body rocked back and forth, as if the motion took the place of tears. Her hands covered her face. Most of the soldiers had left. They had searched through the place again, also the lorry which had not been there that morning, and was the ostensible reason for their return. But she knew, oh she knew, it was because of her, not the elephant tusks. We mess people around, we mess people around, it seared through her. They had torn her suitcases open, strewn her belongings across the rondavel floor: her personal belongings, her used clothing, her green silk blouse – intimately near him as he lay still and dead on the bed.

The officer wanted to give her something to drink, but there was no liquor in the house; he tried to give her brandy from his hip-flask, but she spat it in his face.

She and Auntie Latifa sat through the night like that, with the lantern burning lower and lower. The soldiers who'd remained behind were outside. When the window turned to pale rectangles, Latifa blew out the lantern. Belle couldn't witness the first signs of dawning. She dug her fists into her eyes; she felt as though she was falling into an abyss. She couldn't endure living with such horror.

During the morning his two uncles from Nairobi arrived. Latifa had phoned from the Indian shop, they had set off in the dark.

'We must get rid of the girl,' said one uncle, a delicately built little man in a white silk shirt, spectacles on the fine ridge of his nose. The other uncle was also a businessman and dressed just as formally. He answered, 'She complicates everything. She can make a statement in Nairobi, but then she goes.' Without asking her permission, they'd searched through her handbag and found her air ticket and passport. Paged through her traveller's cheques. 'We'll book her seat.'

'Get her on the earliest flight,' said the other.

'It's going to lead to a hell of a case, miss. I can assure you of that.'

And the other: 'I think you've caused enough harm.'

A sheet was drawn over Hussein's face.

Be the reed-flute, bring a message from the reed-bed;
Give to Majnun a message from the tribe of Laila.
Create a new style for thy song,
Enrich the assembly with thy piercing strains! ...
My being was an unfinished statue,
Uncomely, worthless, good for nothing.
Love chiselled me: I became a man
And gained knowledge of the nature of the universe.
I have seen the movement of the sinews of the sky,
And the blood coursing in the veins of the moon.

She crawled across the floor of the rondavel on her knees, gathering her belongings and stuffing them into her suitcases. How had she managed to do it? she wondered afterwards. Was she still in deep shock as she crawled around the bed where he lay dead? When Auntie Latifa and one of the uncles each took her by an arm and pushed her out of the rondavel, she resisted, but they were adamant. 'Leave him in peace,' one uncle said, slightly more sympathetically.

Only once she was in the car did she think to bid the old man farewell, but it was too late. They hadn't been able to keep her away from the factory. No matter how dreadful it was, she'd pushed her way through the tumbled dry hides; past the wet vat, the work benches with the sewing machines, the lasts, the shelves on which the finished leather goods were. She had pushed past the soldier who was standing guard, and stumbled down next to her bag. 'He gave it to me, he had it made for me,' she pleaded. The sandals were inside the bag. She clasped it to her body and said: 'You'll be stealing if you take it from me.' Latifa said, 'Might as well let her have it.'

She carried it to the car; her suitcases and handbag and camera had been thrown on the seat.

'We'll ring the undertaker from the *duka*, they'll take the body to Nairobi,' said the uncle; the older one who took the lead. 'She can stay in the hotel until we can get a reservation. It's a blessing that the officer said in front of witnesses that the gun wasn't loaded. And when they searched the factory yesterday morning, they could see there wasn't any ammunition in the gun cupboard. Nothing but white people's spite. And how will they punish the soldier who shot him? He'll be court-martialled, get a few years. And we are bereft of Hussein.'

The younger uncle sat behind the wheel. He took a handkerchief from his pocket, shook it open, pressed it to his eyes and blew his nose. He put his hand through the window and pressed Latifa's arm. 'Be strong. We must accept: it was the will of Allah. Our finest son.'

The door of the rondavel was closed. A soldier stood guard, his khaki fatigues scarcely distinguishable from the mud plaster. The pistol in his belt caught the light, and the insignia of the military police made a diagonal white stripe from his shoulder across his chest and down to his waist.

'I must go back to the old man,' said Latifa, 'he's realised there's something happening. He'll be upset; he was fond of Hussein.'

The car took off at speed. Belle was thrown about on the back seat so badly, her head bumped against the roof at one point. But she was scarcely aware of it. She sat hugging the kudu-skin bag to her, pressing her face against the smooth hair.

She was instructed to get out of the car at the hotel in Nairobi, which seemed to belong to the older uncle, or he was the manager. A lot of English people stayed there. She was taken to a room in an annexe. 'We'll send your food to your room. I'm taking your ticket and passport so that I can make arrangements.'

It was only when her bladder and intestines forced her to do so that she got up from the bed and wandered down the passage. She found the women's bathroom and toilet. When she came out of the toilet a blonde was standing at the mirror, outlining her lips and fluffing her hair. A half-smoked cigarette lay in the ashtray next to the handbasin.

She tried to chat to Belle.

'Quite something to get used to, this country, isn't it? I've just arrived from England.' She picked up the cigarette, drew on it deeply, exhaled again. 'A good thing to get yourself an Indian friend, or should I say "protector".' She indicated the surroundings with her cigarette. 'Not quite up to London standards, but for Africa … how should I put it? Outstanding.'

She's cheap, thought Belle, Great-Aunt Issy would have said: Don't associate with common people. She tried to get past her, but the girl stopped her. 'The manager of the hotel is my "friend". Who's yours? I hope they put us together at table in the dining room. Their women don't eat with the men. Come, let me put some make-up on you. My dearie, why do you look so down in the mouth? And the tears? One can really go places in Africa with a "friend", they're crazy about blondes.'

There's probably no harm in her, thought Belle as she stumbled down the passage back to her room with her eyes overflowing at last – she hadn't wept since the night before. No harm, but she's so cheap, now they all think I'm cheap too. That white girls come here to find Indian friends and make use of them. That they behave in ways they never would in their own countries. But he'd surely know it was different with her. Then it hit her: he would never know anything again, ever. Once more she had to dig her fists into her eyes and bite her lips until the blood came, for the black abyss was yawning in front of her. Is it grief, she thought, this black abyss?

She didn't want to go to the dining room, not even for breakfast the next morning before the uncle came to take her to the airport. She tore out traveller's cheques and signed them to pay for her room, but the cashier would not accept them.

'I had to tell his mother this morning. I spoke to her in Mombasa. His sister was very fond of him, I sent her a cable in Lucknow.'

At the airport Hussein's uncle had her luggage weighed. He did not look her in the eye, shoved the documents in her hand and turned to walk back to his car. That's that, said his attitude. All that remained was the irreparable damage she'd caused.

7

The plane was delayed and it was dark when they took off. There were more passengers than there'd been on her first flight.

Food was served, but she couldn't eat. After the trays had been removed, the passengers settled down in their seats; took off shoes, loosened ties, sat back to try to sleep. She sat in a row of two seats, next to the aisle. Through the porthole she could see a few shreds of cloud, and when the plane banked she saw the moon on one side. The clouds and moon disconcerted her. She got up and walked up and down the aisle. But she disturbed the passengers, and when she stumbled over a foot sticking into the aisle, the passenger snapped at her: 'Settle down, can't you?' She took no notice, walked to the lavatory. Inside, she fitted the sliding bolt into the slot. An unnatural white light illuminated the small room which was lined with steel, like a capsule. She saw herself reflected from every angle. She wanted to scream.

A drop of water left by a previous occupant lay trembling on the basin. As the plane roared and shuddered it dashed mindlessly from side to side. She took paper towels from the container and wiped all around the drop. She concentrated on trying to help it maintain its balance. Its unsteady equilibrium. Then she got bored with it, mopped the drop with the towel and shoved that into the disposal slot. She found it difficult to dislodge the sliding bolt again.

Back in her seat she tried to settle down. But she couldn't sleep. Her muscles cramped if she sat still. She had to keep moving. She slipped behind a curtain separating seats and walked down the other aisle. In the galley she asked for water. The steward, pale from exhaustion, poured her some. The air hostesses lay asleep on their backs, one on the floor, one on a bench, legs outstretched. They'd kicked their shoes off, and their toes stuck up, the arms lay limp at their sides. The skimpy blankets had been drawn up to cover them from their knees to their necks, the vulnerable parts. Their yellow hair bunched like straw on either side of faces looking heavenward. Heavenward? Heaven beyond the metal container where the jarring and creaking steel plates beneath their buttocks rocked them to sleep? One woman's mouth had fallen open. As she walked Belle stepped high over their legs. The steward's eyes were open, watching her.

Such innocence, thought Belle. God, such innocence. Such unknowingness.

If only the metal container could tear, shooting them all out into space, like peas from a pod.

She saw an arm stretched above a seat, a head straightening up. She feared the passing of the night. She feared that her feet would once again have to walk out onto the ground, forward, where to?

At midnight they landed at Khartoum and had to disembark and wait in the airport building. They walked along the narrow fenced-off path to the reception hall. Dry, hot desert air and gusts of wind swirled around her.

In the transit lounge, on a low settee covered in plastic, lay a body. She went forward. The man lay with his cheek on his hand, on his side, his knees drawn up to his chest. There was an unmistakable resemblance: the length of the body, the posture. He moved, and the Bedouin shawl that had been pulled over his head fell back; she saw the black, smooth hair, the high-bridged nose, and the dark nostrils. But the skin was old and tanned, not that of her beloved. What had made him come and lie on that bench at that hour of the night, while her plane was waiting for her on the runway, its engines hot?

Or were they beyond time? Was it really he? Her hand trembled, she couldn't cope with the cardboard carton of cold drink she had been given. She spilt great round blotches on the stone floor, and saw the drink evaporate before her eyes. She walked around the bench and sat on the little stool in front of him, against him, and said: Here I am, open your eyes and look at me.

The passengers were called to re-embark and she took her place again. The night passed. A pale grey seeped through the window, then a green glow; she pressed her hands over her eyes, protecting them from the sharp wounding beam of gold – in your breast lie a hundred dawnings.

They landed at Cairo, at Athens, at Rome and then at the destination indicated on her ticket: Luxemburg. Passively, she followed the itinerary Leonora had planned for her. She was on a train, in a compartment full of schoolchildren returning from an excursion. They had been camping, their backpacks had been stowed on the top bunks. The boys wore shorts and the girls short skirts. Their legs were tanned and their sun-bleached hair was combed back. Their legs and shorts and skirts radiated vitality.

Farmyards, forests, meadows, fields, gravel roads, rural villages with one street and the *poste*, the *boulangerie*, the *gendarmerie* flashed past. The train sped by over hills, she saw scenes she recognised from her first French readers: the Frenchman with his beret, resting his bicycle against a wall, turning his head to look at the train for a moment, and then disappearing through a door. A multitude of young hands pointed at a forest flashing past. Behind the trees the grey blur of a building. '*Chateau Thierry,*' the young lips pronounced; they formed the name carefully with their lips. '*Place de naissance de la Fontaine. Vous connaisez La Fontaine? En Afrique?*' And they pointed inquisitively at her kudu-hide bag which they'd pushed on the bunk with their own backpacks. She nodded: Yes, she knew La Fontaine. '*Les Fables, les fables,*' roared the chorus of young voices around her. '*Le lion et le lapin.*' They wanted to take the bag down, to feel it, but her voice became unusually sharp: '*Ne touchez pas, je vous dis, ne touchez pas.*' That, they may not touch. They felt snubbed, and bolted from the compartment with their backpacks and camping gear when the train steamed into the Gare du Nord.

It was precisely the familiarity of Europe that wounded Belle. How much Tannie Leonora had taught her with postcards from Europe. The tower of Pisa leaning so, just think! Children wearing wooden clogs: would you be able to walk like that, SussieBelle? The Seine with the barge, the cabin boy, the bookshops along the Seine. She knew them all. Even the porters at the Gare du Nord with their blue uniforms and black berets were familiar. She felt less lost at Gare du Nord than she had at Nairobi station. She knew what to do because she'd been told so often: First check your heavy luggage in at the *Bagage*, get your ticket, take the underground to the Left Bank, get off at Odéon, go and look for accommodation at these addresses. Then go to fetch your suitcases in a taxi. She had been given street maps which she pored over for hours.

Actually a couple of weeks in Paris, before she left for Geneva to study, should have been a healing experience, Leonora later thought. Wasn't Paris healing? Couldn't she, Leonora herself, testify to that? Paris was healing.

The underground train thundered along. It all rushed past: the white tiles, like lavatory tiles, alternating with the dark, sooty insides of the tunnels that sucked the train through. She got off at Odéon. But when she stood on the pavement outside, holding the kudu bag, handbag and camera over her shoulder, she had to brace herself against the hordes of people streaming to the underground in the late afternoon. She caught the scent of a river, she saw the pavement, the kerbstone, the road, the advertisements, the shoelace vendor, the shoe polish vendor, the bus with the little platform at the back, the conductor with his cap, the streets fanning out from the Place de l'Odéon, the dark grey walls of the *étage* buildings, the small balcony on which – yes, there she was after all – the little woman sat among the geraniums, just like the postcard. She didn't know which direction to take.

She asked a passer-by, '*Rue Trente-et-un?*'

'My dear,' said the woman, 'you're completely off course.'

She had unfolded the map clumsily and pressed it ineptly against her chest, against her knees. She pointed a finger to where the map was spread open.

'I'm not off course,' she told the woman.

The woman shrugged. 'Very well then. You aren't off course. It doesn't concern me.'

The woman was middle-aged, her face uncared-for, her hair stringy and blonde, her shoulders bent by the shopping bag she carried. Her eyes were tired and dull. She looked like Agnes.

'It must concern you,' said Belle, but the woman had already turned away. She heard her mutter, '*Mon Dieu, que cherche cette femme?*'

'You're right,' said Belle. 'What is this woman looking for? I wish I knew.'

The attic room where she stayed was so high up that the timed stairway light went out three times before she reached it, and she had to press the knob again three times. When she looked up from her narrow bed, she could see the sky through the dormer window: blue sky during the day and the stars or clouds at night. Or just the strange glow of the city lights, and sometimes – like a small firefly emerging out of the dark – the light of an aircraft, and as it approached and changed course, the little green light flashing at the tip of the wing, then again the red light.

She felt completely isolated from the other people resting in the sleeping city below her. When she'd mounted the seven long curving spiral flights of stairs, finally turned off the light, and locked the door behind her, there was a moment when she felt free of the world. The porter had carried her suitcases up for her and she drew them nearer and opened them; took out the belongings she had bundled in so desperately as she crawled around the floor of the rondavel. He lying still and cold on the narrow bed, and she creeping and folding and packing. These things belonged to her, but they'd been touched by him. She had not yet dared open the kudu-hide travel bag.

When she ventured on the streets during the day, she followed groups of people moving slowly, looking at a window here, considering the menu of a restaurant there. Oh, the camaraderie, the affection, the intimacy of stretching out an arm and touching the sleeve of another, pulling it a bit closer: look here, look there. Oh, the joy of exploring together. She walked behind them, adjusted her pace to theirs, fumbling in her bag when they stopped, looked up something on her street map, staying in the warmth of their slipstream. She didn't find the language entirely alien. There were sounds that resonated with meaning in her ears.

A child cried during the night. It wasn't quite light yet, when she saw him standing there. Her door wasn't locked. Perhaps she'd expected him.

'Don't despair' he said, 'it isn't over yet.'

'I'm tired,' she told him.

'Sleep doesn't bring rest.'

'I know.' She sat up straight on her narrow bed.

'Answer me,' she said.

Sometimes he walked with her, sometimes she walked alone.

The inside of the arches under the bridges over the Seine reflected flashes of sunlight from the water. The bricks lining the banks of the Seine were warm to her touch. She pressed her hands against the stems of creepers, through the bristly little roots, and felt the earth. Then the shadowing of movement, as though she were drawn along by the water, pulled along by the water. But perhaps it was the wind. Or the flow of the river water at her feet, the riverboat cruising past with the man and woman and child waving.

The cupolas shone on the roofs. She walked and walked, up streets and down streets. She stood at the Arc de Triomphe and saw the streets fanning out, heard the drone of traffic like distant waves of the sea. The sundial moved slowly, as the shadows on one side of the street crept under the buildings and disappeared, and crept out on the opposite side. Before dusk came, the great wheel would turn, the morning had to become evening.

She reached a small square where jugglers, acrobats and musicians had gathered. She saw a man in a shiny black shirt who jumped on a big red ball and tried to balance with his arms outstretched in the wide black sleeves. She watched a girl, dressed in black, like him, give him a small, flat black cushion which he pressed down on his head.

She placed a tin container in front of him, struck a match and the magnesium flame gushed out of it. She called to the people: Come! She rested an aluminium pole and an aluminium ladder against her body. She placed the tip of the pole on the head of the man, pressed the ladder erect, and inserted the foot of the pole through the top rung of the ladder. Quick as a little monkey she climbed the rungs of the ladder, swung across the crossbar and started her tricks: swung and turned over, body between her legs, hanging by the knees. With each jerk of her body the pole on the man's head jerked. His feet trod, trod on the ball, caressed the ball; one hand was on his head to grasp the pole, the other clawed at the air.

The girl was entirely engrossed. Only she and he. Protecting each other with taut exertion.

And once she was on her feet again, the whole construction tumbled down.

Precarious balance.

The girl took the cap from her head and collected coins. Belle gave her all the money in her purse.

Her stay in Paris passed oddly. She didn't get to where she wanted to be, and when she did get somewhere it was not as she'd expected it to be. So much adaptation was required of her that everything that had gone before now seemed shaky. She forced herself, made countless phone calls. The telephone was in the corner of the bistro or pushed in behind the patron's little office, and while she held the phone to her ear, people coming from the toilets would brush against her – the men fastening their flies, the women adjusting their clothes. What she couldn't become accustomed to was the continuous chrrr-chrrr, chrrr-chrrr of an unanswered phone, in an empty house, in a flat no longer occupied, in the living or work places of complete strangers she'd been asked to ring.

Did she believe they could repopulate her world? She sat at a small table with beer glass rings on the glass top, moving the glass, allowing the wetness to spread in ever-increasing circles. The waiter brought a cloth, lifted her glass, wiped the surface under her glass and beneath her elbows; then moved on between the tables. Behind the waiter she saw an old-fashioned mirror with a gilt frame, tarnished here and there. And right next to it an old-fashioned calendar that showed only the date. It might have originated from an old station or an old office, the type that is adjusted by hand. She read the date: *Fevrier* 31.

Had no one noticed it? Or was it a practical joke or a freakish fashion? The people walking in and out brushed past her, and not one looked back and noticed it. The mystery of 31 February. The possible beyond the impossible.

Which suddenly made everything fall into place.

She didn't ever have to ring anyone again.

And she told the mysterious friend who had set the calendar and forgotten about it: Thank you for your clue, or thank you for your answer, or thank you for your warning – no, it couldn't be that – thank you for your answer. *Fevrier* 31.

One place belonged to her, thought Belle. So much of her heart had been given there, and what one gives becomes yours, well, the Bible tells us that. One evening just before closing time, she sat in the Luxemburg gardens, on the edge of the wood and iron bench, as if she was in a hurry and about to walk off, just resting there for a moment. But she didn't go, she just sat there. There were many places where she tried to give the impression: I'll soon be going. But from the pool where the naked youth grasped the naked maiden in his arms to rescue her from the cold water rising about her thighs she would not be driven.

At night on her narrow bed in her lofty room, she wondered: Does he still stand there? Is she still in his arms, slightly resistant with one foot kicking out? Does he still look into her eyes with so much passion?

The beloved rescued.

But the little statue didn't bleed; she was cold, and stiff, made of stone.

Belle walked with grim determination: to the Seine, to Notre Dame. She gravitated to groups, attached herself to groups, French or German or English or Dutch; listened so attentively to what the guide had to tell, the figures and the dates that were reeled off, that he or she would become suspicious and check the list, and with the gesture one would use to shoo chickens from the yard, say: 'Go on, be off with you, get away, you didn't pay, you're freeloading in my group.'

Numbers helped her, and dates and all sorts of information.

She had her film developed because she had to send photos of her brother's grave to her mother. On one she'd immortalised the arm of her beloved, only the arm and the rolled-up sleeve, the hand indicating: Look, Mount Elgon. She trembled so in the street where she held the photo in her hand, that a concierge rose from her chair on the pavement saying in French, 'Sit down, what's the matter?' and pushed her down on the chair and – who'd believe it of a concierge? – fetched her a cup of water.

8

Belle left Paris long before the pre-arranged time. She arrived in Geneva by train, after midnight. She dragged the two big suitcases with difficulty. Agnes had packed the clothes between tissue paper; they were more jumbled now, but the cases were still just as heavy. And the kudu-hide bag had been added. When one of the handles came loose, she hugged it to her protectively. 'I'll carry it,' she told the porter.

The taxi driver was friendlier than the porter. He said, 'I'll try to find accommodation for you, but the hotels are full, you know.'

At the third hotel he tried, he knew the commissionaire. 'We will let her sleep on a sofa in the foyer for now,' he said. 'There'll be a room vacant tomorrow.'

She lay with her legs drawn up, hidden in the shadow of the deep sofa, the kudu-bag and suitcases stowed away between two armchairs.

She watched the bag,. She watched the kudu eye imbedded in the loop attaching the handle to the bag.

She'd drawn her coat over her legs, and her head sank down onto the stiff velvet of the sofa's upholstery. But suspicion stalked her, no, more rapid than stalking, it overwhelmed her: the commissionaire would move the lamp, and the light would fall on her. Not on her, but on the kudu bag. She lay tensed, her eyes open so that the sharpness of the wandering ray of light would snatch the light from her eye together with the moisture of the animal's eye. But the light passed.

Her hand crept from under the coat and sought comfort in the long bristly hair of the handle, which had come loose and came to rest around her body like a paw.

When she awoke it was still half dark, but the commissionaire beckoned. A room was free. It was a small room, high up in the hotel. There was a bed with a stiff white cover and one flat pillow. The sheets were cold, and so stiffly starched they stuck together. She heard a tearing sound as the top and bottom sheets came apart when she got in between them. Her teeth chattered until she fell asleep again.

Another young girl occupied the room next to hers.

'Every hotel has rooms like ours,' she told Belle when they fetched the big breakfast trays, which were put on the floor in the passage each morning after a knock at the door. 'On principle it is better to stay in the cheapest room, even a servant's room, in an expensive hotel, than to stay in the most expensive room in a cheap hotel. That's why our trays are put down here, that's why, when we've finished, we must put them out again. We'll chat later; there isn't enough space for me and my tray and you and your tray in the room at the same time.'

She saw her again when she put the cleared tray out. She was a dancer in the revue *Silly Suzie* that had been running in London for the past three or four years, she said.

'But why are you here now?'

'Holiday,' she said. 'There are a lot of us dancers. We alternate; we all have more or less the same build, so there's no problem with costumes. One doesn't even notice who is away on holiday. That's why the big revues can run for so long. There is one that's been going for 20 years,' she said, 'and how would someone who's aged be able to keep up? So they move us out. New dancers of about the same size, more or less, so that the costumes will still fit. So they keep an eye on you, year by year, one could almost say month to month.'

She pointed at the empty tray. 'I can't eat like that in London.'

She had nothing to fear really. She was not yet 20, she had a retroussée nose and short curly dark hair and bright, brown eyes and lips which, even without lipstick so early in the morning, were red. She had a neat figure; without a bra her little breasts were perky, as if a hand pushed them up from below.

She sat on Belle's bed and stretched her long legs so that she could twiddle her toes.

'Toes are important,' she said. 'If your toes become a problem, you might as well give up.'

'Don't leave,' the commissionaire told Belle, 'I can make the room cheaper still.'

Betty, the dancer, was going out to supper that evening with two Chinese students she had met on the bus from Berne to Geneva.

'Come along,' she said to Belle. 'I promised I'd bring another girl.'

They were quiet, well-mannered young men with small builds and still hands; they were dressed in grey suits with sharp creases in the trousers. Betty asked the commissionaire, 'Where can we go to dance?'

They went by tram. They could hear music as soon as they left the tram. There was a hessian partition around the dance floor and the little tables where they could sit in the open air to be served. Betty's feet started to tap to the music on the plank floor under the table, but her partner was too shy, or perhaps too inept, to venture on the dance floor with his diffident, grey-clad body.

'Come,' said the waiter, who'd watched Betty, 'I'm free now.' She danced with abandon, letting her dress swing wide. The waiter's slender body swayed like a cocktail stick being twirled.

'I'll be back to fetch you again soon,' he said when he brought her back to the table.

While Betty was dancing, her partner, who spoke better English, told Belle. 'The two of us are travelling together, we are going to study in England.'

She thought: I like sitting under the dark blue sky under the strange stars next to the two quiet Chinese students, sipping the glasses of cold drink they order, and not talking much.

Their narrow eyes were half closed, and she didn't know what was hidden behind the lids. She liked not knowing.

Shortly before they were to leave, Betty's partner took a little book out of his pocket and asked Belle, 'Please write your address.' He pointed to her handbag. 'I'll give you my address. Mine,' and his gesture included his friend, 'and his.'

'I don't have a notebook,' said Belle.

'I'll tear a page from my book for you.'

His writing covered the entire page he had torn out. Firstly the address of their college in England, and then, pointing his pen at her, 'I also give you my home address, in case you come to our country.'

But she found it less easy to fill the little page in his book. She didn't know what to write. At last she wrote: Poste Restante, Geneva, and when he continued to wait: Poste Restante, Amsterdam, and then it became easy: Poste Restante, Brussels, Poste Restante, Rome.

'In what order?' he asked. 'When will you be at each place?'

She couldn't tell him. 'How should I know?'

The wooden dance floor moved under the beat of the drums and the stamping of feet.

For the first time he spoke French to her; it lent an intimacy, almost a concerned confidentiality to his words.

'*Sans la Poste Restante, il n'y a rien?*'

She nodded. Without Poste Restante, nothing.

'*Il faut qu'il ait une adresse.*'

'Why?' she asked. 'An address for what?'

'*On ne peut pas rester coupé de son monde,*' he said. You can't live cut off from your own world. His enigmatic eyes were near to her, his lips barely moved. She was astonished at that quiet young man's understanding of her. But I'm already cut off from my world, she wanted to tell him. Much more than that: my people are no longer my people.

'*Ces gens ne sont plus les miens.*' She said it so softly that he could scarcely hear. Those people are no longer mine. And with the uttering of the words, even though in a foreign language – perhaps she wouldn't have been able to say them without the distancing of a foreign language – she momentarily became aware of a new, blinding freedom, which was then banished by desolation so complete, she couldn't endure it.

She began to weep and when the little waiter brought an exhausted

Betty back to the table and held out his hand to her, she went with him and danced until the sweat and tears flowed down her face together.

Belle missed Betty after she left.

'Don't go,' said the commissionaire, 'I'll reduce the rent still more.' But because his intentions were suspect by then, Belle packed her bags.

She found accommodation near Lake Leman. Not on the fashionable bank, not where patios are glassed-in to form luxurious conservatories, where carpets ran in from the pavement under striped awnings, where women hung lined summer jackets over the backs of their chairs, and fingers toyed with long strings of pearls.

She'd seen a card with *Chambre à Louer Deuxième Étage* stuck to the window of an old building, and went up the steps inside.

She found her body a strange burden that she had to carry with her. In comparison with this, dragging her luggage along was a minor chore. A taxi and a porter could do it, although the whole business of finding a porter, getting a taxi, taking out money, and receiving change fished out of the warm dirty lining of pockets, seemed to her an incalculable nuisance. But she couldn't come to terms with the burden of the relationship with her visible self. She even found it painful to take out her passport – proof of the physical presence she was burdened with – and hand it to the woman letting the room, watch her glance briefly at her photo and then the figure in front of her. And to see how the facts of her existence were entered with dark ink in the rent-card by a strange hand.

Here with the short, stocky little woman in her black dress behind her table on the second *étage* it was easier than it had been in the hotel. A quick glance at the photo, then at Belle, then she turned, slipped off her chair, took the key and walked ahead of her.

It was a room on the shady side of the building. The wooden floor was highly polished and scattered with blue and white oval crochet mats with white fringing. The bedspread was of a shiny silky material which, when Belle folded it, slipped from her hands and fell to the shiny floor in a cold little heap. She kicked her shoes off. The blanket was faded, pale green with white checks. She pulled her feet up beneath her and felt the warmth of the old wool against her calves. Later she leaned across the bed and plucked the edge of the blanket from under the mattress, pulled it up over her hips to warm her.

No one could disturb her.

She looked at the space she was going to inhabit. The room was large and so was the furniture. There was a dressing table with crocheted cloths and a small glass jar. Two side-mirrors stuck out like wings on each side, so that by moving them around she could see herself from all angles. If she wanted to.

Against the wall next to the door stood an enormous wardrobe. Her suitcases were pushed up against it. She would have to put one suitcase on top of the other before she'd be able to open the wardrobe because the bedstead was close to it – actually there was just a little gangway between them. And the cold slippery sheen of the satiny bedspread was cold as a fish between her fingers when she folded it; she would never be able to sit on it. She sat on the bed. She played with a couple of woolly threads adhering to the faded green-and-white blanket; unravelled them until she realised what she was doing, then began unravelling again. The window reached down to within a foot or so of the wooden floor, but she couldn't see through it, for it was covered by tightly gathered, opaque net curtains. Long rusty-brown velveteen curtains hung on either side of the window. If they were closed during the day, the room would be in total darkness.

The ceiling was high and a light with three little bulbs under lampshades hung from it. She wouldn't use that, for there was a reading lamp with a silky shade on the table next to the bed, just where the book would be if she wanted to lie on her side and read.

But reading frightened her; she didn't know why. It roused the same fear as the scratching pen making thick black lines of the facts of her life, writing on the form. Words didn't frighten her. Not separate words. She could read words. In English or in the foreign languages gradually becoming less strange. Many simple concepts too, such as: *Keep left* or *No smoking* or *Meals served* or *No further flights today*.

But reading, leading her into the labyrinths of an imaginary life, terrified her. It caused her to panic because it might destroy the clinical, cool emptiness that protected her body like a second skin, and made it bearable and manageable.

She could only find peace in that small, calm detachment. She was antagonistically aware of her body, her breath, the friction when she rubbed her hands against her even colder ankles to warm them. And she felt alienated from the will that caused her actions, like getting up and tidying the bed again, putting shoes on her feet, picking up her handbag and locking the door, putting the outer door on the latch and causing her feet to move, down the street. She wasn't hungry, but she knew she had to eat. She couldn't eat in the room. It wasn't the kind of room where she could cut open a bread roll on a paper bag and peel the silver paper off the single wedge of cheese to flatten it on the bread with her thumb. She did this in the park. Children roller-skated past, but didn't look at her. She crumpled up the papers and threw them in the rubbish bin; the lid was moved back into place, the crumbs remained stuck in her throat.

The street from the park where she'd eaten led to Lake Leman. It was the kind of day when the sun was often obscured by clouds, and then suddenly shone with a feeble milkiness that made the shadows disappear. She kept on walking. Perhaps it was the smell of water somewhere ahead in the mist luring her, perhaps the sounds of the boats hooting whoo-whoo, like owls, as they left their moorings and disappeared into the mist.

It didn't seem strange when she saw Africa, or what Africa had come to mean to her, rise up before her. The dark woman in her pale yellow-and-white sari and sandals and a thin gold chain around her ankle, and the rhythmic movement of her thighs as she walked. She walked a little way behind her thin husband, in his grey suit, who bent forward into the wind, hands folded behind his back. One hand was clasped around the other, she could see the nails and the hands. She moved nearer to where they were standing at the railing on the bank of Lake Leman. Their speech was dark-sounding, and evoked no recognition in her. The woman in the sari had a small red spot on her forehead. They turned and walked away from the railing and from her.

His hands were Hussein's hands, in colour and shape, in the topaz-coloured nails through which the paler skin showed. She groaned. She placed the fingers of one hand in her mouth and bit into the soft flesh of the tips, and her tongue licked the hardness of the nails. Her tongue began to caress her fingertips, the smooth texture of the nails, and the softness of the moist little cushions at her fingertips which became all the rounder and wetter and softer.

At last the hand fell away from her mouth.

She wiped the dampness off on her jacket. The Indians had walked on, along the promenade beside the lake. When they were some distance from her, they started to dawdle along the railing, looking at the grey mistiness over the lake.

She crossed the road, walked under the trees. Only when she'd lost sight of the yellow-and-white sari – perhaps they'd turned back – did she walk back to the water where the mist had come down and a boat bumped against the wooden dock.

But it was only the woman who'd turned back. In the absence of the fluttering yellow-and-white panels of the sari, she'd imagined they had both left, but there in front of her stood the lean, dark man, his hands on the iron rail in front of him.

Perhaps it was the way he gazed across the misty water, perhaps the gentle bumping of the boat against the tyres along the dock and the smell of diesel oil, or the intimacy of his hands suddenly so close to hers – but the grey of the afternoon was swept back and Africa sent her reeling.

She moved along the railing until she was close to him.

'Good day,' she said. Her voice was hoarse, she scarcely recognised it.

He was distant at first and tried to avoid her, then had second thoughts.

'Ah,' he said, 'the lady of earlier.'

A sailor began to loosen the ropes; before long the gangway would be hauled in. The dark man had taken his hands from the railing, he took her elbow. 'Shall we go together?' he asked.

Half of the boat was hidden in the mist. It engulfed the deck chairs; had already covered the white-painted railings, the scrubbed white deck and the figures on the bow.

I voyage out in the glowing sun, thought Belle.

'Shall we?' he asked again.

She shook her head uncertainly.

He must have guessed it from her accent, for he asked, 'Are you from Africa?'

'You too?'

'If we go together,' he said, 'we need not go far. There are many stops, all along the banks of the lake. We can land where we like. We can take trams back, even trains, we can always come back.'

Through the dense mist on the lake she heard the invisible traffic of boats. It was time for the gangway to be taken in. The sailor had noticed them, looked up at them questioningly. His face was wet, his hair damp, drops of moisture clung to his nostrils.

She nodded to him: Yes, we're coming

Now she was the one leading the way on the shifting, drenched gangway. She stood against the rail at the bow; he pushed others aside and stood next to her. He put his arm around her waist, she removed it carefully. The churning of the engine became louder, threw the foam up higher, the dock became more and more distant.

They heard the lowing of other boats, and their boat gave answer. The engines thudded evenly, the boat began to dive slightly. The mist had completely shrouded them. She felt secure among the warm bodies of which she could not see the faces or outlines.

'Not here,' he said where they stopped first. The electric light was harsh on the faces of the sailors, of people boarding and disembarking.

She felt his arm sneak around her waist again.

Only at the third stop did he say, 'Here.' He appeared to know where they were going: a pub with rooms to let. Because he was well dressed, the hotelier gave them a room and the patrons of the bar allowed them to pass without comment, to mount the stairs. He turned the doorknob and they went inside.

There was a hand basin against the wall of the room. He took the towel from the hook, turned to her and wiped the dampness from her face and hair. His touch was not heavy-handed or unsympathetic. He also wiped the moisture from his own face and straight black hair.

But the eyes with which he looked at her were not the eyes of her beloved. The eyes did not overflow with warmth, they were impersonal and calculating, the smile on his lips almost a leer. His fingers on her elbows dug sharply into her flesh. She loosened his right hand from her elbow. She took two of the fingers and placed them in her mouth, pressed her teeth against the nails; her tongue dragged across the little cushions, her saliva ran onto them. He left her to it. With his left hand he undid her buttons, took off her clothes. He undid his own clothes clumsily. She lay on the bed, her eyes closed, his fingers still in her mouth. Only once he pulled his hand away and pressed it to her naked breast, but her breast was unresponsive and he let her take the hand again.

'Is it an obsession with the fingers that turns you on?' he asked once as he penetrated her again. 'A bit uncomfortable, but I don't find it unpleasant.' He came quickly and easily. If her lack of experience surprised him he didn't show it. He was tired then and he lay stretched out beside her, his arm flung carelessly across her. As she lay there she saw the dark brown arm on her white breasts.

At last he sat up and looked at his watch. 'Time to go. I'll take a taxi, you can go by boat, here's the return ticket.'

Her eyes were closed.

He took notes out of his wallet. 'How much do you want?'

She shook her head.

'You don't talk much, eh? Suits me. There's no hurry, take your time.'

At the dock not far from the pub she waited a long time for a boat. 'There will be one,' said the ticket seller, 'there's always another one. It's only the mist delaying the boats.' She walked carefully, hands on the cables on either side, across the soaking gangway, her feet seeking the cross-slats.

'Not outside, it's dangerous, visibility's poor,' said a crewman when she wanted to go on deck. 'Better go below into the cabin.' The light burned dimly in the cabin, she made out more figures like hers, in coats and with wet faces and hair. She could hear them breathing in and out, see their chests rise and fall.

Back in her rented room she removed the slippery bedspread, sat on the woollen blanket and unpacked the things she'd brought from Kenya in the kudu bag. The sandals that she would never wear because she was going into winter; the leather strap that was too wide for her suitcase; the clothing meant for Africa, not for that cold mistiness.

She took hold of the claw that formed the point of the handle that had worn loose from its stitching. She scratched her face with the claw, rubbed her cheek against it, rubbed her fingers across the hairiness, brought the claw to her mouth. She closed her eyes. There was a faint taste of earth and animal, of sun, of Africa on her tongue.

When she walked, she always wore her coat, collar turned up, buttoned right up, but the rain which poured down caught her unawares and she had to seek shelter.

She would later wonder whether it was a coincidence that she had been caught at the steps of the main post office, so she had to enter it. The inside smelled stuffy, with wet raincoats, and water dripping from umbrellas impatiently opened and closed and shaken out. They'd scatter sawdust on the floor later. But the people sheltering there were not there by chance; they stood in queues waiting on the wet stone floor, in the dim wet light.

She moved forward in one of the queues.

'*Passeporte*,' demanded the official.

Automatically she placed her passport on the counter. She was in the *Poste Restante* queue. She couldn't stop herself, for weeks she'd avoided the building. The narrow back of the official was turned on her, his office-fingers paged through the little heap in the pigeonhole under the initial of her surname. He took out two letters, shifted his spectacles back on his nose, pushed the letters to her through the brass bars.

'Not in much of a hurry, are you? They've been here a long time.'

Still it rained. The ink of the words on the envelopes began running in blue streaks before she could reach a café to sit down and tear them open. She was actually shivering with a strange emotion – almost fear – which had overcome her at the sight of the envelopes. Her name and the address were in Tannie Leonora's big round handwriting. Genève, Suisse, with a line under it. In front of her name stood *Mlle*. It was the stamps that upset her. They pushed aside the steamed-over glass walls of the café, erased the misty weather with one stroke. Oh Lord, that little Free State orange tree with an orange frame, the Union Buildings in dark blue and purple, Groote Schuur with the pine trees – even the penny stamp with the little ship in red. Tannie Leonora had pasted the stamps on the two envelopes like a collage. Had she wanted to weaken her? Like this? She felt like pressing the stamps to her mouth, wanted to kiss them and let her tears fall on them. But at the same time she wanted to run back and push the letters back under the copper bars, so that the postal official with his tired, thin hands could replace them in her pigeonhole, or in any pigeonhole, as long as they disappeared.

She placed the envelopes on the table in front of her. The waiter brought the tea she had ordered. She finished the cup before she picked up the letters again and tore the first one open.

The flimsy airmail paper was so transparent, it was difficult to read the closely covered pages, with writing on both sides. She held the menu with its blank side behind the page so that she could read the writing more easily.

Dearest Belle
I am writing to Geneva although I know it will be weeks before the term starts. The others are writing to Paris, but I wanted to be sure that my letter would not miss you.

The words seemed strange to her, formal, as though they weren't seeking to make contact with her. She didn't feel aversion to the words, it was just as though she'd read and spoken those words millennia ago, and she couldn't really be sure what they meant. How long had it been? A few weeks, a few months, a few years? She heard the words of the woman at the metro the first day in Paris: *Que cherche cette femme?* Now it seemed to her: What does this woman who wrote to me want? She doesn't know me.

She read mechanically. All was well at home. She had to recall which home. Her father was no worse. Was he ill? They had heard nothing from her, hoped it had not been too difficult to find Ozzie's grave. Ozzie's grave. She banished the thought of it, forced herself to read further. The difficulty of Nellie's in-laws had been sorted out. At first she couldn't make out what the difficulty of Nellie's in-laws had been. It was incomprehensible that her mother had been so intransigent and that Tannie Leonora had to exert pressure to persuade Hendrik and Philip to help. The sisters were, after all, the same people they'd always been, even though the mother, who'd died so young, had been a coloured woman. Then Belle remembered what it was all about.

And the second letter. *My dearest, dearest Belle* ... No, that hurt, the words started to run in front of her eyes. The letter was shorter, was still about Nellie's problem. Tannie Leonora had taken the two sisters away to work in Cape Town. It was easier for them that way, away from the scandal: they'd been taunted as half-breeds at their old workplace. She was grateful the matter had been settled, because with the increasing immorality cases, the sisters may also have become involved.

The waiter brought her more boiling water, added it to the pot and poured her another cup. She didn't drink it; she folded the letters and replaced them in the envelopes. Face down, so that she didn't see the stamps. She took her handbag and walked to the toilet. When she had closed the cubicle door behind her, she lifted the lid of the toilet. She tore the letters into small pieces and tried to flush them away. The scraps of paper swirled around and around in the pan, clung to the sides; she had to wait to flush again, flushed three times before the last bit of paper and splash of colour from a stamp were sucked down into the sewer.

She sat on the lowered lid of the toilet and wiped the perspiration from her brow with toilet paper. When the supervisor opened the door with her master key, she got up, walked out without arguing, and continued down the street.

In the room she first removed the silky bedspread and then lay down on the bed. She didn't go out in the evening to have something to eat or drink. At nine o'clock the landlady brought her a cup of tea. She couldn't swallow. Neither was she able to swallow the next day, but she wasn't hungry. She remained lying on the bed. It seemed as if her throat had clamped closed. If she tried to swallow, even a sip of water, her throat contracted in a spasm, and the more she tried, the worse it became. Better not to try.

The landlady, who'd removed a second untouched tea tray, asked what was wrong. Belle pointed to her throat. The landlady made a soothing gesture, brought her a glass with bicarbonate of soda, and stirred it until the white powder had dissolved in the water. 'Don't try to swallow,' she said, 'just take a little bit, let it dissolve in your mouth, just melt away in your mouth. *C'est le nerfs*,' she said, and shook her head. '*La flatulence*. You are too young for that.' Little by little she forced the bicarb into Belle's mouth; one hand behind her head, the other holding the glass to her mouth. 'There, lie down now. Tomorrow you will be better. It's just wind. Nothing to worry about. Tomorrow every thing will be fine.'

Then the short stout woman in her black dress left; Belle lay on her bed more calmly. She also slept. And when she woke, she was able to think again. I may as well do something, she decided. I may as well go and register at the university for the course Tannie Leonora planned for me, and provided the money for.

She recalled the words of the Chinese: *On ne peut pas rester coupé de son monde*. Not to live completely isolated from her world, if she had to continue living. The wisdom of age in that very young man! And then she wondered: Was he sent to cross my path? And was Betty sent? Betty from a chorus-line, all interchangeable, all insecure; Betty on her little toes, smiling, insecure.

The rain didn't last long, it was not yet winter. She lived close enough to walk to the university. She registered for the French course, as planned. She should have expected it, but was disappointed that most of her fellow students were foreigners: Americans, English, Germans. She heard more English than French in the cafeteria, in the passages. The groups walked past her, chatting. She made no overtures to them, and was abrupt when they tried to start a conversation with her.

The landlady moved a little table in for her, between the dressing table and the wall, and Belle tried to study. She had registered for the advanced French course, but found she couldn't keep up with the class, she could barely understand what the lecturer was saying in front at the blackboard. She spent hours sitting in her room with the books in front of her, but she found it difficult to concentrate and made no progress. She attended the introductory course, but the work was too basic and bored her. Neither her heart nor her will was in her studies.

I must find work, she thought, even if only so as to keep fixed hours.

For financial reasons too, she would have to find something. Her money was running out. Her class fees had been paid and could not be reclaimed. The cost of living was high, food more expensive than she had ever dreamed it would be. But in Switzerland it was difficult to find work. What did she have to offer? A knowledge of English. Oh, Oupa, if you could see me now, with English as my only skill!

She took a bus to the Palais des Nations where the United Nations was in session. She had avoided the place, she was afraid to come across people from her own country there, perhaps someone she knew.

Now she stood in a queue at the Bureau de Placement to find work, was given a form to complete. Bilingual: Yes. Her turn came – a flood of questions in French. She could not understand. The clerk became impatient, slapped his hand on her form. Those words she could understand: *Bilingue*? Are you wasting my time? It had been ingrained in her so deeply that she was bilingual, she stammered: *'C'est l'Anglais et l'Afrikaans, comme Hollandaise. Je suis bilingue. Ce n'est pas une erreur.'* English and Afrikaans ... she was bilingual ... it wasn't a mistake.

'Next,' said the clerk.

She walked along the sprawling lawns. The gigantic building was glitteringly white in the sunshine, the sky cobalt blue, but she scarcely noticed. She stopped short when she heard people speaking Dutch, turned into a garden path leading nowhere.

One of the girls in the queue had said: 'If I don't find work here, there is always the IRO or UNESCO or FAO to try. They all use English as their written language.'

She tried the IRO, the International Refugee Organisation. The office was in a modern building within walking distance of the city centre. She went to the counter in the spacious foyer, where the stairs ascended with ornate curves, and the ceiling was so high above one's head that it imparted a sense of airiness quite different from shabby old buildings like the post office.

A young girl with beautifully coiffed hair, a scarf knotted at her neck, waited behind the counter; the filed and varnished nails tap-tapped in expectation of her question: 'May I have a form to complete, please?'

'Enquiry about a refugee?'

'No, application for employment.'

The girl was bored. 'There isn't really any work available, but complete it, then we have it on file.'

The form Belle was given to complete consisted of innumerable pages.

'Sit over there,' the girl said, 'there's a pen, and ink.'

She wrote for ages: height, colour of hair, identifying marks, date of birth, place of birth, country of origin, parents' names and dates of birth, grandparents, school, further training, degrees if any, previous employment. It was strange and difficult to re-establish herself as a person with these concepts which had become divorced from her reality.

She took the form back to the counter where the girl placed it in the out-basket.

'Wait,' she told Belle.

Her forms were sent off with the next messenger. After a while she saw a messenger pushing a trolley to a lift. It was loaded with forms that, from a distance, looked just like hers. She watched him. When the lift door closed behind him, the little lights indicated that he had gone to the cellar. It was a strange relief, the laying down of a burden.

But she didn't leave. What she was waiting for, she couldn't tell.

At lunch time a middle-aged woman came out of her office down the passage, putting on her raincoat as she walked. She was thin, evidently English, and took long, somewhat masculine strides. She approached her and said, 'Are you the person who completed the forms? Had anything to eat? Well, come along to the cafeteria.'

Belle stood up and followed her.

When they had sat down, unloaded the tray and placed the tea and sandwiches on the table in front of them, the woman said, 'Just this morning I read about your country in *Time* magazine, et voilà, here you are before me. With your background, yes, I read about your language and your people, and your strange ideas ... I can't understand what you are looking for with us here in busy, influential Geneva.'

'I want a job,' said Belle.

'You want a job.' The woman shrugged as her big strong white teeth tore a piece from the bread roll, and started to chew. 'All the little girls coming to Geneva in search of work ... All the little typing hands, across the whole wide world, on the way to Geneva in their dreams. Where the fate of the world's refugees is to be decided.'

A little of her saliva had come Belle's way during the talking and chewing.

'You mention translation. In our refugee camps there are young men and women waiting for work. They can speak five, six, seven, eight languages. And there is nothing for them. Or not enough. Teaching, you wrote. Who, what, where? How are you going to teach a little Romanian English if you can't understand a word of his language? With your fingers?' She poured the tea.

'But let me have a look. So this is what you look like: one of the Boers *Time* has such nasty things to say about.'

'A lot of it is lies …'

The woman gave a satisfied laugh. 'Why is it then that all South Africans come and defend your country overseas? – "This Russia, that I love in spite of everything".'

Belle felt a strange emotion well up in her, something like rage. She understood the quotation. She moved her empty cup away. 'I'm defending nothing. I have nothing to do with what is happening there. I spoke for the sake of truth.'

The woman lit a cigarette. 'Calm down. Now, if that's the way you feel, first tell me: can you return to your country? You're not a refugee? That would perhaps make a difference.'

'I can go back.'

'Will you be able to find employment in your country?'

'Unfortunately the answer must be yes.'

'No need to be upset.' The woman was feeling warm, started to wriggle her arm out of her raincoat. The cigarette teetered on the edge of the ashtray. 'Your qualifications are adequate. Too good to waste here on typing or filing. In your answers to the questions on interests I don't find much enthusiasm for charitable works or community service. That was a relief. If only you knew how many bleeding hearts we get here, wanting to do their bit for suffering humanity. Fortunately your application was free of that. I don't actually think you have the vaguest idea what our work here comprises.'

She lit a second cigarette, she appeared to relax. She ran her fingers through her hair a few times. She was not beautiful. A sharp, unusual nose, thought Belle. Thick, short grey hair. But there was something about her. Once again that 'something' of Great-Aunt Issy. Now still? Great-Aunt Issy would have said she had class.

'You've probably seen films of the devastated cities in Germany, in the whole of Eastern Europe, even London. But in England they are trapped on their little island. Here the people were driven about like cattle. Uprooted, displaced, lost. They stream in all directions, they are still arriving daily from prison camps in Russia. Parents search for children, children search for parents, husband searches for wife, brother searches for sister. Registers have been destroyed, no one has documents. Five years since the declaration of peace there's still chaos.'

'A formidable task, to simply keep the people alive. Not to mention relocate them, not to mention providing identification. There are children who have known nothing other than camp life – born in camps, now already five, six years old. And the sick and the old ... the United States, Britain, Australia, no country is prepared to have them, now their relatives are not prepared to leave them. Do you understand? Good people. Helpless people.'

'And you wonder what is wrong with me; why I who have a country and relatives and work, come here and waste your time.'

'Perhaps. That is why I wanted to see you.'

'Perhaps another refugee. I'm not that.'

But she was unable to maintain her attempt at a callous tone. That woman was the first to speak to her, really speak to her. And apparently take an interest in her. It touched her deeply. The woman noticed a change in her expression: the lips trembling, but not yielding. She leant forward to catch the girl's words.

'I can go back, but I don't want to,' Belle said almost inaudibly.

The woman exhaled smoke rings, not looking at Belle. 'An *affaire de coeur*, I suppose?'

Then she stubbed the cigarette out and said, more to herself than to Belle: 'The most important lesson one must learn about matters of the heart, is that how the emotion is received, and whether or not it is reciprocated is of lesser importance. It is the intensity of the emotion that is important. And not everyone is granted this emotion. Be grateful that you are one of those granted this experience. The violence of a passion. Then you have experienced everything.'

For the first time Belle put it in words to a stranger: 'He was shot dead because of me.'

The woman had lit another cigarette. She didn't look at Belle.

'Not because of you. Never for such a simple reason. There is actually a touch of hubris in thinking it was purely because of you. There are factors that have probably been building up for centuries. Have you never heard of the inevitable course of history? I should really take you along to one of the camps, then the words "victims of history" will echo in your ears. No, not because of you. Nothing in life is quite so simplistic. Even his genes and your genes and the genes of those who shot him must be taken into consideration.'

She spoke slowly and thoughtfully as if constructing the argument for herself. Belle looked at her. What was she trying to say?

'Is there no such thing as accountability?' she asked.

'Only partial.'

'And the deeds you do of your own free will? Deeds that may have terrible consequences for others?'

The woman shook her head. 'If I could take you to my displaced people in the camps, you'd see what has become of the concept "free will" in our century. No, not only in our century. There've always been victims of the times, not very often perpetrators.' Then she laughed. 'Not that the victims are not sly, crafty, lazy, jealous, envious, I could go on.'

'Man has the free will to act as he chooses.'

'Here in the city of Calvin? I must disillusion you. Free will has fallen victim to circumstances. Do you understand the concept of "expediency"? Dear Lord, I say again: come along to my camps.'

'And what about destiny?' Belle persevered.

The woman gathered her belongings to return to her office. 'All right, destiny I will concede. And your destiny, my child, it seems to me is to return to your country. In any event posts in all these organisations are filled by the quota system. I believe your country still honours General Smuts's promises. If you are so eager to come and work with our refugees, apply again when you're back in your country. Then I'll put in a word for you, I promise you that. And we'll bring you back.'

Before she rose to leave, she turned to Belle. 'I might just add: beware of emotional self-indulgence.'

They walked down the passage; the woman went as far as the lift. 'I must go up.' Only when she was already in the lift Belle thought: I want to speak to her again. She wanted to follow her, but the lift door was already closing. She watched the numbers of the floors as the lift went up. But how was she to know where the woman got out? She walked to the counter: 'Who is the woman I was with in the cafeteria?'

The girl was busy making entries, she scarcely looked up. 'Sorry, I didn't notice.'

'And that office she came out of, whose is it?'

'Which office?'

Belle walked to it.

'You can open the door,' said the girl. 'It's a conference room. See for yourself. There's no one in there.'

She wanted to tell the woman: I didn't tell you everything. It is because he was shot dead that I am able to return to my country. Had he lived, we would have been arrested in my country – it sounded incredible to her – and put in prison. Now I am without him and without my country. And you speak to me about '*Cette Russie, que j'amais toujours.*' Is that not the ultimate irony, extending beyond free will and destiny? With me bereft of him and bereft of my country?

And then she wondered: Why do I still say 'my' country?

In the black impenetrable night she heard the continuous heartbroken sobbing. It came from the compartment next to her, a never-ending weeping.

It was a child's crying which crept down the corridor, entered through the window, permeated through the seams of the rocking train compartment.

She got up, went into the corridor, shifted open the door next door. The blinds in front of both windows had been pulled down halfway, and a peculiar kind of light, not that of the moon, something like a lighter shade of dark, filled the compartment. So she was able to see: the man on the top bunk, on his stomach, with his head turned sideways, his arm in the wide black satin sleeve which hung over the side of the bunk and swung slightly with the movement of the train, back and forth, as though under water. The woman lay on the lowest bunk, her head an untidy bundle of hair as though her hands had combed through it while she tried to fall asleep. A blanket was drawn over her. Under the blanket the vague suggestion of bare shoulders. On the opposite bunk was the child and from her came the crying, the disconsolate sobbing from the wet mouth in the face that was larger than the body.

She picked up the child, supported the big head, pressed her face against the child's, felt how the tears and running nose had left the child's face slimy and wet. The large mouth against her cheek sucked and swallowed.

She sat on the empty bunk, she calmed the child who gradually quietened and snuggled against her neck. But when she tried to put her down again, the large mouth began to cry again, plaintively and continuously.

With the child on her arm she shifted the door open, opened the door to her compartment and found her kudu bag where it rested against the hand basin. She carried it across to the other compartment. Then she sat down, the kudu bag comfortingly against her knee and the child against her shoulder. The child was quiet, the big head heavy against her.

At customs she was still holding the child, her left arm dragged down by the bag. And she tagged along when the parents, obviously familiar with the place, went down one of the back streets near the station and rang the bell at a narrow door.

Belle woke up, her pillow was wet. If only the door had opened, she thought, if only she could have seen the door open and who was standing there.

9

Belle left Geneva shortly after her visit to the IRO.

With her two suitcases and her repaired kudu bag, and her camera and handbag over her shoulder, she travelled to Calais by train. The rain was pouring down there. The taxi drove as near as possible to the goods shed; in the rain she had to pay and drag her belongings in under cover.

'I don't have French money,' she said.

'What have you got?'

'Swiss franks.'

'They'll do.'

Greedily the taxi driver took the coins she held out to him on her outstretched palm. Through gusts of rain she and her stamped, label-plastered baggage was pushed up the gangway into the ferry. The officer at the entrance put out his hand to support her.

The ferry smelled of oil and wet rope. The wind which had driven gusts of rain against her pushed at the boat; she felt her left foot sink, rise up, her right foot sink.

'Careful now,' said the officer, 'ladies' toilet up the companionway to the right.' Her suitcases had been stowed, but she clung to the travel bag. 'When the ferry starts to roll and pitch, it's better on deck,' came the voice of the officer. 'Cuppa tea, thruppence,' she heard at the companionway. 'You'd better, love. There's a long delay tonight.' The tea lady was kind. 'Can't tell when we'll get going.'

Her ticket was the cheapest and did not include a bunk in a cabin or even in the women's dormitory. She found a chair in the dining saloon. She was able to pack her luggage at her feet and would perhaps be able to lean forward and try to sleep, with her head resting on her arms. Passengers continued to enter the saloon. It soon became crowded, and she clung jealously to her place. The newcomers were sopping wet, with them came the smell of damp wool. One couple had a child who sat in its mother's arms, looking around.

After hours the ferry began to hoot, the child began to cry, the huge propeller began to turn, and she heard the mooring rope falling on the quay with an enormous thud. The gangway had been taken up long before. The ferry ploughed into the channel through the rain, pitching and rolling. The steward serving drinks in the bar next to the dining saloon had to watch out for the glasses; the 'thruppence a cup' stall at the companionway landing had closed. More and more people made their way up on deck, only to return soaked through, their faces pale. People sat on the floor, leaning back. A young man gave his seat to the woman with the baby; the baby vomited into the woman's hands until there was nothing left to vomit. The child whimpered feebly until another spasm brought more thin yellow saliva dribbling out onto her clothes. 'Really!' Great-Aunt Issy would have said. Belle smiled wryly. Why had the thought of Great-Aunt Issy occurred to her? Probably because she was on her way to see the country ruled by her beloved Queen.

In the early hours Belle wanted to go on deck. The rain had stopped, but the clouds sped low across the dark water in the strong wind. She found it difficult to get through the door to the deck. The door slammed behind her, she clung to whatever she could, and finally came to stand at the railing. The sea beneath her was black, with small specks of phosphorescence in the swells. The water gave the impression of weight, of heavy blackness pushing against and drawing back from the sides of the ferry. But the ferry seemed to be holding steady. Light drizzle began to sift down on her. She lifted her head, allowing the rain to run down her face, licking it off.

'Fresh up here, isn't it?' said the officer walking past. 'You should be here at sunrise! If it were to clear.'

She had to avoid things like sunrise. The agony seared through her again. The precarious equilibrium she'd attained since her conversation with the woman at the IRO was shattered.

She stayed below in the stiflingly hot and stuffy dining saloon for the rest of the crossing to Dover. She exchanged her money at a Bureau de Change in the customs hall. Her suitcases were stamped, labelled and taken by a porter to where the London train was waiting. She was taken to a seat at a window; he passed her luggage to her through the window. Someone in the compartment took the heavy suitcases and packed them on the shelf above the seats. The train slid slowly out of the station and began to jerk and sway. But it was too misty to see much. Her body jerked and rocked with the motion of the train, which eventually started to travel along more smoothly. With the soothing rocking back and forth, the security of the hour-long journey to London, the walls of the compartment close around her, the calm opening and folding back of the newspaper by the passenger who had taken care of her cases, she dozed off.

She found cheap lodgings in Knightsbridge. The man on the train had warned her: If you don't have ration coupons – with a temporary visa you won't get coupons – it's better to stay in an establishment that serves meals. Just breakfast and dinner, that's enough.

With accommodation and the familiar British money everything felt more manageable. She fed the gas heater in her room with shilling coins. She paid two guineas a week for the room and two meals a day. For the first few days she huddled under her blankets to keep warm and save her shillings. It was a luxury to be able fold her table napkin open in the morning and lay it over her lap, to get toast and coffee, a scraping of butter and a small spoonful of jam from the waitress, even though it was slapped down in front of her, even though the coffee was spilt in the saucer. Once she'd ventured on the streets and got to know the shops, she bought a small saucepan and was able to boil water on the gas heater. She bought a type of soup cube that was not on the post-war rationing list and dissolved it in water. At a bakery, a short distance away, she could buy left-over bread. In the evening she was given a meagre hot meal, usually sausage and mash.

It drizzled almost every day. She slept a lot. Now and then she read the newspapers that were fastened with chains next to the telephone booth in the foyer. She looked at the employment advertisements in a lack-lustre way because she was tired the whole time.

She saw the advertisement for *Silly Suzie*, which was still running. She was seized by an irresistible longing to see Betty again. Betty in the small servant's room next to hers in the elegant hotel in Geneva. Betty who had been so concerned about her toes. She felt excited at the possibility of seeing her again. She and Betty and the Chinese students. Perhaps Betty would be able to advise her about finding work. Perhaps she'd even find work with Betty – altering costumes, darning tears. She would sit with the other seamstresses, and her fingers would be so busy, she wouldn't be able to think. She felt that she had come to England to become a seamstress with the revue *Silly Suzie*; that had always been her destination, she just hadn't realised. She could envisage herself working miracles in the restoration of tatty costumes, with a little stitch here, a small adjustment there. She put it off time and again for a new lassitude had overtaken her, but one morning she resolved: This afternoon I will go and look for Betty at the theatre.

Once again it poured. She waited at the bus stop. The thick tyres of the bus scooped the water from pools, throwing it up to the sides when it came to a stop. The water ran back into the gutters in slow dirty rivulets. The bus was full. She clung to a strap; felt the heat and wetness of the people engulfing her. Their breath steamed up the windows.

At the stage door there was shelter. She was allowed in. The doorman looked at his watch. 'They've almost finished,' he said. He let her through when he saw how wet she was. The passage was poorly lit, the lino trampled by wet, messy shoes. Tattered posters hung on either side of the passage. In the distance she could hear music, but it was muffled, as if the sound was coming through many walls or layers of curtains.

At an office where a woman was sitting at a desk she was called inside. 'Looking for someone?'

She said the name Betty eagerly, but couldn't get any further. She'd forgotten her surname, if she'd ever known it. 'Betty. Betty, a chorus girl.'

The woman tapped her pen on the book in front of her. 'If only you knew how many Bettys we have, and have had and will have again. Which Betty? No really, you surely don't mean it? Well, then you'd better stand here in my doorway, the whole lot streams past when they come off stage. Just stand back a bit out of the way. Then you grab the one you're looking for, right?'

The situation appeared to interest her. 'Many fathers and mothers and older sisters and boyfriends and brothers have stood here trying to identify the little lost ewe-lamb, believe you me, but at least they knew the surname.' She was suddenly suspicious. 'You're not one of those butch women taking a chance, are you? No, come now that I can see you aren't. Here they come.'

The last orchestra notes blared through the doors which had now been opened and curtains which had been drawn aside. The dancers came streaming out. They wore pink tutus and pale pink tights; little shiny pink stars were pasted on their nipples. Their upper bodies and arms were, although powdered white, shining with sweat. On their heads there were creations presumably representing meteorites, shiny quills shooting from out of solid silver helmets. They must have been heavy, for the dancers' necks drooped, as though the headdresses were about to fall, as if, once off the stage, they were no longer able to keep them erect. Beneath the powder and perspiration the bodies and legs looked strangely muscular, out of kilter with the frailty of the little drooping necks and the delicate features beneath the heavy make-up: white faces, red cheeks, black eyebrows, swollen red bows for mouths, slack eyelids. They were all identical. They were completely indistinguishable.

They streamed past her, no one looked at her. Once or twice she felt like putting out her hand, saying: Betty, here. But she drew her hand back uncertainly. Was it Betty? Could she remember Betty's face at all? Would she be able to recognise her face if all the make-up were removed?

But Betty will remember me, she thought with relief. I'm not one of many, there's only one of me. As soon as they've changed, she'll remember me.

She walked down the passage, went to stand near the exit; she waited for a long time, until the first few girls emerged from the dressing rooms, pushed past her to go out. Perhaps it was the poor lighting, but the glamour was gone, their faces were pale, their bodies not even attractive in the winter coats, headscarves and mufflers. They all looked so alike. But she kept looking, examined each face. Most of them returned her glance, but there was no friendly recognition: 'Good heavens, Belle!' Just a passing glance, then past.

The woman had locked her office and came down the passage. 'Found her?' Belle shook her head. 'Oh well, the show must go on, as they say!'

The rain had stopped; black pools of water lay in the streets, glittering as the lights went on one by one.

Why was she so surprised? Belle asked herself as she walked back to Knightsbridge. Why so disconcerted by the anonymity of those girls who went to put down their heavy, shiny space headdresses in the dressing rooms and came out denuded? After all, they had names, surely went back to a room, a bedfellow, a family, perhaps even a child. They couldn't be so very alone in this big city. Was this lack of identity just a mask they hid behind? She thought of what the woman in Geneva had said to her: Do you realise there are hundreds of thousands of refugees for whom we have to provide not only the physical necessities, but also the psychological: they've experienced such trauma they no longer know who they are or where they come from. We have to give their life solidarity. In the camps their displacement is not a mask, but the reality, the quintessence.

Remember who you are, child, Great-Aunt Issy had said.

Who am I?

After the rain the air was fresher. Little clouds of mistiness gathered around the streetlamps. Dusk was falling.

She suddenly thought of Ozzie. How he'd made fun of them when they stood in a guard of honour in Voortrekker dresses and bonnets. One of the girls had fainted. The parents in the audience were concerned because no one knew whose daughter she was. The paramedics had carried her off. Ozzie said: You all look the same, you could dress a doll and put her in your place, no one would know. Put a doll in her place. As Betty had said: They too, in their rows upon rows, were totally interchangeable. But it hadn't been a doll that had loved Hussein. It was she, her innermost self. And she was blessed to have experienced that, as the woman in Geneva had pointed out. A passion that superseded all else: your innermost self – your core identity.

Suddenly from behind her on the pavement she heard: '*Jong, gee die kaart, ek is skoon verdwaal.*' These were the first words of Afrikaans she'd heard since she had left the country. Panic rose in her. She wasn't ready for her people. Perhaps she never would be ready. The Chinese student had said: You cannot exist cut off from your world. But she wanted to live completely cut off from her people. To do otherwise would be to betray Hussein, and the core she had discovered in herself.

The small group of people were now walking to the left and right of her, in front and behind, they chatted across her, they joked and gestured to one another. She felt that she was drowning in the Afrikaans words, that dirty water was rising around her and covering her head.

She took refuge in the verses of Iqbal. There were certain passages that had spoken to her especially, even in Kenya. They must have spoken to him too, why else would the book have fallen open just there, why else would he have reacted so immediately when she quoted from it? They had reached one another through Iqbal, through his words they had been bound together. The night she had left, she had grabbed the book and bundled it into the suitcase with her clothes.

It lay on the table in her room in the London boarding house. *The Secrets of the Self (ASRAR-IKHUDI) A Philosophical Poem by Dr Sir Muhammed Iqbal. Translated from the original Persian.*

The rhythm and images of the poems absorbed her:

Proclaim the secrets of the old wine-seller;
Be thou a surge of wine, and the crystal cup thy robe!
Shatter the mirror of fear,
Break the bottles in the bazaar!
Like the reed-flute, bring a message from the reed-bed;
Give to Majnun a message from the tribe of Laila! …
My being was as an unfinished statue,
Uncomely, worthless, good for nothing.
Love chiselled me: I became a man
And gained knowledge of the nature of the universe.
I have seen the movement of the sinews of the sky,
And the blood coursing in the veins of the moon.

'Give to Majnun a message from the tribe of Laila.' Hussein had spoken of Laila, of Majnun, one evening at table with Auntie Latifa. She wanted to know: Who was Majnun, who was Laila?

Mrs Dove, the char, had already knocked twice to come in to clean her room. She became impatient: 'Open up, love. I've got work to do.' Belle gathered her things. 'Umbrella too, darling,' said Mrs Dove, 'the weather looks bad.'

She was more motivated that morning; she hurried down the street and took the tube to Russell Square. But before she could go up the steps to the British Museum and reach the protection of the colonnades, a strong gust of wind rose and buffeted the heavy clouds, sending a shower of rain down on her. Her hair was dripping, the rain streamed down her face and ran in under her collar. The book was clasped under her coat together with her handbag where they wouldn't get wet. She was blown into the protection of one of the pillars. When the shower passed, she went in through the wide doors. At the counter near the entrance the woman waved her to the rest rooms.

'Dry yourself off first, you can't go in like that.'

She tried as best she could to dry her clothes and legs and face and neck; tugged the roller-towel out far enough to reach behind her neck, so that it came off its roller and got stuck. She felt wet right to the small of her back. But the woman behind the counter allowed her through. The attendant led her down the passage to the main reading room. She tried to explain to the librarian what she was looking for. The Persian poet Muhammed Iqbal. The middle-aged woman who wore her hair in a bun was helpful: 'Our first resource will be the Encyclopaedia Britannica. Always my point of reference. And yes, really, here he is. Dr

Sir Muhammed Iqbal. These Orientals, really! So precious. Dr Sir! I ask you.' She heaved the volume onto a table where Belle could sit and read while the librarian dug out more books for her.

Belle read what was available with close attention: dates, writings, his relationship to other philosophical theories, his quite recent lectures at Oxford.

The dates and facts drifted through her mind, she wrote nothing down. She felt the cold creeping up on her, the feeble heating of the building didn't warm her. She didn't find anything she was looking for, until she turned a page and saw the thick black letters: *Love poets of Medina*.

Then she started to write: In Medina the poetry of idealised love was very popular. The popularity was ascribed to Jamil (died 701) of the Udkrah tribe, the members of which die when they love. The names of some of these 'martyrs of love' lived on and became symbols of the overwhelming power of true love. One of these was Majnun, whose love for Laila drove him insane, and he later became known as The Possessed. His story was preserved by later Persian, Turkish and Urdu poets as the symbol of total abandonment to the power of love. He's held in high regard by both spiritual mystics and profane poets.

The Possessed. Like the man who climbed the ladder against the church steeple in the rain to reach heaven, and tumbled down, thought Belle. Had she been able to tell her Oupa about Hussein, he would have understood. He had said it was good to be possessed by God. Oom Hennie was possessed by God. Be grateful that you experienced the passion, the woman in Geneva had said.

She was shivering violently, no longer able to hold the pencil. Would she ever know what message the tribe of Laila had sent Majnun? Had it caused him to lose his senses? But what was the use? Her beloved had been shot dead and she, Belle, SussieBelle, Tinkerbell was destined to become The Possessed.

She left the book lying on the table, took her handbag and stuffed her papers in it, walked out. 'Found what you were looking for?' She heard but did not listen.

The rain was pelting down now. She didn't know the bus route, she missed the turning to the underground. She kept on walking, until the shop corners and buildings became vaguely familiar. She was soaked through, but on fire inside. Twice she entered buildings she mistook for her boarding house, but the people at the counter didn't know her. At last she reached the right place. It was warm in the entrance hall and she would have liked to stay there, but they led her to the stairs. She had no change for the gas heater; they promised to bring some, but didn't come. She took off her wet clothes, put on dry underwear, lay in the bed shivering until she became so unbearably hot that she threw the blankets off, only to search for them on the floor later and to wrap herself up again.

She finally fell asleep on the floor.

Days passed before she came to her senses. She was in a hospital. The sister brought a visitor. She didn't know him. But something about him was familiar, something about the way he came in, his attitude, his walk, and when he opened his mouth, she knew. She was afraid of him, turned her head away on the pillow. The nurse turned her head back so that she had to look at him.

'And so, girlie, what have you been up to in England? You've been very ill, my dear.'

'How...' she began.

'Oh, so you can still speak your language? How did I know about you? Your landlady rang the embassy: she'd seen your passport. People from the embassy have been to see you. The English winter doesn't suit everyone, and certainly not someone as thin and run-down as you are. But we look after our people and take care of them.'

She remained in the hospital for another two weeks. An official from the embassy came to fetch her and took her back to the boarding house. 'A week to convalesce, then we'll put you on a ship back to sunny South Africa. There's just enough money. We'll pay your rent, we've already booked your ticket and paid for it, you can sign the traveller's cheques for us, we will keep them, we'll also buy the ticket to Southampton.'

'But ...'

'No buts. We've all developed a soft spot for you at the embassy, one of us will fetch you and see you onto the boat-train. And ask the conductor to look after you. And find a porter to get you safely to the boat. You don't have to lift a finger. We'll see to those two big suitcases that have been such a nuisance to you.'

'Why don't you tell me to my face,' said Belle, 'that you won't allow me to escape?'

'That's not a very nice way to talk. We've phoned your Pappa and Mamma. They're waiting for you with open arms.'

10

'I didn't run out of money, Tannie Leonora.' They were in the kitchen of the semi-detached house in Tamboerskloof where Leonora lived. The kitchen window looked out on to the side of the mountain. The sun shone brightly on the fynbos shrubs, throwing light on every little feathery leaf. A sunbird flitted from one branch to the other, burying its little beak deep into the pale bell-shaped flowers that bloomed in delicate profusion.

'I didn't touch the money in the letter of credit with the Standard Bank that Oom Hendrik gave me. They read all my letters, yes, searched through my suitcases! But they didn't get as far as the big flat envelope at the bottom of the suitcase with the letter of credit. Do you believe that, Tannie? I don't.'

They could hear Frikkie talking to her ma in the sitting room. Frikkie had fetched her mother and brought her to Cape Town in time to meet the mail boat. Leonora was also on the quayside. Her father, she heard, was bedridden.

Leonora looked at her. 'If there's so much money left, why don't you go back? There's a mail boat every Friday. No problem.'

Belle opened the kitchen door, stood on the small back stoep. From there she could look down over Cape Town. Could it be a city? This tiny collection of little white buildings at the foot of the big mountain? The row of palm trees along the seafront reminded her of Madeira. Colonial, that's what it was. A small colony at the foot of the continent. To which she's had to sail for two weeks, a captive on the ship, watching the constellations gradually revolve each night until the Southern Cross once more hung in its customary place, as she had known it since childhood.

'I didn't want to come back,' she told Leonora, 'but I had no say in the matter. The woman in Geneva had said there was no free will.' She couldn't disguise the bitterness in her voice. 'I didn't want to agree with her. Now I've experienced the truth of it myself.'

Leonora looked at her thoughtfully. There was something different about Belle although she had only been away for eight months.

'It surely isn't difficult to return. Perhaps after a year, two years.'

'There are ways of going back, Tannie Leonora. I don't know if I'd be able to return in this way again. Europe isn't so special, after all.'

Her mother had decided to look in on Miss Marais, to whom she was, according to Leonora, becoming increasingly attached. Belle didn't feel like joining her. She couldn't understand the friendship, and didn't particularly want to understand it. Leonora had to return to the college for late afternoon classes. Frikkie was going to a photographic exhibition in the city.

'May I come with you, Oom Frikkie?'

Once more she surveyed the small city centre with distaste, the sparse traffic, the lack of street life, the narrow streets; she heard with no sense of familiarity the strings of Afrikaans tossed from one pavement to the other like torn rags. The rooms in which the exhibition was housed were small and whitewashed, with low ceilings and neon lights illuminating the framed black-and-white photos. Most were studies of faces and torsos. People sitting on stoeps, or leaning across front gates, or talking or drinking coffee. None of them looked posed. The camera had evidently caught people unawares – with no chance to hold the head erect so that the jowls would appear firmer, or for the breasts to be lifted from the crossbar of the gate over which they drooped, clumsy and relaxed. One woman's conspiratorial expression as she chatted to her neighbour was repulsive.

'What ugly people, Oom Frikkie,' said Belle.

'Look at your catalogue. Street scenes in a mining town on the East Rand. Poor whites who are no longer poor. Just white. He's damn good, you know, this photographer. But he has it in for Afrikaners.'

'As you always say, Oom: the camera can't lie.'

Her tone caused him to look up sharply.

'Perhaps not lie, but it can certainly distort, SussieBelle ...'

The name was said so tenderly that she felt tears come to her eyes, but she blinked them away. 'SussieBelle, what did they do to you over there?'

'Nothing, Oom.'

Things bothered Belle at home.

The excessive eating. Three meals each day, and then still all the teas. Her journey to Europe was a novelty. She and her mother were invited out: Come, tell; come tell. Up to six large tarts at one of those teas, more tarts than guests. Her mother thrived on all the attention.

The relationship with Grieta. When Belle tried to embrace her, Grieta pushed her away with a nervous glance over her shoulder at Agnes, 'Better not, Miss Belle.'

'What is Grieta's surname, Ma?' she asked one morning.

Her mother didn't know. Her father thought he knew. 'On that form

I had to complete, years ago now, when her man died. What was it now? Apools? September? But that doesn't help. His surname was not her surname: they weren't married. Bit of a mess. Her children don't all have the same father either. Goodness only knows how their surnames will ever be sorted out.'

The word 'mess' again. She put it out of her mind.

In the mornings she sometimes sat with him when she took him his tea. He was still a handsome man, although his skin had a yellow tinge now. There was grey in his hair, but it was still as thick as ever. He combed it high off his forehead, the sides kept short – her mother trimmed it. He was fussy about his haircut, leaning first on one elbow, then on the other elbow. He only got up to shave.

'How long has he been bedridden, Ma?'

'About two weeks. He says it hurts him to walk.'

'I found Ozzie's grave, Pa,' she said. 'You got the pictures, didn't you? I couldn't be absolutely sure it was his grave. It just looks the way a grave does, but it's a beautiful area, with the big mountain and the snow-covered peak.'

They didn't enquire about her stay in Kitale. Their own little lives, she thought, are all that concern them. She was not inclined to mention it herself. She read the newspaper to her father. He was against the government's policies. 'Why I still get *Die Burger*, I don't know. I wonder what Father would have said about this dominee's nonsense. We still needed Jannie Smuts, even if only for another five years. If only he had made it to the '53 elections.'

Father, still Father, thought Belle. He forgets that his father was against Smuts, supported Malan, the dominee from Riebeeck-West.

'Oupa didn't get opinions from on high as he liked to pretend. Oupa also erred. He was so against your going to German South West Africa, and now we see what the Germans really were.'

She sat down in front of him. 'Oh Pa,' she said, and took his hand in both of hers. 'I don't understand anything any more. I don't know why things happen or what I should think.'

She was afraid she was going to cry. She had almost told him about Hussein. He noticed nothing, folded the newspaper so that he could read it himself.

'Shall I go, Pa?'

He said nothing. When she reached the door, he called her back. She turned, expectantly. 'Please take my cup to the kitchen.'

She went to speak to the doctor. He promised that next time the specialist came to Wellington, he'd bring him to see her father. Staying in bed was not a good idea.

She lay on her back with her hands beneath her head for hours. She had to get a job. Schools had already started. It would have to be a private school or a cram college. Anything. Not here. She recalled the trip to the airport in Oom Hendrik's car. At least Johannesburg was a city.

Probably the only place that actually looked like a city, if it was inevitable that she work in this country.

'You should consult your Tannie Leonora about it,' said her mother, 'after all she gave you money ... I really wanted you to come with me to Miss Marais ...'

'All right, Ma,' she pacified her, but in such a way that, even to herself, she sounded condescending. 'I'll go to Cape Town and tell Tannie Leonora, and I'll promise to repay her all the money I wasted, and I'll go and see your Miss Marais. Even though I don't believe that story about her being my ouma ...'

Her mother took her by the hand and led her to the sitting room. They stood among the ferns and pot plants. 'Where did you pick up this nasty way of speaking, SussieBelle? Try to think of other people. Miss Marais is a good friend of mine. Whether she is a relative or not, the friendship means a lot to me.'

In Adderley Street Belle caught the bus to Tamboerskloof. She had come to the city by train, her first destination the Standard Bank to convert Hendrik's credit note for 60 pounds into cash. With the money in her handbag she went to Leonora. She was to spend the weekend with her.

Leonora was in the kitchen once again, she was making sandwiches. 'Make yourself at home, you know your room.'

Belle went first to Leonora's room where she put the notes under the reading lamp next to the bed, making sure they were still visible.

'I have repaid some of your loan,' she said. 'Not all of it yet, but when I find work, I'll send the rest. I've kept ten pounds for the train ticket and a pound or so for incidentals. I will stay with Oom Hendrik in Johannesburg, they have phoned to invite me. Just for the time being.'

Leonora didn't oppose the idea. If that was what Belle wished.

'The money is under the reading lamp. You should put it away, so the servant isn't suspected of taking it.'

'What's happening to you, Belle?'

Leonora had also grown older. Why had everyone changed so much and she hadn't even been away a full year? thought Belle. Or was she now seeing them as they really were for the first time? How old was Leonora? Not yet 50. She was going grey, her face was lined, her hands and nails were neglected, her clothes old-fashioned. But the profile. Heavens, if only she could have that profile. And even when she leaned over to spread the bread she did so with a certain elegance. Even with the streaks of grey in it her thick dark hair was remarkable. Yet there was something different about her, something relaxed.

'Nothing. What should be happening? I must simply find work, that's all. Pa can't support me, and I don't want him to. I have my training. Tell me about tomorrow. I can smell the chicken in the oven. And Ma sent rusks.'

She was to accompany Leonora up the west coast to Saldanha to pick up Philip's son Barry at the naval base.

'I wonder what I should take along to drink? I bought a few bottles of beer, but now I'm not sure …'

'Whether Barry is old enough for that? Come on, Tannie Leonora.'

They left early in Leonora's little second-hand four-door Ford Prefect. There had been unseasonable rain during the night, hitting the iron roof like little chisels the whole night. They'd scarcely turned onto the main road to Saldanha when the sky cleared. The sky was blue and the slight dampness on the shrubs along the roadside vibrated in the sunlight. The tar road glimmered. When she looked back, Belle saw the blue mountain, washed clean, and flat as a table, with its guards each side. She had to concede reluctantly: it was beautiful.

They drove through the fishing village of Saldanha, and were stopped at the big gate to the naval base. Barry's name was phoned through.

'He's bringing a friend for the weekend,' Leonora told the guard. 'I don't know who. My nephew will give his name.'

More cars had drawn up at the gate: parents fetching their sons for the free weekend. Barry was lean and dark, with dark eyes that seemed familiar to Belle – he reminded her of the portrait of her ouma, Emma. As a child she'd often stared at the portrait of the strange woman who had died young: the ouma with the thick dark hair, the frill at the neck, the dark and mysterious eyes.

The friend had a freckled face and red hair. 'Tannie, it's such a mix-up here, it's really great to get away. We're like prisoners in there; and when Barry said I could come along, I jumped at the chance.' He nudged Barry. They only just managed to fit into the back of the car. 'Us two Transvalers have to stick together. They ask why we Vaalies are buggering around in the water. They say we're going to end up feeding the fish. I'd like to see them hunt a kudu. Hey, do you know what, Tannie? My Pa was going to take me on an elephant hunt last winter and do you know what happened then?' The redhead laughed at himself. 'Then this boy got measles. I'm missing out again this year. But next year, just watch me.'

Leonora said, 'We're going up the west coast for another 60 miles. I want to show you Lambert's Bay.' She teased them. 'So that you can see enough fish.'

The redhead talked non-stop, 'You must call me Little Hell, Tannie, it's a family name, from Daniel. Pa and the others say the lions would have eaten me up in their den, so they just call me Kleinhel, like Klein-Jan or Klein-Piet'

The boys helped Leonora to park between the jetty and the beach, as near to the sand as she could get. The smell of sea and fish streamed into the car when they opened the doors. A boat was dragged out, the fishermen in oilskins shoved and heaved. The captain was a swarthy man, the rest in shades from dark to white; as they shouted to one another, the fish lay in a bright glimmering heap in the hold.

'That's not Afrikaans they speak,' said the redhead. 'And those are no white people there. My Ma would say; close your ears, Little Hell, they're rude those words. Ma has a temper you know, Tannie.'

Barry laughed. 'He's like that, Tannie Leonora. But he backs me up against the English. They don't like us here at Saldanha. They call us hairy-backs and rock-spiders. We don't belong in the navy, so they say.'

They drank the beer and Leonora unpacked the food. They sat on the sand with the car protecting them from the slight breeze. Belle said little. The build of a passing fisherman drew her attention. He was tall and walked with a loose gait. His knitted cap was on the back of his head, pushed back so that black curls protruded on his forehead. He had a long narrow nose, a sallow complexion. He turned his head to shout to a mate; his lips were thick and swollen and cracked from sea-water and sun, his voice shrill, his accent flat. Any connection that had started to form in her imagination was shattered.

'This is where Nellie's husband's daughter-in-law comes from,' she said at last. The boys had gone down to the sea. They packed up.

'Actually from a small village a bit north of here. There is a fish factory.'

'Do you still see them, Tannie?'

'Sometimes.' Leonora got up from the sand. She shrugged. She looked across the water. 'No, that's not true. I do. I sometimes invite the girls to visit, they found work in Woodstock. It was a difficult time for them.'

I see him, thought Leonora, yes, I see him, the big man with the rough skin and hands and the calm blue eyes. We walk along the quay together and he shows me the seals at play. His arm touches my breast accidentally and, entirely intuitively, my body responds to him. As my body could never respond to my clever Englishman. That it had to be him, the father of Baby and her sisters …

Her life had become weekends. From Friday evening the restlessness as she drove to the hotel in the fishing village. She had started to sketch, her heart was full and her fingers were ready to give expression to it: a seagull hovering, a rope lying on the wooden jetty. She sat drawing while she waited for him. He saw her, she could tell from his arm movements, the way his shoulders bent forward as he lifted the big baskets, passing them on. They walked to his cottage. He made her tea – his daughters were away, working in Woodstock. What had been her motives to get them away? Why not? His big hands spread the cloth over the table. So calmly. She sketched the interior of the cottage. He washed himself in the small bathroom and took off his salt-water drenched clothes. She stroked his eyelids, combed his salty-wet hair with her fingers, curled her fingers around his ears, and touched his lips. He was rough with her. Was this roughness what she sought? And feared? And didn't wish to find? She knew it couldn't last, and she surrendered herself to it.

'Tannie, you shouldn't have helped them to be reclassified. They say the Danish King had the whole nation wear Stars of David, so the Nazis could do nothing. You should all have had yourselves classified coloured. Then the law would have been meaningless.'

Leonora heard, as if from a distance, the flood of words Belle was pouring over her.

She would have liked to pay attention, it was the first time Belle had opened up, and now her thoughts had wandered, 'What was that, sweetheart?'

'Nothing, Tannie Leonora.'

Leonora tried to patch together what she'd heard: classification.

'One must realise that it was an embarrassment to the brothers up there, they're so keen to get ahead in politics, and,' she tried joking, 'with their Boland blood they're already suspect!'

'Suspected of what? God! The arrogance of these people!' Belle said. 'Is it a sin to be coloured?'

'My dear Belle, don't be so serious …'

'And the passion for what is right, the obsession with the good which Oupa always spoke about? What about that? The obsession with God?'

Leonora didn't reply. She shook out the tablecloth and folded it.

Nobody understands, thought Belle. Not even Leonora. In future she'd say nothing.

They checked into the hotel for the night.

'Perhaps I should have taken you inland. You stay so close to the sea at Saldanha.'

'It's great here, Tannie. We're always cooped up at Saldanha.'

'We didn't even know a bakkie was a boat!'

'What on earth would I have done with you in my tiny house in Cape Town? I thought this was a better idea: I love this coast. You can go for a walk this afternoon, or swim … I'll have a rest. But you go out, go ahead.'

The boys went off to watch the boats which were being dragged out onto the beach, then to the rocks. Belle saw their bounding figures fade into the distance, like dogs let off the leash.

She inhaled the ozone deep into her lungs. The sun was harsh, but the wind started to come in from the sea in little gusts, bringing a surprising tang to the air. It sharpened her senses so that she began to take longer and faster strides; her hands took a firm hold on rocks and cement blocks as she left the beach and started climbing over a construction built out into the sea. She felt the wind damp in her hair, took an elastic band from her pocket and fastened her hair at the back of her neck. She became aware of the relationship of her body to the earth, the rocks, the wind, the sun, the smell of the sea, even the foam spattering over her as she clambered along the breakwater under construction, deeper and deeper into the sea, ever further from the land. Even gasping for breath, or missing her footing on the wet slippery rocks, her foot half in a pool, gave her a physical pleasure she'd long ago forgone.

It was low tide, and wet slippery surfaces of the concrete blocks were forcing her to proceed on hands and knees. Then when she hoisted herself up a last incline, she landed, to her surprise, amongst a great flock of seabirds.

The mewling racket was deafening. Like litter caught in the wind, the birds reeled and fell and soared and swooped around her head. She fended them off with her hands, pressed her ears closed. The movement of her arms disturbed them even more, so that those that had landed took to the air again, waddling clumsily to take off, only to turn back and, with wings spread wide, to squawk and scold. There were hundreds upon hundreds of them. Some sat on the rocks, others skimmed through the air. She saw some of the birds fishing out at sea, dropping out of the air like arrows to dart at their prey. And the horrible stench of guano. Guano Island. Which they were thinking of linking to the mainland, creating a bird reserve. She'd heard of that, perhaps Leonora had told her?

Her climb had left her breathless and she went to sit on one of the rocks with her hands over her ears. Gradually the clamour subsided, although there was continual flapping, like scraps of paper blown in the wind, an ash heap caught up by the wind. Continual diving into the sea after fish.

Gradually she discerned a pattern. A strange pattern. On the right-hand side the white seabirds – Cape gannets, she would learn later – gathered in their colony of thousands. The males hovered above the females who sat on the nests which were no more than scratchings in the rocks and a few twigs and straws and some bark. And then, keeping themselves completely separate on the other side, were the black birds, cormorants. A patch of white, a patch of black. The white birds were bigger, with long necks restlessly probing the air; big pointed beaks seeking a mate's to rub against, and those in the air skirled and dived and wheeled. The black cormorants' side also teemed with birds. Their smaller but heavier backsides waddled as webbed feet staked claim to their bit of territory, the inquisitive heads an extension of the body, the beak hard and pointed with a slight hook underneath. With them too there was a constant flying up and wheeling and flapping of wings and diving into the water.

Even in nature you can't escape it, she thought wryly, white with white and black with black.

As she watched it happened. An immature black cormorant had mistaken his descent and landed amongst the white gannets. Right near to her. She saw it in detail: the white males attacking the smaller black one. He was knocked over, one gannet had him by the wings, tearing at him, another fastened his beak in the neck feathers and he was dragged further into the midst of the white birds. They descended on him mercilessly, feathers flew, entrails began to fly, his gut dragged as he was flung about. A large gannet which had risen swooped down on the struggling bird, and that was the end of him.

The enraged birds then took to the air, hanging like a threatening protective umbrella above the white colony. Some of the black ones rose, fell back again; the sun was behind a cloud, the wind was suddenly colder. Gradually the birds settled down.

Belle struggled back across the cement blocks and slippery rocks; the tide was rising. Where she crawled across the slime on all fours the cold water washed over her ankles, over her hands and upper arms. A freak wave soaked her.

The skirling of the birds grew fainter. At last she felt the firmness and the warmth of the sand beneath her feet, then the tar on the road. She should have frightened off the white birds, waded in amongst them, in spite of the sharp beaks and the furious muscled wings.

She went up the hotel steps. Her hair hung in rats' tails, her wet clothes clung to her body, and she was shivering with cold.

Leonora was sitting on the stoep, and when she saw her, she cried, 'Oh, dear heaven, what have you been up to now, Belle? Soaked through. If you don't take care you'll get sick again, here with us. We don't want that to happen, do we?'

11

Necessity obliged Belle to stay with Hendrik and Rina as she didn't have the money to pay for lodgings while she looked for work in the City of Gold. In the mornings she sat in the back of the big black car with Hendrik while the black driver manoeuvred through traffic jams and road works on the way to the centre of the city.

It was difficult to communicate with Hendrik. Difficult also to avoid the interviews he wanted to arrange for her. It was a release and a minor victory when she said goodbye to him on the pavement outside his big steel-and-glass business centre where the driver dropped them. And could find her own way. No thanks, Oom, I don't want a job in your firm. No, Oom, don't phone that headmaster. I know you have contacts, but I'll manage on my own.

He didn't understand her. The shoulders of the big, heavy body sagged disconsolately as he went through the revolving glass doors, but by the time he reached the lifts, they were vigorously squared again. His bearing announced: Let's get going! There's work to be done! There's no time for hesitating. Buck up!

Where to? thought Belle. To what purpose?

Some days she simply wandered aimlessly through the streets. Eloff Street, across at Commissioner Street, even as far as Fox and Main Streets. She walked for miles, went down stairs to little second-hand shops in basements, touched the wares, and sometimes sat for hours stirring a cup of coffee that grew cold on the formica table. It was all so ugly. The ugliness of the city was a better match for her mood than the affluent suburb where Hendrik lived, the pretty garden, the high walls, the dogs, Rina's concern and the way she followed Belle about.

'Was the little green blouse useful, Belle? Oh, I remember the morning I bought it. Pappie had said: nothing is too good for my little niece. Buy her something that'll knock the socks off those overseas chaps. Not that he'd have liked you to marry a man from overseas, sweetheart, just so that they could see how lovely our Boeremeisies can look. Own up now, was it romantic?'

'Yes Tannie, very romantic. No Tannie, he won't be coming here to visit me.'

The southern part of the city was so ugly that it had a charm of its own. She ate samoosas at a cheap, dirty, shabby Indian café. She sat at the table and ate the samoosas out of the twist of cheap white paper through which the grease oozed in patches. She ate, although she was no longer hungry, and because her chair was turned to the street window, she didn't care when tears ran down her cheeks.

That's all I have left of my great love, she thought, eating samoosas in a dirty slum.

And in the afternoon after five she waited at the entrance to Hendrik's office building, to drive back in the big black car, because only buses for black people went to his affluent suburb. She once stood at a bus stop and the green Putco bus, packed with black workers, rattled past. At a stop a bit further on a black woman climbed aboard, she was hoisted up by the arms and pushed into the already crowded aisle. If it had been her getting on, would they have fallen on her and torn her to shreds like the gannets had ripped the cormorant apart?

In the end it was her cousin, Arnold, who found her a job. He came to dinner one Sunday. 'Teaching, you say? Afrikaans, English, History. I know a chap at the Tech. He moonlights at cram colleges and private schools. And as a newspaper sub. He'll know where they need someone.'

She met Arnold in the cafe at the Technical College in Eloff Street, near the station. He was on his way to a story, his camera equipment was on the floor next to his chair. He took out a comb and slicked back his hair. 'I'll just stay until he gets here, and then I'm off. Here he comes.'

He beckoned to him. 'This is Holtzhausen, this is my cousin Belle. See if you get along. She's looking for work.'

Holtzhausen was a tall thin man and his clothes hung from his body as though from a peg. He was short-sighted and wore spectacles, his fair hair was long and straight. He sat down, took out a pen and wrote her qualifications in a notebook. Careful and precise.

By that same afternoon Belle was employed. And she'd rented a bachelor flat. Work and a place to live in the heart of the city. She didn't need transport. Her flat looked out on a brick wall, her classroom looked out on a shaft. She was buried in the heart of ugliness, and it suited her.

She was paid a month in advance – so that she could get her affairs in order the headmaster said. Head of what? Not of a school. Of a lot of shabby rooms with shabby desks and benches, worn-out blackboards that he'd bought second-hand somewhere, a few collapsing armchairs and a bench in his office where the staff could rest between periods, or mark books on their laps. And a swarm of small, delicate, babbling, chirping, immaculately clean, eager, enthusiastic Chinese children, so eager to learn that they couldn't wait for the lift to the fourth floor where the rooms had been rented, but scuttled up the stairs.

'White schools don't take them,' said Mr Jackson, the 'head'. 'The parents are well-to-do and don't want to send them to coloured schools. I offer a service. And our standards are high, we sit the matriculation examinations.'

Hendrik didn't want to give in. 'It's beneath you,' he said.

She knew how to convince him on his own ground. 'I'm working for the preservation of out mother tongue, Oom, I'll teach the little Chinese to love Afrikaans. Each new speaker is an asset to our nation …'

She didn't show him or the Tante her flat, and they didn't insist on seeing it. Arnold came in his press car and picked her up, with her two suitcases and kudu-skin bag, on his way to a 'possible story'.

He held the lift door open with his shoulder to move her baggage in.

'Buck up, couzzie, you'll have to buy a divan and mattress, and a couple of things for the kitchen on the double. The shops will be closing soon. Hurry up. No time to stand and stare, the pace in Joeys is hectic you know.'

The anonymity of the city also suited her. Without the worry about lodging and food, as she'd experienced overseas, and with the routine of working hours and the security of a steady income, the nagging tension inside her gradually relaxed. Beware of emotional self-indulgence, the woman in Geneva had told her. But, God knew, she didn't go out looking for it. And everywhere she ran into triggers that released her memories again: a curio shop with handbags of leopard or kudu skin; a shop selling silk fabrics, a cerise-coloured sari with gold edging on display; leather sandals gathered on a rope and tied to a pole on the pavement. The little shops were strung along the streets, in Jeppe, in Bree, in Plein Street, in all the cross and diagonal streets. But heaven knew, she had to get out of her room.

One Saturday morning she walked into the crowded Indian stalls on Diagonal Street. Oh Lord, the intimacy of the hands, the smell of spice, the bright colours, the sound of the melancholy Indian voice wailing monotonously from a gramophone record. She bought a bracelet, spice, artificial flowers; a table cloth like Auntie Latifa's damp, unstarched cloth; glasses with little red patterns like those in which Hussein had offered her cool drink. Cooked *chapatis*. She bought only so that she could watch the hands close up. She'd have liked to touch them.

She did not go there again. She wasn't looking for cheap replacements. Despite the temptation to flout the law.

Now that she had money, the city offered a kind of deliverance.

She discovered this one afternoon on her way back from school when her attention was drawn to a bioscope advertisement. Crammed between shops, steps leading down, past a ticket office to a basement bioscope. Books under her arm, ticket between her fingers, she entered the auditorium deep underground, moved into a row of seats in the half-light and sat down. The images flickered on the screen in front of her; she leaned back, took the glass of lukewarm cool drink the girl brought her. The images flickered and took shape; she was absorbed by the cheap romantic story. On the return voyage to Cape Town it was the films shown throughout the day and every evening in the saloon that had kept her going. The celluloid loves and sorrows, the false emotions, life and death, had dulled her like opium. Just as Shirley Temple had dulled her grief when her oupa had died.

Now, for as long and as often as she liked, she could descend into these dens stinking of cigarette smoke and sweaty bodies, to be carried away from herself. She learned how to pick up her things and inconspicuously move away when a man, once even a woman on her own, moved into the seat next to her in the dark, half-empty bioscope. She was familiar with the hand on the knee, the groping higher along her leg. She soon learned how to elude the inevitable overtures in the dark, and shrugged off the insults that followed.

On Saturdays she ascended to the glittering foyers of the bigger cinemas to be carried away. And when she went out to the street again, everything seemed unreal, and this meant she was in control.

She walked to her block of flats, bought food from the Swede's delicatessen on the ground floor, bread from the café, milk, perhaps fruit from the Greek.

Sundays dragged in the heart of the quiet, empty city.

She managed well on the money Mr Jackson paid her at the beginning of each month. She liked the work. She even looked forward to the mornings and standing in front of the rows – there were 40 or more in a class – of cheerful, eager, scrubbed little Chinese faces, slightly yellow, not quite white, with dark little eyes glowing like coals of fire between the tight eyelids.

One little boy in Standard Seven, God bless him, wrote his Afrikaans essays like a virtuoso, like a little Mozart, the way he played with sounds. My Bicycle. She read the essay to Holtzhausen who now and then had a meal with her, or took her out to eat – they never went to the bioscope together, that was her own life. 'Good Lord,' he said, 'those shiny spokes, the speed of the bicycle wheel, the grip of the tar on the bit of wheel speeding by, I've never heard it put like that. We must keep an eye on the boy.'

She began, almost reluctantly, to count on his visits; discussed her work with him. He was always in rather a hurry. She didn't know why he had to take on so much work. He was a widower, Arnold had told her, a bit older than them. He was still paying off the cost of his late wife's illness. Cancer over a period of years. 'And before his marriage he looked after his stepmother. Damned if I'd do it,' said Arnold. 'He's a glutton for punishment.' But she liked him, he wasn't a threat. He shared her enthusiasm for her work. He called her Bella.

'That little Afrikaans Chinese of mine – you should hear him recite *Waghondjies* – it brings tears to your eyes. The serious slanted eyes, the little frown between the eyebrows, and two little fists at his sides that just can't resist the rhythm of the verse! I feel like entering him in the Afrikaans eisteddfod.'

'Don't know much about the eisteddfod business, but there are some forms lying around, I'll bring you one.'

With his hair shiny and smoothed down, new little suit and a bow tie, Belle took him at the appointed time to the school hall where the recitations were to be heard. His parents had been so proud, they'd dropped him at her flat themselves.

It wasn't far to walk, past Joubert Park and up the hill, in through the school gate and then to the entrance hall where a teacher was sitting at a table and taking the tickets and allocating turns. They could hear a boy in a hall down the corridor reciting *Waghondjies*.

'You're much better,' Belle whispered and squeezed his hand.

But a difficulty arose at the table. The teacher looked at them with surprise and disapproval. 'It isn't an eisteddfod for Chinese,' she said. 'They aren't allowed in the hall.'

'And this?' said Belle. She pushed the entrant's ticket across the table, back to the woman. 'Fee accepted and time set and now this?' She felt the rage take possession of her, her heart beat faster.

The woman read again. 'Victor Tam, who would have thought that the child wasn't white? Didn't you hear what I said: it's an Afrikaans eisteddfod, not a Chinese one. For that you can bloody well go to China, isn't that so, poor little mite?'

'For that you can bloody well go to hell, and keep your "poor little mite" to yourself!' Belle heard her voice rising shrilly.

Irrational in her rage, she lost control of what she was doing and her hand swept the woman's box with tickets and money from the table in a single violent gesture. As the woman fumbled about on the floor gathering her money, her breasts nearly fell out of her loose floral dress.

'What on earth is going on here?' The headmaster approached. 'Quiet, please, you're disturbing the entrants.'

Tears trickled from the little Chinese boy's slanted eyes. He started to tug at Belle's hand. She didn't condescend to answer the headmaster. She held his hand tightly, turned around and stalked out.

'They are just afraid you'll beat them all, that's all, my boy, because you're the best, I'm telling you, you are the best.' She wanted to take him to a café, so that they could sit down and have something to drink, but suddenly the thought came like a hand at her throat: what if they won't allow him to sit at a table? Just take his money and then make him leave, like at the eisteddfod? She bought ice-cream in cones and they sat in Joubert Park. He licked and licked, but didn't want to talk.

When his father came to fetch him at the flat, he still said nothing.

'I made a mistake entering him,' she said.

He understood immediately, placed his hand on the child's shoulder. 'It doesn't matter, it's a shitty little eisteddfod and a shitty little poem in any case.'

'You should have warned me,' she reproached Holtzhausen when she saw him again.

'I'm sorry, pal, I should have made enquiries.'
'It's not your fault. What sort of country is this?'
'This is only the tip of the iceberg.'

It didn't end there. The headmaster was a member of the Broederbond and at the next meeting Hendrik got to hear of it. His reputation was affected by it. Belle didn't have a telephone so he wrote her a letter:

My dear child, you are after all our child, our only child. I am asking you nicely: please don't lose control in public. We all have to learn not to do that. These are deep matters. Even if we don't understand, we must have faith. We must trust the vision of our leaders.

She went south a few times, by train, to her parents. Her father's condition deteriorated and he died suddenly. She saw Frikkie, Kowie and Miemie at the funeral. Leonora was away. 'I don't know where she's gone, I couldn't even let her know,' Belle's mother said. 'She never tells me anything, but I think she's in South West Africa.' The brothers sent wreaths, but didn't come … business commitments … pressure of work.

She took a week's leave to be with her mother.

'Your Pa's pension will be discontinued now,' said Agnes. 'The bond on the house hasn't been paid off and there are other debts as well.'

'What do you plan to do now, Ma?' Oh Lord, please not Johannesburg.

'Miss Marais wants me to move in with her. She's also alone.'

Grieta, still tearful, brought the tea tray. They sat on the side stoep. The plants were neglected, some dying, only the hardy, spiky ferns still grew.

'You don't come out here so much anymore, do you?' asked Belle.

'No, I don't,' said Agnes. 'It's disgraceful that I have neglected it so.'

'You've been too busy with Pa.'

Some of the panes of glass in the wooden frames were cracked, others covered in dust and rain spots. The paint was peeling. The canvas on the garden chairs was tearing loose at the seams. There was a smell of dry rot, the plants appealed pathetically to Belle. The paint on the cement at the door had worn thin. Belle recalled summer afternoons on a little stool next to her mother's treadle sewing machine: gathering with small stitches, embroidering lazy-daisy patterns on tray cloths. It filled her with nostalgia.

'You couldn't see to everything, Ma.' That moment, on the stoep, probably for the last time, suddenly became precious. And one of the few times she could speak to her mother honestly. She felt empathy with her. She bent forward, took her mother's hand in hers.

'I wouldn't like to think of you going from one sick bed to tend another, Ma. Miss Marais is already ... how old?'

'Seventy-four or five. Not so very old.' Agnes wriggled her hand free.

The cloth on the stoep table was faded, the fringing matted. Her mother began smoothing the fringing between her fingers. She also looked faded, the hair mousy, with too much grey in the blonde. Her face was thinner.

'You are tired now, Ma, things will look different later.'

'Miss Marais needs me. I'll never know whether she's my mother or not. But she's a good friend.'

'You could work again, take pupils at home.'

'I don't think so. I don't feel like it.'

Then Belle quietly told her something she'd never intended to speak about. 'I found Oupa Greylinck, Ma. He remembered you, but he was very old, he couldn't think clearly. He couldn't tell me anything.'

Her mother looked at her; her eyes were still just as green, like jewels on a faded cloth.

'Yes, that story. I worried about it so much all those years. It isn't really important anymore.' She had let go of the fringing, collected the teacups, placed them on the tray. 'I think life is what you want it to be, now, not what your past was. You should also stop brooding so much, Belle. It doesn't get you anywhere.'

'It isn't always so easy, Ma. To forget, I mean ...'

'At last it's getting easy for me, and I think I've earned it. I want to go and live with Miss Marais and share her life. Her house is the place where I have most nearly felt at home.' The last words were bitter, Belle looked at her in surprise.

'Great-Aunt Issy? Oupa? Pappa?'

'I was always ill at ease because of speaking English. I feel like an Afrikaner with Miss Marais. We think the same way. She's a supporter of Verwoerd, like your Oom Robert. SussieBelle, I don't know why, but I feel that I am myself with her. I don't try to be anything I'm not. I had my happiest moments when I was aware of myself as an Afrikaner. And as a white person. Your Tannie Leonora can't understand that.'

'Oh no, come on now, Ma! You, who were carried through Africa by black people?'

'In their place. They knew their place. Not like those of today.'

Belle got up. 'We must get on with packing, Ma. There are still cupboards and cupboards full.' She tried to restore the rapport between them. 'You're a real old colonial, Ma.' But it didn't work.

'The English were the colonials, not the Boers,' said Agnes. 'It's our country, Belle. It seems to me that you sometimes forget that.'

Belle and her mother went down Koster Street to say goodbye to people. 'The little dwarf died,' said her Ma. 'People like that don't live very long.' The little dwarf who spent the whole day climbing the glistening rungs of the ladders in damaged silk stockings with her long hook.

'And Betta?'

'Betta is still there. She's very fat now. She finds it difficult to walk with the wooden leg.'

They held an auction and her mother sold the house and moved in with Miss Marais. Frikkie took her and Belle by car to the little house in New Church Street in Cape Town. The furniture she wanted to keep had already been moved. Belle was to leave directly from there by train. She had an extra suitcase with things she wanted to keep – Oupa's little tent, Oom Hennie's photo albums, oddments from her youth.

Miss Marais hugged her close. 'I'll look after your mother, dear. We have so much in common.' But her eyes were on Frikkie who'd picked up two silver frames from the piano, and was holding them up to the light to examine them. One was a photo of a young boy, obviously cut out from a group and enlarged. Rather rough-grained, but recognisable. The other was an old yellowed letter, mounted with care.

'Good work, this enlargement,' said Frikkie. 'Let me guess. Little Wilson at the Atlanta …?' He was fascinated by old photos. 'Of what year? Bloody old I'd say.' Miss Marais let the language pass because she welcomed the interest.

'From before the Boer War. He was a rebel, caught and executed by the English.'

'And the letter?'

'From him. He was my friend. Yes, you can read it. Read it aloud, I'm beyond shyness.'

Frikkie gave it to Belle. 'You read, I don't have my glasses.' And when she hesitated: 'There's plenty of time Belle, go ahead.'

Belle read hesitantly, some words were difficult to decipher.

My Dearest…

She looked at Miss Marais, but she encouraged her.

I have to tell you that things have gone sadly with me. I have been condemned to death and tomorrow at eight o'clock I am to be hanged. But thanks be to God, I am no murderer. My darling treasure, you must accept it with resignation, there is one God, who will take care of you.

Dearest, my heart is so full of pain that I can hardly write. But pray to God when you meet difficulty and hardship.

Should you enter into a marriage, my love, I ask the Lord for a good husband, who will look after you and your children.

Keep your eyes fixed on Jesus.

My soul is afflicted unto death. The Lord have mercy upon me.

Until we meet again my own darling heart,

Your most loving Braampie.

Miss Marais dabbed the corners of her eyes with a small handkerchief, Agnes put her arms around the older woman's shoulders, she too was visibly moved.

'Died for the fatherland.'

'Oom Frikkie,' said Belle on the way to the station. 'Do you see: that's how I was brought up. That's how they muddled up our emotions. In your childhood they fasten you with such strong glue to some vague loyalty that when you try to break away, you hurt yourself. And you don't heal easily. If you want to do something because it seems right for you personally, you become completely schizophrenic. I wonder whether other nations are also like that, the French, or the Danes, or the Spanish?'

Frikkie, hands on the steering wheel, straightened his arms, as if he was considering her words. He wanted to speak carefully so he didn't make Belle withdraw again.

But she continued: 'This fatherland that has to be something pure, something beautiful, something noble – it's a myth, a chimera, a mirage. Something like ...' the image rose from some deep recess, 'like 31 February: an impossibility, unattainable, a vain belief.'

Frikkie chose his words.

'I think it must be as the church folks say: love the sinner, even though you despise his wickedness.'

'*Cette Russie que j'amais toujours* ...' her voice was cynical.

'I'm not with you, SussieBelle ...'

'This Russia which I love in spite of everything ... That's what a woman in Geneva told me, Oom. An exile from Russia wrote it in Paris – Russia which, in spite of all his sufferings, he'd always loved and always would love … But it doesn't apply to me anymore, I no longer have any love for my country.'

Frikkie thought for a while. 'Be careful, my dear, one doesn't always know what's going on deep in one's heart, there are all kinds of matrices you carry with you. It's terra incognita in there. But I do agree that those two ladies overdo things. They cultivate their emotions. It's unhealthy. I think it's also dangerous.'

'That's exactly what the woman in Geneva said: beware of emotional self-indulgence.'

'Which woman in Geneva? Tell me about her. Why did she say that?'

'I've forgotten.'

'If that's what you say, SussieBelle.'

That ended the conversation.

When the train steamed off, Belle thought: It's easy for Oom Frikkie to talk, he lives in his cocoon in Worcester, taking his little snaps.

She had less and less contact with Hendrik in Johannesburg and Philip in Pretoria.

After her father died she went to Hendrik and Rina one evening for a meal and to tell them about the funeral. The table groaned with food. 'We must feed up our pale little niece, Mamma, don't you think so?' said Hendrik as he tucked the table napkin into his collar. Then he listened again, asked questions about the funeral. He was touched, dabbed at the corners of his mouth with his table napkin. 'I was really sorry not to be able to be there. There was such an important conference I had to attend on the same day. Negotiations that can mean a lot to our country. They needed my presence. We have to make sacrifices for our nation.'

'It's all right, Oom Hendrik. You all sent such big wreaths.'

'The least we could do. Let me have your Ma's address so that I can write.'

The same young black man she remembered from her first visit cleared the table. When he closed the kitchen door, Rina whispered, 'Frans – yes, I named him, you should have heard the other name! Quite unpronounceable! – Frans had to go back to Nyasaland. You know, there's a law now that they all have to go back. But your Oom Hendrik fixed things up so that he can stay.'

She leant toward Belle across the table, mopping her forehead, which was perspiring slightly, with her handkerchief. 'Such a relief, my dear. I've trained him. And now,' her voice rose, 'now he can't ever leave us, because then his pass will lapse. Isn't that wonderful?'

Belle couldn't stop her words: 'A new form of slavery, Tannie Rina. Congratulations.'

But Rina didn't hear, she'd rung the bell again to summon Frans with the coffee tray.

She put off going to Philip in Pretoria. She kept telling herself: later. I must first acclimatise myself to this city, this existence. She drew the small circle around herself even narrower. The few blocks of shops between her flat and the classrooms with the young Chinese became her world. She became jealously possessive of the blocks. The city belongs only to those of us who remain here day and night, she thought. Not to the Swedish woman at the delicatessen selling the imported sausages and exotic cheeses, for at five o'clock she drew the iron bars on the skewed wheels across the entrance to the shop and locked it, left for where she lived. The city didn't belong to her. And not to the Dutch electrician and his son in his shop with light-bulbs and wall plugs and switches, or to the furniture salesman with his discount furniture standing on the pavement and carried in at five o'clock. Or to the pawnbroker she saw unlocking his door in the morning on her way to school, although he'd told her in broken English: 'I'm here Jo'burg from 50 years, maybe more.'

The Greek and his wife lived in a room above the café. She saw the woman hanging out her washing on the little balcony, she wanted to tell her: You're like me, and I'm like you. But she said nothing as she pushed her money across the counter for the bottle of milk or half loaf of bread. You know the city, she wanted to say, as I know it, when the streets are empty of cars and people. Only you and I, and people in my flats – whom I don't know, whom I don't want to know – hear, when we lie awake before daybreak, the big trucks entering the city again with their loads.

The city belongs to us, we are the inner heart of the city, we can only exist in the hub of the ugly, noisy city. Anonymously. Also the cleaners who live on top of the skyscrapers. The black people who crawl on the floor in the foyer and passages, brush and cloth in hand, tin of polish pushed along little by little, polishing, always polishing in short pants and tops of unbleached calico. And they have to stay here, because, like Rina's Frans, they are fastened to the city by the invisible chain of the passbook. Locked in like slaves who have to polish the city they have built, the passages, the entrances, the floors of the lifts. Every particle of dust polished away so that the black surface shines like a mirror. With a bucket of washing under her arm she went up in the lift, right up, on top of the roof, where she could gaze over the city. She hung her washing on the line they'd erected up there in the dirty, polluted air of the city, and she walked past the row of rooms on the roof, where the flat cleaners lived, until she stood at the parapet. She leant her elbows on the wall, she gazed out.

How strange it was. High above the dark canyons of the streets, where the streams of cars raced and banked up, raced and banked up, always on the way somewhere. From high up on the roof she could see a great distance. Against the pale blue sky on the outskirts of the city, she could see the mine dumps rising up yellow like a Highveld winter, like dried-out maize stubble, heaps of earth, dry as straw, with small black scrambling insects moving on the edge, chains of movement, black coco pans heaping up more and more dry yellow earth.

She was not the only one gazing. Across the narrow gorge of the street, on the roof of the building opposite her, stood a man who, like her, elbows on the parapet, head on his hands, stood gazing. And another one, and to the left of her another one; all over on the roofs black workers stood gazing, outside the rows of rooms on the roofs, against the low walls, etched darkly against the fading light. During the day they wore the 'boy's' uniform of unbleached calico, with red piping on the legs and sleeves, and they polished and they polished endlessly. But in the twilight they were men gazing over the city.

She spoke to Johnny, her cleaner, and asked about his family. He showed her a worn snapshot which he took out of his passbook in his inside pocket. 'My wife and child,' he said. 'In the fields.'

'Such a young wife. You're a lucky man, Johnny!'

'I want them here,' said Johnny.

On Sundays the flat cleaners took off their boys' uniforms. She saw them in the entrance, Johnny and his friends. They hummed. They wore springbok skins hanging on their backs, their shoulders looked knobbly above the tatty vests. Their caps were also made of springbok skin, and they'd inserted large earplugs into their lobes. There were leather thongs round the ankles and their feet were bare. They carried knobkerries and hide shields. One or two had mouth organs. They danced on the pavement, knees and elbows drawn up high, hitting their sticks against their shields, stamping dust out of the cement.

'They are going stick-fighting on the mine dumps,' said a man in the lift, milk and bread under his arm. 'Keeps them happy, gets rid of extra energy. Quite harmless.'

'On the mine dumps?'

'There's native dancing at the mines too, every Sunday morning. For visitors. The Tourist Bureau at the station could organise for you to go. Quite worthwhile seeing it.'

'Thank you,' said Belle as she left the lift. He stayed behind. 'You're welcome.'

Sometimes, but not often, she walked in Joubert Park with Holtzhausen on a Sunday morning. Only when she went to the park was she aware of the seasons, or noticed that the days were shorter. Now the purple stocks were holding their heavy, sweet-scented rows of flowers to the sun, and the thin-stemmed pastel-coloured poppies stood poised, surrounded by their own little circular shadows. The flat blue and purple and white and yellow pansies lifted their faces to her.

She took no pleasure in the seasons in the Transvaal.

'It's boring,' she complained to Holtzhausen. 'Always the sun, and the grass always dry and dusty.'

'But what about our rainy season?'

'So violent, it feels as though you are under attack by the thunderstorm.'

'Surely you're not afraid of thunder?' In a quiet way they got on well together. She began to count on his company.

'Not afraid, but it's so violent. It intrudes on my silence. As the rain in the Cape doesn't.'

'Cape rain? Well now, that I find boring. I delight in the violence: the wham, damn-it-all, bang, crash of thunderstorms.'

He hit his folded newspaper against a tree they were passing. 'And the white flash of lightning, shooting through the dark, oh, that's beautiful!' He smiled at her, an attractive, rare smile.

'I'll have to show you the soft rain on the stripped bark of poplars in the Cape.'

They bought takeaways at the delicatessen, returned to the park, ate in the sun. He fed crumbs to the birds hopping closer across the dry grass.

'Spring grass shouldn't look like this,' she said to break the silence. She stood up and brushed the grass off her dress.

'Come, I'll brush you down too, your trousers are covered with grass.'

Then she said, 'Do you want to come back to the flat for coffee?'

She held on to his forearm as she bent and dusted him off. She'd never touched him so spontaneously before and it seemed to both of them that some border had been crossed. But he said, 'Sorry, girl, important stuff this afternoon. Press announcement at Kliptown, on those congresses I told you about – African National, Indian, coloured, even trade union congresses. Arnold will be there to take photos. Can you imagine? Three thousand delegates.'

'Oom Hendrik would say they're a bunch of communists!'

'Actually, it's more of an American influence. It's said they want to publish a list of human rights, for blacks and coloureds too.'

'Then you can be sure my uncles will be upset. UNO is a dirty word to them. And now you have to sacrifice your Sunday afternoon.'

'I wish you could come along. But I only have one press ticket. The SAPA reports are bound to get through; Arnold suspects that we may get a scoop if we're on the spot.'

'I'd quite like to go,' said Belle. 'But it isn't serious, I'll read about it tomorrow.'

'I can tell you the headline already: *Freedom Charter Released*. But it could be better. If, say, Albert Luthuli was going to be there, it really would be a scoop.' He gave an exaggerated sigh. 'But then the newspaper staff journalists would go themselves and stand in queues to get in.'

They reached the gate of the park. 'How are you going to spend this afternoon?'

'Don't know. Wander around, read ...'

She couldn't prevaricate any longer, or continue to refuse his invitations, and the next Sunday she went to Philip in Pretoria.

He met her at the station. The local train was a few minutes late and he paced up and down the platform until he saw her. He greeted her with a kiss.

'Sorry about your father, so very sorry. Couldn't make it to the funeral. Cases in court, couldn't ask for postponement, had to see it through once the machinery was in motion. Terribly sorry.'

She had to walk fast to keep up with him. 'It's all right, Oom. Thanks for the wreath.'

'The least we could do. Tannie Maude is waiting to see you. Barry is also coming to dinner.'

There were two men sitting waiting in the car parked near the entrance. 'Naude, Potgieter ... my niece, Miss van Velde, from my family in the Cape,' he introduced them. 'They're both from the Rustenburg district,' Philip explained to Belle. 'Friends, both farmers.'

She sat in the back with the younger of the two men. They had evidently been having a discussion since early that morning, and when Philip started the car and drove off, they resumed where they'd left off.

The younger man was talkative. 'Pleased to meet you. I can see you are related. A good man, this uncle of yours. Lived in the city so long, but he still loves the land. And, after all, what's an Afrikaner without his farm?'

'This is news to me, Oom,' said Belle. 'Our family has never owned land. Are you going to buy land now?'

The older man in front was heavily built and turned round with some difficulty to speak to Belle. 'Here in the Transvaal now, every professional man has his bit of ground.'

Belle could see her uncle found the conversation disconcerting. He wanted to end it. 'That other little matter I'll sort out in court this week,' he said. 'As I said, I can guarantee you'll have to pay a very small sum for the expropriation, nothing near the value of the land.'

'What expropriation?' asked Belle.

The stout man in the front sighed. 'Don't worry, my dear. It's all being done by the book. A black spot in the middle of a white farming community. The eviction order was served on them months ago. It is only the compensation that has to be established by the magistrate. All routine. It's very fortunate that your uncle is a leading attorney. And we get a good neighbour.'

The church bells pealed out. The fat man sighed again. Everyone seemed depressed, Philip also sighed. The young man next to her exhaled audibly.

'It bothers us to do business on the holy Sabbath, Belle. But it's the only morning my two associates could get away from Rustenburg. What can one do when there is so much pressure? You have to make sacrifices.'

They drove on, took a wide turn, passed through a gateway into a smallholding. Philip parked in front of the house. The two men got out, they held the front door open for Belle to get in next to her uncle.

'Right then, my friend. Everything fixed up, eh?'

'Everything's fine.'

Philip relaxed as he drove off. 'Sorry about that, Belle. They shouldn't have burdened you with those details.'

'I can't believe that you'd take a hand in the expropriation, Oom.' There was an edge to her voice.

'It's just business, Belle. Nothing to be concerned about.'

'Sooner or later someone will have to be concerned about it.'

Philip rested his hand on her knee soothingly. 'But not now. And not you. Right?' He concentrated on the road, but before they reached his home, he warned her, 'It's a busy day today. We have an important guest. We won't be able to pay you as much attention as we'd like. Your Tannie Maude gets so hot and bothered.'

But Maude wasn't hot and bothered. She kissed Belle and took her through to put her bag down and wash her hands. 'We worry so about you all alone in the city. Your Oom is under a bit of pressure today. All kinds of things are happening. Take no notice.'

Maude's skin was cool, her perfume a light citrus scent. But there were two red patches on her cheeks.

'What sort of things, Tannie Maude?'

'Politics, Belle. Your uncles are knee-deep in politics. The guest coming to dinner today is a senator. He and a few others are pulling strings to have your Oom Philip nominated as member of the new enlarged Senate.'

'Do you find that disturbing, Tannie?'

Maude had sat down on the bed, her hands pressed down on the bedspread on either side of her. 'I don't know, Belle. It is an honour. He'd be the youngest senator. He has worked hard for the Party. But I don't know, Belle. I just don't know.'

They heard the front door open. Barry came charging up the stairs. He grabbed Belle. 'At last.' He was no longer the young naval cadet of the weekend on the west coast. He looked grown-up. 'Come to the garden, my sisters are waiting there. I'm studying medicine, only come home on Sundays, and everyone makes a fuss of me.'

There were two extra guests at table, not one. The arrival of the second one had startled Philip, but he soon recovered. 'This is an honour. Can we have another place at table, please, Maude?'

The conversation was lively. They discussed the enlarged Senate from all angles, considered possible candidates. Philip laughed modestly, but was persuaded to open a bottle of champagne that was already on ice. He was clumsy with the cork and Barry had to loosen it.

Belle had a couple of glasses of wine, and her cheeks felt hot when she, glass in hand, half rose and said, 'Has no one ever read about Rome? Does no one realise that packing the Senate is the beginning of the end? The fall of the Empire. Not to mention the injustice to the coloured people. That is after all the only reason for all these new senators: to vote the coloureds off the voters' roll.'

As she spoke the champagne cork shot out and a pale froth spilled over Barry's hands. Perhaps the sound of the cork had muffled her words. But no. Silence while Barry wiped his hands and began to pour.

And then, with a pretence of playfulness, the important unexpected guest said, 'It seems you have a free-thinker in your family, Philip?'

Barry straightened up with the bubbling bottle of champagne. 'You're telling me, sir! A nest of communists, those Boland relatives of ours, you have to be careful of them.' Then he took fright at the pale face of his Pa. He tried to make amends. 'It's only my cousin back from overseas. Give her a chance, she'll come round.'

Maude rang the bell. Plates were cleared, the dessert served. Conversation resumed, on an impersonal level. But the spirit had left the gathering. The guests didn't linger after the meal.

Philip escorted them to the big dark cars, came back to the dining room along the garden path. He was the tallest of the brothers. With his thick dark hair, slight touches of silver at the temples, he looked distinguished. Could have been an ambassador, thought Belle. But his hand shook as he poured himself a glass of port at the sideboard.

'Hendrik warned me that you were wilful,' he told Belle. 'It wouldn't surprise me if your infantile remark at table were to cost me the position of senator.'

And to Barry: 'You did your best to embarrass me, didn't you? You know very well what I mean.'

'Come on now, Philip.' Maude pacified him as though she was accustomed to doing it. The two young sisters were all ears.

Later Barry took her to the station. 'He meant the scandal of Tannie Leonora standing in front of parliament wearing a black sash. And giving the newspaper her name because she wanted at least one Afrikaans name to appear amongst all the English ones, she told Pa on the phone. I heard him ask her: "What do you think you're playing at?" Apparently she answered: "Subversion, Boetie. Subversion." That enraged him even more.'

Belle smiled for the first time that day. 'Tannie Leonora protesting against the senators with a lot of Black Sash women? I didn't know.' Like his mother, Barry tried to pacify her. 'I don't like to be on bad terms with my Pa. But I can't convince him. I can see his point of view too. He explained it to me: they have to pack the Senate to have a majority. Otherwise there will be a mess.'

'Oh well, it doesn't concern me,' said Belle.

The train was already waiting. It hissed and rumbled. They hurried, but once she was inside, and let the window down, there was time to talk.

'You're a Transvaler now Belle. You must understand: it isn't the coloureds themselves they're against, it's their right to vote.' The coloured people's vote. How well she remembered the phrase from her youth. For sale in exchange for a bottle of wine or a little money. Everyone knew the story of Bruckner de Villiers walking through the coloured neighbourhood in Stellenbosch tossing ten-shilling notes over his shoulder so that the whole location followed in his wake. And then he didn't make it against Fagan. Only 30 votes short. Barry stayed at the window. She told him. He laughed. Then he said, more seriously, 'There are a hell of a lot of blacks here in the Transvaal, Belle. People feel differently.'

A young man in a passing group waved to Barry, he returned the greeting. His face seemed familiar to Belle, but she couldn't place it. 'One of Greylinck's brothers,' said Barry. 'There's a whole bunch of them – you remember that crazy guy who came along for the weekend at Lambert's Bay? Daniel-hell or something like that. Well, that's his brother. They look alike.'

'Greylinck is an unusual surname,' said Belle. She struggled to keep her voice neutral. 'You never introduced us properly that weekend.'

Daniel Greylinck, the dribbling old man under the silk shawl. His brother, Piet, had no children. Then Kleinhel must be the grandson of the younger brother, Jannie, who'd married 'beneath his class', the one who'd been in the rebellion? That figured. It could be. And she hadn't known.

The train began to move. Barry waved, then turned around to leave. She leaned back on the seat. Why allow herself to be upset by this? His grandfather Jannie was probably dead, and his great-uncle Daniel in Kenya was probably dead too. And Auntie Latifa too. And Hussein was dead. Then let the dead remain dead.

The train moved slowly past the little stations, picked up the hundreds of black people who stood waiting in the veld beyond the platform. They climbed aboard and kept on climbing aboard; she'd never seen as many black people as on this Sunday afternoon on the slow train to Johannesburg. Wrapped in blankets, although some were wearing suits; some with hats on their heads, some with Sotho hats. Some women had bead anklets reaching right up to the calf. They had white clay on their faces; the hair combed high and caked with red clay, towering against the blue sky like a medieval headdress.

As the train picked up speed and steamed past those left at the station, she heard greetings and shouts in many strange languages. Late winter afternoon in the Highveld and chilly. The train sped on, pursued by its black shadow. It would be completely dark by the time they steamed into the Johannesburg station. She'd grab her luggage and climb the steps to the streets where the lights would be on, she would walk past closed shops, and look away if a police vehicle stopped with a screech of brakes and a wandering black man without a pass was bundled in. She would enter her block of flats, press the button for the lift in the shabby foyer, enter the lift, allow the door to close behind her and take flight upward.

She knelt at her window. The curtain had not yet been drawn. Strange shapes and figures in red and yellow and blue were reflected on the wall by the neon advertisements across the street. She was transfixed. She was familiar with the patterns of rings and shadows and the images of human figures, oddly misshapen, still moving. And were she to open the window, she would hear the throb of jazz. It was a dark, monotonous dull throb, like that of drums. She never heard voices, only the regular beat. Even when she woke at night, it still throbbed. Sometimes she heard shuffling, as if feet were moving across a dance floor, but that couldn't be, she imagined it. But that night the rhythmic, repetitive throb was louder, even when she covered her ears.

She started to sway on her knees in front of the window. Her hands over her ears, from side to side in time to the throbbing. Let the dead remain dead.

Yet this kept running through her mind:

I have seen the movement of the sinews of the sky,
And the blood coursing in the veins of the moon.

12

Even during holidays Belle no longer left the city. Holtzhausen was the only person she saw regularly, but even he did not know her intimately. She saw the family on special occasions.

Arnold phoned her at school, said he was to marry a girl from Boksburg.

'Come to the wedding, Belle. It's going to be fun. My Lulu is a real doll. And the old man actually helped me to buy a house in Brixton.'

'Oom Hendrik?'

'No, my Pa. Can you imagine that? With the proceeds from his snaps!' She didn't go to the wedding, but she saw Frikkie and Kowie when they stayed with Hendrik for a few days after the wedding.

'SussieBelle,' said Frikkie, 'we miss you.'

She was astonished at the stream of memories that the sight of him evoked in her. It was his first visit to Johannesburg and he found the city exciting. Especially the city centre where he took roll after roll of film. In Joubert Park, where Belle had taken him – it was near to her flat – he photographed young and old, white and black, foreigner and Boer.

'Wherever you look, the pictures come streaming towards you,' he said. 'But I haven't yet been able to fathom the soul of the city, Sussie-Belle.'

He was the first of her relatives she took to her block of flats. Up in the lift and then to the roof by way of the cement steps.

'There you are, Oom Frikkie. There's the soul of the city.'

His straight grey-streaked hair stood on end with zeal and enthusiasm, and she no longer noticed the deep lines between nose and mouth, the hollows under the cheekbones. She was swept along by his excitement. He strode across the rooftop, looking here, then there, focusing the camera, taking pictures, leaning over the wall, shooting the streets from above, then sinking down on one knee to get a different angle. The wash lines were behind a fenced enclosure and each resident had a key to the gate. A few bits of clothing were hanging to dry.

'SussieBelle,' he asked, 'have you got your key on you?' She nodded.

'Go in and pretend to be hanging up washing, there, that white shirt.' She did it. No one called her SussieBelle any more.

'Press your face against the wire, look straight at me.' She did so.

'I still have your camera, Oom,' she said.

'Do you, SussieBelle?'

The light changed. He pushed her back into the wire enclosure. The angled sunlight cast strange shadows, the buildings rose out of the canyons behind her.

'My God!' he kept gasping, 'My God!' He worked rapidly. Darkness was gathering. She saw the flat workers looming out of the dusk on the surrounding roofs. 'Photograph them, Oom Frikkie.' He used a zoom lens. Still repeating, 'My God!' He set the camera, took time exposures of the neon advertisements which had started to flicker. When it was pitch dark, they walked down the cement steps to the foyer where they had to wait for the lift.

'I can make you a cup of coffee, Oom Frikkie.'

He patted her shoulder. 'Another time, Belle, another time. Not that I don't want to. Kowie will be biting her nails because I've been away so long.'

He took a taxi back to Hendrik's house.

I could have shown Oom Frikkie the projector, Belle thought.

There was no intimacy between them during the farewell family meal at Hendrik's. They chatted about impersonal trivialities. 'Another time, Belle,' he promised, 'another time I'll come.' But she knew they were only words.

The wealthy father of one of their Chinese pupils had presented the school with a projector and screen. No one else on the staff wanted to take charge of it so Belle volunteered. The first film she showed was of a prescribed novel, *Great Expectations*. The reel broke; her fingers were clumsy in the darkness as she battled to get it going again. In vain.

It was Friday afternoon. 'If I take the projector home, I'll ask someone to teach me how to operate it, then I can practise,' she said at school.

'Why not? Get one of the bigger boys to carry it across to your flat.'

She rented films at a record shop. There was a great variety to choose from. That weekend she watched something different each evening in her flat. When she struggled to school that Monday morning, projector in her hand, and had to go back for the screen, Mr Jackson said, 'Why not keep it at home? It's nearly exam time, we won't be showing any more films. The boys can fetch it, should we need it. In any case there is no storage space here.'

And so she could watch films whenever she chose.

The school had rented two additional classrooms and a young teacher was appointed to teach typing and shorthand. She was a lively chatterbox with a mass of curly hair and everyone called her by her first name: Sandy. A secretary had also joined the staff. Belle took a liking to Sandy. In a strange way she reminded her of Betty. So long ago. In another incarnation. What had happened to Betty? Like Belle, she'd be in her thirties now. Would she still be able to dance?

She heard the secretary tell Sandy: 'Miss van Velde is a bit eccentric, but you can rely on her.'

'Eccentric, my eye,' said Sandy. 'Look at those lovely legs. I'll sort her out.'

She didn't let on that she'd overheard them. When Sandy dragged her off to a fashion show, she went along. Belle bought a few things, pleased that Sandy cared enough to say: 'Buy this, buy that, it's stunning on you.' Although the clothes were left to hang in the wardrobe.

She even went on a weekend excursion with Sandy. Neither had a car, but they could take a bus as far as the turn-off to the guest farm. Half an hour's drive from the city in a north-westerly direction. Then a short walk along a gravel road, carrying their weekend cases. Her courage failed when they were shown to the rondavel they were to share. Dear God, how vivid the memory still was! The cement floor, the thatched roof, the narrow window, the smell of reeds, the chill around one's ankles. The single spider swinging on its thread like a pendulum and quickly killed by the host.

Sandy basked in the sun at the pool. Belle lay on the single bed against the curve of the rondavel wall. The tears ran down her face. She was unable to stop them. It was the first time she'd been in a rondavel again. But she didn't want Sandy to see her like this. The eccentric teacher from the Chinese school in tears! Later she took a book and went to sit with Sandy. Watched her diving and splashing in the water. A young man in the pool stayed close to her, came to sit on the grass next to her, pretended to help dry her hair. But he was also interested in Belle: he chatted about the book she was reading. For dinner that evening Sandy loosened Belle's hair, fastened it back with a comb, dabbed powder on her cheeks, put a touch of lipstick on her lips. This is grotesque, thought Belle. But she didn't demur.

To her surprise she felt a strong urge to return to the place a few weeks later. It was so easy: just catch a bus on Saturday afternoon, be dropped at the gravel road half an hour later, walk the short distance to the farmhouse, then down the footpath to the rondavel. She didn't tell Sandy that she returned time and again. And spent a whole week of the holiday there, when Sandy had tried to persuade her to go to Durban. It was cooler and she was bathed in tranquillity as she crossed the threshold of the rondavel. She became familiar with the few pieces of furniture, quickly unpacked her things. She spent hours lying on the narrow bed staring at the thatch, trying to follow the pattern in the thatching, working out how the domed roof was plaited, the web shaped between the uprights. She lay and watched how the sun, shining in through the narrow window, moved along the curve of the rondavel wall; how the whitewashed graininess was lit up, each tiny unevenness given its own little shadow, and then had it taken away again so quickly; how the pattern of light reached the wardrobe mirror at last, just before sunset, and the blinding copper-bright sunlight reflected onto her. And then it was gone. She sighed deeply, put on her cardigan and went for a walk. She knew the footpaths. First she'd walk along a marshy hollow, watch the birds coming down to drink, then she'd climb up the ridges to where there was still sunlight. She returned at dusk.

She didn't talk much to the hosts or the other guests, and slept long and deeply. She told Holtzhausen about her weekend excursions; he noticed that she was looking better, and went on with his weekend work.

Leonora was going to Lourenço Marques on holiday. She invited Belle to go with her, but Belle made an excuse.

'Your excuse is feeble, Belle,' she wrote. 'I'm going with two friends, you would like them. We're spending a few days in Johannesburg on our way there. Will you fetch me from the station? I'm coming specifically to visit you, not to see my three boeties.'

Belle booked her into a small hotel near her flat. 'My place is too small, Tannie. There's only a single bed.'

'There was a time when you'd have said: I'll sleep on the floor, Tannie, you must stay with me.'

Belle didn't answer.

So Leonora only once had a quick cup of tea with Belle who couldn't endure having her aunt scrutinise her bed-sittingroom.

'I know it's dreadful, Tannie. But it suits me.' It didn't occur to her to mention the projector and screen.

'Your mother isn't getting any younger, Belle. Miss Marais needs a lot of attention, she's often sick. You should come to Cape Town again.'

'After Pa's death I told Ma it was ridiculous to exchange one invalid for another.'

'You're hard, Belle.'

She didn't cook for Leonora. They ate out, usually at Leonora's hotel, where she insisted on paying.

If only she could sit down on the floor and rest her head on Leonora's lap as she'd done as a child. If only she could talk to her. But what was there to say? Too much time had passed. It was no longer so very important.

'I love you, Belle,' Leonora said when it was time to go.

She was standing at the train window and Belle was on the platform. Leonora saw a variety of emotions – boredom, relief and then suddenly something intense – cross Belle's face. Was it fear of being left? Fear that the darkness would descend again? What is it, child, for God's sake what is it? And at that moment Belle grasped Leonora's hand, went to stand dangerously close to the coach, pressed the hand to her cheek. Leonora felt tears come to her eyes. Then Belle released her hand.

Was Leonora also thinking of the parting on the Wellington station, almost eight years earlier, when her fingers had been the last to touch Belle's hand? Then the train coupling lurched, the conductor's whistle sounded shrilly, steam gushed between platform and carriages, the window at which Leonora stood began to move, and the distance between her and Belle increased.

13

Several years passed before Belle visited Philip and his family again. By then they'd moved to a larger and smarter house in Waterkloof. She was in her thirty-fifth year when Barry contacted her on the school telephone.

'Come on, Belle. It's high time we all got together again. It's Pa's birthday. Oom Robbie and his children are coming from Potch. If you don't say yes, I'll come and bang on your door until all the neighbours threaten to call the police!'

Barry, now qualified, was specialising as a paediatrician, and he spent all his time at Baragwanath Hospital. He insisted on fetching her. 'Unfortunately Oom Hendrik isn't coming, Tannie Rina isn't well.'

'I'll come by train,' said Belle. Barry was spending the weekend in Pretoria and he fetched her at the station. The house was situated high on Waterkloof Ridge, with a beautiful view and green lawns. Two young girls and three little children were running about like colourful butterflies among the shrubs. The little ones in their pretty Sunday dresses screamed as the two older cousins tried to catch them. One little one tripped and fell flat in a border of purple and yellow pansies. She struggled to get up, rubbed her eyes with dirty little hands. 'You pushed me.'

'I didn't.'

'You did.'

'The three little ones are Oom Robert's,' said Barry, 'and those two young ladies are my sisters. Can you believe it?'

The grown-ups stood on the patio, drinks in hand. Belle's arrival with Barry interrupted their conversation. Robert put down his drink, pressed her against him. He wasn't quite sure how to behave towards her.

'None of us is getting any younger, eh?' He began to work out when he'd last seen her.

The years had taken their toll from Robbie too, the youngest, Leonora's favourite brother, with the fly-away quiff. His hair was thinner – was that grey there in the blonde? He was leaner than his brother Philip, shorter and his face thinner, his nose and chin sharp and his lips thin. He used his hands expressively when he spoke. His remarkable blue eyes were dark that day, blazing with conviction, pent-up energy and dynamism. Something ruthless as well? Maude was cool and beautiful as ever; her perfume with an undertone of citrus. She and Estie, Robert's plump young wife, were on their way to the garden. 'We'll pick flowers for you to take home too,' she told Belle who was standing with Barry. Philip had apparently forgiven Belle's provocative outburst during her previous visit. He had subsequently made it into the Senate and had bought this splendid house with the profits from the expropriated land – advance knowledge about a development always yields dividends.

He kissed her, and looked at her closely. 'Still all alone there in the city? That's no good!' he teased.

'And here we go: talking politics again … there's no stopping your Oom.'

She listened. It was difficult not to listen to a voice as strident as Robert's. 'Can you believe it, Philip, in Potchefstroom, in my Political Philosophy class, where my students are taught to think for themselves, this "winds of change" nonsense reared its ugly head. A little twit thought to instruct me …'

'That Harold Macmillan came here to stir things up … Father would have said: the hypocritical English.' Philip drank whisky these days, he was on his second.

'I said to him: If the other countries in Africa fall like card houses – the domino-effect, and all that – let them go ahead. Let the English, the Portuguese, the French and the Devil knows who else, pack their bags and go. We know what's best for our black people and, by God, we're going to stick to our guns. We're damn well giving our blacks the vote, not taking it away.'

'Boetie, you know as well as I do: the vote outside of the Homelands is what they want.'

'What they want and what they'll get are two different things. The pass laws create difficulties, I know. But the passbook is essential. They must just put up with it.'

Maude and Estie had returned from the garden, they came to call the others. Maude put an arm around Belle's waist. 'Leave the men, they've raised politics to a fine art. Everything discussed: nothing solved.' She called to the girls in the garden. 'Come in now, children, it's lunch time.'

And to the men: 'No politics at table, that's an order. We're celebrating a birthday.'

As they went in, Robert took Philip by the arm, 'Just never waver, my Ouboet. Be resolute, then we can challenge the whole world. As Verwoerd says: stand firm as granite.' Then a friendly: 'Come and sit next to me, Belle.'

Belle was exhausted by the time Barry took her to the station that afternoon. He stood at the window of the train, waiting for it to leave. They watched the people crowding in, some running to catch the train. At the same moment, they both thought of the previous time. 'That Greylinck brother, Jan, I saw him again the other day.'

'I wanted to hear about your …'

'No, not Little Hell, his brother, he's in the intelligence service, high up,' said Barry. 'He told me he was just back from Kenya. His Oupa's brother had died at a great age. Your name was mentioned.'

'My name was mentioned?'

'He had to go and sort out old man Greylinck's affairs, he had died intestate. His estate comes to them now: it's apparently worth quite a bit.'

Belle held the fingers of her right hand in her left hand. She breathed slowly. 'My name?'

'According to him, Indian squatters had taken over the place. He had to get the police to get rid of them. Apparently they've had a good offer from a neighbour.' He looked at her questioningly. Her face was pale. 'Does it worry you, couzzie?' He trod on his cigarette butt and then kicked it over the edge of the platform.

'No, but I'd like to know what was said.'

'Apparently the Indian woman claimed you'd given your word that they could keep the place. I didn't even know there was any connection with you.'

'My mother was a Greylinck, she grew up with the old man. He may have been my Oupa. I was with them when I visited Ozzie's grave. The Indians should have got the property.' She spoke softly, the train was moving, Barry disappeared among the people.

She was pleased to be alone in the compartment, for her body was trembling. She clamped a handkerchief between her teeth to stop them from chattering. Then she felt like laughing, laughing and laughing. They'd resorted to the law, the police, the soldiers with searchlights … it seemed so funny to her, because the old man had died at last. God, but he took long time to die. And her laughter was no longer laughter:

it had given way to tears. Auntie Latifa, did you curse me when the soldiers came again to chase you away? And who else was with you? More nephews from Mombasa? Nephews with tall, lean bodies and dark eyes and a scar on the right forearm and big hands which could form a cup for you to drink from?

Where did you bury my oupa, Auntie Latifa? In that garden that was so overgrown? My mother's garden? She who caused so much damage as a child, just as I did as an adult. I knew my visit would cause harm when I stood in the room with you. Why didn't I leave straight away? Why didn't I walk out into the veld, just to get away from you and from him? Because I too have suffered damage, Aunty Latifa, dreadfully serious damage, more damage than just having your home taken away because Hussein died before he could persuade the old man to draw up a will. Much worse damage, for I live as a stranger in my own country.

Her tears had dried. She pushed the thoughts away. Shut off the memories, closed her eyes.

The train rocked, her head swayed with the movement. She must have dozed off, for when she woke it was dark and the train had drawn up at the Johannesburg station. Most passengers had left the train. The wheel-tapper peered in through the window. 'Jo'burg, Miss.'

Still befuddled from sleep, she got out, and she had to hold on to the escalator rail. The enormous main hall seemed strange to her. Where had the people gone? Even the ticket offices were closed, the shutters in front of the stalls pulled down. When she looked up the ceiling was high and deserted, the walls strained and groaned to support the high, yellow-painted dome. Then the walls began to tremble. Dear God! The walls, like her, were not strong enough. Who could expect such strength from these thin, ornate walls? The walls moved into outer space.

A railway policeman approached her. He said roughly: 'Don't loiter.'

She was surrounded by black women on their knees scrubbing the tiled floor. They slopped water on the floor and then wiped it in ever-increasing circles around their bodies, but before the water was wiped away it caught the red of a neon advertisement. The black women were wiping blood around in pools with their floor-cloths.

She found her way to the Eloff Street exit, past the Tourist Bureau where animal heads were mounted above the locked doors, as trophies or to lure. The kudu, the eland, the springbok, the beautiful, beautiful animals. Their glass eyes reflected the light of the neon advertisement.

They bent down from the wall, descended to her. She touched the rough hair on the skin of the neck, pushed her fingers through it so that the hair folded open in ridges against her fingers; she moaned in recognition of these friends from so long ago.

Then she sighed and followed the path so well known to her, back to her flat.

A week later, on a Sunday evening at dusk, she walked across the street from the Greek café to the entrance to the flats where she lived. The door of the lift stood ajar. There were two men who seemed to be holding the door open for her. She stepped in and pressed the button for the fourth floor. The lift swung into motion. When it stopped and the door slid open, the two men moved forward to get out and she felt to her dismay a hand on each of her elbows. It's the wrong floor, this is only three, she wanted to say, I need to go to four, but they took her out with them. To a flat door which they opened quietly. The one had a revolver on his hip, the other carried an enormous torch. They kicked down an inner door and took her along with them. The beam of their torch flooded the room and they said: 'Look at that! Take a good look.'

Two people were impaled by the beam like insects. They lay on the bed staring up in astonishment. Then the man said aloud: 'Oh, God!' and he drew the sheet up and tried to cover the naked woman lying beside him. She tried to fend off the light with her hands.

'Caught in the act, with a witness to testify,' said the man with the revolver at his side. 'Come on, get dressed. We haven't got all night. Charge: contravening the Immorality Act. It's the law, man.'

The man, who was dark-skinned, sat with his back to the detective and put on his clothes. Then he walked around the bed and tried to shield the white woman from the police's eyes with his body. When she'd dressed, she said to the man, 'Can I have a drink of water?' The younger detective put down the torch and brought a cup of water from the kitchen. She told the man: 'You drink first.' He swallowed and then he held the cup for her, both his hands encircling it as he brought it to her mouth. She drained the water. 'Thank you,' she said to the younger detective. They were taken down the passage.

'Now where are you from, Miss?' the older detective asked Belle. She pointed to the flat directly above.

'We'll escort you home. You'll be subpoenaed. Stroke of luck, having an eye-witness.'

In the lift the white woman stood against her. Tears had left silver snail traces on her cheeks, but she made no move to wipe them off. She had tried to tidy her hair when she dressed. Even in the harsh light of the lift she was pretty, but no longer really young. The man was very swarthy, like a very dark Indian. He stood with his shoulders bowed. Standing upright he would cut an imposing figure. The two didn't look at each other, but Belle noticed a movement between them at hip level. The one hand sought the other, curled together as though the brown and white fingers would grow together. Forgotten images arose in Belle: a white cashew nut with a brown membrane around it. She got out when the lift door slid open, unlocked her flat door. When she looked back, the lift was still there, the door held open.

'We're seeing you home, lady,' said the detective with the revolver.

'Fuck you,' said Belle. The next day on the way home from work she went to the nearest record shop. They knew her, left her in peace to make her selection. She chose two long movies, two reels each, put them in a cloth carrier bag she had with her. The girl behind the counter wrote down the names and numbers, scratched behind her ear with a pencil. 'Long time no see. But haven't you had these already?' She had a retroussée nose and reddish frizzy hair: Great-Aunt Issy would have said, 'A touch of the tarbrush.' It's only your hair that gives away your secret, I won't betray you, thought Belle. She was generously endowed and there something wanton about her walk as she turned from the counter to take out a bag. Your walk also betrays you, thought Belle.

The four reels in the bag were heavy. The traffic thundered past her.

The word 'betray' kept echoing in her mind. Had someone been spying on the woman and her visitor for long? Someone paid by the security police? There were so many stories going around about the security police. Belle felt she couldn't swallow, just as she'd felt long ago in Geneva. Her throat was not only dry, but the muscles were in such a spasm that they wouldn't be able to move. She would have liked to have something to drink at a café, but she wouldn't be able to swallow.

The short passage from the lift to her flat door was endless. Who'd watched the pretty woman and betrayed her? Where were the eyes hiding? Behind which flat door, behind what bathroom curtain, cluttered with boxes of washing powder and bottles of Jik?

Only once she was inside, the door locked behind her, the chain in place, did she feel safe. She drew her curtains and set the screen up against the far wall. The projector was on a table next to her bed. She put a cushion on the floor and sat on it, her back against the bed. The projector began to run, the flickering black-and-white figures on the screen took shape, at first vaguely, but becoming clearer, as her attention focused. The sound was low. She followed the frivolous story avidly. When the one reel had finished, she replaced it. She sat on the floor again. The film ended with the second reel. She got up and the little room about her was bearable again. She felt like a cup of tea, her throat was no longer in spasm. She opened the curtains. The colours of the big neon advertisements across the road were coming alive. It was late.

But it wasn't too late for the law. A knock on the door and a man handed her a paper.

'Subpoena, Miss.'

She read it in disbelief. The next morning at nine o'clock she had to be in Court C at the Magistrates' Court, as a witness in the case State v. Williams and also State v. Nahore.

'I was forced into the flat by the detectives,' she said.

'Just say so in court.'

'I work.'

'Let them know you've been subpoenaed, then it'll be okay. Remember you must wear a hat.'

'The children can do revision,' said the headmaster the next morning when she phoned him from the delicatessen shop.

She walked to the Magistrates' Court. It was quite a distance, she had to ask the way a few times. Small groups of black and white people gathered at the steps as if they were waiting. A car skidded at high speed into the parking area with a reserved sign that said PRESS. Doors slammed and a reporter emerged. Followed by a photographer with a camera around his neck.

'My God, Belle!' It was Arnold. He'd put on a lot of weight and sported salt-and-pepper sideburns. He swung his camera bag back over his shoulder, drew her to him and gave her a damp kiss. 'My Van Velde cousin,' he told the journalist. 'What brings you here?'

At first she didn't want to answer him, but he took her by the elbow and walked into the building with her. 'I'm a witness in a case.'

'Which court?'

'C Court.'

He and the journalist exchanged a meaningful glance. It was as though they consulted silently, and then gave in. 'C Court. Immorality case. Saw it on the roll. How the hell did you get involved?'

'In my flat building, the police dragged me along. God knows it's not that I want to be here.'

She was irritated that he didn't loosen his grip on her arm. To her annoyance she felt her throat beginning to contract, her lips start to tremble.

'Just take it easy, Belle, take it easy. I'll see how the morning goes. Maybe a story there with you. I'll look in.'

She was thankful when the reporter started getting impatient and Arnold had to leave her.

The official of C Court took her to a bench in front in the courtroom which was smaller than she had expected, almost like a classroom. He explained the procedure to her. He showed her where the prosecutor would sit and where the defence and accused would be. The prosecutor bent over his table to add something to the charge sheet. He looked up at her once to sum her up, and continued to write. There were many delays. At last the accused were brought in. First the woman; she and the man were being tried separately. She was wearing the same clothes, but looked tidier. Her eyes avoided Belle. She thinks it was I who betrayed her, thought Belle.

The proceedings were drawn out. At last she was taken to the witness bench. She had to raise her hand to take the oath. She couldn't utter the words, but the magistrate was satisfied when she nodded her head. Why would she lie? The prosecutor looked at her.

'And you, Madam, came down the passage and followed the police into the flat.'

She interrupted him: 'I was taken by the arm and dragged along.' Her words sounded shrill.

'In any case, you were in the flat when the accused was arrested.' She said nothing. He repeated the sentence. The magistrate said: 'Come now, Madam, we are waiting.'

She had no option, she nodded.

'What did you see? The light was bright enough – it was actually a searchlight, wasn't it? And you saw the accused A, unclothed, or partially unclothed with accused B.'

'Objection,' called the defence attorney. 'The witness is being led.'

'Objection sustained,' said the magistrate.

'Very well, I'll rephrase that,' said the prosecutor, 'and I'd appreciate the co-operation of the witness. When you stood in the passage of the flat and saw the accused in the strong searchlight, what was the condition of her clothing?'

'Objection!' called the defence attorney.

'Objection overruled,' said the magistrate. 'We are waiting for the witness. We are waiting, Madam. I repeat the question: What was the condition of her clothing?'

Belle didn't reply. She wanted the woman to look at her, she wanted her eyes to tell her that she had not betrayed her, but the woman stared at her hands on her lap.

'We are waiting, Madam,' said the magistrate again.

'I was there against my will,' said Belle, 'why should I answer?'

The prosecutor stood up. 'Because you were subpoenaed and because the state requires it.'

The defence was silent.

Take it easy, Arnold had said, and then it'll be over sooner. Now her voice was barely audible: 'They forced me into the room.' Then her throat went into spasm again, her face was distorted and she made no effort to conceal it. She grasped the wooden railing, she was cold and she shivered. She barely managed to utter: 'I don't have to speak.' There was consternation among those present in court. The magistrate looked at the witness, and then at the clock that was moving on to nearly twelve o'clock. He tapped his hammer on the bench. 'We adjourn until two o'clock. This will hopefully give the witness time to recover. And I must remind her that she is under oath.' His voice was sharp. 'And that giving evidence is not optional.'

She stayed sitting in the court, even when the official explained that she could leave. She had to decide whether or not she would speak. He had said it wasn't optional. They couldn't force her mouth open and cause words to come out. She was still considering, when she heard a commotion at the outside door, it opened and – good God, what were they doing there? – Hendrik and Philip came in. They were clearly upset.

'I had to phone them,' she heard Arnold say. 'This story is going to make the newspapers, the Ooms can sort it out for you. It's the name, Belle. The journalists are already sniffing at it: *Reluctant witness. Van Velde refuses to testify.* Those two will go to jail anyway, that's the law. If you don't play along, they'll lock you up too.'

Hendrik stood right in front of her, the gold watch chain across his stomach shone so that she couldn't take her eyes from it. He leaned forward as if afraid the walls would hear. 'Listen to Arnold: if you won't speak you'll be jailed. There is no option of a fine, even if Philip and I would pay.'

'It would serve her right if we let her end up in jail. She's more than wilful, Hendrik, she's malicious.' Philip was livid.

'There's not much time before two o'clock. Are you going to pull yourself together or not? Contempt of court carries a minimum sentence of a year, do you know that? What in the name of heaven have you got to do with this mess if, as Arnold says, you simply live in the same building?'

'Nothing to do with me, except that I was dragged to go and watch their dirty work,' said Belle

But Philip wasn't listening. 'I'll tell the magistrate: health reasons. I mean, just look at the child, look at the rings under her eyes. Only the day before yesterday I told Maude: living alone in the city like that is asking for trouble. We'll get a medical certificate. This afternoon. I know someone. Tomorrow she'll be fine.'

They got her to the car against her will. In the corridor a camera had flashed, once, twice. They pushed her into the car. Philip sat in the back with her as if he was afraid she would try to escape. 'Of course it would be better if she spoke today. Arnold's right about the newspapers. I swear it'll be in *The Star* this afternoon.'

The mention of *The Star* disturbed both Ooms. Hendrik, who'd got in behind the wheel, threw up his hands, his cuff links shining like little suns. He sat sideways. 'Move over, Oom,' said Arnold, 'I'll drive.' He started to reverse.

Philip also talked with his hands – it concerned the meeting that evening for which he had come to Johannesburg. 'She's an embarrassment ... people feel strongly about fornication across the colour line ... and my own niece, conniving ...'

Suddenly the implications of the camera flashes dawned on them. 'If it isn't already too late.'

'Both of us in the pictures ...'

In their dark suits, with the white cuffs flashing as the hands gesticulated in distress, the sharp voices pecking like beaks, the ooms brought to Belle's mind the gannets that had attacked the cormorant at Lambert's Bay.

The car jerked to a halt at a red light. She touched Arnold on the shoulder questioningly, he was her contemporary, he had no axe to grind. He looked back at her. 'That's so. It doesn't make a scrap of difference to the accused whether you testify or not,' he said. 'They're obviously guilty. If you won't speak you'll go to jail along with them.'

Belle thought: I'd like to embarrass the ooms. Still more photos, newspaper reports. And their sacred surname. But then she reconsidered: Arnold won't lie to me. A year in jail just to spite the ooms? Newspaper reports, photos, movie images of life in jail flashed through her mind. No, not even to get at the ooms.

In the doctor's surgery she was given a sedative, her blood pressure was taken, she was given an injection and taken back to the magistrate's office. The case was soon over. She confirmed what they asked her to confirm, without emotion, in monosyllables or by nodding her head. She didn't look at the woman, or at the man when he was brought in for the second case. She wouldn't have managed to speak if she'd looked at him. The woman was sentenced to six months, the man a year. When the woman was led away, down the steps to the cells, she gave Belle a long glance, as if weighing her up. Then Belle met her eyes. I'm not sorry for you, she thought. You had your love, your punishment is six months of suffering, my punishment is a life sentence.

Belle resisted strongly when Hendrik said that he wanted to take her home with him. With more anger than she'd shown the whole afternoon, she wanted to get away from them, to get out of the car.

Arnold said, 'Oh, Oom, let her go back to the flat. She'll be okay.'

Hendrik looked at his watch. Then his thick fingers took out his wallet. 'Perhaps that would be best. Mammie stayed in bed again this morning. One doesn't know what the evening newspapers have got hold of, although it would be very irresponsible of them … You must realise, Arnold, it's a great embarrassment to us. Here's some money, take a taxi to her flat.'

They spoke as if she was no longer with them. 'It isn't an embarrassment, Hendrik; with the meeting at your place this evening, it's a bloody catastrophe,' said Philip.

'I'll look after her, Oom.' Arnold's eyes were sharp and bright. This was one hell of a story. Which he couldn't use. Belle: still waters run deep. He didn't know what they'd injected her with, but the fight had gone out of her now.

He helped her out of the car. The Ooms got out to kiss her on the forehead.

'All we have left of Ouboet Stuart,' said Hendrik.

Quite forgetting that their Ouboet Stuart had gone to fight for Jannie Smuts, thought Arnold. He realised: They edit their memories, they're sentimental. But he wasn't in the habit of entertaining such deep thoughts; he shrugged them off.

There was a good bit left of the taxi money when they were dropped at the flat. 'Have you food at home, Belle?' he asked. 'Come, let's get you something at the deli.'

She shook her head. She had enough.

'Bread, milk, stuff like that?'

'More than enough.'

'Then I guess I'll leave you here. I must get back to work, they'll be wondering what happened to me. Shucks, if only I could've taken a photo of you: the unwilling witness, niece of the powerful ... little crack in the granite? There now, I'm teasing you, don't get all upset. Run along now. You look exhausted.'

He saw her to the lift and waited until the door had closed. Then he set off, whistling, stopped to buy a hot dog at the deli and walked down the street eating it. He savoured the tang of mustard; the taste of the sausage and melted butter that he licked from round his lips. He should have more regular meals, he told himself. Drinking at Frankie's with the boys after work was taking its toll, sooner or later he'd develop an ulcer.

It seemed as though the woman was still in the lift with Belle. When it reached the third floor, the doors slid open. Who could have pressed the button? Nobody got in or out. It was an eternity before the door slid closed again. On her floor, the fourth, she got out. She felt that she was being watched, her fingers were clumsy with the key. She locked the door behind her, fastened the safety chain.

She made herself tea, but forgot to drink it. The afternoon drew to a close, it was getting late: she could tell by the droning of the traffic. When she looked down the traffic was one long segmented snake, shining where chrome reflected the light. She closed the windows and drew the curtains.

She had betrayed the man and woman.

She took the projector out of her cupboard mechanically, the little stand with the long steel neck. The white screen was rolled up and pushed down in a narrow slot, like a pinned-down arm. She released the little steel catch, allowed the steel neck to rise in its slot, somewhat jerkily and then evenly, then carefully pulled the white screen up to fix it to the catch. She put the projector on the table, took the first reel from its container, threaded it and switched on. Once more the pale, flickering figures appeared on the screen, the people began to talk, softly at first and then more loudly. Slowly she sank into non-existence through the lives of others, their loves, their conflicts. The hard, tight knot under her ribs started to relax. She lay on her bed. The whirring of the projector on the table next to her didn't disturb her, it lulled her into the old familiar non-feeling, non-thinking. She would be able to sleep, she would be able to surrender. The second reel was halfway when the knocking penetrated her consciousness. She recognised the knock and at first she was reluctant to open the door, but then she did it after all. The shaft onto which the passage faced was pitch dark, the passage light shone feebly in the corner. Was it already night? It had been afternoon when she came home.

'May I come in?' asked Holtzhausen.

She stood aside. He looked at her, then at the screen on which the shadowy figures were gesturing, and it seemed that something dawned on him. He walked to the screen, lifted the catch out of the slot, and the white screen curled itself up. With the screen gone the figures writhed on the wall, faint and distorted. The conversation emerging from the projector sounded odd in the room, like the words of people who had left, or died. Holtzhausen bent over the projector and stopped the slowly turning reel, switched off. Then the room was dark.

He said, 'This must stop. You can't lock yourself away in this twilight world. I don't know why you do it, but you must stop.' He turned roughly to face the window. Because the room was dark, the city lights and neon lights of advertisements seemed brighter, like radiant traces of ore discarded somewhere on a dark landscape, but surprisingly close. He continued harshly: 'If the lights were dimmed behind each one of those windows, and a machine were to inflict this quasi-life on the inhabitants ... Think of it: behind every window, in every building, in every house the thousands, millions of people leading sham lives. What would become of the world around them? You must stop, Bella. You must become part of life again.' He sat down on her bed. The neon lights seemed brighter than ever as they flashed colours into the room.

'I'm more part of life than I want to be,' said Belle. 'I don't know why you're angry with me tonight.'

'I'm not angry. I love you, Bella. Arnold phoned me at the college and told me you had a rough day in court, he thought you needed me. I came as soon as I was free.'

'I shouldn't have testified against them,' said Belle. 'I will never in my entire life forgive myself.'

He drew her down to sit on the bed next to him, then lifted his hand and stroked her hair. His other hand sought hers on her lap.

'You didn't have a choice, girl.'

'If I had refused to speak, they wouldn't have been able to force my lips open.'

'Poor Bella. One alone against the whole draconian setup.'

He didn't say it to mock her, but tenderly. He put his arms around her, let her rest against his chest. 'Relax, my love. Yes, "my love" – although neither you nor I was prepared to acknowledge it.' His fingers were in her hair. Then he lifted her head and his mouth sought hers and he kissed her. He held her face in both his hands and no sooner had his mouth left hers than he came close to kiss her again, as though he had long yearned for her.

The human warmth, the protection of his arms, touched her; the caring, the caring for her sake, was a shelter. She didn't resist when he took off his spectacles and folded them and put them on the little table next to her bed and then lay back on the bed. His arm was around her, she was tired, she lay back with him. The depression in the pillow, where her head had rested while she lay looking at the screen, was still warm. Had the shadows that had filled her room been banished, or were they still with her? Were there now other shadows? She was aware of his mouth, his lips. Slowly her lips – dead for so long, how long, ten years? – returned to life. She didn't object when his fingers began to undo her blouse clumsily. Her breasts came to life again under his hands. He stroked and caressed them, sucked at her nipples. They responded of their own accord. Her body was passive. What had to be, had to be, she thought. She wanted the taut feeling in her to relax. She felt: I've been alone for so long. Her body began to seek his too, she helped him to undress her. He took her carefully, tenderly, almost with reverence. He kissed her over and over – on the eyes, the face, cheeks and ears, then at last the mouth again, long and deeply as if he wished to know her totally. Then he turned on his back, his arm still around her, his hand on her breast.

'It's nearly ten years now since my wife died,' he said. 'I thought I'd never feel like this again. But today, when Arnold said: Your girl had a hard time, I knew: She is my girl, and she is not going to be alone when she has a hard time.'

She lay with her head on the pillow. Had he touched her cheek, he would have felt the tears. She said softly: 'I shouldn't have testified against them.'

But he didn't hear, for once again he turned to her, his kisses became more insistent and fervent, and his seed entered her a second time.

14

It was inevitable that they would marry. Before Belle had told Holtzhausen that she suspected she was pregnant, he'd asked her to marry him and move into his house in Westdene. Without delay. Events in the country had motivated his insistence on the marriage.

One Tuesday evening about three weeks after the court case, he arrived late for the supper she'd invited him to. So late that she'd opened her door a few times to see if she could hear the lift coming. She wandered around in the flat. At last he came. He closed the flat door behind him, put his arms around her, his face against her cheek. His face and hands were ice cold. He looked exhausted, and in a way she had not seen before, dismayed. He didn't want to eat so she made coffee; he spoke with difficulty.

'I was out on a story with Arnold this afternoon. They call it a story. Have you ever been in a mortuary, Bella? Of course not. How could I suggest it? Have you ever seen death? The cold distancing, the finality?'

He took a mouthful of coffee.

I have seen it, she thought, but she said nothing.

'Fifty bodies laid down next to each other. Fifty. Name tags fastened to some of the ankles; they don't know the names of the others yet. Cold finality hanging over fifty bodies. What is past of their wretched lives is past. And there are still more. In the hospital mortuary there are more, but they wouldn't allow us in there.'

'I thought you were taking a late class.'

'There weren't enough reporters at the newspaper. Arnold said: take leave, make an excuse, but come. Have you seen the afternoon paper?'

She shook her head. He took her hand, held it around the coffee mug to absorb the heat, then put it against his cheek.

'They stopped us at the location, we weren't allowed to go in. Have you ever heard the name Sharpeville? It's the name of the location at Vereeniging. The police shot at people. Since the night before last. They were protesting against the passbooks. The police stopped us, we weren't allowed in. And I,' his voice was self-reproachful, half surprised, 'I had only one thought: Were you safe? Had the violence spread to the city?'

He looked at the flashing neon advertisements outside, at the dark shafts between the buildings. 'It could have happened so easily. The thousands of natives who began gathering the night before last … the workers who live on the roofs above us here … only 60 policemen on duty at the police station, also just youths, also afraid. They started to shoot, it got out of control. When the crowds fled, they kept on shooting. The dead were wounded in the back.' His voice was no longer so compassionate, but incredulous. 'In the back! And when I could feel all the violence and hatred and the sticks and fists hit our press car like hailstones, and I saw the firing squad drawing up, the Saracens, I had only one thought: Were you safe? At the newspaper they said the city is quiet, you can knock off.'

She fetched the food she had prepared from the stove.

He went to the bathroom, and washed his hands. On the mirror above the hand basin, she'd written in soap: *I should not have testified*. He didn't pay much attention to it, but absently took the corner of a towel and wiped the words away.

He heard Belle take the plates through and put them on the table. He said nothing about the words on the mirror: said little while they ate, he was too tired. But because he was afraid he had upset her too much with his stories, he said as he pushed his plate aside, 'It's nothing to worry about, Bella. As the newspaper says, the police have everything under control. And the city is quiet.'

She was on her way to the kitchen with the dishes; she turned around. 'That's not the point, that's not the point at all.'

He didn't understand her.

He remained sitting while she washed the dishes. Her school books lay to one side on the table. *I should not have testified* was scrawled right across a double page of a classwork book, over the small neat handwriting that covered the pages. The letters ran, red and poisonous, across the neat writing. He closed the book, saw the name on the cover: Victor Tam, Std 8.

'Bella,' he said, 'Come and sit down.' He spoke calmly in his customary voice. 'Listen carefully now. It's no longer right that you should stay here alone in the city. We must marry. I have a house in Westdene as you know. We can begin a new life there.'

She sat on the chair at the table next to him, played with the red pencil that she rolled towards her and then away again. She spoke softly. 'I'm not happy in the flat any more. I don't take the lift anymore, so I have to climb the stairs.' She frowned. 'I have a thing about the lift; I feel unsafe in it. That someone is watching me. I also thought I should move.'

'Move to me.'

'Yes,' she smiled fleetingly. 'You're right about a new life. I think there is to be a new life.'

Holtzhausen insisted on meeting her family.

At her own request – much to the joy of Hendrik and Rina – Belle took him to have a meal with them. Hendrik was impressed by the tall quiet man dressed in grey, with the thick glasses and the straight fair hair that fell forward rather untidily however much he combed it back.

'I feel like a father to her, she is all we have left of our oldest brother. We have no children ourselves, so you'll understand.'

Holtzhausen didn't impress him as a strong nationalist or a political figure, but as an educator he was someone with his own status. 'Not a teacher, a lecturer of teachers, albeit in technical education,' he explained to Philip on the telephone the evening after Belle and Holtzhausen had left, and Philip relayed the news to Robert in Potchefstroom. A good thing she was to change her surname, the ooms assured one another in turn on the phone. She appeared to be unstable. Especially politically. And with things the way they were at that time, such a powerful mustering of the ruling political party, such an enormous upsurge of national feeling with the declaration of a republic in view, so much at risk – especially considering the part all three were playing in developments – a good thing that her name would no longer cause them any embarrassment. Who could tell which one of the three of them would play an increasingly important role in the future of the country? The name should be kept immaculate, free from even the shadow of stain. Leonora with the Black Sash women in the Cape had done enough damage already. And this one was up to the same tricks as Leonora, that was obvious.

Hendrik and Rina – Pappie and Mammie again since Belle had agreed to move back in with them temporarily, at Holtzhausen's request – were organising the wedding at their home in Northcliff. A small wedding, the couple insisted.

Mammie bought the trousseau. 'No need to economise on it,' Pappie said generously. 'Our daughter won't leave the house empty-handed.' The little house in Westdene didn't measure up as far as he was concerned, but something could be done about that.

Only Holtzhausen knew about the pregnancy. He had sorted out matters with her headmaster himself, recommended someone to fill her post temporarily. Belle felt nauseous all the time and had to conceal it. The greatest test came when the bridal gown had to be bought. Mammie didn't know what to do with this unenthusiastic bride who was no longer so very young, no longer particularly pretty, and never uttered an opinion.

'Something simple, but good,' she said nervously to the saleslady. Her hands fluttered around, her feet in the little shoes with ankle straps and tiny heels trotted from the rows of dresses on display to the fitting room, each time with more dresses over her arm.

'It's lovely, not that one, this. We don't want white, do we? Oh, what this green does for your eyes! Do you remember, dear child, the little green blouse I bought you before you left for Europe?'

She watched with horror as big, shiny tears started to run down Belle's cheeks.

Belle shook her head, rejecting the green dress. At last they settled on a cream-coloured suit with a narrow skirt.

'She'll carry roses – apricot-coloured roses from my own garden. Oh, I can just see her already. The weather will still be pleasant: autumn. The golden leaves falling, oh, you should see my garden in autumn, it is so, so pretty, the leaves will fall upon the bride's golden hair, I'm sure, oh, I'm so very sure we'll be able to have it outdoors.'

It was impossible for Leonora to attend the wedding; she tried, but couldn't get leave. She phoned repeatedly to speak of her regret and to wish Belle luck. Agnes wrote a long letter:

> *How sorry I am that it is impossible for me to come to your wedding. Miss Marais is having difficulty with her chest. She is in bed with a nasty attack of bronchitis. I have asked her friends if anyone could help, but each has her own obligations. A nurse will come here each day, but I can't leave her alone at night. No, I'm afraid you will have to stand at the altar without a mother just as I did. But you are surrounded by your family, which is more than I was granted. I am sending you a tablecloth, which I embroidered, it took years to make. I hope you like it.*

Belle was glad that the wedding would be small. Her affection for Holtzhausen was passive, but she felt secure with him. He was thoughtful and loving. When they were alone his hand lay tenderly on her stomach. Then she covered his hand with hers. We will get along well together, she thought.

The dominee married them on the side-stoep of Pappa Hendrik's house. Big banana leaves rustled against the veranda, the leaves of the deciduous trees were changing colour: rich red and gold and light rust. The sky was bright blue. Although the grass was already dying, there was still colour in the shrubs. Potted ferns grew on the stoep. Only the closest family members were present. A chill wind had come up, a precursor of winter. Holtzhausen seemed unfamiliar to Belle in his specially bought dark grey suit, his hair so neatly combed, his face so smoothly shaved. She had lost weight, and the skirt still fitted well, no bulge in sight. But she was pale. The apricot roses on which Mammie had insisted drew colour from her face, made her look rather sallow. She also felt bilious.

She liked Barry best of all her Transvaal relatives. He came and joked with her after the ceremony when the ring was on her finger and the register had been signed.

'Wanted to introduce you to my friends, but this guy got in ahead of me. Still waters, hey, old couzzie?'

She just smiled.

'Looks like we frightened you at table that Sunday, so you decided: now I'm getting out of this family!'

He took another glass of champagne from the tray Frans, in his white clothes, was offering around. Drank a toast to her.

Holtzhausen came to stand next to Belle, his arm around her shoulders. He felt that she was shivering slightly. 'Let's move inside, out of the cold.'

'We can leave as soon as you like,' said Belle. He nodded. But the silver knife with a bow tied on the handle was shoved in her hand, and with his hand over hers she had to cut through the thick hard icing on the fruit cake. It crumbled stickily under the knife. The slices of cake were arranged on little silver plates with doilies, and then offered around by Barry's two sisters, dolled up for the wedding. At first they had been disappointed at not being bridesmaids, but they were delighted to be very much part of their first family wedding, and, what was more, a wedding with something different, something secretive, something of a story book about it. They were still young enough to take some of the sweet dark brown crumbs with the bits of fruit and cherries and pop them into their mouths when backs were turned.

Belle didn't have any cake. Rina noticed. She suspected more than she let on, but she'd never sadden Pappie by telling him.

'Don't worry, my darling, she'll get all that is left of the cake. You must both take some,' she told Barry's sisters. 'Put it under your pillows, then in your dreams tonight you'll see who you'll marry. There, we'll wrap it in these serviettes.'

The two giggled, but they'd do it. That night, in their pink and white bedroom, with the Dolly Varden dressing-table, the plump, frilly cushions on the chair, and the teddy and doll on the shelf, they would slip the securely wrapped pieces of cake under their pillows. Their curlers and rollers and steel hairgrips would prick their scalps painfully, as they lay on their backs, hands behind their heads. But instead of discussing possible boyfriends, they'd talk about the grown-ups. Belle who'd so very nearly been an old maid. And Tannie Leonora, whom they so seldom saw. Their mother said she was the beauty of the family, but she seldom came to the Transvaal. Their father said that Oom Stuart had said, when she was young, that she never had 'it'. 'Sex appeal'. Odd words to hear from their father's lips, he was such a square, but those were also square words: who ever spoke about 'sex appeal' any more?

Their mother said Tannie Leonora had never been prepared to sacrifice her independence to a man, and she didn't blame her.

Their pa said she'd been bloody-minded since childhood. He didn't know they were eavesdropping. Then their mother said it was very simple: she was of the generation whose young men had died in the First World War. They knew about the war from films and history books. Belle's brother had been killed in the Second World War, so maybe the young men of her generation were also all killed. And that was probably why she married such an old drip. Gradually the discomfort of the curlers became more bearable and they dozed off, each thinking secretly: she had to, she just had to, dream of *him*, but she'd die rather than say his name out loud. The older, more serious girl of the two, would think: I'm glad there isn't a war now. There should never be war again. Never, ever again. Rather peace, like now.

Had they stayed awake, they would have heard something else: Their ma, who had been such a young bride and mother, scarcely of age when Barry was born, sat up straight in bed. She watched Philip prepare for the night. He was becoming increasingly devious, she thought, probably also cleverer, but she wasn't sure of the cleverness. And if he referred just once more to his niece's instability, she would scream. He did, and she didn't scream, but said in a quiet, dangerous tone: 'Don't say that again. Perhaps Belle's instability is preferable to the stability you and your brothers pursue so assiduously.'

Philip would know what she meant. It deflated like a punctured bicycle tyre all his romantic inclinations which had been building up since the late afternoon, inspired by his wife's charming appearance at the wedding.

'Night,' he said as he got into bed and drew the blankets up around him. 'It is, after all, my career.'

'And it doesn't concern you in the least,' she said, 'that my friend's son is in jail because of your so-called stability. And that, to keep the peace, I may not mention it in my own home. One thousand and nine hundred detained since the twenty-first of March, with no question of charges or hearings.'

'Communistic filth,' he shrugged it off, and then turned on his side disconsolately to try to sleep.

He would not admit it to her, but he was sleeping badly. As he tossed and turned the desire in him became increasingly obsessive, not for the body of his slim, well-groomed wife in her cool, apricot-coloured silk nightgown, but for someone earthier, fleshier, rougher. Someone like … Where had the thought come from? From wretched Leonora's whining about the identity cards? Someone like … like Nellie. Suddenly and intensely he longed to curl up next to someone like Nellie once more, as he'd done as a little boy, desperate after his ma's death. Just thinking of Nellie's soft, yielding body, the smell of her hairy armpit in which his head could nestle, the pressure of her big, ringless hand on the small of his back, gave him an erection.

At last he rolled over to Maude. Reluctant, half asleep, but she did have a charm of her own.

Gradually Belle got to know her husband. The pregnancy brought a forced intimacy, which would otherwise have taken people of their age a long time to achieve. Both had spent a good deal of time alone. Belle had never lived in such continuous intimacy with a man.

Schalk, for that was Holtzhausen's name, although no one called him by it, would never hurt her. Neither did the possibility of being hurt by him exist in her. She felt no guilt about it. She could give him what his sick wife could not: a child. And security.

Rina had the trousseau which she'd bought sent ahead to the little house in Westdene. Belle herself had been taken to her new home after the ceremony with only the two suitcases with which she had originally set out from the Cape. Only the kudu-skin bag had been added.

'It's an unusual bag,' Holtzhausen remarked when he carried it in. 'It probably has a story?'

She nodded.

'Well, one day I'll get to hear it, I hope.'

He never referred to the words written on her bathroom mirror and Victor Tam's exercise book.

In the few weeks after that night in her flat and her move to Hendrik and Rina's, she'd been to his house with him once. He picked her up after school. A late summer thunderstorm was building up. The light faded to darkness as the clouds banked up over the city. The secret anthill activity in buildings, in shops, in blocks of flats, in offices had suddenly become almost feverish. The gathering darkness had caused people to hasten, to seek shelter. As arranged, Holtzhausen had stopped at a yellow line and hooted three times. She heard him from the little balcony and went down the steps. Exhaust fumes spread darkly over the already darkened streets. During the previous few weeks, after the shooting at Sharpeville, there had been an almost frenetic aura of tension hanging over the city, something like a web of fear.

'The weather looks threatening,' he said.

Past Auckland Park and Melville up the road to Westdene. The sun was shining there. An impression of openness and light and space. He stopped in front of a smallish house on a small erf, and when they got out he first turned around and looked back at the city.

'So peaceful, almost rural here, but just look over there.'

The heavy thunderclouds tumbled in great swirls over the city. Between the dark masses trails of lighter clouds curled, causing the black to look even blacker. Then the first lightning zigzagged, lit up the congested skyscrapers of the inner city for a few seconds, and then the thunder followed.

Doomed city, thought Belle. Like something in a Blake etching. She wasn't afraid of lightning. And the clap of thunder, shortly after, for the lightning had struck nearby, evoked a strange excitement in her. She remained standing in the street, even when Holtzhausen wanted to go in. She had an irresistible urge to see the storm, to hear it.

He took her elbow. 'Come, over there, where the clouds have lowered so evenly, the rain is bucketing down now. Look, you can see it coming this way.'

The light grew dimmer, almost dusk, she felt drops on her head and hands. He unlocked the door and they stood in the passage. It was warm and smelled fusty.

'You must have a good look, Belle. Everything is as Moira left it, I haven't changed much since she died. But you can do as you please.'

He was nervous, the little rooms now seemed so small to him, so plainly furnished, so full of catalogue furniture. Even the colours of the cushions Moira had covered before she took ill did not seem attractive. Too shiny.

'This was our bedroom, but it faces south. We can use the back room, I have slept there myself since she died. They're the same size.'

Belle said nothing. The room with the double bed, the dressing table in front of the window, the side mirrors, the closed lace curtains, didn't appeal to her. Nor did the satin bedspread. But she should think of sun for the nursery.

'The back room can be the nursery. This one is fine for us.'

She wondered how she'd sleep in that bed. Where his first wife had died.

'Don't look so worried, it's all fine,' she said.

Yet he must have noticed something for, without her knowledge, he had the old things taken away and sold on an auction. Her divan was brought from the flat, and another bought and put next to hers. He took her to a furniture shop to buy a plainer wardrobe and dressing table. She was grateful to him for that.

The Ooms' wedding presents were from Ansteys. She could exchange them. She chose a plainer dinner service, and got a couple of saucepans as well.

'And this?' she asked the first afternoon, when she saw an eight-sided black box on the dressing table, which had been cleared of toiletries. The sides of the box were worn, but it was still sturdy.

'Open it,' he said

She lifted the lid. The box was lined with purple velvet and inside was a concertina.

'Take it out,' he said. She put her fingers through the leather loops and pulled. She was certainly doing something wrong, for it sighed a few false notes and collapsed again.

He took the concertina from her, pressed his fingers, and the melody came tripping out. 'Soutpansberg Waltz, girl. I'm going to have you dancing!' His tall body swayed from the waist as he pulled the concertina out and pushed it back, pulled and pushed; his fingers pressed the shiny round buttons mechanically, his eyes looked beyond her. She couldn't help it: she started to cry. He put the instrument away. 'It can wait till later.'

It was mid-term and Holtzhausen had to work after the wedding. Belle stayed in bed late after he had left for the college. She did the housework herself, just superficially. In the evening he helped prepare the meal. He was by nature a quiet man. They adjusted calmly. In the evening they sometimes sat on the little back stoep and he played her lingering tunes. The house was on a slope and they could see a long way. This must have been where he spent his evenings alone, when he wasn't working, she thought. There was something sad about it that softened her heart towards him.

Sometimes when the sky was clear they saw a moving speck and followed its course. 'Oh, I felt so sorry for that little dog Laika, up there in the Sputnik,' said Holtzhausen. 'More than when Gagarin was sent up. The little dog was so totally defenceless.'

During her time in the flat she had scarcely been aware of the Sputniks, but now she watched them. The human lives moving up amongst the stars seemed comforting in some strange way, even exciting.

Gradually she also got to know her husband's friends. She discovered that her cousin Arnold was merely an acquaintance, and this pleased her. She wouldn't have got on with Lulu, his wife, who was much younger than her.

She was surprised when Holtzhausen said one morning, 'I've invited a colleague home this evening, Jack Boonstra, a coloured man from another college. We met, guess where? The only possible place. In a bookshop. He's looking for a book I can lend him.'

She'd said: That's fine, and prepared supper in advance herself. Boonstra arrived on foot, dripping with perspiration.

'But there are buses, man,' said Holtzhausen as he invited him in.

'I didn't walk from the city, just here from Kingsway, where the Putco buses run.'

The Putco buses, filled beyond capacity with black workers, were difficult to associate with the refined and highly civilised Jack Boonstra, but Holtzhausen left it at that. After supper they chatted a while and then Holtzhausen gave him a lift back to the city. Up until then Belle hadn't met any of the neighbours, but the next morning she'd hardly set foot in the garden when the neighbour's door opened and she came to the fence. She was a thin woman with a leg that dragged, she was wearing an apron.

'I've been hoping for a chance to meet you,' she said. 'I couldn't believe my eyes when I saw a coloured man going inside with your husband. I thought he must be a plumber or something, as I said to my husband. But he stayed rather late.'

'He's a colleague of my husband's,' said Belle, 'he had dinner with us.'

The woman shrugged. 'I thought so. You'll soon find out the people around here don't like that kind of thing.' She shooed off the little dog at her feet. 'We're a bit nervous here. It's a mercy Sophiatown over there was removed boots and all, you took your life in your hands driving to Florida. Such a stink when the wind blew this way.' She leaned over the fence, spoke so that the black woman hanging up her washing wouldn't hear.

'Us ladies have a shooting club. We practise once a month. I don't suppose you'll want to join?'

Belle couldn't follow the logic; she placed her hand on her stomach. 'I'm four months pregnant.'

'You don't say.' The little dog charged at the postman and the woman had to go to the gate.

'You should bring your colleague again,' she told Holtzhausen that evening. He nodded. Jack Boonstra came again. Holtzhausen lent him more books; they didn't discuss politics, sticking to education. Then one evening Jack in turn brought a few books that caused Holtzhausen to look up in surprise.

'This is forbidden stuff, man.'

'How do you mean "forbidden"? Are we living in the Middle Ages?' A challenging tone had crept into his voice. 'If you don't want to keep them, too bad.'

Holtzhausen looked at the titles again. Books about Russia, communism, books by exiles overseas, *The Scourge of Apartheid*, etc.

'Not my field. I'm not complicating my life. Not with a wife and a child coming. You can end up in jail because of those books.'

'You don't say!'

'Come on, man,' Holtzhausen said, his hand on his shoulder. 'Sit down again. Let's talk. I dislike it just as much as you that something should be forbidden. But getting involved … I don't think so. I'm not going to beat my head against a granite wall. I have priorities.'

'I also have priorities,' said Jack. 'And, like it or not, these are mine.'

He stroked the books that had been put on the table. 'It has to be our priority. What is left for us otherwise? I've never told you that I'm married, have I? I also have a child and my wife is pregnant.'

Then he sat down. He accepted a glass of sweet wine from Holtzhausen. 'If I were black the police could pick you up for giving me wine.' He touched his cheek. His skin was quite dark. 'The police have confronted me in front of my schoolchildren and turned out my briefcase to see if I had liquor on me. "Kaffir, show us your booze." Would you be able to take that?'

'I do relief shifts on the newspaper. I know about these things,' said Holtzhausen. 'Do you think it doesn't bother us?'

'Bother is a bloody pale word.'

Holtzhausen ran his fingers through his hair. 'So tell me: what can we do? Just tell me what.'

'Quite a lot. A bunch of whites are also in jail. Quite a few surprises when Erasmus released the names. My God, more than 2 000 in jail and not a single one brought to court and charged!'

When Belle was seven months pregnant, she paged through the *Rand Daily Mail* which Holtzhausen sometimes brought home. She was not a keen newspaper reader and only looked at the headlines. But that evening a heading at the bottom of a page drew her attention: *Alleged Neglect Causes Miscarriage*. With the subheading: *Williams Lodges Complaint Against Warders*.

Her fingers were clumsy. She folded the newspaper to read the report more easily. Now and then her left hand let go of the newspaper and touched her stomach. The baby was constantly moving and kicking. She read:

> *Anne Williams, detained under article 16 of the* Immorality Act *was two months pregnant when she went to jail. At four months there were signs of a threatened miscarriage in her cell. She told those in the cell with her that she was bleeding intermittently.*
>
> *The wardress was informed, but neglected to call the doctor at once.*
>
> *'I was forced to go to the exercise yard with the others, was forced to keep moving. When the doctor finally came it was too late to stop the haemorrhage. I was taken to hospital, but lost the baby. If I had been able to lie on my back at once, with medication, the child would have been saved.*

Her sentence of six months had been served, and she had laid a claim against the Prison Services for neglecting to provide medical care.

She should lay a charge against me too, thought Belle, because I testified. How can my child live if hers has died? Up until now, the idea of motherhood had seemed too strange for her to grasp; then it became repulsive. I am an accessory, for had I not testified, the case would have dragged on and on. There would have been so many newspaper reports, so much sensation, they would have had to let her go. My cowardice cost Anne Williams her child. Or my perverse jealousy? But she rejected that thought. She began to weep softly. The baby in her womb kicked incessantly. What love will I be able to give her, thought Belle, if all I can feel is guilt?

The baby was born in December, a little girl. Because Belle was in her thirties and had developed high blood pressure, she was given an early

Caesarean delivery and the birth was not traumatic, Belle recovered slowly and stayed in hospital the full 14 days. She showed little interest in the baby. Holtzhausen tried to cheer her up. 'We must think of a pretty name. She's so lovely.' He rejected his mother's name and also his stepmother's. Belle didn't fancy Agnes. She suggested Leonora.

Having the baby named after her touched Leonora deeply.

During the school holidays she took the train to Johannesburg. She went to stay at the Melville Hotel, which was within easy walking distance of Westdene. Hendrik protested, but she told him: 'Man, I'm a seasoned traveller, don't you be taking offence now. I like to be independent.'

She helped bath the child in the mornings, she helped with the laundry, she even tried to cook. In the afternoons after lunch she told Belle and Holtzhausen who saw to the child at night: 'You have such broken nights, have a rest now, I'll take her out in the pram.' Then she walked along the uneven streets, uphill and downhill, in the peaceful rural suburb of Westdene. Before long the baby would sleep. She stood looking across the hills for a long time. To the north lay the hills of Northcliff, to the east the outline of the city. So different to the Boland, she thought, the high, sharp air, the different shade of blue, and the ever-wandering clouds.

Sometimes she sat on a rock, the pram turned away from the sun. Once when the baby became restless, rocking its little head from side to side, she hesitantly put her little finger between the tiny lips. She was amazed at the strength with which they sucked and how the sucking motion of the throat went deep into the taut little body. It touched her. I'm bound to this child, she thought, more than just by my name.

Despite her help Holtzhausen was pleased when she had to leave after ten days. She went first to Hendrik for an overnight visit, then to Philip in Pretoria, and then Philip would take her by car to Robbie in Potchefstroom. It had become too easy for Belle to hand the baby to Leonora and to say: You cuddle her, Tannie, my back is tired. Holtzhausen worried about Belle's relationship with the infant.

The family planned the christening for shortly before Leonora had to leave for the Cape again. A long letter arrived from Agnes. Apparently Miss Marais was on her deathbed. With a long severe winter behind her, she had never fully recovered from the bronchitis. Agnes wrote:

I am very thankful that all went well and that I am now an Ouma, but at present I don't see my way clear to come to the Transvaal. I would not forgive myself if Miss Marais were to pass away while I was not with her.

I'll send the christening robe in a few days. Miss Marais's friends so encouraged me to make the robe, took such an interest, they even wanted to help with the insertions, I couldn't disappoint them. But it is all my own work.

The little christening robe that arrived soon after was magnificent.

The brothers sounded Leonora out concerning Belle. 'I'm worried about her,' said Hendrik. 'Try to find out from her, she's always been so close to you. There's something the matter with her.' It concerned him that even on the phone, which, after considerable persuasion, he had had installed for them, she sounded curt and distant. She couldn't be offended because of the phone, but with a birth one never knew ... He felt very tender towards the baby, but tried not to phone too often. What had happened to merry, loveable SussieBelle? Stuart's only living heir. Perhaps post-natal depression?

All three brothers and their wives were at table in Philip's house in Pretoria. Robert had brought Leonora back from Potchefstroom for the christening and would stay over for the ceremony. They were all enjoying the afterglow of good food and wine; Hendrik's cigar smoke hung over the table. The conversation kept returning to Belle. They appealed to Barry. He was a physician, he would be able to advise them.

'No psychiatrist or analyst will be able to help her against her will, and if she is not prepared to talk,' he said. 'We don't know the reason for her depression, if she is in fact depressed. Give her time, the first few weeks after a birth are difficult for women. Things will sort themselves out, you'll see.'

Like the wedding, the christening was held at Hendrik and Rina's home. Leonora was asked to carry in the baby, by then barely a month old.

Maude thought she had never seen Leonora looking as gentle and beautiful. What an effect a baby had on one, on all of them. Even her two wilful and rebellious daughters were touched. Rina, her poor childless sister-in-law, wept openly. Arnold and Lulu were there with their first-born, almost two years old. Lulu was pregnant again. Hendrik had to blow his nose and press his handkerchief to his eyes. The nose-blowing set the toddler crying, but Lulu carried him out.

But the mother, dressed in her wedding outfit, was stony-faced. And Holtzhausen, also in his wedding suit, looked more worried than happy.

Leonora carried the baby carefully into the lounge and laid her in

Belle's arms. She walked slowly. In the gardens of her youth her arms had caught up babies and toddlers and held them up to the trees and plants and blue sky with ease. Now those arms had become uncertain. And she didn't want the moment to pass too quickly. She stood aside, her face turned away to hide her tears from the others. She too, childless.

Philip, the eldest of the brothers, stood as though carved in wood, his sharp nose, his lips and chin motionless.

Robert, the youngest, had put on weight and was balding. He kept his few remaining strands of blonde hair long and combed them over his bare pate. So clever, yet so vain, thought Leonora, glancing at him frequently. She noticed his hand starting to fidget, and then succumbing to the urge to smooth his hair again.

The women were like flowers in a wind-still garden, stately, heavy flowers, she thought. The young girls like blossoms. How tender the line of cheek and chin, how pretty the soft lashes, the shy, hidden eyes, the moist lips.

The shadows of the shrubs next to the stoep lay in quiet patterns, as if drawn indelibly. Then the coldness of the drop of water on the baby's little forehead reached those new little nerve receptors and she howled.

The brothers and their wives gestured to Leonora: 'Take the baby from Belle.'

Leonora, little Leonora, tiny, tiny Leonora.

Hendrik blew his nose again, violently. The next day he took out an insurance policy for little Leonora, on his own life. A large policy.

Leonora stayed with Hendrik another night, then left. She held the baby in her arms for a last time, then handed her to Belle. 'She's yours, SussieBelle. Love her.'

15

There were iron posts with rings opposite the magistrate's office in Marshall Street. The posts dated back to when horsemen had dismounted there. She lifted the rusted ring, let it fall back. It made a dull clanging sound. She was free because the child was with a day-mother.

The constable stopped her at the door leading to the gallery of C Court. She was not wearing a hat and had to place a handkerchief on her head. White people were seated on one side of the gallery, black people on the other. Would Nahore, had he been there, have to sit with the black people? wondered Belle. She looked, but saw no one who looked like him. She hadn't seen his name amongst the detained, but Anne Williams was listed. Perhaps he had left the country after his year-long sentence.

A woman of her own age stood in the witness box. She wore a long unbuttoned cardigan, and she clasped the front welts across her chest. Her hair was mousy, looked dirty and unkempt and was fastened in a ponytail with an elastic band.

The prosecutor read from a document, tapping it on his left hand from time to time. He was a shortish man with dark hair.

The group had been charged with contravention of the Act on the Suppression of Communism, and attempting to promote the activities of the banned Party. The trial had been running for several weeks. She'd read about it the night before, and that was when she'd seen the name of Anne Williams listed amongst the detainees.

'And after that?' the voice continued. 'What happened after that? The unidentified person gave you an envelope, an oblong envelope, please note, of an unusual size and said you should post it. And then?'

'I posted it.'

'Immediately?'

She shook her head

'And why did you not post it immediately?'

'They said I was to wear a raincoat and a headscarf and go to post it in another suburb.'

'And that did not make you suspect that you were involved in illegal underground activities ...'

'I object. The accused is being led. Unsubstantiated allegations are being tossed about arbitrarily.' The defence took a sip of water and sat down again.

'Objection sustained.'

The magistrate shut his eyes, he seemed to have sunk into a subjective reverie. Yet, as Belle observed him, the pencil in his hand continued writing or marking the paper in front of him.

'And when you were arrested with the envelope concealed under your raincoat, can you recall the words you said to the person taking you into custody, who was allegedly your lover?'

The woman straightened up, her hands let go of the cardigan and held on to the edge of the witness box. She looked sideways. The women on the bench in front of and next to Belle followed her glance.

A lean, fair young man sat on a chair in a row of empty chairs along the wall. He looked at the girl in the witness box boldly, almost playfully challenging. State witness.

She spoke more clearly than before. 'I told him that I regretted that I had ever allowed a traitor to touch me. I spat in his face.'

'A traitor? What do you understand by the word "traitor", madam?'

'Someone who betrays those who trust him.'

'Or betrays his country? Come, answer me, madam. Someone who betrays his country … is he, or rather she, a traitor?'

He didn't await a reply, but sat down.

'No further questions.'

The magistrate adjourned the court for tea. Belle walked out with the women who had been sitting on the bench near her. She followed them to the café, sat at a vacant place at one of the tables, and ordered, as they did, a cool drink. The women chattered like starlings about the lean blonde man on the chair in the empty row. His challenging, playful smile. The evidence he'd given.

'I was flabbergasted!'

'I was shocked when he walked in.'

'I liked him so much!'

'He had me completely fooled!'

'Hell, what a terrible blow. What else is going to come out of the woodwork?'

Belle concluded that the young man had infiltrated their cell, in service of the Security Police. Anton Ludi, agent Q017. And now he was testifying against all those who'd been arrested.

'He knew everything.'

'I was devastated when I heard Bram Fischer had jumped bail and disappeared. Now I'm beginning to understand.'

'I feel lost without Bram.'

'He made fools of them at the Rivonia Trial.'

'He'd probably have acted in his own defence.'

'Like Nelson Mandela last year, God, I can still hear that voice …'

'They say Fischer is in hiding somewhere in the city.'

Middle-class women like her who sat in court every day. She learned that two of them had husbands and one a son behind bars. She was gripped by it all. She was too excited to finish her cool drink, quickly paid at the counter and followed the group back to court. The handkerchief once again on her head. The young man was back in his place. They led in a second mousy-haired woman, also about her age. She was sworn in. The prosecutor presented the evidence. He cross-examined her. He obviously already knew everything.

'On the eleventh of September last year you rented a safe at the X-bank in your own name because you had been instructed to do so by the organisation, and a week later, on the eighteenth of September, you deposited a parcel of money in it ...'

The allegations followed one after the other in quick succession. The defence rose time and again: 'Objection, that is not an illegal activity.'

'Objection, the accused had no knowledge of the contents, and still does not know to this day.'

'Objection.'

'Objection.'

Some sustained, some overruled. Ad nauseam. 'Lift your head, Madam.' 'Speak more clearly, madam.'

Belle returned the next day. She had tea at the same café the women went to. She plucked up the courage to ask one of them: 'When will Anne Williams be called?'

The woman looked at her sharply. 'Do you know her?'

'She's my friend.' Belle lied.

The woman relaxed. 'No one can tell, depends on the magistrate's roll.'

She ate hot dogs with the women that afternoon. She'd asked Holtzhausen to fetch the child from the day-mother. When the court adjourned, the prisoners and witnesses thronged together at the wooden partition, and the visitors rushed down the gallery steps, just to touch an outstretched hand, hand over a few oranges, pass a note, or get a message.

Her hours at home were spent waiting for the next day. Saturdays and Sundays dragged. Holtzhausen gave no sign that he noticed anything odd about her.

Especially when women were in the witness box, her excitement became so great she could barely contain it. Her lips uttered the words with them. She willed the answers into the mouths of the accused.

'You were asked to fold a pack of 300 pamphlets and place them in envelopes, to address them and post them in different post boxes, with all the folding and enclosing, you never got to know what was written in the pamphlets?'

'You were asked to buy food and deliver it to a certain house in X Street, and you never wondered why they did not go and buy food for themselves?'

'You were told of an account in the name of a certain Mr X. You never thought of a connection between this Mr X and a fugitive?'

'You were asked to take a suitcase, obviously containing secret documents, to a certain café and a person who would sit at a table next to yours would have an identical suitcase and would place it next to yours. And when leaving you would take his and leave yours. You are a woman …' At this point there was laughter from the gallery, and they were silenced. 'Were you not tempted, when you got home, to open the second suitcase and peep in it?'

What intrigues had been enacted beneath the surface of everyday life! Of which she had known nothing. Belle's excitement mounted. Every deed had a counter deed with a totally alien meaning. She longed to see Anne Williams in the dock. But she was also afraid of seeing her.

Tea time and lunch time in the little café with the rickety tables became tenser than the court sessions.

'We need an address,' said a woman at her table one day. 'We must have an address that isn't under observation.'

Before she could think twice, Belle had torn a page from her notebook and written her address on it. 'Take it. Please.'

Something in her expression appealed to the woman who had spoken, but she returned the paper. 'We don't know you. You've seen what happened, how we were betrayed.'

She was shattered. 'How can I convince you?' she asked.

'You can't convince us.' Yet the woman put out her hand, took the piece of paper again, and when they got up to walk back, she slipped it into her handbag.

One day shortly after that a policeman entered the café during the lunch recess. He touched his forehead with the fingers of his right hand, took off his cap, and said in a deliberately friendly manner, 'Sorry ladies, we have to check up on what the prisoners have let you know in the notes given you in the court just now. Handbags open, please.' He started searching handbags from table to table. 'And pockets.' The women emptied their pockets. He read a few folded notes, nothing suspect. He confiscated Belle's notebook, and, from the woman's handbag, the page torn out of it with her address written on it.

The woman tried to stop him. 'She's not one of us.'

'Sorry lady, that means nothing to me'

The woman who had refused Belle's offer pressed her fingers against her wrist, 'Now you're also under suspicion.'

It gave Belle secret gratification. *Now you're also under suspicion.*

416

She couldn't stay away from the court, not only because of the cross-examination, but also to see the blonde man. She'd dreamed of him one night, that he'd come upon her in a room and was holding her by her upper arms, and as she spat at him she wriggled her arms free and threw them around his neck, nestling her body against his.

Another night she dreamed that she saw him in white trousers and a white shirt, with a flag-bearer's harness. The Union flag hung from the flagpole he held. He marched with knees raised so high they came to his chest and his hands were clamped to the flagpole at his groin. The flag unfurled slowly – blue and white and orange – and began to take the wind with lazy, graceful movements. She cried in her dream, it was so beautiful.

Hendrik was furious. 'Hello, darling,' he muttered to the four-year-old Leonora who was playing on the garden path of the Westdene house. He pressed the bell angrily. 'She's not deaf, damn it.'

When Belle opened the door, he wasted no time. 'Stories have reached me, Greylinck of the Security Police, if you must know. They're still looking for that damn Bram Fischer, and now you are also in this business. How the hell you, as the mother of a young child, can get involved in these things, God alone knows. Yes, I'll have some.'

He took the cup of tea and a cupcake with a cherry. He sat on the edge of the chair, stirred in sugar, swallowed. His knees were wide apart, his belly taking up more and more space, Mammie wanted to put him on a diet, but when he was so agitated, what could he do but eat?

'You, here.' He swung his arms around in the room. 'An address for money arriving for the agitators. From overseas. It's beyond my comprehension.'

'They didn't want to take the address.'

'Thank God for that. But I'm warning you, leave those people alone. Stay away from the court. What were you there for anyway? Hasn't there been enough trouble already?'

I have a good mind to leave her to be locked up, he thought as he left at last, placated by Holtzhausen with little Leonora, who called herself Leo, on his arm. Such a sweet scene always softened him.

Those damned security fellows were so keen, once they got a hold on someone they never let go. They dug and dug. And Greylinck's information about Belle's involvement with the Indians on her Oupa's farm gave them something definite to encourage their digging. God help her:

he was sure there'd been a file on Belle somewhere ever since she'd been reluctant to give evidence in that case. And once there was a file, they kept an eye on you.

She was pleased when the young blonde man was in the room with her – she knew it was the café, but she couldn't tell how he'd entered, for there were no windows or doors. And when he drew back the chair and sat down at her table her heart leapt. Because he pushed his briefcase in next to her, she felt it brush against her legs.

When I leave, you must pick it up, he said, and when the clock in the post office strikes three, you must be standing at the Poste Restante counter. Someone will take it from you there. Do this for me.

Her heart was beating so hard she thought he would be able to see it through her blouse. He squeezed her wrist. Don't worry, just do it. Then he left.

She remained sitting for a short while, and then she too left. Without the case, which had been left under the table. Out in the street she stopped. She couldn't leave the case. She turned back to fetch it. She criss-crossed the streets, walked against the traffic, and was knocked down, the driver swore at her.

She stood in the post office. The clock began to strike. She knew the way to the Poste Restante counter, she was there before the striking ended. Thanks, said his voice. He stood next to her. He took the case from her hand. His mouth laughed, but not his eyes. We know all about you. And about your ivory poacher-lover.

Sounds of pain gathered in her throat, but she couldn't get them out. Your oom knows everything, and if you feel like offering to be an agent for the enemies of your country again, you should think twice.

Then he bent over and said: Thank you, my darling, for the case. He kissed her on her mouth.

When she woke, she could still feel his lips on hers.

There was a file, and when Belle's name came up again, in spite of the married name, Jan Greylinck wrote to a colleague in Nairobi asking him to investigate.

He took the information to Hendrik's office, thrust it across the desk.

'Read it. The whole business is there. Your niece's statement tells us a great deal. The statements of the English soldiers tell us even more. A clear case of immorality, and an accessory to attempted transport of illegal ivory.'

Greylinck was short and thin, his face lean and pointed. He looked to Hendrik like a rodent.

'We'll keep it out of the newspapers. But I warn you: if there is ever an attempt at subversion again, everything will come out.'

And Hendrik knew, he too was now in their hands. And Philip. They would be used, even in matters they did not want to be involved in. The future suddenly looked dark to him. He was thankful when Greylinck left and his secretary brought him a cup of tea.

He had to phone Philip. Philip could speak to Robert.

And it had been he himself who had paid for her ticket and seen her onto the plane. Poor Belle, poor, dear SussieBelle. He resolved not to tell Mammie, nor, for the time being, Leonora.

16

After Hendrik's visit Belle no longer went to the courts. But her child was in permanent day-care and she went to the city each day. She left the bus at the Loveday bus stop and then walked into the city. She wandered in Fox Street and Simmonds Street and Pritchard Street. She knew the entrances, the little lights shining even though it was daytime, the little yellow and red lights going on and off, lighting the advertisement in a teasingly alluring way: a girl in skimpy clothes, fringing on her dress, protruding breasts, or the face of the hero, his eyes fixed, a cigarette between his fingers.

A few steps down, then the ticket office, with the short, fat woman in her black dress, who tore the ticket from the roll of pale blue strips, dragged the money towards her along the counter and pushed the ticket out through the narrow brass railing. She too had a cigarette in the corner of her mouth, the ash drooped, and her yellow teeth barely moved when she said, 'One?'

Belle knew the way around the dark corner, she steadied herself against the wall step by step. It was pitch dark around her, and then around the last curve: a voice soulfully declaring love, or the high-pitched voice of a comedian, or the screech of brakes as a car was stopped, or the whistling of bullets, unreal in the dark. Until she blindly pulled away the heavy curtain in front of her and the faces and moving bodies and vehicles on the big screen beamed down on her.

She pushed into a row of empty seats, waited for her eyes to become accustomed to the dark. The cinema wasn't full, here and there little groups of backs. A girl shuffled down the aisle, flashed the light of her torch on the wooden shelf in front of Belle, saw it was empty and whispered: 'What kind of cool drink?' Belle sighed: 'Doesn't matter.' When the glass on its saucer was put in front of her, she lifted it and sucked at the straw, her eyes glued to the screen. She stayed to the end, and remained sitting as the advertisements began to drone. Sometimes she stayed until the film started again, and sat through it to the end a second time.

When at last she went back out on the street, she had to blink against the bright light. Her head ached, she felt lost and a bit dizzy. Day after day she went to the café-bioscopes in the basements beneath the big, noisy city. She alternated between them. Sometimes she forgot that she'd already seen the film; only realised this halfway through. She yearned for the tepid, sticky cooldrink, sucked through the straw in the dark.

Sometimes a man from a few seats away would move nearer. First one seat from her, and if she didn't move, right next to her. His knee pressed against her knee; his hot thigh against her thigh, started to rub up and down. It didn't concern her if his breathing became heavy.

Sometimes it was a woman who moved in next to her, whose thigh began to press against hers, tentatively at first, then increasingly boldly. Sometimes the woman's hand began to massage her thigh, she would lean forward so that her hand could move further up in her groin. Belle pushed the hand away without even looking down.

Or the one who had tried to loosen her hand from around the cooldrink, and draw it nearer, but then she wriggled her hand free of the grip, and sought the rounding of the glass again, her eyes fixed on the large flickering screen in front of her.

Until one afternoon, when a woman next to her put the seat down, sat and started to grope at her and she saw the short, stocky little woman in black who sold the tickets standing there. The girl who served the cool drinks flashed her torch on them, they were caught in the light like insects.

'Shame on you, this isn't a brothel! Disgusting!' The fat little woman dragged Belle from the seat by her sleeve and pushed her up the steps in front of her. 'Get out! Shame on you!'

Then she looked at Belle inquisitively and said to the cool drink girl: 'Why does this one look so dim, doesn't she know what's going on?'

For Belle was not upset, she just regarded her, her hand still around the glass. She was straining to get back to the steps.

'Hell, you can't put her out on the street, they'll knock her down or rob her.'

She tried questioning her. 'Where do you live, lady? You got family?' More patrons arrived and she had to return to her little office behind the copper bars, but she kept an eye on Belle.

'Here, let's have the glass, come on, give it here.' She loosened Belle's fingers, took her handbag from her arm.

'The woman's crazy for the movies, she doesn't want to go out again.'

'She's dressed quite nice,' said the cool drink girl. 'She's not like the other one. Let's see in the handbag who she is.'

But the woman got no reply from the house she phoned. The name and phone number were on an account stuffed in the handbag – grabbed out of the letterbox and stuffed in on the way to the city? The woman allowed her to sit in the back row again. 'But you watch her, you hear, I don't want the place to get a bad name. I'll phone again later.'

When Holtzhausen got home, the phone was ringing. He left Leo with the day-mother and drove to the city. But he could only find parking some distance away and he ran the last few blocks to the address given to him over the phone. He was seriously alarmed.

The ticket-seller was surprised that such a decent-looking man came to claim the woman. He looked confused, looked at the posters on the wall uncomprehendingly, at the lights, at the steps disappearing down into the darkness.

'Don't you know café-bio's? Dearie me. Come, I'll show you.' She drew the door closed behind her, took a torch and walked ahead of him.

'Bella,' he said when he saw her in the half-dark sitting on the last seat of the back row, her eyes glued to the screen. 'My dearest, Bella. Come with me.' He had to speak over and over again. She rose unwillingly, walked up the stairs with him. He gave the woman a tip. 'For the phone calls.'

'Thanks, man, now don't be too hard on her, she wasn't no trouble. It was that other slut. I think she got problems.'

He had to drag Belle outside, in amongst the people on the pavement, wait at the red light, walk across when it turned green, block after block through the dark canyons between buildings where the sun never reached and an icy wind blew, to where the car was. He didn't speak and she didn't speak. Later he tried a few times, but she seemed not to hear. When he put his hand on her knee reassuringly at a traffic jam, she didn't react.

He picked Leo up. She sat in the back, she was used to her mother being silent. She chattered at table and ate the food her father gave her and went to bed as he told her. Belle didn't eat.

In the night Holtzhausen woke with a feeling that all was too quiet. The second bed was empty. He put on his coat over his pyjamas, it was winter, and cold. He walked through the house, to the kitchen, to the bathroom, to the lounge. Then he saw the front door wasn't locked as it had been when he went to bed.

He walked down the garden path, began to run. But where to? 'Bella,' he called softly, he didn't dare call more loudly. He walked up one street a short way, then another; at last chose the road leading to the ridge. Instinctively he knew Belle would want to get away from the more densely populated areas. His breath raced, blew white clouds in front of him until his lungs began to ache. He should rather walk. He turned up his coat collar. God, had Bella left the house in her night-clothes? He began to run again, called more loudly, had to walk again. He had left the house without his spectacles, he wouldn't even be able to see her from afar. 'Bella, Bella … Bella, Bella,' he called, but his voice sounded fearful and thin.

It was a cold clear night, moonlight. Time and again he thought he saw Bella on the ridge, and stumbled there, but each time it was a rock.

It was still pitch dark when he found her. He took off his coat and wrapped it around her. His teeth began to chatter from cold, but she appeared not to feel it. She resisted putting her arms in the sleeves of the coat. He hung it around her shoulders. He made her walk as fast as he could, and while walking rubbed her hands. The door of their house stood open and the child was crying, the cold was seeping in through the front door. He turned on heaters, put milk on the stove to make coffee for them and cocoa for the child.

Belle drank the coffee, her two hands around the cup as around the glass in the café bioscope. She didn't protest when he took her to the bedroom and had her lie down and covered her with blankets.

He didn't sleep the rest of the night. God in Heaven, he couldn't lock his wife in the house during the day. He could take the child away to be cared for, but he couldn't lock the house like a jail. And at night, when she could open it from inside. He would have to get help, he had no choice. Hendrik would have to help. All those weeks he'd known something was amiss, he'd tried to manage on his own. But now it would be foolish to leave Bella on her own, even for the short time it would take to get Leo to her day-mother.

He put drawing books and crayons on the kitchen table, had Leo sit there.

'Come, sit next to Mamma, tell her to eat all her food. Draw something pretty for her, don't go away from Mamma.'

He phoned the college. 'I'll be late. Yes, I know it's exam time.'

He phoned Hendrik. 'I have problems.'

The tone of his voice and his refusal to give further details warned Hendrik that something serious was afoot. He walked out of a meeting, got the car out of the basement garage, and drove to Westdene himself.

'Bella doesn't react. Last night she walked off to the ridges. It's too dangerous, I can't leave her and Leo.'

He poured coffee. Hendrik was bewildered, helpless, too shy to enquire about intimate matters. He said: 'Shall I ask Mammie to come?'

Holtzhausen paced up and down in the lounge where they were talking. They couldn't discuss it in front of Belle. 'I don't think she'll be able to cope with it.'

That was deliverance for Hendrik. 'I'll phone my doctor, he can give her a sedative, so that she'll sleep. You say she didn't sleep last night.' He seemed to be pleading with someone. 'Perhaps things will be better once she's rested.'

'The students are writing exams, I can't stay away.' Holtzhausen's eyes were tortured with doubts, worry, despondency.

'My business can't wait either, but as I always say: Belle comes first.' Hendrik was sitting with the telephone directory balanced between his fat knees. 'Now, first of all the doctor.'

Belle didn't submit easily to the injection the doctor wanted to give her, it ended up in a struggle. Holtzhausen had to help hold her. When she was asleep Hendrik had Mammie come, and he and Holtzhausen could leave for work. Little Leo kept Mammie company.

The next night she walked off into the ridges again. The doctor had prescribed sleeping tablets which Holtzhausen had given her at bedtime, but she held them in her cheek and spat them out later in the bathroom. Once again Holtzhausen was late for work because he had to wait for the doctor. Again Mammie had to come to sit with the sleeping woman, still and pale as marble; had to look with incomprehension at the smooth white mask over the face. When it had happened three nights running, and Holtzhausen was dead tired, and Hendrik worried about Belle all day and lay awake at night, even lost his appetite, the doctor recommended that Belle be placed under psychiatric care in a nursing home.

'Only the best,' said the deeply disturbed Hendrik, 'only the best.'

In the afternoon they took her to a private institution in one of the side streets of Orange Grove. Seen from outside the building looked like a large, somewhat neglected Victorian residence. Only the notice on the wire fence, *Trespassers will be prosecuted*, indicated that it was not a private home. There had been some attempt at keeping up the formal garden, the roses had been pruned, but now, in winter, the garden looked dreary.

Hendrik held Belle by one arm, Holtzhausen by the other. She stumbled when they had to go up the first step to the veranda, but they supported her. Hendrik swallowed anxiously as he pressed his white finger with the neatly filed nail against the polished yellow brass bell. They heard the bell ring far and deep, but the door was opened almost immediately. A woman in a nursing sister's uniform invited them in. The entrance hall was dark and cold. A double door led to the rest of the house, but they were taken to the reception room to the left of the door. The sister sat down behind a big heavy desk, so highly polished that the pencil she held at an angle between her thumb and index finger, while she waited for their details, reflected as a line on the surface. When she began to write, the pencil reflection disappeared. But her elbow, the folds in the sleeve of her thick cardigan, were mirrored on the surface.

Because Hendrik was too emotional, kept dabbing the corners of his eyes with his white handkerchief, had to swallow before he could utter a word, Holtzhausen spoke. Just her name, date of birth, address, next of kin, telephone numbers. Their GP had already made a provisional diagnosis: endogenic depression. The psychiatrist – the best, nodded the sister – had already been allocated to her.

She moved the papers back, closed the file, rose. 'Leave the little lady with me now. She's in good hands. You can give the suitcases to me,' she said.

Belle didn't turn her head to watch them as they walked away slowly, reluctantly turned the doorknob and went out.

Hendrik struggled to start the car. 'Just a few days, my boy. Just to give the child a chance to settle down.' He had to let go of the wheel to take out his handkerchief again, he blew his nose hard. 'It gets to one.'

Holtzhausen said, 'Let me drive, Oom.'

Is the man made of stone? thought Hendrik. Oh dear Lord, poor darling SussieBelle. Better not to think. His green-eyed SussieBelle.

Child of his heart. At the house they picked up little Leo, who was to spend a few days with Mammie. The child was fond of them and went willingly.

Visitors were not allowed the first evening, the sister had said. The patients needed to be calm. The second night the spouse would be allowed to come.

Holtzhausen forced himself to eat something. Under the harsh fluorescent lighting the kitchen looked neglected and inhospitable, as if people hadn't lived here for some time. He fried an egg and some sausage, sliced bread. He had to wash the food down with coffee. Usually he was a tidy man, but he didn't trouble to wash the dishes. Why would he?

He took his concertina from its box and stroked it. A few odd notes came from it as it fell open. As if it was trying to speak to him. It was too cold out on the back stoep. Where could he sit and play? Not under the white fluorescent lighting, not in their bedroom with the two unmade single beds, not in the child's room. Neither did the small sitting room attract him. There was no place in his own home where he wanted to be. At last he switched the lights off and went to sit in the child's room. The streetlight shone in, but he didn't need to see, his fingers knew their way. He sat in the armchair where Bella had sat to nurse the child. Bella? Who was she? What was she? Bella behind the wooden doors, with strangers tonight.

His hands moved and his fingers found the buttons of their own accord, so that the sound that emerged was not what he had intended, but a strange faltering melody – as if the sounds wished to comfort him, reach out little hands and stroke his face. Is it my fault? he thought. What sin did I commit against Bella, sinning when I don't know I'm sinning? The pain his first wife had suffered was bearable, he could look after her, give her medication, even injections. It had been difficult, but not as difficult as this. Her he could cradle in his arms the whole night long, and help her bear the pain, and in the morning he would get up exhausted, but whole. But with Bella nothing was clear. He didn't know how to help her. At last he replaced the concertina in the box, went to the bedroom in the dark and lay on his bed. Later he slept.

At the college the day went by mechanically.

'Yes, I'm going to visit her this evening. Yes, I'll give her your regards. Right, Tannie Rina, give the phone to little Leo so that I can talk to her. Well, thank you for everything. I'll let you know, yes.'

He stopped the car in the parking area. He slammed the door shut, walked up the steps and rang the bell. Another nurse. Still young. Quite pretty. She stood in front of the big wooden double door. Dear God, it was an old-fashioned door key she was looking for on the ring she had taken from her pocket. She unlocked. 'Come,' she said. She turned around, bent, locked the door behind them. He should have expected it, the doctor had probably said she ran away. He followed the nurse, their footsteps loud on the old-fashioned mosaic passage floor. Another door, where a stout coloured woman sat at a little table knitting. She stood up, took a key from the key ring on the table, unlocked the door, let them through, pulled it closed, locked it on her side. He heard her chair legs creak as she sat down again. There was only a dim wall light. He saw closed doors on either side of the passage. And then he heard new sounds.

A soft moaning. Sudden, barely human laughter, stopping just as suddenly. Voices speaking. A whining – it couldn't be, but yes it was … an old person's voice: *Ma-ma. Ma-ma.*

The nurse had stopped at a door which she unlocked with her own key. Locked behind them again. There were two lights hanging from the ceiling, one near them, one further away. With old-fashioned white glass lamp shades. Yet the light wasn't bright, a darkness hung over the room. There were two rows of beds, with drawn-back curtains on iron frames around them. Three beds on each side. On some beds the women were sitting up; one swayed from side to side, held her arms in front of her, as though rocking a baby. Other women were lying down; one lay on her side and plucked at the bedspread.

'Here, sir,' said the nurse. And there right in front of him, where he hadn't noticed her, on the first bed, lay Belle. The nurse drew up a chair. She glanced at her watch. 'I'll give you half an hour, don't upset your wife.' He heard the door being locked behind her.

He went to sit next to Belle. The bedspread was drawn up over her, she lay absolutely still on her back. Her hair had been combed with a parting in the middle and lay flat against her head on either side. Her eyes were open. Her arms were under the bedspread, and he saw, to his horror, leather straps fastened on either side of the bed. She looked at him, a docile smile reached her lips. She seemed far removed from everything, as if nothing concerned her.

The woman in the bed next to her pushed herself up on her elbow. She was a big woman and the loose breasts under the nightgown were pendulous. She looked at Holtzhausen inquisitively and then at Belle.

'She gives no trouble, this one,' she said. 'She's quiet, she doesn't make a fuss.'

Holtzhausen took the end of one of the leather straps in his hand. 'And this?'

Even she could hear the horror in his voice.

'That's for when they take us for shocks. It doesn't bother me, but some resist, then they have to be strapped down before they can be pushed out. Like that one there …' She indicated the woman sitting up with her arms crossed, rocking back and forth. 'Your little one is quite meek.'

Holtzhausen couldn't believe what he was hearing. 'Madam, I have no idea what you're talking about. What shocks?'

'Electric shocks. It jerks your body a bit, but I don't mind that. It switches off the thing bothering you, shocks it dead in your head. When that happens, it's good. You wouldn't believe what the thing in my head made me get up to. The day before I came here, I painted my whole kitchen with black paint, even the fridge. I know it's not right, but I couldn't stop myself. Let them shock me, I say, let them shock me, even if my body jerks so that my feet fly up in the air, let them shock me.'

Holtzhausen had drawn the bedspread aside and took both Belle's hands in his. They were cold, but rather damp. He lifted them and kissed the fingers, turned them over, kissed the palms. He bent down and pressed his cheek against hers, then kissed her on her forehead.

'Speak to me, Bella,' he said. But she didn't utter a word.

Before the half hour was over, he knocked loudly on the inside of the door. He wanted to get out of there. The nurse opened the door, looked at Belle, saw she was lying quietly as before, led him out, knocked in turn, so that the fat woman unlocked, unlocked the last big wooden double door that led to the entrance hall.

'Where's the sister?' asked Holtzhausen

'She's off duty.'

'Where can I speak to the doctor?'

'The doctor or the psychiatrist?'

'The man who is treating my wife.'

'Probably at his rooms.'

'No, now.'

'I won't disturb him at home now, the patient is quiet.'

Hendrik had already locked the house for the night and he was in the bathroom, when Mammie heard the violent knocking at the door. And Holtzhausen's voice shouting.

Alarmed, she opened the door. She called to Pappie who put on his dressing gown and slippers and hurried down to the lounge. Holtzhausen sat on the sofa, his shoulders bent, his head in his hands. His body shuddered as he sobbed. Mammie put her hand on his shoulder awkwardly, she looked at Pappie hopelessly.

They were both helpless before the grief of the man they accepted as their son-in-law, but scarcely knew.

Then Mammie held his head, bent it back a little, and placed the glass of brandy Pappie had poured to his lips.

'Swallow,' she said.

The liquid burnt through his mouth and throat right to his innards. It brought a degree of objectivity, of control.

'Belle?' asked Hendrik.

He nodded. 'She's under lock and key and there are leather straps on her bed. They are giving her electric shocks to burn out whatever is the matter with her.' And in response to Hendrik's question: 'No, she didn't speak to me. She lies there like a lamb about to be slaughtered.' By then Rina was also crying. Her dainty cotton handkerchief was wet through, they caught the scent of lavender.

'Do they have the right to do that?' asked Holtzhausen. He'd taken off his spectacles which had misted up, his eyes looked glassy and distant and dull. A deep frown creased his forehead.

'I think we gave permission for the doctor to treat her as he saw fit.'

'But shock treatment!'

'I've heard of it being used with success. Anything to help our dear Belle.'

' Must we accept it, Oom Hendrik?'

'God knows, I don't know.'

It was after ten already, but Hendrik phoned Philip in Pretoria.

'Now don't ask questions,' he said, 'just give me Barry's number at Baragwanath. Yes, it's about Belle. Why do you ask? You surmise? I'll let you know tomorrow.'

Barry reassured Hendrik, the phone was handed to Holtzhausen. Now that he had the name of the psychiatrist, said Barry, he would phone him early the next morning. Perhaps it was for the best. It's dreadful for the relatives, doctors differ about it, but good results are achieved. No, personally he didn't like shock treatment. Just leave it till the next day. Yes, he would phone early, before a possible repetition. It was difficult to intervene, but for Belle's sake. He thought the damage was of long standing, perhaps for the best, drastic and fast.

His even voice calmed them. Hendrik poured another small shot of brandy, Rina made up a bed for Holtzhausen in the smaller guest room. Not to disturb little Leo. Relax now, Belle is safe for the night.

He stood by while she made the bed. Usually a quiet man, he then needed to talk.

'You know my ma passed away. I told you before the wedding that I have no close relatives. She died at my birth. As soon as I could think, I knew already: had it not been for me, she would have lived. My pa married again, but was unhappy. I reproached myself even for his unfortunate second marriage, and then for my first wife's cancer, and now Bella. It seems to me I bring women misfortune. If I hadn't made Bella pregnant, she wouldn't have married me. Now you may as well know: she was pregnant when we were married.'

'I knew that,' she said. Shaking out blankets and sheets hid her face, also hid him from her. 'You don't bring women misfortune,' she said, 'you care for them when misfortune strikes. You are a care-giver, Holtzhausen.'

The bed was made. She lifted her plump arms and Holtzhausen bent his head and laid it on her shoulder. She held him in her arm, stroking his straight greasy hair with the other. He smelled a bit of sweat, and of oil, not unpleasantly. He put his arms around her soft upper body. She felt a strange flutter in her body, a pleasant feeling, she pressed her cheek to his head. A tiny bald spot on the back of his head touched her even more; she rubbed her cheek on it. Then she took fright at the emotion coursing through her body. She pushed him away from her, he blinked his eyes as he straightened up. He looked bemused, as if something had touched him too. Poor motherless soul, she thought. And poor childless soul I, her thoughts led her on relentlessly. So we comfort each other.

'Pappie is probably in bed already. I'll bring you pyjamas, although they'll be too big.' She smiled. 'Fold the pants double.'

Belle wasn't discharged from the institution for another two weeks. The course of shock treatments was completed. The psychiatrist refused to budge, the family had, after all, signed. Barry, although not in favour of the drastic treatment, was unable to intervene. When Belle was discharged Holtzhausen took her to Hendrik and Rina's house. She looked drained, but calm. She was very quiet. She sat in front of her window for long spells, gazing out with a book on her lap. An old book, which she closed if anyone approached – it looked like a book of poetry.

During this time there was much unrest in the country. Those who could afford it and were able to get passports emigrated. The property market dropped. The house in Northcliff next door to Hendrik and Rina came on the market, and Hendrik picked it up for a song.

He took Holtzhausen into his confidence. 'Look, man, I want to buy it for you. No, don't argue, it's more for our sakes than yours. Belle is recovering and it'll be good for her to have a house to see to. And it will mean so much to Mammie to have Belle and little Leo so near us. Think about it. Consider it. For my sake and Mammie's.'

He knew how well Mammie got on with Holtzhausen. Sometimes in the early evening he would play his concertina for her on the side stoep: the songs she knew and liked so much. Belle wasn't interested in listening. Hendrik felt that Holtzhausen had been given a heavy cross to bear.

Holtzhausen considered and accepted the offer, and they were able to move in quite soon. The previous owners let them have a lot of furniture. It was perhaps just as well to start living in a strange house. No reminders of his first wife. You are a care-giver, Rina had said. He treasured the words in his heart.

Hendrik could mean so much more to little Leo. The child had no oupa. She seldom saw her own ouma from the Cape. Agnes came to visit a few times after Miss Marais died, but the high altitude, she said, affected her heart. Leonora came more often.

Belle gradually became stronger and began to take over her own household; although Rina still sent a dish over from time to time; although Belle had to go shopping with Rina, because she didn't drive; although, as Leo grew up, Hendrik's driver more frequently had to take her to her extra-mural activities at school.

Belle became particularly adept at making little snacks – small chicken pies, angels on horseback, stuffed olives with anchovies in them, tiny, dainty white bread sandwiches, or little rolls of bread around spears of asparagus. Rina was becoming less handy. And she took pride in serving something attractive and tasty when Hendrik's Broederbond-friends met at their home. The afternoons before these meetings Belle, apron around her waist, would be frantically busy in Rina's kitchen. She'd blow impatiently at the hair that fell forward over her face, press the backs of her hands against her flushed cheeks, keep an anxious eye on the wall clock, cool her hot hands in a basin of water with ice blocks.

You're a tower of strength to me, Rina would say. I'd never be able to cope with the snacks and the meetings on my own anymore. As a sign of his affection and appreciation Hendrik bought Belle and

Holtzhausen, and of course little Leo, at high school by now, one of the first and biggest television sets to come on the market.

Then Belle no longer sat in front of the window with a book on her lap, she sat in front of the TV. She drew her knees up almost to her chin, and sat curled up like that in the old armchair left by the strangers. She no longer had her hair cut, but fastened it loosely in her neck. She paid half-hearted attention when Leo asked for help with her homework. She willingly took time off only for the snack-making afternoons at Rina's. Her fingers worked nimbly with the little triangles, the little wedges, the thin-sliced bread that was spread with a filling, rolled up and then sliced to make little savoury oxwagon wheels that nestled in the shredded lettuce. She even designed a little bread-wheel with the four colours of the old republican flag in it – using a touch of salvia to get the blue. She made miniature torches cut from brown bread, with a strip of tomato peel as the flame. She loved making the torches with their little red flames. She took pride in them.

17

In Cape Town Leonora felt duty-bound to keep in contact with Agnes. The child Leo was a bond. She said nothing about her sadness over SussieBelle, so quiet, so inert, so unyieldingly introverted.

Miss Marais left her house and her financial assets to Agnes, and Agnes continued living there after her death. One afternoon each week she and a few friends from Miss Marais's time worked together at their hobby, art needlework. When Leonora visited now, the house was strangely quiet and peaceful. Miss Marais had suffered during the last months and her asthmatic calling from the bedroom had frequently interrupted the conversation.

'Are you adequately provided for Agnes?' Leonora ventured to ask.

'Yes thanks, not a lot, but sufficient.' She didn't want Leonora to know that it took skimping and saving to afford the fine linen and embroidery thread. She didn't mention that she took orders for needlework. She liked to spread open the tablecloth she was working on to show Leonora, smoothed the cloth, lifted the corners, spread it open over the back of her hand, stroked it so that Leonora could admire the fine stitches.

'But that's a work of art, Agnes.'

'It's a blessing from God that my sight hasn't failed.'

So I'm the only one still unfulfilled, thought Leonora, while Agnes lovingly gathered the cloth, folded it, put it away in tissue paper. I'm the one Aunt Issy would not have 'esteemed'. In spite of the fact that I've worked my whole life, never had to look to a man for support, and now, close to retirement, have been asked to stay on in a part-time capacity.

Her cosy house suddenly felt oppressive. I must reach beyond the walls. I must travel again.

She was alone too much. She read a great deal. Often Eliot. Her generation's Tennyson, she thought wryly. What a massive change in perspective from *The Lady of Shalott* to *East Coker*:

As we grow older
The world becomes stranger, the pattern more complicated
Of dead and living.

A pattern which had remained hidden from her. She tried to banish SussieBelle from her thoughts. SussieBelle didn't speak to her.

One Saturday morning she got in the car and drove to Worcester where Father, Mother, Vicky and yes, also Aunt Issy, were buried. And Grandma.

The main street of the town was busy. It was the Saturday morning bustle. There were many more shops than she remembered. She had not been here for a long time. Many more tall buildings, many more people. She didn't stop anywhere, but drove through the traffic, through the groups of coloured people in their bright clothes, shopping bags in their hands, who had been brought to town from farms on lorries. At a fish shop next to a bar with an off-sales there appeared to be trouble. The people crowded around the two who were fighting, looked over the shoulders of those in front of them, pushed each other out of the way to get a better view. The children sat licking ice-creams, unperturbed.

She drove out of the town to the cemetery. The concrete wall around the cemetery was ugly. Was it always so stark, so treeless? Did mourners not notice the ugly surroundings? Were their eyes filled with tears, did they look out at the dull blue hills surrounding them as they tried to join in the mournful hymn the dominee had started to sing?

She followed the footpath in the direction of the graves she was looking for. Sooner than she had expected, she reached the familiar gravestones. Was everything closer together than she had perceived it as a child? Mother and Vicky shared a gravestone: a narrow, upright piece of white marble on which their names and dates had been engraved. And against the marble, still just as moving as ever, leaned the more than life-size white marble angel. Her right elbow rested on the marble gravestone and her cheek on the palm of her hand. Her left hand hung passively at her side, and from her fingers a wreath carved from marble drooped and was pressed to the robe covering her left thigh. The Weeping Angel. So it was described in the little advertisement brochure sent them after the deaths. It was at her insistence that Father had ordered the stone. It had to be brought from Italy, took ages to come. But it was an adornment to the graveyard.

Mother and daughter in graves next to each other. Unbidden, the old habit returned: she wrapped her handkerchief around her finger and wiped the dust from the ridges and hollows of the stone features and fingers, and the stone flowers. The stone was a dirty grey, the dust and dirt packed in the hollows and curves. They would have to have it cleaned. The angel still charmed her as it had when, as a young girl, she'd insisted to Father: This one Father. Mother would have liked it and Vicky too. Overcome with grief, he had agreed. His own gravestone was square, as tall as the one next to it. But without the angel; plain. The graves had gravel on them and a low stone wall surround. Aunt Issy and Grandma were in the older part of the cemetery, next to the grave of the grandfather none of the children had known.

She took the familiar path to it. Grandma's gravestone was an open Bible, opened at a text. The black letters of the text had run, as if seen in rain. Or through tears. For Aunt Issy there was only a name and date beneath Grandma's Bible. Flowers would not last in the heat, yet she wished she had brought some. Father had been particular about flowers on Mother's grave. Right up until his retirement. She sometimes wondered why Father, a man who appreciated simplicity, had agreed to the angel. Perhaps because of Vicky.

Ants had started to crawl up her feet and legs. She rose from the low granite wall and stamped her feet. Slapped at her legs. Actually there was nothing for her to do at the graves. All she could do was to stand the empty vases up again and support them with gravel. Mercifully someone had removed the dead flowers. It was lunch time. She drove to Frikkie's house, turned in at the road passing behind his house, as she had always done, and stopped in the shade of the trees. Frikkie had bought the old-fashioned house during the years when property was cheap. At that time it had been on the outskirts of the town. To his delight the area had not yet been built up. His studio was in the attic which was reached by an outside staircase. In the summer the house was cool, even the attic with its thatched roof.

She knocked at the back door. A little dog barked inside, but no one opened the door. The back stoep had an air of neglect; peeling paint and plaster, broken baskets, a broken canvas chair.

She heard someone come down the outside steps. It was Frikkie. He hugged her. 'Surely not you, surely not my old Norie!' He was in khaki pants and braces, shirt without collar, top few buttons undone, sleeves rolled up. She pressed her head to his shoulder for a few moments. Then she looked at him. His cheeks were unshaven, he had a sparse goatee, pepper-and-salt. His hair was also pepper-and-salt, thinning; widow's peaks either side of the forehead where the skin was paler than the face, and where she saw drops of sweat glistening. His hair above his ears and at the back was still thick, he combed the hair on the middle of his head back with his fingers. There were rings around his eyes and his cheeks were sunken. The hairs on his chest were grey. He was stooped – from all that bending over the camera? He wasn't really old, scarcely 65. What did he see in turn? she wondered. His sister, become hardened? Grown old? Bony? Did he recognise something of the girl in the green garden of their youth?

He unlocked the back door and led her in. It was cool in the kitchen, also in the dining room where he drew up a chair for her and said: 'I'm on my own. Kowie has gone to Miemie, she's lending a hand with the baby today. Miemie battles to cope, her husband doesn't help much, he has to supervise sport at school most of the time.' He fiddled with the door of a wall cupboard. 'Thirsty?'

'Not wine. It's too hot.'

'Beer?'

'Please.'

The beer wasn't really cold, but it quenched her thirst. He drank his first bottle down quickly and opened a second.

'You know about Belle, don't you Boet?'

'Yes, I know.'

'Hear from Arnold?'

He nodded. They didn't say any more. Well, Arnold knows as much or as little as we do, thought Leonora. Yet she would have preferred to tell him herself. In her own way. The wall clock began to strike. The four quarters and then a heavy vibrating sound. 'So you kept the clock,' she said.

'At the auction the thing looked at me so reproachfully, I could have sworn it was breathing. I had to pay up half a guinea, and God knows, I didn't have much. But I don't regret it.'

'But you could just have taken it.'

'The stuff had already been listed.'

'I'm glad you kept it. I don't know if I would have wanted it myself: those endless quarter hours and that striking. It brings everything back so.'

He put down his empty bottle, stood up. He went to the kitchen and she went along. 'Kowie has put out sausage and eggs. I'll fry them for us. You can fetch the bread, the butter and stuff is in the fridge.'

They ate at the kitchen table. The sausage was thick and fatty and still a little red on the inside. As he pushed his fork in, pale red wateriness flowed out and dammed up on the plate. He took bread and wiped it up with the crust. The yolk of the egg was also runny. She could see he wasn't aware of what he was eating. She ate more slowly, looked around for a table napkin, then got up and tore off a paper towel, pressed it to her mouth. 'It's nice sausage,' she said. He shared between them what was left in the pan, which was drier, browner, almost burnt; scraped crusty bits from the pan with a kitchen spoon and poured the gravy over their bread.

Suddenly her mood lightened. She regarded him with the old look. Her eyes are still bright, he thought, this is how she looked at me when we were young. It's so long ago. Still he felt the old affection for her, his little sister, always standing up for him, so torn between understanding for him and sympathy with Father.

He said: 'We're taking too long over the food, I want to show you, in the studio. I'll make coffee there. I'm busy with amazing stuff, Norie.'

Something in his voice was urgent. Was their short time together, without Kowie, as precious to him as to her?

They left the plates and pan on the table. He walked ahead, by way of the outside stairway up to his studio. She had to brush the oak branch aside, the tree had overgrown the steps in places. The roughness of the bark, the tender greenness of the leaves were familiar to her from the time of her youth. 'It's a tree house up here, Frikkie.' He moved a branch out of her way. 'I could never bring myself to prune a tree, I didn't even want to help Father with his roses.'

'But you surely don't bring the people you photograph here.'

He laughed his old laugh, which she'd almost forgotten. 'I bring very few people here. Until last year I still rented the place in the main street.

With sofas and shawls and pillars and backgrounds. Metaphorically speaking. The whole caboodle.'

'And now?'

'Heavens, Norie, I'm old, past a man's retirement age. I've done my duty by Kowie, the children are grown up. Now at last … now at last, I can seek that which I have longed for all my life. Do you know what it's like to wait, and wait, and wait?'

Is he drunk? thought Leonora. Is he crazy? Father had said it's a good thing to be obsessed, to have a passion. But Frikkie? His voice had hardened, had something cruel in it. 'A lifetime of hard labour.' Had he really said that? 'Willing, joyful loyal to your belief. Joyful, yes. But time goes by, so much is still demanded. Not she demanding it, but my work … the relentlessness of time passing …'

He used both hands to open the attic door. The studio was untidy, messy, disorderly, overcrowded. The light came from two dormer windows on either side. The far side was partitioned off with plank, with a door above which a red and a green light had been installed. A darkroom. There he would also have water and washing basins. Cork display boards were nailed to the other three walls. More display boards stood on stands away from the walls, so that the display area was doubled. Photos had been attached to the boards with drawing pins. The many photos – failures? – which had been thrown on the floor, kicked under the display boards as if he had ripped one off and thrown it down when he had something better to replace it, increased the disorder. It looked as though he'd tripped over the photos at times, kicked them aside, so that they lay heaped up like fallen leaves.

'I want to look slowly and carefully.'

'Take your time.'

On a distant board, yellowing under their plastic covering, the acid eating into the paper, were the photos which had hung in his room in the pastorie. Dozens of shots of Kowie's cheek from different angles. Still his love. An aching impotence scorched through her. The slanting cheek, the indescribably tender line of the curve of the cheek falling away with a small shadow into the hollow of the eye, and the light blush – a subtle deepening of tint on the cheek; a delicate lock of hair throwing a soft shadow over eye and cheek. And there were other photos of her which she didn't recognise: the glossy hair as the head bent forward, the slight smile on the lips which, with the downcast eyes, gave the impression that something distant and very beautiful was on her mind, or was only just dawning on her memory. A moment captured, never to be repeated.

'Yes, they go back all that time. But it goes much further than Kowie, much, much further. It is her face that gave me an indication of the fleeting, the elusive something we cannot grasp. And I pursue that. In everything.' His arm drew a wide circle to include the length and width of the attic.

She walked slowly from image to image. The grain of tree bark, the thickening of a leaf on a twig just before it dried and fell, the aureole surrounding the waving stamen of a mesembrianthemum, the movement that had frozen in the halo. Reflections on water. Bare branches. A few nude studies.

'What you photograph is manipulated,' she said at last. 'What I see here is not real.'

'That's true,' he said. 'I'm not in search of reality. I capture the moment of super-life. Of ecstasy.'

'Whose ecstasy? The observer's? Then it's subjective, distorting.'

'Creative rather. A new insight. But let's not bicker. Look at these.'

She took the pile he'd picked up from a shelf and handed to her. When she saw who the photos were of, she looked at him in amazement.

'They're incredible. SussieBelle? When? Where?'

'On the roof of her block of flats. When Arnold was married.'

'She looks possessed. How could you? It was cruel, Frikkie.'

He laughed. 'Agnes said I was a monster. To sacrifice compassion for a photo? I ask you; does the camera lie, or does it expose that which is hidden? Does it discover? You answer that for me.'

'You mean, had we paid attention to SussieBelle then?'

'Exactly.'

'But you paid no attention.'

'It is I who failed ... I have often reproached myself. She invited me to her flat, I didn't go.'

She spent a long time looking at the photos. 'Strange discords in Belle, all in irreconcilable contradiction, almost schism. On my last visit I saw Father's little concentration camp tent and the Indian's kudu-skin bag lying side by side in her cupboard. I think she was a victim, perhaps even a sacrifice.'

He took the photos from her. 'It's past, Norie.'

He also showed her the photos he had taken of Oom Hennie many years back.

'The poor old man.'

'Perhaps the blessed old man,' he contradicted her.

They stood at a dormer window and he drew up two chairs.

'Sit down, Norie, forget about the family now, I need to talk. You will just have to listen. It's providential that you arrived today, I want to express my thoughts in words. For once in my life.'

'Speak, Frikkie.'

'Do you remember the furore that time? I would have abandoned photography as Father wished, to take up the Classics. He, and also the professors, thought I had aptitude. Then I had such a strange experience. One afternoon I went for a walk on the slopes of the mountain near Stellenbosch. A lovely afternoon. I felt good, everything was fine. On the way back I looked in on a friend who shared a house with an artist. While I was waiting, the artist walked in carrying a canvas he had painted that afternoon. More or less the same mountain slope I had come from. Oh, but the difference. Tiny yellow and orange soil particles swarmed on the footpath. The flowers next to the path cried out with exuberance. With joy. The grass seemed to be swelling before my eyes, drawing in moisture after the rain. There was only one tree, barely in bud … its branches are still imprinted on my mind. Then I realised I had not seen before. The way I had been looking, I might as well have been blind. I had forfeited too much. Was it only the artist's talent that enabled him to observe so much? Was it only granted to the chosen few? I had no drawing or painting talent. Then I realised: on that picnic when I had taken the first photos, I had seen as he, the painter, saw. Seen people. Then I knew: I didn't want to go through life blind, I had to exploit the medium available to me to the utmost. Hence the photos.'

'Boetie,' it was her childhood name for him, 'may I be honest? It isn't the same. You are not looking with a living eye, but a mechanical lens. You manipulate.'

'The eye is also a lens.'

'But the person painting controls it, not an apparatus. The painter interprets, he doesn't simply reflect.'

But he persisted. He touched one photo after the other. 'Look here. Look here …' He took images still wet and dripping out of the darkroom, held them in front of her. 'Have you ever seen anything like that?' He put the images down, went to sit next to her. 'It's in the eye Norie, really seeing. We don't see. But why does this distress you?'

'I too tried to see.' She told him of the night in the desert, how she had become afraid. 'I fell short, Frikkie. I could not. Then my life, not yours, was a difficult road leading nowhere. A halfway-love. Halfway to humanity, halfway to God. I envy you what Father would have called your obsession.' She began to weep softly. The room around her with the rows and rows of photographs seemed to her like a battlefield. The shabby old photographer a warrior, still a warrior on his steed. And she? An elderly lover. A barren woman after whom a child had been named. She told him about Leo, but it didn't interest him much.

'My whole being told me: man can see. You have probably read about mescaline, and LSD. Just as aspirin dulls your headache, so these substances influence your brain's, let's call it, filter. For it's not the eyes that don't see, it's the brain that doesn't admit all that the eye sees. It came my way by coincidence: a doctor friend who was interested in these drugs, injected me. She stayed with me to monitor my reactions. God, then I saw, more than the artist had seen that spring afternoon. Since then I know and I will seek and keep on seeking. That one time was enough, then I knew.' He placed the plates on the table, drew a chair near to her, and said: 'Listen Leonora. I must tell someone. I have seen how the light surrounding us breaks up into milliards of particles, in colours and shapes. Before my eyes, the colours formed hundreds of patterns, and regrouped to make others, stars and triangles and circles and patterns within patterns. And they are all present here, in the light around us, and we don't see it. Here, now. It drives one mad.' He was very moved, and he held his head in his hands.

'And then I saw how nature dies around us. I picked a leaf and the stem died in my hand. I saw the life flow from it, the green grow brown. Slowly, slowly, the edge began to curl up and dry. My hand was also repulsive, also in the process of dying.'

He spoke so softly, she could barely hear him.

'We should not see it, Frik, that's why we don't see it.'

'And then – where it came from, I don't know – I was under water and I felt quiet and peaceful and heavy; I was a heavy stone in a mountain stream, and a fine rusty brown moss covered me; I saw a long thin green plant droop over me, but the stream wasn't moving, the bending of the plant was without movement, it just was. And through the amber water and the green fibres of the water-leaf came the amber sunlight. A perfect moment of existence. Balmy, the same temperature as blood, silent.'

It was as though he awoke from a swoon. He sat up. 'Well now, sister dear, I could go on like that. Of course we must see it. And water. I can tell you about water. What do we know about water? I have seen water streaming in pipes underground and through buildings, and the water became fire. A framework of fire in which we live. What do we know about water? Christened with water, christened with fire?'

Drink of the water. Drink of the fire.

My brother is raving, thought Leonora.

'It's getting dark,' she said. 'I think we should go back: next thing we'll tumble down the stairs.'

Kowie was cooking in the kitchen. 'I'm so pleased to see you, Leonora, it's such a pity the family is losing touch. Everyone seems to lose touch with us, it seems to me no one cares. I was so pleased to see your car, I guessed you were up there with Frikkie.' She kissed Kowie on the cheek. 'Stay and spend the night.'

Leonora noticed how solicitous her brother was of Kowie, well past her prime, stout, a permanent petulance at the corners of her mouth. He helped her, laid the table. No, he wasn't hen-pecked, she thought, rather dedicated. Not hard labour – she felt a slight envy – just surrender. It seemed as if his heated words had brought him release.

A passion for something, Father's words recurred.

She slept peacefully that night.

The next morning when Kowie had gone to church – apparently she usually went on her own – he said, 'Let's sit in the backyard, in the shade.'

'You look more relaxed,' he said. 'Do you want to talk?'

'I feel more relaxed. How should I put it? The solitude, call it the desolation of being imprisoned in myself, has eased. In my small space I feel calmer, even sheltered.'

They lay back in old-fashioned deck chairs – she remembered the chairs from the days in the green garden at the pastorie. The canvas was bleached, worn through in places; had started to come apart at the seams.

Frikkie took an envelope from his pocket and unfolded a few thin pages of yellowing paper. She recognised the handwriting with a start. 'Do you remember, or were you too young, how Mother wrote and wrote in the short time between the two 'flu attacks? Aunt Issy said she had exhausted her strength writing, that was why she died.'

'I remember Mother at the little table in her bedroom, in a dressing gown, her hair in a roll, not pinned up but loose over her shoulder, such thick, dark hair. All the children, and not a grey hair.'

'Do you remember how Father read aloud what she had written: *A Vision?*'

'I was heartbroken about Vicky; I listened, but it didn't touch me.'

Frikkie held the thin yellowing pages with the faded script very close to his eyes.

'A Vision,' he read. 'I won't read all of it, you can take it home. Actually typically Victorian, her portrayal of heaven. It was amongst papers of Father's and a few old photos Stuart sent my way. At the time I wrote it off as Victorian sentimentality, but listen here: she lay there sick and as she said, "half in stupor", when she heard a voice say:

"Come. I will show thee the realms of the blest." In an instant of time, I know not how, I found myself in a place which for the grandeur and glory and the brilliance of it's light so dazzled me, that I was well nigh bewildered nor can pen ever describe the vastness and the wonderful glories of those mansions fair. I thought of all the beautiful scenes I had beheld on earth – sunrise and sunset and rainbow. It was all this and much more.

'Think of the light patterns I told you about,' said Frikkie. 'This vision differs very little from that of mescaline users.' Then he read on:

'Floods and floods of golden light tinted with the most exquisite colouring. Its streets seemed to me to be laid with blue stones the colour of our clear sky and this overlaid with gold so that the blue still showed itself. And as I thus stood not knowing where to look, so overwhelming was the sight, I turned aside and my eye fell on a spot of surpassing loveliness, it seemed to me a garden of lilies where flowered also the roses and beautiful flowers, but the lilies specially drew my attention, some so tall that they looked like trees.'

Frikkie leaned forward in his chair: the sun shining through the leaves hindered his reading. What wonderful play of patterns of sun and shadow over his face and arms, over his hands, thought Leonora.
'Just listen to this.' He read rapidly, excited:

'…it came to me that the things which men on earth consider as most perfect are but faint and imperfect reflections of the heavenly. Oh, those heaven-grown flowers with their perfume as rich as roses as the gentle breeze wafted it to where I stood.'

'This frail, exhausted wife of a dominee experienced, in 1918, what scientists and philosophers would describe half a century later … Just think of Huxley. It astounds me. He wrote that in the Middle Ages monks and nuns after hours of fasting and chanting had seen such visions. Perhaps she was in a similar condition after her illness.'

'There were negative perceptions in your case: the leaf dying ... your fingers hideously ugly ...' said Leonora.

'Exactly,' said Frikkie. 'What did Mother experience then? That her garment, her figure were too ugly for those surroundings. As if in her too there was revulsion with self:

> 'I remembered my travel-stained garments. So mean and dirty did my dress appear to me, when I looked at the pure white raiment of the Saints, that it was to me as if I was clothed in nothing better than sack cloth, so that for very shame I fled from Him, whose eyes would surely see me hidden though I was behind the cloud. Down I went through endless spaces, whirled along as it were, until I found myself upon my bed, wearied and worn as from a long and toilsome journey. And as I there lay thinking to rest myself a strange feeling came over me and my heart began so to throb and beat, it was as if the Spirit would burst its bonds and return to whither it had just been.'

'Note that: with her too the revulsion at self.'

'Do we need a drug to be able to understand today?'

'Perhaps the crust of the world around us has hardened so much that we need something like that.' He smiled. 'Just some cleaning materials to scour away the encrustation. Just a chisel to lift the window latch that is rusted fast. Anyway, that's how I see it. That we could really just know what seeing means.'

Frikkie banged the sides of his head with his open hands. Then he waved his arms to indicate the tree, the leaves, the branches, the sun, the fine grass at his feet, the blue sky, everything. 'How blind we are, how much we miss! As little as this ant on my leg can see the glory of the oak tree, that's how little, just as bloody little, we see. It gets to me.'

'And the camera?'

'Enlarges, enlarges to infinity, perhaps further. Tries to capture a moment, tear away veils.'

'The microscope?'

'Also tries to remove veils. For the initiated who understand its language. But the microscope is different, it requires no creative leap of the imagination.'

Leonora twirled a piece of salvia between her fingers. 'I picked it and now it is done with. It's finished. I feel that's what the camera does. When a moment has been photographed, that moment has already passed. It's dead. Whether it is a cheek or a shadow on a wall or a leaf.

It's counter to life.' She hesitated. 'There's another danger. I see what another person has decided I should see. So my perceptions are never my own. That oil painting of the artist, it continues to exist in your mind in another way. That you told me yourself.'

'There we differ, my dear Leonora.' She had annoyed him, she realised. 'I photograph to see for myself. I don't give a damn what you, or anyone else, sees. And what I photograph doesn't lie. Think of Belle, or does it hurt to think of Belle?'

After lunch Frikkie and Kowie took Leonora to see the grandchildren. Miemie was a plump, friendly young woman with her youngest, a little boy, on her hip. The little girl was riding a tricycle on the front stoep, deliberately bumped against her oupa's leg. 'I don't believe in these exotic names, Tannie Leonora. My eldest son is named after my Pa, Frederik. We call him Fred. The little girl is named after my Ma: Jakoba. My little Kobatjie. And the baby is Josias, after Oupa. Please sit down, Tannie Leonora, now tell us about Arnold's family. You saw them last. It's so nice that they've got three, just like us. Is their baby pretty?'

'I haven't seen them recently, Miemie, the baby must be quite big.'

'But tell us, Tannie.'

She told what she could remember. She pressed a banknote in Miemie's hand for each child's piggy bank; she lifted their little faces and kissed them, they were after all her flesh and blood. She scarcely knew Miemie's husband, Stoffel. He was a primary school teacher and was taking a Sunday school class that afternoon. Fred had gone with him.

'I'm sorry I've missed them, give them my love. But now I have to go.' She had Mother's *Vision* in her handbag.

'Please come again,' said Frikkie.

She said goodbye to him once more. 'Thanks, Frikkie, for everything, I won't forget it. And take care of yourself.'

Before she switched the engine on she said, 'I think we should have the gravestones cleaned – Father's, Mother's and Vicky's, and also the others. The old people set store by things like that. If you can organise it I'll send my contribution. And let the three brothers know.'

'Forget about the brothers. Let's the two of us take care of the dead. The brothers are much too busy building the volk.'

Where did the thought come from, like a slight scent on the breeze, that he was eager for her to leave, that he was not displeased that she was leaving? Had she disturbed his precarious balance? It would sadden her if that were the case.

The wine Frikkie had served the previous night had made her thirsty. As she drove over Du Toitskloof pass in the late afternoon, she stopped at one of the view sites. There were no other cars and this pleased her. The leucodendron, the scrub, the buchu shimmered in the light, she saw a cobweb ablaze with light. God Almighty. Then what she had once read was true: what counts is not *what* life is, but that life *is*. It seemed as though she heard a rustling, but there wasn't a breath of wind, the mountain shrubs were motionless. Somewhere near, she knew, there was a stream. She walked along the mountain path, some distance from the road. Then she heard the sound of water. She bent down next to the stream, had the water flow over her hands, cupped her hands, bent forward and drank. The feeling of unity between her body and the mountain water overwhelmed her. She closed her eyes and felt how the cool water was absorbed by the inner membranes of her mouth. One hand lingered in the stream. The water flowed over it, washed over the heel of her hand in little wavelets and then flowed smoothly again.

Almighty God, she thought again. The golden brown of the water coloured the large, round stones lying on the sand, saturated and heavy and still. A thin watery green blade of grass drooped over the stone in the flow of water, hung motionless over the rusty brown dappled stone for an eternal moment. She felt that she was entering the stone, she was the stone, and all was well. She wondered in a vague way, without disquiet: How had Frikkie, yesterday afternoon, known about this stone, at this place? That moment and this moment are completely intermingled, there is no time or distance or separateness.

PART FOUR
Leo

1

At first the grown-up Leo didn't really impress Leonora. At the Cape Town station, Leo with her suitcases full of new clothes – Rina had kindly done the honours again – and her hockey stick, was rather traumatic for Leonora. She'd last seen Leo four years earlier as a gym-slipped schoolgirl.

She was anxious from waiting and worrying about how she'd find her amongst all the people and luggage. But she did find her, or rather Leo grabbed her arm.

Leo doesn't take after her mother, or our side of the family, thought Leonora. She takes after Holtzhausen. She had thick spectacles, for she was short-sighted like her father. Her hair was thick and fair, but mousy rather than blond. I must take her to a good hairdresser, she resolved. And as for those thick spectacles. But she has a good figure, a little puppy fat, but that'll pass. Not bad legs. A nice smile, when she does smile. But the posture. *My dear!* Aunt Issy would have said. The shoulders were hunched nervously and the head thrust forward, as if aiming the hockey stick.

But the child greeted her enthusiastically; she indicated the hockey stick. 'I'm goalie, Tannie. I can see well up close.'

Leonora found the meeting emotionally draining.

She was relieved when she had seen Leo and her luggage onto the train for Stellenbosch – she no longer drove such long distances herself.

At last the local train steamed out of the station.

'Your little room is ready for you at my house, dear, come as often as you like.'

The decision to go to the University of Stellenbosch after matric had been taken by Leo herself. Her father accepted it with some hesitation. Sometimes he longed for his old, simpler surroundings in Westdene. He'd secretly hoped that his daughter would attend the Randse Afrikaanse Universiteit, so very near to Westdene. It would have been a link with the past.

But the three ooms had enthusiastically approved of her decision to attend their Alma Mater. She would be the first of the fourth generation to become a 'Matie'.

'We'll contribute. We'll help you, Holtzhausen.'

'It's my privilege,' insisted Hendrik. His business interests were flourishing. Sometimes he had doubts about foreign transactions that were increasingly channelled through his financial undertakings – payments and invoices did not always correspond – but what alternative did the government have? The crippling sanctions had to be broken, he rationalised. He consoled himself: It is for the Nation, for the Nation. And tried to banish Greylinck from his thoughts.

'It will do her good to get away,' Philip's wife Maude told her son Barry. 'She's like a little old granny already. It breaks my heart: ever since she was tiny she's been the buffer between her poor mother and the rest of the world: "Yes Tannie, Mamma will have another slice of cake; no, Tannie, the cuttings didn't grow, we'll come to get more." Even concerned about Rina: "Put on another jersey, Tannie, it's chilly out."'

'She's a strong girl, that Leo,' said Barry. 'I'm not worried about her. She'll be fine, just give her time.'

The fact that Leonora, who took such an interest in the girl, would be near, for advice, for weekends, settled the matter. Leonora was still fit and active in her mid-seventies.

And Ouma Agnes. Of course, she was also in Cape Town.

Leo took Tannie Leonora at her word. She came to stay, at first every other weekend, later less often. Leonora began to look forward to it. Later she brought along a boyfriend, who even stayed the night once, sleeping in the lounge. 'A Tokkelok, Oumatan,' as she had called Leonora in childhood. 'But he's not the usual sort of theology student, he's different.'

And after Hendrik had taken her to the optometrist during the first July vacation, and paid for the contact lenses, Leo was also different. Her head was no longer dragged forward by the heavy lenses, her shoulders relaxed. Her neck appeared longer and graceful with the stylish hairdo. She'd lost weight and walked gracefully, head back, an eager expression on her face.

She's actually almost pretty, thought Leonora. Perhaps my eyes are failing. Perhaps love is blind. She had grown very fond of Leo, and Leo of her, but things went less well between Ouma Agnes and Leo.

'It's tough having two oumas in the Cape,' Leo told her roommate, a Boland girl, as they sat in the common room one afternoon, waiting for the coffee to arrive. 'You always feel you're neglecting the one, because you'd rather be with the other. And I don't think they really like each other. Oh, it's a long story, I can't tell you all. My Ouma was married to my Ouma-tannie's brother, that's how it came about. I never knew my Oupa, but after his death my Ouma went to live with the woman she thought was her mother, but then again she thought not, but then when the woman died she left her house to my Ouma who still lives there.'

'And your Oumatannie also has a house in Cape Town.'

'Not far from my Ouma, just up the hill in Tamboerskloof.'

'Then you'll have two houses one day,' said her roommate, 'if you're the favourite of both of them. Two houses in a beautiful part of Cape Town!'

'Capitalist! Talking about inheritance already!' said Ernie, an anti-establishment brunette. Her boyfriend was at the University in Cape Town and the dreaded word NUSAS had already been associated with him. He was a dissident. She straightened up on the sofa, and held out the magazine she'd been reading. 'You belong with the *momios* in Chile! Go on, read! Read aloud so we can all hear.'

Leo picked up the magazine and glanced at the article Ernie had been reading. Other girls encouraged her: 'Go on, read.' They were bored and the coffee hadn't arrived. Leo had even taken elocution lessons. Another contribution from Hendrik: 'Do all you can to enrich your life, sweetheart. Use your opportunities, they may never occur again.'

She read:

A lost civilisation has been discovered in the Atacama Desert in Northern Chile. Among other things, mummies were found, preserved in their sand-coloured binding, as proud and erect and rigid as in their lifetime, they were brought to the surface by bulldozers. To the light. To a world centuries removed from that in which they had lived. Anachronisms. Belonging in the museums where they have been placed.

'No, don't stop, you're getting to the point,' Ernie urged her. Leo sighed dramatically and read on with exaggerated gestures:

Thus is the ruling class – the land owners, the industrial masters, the wealthy, living on interest, actually all those artificially privileged – those enjoying the 'status privilegio'. So states the socialistic government in Santiago. They are mummies, 'momios'. The only place for them is in a museum.

'Like us here at university, at our fathers' expense, or on inherited money, privileged, anachronisms, *momios*.' The girls were familiar with

Ernie's diatribes. Her father was the wealthiest of all. And on top of that she won scholarships by the dozen, for she was clever.

She took the magazine from Leo and read on:

'Momios' have typical attributes. They look, but don't see. Hear, but don't understand. They regard the world with a cold eye. And people they look upon as their social inferiors with something of 'odio' which means hatred. If not actually hatred, with scorn, contempt, disdain, which can be as deadly as hatred.

Leo sighed in boredom. 'Okay, so it's politics again. But this *momio* works for what she gets. Not everyone is as clever as you.'

'Work as a privileged white with everything in your favour, free schooling, automatic bursaries if you are going to do a Higher Education Diploma – that's not working. Not anything like a black child has to work to get anywhere.'

'Okay, so it's my fault. The whole education thing. Hell, I was 14 years old when the Soweto schoolkids began marching and burning.'

'My father says it's useless to give our Ella money for her children's school,' said Leo's roommate, 'they just go on strike and burn down everything. I said it was really weird that black children had to buy books and we got ours free. Then he told me it wasn't weird at all, he was paying taxes for them.'

'Ernie, you can't say we don't care about them,' said Leo. 'My ma's maid cried so when they were marching that we said she could bring her child to us. We let her stay in the garage the whole week. Okay, winter and a cement floor, but she said she slept on cement at home too. And we gave her a rug.'

The girls lounging about on the dark green carpet in the rust and green common room held their mugs of coffee in cupped hands and drank lazily, they listened to her inattentively.

'I sometimes played with the baby a bit, quite odd to carry the black child around.'

'You don't say,' said Ernie.

'Ma gave Lilian two white towels and a scissors so that she could make nappies. We weren't unsympathetic.'

'Goodness,' said Ernie again, 'probably tatty old towels.'

The girls began to saunter back to their rooms. Their ideas largely, sometimes entirely, reflected the political views of their boyfriends. To differ from your boyfriend was the equivalent of rejection. It was because of her UCT boyfriend that Ernie held those views, everyone knew that.

Ben Deetlefs, Leo's theology student boyfriend, was conservative. He'd suffered a negative experience when he went to a squatters' camp just beyond Philippi to try to take a Sunday school class. Confidentially he confessed to Leo: 'I was called the most filthy names, names I can't repeat to you, and even had stones thrown at me!' It evoked in him a self-righteous but raw sense of martyrdom.

'We also have to put up with a lot,' Leo then said to Ernie. 'Eat at some ungodly early hour in the evening so that the kitchen staff can go home.'

'Gives you more time with Baas Ben.'

'Oh, shut up. You're just as much a *momio* as us. Even more so.'

'And you're surprised they chased Ben out of the squatters' camp!'

The squatters' camps. No one liked to think of them. Because she travelled to Cape Town by train when she went to Tannie Leonora or Ouma Agnes, Leo realised that she had no idea what the squatters' camps along the main road were like. She was inquisitive to see them, but she couldn't persuade Ben to take her there.

Some things, she had to admit, she just couldn't accept. Nobody could expect her to accept them. When the bulldozers demolished the squatters' shacks in the bitter winter weather and they showed it on TV, she preferred not to look. And she agreed wholeheartedly with most of her friends having coffee: The squatters shouldn't be here in the Cape. What were they doing here, without work, without homes? And cheeky as well. Just think of Ben's experience. If Ernie wanted to talk about 'odio' …

Leo obtained her B.A. degree, was doing her Higher Education Diploma, and considering continuing with Honours. She still enjoyed taking the train to Cape Town for weekends, or increasingly frequently just for the day, if Ben wanted to do something special on the Saturday evening and she had to return by the afternoon train.

Something special? By that time she knew all about his 'something special'.

As she sat in the empty compartment rocking its way through the green marshy pastures, with arums here and there, it was not politics, or whether she was a *momio* worrying her. Not the crowded workers' cottages or the empty first-class coaches in contrast with the third-class coaches, so full that people hung out the windows. She was examining her short fingers with the bitten nails. To bend the fingers like a little claw, to examine, straighten again, bite off a bit of cuticle, wipe the wetness on her dress, to examine again. There was a deep frown on her forehead. Ben Deetlefs wanted her to buy 'The Pill' from a chemist in Cape Town. Not yet an ultimatum, but still. It brought her feelings towards him to a head. If he wanted her to be on the pill – and they'd debated that endlessly – why shouldn't she go openly to a Stellenbosch pharmacy? Or go to the students' clinic? If his conscience allowed her to take the pill and yield to his needs, why the hypocrisy? Was Ben, the trainee theologian, essentially a hypocrite? And on top of that his stupid reasoning: because it would be his birthday in a few weeks, buying the pill would be her birthday present to him. The loveliest, the best birthday present of his entire life!

Apart from her slight disapproval of his shirking army duty, or postponing it, in the hope that the conflict on the border between South West Africa and Angola would be over before he had finished his studies, she wasn't really concerned with the war. There was considerable feeling for nation and country in her heart – it wasn't for nothing she'd reached the rank of President's Scout at school, to Hendrik's delight – but she was honest enough to know: this disapproval of Ben's shirking was probably merely an excuse she had fabricated to divert attention from the real reason: she was tired of him. And of his raw martyrdom since he was chased from Philippi. His clumsy efforts on Saturday evenings in the dark bushes behind Coetzenburg (he didn't have a car) had not succeeded in kindling a flame of desire in her. Not even if she added Friday and Sunday evenings.

She was eager to have someone arouse a reckless flame of desire in her.

She began thinking of leaving the campus and the boyfriend at the end of the year. Of applying for a post. So that she could spend her own money, think her own thoughts.

So she could begin living.

But the Honours degree still attracted her.

And the gnawing doubt: would Hendrik get around to giving her the promised car? Promised for her twenty-first birthday, but not mentioned again. He would come up with it, she knew he would. The train rumbled into the Cape Town station.

On this particular Saturday excursion she experienced something new. She was standing in the office of the United Building Society in St George's Street, completing a form, when she heard a new sort of noise: black schoolchildren marching up Adderley Street, being dispersed with teargas and truncheons, and she heard the dull thud of rubber bullets. A fleeing child burst in through the door of the UBS and hid behind her legs. Involuntarily she held her raincoat to hide the child. A constable, truncheon in hand, looked in, saw nothing, rushed up the stairs to the next floor. Shame, she thought. She felt rather that heard the panting child behind her legs. She, too, trembled slightly.

She was annoyed that Ben who came to fetch her at the Stellenbosch station late that afternoon – no, she hadn't bought the pill – took so little interest in her 'adventure'. He pushed his bicycle and walked her back to the residence, disgruntled.

'See you at seven,' he said as he got on his bike and rode off.

In their room her roommate was sitting with the latest *Education Gazette* and said, 'Gosh, we must apply for posts. I'm telling you: forget about Honours. Then you'll be shot of Ben too, without any drama.'

Her roommate knew Ben was getting difficult, talking of student marriages, better to marry than to burn, but she wasn't burning at all, far from it. Her roommate had been telling her for ages: Leo, you can do better than Ben. At first she couldn't believe it when he dated her, walked her up and down Lovers' Lane and poured his ambitions into her willing, humble ears. But with her contact lenses, her new hairdo, her slimmer body and her new self-confidence, she no longer felt like being humble. She had lost her interest in hockey, and what irritated her most of all was that Ben took this amiss, because he had thought hockey would be an asset for the wife of a dominee and for his future parish.

Leo applied for a post at a school in the centre of Cape Town. She went to the interview by train. She didn't get the post – no experience – but was offered a temporary post for two terms at the same school. She made a final decision not to buy the pill. He would just have to keep on burning for the last term.

'I'm not going to do Honours next year,' she wrote to her parents. 'Neither will I be coming home for the long vacation, I've got a post. I'll stay with Tannie Leonora. We're going to clean up Ouma Agnes's house, and I'm going to move in there before school starts. Another teacher will be sharing the house with me,' she fibbed, not to be sneaky, but because she loved her parents who would worry about her being alone in a house.

She lied to Ben: 'I've got a post in Calvinia. Let's rather break up. Then you can find yourself another girlfriend, who'll give you that birthday present you want so badly.'

She wrote to Oom Hendrik and Mammie that she could now support herself and thanked them so touchingly for all their financial assistance that oom Hendrik immediately sent her a cheque for a little car. Also as a gift for her twenty-first.

She danced around the residence passages with the cheque pressed to her chest.

She was so excited she could scarcely swallow.

'*Momios* must have motors,' said Ernie rather enviously.

Yet something strange was happening to her.

She no longer enjoyed walking around on her own in Stellenbosch. Earlier she had used every opportunity when Ben was working or at rugby practice to explore the town.

Now she felt vulnerable. She'd wander down a back road and then suddenly, as if under a microscope, see a scene in front of her, as clearly drawn as if it were the first time she really saw: a wedge of sunlight falling between two rows of damp, dark semi-detached houses, a pool of water between the two reflecting a strange blue oily colour. But then an old coloured man, bent over a broom, strained forward and dragged his feet through the water as he tried to sweep up the leaves. Could he have been drunk? She thought of the words of the omniscient Ernie: The coloured people, especially the old ones, try to find a job at the little houses they once lived in themselves, before expropriation. They simply want to be on the property again.

And the ragged coloured child, thin as a skeleton, sucking pineapple skins she'd found in a garbage bin – why had Leo never seen her before?

She walked away quickly. She suspected she would see worse things if she continued looking. Or was she like the *momios* looking, but not seeing? Ernie's mockery had hit home.

She sat in a library waiting for a book. On the table in front of her lay a copy of the encyclopaedia *Algemene Winkler Prins*. She drew it closer, paged through it; her finger strayed to the letter m, stopped involuntarily at 'Mummy'. She read:

> *Mummy, a corpse preserved from decay by embalming ... The preparation of the mummy was a religious activity of the Egyptians ... A mummy mask was laid on the face; specific body parts (eyelids, lips, etc.) were sometimes gilded.*

She stood up, fetched Volume 1 from the shelf, paged to 'Embalming': according to the somewhat unclear description of Diodorus, the

Egyptians would first empty the skull and then fill it with aromatic matter, as well as asphaltum. The corpse was then laid in a bath of nitron and then bound. The corpses of poor people were treated in less costly fashion; they were pickled.

Who did she know who was a mummy? she thought. Rina who was so sweet? The ooms who worked so hard? Barry? Her mother? Never, ever her mother.

Her heart ached when she thought of her. There was a story about her mother that she had been told in part.

'Your Mama had a romance,' Tannie Rina once told her. 'It caused her dreadful harm.'

'But what about Pappa then?' she'd asked.

'No, darling, it was long before your Pappa. Everyone's nervous system is different. Your Mamma was frail.'

Philip? Maude? Robert? His faded little wife, Estie? Anachronisms? Part of a ruling class taking its advantages for granted?

Pickled?

Could a heart be unpickled?

It's different here from Johannesburg, thought Leo. Things she'd rather not see were closer in the small university town, unavoidable. She tried to change the trend of her thoughts. Pity her roommate was going to teach in Worcester, but she'd make other friends in Cape Town. As she walked, in late spring, through the trees, still wet, but sun brightened in places, where the tight little buds were shedding their covering, and the thin oak twigs caught the sunbeams as they trembled, she forced herself to anticipate with excitement the life ahead of her. An excitement somewhat dampened when an old coloured woman appeared staggering from under the trees and asked for money, which she refused, for drunkenness should not be encouraged. Or when a group of coloured children confronted her and asked for money for bread, became insolent, pressed against her, surrounded her. Avoid eye contact, she had read somewhere …

Just think what had happened to Ouma Agnes.

Agnes had come to a gruesome end. Why did the unfortunate woman have to suffer this fate as well? Holtzhausen, greatly disturbed, asked himself in the mortuary at Salt River. With doubts spilling over him: Had he looked after his mother-in-law adequately? With Belle as she was, and Leo to be brought up, hadn't they neglected her rather shamefully?

Leo was in her fourth year at Stellenbosch when she was called to the phone one Sunday morning. 'Hurry, it's a trunk call.'

It was her father. She could hear he was upset. 'I'm flying to Cape Town today: your Ouma Agnes has died.'

'And Ma?'

'She's staying here. You must let your Tannie Leonora know. Take the first train to Cape Town. I'll meet you at Tannie Leonora's.'

'But Ouma Agnes?'

'They've taken her to the mortuary. Try to stay calm, darling.'

The words worried her as she rattled along to Cape Town in the empty compartment. Ben couldn't go with her, he was taking a Sunday school class. Keep calm now. She felt guilty about Ouma Agnes. She felt little empathy with the thin little woman who clutched her arm with such a strong grip. Or moved her fingers up and down on the inside of Leo's arms. As if she were absent-minded, but – Leo shuddered – wished to become intimate.

She was stingy too. Never a biscuit or any fruit in the house, she was surely not so very poor. And there was a nasty atmosphere in the house, as if it was already inhabited by a corpse. The portrait of the rebel. His framed letter, still regularly dusted. A couple of geraniums – the only things that flourished. No cat or dog or other companion. And the endless embroidered cloths taken from boxes in the cupboard and unpacked to show her. Some were beautiful, she would have liked them, but Ouma Agnes was obstinate, didn't want to give them yet. The stitches in the last cloths, when her eyes began to fail, were skew and uneven.

They all neglected her, thought Leo. One would think her mother was not really her child, yet she was. But when Ma withdrew from life, it was as though she had an aversion to her own mother – actually to all her family. At least Ouma Agnes didn't have a smell, like so many old people. The house was just stuffy. Everything closed, everything turned inward, no window open, the doors locked. And so much old-fashioned junk.

'I'll wait for you so that we can go to your Ouma's house together,' Leonora had said on the phone. 'Yes, I know; the neighbours phoned me.'

Such darkness in her voice that Leo was too afraid to ask for details. Keep calm, darling, she had heard her Pa say. There was a bus to Tamboerskloof comparatively quickly for a Sunday morning. Tannie Leonora opened the door as if she had been waiting. Her face was grey.

'Sit down, so that I can tell you.' She drew Leo down next to her on the sofa. 'Be brave, my precious. Your Ouma Agnes was murdered. Early this morning the neighbours heard their dog barking in an odd way. All along the fence. They found the body at the woodpile. Strangled with her own wash-line. They suspect it was the gardener. But they'll catch him, they'll catch him.'

'She never had a gardener, Oumatan, she was too ...'

She swallowed the words, but Leonora said them: 'Too stingy, too economical, call it short of money. But the poles of the wash-line had collapsed, she had to have holes dug. She just took someone of the street. That's what the neighbours say. When they drove off on Saturday afternoon the kaffir was working. When they returned all was quiet. Only this morning the dog began to bark. Poor Agnes.'

Tears ran down Leonora's cheeks, mixed with wet mucus from her nose. Leo gave her a tissue. She wiped it across her face, her hair hadn't been combed, she tried to swallow her tears. 'She was so radiant when she entered our house, and that she should come to such an end. I neglected my duty. I never felt affection for her. It was sinful of me.'

Leo thought of a photo she had seen somewhere, which Oom Frikkie had taken of Ouma Agnes in a white Voortrekker dress and bonnet.

'She looked so lovely in her Voortrekker dress, Oumatan. Something so different about her, something, as you say, aglow.' While she had been unable to weep for the Ouma as a little old woman, her tears now flowed for the young one. 'And it all came to nothing.'

Her father took a taxi from the airport. This was such an unusual extravagance that it nearly overshadowed the enormity of his mother-in-law's death. While they were greeting him on the stoep, the police phoned for the third time. 'We're coming,' said Leonora, and to Holtzhausen who was taking his suitcase from the taxi: 'Keep the taxi. The police are impatient. We didn't want to leave before you arrived.'

The taxi stopped in front of Agnes's house. Two police cars were parked next to the street. The neighbour, already questioned, stood on her stoep holding her child's hand. She wanted to speak to Leonora, but Leonora just greeted her and walked on. The close smell of the narrow, linoleum-floored passage was strong, in spite of the open door.

The police had removed the little vases and cloths from a table in the lounge, drawn it nearer to the window, and the sergeant was sitting there writing. They were asked to sit down.

'Obviously murder and robbery. Sign here for the autopsy, please.'

He looked at Leonora, but she indicated Holtzhausen. 'He's her son-in-law,' she said.

'We have to establish whether she was also raped. These old women, it makes you sick. Clothes show signs of a struggle. Could have been as the wire was tightened, a sort of desperate effort for air.'

Leo's stomach turned. Leonora drew up a chair for her.

'Is it necessary,' she reprimanded Holtzhausen, 'that she should be here?'

'By rights she's the only blood relative,' he said defensively.

The sergeant slapped his hand on the form he had completed.

'Why these aunties, living on their own, must take in kaffirs from the street is beyond me. The neighbour says it's from stinginess, she pays little. She reckons the deceased had perhaps also argued about the payment when the job was done, then he let rip. You must look around, see what's missing. Then the identification. One of the cars here will take you to the mortuary. Sir, perhaps you'd better come.'

Holtzhausen took his hat. Pappa doesn't know Ouma, thought Leo, how many times has he been here? Actually none of us know her.

'Should I come along?' asked Leonora. But Holtzhausen pressed her arm. 'It's all right, stay here with Leo.'

'Please check what's missing. Here's a pencil and paper, a list will help us. Radio, TV, stuff like that. Jewellery, money.'

The police car travelled fast and smoothly, the driver sat with his elbow on the windowsill. There was little traffic on a Sunday morning. Holtzhausen didn't know Cape Town. Nervousness caused his stomach nerves to contract. Yet he pretended to take an interest in the surroundings. City centre, past the parade, there was the Castle which he recognised from pictures.

'Not far now,' said the driver, 'to the office in Salt River.'

The nervousness increased, even his throat muscles felt tense. The driver turned in at the gate deftly, parked, opened his door. Holtzhausen followed him up the steps.

The man nodded to the guard. 'They're expecting us. It's about this morning's body.'

'Straight through.'

Now the smell of formalin increased. The doors on either side of the passage were tightly closed, yet the smell seeped through somewhere. His thoughts jerked back to the day after the Sharpeville shooting when he'd seen the bodies lying in the mortuary. Yet that was different, they were unknown to him. Now his own wife's mother. The policeman knocked at the last door, opened and they entered. A man in a white coat was bending over a table, straightened up. The smell was as strong as ether.

'Just the face,' said the policeman. 'All that's necessary.'

The man in the coat reluctantly drew the sheet up over the exposed body of the old woman. Not before Holtzhausen had seen her; the yellow, sunken belly, two knobbly hip bones, two widespread bare legs which the man pushed together with his hand, the sunken shoulder hollows, the deep cut in the chest.

'The doc is taking samples from the lungs,' said the policeman.

The dried blood was dark, almost black. The laboratory assistant pulled the sheet up to the chin. He tapped first against the one cheek, then against the other with the palm of his hand so that the head would lie right, for it had fallen to the side. A stiff, contorted fall, for rigor mortis had already set in. An obstinate fall. He held the head in both hands so that it looked up. Then he let it go.

'Not a pretty sight,' said the policeman.

It looked as if the face had been inflated from the inside. The eyes were open and stared at the ceiling. The absence of expression in the eyes caused the green of the corneas to be sharper and brighter than in life, like emeralds. Had she such green eyes? wondered Holtzhausen. Why was there not fear or horror in the eyes, only the hard emerald? The skin was so tightly drawn over the cheekbones it looked as if it might crack; between the nose and the upper lip there was swelling; right around the mouth it seemed puffed up, as if in rage. Oh God, the tongue. That could not be pushed back in by the pathologist, it was protruding halfway out of the mouth, like a seeking, swollen monster.

'Look here,' the assistant said to the policeman. He lifted the chin and pointed to the deep red circle around the throat. 'We had to battle to get the wire loose. Couldn't have been tighter if he'd used pliers.'

'Is this your mother-in-law?' Holtzhausen nodded. 'No need to tell your wife or daughter, but they abused the old women horribly. Raped to a pulp. This way sir, here's the toilet.'

Holtzhausen had pulled out a handkerchief and held it to his mouth. He stumbled to the lavatory.

'My ouma didn't have a TV, only a little radio. My father may still have the serial number, he bought it for her. Perhaps he kept the papers,' said Leo. Thrown from an upturned dressing table drawer, underwear lay strewn over the floor; old-fashioned underclothes, darned, even patched.

These shabby underclothes brought Leo to tears for the second time that morning. She swallowed her tears and wiped her nose on her sleeve, she couldn't bring herself to use one of her ouma's worn handkerchiefs. Actually it caused her to shudder; she began stuffing the things back in the drawer. Something hard, with corners, in her hand; it was a small box. She opened it. On a piece of cotton wool lay the brooch, the pretty green emerald stones on the small gold bar.

'Look, Tannie Leonora, do you recognise it?'

Leonora took it in her hand. 'She was really attached to it. When she was younger she used to wear it all the time.'

Leo liked it: 'I suppose it's my ma's now. I'll keep it for her.'

'You can put everything away, the fingerprinting people have finished.'

There was a mess in the dining room too.

'She had good silver cutlery, that's missing,' said Leonora. 'With vV engraved on the handles.' How Aunt Issy had insisted on that, she remembered. 'That's class, my dear.' 'Perhaps that'll help you. Should he try to sell it …'

She began picking up the clothes and underwear scattered all over the floor as drawers were yanked out and overturned.

'Come, let's tidy up, dear, as far as we can. Then it will at least look better. Agnes was particular. It would grieve her …'

It was disturbing, the way death exposed a person. Such a private person really, and now they could walk around, tread between her most intimate possessions, now she was defenceless.

'May I make tea?' Leo asked the policeman in the lounge. He saw the brooch in her hand. 'Put that down please. Assets must be frozen. Then the heirs can … But go ahead, make tea. It'll be nice. Yes, you may water the geraniums. But we're going to lock the house, then they'll die in any case.'

They didn't find a will. Winding up the estate took ages. Miss Marais's nieces and nephews tried to claim the house, but it had been left to Agnes legally. Belle was the sole heir. But Belle was sickly and wasn't interested. The house stood empty. Leonora half-heartedly suggested to Leo, 'The two of us had better tidy up, I'll help you. Then your mother can let the house. It will be an income.'

From the bit of money which also went to Belle, Holtzhausen paid the rates on the property. Now and then someone would rent the house. Then Leonora was ill for a while and the place became even more neglected. The walls needed paint, the little garden was overgrown, the front gate sagged.

Agnes was cremated. What became of the ashes no one knew.

The brothers in the Transvaal were grateful that Holtzhausen had taken on the task on behalf of all of them. Hendrik sent a car to the airport to await his return flight, went across to his house that evening. While they were having a drink, Philip phoned from Pretoria. Shortly afterwards Robert rang from Potchefstroom.

They were inspired less by sympathy for Belle than horror at the murder. Not one of the three had known Agnes well. To Belle, they knew, she had meant little during the past years. But the deed reached deep into their innermost being and thoughts.

'Just a criminal element,' soothed Hendrik.

'Much more than that. If a poor old woman in her own backyard … with a washing line …' Philip couldn't say any more. 'What about respect? Helpless old women. These murders are increasing at an alarming rate. As if the black creatures harbour a deep hatred against old white women. There's no gratitude. Just hatred.'

'Our Achilles heel,' said Robert, 'The black people among us. On our pavements, in our gardens. That's why Verwoerd was so right: separation. For the sake of everyone. Them as well as us.'

These things didn't concern Leo. One day, she thought, she'd fetch the little green brooch for herself. A young man had once grasped her by the arm and said: Hey, green-eyes!

But more than Ouma Agnes's house, Tannie Leonora now needed her care.

Did the new responsibilities cause the final distancing between her and her theological student? Not at all, Leo would proclaim. I simply couldn't take his little mannerisms anymore. Dictatorial. And – at last she uttered the ultimate word – stupid. I'm not stupid, she sang, I'm clever, I have a house, I have a job, I'm going to get a car. Life lies ahead of me.

Ben Deetlefs, student days, finis.

The day after she had finished writing exams – who'd wait for a Higher Education Diploma ceremony, anyway? – she took her belongings to the station by taxi and moved in with Tannie Leonora, in the room still always regarded as hers. She resolved: Oumatan's health is much better. She and I will have the greatest and jolliest summer holiday we have ever known. She kept her word. She took Tannie Leonora to the sea, shopping, she put up a small Christmas tree in the lounge. New Year's Eve she took her to the theatre, and together they drank champagne in the foyer.

'It's my real twenty-first celebration, Oumatan,' she said.

Her blonde hair shone, her cheeks were red, her lips slightly open and moist. In the glow of the green eyes Leonora saw the expectations of her own youth mirrored. Oh, the innocent young shine in the eyes, thought the seventy-eight-year-old Leonora.

There was only once an uneasiness between Tannie Leonora and Leo. It happened on the Camps Bay beach, after Leonora, exhausted after plodding through the deep sand to reach just the right rocks, sank down on the sand and said: 'No really, now I'm going to sit for a while. Come and sit next to me.'

Leonora began to feel uncomfortable sitting with her legs stretched out in front of her. She was wearing stockings and walking shoes and she tried to draw up her feet under her so that she could sit sideways, not too uncomfortable to look at the scene around her. The sea blue as agate, shiny blue in the distance, and a fishing boat, the oars resting, bobbing on the quiet blue water behind the waves. For a moment her eyes stung, and she moved her gaze up to where the small lapping waves drew foamy membranes over the wet sand, and then soughed back and came again, soughed back and came again – the fresh smell of the sea a balm. Behind them the palm fronds lay still against the blue sky. And Leo relaxed in her bikini next to her, flat on her stomach, her chin on folded arms.

'Will you please rub oil on my back, Tannie?' she asked.

Leonora took the oil, spread it on both palms and began rubbing on the young skin. The smell of the tanning oil was stronger than the sea smell: that and bending forward made her a little dizzy. When she had finished rubbing she said something she had been wary of saying before: 'Let me call you Norie. You don't seem like a Leo to me, Leo is a boy's name. When I was young, they called me Norie.'

This caused Leo to turn quickly, and grains of sand stuck to her oiled back. She pushed back her sunglasses.

'Where did you get that idea? "Norie". I don't feel like a Norie. It's so, sort of slummy. No, I don't mean it like that, it's just too – what can I say – old-fashioned for nowadays. Like Bessie or Daisy or Nellie ... do you understand, Tannie? I've always felt like Leo, since I was small.' She put her glasses on again. Lay on her back. 'Please put oil on my tummy, Oumatan.' She closed her eyes. 'Perhaps I had to make a racket because my Ma was so silent!' But she said it so softly that Leonora could not be sure she had really heard it.

Leonora, the oil rubbing done with, leaned back, both arms stretched behind her. She tried to support her body. Her days of sitting on the beach were really over, she thought. Tonight she'd know all about it: rheumatism, fibrositis, arthritis, the whole lot. But she didn't want to oppose Leo.

She wished Leo would meet someone her own age on the beach. 'Gosh, Tannie,' she had once said, 'you notice a dishy guy, you think now's the time to go into the water, which is hellishly cold, to get to know him. Then what? Then a bunch of toddlers comes after him: Pappa, Pappa, wait for me, Pappa ...'

They had plenty of time to chat. Leo was surprisingly willing to listen to all her Oumatan had to tell about the old days. About their childhood in the pastorie, about the Magic Lantern. Aunt Issy ...

'What would you say, Tannie, is the most important thing in life? You could have married, children, things like that. But what is your first priority?'

Involuntarily Leonora thought of Frikkie. Of her Oom Hennie, of Agnes, even of Braampie Nel. Also, and this surprised her, of Belle.

'Perhaps to have a passion in life. A passion that overshadows everything. Your great-grandpa talked of the Holy Passion.'

Leo side-tracked, for something she didn't like had crept into Leonora's voice. Something that seemed to evoke the image of her ma.

'And your passion, Oumatan?'

'No, darling, I never had one. Not in the sense your great-grandpa meant. That's my tragedy ...'

There was then something so powerful and raw in Leonora's voice that Leo shied away from it.

'I have many passions,' she said, her tone deliberately light-hearted. 'I'm mad about John Donne, I'm mad about Breyten, I'm mad about the Beatles, and,' she picked up a piece of dried seaweed, touched it to Leonora's cheek, 'I'm mad about the Golf I'm going to buy!' She grabbed her by the arm. 'Now you and I are going to have a beer. How's that? My treat. Here on the pub veranda.'

2

Dear Frikkie, wrote Leonora.

> *I have heard from your granddaughter, Koba, that you are not in good health. So I'm writing to ask how you are, and to let you know this and that.*

Think of me as a lonely old maid.

I so long for Father these days. I want to kneel on the floor next to his chair in the study and feel his hand resting on my head. I've recently spoken to Leo about obsession, fervour, holy passion. Probably these discussions brought Father so clearly to mind. Do you recall his words about Oom Hennie, the poor, mutilated, confused Oom Hennie? And, just think, once Father told me that he envied him because Oom Hennie, more than any of us, had experienced the most holy of all when he saw God in the eye of the lion. And that Oom Hennie had known the Absolute before the destruction. Beware of unbridled passion, he said to Belle in the days of the Voortrekker wagons. He warned against misdirected passion. And when I now consider where that passion has taken our people, his words were those of a prophet.

I long for Father because, looking back at my life at this age I see very little in it that would have pleased him.

And yet I console myself: one simply lives according to one's daily guidance. Not always though, sometimes against the light of your day.

The Boeties accused me of disloyalty in my relationship with the sick Englishman. It is so long past, I no longer speak, or even think of it. It would comfort me if the sick Englishman had been able to inspire unselfish passion in my life.

There were others I haven't told you about. Is this just the need of a single woman to expose herself? To whom can I confess, if not to you? Even in my late seventies. I look back on my short-lived relationship up on the west coast, as an art lover would like to look at a distant miniature drawing. Not with guilt – he died long ago— not with rancour, only with silent fulfilment. A limited fulfilment that I was granted. The big man with the rough skin and hands and the quiet blue eyes. Then – yes, it was the fisherman father of Baby and her sisters – he brought a sweet peace into my life. In the mornings I walked to college and looked down from the hillside on to the calm water of Table Bay and blessed him in my heart: fare well today. Even the meaning of words had changed: Fare well my seafarer. And in the evening when a red glow lay over the water, I thought: Now you return, peaceful, drenched in the expanse, the peace, the godly nearness on the quiet eternal sea. The Lord Himself called fishermen to Him. On stormy days I was afraid. I stood in front of the class and the rain drove against windowpanes, it grew dark, lightning flashed. May we switch on the lights? asked the students. Switch on, I said, but my heart was dark with fear. I walked home in the pouring rain. The incline I walked up swayed and moved and became waves. I slammed the door behind me, stood with my back against the door, for I wanted to continue being part of the storm. For the storm was also in me. Maybe it was nothing but the passion of the late forties. I'm embarrassing you, Frikkie, I probably won't post this letter. In any case, I knew it wouldn't last. But let's allow it to burn itself out, I thought. Was I sometimes afraid that people would talk? Aunt Issy's teaching had left its mark! Then I told myself: and if they talk about the woman who drew, that autumn, that winter ... and visited the fishing village so often ... what did it matter?

You would have approved, because I know you consider the love between man and woman the highest passion granted to humankind. I can hear you say that. You had experienced it already as a boy, the day of the picnic, with Kowie. In spite of my sharp words I envied you.

But I don't agree with you.

Is the highest passion in life then that devoted to a cause? I faint with horror when I think how fervour for a cause has warped our three younger brothers. Here I am repeating what I have already said. I must gather my thoughts.

I return to Father's passion for God. About the ever-elusive, ever-pursued uniting with, flowing into God? Even Father could only vaguely surmise it, and failed to achieve or retain it. How dare I say that?

I keep visualising Oom Hennie with his martyred, distorted body. Were those tortured limbs, scorched by Holy fire, really visible proof of a meeting with God? You spoke of the blessed Oom Hennie. Only if his spirit could rise above it. But he wasn't able to find peace. Remember the story of Karel Kumm we were raised with? There is water all around you, scoop it up. Only later did I understand Father's plea on his deathbed: Water. And you told me yourself: Drink of the water; drink fire.

Mother's faith was quieter. I think, if I can recall my memories over eight decades – but I hesitate to write it – that even her 'Vision' you read to me, was after all Victorian romanticism. Written in the idiom of her time. Does one only recognise the idiom in retrospect? Does time have to pass before we know it?

Who am I to talk, you will say. Without chick or child, drifting.

All I can boast, to misquote St Paul, is that I know what I've missed.

Therefore, Frikkie, I long for Father. To tell me: Your little drifting boat too, lies in the palm of the Father's hand.

If only I could believe it. Have you noticed, Frikkie, how these days the young people, in search of something greater than themselves, of their own holy passion, turn to the creation? What else is this devotion to animals and plants, the worldwide Green movement, than the urge to preserve? Working until the sweat pours off you on Sunday mornings to wash oil-covered penguins. *Wash me in the blood of the Lamb* ... It strikes me as peculiar, but I can understand and appreciate it. Do you also notice how differently we were disposed to our world? It was a strange, unused, undiscovered near-wilderness. If we climbed a ravine, we were the first people who had set foot there. If we walked on distant beaches, in the mistiness, the prints of sea birds and little shell creatures were like music notes on the wet sand, and the wavelets at our feet the music.

Now the young people pick up plastic in their pools. It appears to me they seek a creator by first trying to save the creation.

We had to tame our own wild world and set limits and make it our own. Today they cherish the tired creation in their arms, trying to protect and preserve it.

Why are there tears in my eyes now? I digress. Nostra culpa. My thoughts wander. I sit writing and it is growing late, I fear going into the night.

One night I went to the Methodist church. My English strain again you would say, but I wasn't wearing a hat, had sandals on my feet, and would have been too conspicuous in our church. I moved into a pew. The people were singing. Next to me was a coloured woman in working clothes, obviously a char. She held the hymn book out to me. I took one side, she the other, my manicured white hand, her rough brown scrubber's hand – a short little woman, fingers arthritic, knees too, probably. And we sang:

> Bless these hands and let them move
> at the impulse of Thy love
> Take these feet and let them be
> swift and beautiful for Thee.

When I sat down, for I was suddenly tired, I saw her legs and feet. Elasticised stockings covered the varicose veins, and the feet in white tennis shoes with a hole cut for the little toe, which protruded from it, sore and swollen.

Here is the Lord, I thought. He isn't in Father's Holy Obsession, but here next to me.

Should I wish to be bitter, I must add that she would not be allowed in my church. Last week the caregiver of a deceased 'madam' was refused admission to the funeral. You know it is the same in your town.

May God have mercy on us.

Now I ask you: what is left for your drifting sister? To stand by the child who bears my name? No longer a child. She is a young adult, but in our old eyes a tabula rasa. She is so innocent. Yet I think that she too is searching. May the Lord help her. May the Lord help her mother too – I would so much like to help her, but she doesn't speak to me and I cannot forgive our poor torn-apart country that.

It seems to me Father lived in an age of innocence. But his innocence wasn't innocence, rather ignorance or denial of knowledge. I longed for Father, but now I'm no longer longing. We have come further than Father was and we can look back at them and judge them if we dare.

Who will judge us?

Look after yourself, Frikkie, although you may never read this letter. And get better soon, I can't manage without you.

Leonora.

P.S. So absent-minded, typical of an old woman. Forgot the whole point of the letter. A young ex-colleague visited a mission station in Malawi and came to tell me of it. There is a small prayer room for the missionaries, and in it she saw plaques on the wall in memory of children who died in the mission field. She told me one of the earliest plaques was for Baba (Leonora) van Velde, 1904. Then I thought: Oh Lord, have we forgotten about that baby? Also named after Father's and Oom Hennie's Mother, just like me.

Born the same year as I was.

And she went on to say that stories are still told at the station about the baby's father. The one story is that he was sitting in the veld reading his Bible, and a lion came and laid its paw on the Bible as he was sitting there reading. Then the lion turned and walked away. The other story is that the lion savaged him.

Which story was true? she asked.

Frikkie, I thought: perhaps they are one and the same.

A terrible truth. A blinding truth.

3

Leo loaded broom and dusters and cleaning materials and cloths in Leonora's car. She covered her short stylishly cut hair with a scarf. Her cheerful mood evaporated when she stopped in New Church Street in front of the row of semi-detached houses. Her house – it was really and truly her house – was on the corner. It was built on the rise, with the front gate and garden path and stoep on the level of the street. The garden wall dropped sharply and the back gate opened on the side street.

The place looked dark and neglected. A palm tree grew in the little garden to the right of the path, and the wind dragged through it disconsolately. It was a grey day; old newspapers and leaves lay blown against the gate. She kicked them aside and lifted the latch and pushed the gate open. It creaked against the dry hinges. The leaves crumbled as she kicked them aside, a mistiness began to descend over Signal Hill. She shivered. She noticed Leonora also shivered. She diverted her thoughts from the backyard and the neglected little lean-to room that used to be the servant's room, then a storage place for wood and junk where her strangled Ouma had been brutally dragged.

'We're not going to the backyard, Oumatan. Not before everything is sorted out, all the ghosts swept out and dusted off.'

She spoke light-heartedly, but something strange kept gnawing inside her. Leonora didn't look her usual self either.

Once or twice the neighbours had let them know of a single person looking for a room and the house had been partly inhabited. Perhaps for a few weeks, maybe longer. But no one had cleaned up.

It was a windy day in January. Dust everywhere. More newspapers came blowing down the street. A palm frond had been blown in from somewhere and lay across the path. Leo picked it up and threw it on the desiccated lawn. On the stoep leaves piled right up against the front door. The little mat was old and worn. The passage was dark and the smell of disuse hit them. It smelled of death. Dead rat or dead cat or dead person. Leonora shifted past Leo, she was, after all, more familiar with the house. She sent the blinds in the kitchen shooting up with an arm movement that had become small and feeble, pushed open the shutters and opened the window as wide as it would go.

The bright light streamed in. Leonora sat down at the table. She looked like Ouma Agnes, the same stooped posture. This upset Leo. It could not be; may not be. She took a cloth from the basket, lifted both Leonora's hands from the table with one of her hands, wiped away the dust with the other, wiped and wiped the months, the years of old hands, from the table. She took out mugs and coffee. While Leonora was drinking, she took a plastic bag and tipped the dead geraniums and their pots into it, cleaned the windowsill, brushed, rubbed.

'You could have kept the pots.'

'I'll buy some myself, Tannie Leonora.'

The dining room didn't get much sun in summer: the kitchen would get morning sun.

'They say people's vibrations enter the walls and furniture. I'll get rid of everything. I'll buy paint and employ a workman.'

'I'll not leave you here alone with a workman, my girl. I'll come and sit here every day, whether you like it or not.'

'Okay, Okay, Tannie. I'm not afraid of them, not of a workman and not of the old ladies either.' Then she looked about her helplessly. 'Oumatan, tell me, where do we begin? I really don't want the stuff, I want my own things.'

'You won't scorn the money, child. Second-hand shops will be only too eager …'

The last tenant had left behind dirty dishes, stale bread, glass pots with scraps of jam on the bottom, anchovy paste. Leo threw the whole lot out.

I shouldn't have brought Tannie Leonora, she thought. It's difficult for an old person to clear up another old person's life. She drew out a chair. 'Stay sitting here, Tannie. I'm just going to do the kitchen. I can get some of my friends to help with the rooms. We'll have a ball with all the old clothes.'

She knew immediately that she had said the wrong thing. But what was she to say? It wasn't her fault people got old and died. She couldn't go and sit amongst the ashes until she kicked the bucket herself.

'We'll be careful, Tannie,' she said more gently. 'We'll keep all the embroidered cloths safe. We'll take the better things to an old age home. I promise you, Tannie, we'll be respectful.'

Yet Leonora insisted on going through the rooms herself; put aside something here and there that she knew had been precious to Agnes.

She gave Leo the little emerald brooch still lying where they had left it. It no longer seemed so beautiful to Leo, but she took it. Leonora took two silver frames for herself: the one with the mounted letter of the rebel and the other with his photo. She didn't want to leave them to the mercy of the young people. To her there'd always be something poignant about the two things the two women had been so attached to. But where would they go when she died? With her portraits, where would they go? She couldn't find a picture of Stuart. Or wedding photos or childhood photos of Ozzie or SussieBelle. Frikkie must have taken some. Perhaps packed in the boxes on the wardrobe. She didn't have the strength for it. She thought wryly: they also have sale value. She had heard that people bought ancestors, and deceased little brothers and sisters. Especially people restoring old houses, people who didn't have their own ancestors to hang on the walls.

Father, she thought. Tears came to her eyes. Father. Her beautiful portraits of Father and Mother. What would become of them? One couldn't burden the young people with the past.

She wiped her eyes carefully with the little lawn handkerchief, pleased that she'd sprinkled a little cologne on it. It refreshed her. She looked up when Leo came into the kitchen with a big flat box. 'Found right at the back of the cupboard, Tannie, under old shoes. We must have a look what's inside.'

Leo loosened the cover from the box corner by corner and lifted it off. She carefully unfolded the old yellowed tissue paper. Hidden beneath layer after layer of tissue paper lay a dress of green taffeta. Sunshine slanting in through the kitchen window glowed on the green fabric.

'What on earth?' said Leo. She slipped her hands under the shoulders of the dress and carefully lifted it out of the box. Fold after fold, as the dress had gently been lowered into the box, with the thin, dry, yellowed tissue paper between each fold, the bodice, the waist, the skirt were lifted out. The pieces of tissue paper drifted soundlessly through the particles of dust to the floor. More and still more taffeta, a long skirt, a full skirt, metres and metres of taffeta. It hung over Leo's arm. The hem, slow to move, lay in great double folds on the last layer of tissue paper.

Leonora had lifted the box from the table, she helped Leo spread the gown out on the table: to flatten the bodice, lift out the long sleeves. The bodice coming to an elegant little point in front, the piping carefully stitched in between the bodice and skirt, lay across half of the table, the skirt cascaded over the edge of the table to the floor.

Little covered buttons were sewn from the neckline to the pointed waist and fastened with neat delicate loops of green taffeta cord. Exquisite needlework, exquisite the glow of light on the pristine green shot silk.

Leo bent to touch the folds that had slipped free of the tissue paper and leaped to life.

'But what on earth … ?' she said again. She fingered the hem. Dust, perhaps dried mud, stained the fabric. The remains of red soil partially sponged off spread like a blight right round the hem of the otherwise perfect garment.

The sun was suddenly gone, the glow of the dress faded.

'The Voortrekker dresses were made to this pattern in 1938,' said Leonora. 'You've also seen the photo of your ouma in the white dress. Exactly like this one. But I knew nothing of a green one. Come, let's pack it in again, then it can go in the dustbin.'

Leo stroked the silky green of the taffeta. 'You can't buy this material nowadays. I'm going to unpick the skirt. For a throw on a divan or a cushion cover …'

'Rather leave the dress in peace, child,' said Leonora. 'Throw it away. What is past is past. Do it for my sake.'

Leo agreed reluctantly.

Leo got a lot of money for the rickety brass bed that had been brought from the farm and on which Miss Marais's father and mother had slept and died, and she too had died. She got a little less, but still a surprising amount, for the sagging walnut bed with the high headboard and foot, on which Ouma Agnes had slept in the second bedroom. Also for the walnut wardrobe and dressing table with its many little drawers and adjustable mirrors. And the washstand with the marble top and the porcelain basin and jug. It surprised her, because they all seemed shabby and ugly to her. Later she saw them, sandpapered and repaired, on pavements in front of second-hand shops in Kloof Street, exorbitant price tags fastened to the legs.

With my compliments, she thought.

She used the money to have the rooms painted and built-in cupboards installed. She slept on a divan with a woven cover and a lot of cushions. She would have a TV room with easy chairs and a cassette and record player and amplifiers. She kept the single table and kitchen chair that didn't seem too unattractive to her. The second bedroom was empty. She wondered, with pleasant anticipation, who would move in there and when. It had been her Ouma Agnes's room, small and dark with an overgrown east-facing window. The walnut furniture had filled it from wall to wall. Empty, it suddenly seemed full of possibilities.

The piano?

'Keep it,' said Tannie Leonora.

'It belonged to Miss Marais and she was nothing to me.'

'Agnes thought she was her mother. She might have been your great-grandmother.'

'That's a bit far-fetched, Tannie.'

Yet she kept it and decided it lent flair to her lounge. She didn't buy the music centre for the time being. In her imagination she saw the long white fingers of a gifted boyfriend playing on it, arty friends on the big studio cushions on the carpet. She shivered with excitement.

Wait until after the Christmas season to buy your little car, Hendrik had advised. You might come across a bargain.

She bought a Volkswagen Golf.

She bought clothes. She employed a char.

She drove to school exuberantly in her new car for her first day.

It's not a bad thing at all to be a *momio*, she challenged Ernie in her thoughts. Ernie had gone to London. Left the country. Following her boyfriend.

Initially she parked the new little car in the street under the streetlight outside her bedroom window.

'I really can't face the uphill side street and the impossible corner I have to take and parking on an incline while I get out and push open the iron gate,' she told a colleague. 'The char who comes on Saturday mornings puts her things on the back stoep and uses my bathroom. She's clean, I can't let her go to pee in the mess out at the back.'

She never went into the backyard. She was too busy teaching, and in any case wanted to clear the front garden first.

For a full term she enjoyed her new life. Two more-or-less boyfriends; she even began taking the pill of her own volition. Some evenings on the white woolly carpet and the studio cushions became quite steamy, she would grab a piano leg for support, dig her nails in it while she experienced the pleasant pain. She didn't recognise her blood-red cheeks and shining eyes and tumbled blonde hair when she went to the bathroom and looked in the mirror. Especially not the expression in her eyes. Flames of lust, she thought. No, actually they just looked tired.

In the night on her bed she mused half-nostalgically: My mother had a romance so different to this. If I never see him again after this evening, it wouldn't really bother me. She began to feel heartsore. Then decided it must be post-coital depression – the latest *Fair Lady* magazine was full of it – and she laughed aloud. We conduct our sex lives according to magazines. Wow. At least Ma was more original. Although it took its toll of her.

But one evening she heard something.

She presumed it was in the backyard that was still overgrown: she never went out there because the khaki weed and blackjacks stuck to your clothes and stockings and took hours to remove. A heap of builder's rubble was overgrown with rank yellow kikuyu grass that got too much water and not enough sun, a pool of slimy water was dammed up in a piece of hollow corrugated iron. Then the old fallen wash-line pole – reason for her ouma's death. And the old garage? No car had ever stood in it, that was for sure. Made of corrugated iron, like the lean-to wood store next to it where her ouma's body had been dumped. Would the door that was hanging askew be able to open? Her Golf was still parked out in the street.

She heard it from the back stoep: a shuffling as if a crate or a box was being pushed about, and then it was quiet again. Then more shuffling. She went cold right to the marrow. There was no light on the back stoep. The murderer has returned, she thought. They'd never caught him. She was terrified. She stood on the back stoep, too afraid to move. She saw the rubbish heap, she saw the garage door clearly. She peered keenly to see if there was the least movement of the derelict wood store door. Stared, but saw nothing. Then she calmed down. Perhaps there were rats. She'd buy rat poison. It was autumn already, she should have got around to sorting out the backyard and getting her car under cover long ago.

For the first time she was afraid inside her little house. She pushed a kitchen chair under the knob of the back door, and another on the inside under her bedroom door. The windows were latched. She lay on her bed and watched the lights of the cars in the street outside splash past on her bedroom walls.

The next morning before school she armed herself with an old broomstick and went down the steps. She cleared a way through the rank kikuyu and nasturtiums; she hit at a few nasturtium leaves just to see how the drops of dew shot away. If she had time, she would have cupped the leaves in her hand and collected the drops to a shiny shivering piece of mercury, as she'd done as a child. She walked to the door of the lean-to and pushed it open. In the near dark she saw the white gleam of a black boy's eyes. The glint of a flick knife in his hand, his other arm pushing a coloured boy behind him protectively. Further back, on a heap of sacks, lay another coloured child, younger than the other two.

'What the hell is going on here?' she asked.

She realised at once that she had it wrong. She was under threat, not the children. The black boy had grasped her hand so tightly she was forced to let go of the broomstick. It fell and was grabbed by the second child. The flick knife moved, came to rest against her throat.

Hang on a minute, steady now, she wanted to say, but couldn't utter the words.

His face was near to hers. The lips were thick and as they folded back, cracked; there was spit at the corners of his mouth. Was the man who had strangled Ouma as close to her? Could she see his breath going in and out as his chest moved, had his spit dropped on her? She didn't think of screaming. With his face so close to hers it would have been difficult. She was being pulled inside and pushed down on the heap of sacks. The younger child pulled the door shut behind them. There were thin splinters of light between the wooden slats. It stank so that she felt she was smothering. Still she wasn't afraid. Was it the empty chips packets lying around, the couple of orange peels and milk cartons, that suddenly made of them children, not perpetrators of crime?

Until she saw the bottle of thinners.

The thinners introduced a new element: animal irrationality and probably violence. Physical fear, the fear with which she had been brought up, the fear of black hands on her body, moved like nausea from her ankles to her stomach. She couldn't swallow, she could barely breathe.

The eldest boy spat at her: 'We're many, we know about the old woman murdered here. You report us, we watch you, we burn your house.'

She tried to collect herself. She raised her head, looked at the boy's ragged clothes, the men's pants fastened with string, the vest, the big Adidas shoes. He stank. All three stank. The wood store stank.

'If you report us, we got you. You move away we watch where you go, we always come after you. We get your friends too an' your aunties.'

She had, by pressing her hands on the sacks behind her, tried to move away from the light but sharp touch of the knife blade.

'What the hell is going on here?' she asked again.

The middle one answered her, 'Missus, we jus' stay here, we got no place.'

'You can't stay here,' she said.

The eldest turned to her again. 'Bitch,' he said. He took her arm and turned it so sharply behind her back that her face turned grey from the sudden pain. Then he let go of her.

'Go phone the cops, we not afraid. We chop you dead, hey.'

'But she's a missus,' the middle child said.

'She's a bitch!' He spat on the knife, wiped it on his pants.

'She after us, hey, she better not!'

The child lying down wasn't more than six or seven. Heavens, the same age as Robbie's Bennie when she had last seen him at Potch. His body jerked on the heap of sacks as he succumbed to a bout of coughing. It choked his lungs, tore through his innards, his eyes bulged. Leo had the strange feeling that she had to restrain herself from helping the child. She wanted to hold his head and support him.

Later she thought wryly: was it the first stirring in her pickled heart? She had never before felt like that.

Yet she was still filled with repugnance: she tried to hold her breath, so that the germ-laden breath he was spewing out didn't get to her clean lungs. The yellow snot covered the corners of his mouth where the back of his hand had smeared it. The middle child was the most compassionate. He scrabbled beneath the mess and got an empty plastic orange juice bottle. He shook it upside down so that the few drops of liquid in it fell out. Then he took the bottle of thinners, made a fist over the mouth of the plastic bottle, and carefully dripped thinners through the fist which he gradually released until it formed a funnel. When the bottle was half full, he placed his thumb on it, shook it once so that the vapour began to rise, and gave it to the child who was lying back exhausted.

'G'on, cool it,' he said. The child took the bottle, placed his mouth over the opening and breathed in. Then the hand pumped at the bottle in and out, and the thinners washed about in the bottle; the vapour rose, fell back, was pushed up, fell back, was pushed up so that he could breathe, breathe, breathe.

Eventually he lay back in a swoon.

'He okay now. Leave him wi' his bottle,' said the big boy.

The thinners had completely calmed the child. His eyes were closed, there was even a little smile on his lips. The eyelids had long black lashes which curled innocently on the grimy cheek. He lay quietly with his paainie like a child, fallen asleep with his bottle in his mouth.

'Don' worry, he on a trippie.'

'You can go,' the eldest told Leo. 'But don' worry, tonight we here again. Remember; you squeal, we burn. The p'lice take us, our pals come work yo' case.'

'I won't squeal, but the child's sick. I'll take him to the doctor in my car.'

'Nev' mind, we got our own doctor.'

They pushed her out the door. She had to get dressed and go to school. She drove through a strange city. The streets looked different, the people, the buildings. The groups of children at the traffic lights called out to her. Did no one hear the calling? she wanted to ask the people around her. Avoid eye contact, she heard from afar. Of course, then you don't really see them. Look! she wanted to shout. Pull off your blinkers and look!

Throughout the winter months the children were there. When she slept in her warm bed, heard the rain spatter on the corrugated iron roof, the wind howl through the palm tree, the cold seep in through the windows, she thought of the children. Thought of the child who coughed, who sniffed thinners and glue and who knows what else. She spoke about it obliquely in the staff room, about runaway children, and heard various names for them. Traffic light kids, because they crowded around cars that stop at traffic lights, were sometimes given money. Street children, because they slept in entrances to shops, in alleys, under bridges. Why? she asked. Every child surely had a mother and a father. It was those who had a tough time at home, who were beaten or starved; those whose father had disappeared and the mother drank – they took to the streets. A child of eight, nine took to the streets? Younger still, even of five, six, seven. One teacher, whose wife was a social worker, said: There's a child of ten who has been on the streets for five years, last saw his mother five years ago.

Could she leave food for them, give them blankets? Stuff she put out for them was left untouched. They think I'm testing them and will accuse them of theft if they take it, and wondered where she had come upon that insight.

The children, especially the little ones, did well at the traffic lights, said the social worker. Ten, twenty rand a day. The older children kept the little ones to push them in front, they looked after them. A handicapped child was sought after by the older ones. Or with a cough, she thought. How long could he survive? On a rainy night she stood outside on the stoep for ages and tried to listen: was the child coughing? She never saw them coming or going. It made her physically ill when the rain hit on the corrugated iron roof like nails. She no longer took pleasure in her musical evenings, she no longer yielded in the thick long piled carpet, her hands no longer grasped back for the piano leg. She pushed men's hands away from her.

'You're somewhere else, girl,' said her friend, 'Come back.'

'I'll bring a workman and come and help you clean the yard,' said another friend. 'You should be able to make use of your garage.'

'It's easier to just park in the street, nearer when it pours. I scarcely open the umbrella.'

'You could let the garage.'

'Oh, don't nag.'

Afterwards she didn't know whether the children were there or not. But in her mind they were there. She never fell asleep without them lying with her.

She couldn't rid herself of the image of the child with the long lashes, sleeping with the paainie in his mouth. Sometimes she thought of getting a chain and lock and locking the yard gate. When they were out. Or when they were in. To put a stop to it.

Sometimes she thought: I don't know if they are here. But if they aren't here in my shed, they're somewhere else, and perhaps worse off than here.

She experienced something like the 'odio' Ernie had read about. She couldn't say it was directed at them, for they hadn't harmed her. It wasn't directed at her, for neither had she done them any harm. It was against the entire society she lived in. An 'odious' society. It was something she'd never thought of before. It consoled her when she read of street children in other parts of the world. But it didn't really console her. Before the first winter term had passed, she had to apply for another position. She got a post at a coloured school.

'Another bleeding heart,' mocked her friend, 'but don't worry, you have a car, it won't be too difficult for you. Myself? No ways.'

And then, on a Saturday evening, not yet very late, there was knocking at her back door, hasty and hard.

The middle child stood there. 'We got troubles, missus, we dunno where we mus' take him.' He twisted his jersey between his hands – the front panels hung down, almost reached his knees. 'We think he nearly gone.'

She pulled the child into the kitchen. 'Let go of the jersey, look at me. Who is nearly gone? Is it the little one, is he sick?'

'He dyin' missus.'

She grabbed a torch, threw on a raincoat, pushed him ahead of her and went down the back steps. The door of the wood store stood open, she shone the torch round. The big one wasn't there. The little one lay on the ragged sacks, he didn't cough. She felt panicky, he seemed to her to lie so limply. She felt his hands, ice cold; she put her head to his chest to listen, his heart seemed to be beating. His eyes were closed, the fingers slack, not far from his hand lay the bottle.

'Why did you say he was dying? He's on a trip.'

'Isn't no trip, he like that from mornin'.'

She pushed her hands under him. 'Help with his legs,' she told the child. 'Let's get him up the step.'

'An' then?'

As she bent to the floor she looked around. 'Where's the other one, the big one? Has he left you now?'

'He at the robots, missus, he didn' leave me.'

They laid him on her bed. She phoned the coloured teacher she knew best and whose wife worked at a clinic.

'What should I do? The child seems to be in a coma.'

'We'll come.'

The Septembers had to drive a long way, they lived beyond Athlone. For half an hour she paced up and down in her house, to the bed, to the front door, to the bed, to the front door. She sat the middle boy down at the kitchen table, made coffee, sliced bread for him.

When George and Ivy September arrived, they put the child in their car and raced to the hospital. The streets were wet and the neon lights drew red and yellow lines across the tar. The child was pushed away on a trolley, the needle already inserted in the arm. The tube between his arm and the upside-down bottle, held high above his head by the nurse, jiggled along passively. They were told to stay to complete forms. They struggled to keep the middle child with them. The teacher held him by the arm, forced him to answer questions.

'The sick child's name, his surname?'

'Dunno.'

The teacher jerked him by the arm. 'You're going to tell us, this evening we have to know.'

'Jesoppie. We call him Jesoppie.'

'That's not enough.' He jerked him again. 'For God's sake, we're trying to help him.'

There was coming and going at the emergency entrance. The people writing were in a hurry. An ambulance stopped and a black man, still as a block, was wheeled in on a stretcher. The blanket over him had a dark stain, and as he was pushed past the stain spread visibly. A nurse lifted the blanket to allow his arm, which was slipping off the narrow trolley, to lie more comfortably.

The child forced the words out: 'His bra's Ampie Gal. He was with us first, but he taken to jail. Jesoppie's Jesoppie Gal.'

'Did he go to school?'

'No, no, no.' The child's chin pressed down on his chest, he shook his head. 'Did'n have no school.'

'His bra?'

'He say about the teacher hits him, of the Tang.'

'At Rynheuwel?'

'Maybe, dunno, dunno of the Tang.'

The child was terrified, he began to shake. 'Dunno, dunno, dunno,' he said. 'How I mus' know?'

Leo put her arm around him. 'Okay, now, okay.' She pressed his dirty crinkly hair against her with the palm of her hand. 'Okay, okay.'

The child nestled his head against her clothes, he sniffed noisily. Probably snot, thought Leo, but to her surprise it didn't bother her. She put her other arm around his shoulders. The child was skin and bone, he'll be the next one to go, she thought, but I'll see to it that he doesn't die. 'Okay, we're going home now.'

George September told his wife. 'I know who the Tang is, I also know which school it is. We'll have to track down a parent.'

'That's at least something to go on,' said Ivy. 'We can't wait till Monday, it's Joey's area. I'll phone her tomorrow morning, maybe she'll take me herself. On the holy Sabbath.'

Leo felt something like an umbilical cord linked her to Jesoppie, who had been wheeled away down the chill, impersonal corridors, and to the child pressing himself against her body. She moved away from him a little to be able to speak better.

September had completed the forms as best he could. 'Tomorrow, or Monday at the latest, I'll bring more details,' he said and pushed the form away. 'It's like a needle in a haystack …'

Leo's hand was involuntarily rubbing the child's scalp, it calmed him.

'I'll come and pick you up,' Leo told Ivy September. 'I'll bring this one along too, he'll be able to get in where we can't.'

'But …' she objected.

'I'm coming along.'

'You know where we stay?'

'I have a map.'

'Let her come,' said the teacher. 'Perhaps she should have come long ago.'

The black boy must have been waiting for them on the back stoep, because as soon as they were inside the knob of the back door began to turn. She opened the door. He gave the coloured child a bag of food.

'There, g'on.' The child took it from him and took out a soggy hamburger, began to eat with great bites.

They spoke, but their words were incomprehensible. She was tired.

'Go to bed now, I want to be away before nine tomorrow morning.'

The big one looked at her and at the child. It seemed the one eye turned to her and the other to him, so wild was his look. The child explained in words she couldn't understand. She closed the kitchen door behind them, she heard their talking going down the steps, into the lean-to in the dark.

But before nine o'clock the child was on the back stoep.

'I don't even know your name.' He got into the back. He mumbled something. 'Okay, Apools, Jesoppie made it through the night, but it doesn't look good.'

Before now, she hadn't been any further into the coloured area than to the school and the headmaster's house – he was a Mr Abrahams. Now she drove further. She kept an eye on the streets on the map. The houses looked much the same as in any other middle-class neighbourhood, only discarded papers were being blown across the sandy streets and stopped in the gutters, lying there along with empty tins and debris.

She'd barely stopped when Ivy September closed her front door behind her and walked down the garden path. She got in next to Leo. 'My husband phoned – let's call him Tang – last night. He remembers the Gal child. My husband gave him a tough time, so he gave in and said he'd meet us at the school this morning so that we can go through the books. Unfortunately my husband is taking a Sunday school class.'

The school was in a poor part of Manenberg. Small brick houses on bare, windswept yards; wrecks of motor cars pushed into the yards over flattened wire fences; corrugated iron lean-to's against houses, stones on the flat corrugated iron roofs. Where the buildings were close together, burglar-proofing at doors and windows showed that business was done there. At a few buildings the burglar-proofing was slightly ajar so that a client could pass through and come out with a loaf or a bottle. And against the walls were damaged advertising hoardings.

The school buildings were flat prefab. The Tang's bakkie – he explained that he did transport work during holidays and weekends – was parked in front of the entrance. A few children had gathered at the fence to see what was going on. They were dressed as if on the way to church. Their clothes shone like dolls' clothes, pink and yellow and white satin and lace. The school door was open, they walked in. First door left, the Tang called to them. A small man, with reddish hair, freckles showing through his whitish skin, as if he was half albino. His eyes were small with red, swollen eyelids behind thick spectacles. There was something ugly in the eyes. His fingers touched the pages of the book in front of him with distaste.

'The bloody Gal kid. I went five years back in the books and I can't find him.'

'Give here,' said Ivy September. She opened the book and put her finger on the first page, moved her arm so that the finger went up and down along the rows of names. Later, when her back got tired, she drew up a chair and sat, but went on paging and searching up and down the rows.

Gal, Ella, she found. Apools tugged at Leo's arm. 'Ella was his auntie.'

'That was eight years ago. What else? Let's try the address.'

The auntie was still young, heavily pregnant, a child on the hip too. She came to stand at her gate when the car stopped. The floral dress was pulled up so high in front that her knees were bare. Legs like sticks and the big bulge in front.

'I don't like to talk. 'Cause why, my man doesn't like that I talk. He don't like my people. He don't like people in jail at all. We stay in my pa's house, yes. I'm not churched, but my pa don't mind, my pa likes me. I'll give the message to my pa, yes.'

But it was the pa's younger brother who came to claim the body of Jesoppie two days later. He came in his working clothes, in a blue overall, he was a packer in a warehouse. He held his cap in his hand, and cried when he saw the body. He came across Leo in the hospital entrance, the tears were still running down his face. He took a handkerchief out of his pocket and wiped his face.

'We've been missing the child so many years,' he said. 'His ma left my brother and ran off with a rubbish, they're in a sacking house on the flats. It's because of the stepfather the kid and his bra ran away.'

'And his pa?'

'His pa drank. He beat the kids. But now he's dead. God rest his soul.'

'And you didn't even try …' There was a hypocritical tone to the brother's voice that turned Leo against him, but she had no defence against his next words.

'It's the forced removals, missus, that split up our families so. Some stayed good, others went bad. God, missus, don't blame us, it's the times …'

But the child still had to be buried. Carted away through the streets and thrown in a hole? God, thought Leo. No.

There was no one in the lean-to when she came home from school that afternoon. But by now she knew where they would hang out. She drove up and down the streets until she saw Apools.

'Get in.' she said.

'But, missus ...'

'We're going back to that auntie, and she or her pa must tell us where Jesoppie's ma lives on the flats.' She felt the urgency in her would slice through circumstances like a knife. But Apools had to show the way to the auntie's house.

He found the house without much difficulty. The wind was blowing and the papers and plastic bags pressed and bulged against the fences, windblown newspaper beat against the wire with a despairing sound, empty milk cartons swirled around in a gust of wind. The pregnant girl came to the door. The child spoke to her and she said a few words to him which Leo didn't hear, but satisfied Apools, for he came back to the car.

'I'll get 'im, missus. Missus mus' go along here.'

They turned off onto a sandy road. The car bounced up over an unexpected ridge in the road. There weren't many people or children, beyond them were the sand dunes behind which, presumably, lay the sea. The sea? That concept seemed to Leo irreconcilable with the desolation she was struggling through. The steering wheel jerked from one side to the other. When the front wheel got stuck, it strengthened her will; she pumped the accelerator, put the car in reverse, got free, drove on again. Then there were animals: skinny goats, a cow; children with sticks trying to herd the animals in the sandy wilderness.

'Over that hill, missus.' Apools sat on the edge of the seat, his hands on the dashboard. He peered keenly, looking out for something he recognised. The road was no more than an indistinct track. Their surroundings became more bushy: wattles, thorn bushes, and she saw corrugated iron shacks that had been knocked together, only a few, the rest were made of sacking and black plastic, stretched it appeared over bent branches. The yards around some of the shacks were clean, others were a mess of plastic bags, tins and bottles. In one there was a wash-line on which a few pieces of clothing ballooned out grotesquely in the wind.

She put the car in first gear and drove slowly up the incline. A dog came dashing out barking; she drove on. There were more people. Then downhill again. It wasn't the rainy season. Where had the water, lying in slimy puddles, come from? There, out of the wind, the water barely moved. All around the mud had been trampled by animal hooves. Where could they drink? The rubbish was dammed up – tins, bottles, papers, plastic, sewage waste rose in reefs on the shallow water. It stank.

One of the group of sacking shacks, half hidden behind bushes, was the one they sought.

In a language she couldn't understand, Apools asked a woman carrying wood on her head, who scarcely turned to listen, as if it didn't concern her, in which shack the Gal woman lived. Children bundled out of the nearest shack and tugged at her clothes. As they walked on with the woman, their heads turned and the little eyes remained fixed on the car and its occupants.

'The secon', missus, but she a vi'lent woman, missus mus' watch out.'

The woman with the wood called toward the shack, but there was no reply. Leo pushed Apools ahead. 'I can't just go in there, tell her she must come out.'

But no sound came from the heap of black plastic and sacks. It was so quiet that the woman threw down her wood, came across and bent to draw open the piece of sacking that was the front door.

She turned around, blew her nose into the sand with her fingers, and said something to Apools.

'She passed out, missus.'

'Then I'm going in.'

She bent and pushed the sacking aside. She had to wait for her eyes to adjust. She remained bent over, her back began to hurt and she crouched down, she shuffled forward on her knees. Over crumpled plastic and sand pushing ridges under her knees. God, the stench was worse than in her wood store. Did they shit and pee right there? The unaccustomed words came spontaneously.

She started to see. A primus stove and a saucepan, a galvanised iron bucket without handle, two dirty plates and mugs. On a pile of sacks lay a person. It had to be a person, because the head was held up by a hand and the eyes looked at her, red, glassy, too far gone to show rage or hate or even embarrassment. The supporting hand gave in and the head sank down again. It was a coloured woman with thick, uncombed black hair. Her face was thin and the hand and arm looked skeletal.

'Go and find the woman who was carrying wood,' Leo told Apools.

'Missus mus' watch for missus's car, the kids aroun' it like flies.'

'Go on, call the woman.'

The woman, when she came, thought Leo was a social worker. She spoke a few words of English. No, the woman's man had left her, there was no one to look after her. She sold her body for a mug of wine. There were lots of men at night.

Dear God, thought Leo, Where have I been my whole life? I know nothing.

She heard the younger brother whine: It's the forced removals, missus, some stayed good, others went bad. Everything was upset.

'Help me put her in the car,' said Leo. 'Her child is dead. I'll take her to the clinic.'

Jesoppie would be buried without his Ma.

At school she told the headmaster, David Abrahams: 'The child and the mother haunt me. Apools doesn't want to tell me anything, he just says he doesn't have a pa or ma. The bigger one is a black child. His name is Mzamo. He came from the Transkei to Cape Town with his oupa to look for his ma. But they couldn't find her. His clan name is Kasi and his ma was Thobeka. The bus dropped him and his oupa at the Kieck hostels in Guguletu, but no one knew of a Kasi. Then they went to Site B in Khayelitsha in the bush where the people live in the corrugated iron shacks, but no one could tell of a Kasi. Other people let his oupa build a kaia in their yard, but when his oupa died, they kicked him out, because they could take the oupa's kaia and let it. Then he went on the streets. That was four, five years ago. These places were just names to me, but now I've been there myself. Now I know.'

'I don't want to put you down, Miss, but I must say you white people know very little. You know nothing.'

'Mr Abrahams, I want to help. Jesoppie's oom said it was the times. If it is the times, we must try to change the times. Mr Abrahams, we can't play with the lives of children like that. God knows, we can't.'

Did she see the same expression in his eyes as in her friend's: another bleeding heart? Probably he thought: It's so easy to make them feel pity. Pity is of bugger-all use. Take them to a squatters' camp even once and the tears flow. But what's the use of tears? Tell me: what is the use of tears?

4

Leo had a radio in her Golf. She listened to news from Radio Good Hope on the way to and from school. Every half hour. Outbursts of resistance were increasing throughout the country. She listened to reports of violence, arson, unrest. For the first time since Sharpeville, a state of emergency had been declared in 36 magistrate's districts in the

Eastern Cape and on the Rand. She discussed the situation with her colleagues in the staff room. They said the police had been given very nearly unlimited power: arrest, search, detain without trial. 'We should have expected it,' they said when the state of emergency was extended to Cape Town. The tension in schools increased. Coloured schools began acting in solidarity with black schools.

Leo parked her white Golf in the school grounds, and she had scarcely crossed the threshold when she became aware that something was afoot, that a storm was brewing. Mr Abrahams was waiting for her in the entrance. He reminded her of Oom Hendrik. Stout, and always wriggling his shoulders about as if he was trying to make his well-tailored suit fit more comfortably. A Muslim tailor in Schotsekloof made his clothes. He was in the habit of smoothing his little moustache with two fingers of his left hand. That morning he was disturbed, under pressure. His fingers were incessantly at his moustache, sweeping against the short greyish hairs, flattening them.

'I tried to phone you at home, Miss. You'd already left. Perhaps it would be better for you not to be here this morning.'

'Why? Who on earth would take my classes?'

'You may be injured.'

Then she heard the sound of controlled uproar coming from the school hall. She looked up and down the passages. No children hanging around, walking to classrooms chatting, their satchels on their backs.

'I've had a feeling since yesterday afternoon that something was up,' she said.

A small group of senior black boys from a different neighbourhood had entered her classroom, without a word of apology, and told her to go to the staff room, they wished to speak to the children. They went from class to class, the staff members told her. The next day was to be the great boycott.

'I couldn't stay away,' she told the headmaster now.

'They won't allow us in the hall. They have their own leaders. I think they want to march.'

The chanting was growing louder.

'Get out of the way,' said Mr Abrahams. He pushed her through the nearest open door, the secretary's office. Next to her at the window stood Fay Mentoor, the Standard Seven teacher. The secretary turned around and shouted to them: 'Oh my God, here come the police!' Mr Abrahams pushed past. At an angle behind him Leo saw two police vehicles entering the school gates, and five or six armed policemen got out. They stood in front of the school entrance. Two Casspirs were slowly approaching along the road.

'Somebody from the school must have phoned them, some bloody informer. Someone tell the kids, quick.'

Fay Mentoor walked away quickly, to the hall.

The Casspirs blocked off the road. Policemen with sjamboks swarmed over the school grounds, they approached across the quadrangle in groups. They yanked the hall doors open. Then a couple in camouflage arrived, armed with the ominous guns that shot the containers of teargas. Mr Abrahams stepped forward to try to stop them, but he was pushed aside. The teachers standing in classroom doors heard the first hissing of the gas containers.

The hall doors were slammed shut, but not before clouds of teargas swirled out. The chanting had stopped. Then the children streamed from the hall, tried to clear the air around them with their arms, put hands in pockets, groping for a stone to throw. But their eyes were streaming, they couldn't see and the stones went wide. They heard a window break. Most of the children had been cornered in the hall, they huddled with shirts or school dresses covering their faces. Among those who had rushed out was a youngster from Leo's class, no older than 14 or 15, a clever boy. The stone in his hand had fallen on the floor, for a policeman had him by the arm; he jerked him so that the boy writhed in pain, and then he attacked him with the sjambok. Across his back, his buttocks, his head. Fay Mentoor and Mr Abrahams, who had been pushed aside by the police, tried to protest, but their mouths opened helplessly, what could they say? They saw the blood seep through his torn shirt in red streaks, although the boy had been brought to his knees. The expression on the policeman's freckled face was one of such naked brutality that something in Leo snapped. She stormed across the quadrangle to the policeman, jerked at his arm and screamed, 'What the hell do you think you're doing? Do you want to murder the child? Come,' she shouted, 'hit me. Have you hit a woman yet, you little shit? Do it now.'

He shook off her grip and pushed her so that she fell on the cement of the quadrangle. But she didn't stay down. When he lifted his sjambok to set upon the boy again, she clung to his arm. Her hands and elbows were grazed from the fall and started to bleed.

Mr Abrahams had come to them. 'Let go of the woman. She's a teacher. I'll lay a complaint. I'll lay a complaint about this whole bloody morning. Where's your warrant to enter the school grounds?'

'Fuck off.' He threw her down again so that she fell on the cement.

But before she could get up another policeman had her by the arm and he pushed her out of the school door. He walked her to the nearest police van, opened the door and threw her in.

'Be careful of this woman, she's a tiger.'

She lay on the floor of the van, panting, she tried to wipe away the blood with her dress. If only she could have got at the second one.

The van door was opened and a few school children, shirts torn, eyes streaming, were pushed in. As their burning eyes adjusted to the van after the bright light outside, they recognised her and began to shout, half incredulously: 'Miss, hell, Miss! You helped us! Look at the blood on your clothes, Miss! Did you see how she tackled the cop?' They touched her, were pushed against her as others were bundled in, tried to wipe the blood from her, told the others, 'She's in the struggle with us, she's a comrade.'

They joked around her, one started to sing, the others chanted along. The feeling of excitement was infectious. She began to feel it, joined in the singing, although she didn't know the words. She felt excited, wanted to spit at the police.

At last, protesting, but with a touch of pride as he adjusted his jacket, Mr Abrahams was pushed in. And more staff members and more pupils. The children smelled of teargas, some were crying in pain, or they coughed. But they still sang. The new ones arriving weren't satisfied with chanting, they shouted. The stench from their clothes reached Leo's eyes, they began to water, later it hurt to breathe. Despite the air coming in through the barred windows it was stuffy in the crowded van.

More police vans arrived, and they were also filled. Singing and jeering echoed from each van. One hundred and seventy of the pupils and staff were arrested that morning.

When the first police van started off, a stone hit the driver's cab, and the driver took out his pistol and began to shoot. Into the crowd. Their van stopped and the policeman next to the driver shot teargas at the charging, stone-throwing children. Too many to load in. Some gas came through the bars.

They didn't see a child fall, to be picked up and carried by peers.

Mr Abrahams, no longer cool and tidy, carried along by the singing, took out his last handkerchief, shook it open, and passed it to Leo over the heads of the children. 'Press it to your eyes, and those of the children next to you.'

The children drew away, they took pleasure in their streaming eyes,

'You keep it, Miss.' They were proud of her. Protective. One of them took half a lemon from a pocket, passed it. 'Hold the hankie over the lemon, breathe through it.' She did that, it brought relief. She passed it to the next child.

She found the short drive to the police station a satisfying experience, with children thrown against her on the turns, or thrown about by bumps over holes in the road so that she had to help hold them.

But it turned bitter in her mouth when she was parted from them and locked in a separate cell because she was white.

The rest of the day they remained locked up, but at dusk, after half a day of wrangling, an attorney, who had been called on by the deputy headmaster, obtained their release.

None of them could understand why there was no charge against Leo for her attack on the policeman. But it didn't detract from her deed. The next morning in the staff room Fay brought her a cup of tea. 'You put us to shame, hey. Now you're part of the struggle, comrade.' But she said it softly. Suspicion was rife about exactly who had informed the police of the meeting. Some believed it was a pupil, but a few of the staff were also suspected. Again Leo experienced the sweet feeling of camaraderie. That she was trusted.

'You're brave, hey?' said Fay. 'A real fighter.'

'I got so fucking mad, I wanted to tear at his flesh, I wanted him to feel ... No bravery at all, just, just ...'

'Rage.'

'Yes, rage. And wanting to smash this horror we are living with.'

The horror continued. School boycotts – she became accustomed to standing in front of a class of one or two. Should she boycott, should she come? Mr Abrahams said, 'Come. We can make better use of you if you aren't suspected of instigation.'

'Make use of?'

His fingers stroked his moustache. 'I surely wasn't mistaken in the police van? You do want to be involved in our effort?'

'Fay called me comrade,' said Leo. 'It made me very proud that she did that. Yes, I'm part of the struggle, if you want me.'

Boycotts, marches, instructions spread from school to school: stone police vans, overturn buses and burn them, and put up barricades as soon as the Casspirs enter the townships. The children were fighting their own bush war.

Hundreds of them were rounded up and incarcerated, or simply disappeared.

When the schools were closed and it became a new struggle for children and parents to try to occupy the closed schools, Leo went with Fay Mentoor to trace parents, pay fines, arrange for bail. She got to know the prosecutors, the attorneys, the advocates who could be approached for legal aid. She knew exactly which magistrates were more compassionate. Whether her presence in court had a favourable or negative effect on the outcome, or any effect at all, she didn't know.

'Don't worry, comrade,' said Fay. 'The cops are careful if there's a white face watching.'

Tracing children who had disappeared was heart-rending work. They drove from police station to mortuary to hospital in her Golf. No names were given of children detained without a hearing.

'It's very hard for a parent not to know whether a child is dead or alive, or in jail,' a mother told her.

'Don't lose hope!'

Neville Baatjies, the young Maths teacher, helped with the task of tracing. He was a hero amongst the children: when school was still running, he would roar past the hordes of children in the afternoon on his motorbike with his yellow helmet. He could reach where others couldn't go.

Leo's was required to help at weekends too.

Every week, large numbers of children died, especially black children. The children were aggressive, burned tyres, set buses alight, threw stones. They were fired on. Rubber bullets that hit the head, killed. When the stomach or lungs were hit, organs were damaged and death resulted.

'Should you see a group of children in a train or bus on a Saturday afternoon, neatly dressed in their school uniforms, you can be sure they are on their way to a funeral,' said the people.

Mass meetings at the graves of these children were prohibited. So too speeches, the showing of flags, singing. Casspirs kept watch.

But no law could stop people from burying their children.

Mr Abrahams brought an important message to all the staff members he trusted, especially Leo.

'The presence of white women in court, we have found, does make a difference,' he said. 'At funerals we want a living shield of women, also white women, walking in front of the black funeral-goers, arm in arm as in a march, to stop the soldiers from firing. The soldiers will think twice before firing on white women. The Black Sash women agree.'

The difference again, thought Leo. Would she remain 'white' forever? Useful because she was white and could taunt a soldier without getting beaten with a sjambok; because they reckon a 'white' woman will be able to stop a bullet from a gun?

But she went. On Saturdays, on Sundays. She entered the black townships, where the funerals took place, illegally. She joined arms with the row of women, she walked, she chanted. Twice she was arrested, loaded in the police van and driven off. The second time, while she and a few other women, some of them black, were waiting to be charged in the police station, she said to a black woman, 'The song we try to sing with you, I only know a few of the words *akuhlanga lungehlanga* ... Please write the words down for me, I want to learn them.' She took paper from her handbag and the woman wrote the words, the paper supported on Leo's handbag.

'And the meaning?'

'I can't really tell you in English. I'll ask my sister to write the English for you.'

Both times Leo paid the fines. She had been advised to have money on her when she went into townships. She remained in the police station with others overnight once, appeared in court briefly, was then released. She blinked when she got out on the streets of Athlone, so busy on the Monday morning. Neville Baatjies stopped his motorbike next to her. His boots dug into the gravel road. 'Wanna lift? They can't see whether you're black or white under the helmet.' Her hands and feet and body were shivering slightly when she walked up her path. Neville didn't go in, took off at speed. She bathed, put on clean clothes and lay on her bed. She only got to school at eleven o'clock. A week later Fay brought her the English words of the funeral song. She read it so often that she later knew it by heart, Xhosa as well as English:

Akuhlanga lungehlanga,	*It is a happening,*
Dade, nani bazalwana;	*Brothers and sisters;*
Lo mntu usishiyileyo,	*The person who has left us,*
Nguye ogodukileyo.	*Has gone to his home.*
Akuhlanga lungehlanga,	*It is a happening,*
Kunje kuzo zonk' iintlanga;	*So it is with all generations;*
Kungumthetho ubaliwe,	*It is the law that is written*
Sisigqibo sigqityiwe.	*It is a decision carried out.*

Akuhlanga lungehlanga,   *It is a happening,*
Yonwabani lusatshana;   *Be satisfied children;*
Nizilungise' okwenu,   *Prepare yourselves,*
Xa nibizelwa kokwenu.   *When you are called home.*

Akuhlanga lungehlanga,   *It is a happening;*
Noko ngathi kubuhlungu;   *Even though it is painful;*
Lo mmiselo wuqondeni,   *This covenant you must understand*
Lo mmiselo wuqheleni.   *You must accept this covenant.*

Leonora was aware of Leo's activities. She vaguely knew Leo was doing something in aid of black children.

'It reminds me of my Black Sash days, child, when I so annoyed the ooms in the Transvaal with my black fabric draped over my shoulder in front of the Parliament buildings.'

'It's actually not quite the same, Tannie,' said Leo.

'Oh, and what about old Skottel and Maggie, just about every Friday they're at my front gate. I heat up a bowl of food, or keep a bit of fish for them. It wouldn't be the same without them.'

Skottel and Maggie were two homeless people, Leo knew, who begged for empty bottles and exchanged them for a shot of liquor; who, thin as rakes and tough as nails, lived up the mountain slopes – Skottel always going ahead and Maggie protesting behind him. Free as the birds in the sky.

'It's not quite the same, Tannie,' Leo said again. 'But how can I explain?'

Leo felt as though she was living in two different worlds. One country but two different worlds.

One weekend in December family obligations claimed her time. Frikkie had passed away. Leo was asked to collect Leonora and Koba – Miemie's daughter, Frikkie's granddaughter – and take them to the funeral at Worcester in her Golf.

5

The feeling of living in two worlds was overwhelming. She drove in the same car along the same N2 highway past the black townships, but she was moving in an entirely different frame of reference. It made Leo feel schizophrenic. Even words had different meanings.

It was a boiling hot summer day. The smoke from the water-cooling towers was a fixed misty black blot against the pale blue sky. The heat lay over the plain; at times the mirages shimmered, touched the tops of the Port Jackson trees, shivered over the grey ash heaps and rubbish dumps.

Seen from the old point of view, she realised: It's dangerous on the way to the airport. Especially under the fly-overs one had to be on the look out for groups of children or youths with yellow Checkers bags, which might hold bricks or stones. They hurled these missiles from the fly-over down onto passing cars.

There were soldiers with guns on every bridge. There was even talk of wearing crash helmets on that road.

In that frame of reference she was a target for the children. Now and then a Casspir drove past on the gravel shoulder of the road.

'What a hideous monster,' said Koba in the back of the car.

Leo, who was driving, said nothing. Leonora, next to her, also remained silent. Leo doubted she had noticed the Casspir, for she was sitting with her eyes closed. 'It's a long way round to pick up one person at the airport,' said Leo. She had to swerve. 'Lots of traffic for a Saturday morning.'

'Not so much.' Koba was always otherwise. 'One probably should bear in mind …

'One person just makes the difference.' So Tannie Leonora had been listening. 'Your father's car can't take five.'

'I wonder who'll come with us.' Then another idea occurred to Koba, 'I wonder whether Pa will inherit enough from Oupa for a new car.' No one answered her. She said to the passing road: 'Maybe my brothers and I will also inherit. I'm tired of relying on lifts.'

She was a few years younger than Leo and worked at a hairdressing salon. They had little contact. Her great-aunt Leonora also saw little of her. They never saw Fred, the older son, a professional photographer whose work met with acclaim overseas, much to the disgust of the Ooms in the Traansvaal.

'If I inherit enough money from Oupa, I'll start my own salon. How do you think it'll sound, Tannie? Chez Koba. I think I should make it Chez Jacqueline.'

After a while she leaned forward and tapped Leonora, who seemed to have nodded off, on the shoulder. 'Is it true, Tannie, that Oom Hendrik is coming with a chauffeur? A black chauffeur or a white chauffeur? He's very rich, hey?'

No one answered her. She kept herself occupied with a nail file. To everyone's surprise the family had heard that Belle, or Bella – as Holtzhausen called her – was coming with Oom Hendrik in his car, and perhaps Holtzhausen might be coming too. It was a long time since Belle had travelled so far. Leo had prepared a room so that her parents could stay for a few days if they wanted to. They had never visited her. A couple of days extra would surely not make any difference.

'Oom Hendrik misses Tannie Rina so much. I'm thankful Belle is coming. It's a long way for him.' Leonora's head nodded again: she appeared to have dozed off.

Rina's death about a year earlier had made Hendrik increasingly dependent on Belle and Holtzhausen.

Although there had been warnings on the radio that morning, the drive to the airport was uneventful. Probably because of the Casspirs in increasing numbers at the Crossroads squatters' camp. 'It looks miserable there, hey Leo?' said Koba from the back. 'You're a kaffir lover, but I bet you've never set foot in there. Ugh! There are plastic bags blowing around all over the place. You'd think they'd pick it up. I suppose it's probably just as messy at your school.'

She got no response. Leo turned in at the road to the airport. There was tight security at the entrance to the parking lot. Leo showed her ID and they were admitted. All around them doors were slammed and locked, and car bonnets were given a farewell pat, streams of people converged on the terminal building. Now that they'd made it safely over the part of the road described in the newspapers as dangerous, everyone was back in a holiday mood. In the waiting hall for arrivals from Johannesburg Koba spotted her father at once and greeted him noisily.

'Who should actually sympathise with who?' said Leo. She shook hands with him, Leonora kissed his cheek. Stoffel, Miemie's husband, was a tall chap and had to stoop to Leonora. Koba clung to his arm.

'Oh, we are all pleased for Oupa's sake,' said Stoffel, 'he suffered so much towards the end.'

The plane landed, turned on the tarmac, and taxied up to the building laboriously. At last an official with yellow markers guided it to a halt. The steps were taken closer and the silver tube began to leak people. The passengers reached the entrance in groups. The great-uncles, Philip and Robert, blinking as though slightly disorientated, entered the arrivals hall. Philip had grown stouter, but Robert, who'd retired from Potch, was bald, thinner and nervous.

Philip kept an eye on his son Barry, who had arrived with his two children, as if it made him feel safer. There were so many stories about the Cape Flats. Who'd thought to build the airport in such a vulnerable position?

Leonora took a brother's hand in each of hers. She couldn't speak, just shook her head, then drew the hands closer and pressed first the one brother's hand and then the other, against her cheek. Both were uncomfortable with this show of emotion.

'Come now, Leonora, no need to overreact,' said Robert.

Barry had told his teenage son and daughter, Phil and Emma, to see to the luggage. Leo went with them, she liked those two.

Barry hugged Leonora. 'I can imagine how you must feel, Tannie. You and Oom Frikkie were so fond of each other, I know. We really wanted to come.'

Barry looked well. He was a doctor, but saw to it that he had weekly recreation; he was tanned and looked healthy in his sports shirt and trousers. In his brown eyes – Mother's eyes, Leonora always said – there was understanding, empathy.

Leonora couldn't stop the tears welling up. Now she was the eldest, the hub of family affairs, but she didn't feel up to it, she'd rather be alone somewhere. She dreaded seeing Belle who, so she had heard, had arrived the previous day and was with Miemie.

Phil and Emma, brown curly hair, brown eyes, tanned like their father, came pushing the trolleys loaded with suitcases. Stoffel took one from Emma.

'You're coming with us, Oom Barry,' said Leo. 'We'll take his suitcase, the car isn't parked far away.' Barry sat in front with her, but often turned back to grasp his great-aunt Leonora's hand and press it.

'Things are stirring in our country, hey, Oom,' said Koba. 'When I open the newspaper in the morning, I say to myself: Give us this day our daily angst! Actually one of my clients said it … I thought it was cute.'

'I don't know about cute, but it's certainly stirring.' Leo didn't conceal her impatience with Koba. 'I think PW Botha now feels like a bull in a crush-pen, tossing his horns every which way.'

Barry gave Leo a sideways glance. He wanted to weigh her up. With his own father and Oom Robert he had long since stopped discussing politics. It was better that way. As he had said to Belle – light years ago – it's better to hold your tongue. Never to speak up. Had it been cowardice? God grant that he didn't become embittered.

He risked it: 'I think PW is going too far.'

'He's pathological about his "total onslaught", Oom. He should rather force us to open our eyes to what is happening around us. We notice nothing. As even Koba remarked: most of us don't even know what is going on behind the sand dunes.' Leo was immediately irritated with herself; she had resolved to say nothing, now she was getting worked up again.

'It's difficult to know if you're not allowed to see. We're kept in ignorance. I don't think we realise the extent of our ignorance. But these Casspirs' – there were a few half-hidden in the bushes – 'we can't miss.'

'Politics, politics, politics.' Koba took the nail file from her handbag and began to file. They were driving along the road that passed the University of the Western Cape. 'They look well-dressed to me.' She pointed at a couple of students hitching at the roadside. 'And damn cheeky.'

'I wish you'd stop talking about "them" as if you were referring to another species.' Leo's voice was, even to her own ears, a bit too sharp. But she didn't care. She would like to take Koba by her shoulders and shake her and shake her, but it wouldn't make any difference. She'd realised long since: Koba was stupid.

Leonora wasn't with them: her head had fallen forward and swayed with the movement of the car. Now and then the head would jerk and they heard a little snore, then it was quiet again. They drove on in silence. Barry leaned over to the back to arrange Leonora's hands more comfortably on her lap. Leo felt the lump that was settling on her stomach ever more frequently; she would find it difficult to part with Oumatannie. Without her so much would fall apart.

The changing of gears as they started climbing the pass woke Leonora. She lifted her head, looked out the window at the valley lying to her left.

'How lovely,' she said. 'Over all these years I've always found it so beautiful. As expansive as the Lord's mercy ...' she murmured, but Koba chipped in: 'Oh, no, Tannie, too many mountains. Oom Barry, they say Transvalers feel claustrophobic here between our mountains. Is that right?'

'Never. I find it difficult to leave the mountains.'

'But you are staying to visit a while, Oom. You and the children can come and stay with me; when Ma and the rest have left, we can climb Table Mountain.' Leo began planning. She would invite Neville along. She thought Barry was the only one of her ooms who would accept her friend.

It was just after twelve when they reached Worcester, the birthplace, the town of Father's parish, the town where Mother had died, where Frikkie had lived.

'You know my mother,' said Koba. 'She and her ladies – I'm not allowed to call them maids any more I suppose – will have everything ready.'

'Are we to drive to your house or your oupa's?' Leo was abrupt.

'Drop me at my ma's, but the dining table at Oupa's is bigger, we'll eat there. I want to change into a dress. We're all going to church together from Oupa's house.'

Leo sensed a slight anxiety taking hold of Leonora after they'd dropped Koba, driven to the outskirts of town and turned in at the gate of Frikkie's yard. As if something in her had started to tremble, as if the cells of her body lacked the resilience to cope with the emotions overwhelming her. 'Oom Barry,' she said softly, but Barry had already taken Leonora's hand in his again. She had deliberately avoided driving past the old church where her great-grandfather had preached. The old rectory, where he and his family had lived, had been demolished, something modern was built there; that too she avoided.

Members of the family stood together in a little group under the oaks behind Frikkie's house; they made room for Leo to park. She stopped between Stoffel's car and Hendrik's big shiny black limousine with the Transvaal number plates. The driver was nowhere to be seen; the bucket and cloths he'd used to wash away the journey's dust stood to one side.

I'll leave it to the great-uncles to see to their sister, thought Leo. She didn't see her mother. She greeted her father hastily, then entered the house through the kitchen. Her mother and the others were to have arrived the previous day. She hadn't been at Miemie's house. Was she resting? Had she decided to have a rest at Frikkie's house?

Two coloured women were working in the kitchen, one at the stove, one washing dishes. She nodded to them, but she didn't know them.

The passage was half dark, cool. It ran the length of the house, with rooms leading off it. But all the doors were closed. Behind one of the closed doors was the coffin. Brought by the undertakers that morning so that the brothers from the Transvaal … Leo would rather not think of it. As far as she could remember from a visit with Leonora, the bedrooms were at the front of the house. Where was Miemie? She had to be there, it was her father's funeral. But now she wanted to see to her mother, if only one of the doors would open. Then she turned a doorknob and a large square of light, with the oak leaves dappling it, lit the room. The blinds were up. The little squares of the windowpane shimmered as the oak leaves moved and suddenly let light through, only to cut it off again. Belle lay on one of the beds from the old pastorie. Her eyes were closed; she had taken off her dress and lay in her petticoat, a light blanket over her legs.

The sight of her mother brought tears to Leo's eyes. She knelt next to the bed. 'Ma,' she said, 'it's me, Leo.' The eyes opened. Such pretty green eyes with little golden flecks. She'd been the green-eyed girl. Does she recognise me? Does she love me, worry about me, care for me? The questions rushed through Leo's mind. Then she saw in her mother's eyes a kind of vacant look that made her even sadder. Don't Ma, she wanted to shout. Fight, Ma. Don't let them deprive you of your being. I'll fight for you, Ma. God, I'll take our country and shake it to its senses so that you can live again. But she said nothing.

Belle lifted her hand and drew Leo's face nearer. Leo kissed her lightly.

'Are you tired, Ma? We're all here. I'll help you dress. Tannie Leonora is outside with the old Ooms. I must still go to greet them, I just ran through to you, Ma.'

Belle straightened up, rose from the bed and reached for her clothes. Her smile was small and sad. She reached out to touch Leo's hand again. 'I'm glad you came.'

'Ma, you must visit me too. Please. I'm not going to let you go off again right away.'

Belle nodded. 'We must tell your Pa.'

Her Ma's thick fair hair was flat from being lain on and slightly damp with sweat. Leo stroked it, saw how grey it had become. Also thinner. Otherwise she had not changed much; perhaps put on a bit of weight. But her colour wasn't good. She would take her Ma to a doctor, she resolved.

Miemie had gone to her house to fetch more cutlery and an extra tablecloth, and she and Koba returned together. Leo and Belle came down the passage to greet those they hadn't yet seen outside in the shade of the trees. A chair had been brought out for Leonora. Belle sat on the chair beside it. For a moment everyone was astounded, because Leonora evidently didn't remember who Belle was.

'It's all the new faces, Oom Barry, she's confused,' said Leo. 'Your two nice young people, and Miemie's children who she doesn't really know. And the three brothers after such a long time, and to see them as old men now … Hell, Oom, growing old is the pits, isn't it?'

'Not really so very old,' said Barry. 'Oom Robert is scarcely 70!'

For Hendrik too, a chair had been brought out. Leo knelt next to him. He stroked her hair.

'Oom, the Golf is still going well. I love it. And I'm so grateful to you, Oom.'

He smiled slightly. 'Mammie egged me on. "Leo will only be young once, Pappie," she told me. "Why not give it to her?"'

'Oh, Mammie had a heart of gold. It must be very difficult for you without her.'

'I do have your ma. Right next to me. She's kind to me.'

'As Oom has been kind to us.'

'Money is nothing, my child. It's understanding that's important, and that I found difficult. Mammie understood better, I think.'

'And with yourself, Oom, are things going well?'

'The business just has to keep going under its own steam. But I'm still involved with many matters. The country needs me.'

'Of course, Oom.'

'As long as I keep my strength.'

'Of course.'

She wasn't going to argue with him, that she had resolved. She would not succeed in convincing him of anything. She'd just confuse him.

Stoffel was still carrying chairs out, to add to the stacking chairs he'd brought on his bakkie. Josias, his youngest son, helped him. Phil and Emma, who had met their cousin for the first time that day, helped. They put up a trestle table, covered it with a starched white tablecloth. Miemie was busy in the kitchen where she was slicing cold meat; potato salad, beetroot salad, tomato salad; all arranged and finally garnished. The servants brought plates and dishes and also fresh buttered bread and packs of serviettes to the trestle table. Red and sweaty after all the activity, Miemie tried to herd the people. 'We're eating outside, it's better so, it's just a finger lunch, it's because … it's just …' She got stuck. Pulled herself together. 'We'll have a proper meal tonight. Inside.' She didn't say what everyone could hear in her words. Inside lies the old man, Frikkie, in his coffin, balanced on two chairs in the dining room. The eldest living member of the big family now gone. Shortly, when they'd eaten, before the undertakers came to screw down the lid, they would walk past the coffin one by one. For a last look. For a last farewell. Miemie babbled on, 'You asked me to order flowers for you. They're fresher locally, and cheaper. There are beautiful wreaths, I put them in the dining room, I hope that's all right.'

'Come, I'll dish up for Tannie Leonora and Ma. Here are serviettes, then we'll take the plates on our laps.' Leo took two plates and served meat and some salad. Took a fork for each. The others followed. The younger ones served the old ooms who were sitting.

'Something to drink?' asked Philip. His face was red, Barry helped him take off his jacket. He loosened his tie a little.

'I don't think wine now, Pa. Perhaps a beer, Stoffel?'

'There's plenty of everything.'

Something was bothering Philip. Beer in hand, he looked around, asked the question out of the blue: 'Does anyone know what became of Nellie?'

Miemie perceived this as criticism. Should she have let her know? She looked at Leonora, but she gave a slight gesture, as if negating the question. 'Probably passed away.'

'It's really a long time ago, Oom,' said Leo, to whom her oom's words sounded like a line from a poem. 'I'm sure she must have passed away.'

Leo was looking for her father. She saw him coming around the corner of the house. Always slightly withdrawn, always unsure of his welcome. And where was the driver, and was he black or white? That is typical of this country, she thought. What can we do about the driver before we know whether he's black or white? She dished up food for her father, took a bottle of beer to him.

'The driver, Pa?' The question of the driver suddenly concerned her more than Oom Frikkie inside. 'Should I take him some food?'

'He walked to town, I gave him money to buy a meat pie and a coke or something. That's how we managed on the way here too.'

'Hell, Pa.'

'It's a family gathering here, Leo.'

'I'm glad you came, Pa. I'm pleased to see you again.'

Her father was wearing a light grey suit, his heavy spectacles were slipping down his nose because his face was sweating so much. His hair, which was combed back, was completely grey, but still thick. He'd had to get false teeth and they still bothered him, he was inclined to suck his lips in as if trying to get the teeth in position, as though they were a little out of line. This irritated Leo, but what could she say?

Before they had finished eating, Fred, Miemie's elder son – a photographer like his Oupa, a tall, lean chap – arrived from the city. He drove the car into the yard in a cloud of dust. He took camera cases out of the car.

'Made it. Yes, Pa, my throat is crying for a beer. Pass one here.'

How lovely Emma is, thought Leonora as she watched the young people. With Mother's dark eyes, with the thick dark hair, like Vicky had, but who would still remember Vicky? She must tell this pretty child about Vicky. For a moment she felt a slight heat in her cheeks, a slight shyness, as if she was young again. Would she be able to tell her about Adriaan who had touched Vicky's breast the day before she fell ill? Had anyone yet touched this child's breast? How glad she was he had touched Vicky's breast before she died and that there had been a new glow in Vicky's eyes that evening. So short-lived, because within hours the head was tossing feverishly on the pillow and the pillowcase was wet through, and she and Aunt Issy had to change sheets and pillow cases and blankets all the time, all the time, until she had died. And would never know of her, Leonora's and Adriaan's betrayal.

'Tannie Leonora,' said Leo. 'Please try to eat something, just a little.' Leonora took a piece of cold chicken from the plate in her fingers, but found it difficult to chew, the chicken was too dry for her. She chewed and chewed and at last there was a little dry fragment in her mouth, which she, looking around to see if anyone was watching, placed on the side of her plate.

Belle sat looking ahead with a blank expression. She ate, and even allowed Leo to fetch a second helping. She wiped her mouth carefully with the paper serviette, crumpled it and put it on the dirty plate. She gave the plate back to Leo.

Dear God, Leo asked herself, what could one do with these two weirdos? Then she thought, reproaching herself: I love them and they are nearest to me.

She linked arms with Holtzhausen. 'Another beer, Pa?'

He shook his head. He was regretting the previous one. Wondered if he would make it through the church service. His prostate was bothering him.

By one o'clock Miemie started chivvying them.

'You must go and get ready now, at half past two the cortège is leaving, the undertakers are coming just after two ...' She stopped, she couldn't utter the words. 'To shut Pa's coffin. Our family will drive across to our house to get ready. The women can change in the room with Belle, and then there are two more rooms for the men. Come on, Josias, you show them where. Your Oom Arnold went to lie down in the attic, he's exhausted. I'll send up something for him to eat.'

The first room was where Frikkie had lain on his sickbed for so many months. Arnold had slept in the next room during the past weeks, on the nights when he wasn't keeping watch at his father's sickbed. Miemie and her helpers had spring-cleaned the room after he died. The bed had been stripped, there was a water carafe and a glass with a beaded doily over it on the bedside locker. And his Bible. There walls were covered with photos of Kowie, as a young girl, as a mother, as an older woman, even as a very old woman shortly before she died. Some mounted in the old narrow black frames, others mounted in a more modern style, some simply glued to cardboard.

Strange how Frikkie had passed his passion for photography to his own son and then Miemie's son, thought Hendrik as he put on the clean shirt he'd brought from the hotel that morning. He and Mammie had not been blessed with children. If he had a son, would he've liked him to follow in his footsteps? The thought pained him. No. A hundred times no. He could manage to carry on, stumble on without Mammie. His eyes were full of tears. He struggled with his cuff links.

His brothers Philip and Robert … the Three Musketeers, he suddenly thought, yes, they'd called themselves that when they were growing up in the pastorie. When last had he thought of that? Aunt Issy had read the story to them. He must ask the others about that, but these days the relationship between them was troubled. And when they'd driven down the main street the day before and seen old Perry's shop still there, with the long stoep and the overhang just as before, the memories had pierced him: Philip and Robert, who with inside ankles fastened together ran three-legged down the long stoep and sang: RobbiePhil, Robbie-Phil. Never HenniePhil – you're too fat, you're clumsy, you make us stumble, and now you're blubbing again, cry-baby, cry-baby … And old Mister Perry who took him by the arm and pulled him into the dark shop and told his other customers: come, just listen how this boy can add, but the sums weren't so difficult, he would rather have run three-legged. It was Aunt Issy who'd called them the Three Musketeers, never the other two. Did he have to acknowledge the truth to himself here next to Frikkie's coffin?

Robert and Philip didn't need to change after their flight; they just combed their hair in the room next door, washed hands and faces in the basin on the washstand. Hendrik heard how one brother sloshed the water from the basin into the slop bucket, then how the other poured fresh water into the basin. The evocative sound brought their childhood back sharply. He felt, in spite of everything, renewed affection for his brothers.

When he was ready, he sat on the bed for a few minutes. To prepare himself. The other two waited for him at the door. They were the first to go to the coffin in the dining room. It was also fitting that the three of them were there on their own.

Too many flowers. The scent was too sweet and too heavy. Philip took his arm as support. Anything troubling you? asked Hendrik. Philip shook his head. His colour was high.

'I'll be next to be carried out feet first. That's all that's troubling me.'

On the flat satin pillow Frikkie's face was yellow and angular. The skin looked hard, as if the stuff they had injected had solidified under the skin. He'd never seen Mammie like that, he couldn't. Belle had understood and she had gestured to them to close the coffin. Afterwards Belle had given him a small brandy, it still worried him that he had gone to the memorial service for Mammie with brandy on his breath. Although Belle had repeatedly insisted: It was medicine, Mammie would have understood. She was entirely devoted to him and Mammie.

The closed eyelids looked solid, shut tight. Never again would they see what they'd been focused on for a lifetime: the small, the beautiful things. Hendrik lifted a hand and touched his brother's forehead, withdrew from the cold contact. He shuffled on so that Philip could approach.

And Robert.

Robert didn't look at the corpse for long. Frikkie is well out of the mess, he thought. Frikkie with his Kowie had turned out better than Father expected or Aunt Issy predicted. His children didn't amount to much. Arnold prematurely aged – what had his chasing around for the newspaper gained him? Learned to drink too much. He was suspicious of the resting in the attic, the pale face, the damp hair. Was probably blind drunk. Miemie who sorted him out. Miemie's kids didn't look too bad.

Children ... once again it was gnawing at him like a cancer. If only it were cancer ... His Benjamin ... named after him. Bennie. His lastborn. He didn't really have strong feelings for the girls and he hadn't brought them. But how proud he would have been of Bennie ... But he'd thrown his life away. Went with his pals on Border duty, and messed around with the shrivelled up old black woman. Then lost his head. Bush madness. Fucked up. And soon to be court-martialed. God, thought Robert, is this where a life in service of my nation has brought me? Then fuck the whole nation. Just leave Bennie alone. Bennie wouldn't speak to him, not even in the cell.

He gave the coffin one fleeting glance. They called this grief. When an old man snuffed it. He'd come – how would Aunt Issy have put it? – to keep up appearances. His brothers didn't yet know. It had been kept out of the newspapers. But the newspapers would get hold of it, that he knew. As he moved on, he noticed that Philip didn't linger long at the coffin either. Philip's heart was no longer in national affairs, not since he hadn't been elected to the President's Council. And took it amiss that he, Robert, was elected. Philip's two daughters had married well – well as far as money was concerned, but not men with national pride. Modern men, call them by their name: traitors, colluding with kaffirs. Members of the Progressive Party. He felt like spitting on the name. While his Bennie …

Leonora smoothed Frikkie's hair, which was slightly dishevelled on one side. Where had that little sign of life come from, was there a breeze? Was it a farewell to his sister? The wispy grey hairs on the cold head rose again. Were they trying to tell her something? Frikkie, she began to lament, what are you trying to say? Open your eyes. She clung to the side of the coffin.

'Come, Tannie,' said Leo. 'We're going to be late.'

Belle looked at the oom in the coffin with impersonal affection. He had given her the camera, tried to teach her to take photos. All she had from it was the arm of her beloved on a snap she'd torn up long ago. I loved you, Oom Frikkie, she spoke silently. Why didn't I ever tell you? I very nearly did once: that evening on the roof. She bent and kissed the cold forehead.

The wreaths were stacked against the fireplace; a vase of flowers stood on the mantelpiece; more wreaths and sheaves were piled on the dining table, which had been moved aside to make room for the two chairs supporting the coffin. The summer flowers had a heavy scent. Sharp in contrast, a bitter, sandy smell rose from the cypress twigs, inserted in the round bases for greenery. There were a few late narcissi, their sweet aroma of death rose above the scents of the other flowers. The women who had made the ordered wreaths had got up at the crack of dawn, taken the flowers, which had been kept in deep water the whole night, from the buckets and baths, and got to work breaking stems, inserting. Skilled creators of wreaths.

A bee hovered around one of the Saint Joseph lilies in a sheaf lying on the table. The buzzing was irritating. Miemie's youngest son, Josias, tried to get rid of it, flapped his handkerchief. The bee settled on the nose of the corpse. 'Oh my God,' said Miemie. She went so pale that

Stoffel took her by the arm. He had her sit on a chair. The bee flew off. Those who were afraid of bee-stings ducked, attention taken away from the body, the finely drawn grief broken.

The older people stood aside. Then the children went to the coffin, Arnold and Miemie. Then the grandchildren – Miemie and Stoffel's children took priority. Koba wore too much make-up, thought Leo, the tissue held to her eyes was for effect. But her older brother, Fred, looked interesting. She'd like to speak to him. As long as he didn't come messing around at the coffin with his camera. He did just that, they had to stand back. He took a photograph of the corpse – that was all it was, a corpse. So why did she need to swallow back tears? What the hell! What complications had she allowed herself to become involved in? Family, family …

Neither of Arnold's children had come to the funeral. Too expensive, he'd said. Arnold is shattered, Miemie had told Leo over the phone, he sat next to the deathbed for a week. He looked pale and exhausted.

Philip's granddaughter, Emma of the thick dark curls, had big brown eyes, almost misty. She'd edged up to the coffin, hesitant to look, yet wanting to see: it was the first dead person she'd seen. It no longer looked like a person to her, she felt panicky, she looked up, sought her father, her brother amongst the strangers for reassurance, and saw Josias's eyes on her. There was a fleeting glance of acknowledgement, almost a smile in her eyes, then her lashes were lowered on her cheeks again. Josias caught his breath. His legs went numb. She's a princess, he thought.

A shy but determined cough at the door. The gentlemen in black had come to take over.

Miemie wept, took a last look at her father in the coffin. Arnold held her arm. Was it because he was unstable himself and needed his sister's support? Miemie wouldn't acknowledge it, but she smelt liquor on his breath. Arnold should never have gone to the Transvaal, she thought protectively. She held his hand, hooked around her elbow, with her other hand. She wouldn't let him go back, she resolved, not right away.

Another crisis, thought Leo when she went out and saw Hendrik speaking to the driver. He asked for the keys, he'd drive himself. He explained to the black man that he should wait there, or he could go back to the hotel. The man took a comic out of the car and walked to the garage. With a shrug.

The church bell began to toll when the cortège turned into Church Street. There were a good many cars parked along the street, the verger was kept busy. Leo had to park a little distance from the church in a side street. The bell tolled its heavy dark sounds. 'D'you know, Oom Barry,' she said before she rolled up the window and got out, 'that tolling gives me goose flesh. I've heard it in a church chock full of black people, we were only a very few whites, a memorial service for Neil Aggett. One toll for every detainee killed in detention, then silence. The tolling went on for ever; just when you thought it was over, the dark sound came again, more that 70 times … it was horrific. And the whole time the black people chanted, so softly, deep in the belly. I didn't feel afraid, I just felt: here is grief I'm not sure I can cope with. It was endless – more and more tolling and more breath expelled from the chest.'

They waited for the church-goers in the street to pass, then got out themselves. There were several old people, who'd been children during Father's term of service. Here and there someone who knew the ooms, who had come to see what had become of Father's descendants, nodded.

The family gathered in the entrance, walked to the front pews together, shifted in. It was hot, three o'clock in the afternoon, the yellow in the coloured windows diffused unbearable heat. Somewhere the glass of a watch, or a bracelet, caught the light, and strange flashes shot from them. The coffin had been laid in front of the pulpit, the sheaf from Miemie and Arnold on the lid. The handles hung shining and heavy. The six bearers – Arnold and his brother-in-law Stoffel, Stoffel's sons, Fred and Josias, Barry and his son Phil – moved in with the rest of the family. Even there the scent of the narcissi on the coffin was strong.

The young dominee spoke of a son of the parish who had died, of the descendants of the beloved old minister who had gathered there to bury him.

Koba was battling with her hay fever, the tissue was sopping. She blushed blood red with embarrassment.

Leonora had taken her hymnal out of her handbag; she was looking for the hymn given on the little pamphlet. She tugged at Leo's sleeve, whispered loudly, so that people looked in her direction: 'The words don't match, they're not the right words for that number, it's all wrong.'

Leo, who never set foot in a church, remembered what she'd read in a newspaper. 'It's a new version, Tannie, hush now. Just sing from the pamphlet.'

'But it's not right, dear, I want to sing the Afrikaans words.'

'Tannie, it's the new Afrikaans words.' She pointed her finger at the words on the paper: *Gesang 292, Rus, my siel, jou God is Koning, oral voer Hy heerskappy*. 'Tannie, that's Afrikaans.'

'But it's not hymn 292. It's hymn 22.'
'There are new numbers now, Tannie, just sing.'

It was shortly before four when the cortège began to leave the town, headlights on. The sun on the headlights shot out shards of fire. Smooth and oiled, the hearse made slow and stately progress through the streets of the town, the only slight bump came where the tar met the gravel road. The coffin was firm on its stand, scarcely moving. After the hearse, also with the slight bump from tar to gravel, came the undertaker's long black car carrying the surviving children. The twins: Miemie well-groomed, on a high that afternoon, satisfied with the flowers, a little uneasy about the evening meal; and next to her Arnold, her beloved Boetie, decrepit, his head hanging forward. She nudged his knee: Don't go to sleep now. Stoffel sat in front next to the driver (white, in a morning suit); her heart overflowed with joy at the thought of her husband, so willing to let her have her way, so reliable, her tower of strength.

Hendrik took the wheel of his own car which was just as black, just as shiny, just as long. Leonora at his side, her two brothers behind. The brothers from the Transvaal didn't speak to one another much. There was a distance even between the two inseparables, no one could deny it.

The next car, Stoffel's, was driven by his son, Fred; he drove nonchalantly, window rolled down, elbow on the sill, hand resting on the roof. Not much respect, thought Holtzhausen, sitting in front next to him, but he didn't say it. In the back Belle sat between Koba and Josias, Koba at the window.

'Oh, close it, Fred,' complained Koba, 'what will my hair look like, we're being blown away in the back. You're not on the tar any more; you may not mind the dust, but we do.'

He dropped his hand, began turning the window up reluctantly.

Leo, in her car behind him, with her Oom Barry next to her and his two nice-looking children, Emma and Phil, in the back, had closed her windows long since.

Barry looked back. 'Quite a lot of cars in the cortège. Usually people just go to the church out of curiosity …'

'Probably for the sake of old Father.'

'Leo, my child, don't underestimate your great-uncle Frederik. In his day he was a highly regarded man. One of the first to be called an art photographer. I noticed people from the press here. Note books, cameras, all of that.'

It happened as they drove past the coloured peoples' township. Out of the blue, at four o'clock on that hazy, dusty midsummer afternoon.

Only the white driver of the hearse saw it but he lied to save his skin. Two coloured children on bicycles on the gravel road; he dared not hoot, it wasn't done. They were impudent, mischievous, didn't get out of the way. A few seconds of taunting, and on a small incline the hearse picked up speed to overtake them. The cyclists were confused, slid in the sand. The two bikes collided, the back wheel of one became entangled in the front wheel of the other, and the children tumbled in the road. The right front wheel of the hearse caught the entangled bicycles and dragged them along a few metres; the children too. One of them had a foot caught in a pedal.

The people in the front vehicle were scarcely aware of the incident, when the stone hit the side window of the second car. The window shattered to pieces, the stone hit the right-hand side of Koba's head. She screamed, screamed louder still when she took away her hand which had flown to her head and saw blood streaming from her fingers.

It was a miracle, everyone said later, that there hadn't been a pile-up. Fred had the presence of mind not to brake sharply. A bit further up the incline he pulled up. Leo warned her passengers and braked. 'Drive on, don't stop,' someone shouted from a car behind her, but she stopped.

Barry had got out and opened Koba's door. He pressed his handkerchief against her head. Within seconds it was soaked. 'Belle, you and Josias must get out, get in with Leo, right away. Hurry, you don't know what might happen.'

Josias helped Belle in next to Leo, and he got in next to Emma.

'Turn, Fred,' said Barry. 'Right here next to the patch of sand. Drive back along the shoulder, we must get Koba to a hospital.' He was silent for moment. 'I'd like to attend to the children.'

'They're okay. The one's leg was bleeding, probably just a scratch.'

'Thank God.'

Fred's attention was focused on driving the car. The road wasn't wide, and although the cars in the cortège tried to move aside to let him through, he had one wheel on the road and the other on the sloping ridge on the other side most of the time. Finally he passed the last car. The people stared through the back window nonplussed. Another car turned out of the cortège.

Only the one stone was thrown.

People crowded along the fence of the coloured township. Not a single hat was removed in the usual token of respect for a cortège, no one stood with head bowed. No more stones, but the aggression was tangible. Fred drove to the hospital, where the sister examined Koba. A cut of five centimetres on the right-hand side of the head. The hair would have to be shaved to disinfect it. A few stitches. Koba groaned. 'Hold still girl, you should be grateful it wasn't your face. The hair will soon grow again. Come, steady now.'

Koba began to sob jerkily, she was injected. The sister said, 'We'll keep her here tonight, we must keep an eye on her for concussion.'

Fred wasn't very sympathetic. 'It's no great drama Koba, it's nothing terrible, calm down. Come, Oom Barry, we'll go back.'

'Home?'

But Holtzhausen, who'd remained sitting in the car, insisted: 'To the cemetery. One doesn't know what else may have happened, and there's the drive back, I'm worried about Bella.'

'Right,' said Fred. 'But by this time the other car that turned back will have been to the police. Believe me, the police will be in the township by now.'

Was there satisfaction in his voice, or concern, or dismay? Barry wondered. One always wondered about one's family. Something must have led to the stoning – or was it resistance to the great injustice that was at last bubbling up like black water out of the earth, demanding burnt earth and burnt bodies? And blood? God help us. He couldn't endure it any longer. Or expose his children to it. Why was he leaving the country? Self-preservation? Revulsion? Perhaps. Or was he simply still the Pilate he'd scorned since childhood: I wash my hands? All he knew was that he'd had enough.

The burial was nearly over when Fred drove past the other parked cars with dust flying, stopped next to the cemetery, trod on the wire fence to let the others over, and then joined the rear of the little group at the graveside.

The slow hymn hung over the hot afternoon; the minister's tenor dragged the voices of the bearers, the women, the old men with him:

When we enter death's dark vale,
even loved ones come no more;
but He, the faithful friend in need,
guides us to the unknown shore.

He closed his book, said his final words. Miemie was supported by Stoffel, shuffled forward, scattered flowers on the slowly lowered coffin, then the others followed. The green straps were caught up, there was a screeching sound from the pulley, but the black-clad coffin escort bent down, adjusted something, quickly applied a little oil from a Three-in-one can which he took from an inner pocket. The people began to turn away from the open grave; they stepped carefully over the uneven ground, back to the cars. The first cars moved off.

Miemie, with Fred and Stoffel, was concerned about the meal; hoped everything was in order at home. She tried not to hear the sods being shovelled onto her father's coffin behind them. Would the pastry be burnt? Her son would have to help move the table back; get the chairs on which the coffin had rested out of the way ... those were stones, not sods falling on the coffin. Those coloured gravediggers didn't give a damn; she should have had her sons fill the grave.

She wanted to cover her ears to block out the sound of the stones.

Only when they were driving past the township and saw two police vehicles there, it hit her. 'My God, I forgot about Koba.'

'It was no more than a scratch, dear, Barry will see to it.'

And Leo told Barry, in the car with her again as she reversed jerkily across the grass: 'Oom, shouldn't we go and see if those children were hurt? I don't entirely believe the undertaker's story ...'

Barry looked back uncertainly to where his children and Josias were sitting. 'After one incident feelings usually calm down. I wouldn't like to go in there with the children ... the police are probably there already.'

'We'll leave it at that, then,' said Leo. 'If the police are there, the stone-thrower and his mates have been found already, they're sitting in the cells and are being "questioned". I know all about the questioning.'

Yet she couldn't leave it at that. She turned off into the entrance to the township, where they were stopped.

'I'm a medical doctor,' said Barry

'No one is allowed through, sir, the police doctor will soon be here. Drive on, there's nothing you can do.'

It was the sight of the police vans in the township that had upset Miemie. The guests were forgotten. She forced the driver in his black clothes to drive to the hospital. Only after the sister had allowed her to see her sleeping daughter was she satisfied. The bandage looked horrible, but the sister held her elbow: it's only the sedative making her sleep like that, leave her now.

The dinner she had planned for so long, even before her pa's death, ended up as a strained affair. Nothing wrong with the food. The enormous chicken pies in the oven dishes were a beautiful golden colour, slightly brown at the edges, as if caused by a light brushing of butter; the clove and nutmeg aroma rising from them gratified every nose. The rice was fluffy and white and steaming, under a scattering of parsley. Roast potatoes lay, golden-brown, in the dish with the irresistible promise of soft flouriness beneath the crisp surface. The tender, tasty baby peas played hide and seek with the serving spoon; and the little carrots, sliced finely, soft as butter, were sweet as honey with just a tang of roasting.

Hendrik, aware of the solemnity of the occasion, helped himself with pleasure from the dishes offered him. Eating well, so he believed, had never harmed anyone. He sat at the head of the table in the big old-fashioned room. It should really have been Philip's place, but Miemie had decided otherwise.

He encouraged Leonora: 'Eat now, my dear. Frikkie is at rest. Yes, pour some, Fred, another little glass.'

He handed dish after dish to Philip on his left – the seating was arranged by Miemie, it was her moment of glory, she was entertaining great men of the nation. She and Stoffel too, thank the Lord, held the right views; she wasn't entirely sure of Fred.

Even Philip nodded his approval to Miemie at regular intervals: excellent … the Boland kitchen … excellent … the bean salad, the onions in egg sauce … when had he last? His lips were greasy, he wiped them with his serviette, but also licked them clean. Actually Edna and her ma, old Alet had done the cooking, but Miemie let it pass. She immediately banished the treacherous thought – were Edna and old Alet then Bolanders?

The young people were seated at the other end at an added-on table – one tablecloth folded over the other, only a slight dent betraying the join. No one thought of Koba.

Phil and Emma and Josias sat at the foot of the table, crowded tightly together, Emma in the middle. Emma was to serve the two young men, but her elbows were pressed so close to her sides that she had difficulty moving the spoon from the dish to the plates next to her, especially to Josias's plate, because he was to her right and she was dishing up with her right hand.

'Take the spoon in your left hand, clot,' said Phil. No, she had to serve like that, she had to try. They giggled until a dollop of chicken pie landed on the tablecloth. Josias scooped it up with his knife, lifted his plate, held her wrist so that she emptied the spoon on his plate. Beneath the teasing he was aglow. He sensed something in her too. When she looked at him from under those lashes with those misty dark eyes, his legs felt numb again. She shook her hair back, but it kept tumbling forward when she bent. She had her hands full serving, and she tried blowing her hair away from her face, but didn't succeed.

'Please brush my hair away from my eyes,' she said to Josias. He did it, and as his fingers touched her forehead he felt himself joined to her forever, like the slave in that story. Or was it a goose? Or children? He thought: I would die for you if anyone tried to harm you.

Emma's father had finished eating. He refused a second helping from the dishes offered around again. Held his hand over his glass.

'Oh, come on, Barry,' urged Miemie, who was sitting next to him, but he gestured with his hands: enough.

'I'll always remember this feast,' he said. 'Where we are going I won't have such meals. I was really very pleased to be able to come today. And to bring Phil and Emma. So they'd know something of their ancestry. And enjoy delicious food.' He laughed.

'And where on earth are you off to?' asked Miemie, her eyes still on the dishes being handed around.

Phil again had the injured expression on his face, which Leo had noticed at the airport. He looked at Barry once, then dropped his eyes.

'I'm going to Canada. I've got a five-year contract with a hospital in Vancouver. Option to renew and settle there. Call it by its name: our family is emigrating.'

Even those still eating put down their knives and forks. The other brothers stared at Philip in total amazement, reproach and incomprehension.

'Did you know about this, Philip?'

'Of course I knew. I can't understand him, his private practice is flourishing, he's earning a lot. I don't know what's got into him. And still less what has happened to his feeling for his nation.' He spoke hastily, as if to mask his pain with annoyance.

Miemie, feeling partly responsible, because he had told her first, was speechless. Emigration was a dirty word to her. Like Joiner.

'Come now, Ma,' said Fred. 'The man has a right to his own life.'

It's his wife, thought Miemie, his wife's people had left Rhodesia, those people were jumpy.

Barry indicated the enormous, half-finished dishes of food on the table in front of him with a wide gesture. 'All of you saw what happened this afternoon. Evidently it didn't worry you much. It worried me. And finalised my decision.'

'Heavens, Barry, we aren't made of stone.'

'Right, but you accept the violence. I don't want my children to learn to accept that. I want them to have a carefree youth. I'm going to give them that.' Either the wine, or the opposition he sensed, and the start of – could it be alienation? heightened Barry's colour. Yet he poured himself another glass of wine.

'Oh, come now man, you're not a coward,' Stoffel tried to placate him. 'Well, we've not solved our problems, and we're given hell from overseas, but I can face a struggle. We've fought before.' Stoffel began to eat again, as if the matter were concluded.

The nerve in Robert's cheek was jumping. Robert, supporter of Verwoerd, the man on the President's Council – *Benjamin, my son Benjamin!*

'I've said it all along, we must have our Boer homeland. What Barry says is right, the mess the country is in now is unendurable. We must separate. We must fight for being apart.'

Barry sighed. 'Not again, Oom. It's the end of the twentieth century, we can't remain apart, we've discussed it so often. Don't you remember, Oom, the times we've spoken?'

Benjamin, my son Benjamin!

'Or is Phil afraid of doing border duty?' Robert couldn't stop himself, it had slipped out before he could think. Was it bitterness about Benjamin that had to find expression? That made him want to attack, destroy?

'And Josias, what about you? You're also old enough for the army?'

'Just hang on, Oom, leave them alone.' Fred took a sip of wine, spoke soothingly. 'I know how you feel. I have the same problem with my folks, always harking back to the past. Boer Republics. Those of us living in the city feel differently. I get on well with my black colleagues, they're bloody good, come and have a look where I work. You can't want to keep them down. We're not going backward, we're going forward.'

'Potchefstroom is also a city Fred, don't patronise me.'

'All right, all right, then let each just go his own way. I'm staying here with the blacks, provisionally anyway, as long as I don't get a stone thrown at my head!'

His little joke fell flat, Miemie began to worry about Koba. Fred regretted his flippant remark; he sensed her concern. 'Relax, Ma, Koba isn't serious, thank God.' He jocularly made a sign of the cross on his chest, a gesture that displeased both his ooms and his parents. 'Let's relax. And now the ooms from the Transvaal must tell me: how do they view the business this afternoon? A stone thrown at my sister's head? Here in a peaceful rural area?'

'Deliberate, insolent aggression,' Robert said immediately.

'Result of too many concessions,' Philip said. 'Give a finger and they take the whole hand.' He had never been in favour of their Tricameral Parliament, probably because of the President's Council which had meant the end of the Senate. And the end of his career as senator. 'And I can't see your cosmetic councils achieving much either, Robert.'

Fred held his fork by the handle, turned it round and round, traced lines on the tablecloth. His ma feared he would leave marks, it was an extra-large damask cloth she'd borrowed, but she restrained herself from reprimanding him.

'Not a symptom of a deep, unexpressed frustration, Oom?'

'What frustration? They've never had it so good.'

Robert's face suddenly seemed sharp to Leo, like a rodent's.

'Well then, we'll leave it at that,' said Fred and put the fork down, to his mother's relief.

But Barry didn't want to leave it at that. 'You talk of frustration, Fred, I'm speaking about gradually slipping into chaos. Will things improve? One can't clean a bath if the tap running dirty water isn't turned off. And no one cares a damn about turning off the tap – truly a task of Sisyphus, just use stronger cleaning agents, more force, stronger hands scrubbing. Until the cleaning agents begin to erode the hands. Therefore I say: No more of this. It's mental suicide to stay here.'

Stoffel, who'd drunk quite a lot of wine, tried to save the day. 'Barry, don't take this afternoon's business so seriously, the police are in there already, it's over man, past, maybe just a bit of Saturday afternoon drunkenness.'

'Exactly,' said Barry. 'Over. Till when? Just stronger cleaning agents. In my experience the hands have already started to erode. I want my children's hands to stay whole.'

The pudding was set out in bowls on the sideboard; everyone helped themselves.

The members of the big family around the table were about to take up their spoons and bring the first scoop of orange mousse with the crisp crust of the apple tart, and the tartness of the filling, the tang of the sweet, brown brandy tart, to their mouths, when a loud high scream was heard from the kitchen. They put down spoons, looked up. After the scream came wailing – the age-old wailing of a woman who, helpless against the onslaught of life, throws her apron over her head and calls upon the heavens.

Miemie pushed back her chair so that it fell over, indicating with a gesture of her arm that the others should remain seated. She hastened to the kitchen. They heard the thwack of a hard slap, then the keening stopped. Before Barry could get up to help Miemie, before Leo could rise from her chair, Miemie was at the dining room door again, a bright red spot burning on each cheek.

'Hysterics,' she said. 'Everything is always a great drama. As Stoffel said: Saturday drunkenness. Edna's son came to tell of a stabbing in the township. I said they could go. No, Barry, they've been to the doctor already. We'll clear the table. Come, come, eat. Come, Belle; come Oom Hendrik, Oom Robert; come, Tannie Leonora, don't scorn my puddings. Eat. Come Leo. What about you, Fred?'

They finished the meal in silence. The tension caused by Barry's news and the keening which had intruded like a presentiment of evil in the house – not to be glossed over by Miemie's efforts – on top of the funeral had completely drained their energy. Weariness with arguments that led nowhere, the ominous realisation of an ominous future, came down on them.

The older ones' heads were nodding, they needed to go to bed.

The group staying over with Miemie were taken in Stoffel's car. They came upon Arnold in the back of the car, actually heard his snoring before they saw him. Miemie moved in next to him, took his head on her lap.

'My Boetie is so tired,' she said, 'kept watch next to Pa for so many nights. I'm taking him home.'

The car stank of liquor.

'I'll come and tidy up tomorrow,' said Miemie. Belle went to sit next to her in the back, and Holtzhausen got in the front. Hendrik took his two brothers and Barry back to the hotel. The young ones would walk back to where they were staying.

The young ones?

'It's amazing,' Leo told Fred, 'to realise only now that it was my own cousin who took the photo that was so much acclaimed overseas. Congratulations, even though belatedly.'

'Thanks, Leo. A lucky shot.'

'It's quite something, isn't it, the way you guys catch the whole damn thing, without the bias journalists are always accused of. Photos can't lie.'

'Don't be so sure, one day I'll show you how we can slant things when we feel like it.'

They lingered at table. He was Leo's only contemporary at the funeral, except for the wretched Koba. He'd recently returned from Europe, Miemie had said, that was why he and Leo hadn't come across each other before. He had inherited his Ouma Kowie's rusty brown hair, his hair was quite long and curled in his neck, his eyebrows were thick, and there were a few pale freckles across the bridge of his nose. In turn he studied his cousin appreciatively. From her ankles to her short fair hair. Ankles that met his approval. And the lively greenish-blue eyes.

Leo thought of something to say. 'Quite an evening, hey? First Oom Barry's news and then the bloodcurdling scream, as if to underline it. How does the saying go? Voices prophesying doom – something like that. Strange end to the day.'

'Oom Barry should be left to do his own thing, I don't have a problem with that. It's his life.' He took her hand playfully. 'Hey, leave the dishes. Tomorrow is another day. Oupa's photos interest me, come to the attic with me: we can look through his stuff.'

'You're married, aren't you?' she said as she climbed up the steps to the attic ahead of him.

'Divorced.' He shrugged casually, as if talking to himself. 'Made the mistake all artists and photographers make: married the model. I travel around too much, too many other interests. She just couldn't understand. So she walked out on me. Finis.'

'Children?' asked Leo. He couldn't be much older that her, yet she had seen flecks of grey in his hair and even his eyebrows. He had beautiful hands, articulate hands, he spoke with them.

'Fortunately not.'

They pushed the door open and went into the studio, saw the camp bed where Oom Arnold had slept that afternoon. He picked up the bottle on the floor next to the bed, and shook his head. Put it down again.

'That oom of mine is in a mess,' he said. 'It gets to my ma. They're twins, you know. Maybe it's frustration with his job. He had aptitude, but not Oupa's talent. Oupa was outstanding, you know.'

'And you?'

He mocked. 'Just as outstanding.'

'Wait,' she said, 'bend your head.' She carefully gripped a single grey hair standing up in a curl from his left eyebrow, and quickly pulled it out.

'Ouch! What was that about?'

'Just an impulse.'

With the touch of her fingers to the ridge of his eyebrow, the intimacy of the slight dampness of his skin, she felt a response in her body, sudden and unexpected. She sensed it in him too. She turned away, walked to the display boards with photos, adjusted one that hung askew. The attic had an air of desolation, of neglect, of something past. He followed her, he was the type of man with a physical presence one would always be aware of, she thought, and she was a little irritated by that. Yet she stood so that his arm, indicating a photo across her shoulder, rested lightly against her.

'We must make something of this, perhaps organise a retrospective exhibition.'

She nodded.

'A bygone era. Gentle decay of the late bourgeoisie.'

She thought of the afternoon and the stone and the hundreds of other stones and the burning and the fear. And his photo which had shown the world the black woman carrying her dying child away from the Casspir.

He sat down on the camp bed and gestured to her to join him.

He took her hand and absently stroked it with his rough, long, thin fingers, from her fingertips to the wrist. He looked thoughtfully at what he was doing. She found the tension the slow stroking sent through her body difficult to endure. Then he put her hand down, and as if something had been confirmed, continued to chat.

'Well, the ooms have to come to terms with the stone against my sister's head. What did they call it: Deliberate? Impudent ? Aggression? Result of too many concessions? Our dear parents have no idea of the deep inarticulate frustration. Come and help me, let's pick up some photos and try to arrange them.'

The three youngest were left behind in the dining room with nothing to do. It was too early to go to bed. 'Let's take the glasses and pudding dishes to the kitchen,' Emma suggested. 'Just look at all the serviettes lying on the floor.' She began picking them up.

Phil soon grew tired of it. Emma washed the glasses and dishes, and Josias clumsily helped dry them. He took the wet dishes from her carefully, shy of touching her fingers. 'Gosh, it's hot in the kitchen.' Emma wiped her forehead with her fingers, shook her hair back again.

Like a pony, thought Josias, just like a lovely pony with a black mane. He couldn't believe she was going to go away, it couldn't be. He too had forgotten about his sister, about the drunkenness in the township, about the keening in the kitchen.

'Would you like to see my pigeons?' he asked.

Phil had fallen asleep on the sofa in the lounge.

She nodded. They went, quietly and seriously, out by the front path, then turned back, past the attic steps, heard Fred and Leo talking and laughing up in the studio, walked round the back of the garage to reach the pigeon loft. The sky was cloudless, dark and far, with the dryness of summer, the stars sparkled like diamonds. Suddenly they saw the moon, big and round and yellow, rising from behind the mountains, it seemed as though the stars made way for it.

Josias heard Emma catch her breath.

He stammered, 'I'll always think of you when I see the full moon. Always and always.'

'And I'll think of you.'

'It's always cloudy in Canada, you won't be able to think of me often.'

'I'll come back, I know I'll come back. Do you think I look forward to all that cold and snow? I'll just finish school there, then I'll come back.'

'Then I'll be in the army when you come back,' said Josias.

The dreadful net of the army, and the even more dreadful prospect of refusing army duty and going to jail, loomed up to both of them.

'Actually I want to go to the army,' he said. 'After all, it is my country.' He became bolder. 'I just wish we could live on another planet, just you and me.'

'On one of the stars, let's choose one for us,' she said.

He pointed at one. 'That one, no, that.'

She also tried to point. 'How can I tell which one you're pointing at? There're thousands. You'll see, we'll miss each other on the stars. What on earth can we do so that we don't miss each other on the stars?'

She laughed at her words, so did he, but their laughter was forced and nervous as if something inside them took their breath away.

As they were standing there, he put his arms around her awkwardly. She stood stiffly in his embrace, her head bent, she dared not lift it, then his mouth was near hers. She had so often dreamt what it would be like to stand in a boy's arms, pressed against his shoulder, her cheek on his chest, and then the first slow lifting of her head, his lips on hers. And there she was, standing stiffly, too afraid to move.

Perhaps he would kiss her this evening, it would be her first kiss.

Perhaps he wouldn't kiss her, and then, she knew, she would cry into her pillow. Not only for this evening, but about always, for in her heart she knew she wouldn't be coming back.

She could hear him breathing. But then he took his arms away from her. He opened the door of the loft, had her bend down and pushed her in ahead of him.

The pigeons, their sleep disturbed, came to rest on her shoulders, her head and hands, pushed against her chest with fluttering wings.

Josias grabbed at the pigeons. 'They're my oupa's and my pigeons, we used to come here every afternoon … my oupa and I …'

He was the first to show he was heartbroken about his oupa that afternoon, thought Emma.

He tried not to show it, but his voice was rough as if he was struggling not to cry. 'Every afternoon … he'd say the pigeons should fly up to heaven on his behalf when he died.'

She held a couple of pigeons against her. She had to hold something, her body and hands reached out for something warm and pulsing to hold. Josias tossed a pigeon away and grabbed another, which fluttered and resisted, the little feathers got up his nose. It became a compulsive game. When the pigeons slowed down and settled on the roosts, he waved his arms to chase them up again, come, come, come, he didn't want it to end.

When she was tired of playing, she leaned back against the roost. He came nearer and put his arms around her, but more firmly this time. Her face was full of pigeon feathers. He blew the feathers away and leaned forward until he could feel her lips beneath his mouth. It was a bit spitty, he thought, and that excited him. He kissed her, he did what he thought a boy would do to kiss a girl. He drew back rather shyly.

The whole way they walked back to the hotel he only got up enough courage to take the pigeon feathers out of her hair. The feathers stuck to his fingers.

And she cried into her pillow after all, because he didn't kiss her when they said good night. Maybe he was too shy in the bright light on the hotel stoep, she thought. And he was going to the army, and she wouldn't be coming back.

'Stoffel,' Miemie said to her husband in the bedroom that night, reassured after they had been to the hospital again and found Koba sleeping peacefully, 'Stoffel, that cousin of mine from Johannesburg is a bit funny. D'you know what she said to me? After the funeral and everything. Like it's been worrying her all day: "Was Amy's baby a boy or a girl?" Amy's child? I don't know any Amy, I said, but she kept on: "Amy who was expecting Edward's child. Edward is married to Angela and he so badly wants a little boy." Then I twigged it was those people in the soapie I also watch sometimes. But she talks like they're real people, she'd missed it on the way here, so she wanted to know, it worried her.'

Stoffel was accustomed to his wife's need to talk just when he wanted to sleep. 'Shame,' he said as his eyes closed. Yes, it really was a shame, thought Miemie. Didn't she have any other friends? That SussieBelle who'd had such a privileged childhood, who was actually richer than her and Arnold and cleverer, and went to university, and overseas. What could she show for it now? Pleasantly self-satisfied, she settled down to sleep.

But she couldn't fall asleep. She was overtired, she thought, but knew that wasn't the truth. At last she leaned across Stoffel, shook his shoulder. 'I lied this evening, Stoffel. It wasn't a stabbing that made Edna scream like that. The child came to tell her the police had taken her son and three others from the township. About the stone-throwing. They were taken to the cells. I couldn't tell that, could I? They still had to have their pudding. How could I spoil the pudding?'

Now that her conscience was clear, she lay back with a sigh and fell asleep.

6

By Sunday morning Koba was no better. The doctor phoned: she wasn't sleeping, she was in a coma. He suspected haemorrhaging between the skull and the membrane of the brain. She was transferred to Tygerberg Hospital by ambulance. Various neurologists would be consulted; they'd have to decide whether or not to operate.

Miemie and Stoffel were at the hospital early on Sunday morning. They stood by, dismayed as the narrow bed was wheeled into the ambulance, the door slammed, and the vehicle left for Cape Town.

Stoffel told his elder son, 'My God, Fred, you know I keep a pistol taped under the dashboard, why the hell didn't you fire a couple of shots? When the stone hit you, you could have fired into the bunch, the more you hit the better. But no, you're a kaffir lover, a Commie, even when your own sister gets a stone thrown at her.'

Josias spent hours in his pigeon loft. That's why he didn't get a first-class matric pass, his ma complained, she'd confused the dates, because by then the exam was long past.

Josias was pining for Emma. He had no appetite. Miemie and Stoffel discussed it in their bedroom at night; who would have thought he was so fond of his sister?

Hendrik, Holtzhausen and Belle went to Cape Town, but stayed at the Mount Nelson Hotel. They only stayed for two days. Hendrik had flowers sent to the hospital on behalf of all of them, but the nurses put them on a little table in the corridor; the poor girl was unaware of her surroundings.

When Leo asked her parents to stay with her, Belle said, 'No, dear, I'd better stay in the hotel with your oom. He'll be lost without us. We'll come to tea with you this afternoon.'

Belle took little interest in the house although it actually belonged to her, and this was where her mother had lived and died. It meant nothing to her. Holtzhausen, who still had the unpleasant memory of the Sunday after the murder of his mother-in-law, visited his daughter reluctantly, but was relieved: the house was so changed, all the old furniture had gone, the dreaded recollection faded. He stood on the back stoep and looked at the garden. Still just as neglected, he thought.

Hendrik didn't feel at home in the house; he was too big for the chairs, too stiff to sit on the low couch. They drank tea, ate a piece of store-bought tart, then left. Leo had dinner with them at the hotel that night; early the next morning they left for the Transvaal again.

Barry and his children's visit to Cape Town was more successful. Leo arranged for Neville – a coloured friend, Oom, only platonic, don't worry – to take them to climb Table Mountain. Up Platteklip Gorge. The children went up like mountain goats. Barry and Leo and Neville climbed more slowly, they discussed political affairs. Barry listened to Neville and his ideas reluctantly, he wasn't sorry to be leaving so he didn't need to become involved in their so called 'struggle'. Had they stood still, they would have been able to turn and look down on the hazy flats, shimmering in the heat, which extended south-west of Devil's Peak, and could have brought the low, fort-like building of Tygerberg Hospital as well as the ever-growing fungus of the squatters' camp into view, as though in the lens of a camera.

Koba still lay in Tygerberg, skull shaved, inert as a block of wood.

Black women walked across the road separating the Port Jackson bushes from the squatters' camp, carrying bundles of wood on their heads to the shacks that shot up daily like mushrooms.

'Do you know, Oom,' said Leo, 'when it became too bad, when the shacks were demolished daily, only to be built again during the night, the people went underground, literally underground: dig a hole and cover it with a plank of corrugated iron or plastic. A hole can't be demolished. Doesn't it move you?'

Leo pulled a twig from an aromatic bush – buchu or something like it – so roughly that her fingers were scratched and a line of blood oozed out. 'Smell that, Oom. Smell it. Doesn't it touch a chord in you? It's your country. Just keep on smelling it. Where will you smell that in Canada? I hate it that you're leaving, we need you here, Oom.'

When they stopped to rest and drink from a spring – the youngsters had gone ahead – she went to sit on the ground next to Barry. She filled her hands with earth and pebbles, poured it from one hand to the other. 'It's my earth, this is me. That frozen business over there is not for me.'

Neville had swung the backpack from his shoulder, took out cans of beer. 'Have a beer, boss,' he mocked as he opened it and the liquid bubbled up. There'd been unvoiced antagonism between Neville and Barry the whole morning. Leo couldn't understand it. Barry who had worked in Baragwanath Hospital for so many years. Was Neville perhaps the first educated coloured man he had spoken to? It was incredible. It made her behave aggressively.

'I think you're also doing the country an injustice, Oom. You've been trained here, you have had all your experience here. And now?'

'No, wait a minute, Leo,' said Neville, who lay stretched out on the ground. 'Many of our black people have also left voluntarily. In protest. We don't blame them. You can't blame your uncle.'

'His leaving isn't in protest.' She felt like saying it was to retain his comfortable lifestyle, but didn't.

'Oom Barry, Neville is a very special person. We are colleagues. Neville will take risks for my sake, and I for his. He has suffered, I haven't suffered. He doesn't hold it against me. May I tell him, Neville?'

'Skip it, Leo, what's done is done.'

'His brother is paralysed. A shot fired into a crowd. Fourteen years old and he'll never walk again.'

Neville hit the bushes in front of him with a twig. He was embarrassed, felt he'd been put in the wrong by having a personal motive ascribed to him instead of the more important moral considerations.

He said, 'To misquote Stalin: one boy lamed is a tragedy, one thousand wounded is a statistic. But I didn't come here to be held up as a martyr.'

Leo pushed against him playfully: 'Now you're being perverse. We only know the statistics. It's important to know the people. And it's important that resistance should come from inside, from within our own ranks. Our uprising is not only for the sake of Neville's people, it's also for the sake of our own people, to open their eyes. Once one's eyes have opened, and one can see for the first time, something wonderful happens. It's an undeserved privilege to be accepted as a comrade in the struggle. It's something indescribable, Oom. I'll never forget the first time one of my coloured colleagues called me comrade.'

'She's quite something, hey,' said Neville, teasing. 'Got to control her, man, nothing like the newly converted.'

Barry wondered what was hidden behind Neville Baatjies's joking. Was it bitterness he was hiding? Was the jocular teasing a front? Did he trust them? More importantly: did he trust Leo? The thought plagued him. Could he then trust Neville? Trust his people? Now they made use of whites, but later? He thought of 'later' with revulsion.

Leo was still talking. She was so vulnerable, he thought. Leo in her enthusiasm, her total commitment.

'You must understand, Oom: the more difficult it is to see evil in your own people – it's not easy, it hurts – the more valuable it is. It's nothing very marvellous to try to reach light from the dark. If you're suffering yourself, it's natural that you should fight for better conditions. But if you aren't suffering yourself, if you just are aware that the light around you is a false light, and can't endure carrying on in that false light, then you have a tougher battle, first through the dark, then to a purer light. A friend once told me we whites in South Africa are mummies – anachronisms that belong in museums.'

Barry was fit, his pulse rate had barely increased from the exercise. He climbed without a hat, was pleased to feel the sun on his tanned skin. Fleetingly the bitter thought: Where would he find sun in Canada? Tan under infra-red lights? He'd miss his sport. Perhaps ski with the children?

Leo was still speaking. 'When you think how spiritually warped our people have become, just to retain political power, then you're actually doing them a favour by helping them to see.'

'Then you're still a racist, Leo. I'm disappointed. Still "your" people, you still separate from me.' Neville sighed exaggeratedly.

Barry heard the pretence in the sigh, was suddenly disappointed that he'd allowed himself to listen to the argument. It spoilt the morning. Fleetingly the image of Belle rose before him. As a young girl at table with his father: her brave, useless words. He took another mouthful of beer.

'You mean that the people in control will be hit harder if one of their own people took the stone and shattered the false mirrors in which they were looking. Is that right Leo?'

'Not quite. Someone spoke of "the power of re-entry" which is important if the resistance is to be meaningful. But it presupposes that the borders around groups remain intact. I envisage something more open. To use a corny word: just plain humanity.'

At one point, when Neville had gone ahead to Phil and Emma, she said, 'I also have a feeling for my nation and country, no matter how oppressive it is. And it's terribly difficult to have to ask: were nation and fatherland just chimeras? Something we had been made to believe? My only way to cope with it is to try to help bring an end to the injustice they are inflicting on others.'

'Reason enough, Leo,' said Barry. 'But is suffering humanity itself not the main concern? Now I speak as a doctor. When I sew up a wound, I only know: I am helping this person to suffer less. No national pride or national penance or anything personal like that is involved. No specific nation, simply people. That's why I can leave.'

'Oh, I know my thoughts are confused. You're right, it concerns humanity. The human being himself. But while these structures are in place people will continue to suffer. We are battling against the structures.'

Fred, who had visited Leo a few days after his return to the city, also went climbing with them one Saturday morning.

'This cousin of yours is a firebrand, Fred, you'll have to keep an eye on her,' said Barry. He winked at Fred, he suspected his words were unnecessary, he sensed something between them. It made him feel old.

'Second cousin,' said Leo, blushing, and that confirmed his suspicion.

But Fred put his arm around her shoulder. 'Not named Leo in vain. Trust me, I'll look after her. We're in this together.'

A departing ship sounded its horn in the harbour. Barry, with sudden self-hate, heard it and wished he was on the ship, on his way, leaving forever.

7

Every Wednesday afternoon and every Sunday afternoon Miemie and Stoffel sat next to Koba's bed in the Tygerberg Hospital in Bellville. She lay in a two-bedded room, but the other bed was empty. Somebody would be coming, said the sister, but the bed remained empty week after week.

Miemie and Stoffel moved the straight chair from under the second bed and put it next to the one at Koba's bed. They didn't speak much. Sometimes Miemie leaned forward to touch Koba's right hand, which made a bump under the cover. Sometimes Stoffel did, while sighing deeply.

Koba's head lay flat on the mattress, without pillows. In the large vein at her left wrist a pipe had been inserted. The plastic bag with the coloured liquid hung next to her bed fixed on a tall steel stand. The liquid ran, very slowly, into a small funnel, formed a drop, which went down the transparent pipe slowly. Sometimes a nurse entered the room to prod at the bag and check how much was still in it. Should the bag run dry and an air bubble reach the vein, Koba would die.

Miemie and Stoffel watched the liquid falling into the pipe drop by drop, running into Koba's blue vein.

Under the bed, on the side where they sat, hung another plastic bag fixed to a pipe. The liquid Koba's body discharged ran into this. Drop by drop the amber urine fell in the bag.

Strange, thought Stoffel, water running into the body and water running out of the body, just slightly discoloured – is that what life was?

Koba's eyes were closed. Her hair had been shaved and there was a white bandage around her head. On the day of her arrival at the hospital the doctors had decided to drill through her skull, lift a part of it, to look. Could they remove the blood? Remove all the blood?

She hadn't regained consciousness after the operation. The doctor said: You must keep hoping. The time of miracles has not passed. On a Wednesday afternoon of the third week they had sat there, Miemie told Stoffel, 'Our child is going to die. The Lord is not going to grant us the miracle.'

But Stoffel wasn't paying attention. He had risen and was standing at the window. The window could not be opened or closed, it had a slightly smoky colour, the world outside looked strange. Koba's room was on the fifth floor, he could see far. He looked out on the N1 highway which passed the Carl Bremer Hospital beyond the low hills; the cars passed like silent vehicles in a dream, small, flat, dark. Had he been able to see further, to the level of the sea, to the horizon, he would have seen the flat, dark outline of Robben Island.

Each afternoon the world seemed unreal to him through that window. When he went up the wide steps at the entrance to the hospital, went up in the lift, and walked down the twilight corridor with the low ceiling, he left reality behind. He was filled with fear when he pushed open Koba's door, allowed Miemie to enter first, followed her, and once the door closed behind them, they were enclosed in this strange glass space that admitted no sound from outside. Secure, with the presence of death their only companion. Was the perceptible presence of death, he wondered, a pre-condition for this quiet seclusion of spirit? And of body? Outside the wind howled, the heat lay heavily, there was a sudden cold snap, but inside, the air remained tepid around them

Miemie sat on the edge of her chair, strained, tension in her face and the tight line of her lips.

'Our child is going to die,' she said again, 'because I lied.' Her face had become puffy during the past few weeks, her eyes smaller.

He heard. He replied with divided attention, 'Oh, my love, it was after a tough day, what you said didn't harm anyone. You must forget about it, you mustn't blame yourself for Koba's condition.'

She laid her head on the bed cover, on the shape of Koba's right hand. 'My little Kobatjie.' But there was no response from the motionless body on the bed. The previous time when they'd come in, Koba's eyes had been open. They had hurried to her, delighted, made little sounds of affection. The eyes had looked, but not seen. They found it almost worse, the staring eyes without any recognition, the closed still eyelids were almost preferable.

Then Miemie looked at Stoffel, a frown on her forehead. She whispered almost conspiratorially, 'When people sympathise with me, and say it's God's will, my thoughts run this way and that. Then I don't know what to say. Because it always comes back to the lie.'

He turned away from the window, and came to sit on the chair next to her again. 'Then rather talk,' he said, also whispering. 'It's better than the silence.'

'Even if it was Edna's child throwing the stone, he surely couldn't have aimed it at Koba. Just thrown in amongst all the cars. It must have been fated that the stone hit Koba. I could accept that, I think, from the hand of the Lord. In these troubled times.'

The frown on her forehead deepened. She pulled her skirt, which kept creeping up, over her knees, laid her hand on Koba's again. Still whispering, as if Koba, lying there, would be able to hear; as if it were in the old days when they whispered in the bedroom at night so that the children wouldn't hear.

'Why didn't I just say that the police had four children, one of them Edna's, in the cells because of the stone that had hit Koba? Because it would have dragged us all into the incident? Was I afraid that one of the family – perhaps Fred, yes, Fred would do it for his sister – would rush to the police cells and create difficulties? Was I just not wanting to create difficulties?'

Stoffel took her hand and stroked it. 'Quiet now, dear. We all do things we can't understand. You were overwrought, you'd just buried your father, you had to attend to a house full of people.'

'But Edna is staying away from work, sending messages does no good. And old Alet doesn't come to do the washing on Mondays any more.'

'You know what they're like,' Stoffel said.

No, I don't know, she suddenly thought. I don't know at all. After all these years.

But she was tired from all the thinking, and all the talking. She told Stoffel, 'We might as well go.'

They got up, but before they could bend down to kiss Koba's forehead, the door opened and the nurse brought in a big arrangement of flowers. All the colours of the rainbow, light pink gladioli, long-stemmed yellow roses, blue cornflowers, pale pink roses, lilac larkspurs, light yellow asters, single and double, little white flowers like fine rain, green foliage. A motionless silence lay over the flowers, as if they were artificial. But they gave off a faint perfume.

The nurse placed the flowers on the table next to the second bed. 'They won't get in the way here. To the unknown patient,' she offered a little joke.

Miemie read the card. 'From Hendrik, Bella and Holtzhausen, again,' she said. 'It must have cost him a fortune.'

Then she began to cry.

'Sorry,' said the nurse, 'I didn't mean to …' She handed Miemie a tissue. 'You've been so brave until now. Don't let a few flowers upset you.'

She leaned on Stoffel's shoulder. 'So many lies,' she sobbed, 'and I didn't know.'

8

On the mountain Fred had told Barry: 'Don't worry, I'll take care, Leo and I are in this together.' Yet she sometimes wondered whether they really understood each other's motives. But she tried to banish the doubt from her mind. He was often out of town. In addition to his normal job with an advertising agency, he took commissions from overseas for news photos. With the latest strict boycott of journalists and photographers, the taking and smuggling out of riot photos had become a dangerous art. Photos of police brutality were high on the list of overseas priorities.

'I have to be where the action is,' he told Leo. 'And if there isn't news, I create my own news!'

Once at dusk he said, 'We're going to Tygerberg this evening to see Koba in hospital. Duty, my girl, so I can tell Ma I've been there.'

The visit distressed her. Neither he nor she went again.

In Oupa Frikkie's attic the afternoon after the funeral, prompted by his famous photo of the black woman with the dead child in her arms, Leo had asked him, 'Tell me, would you, had you been able, have wanted to photograph the boy who threw the stone at Koba?'

'Why not?' was his reply. 'One hell of an action shot, hey? Funeral procession, oppressive heat, hearse taking the white patriarch to his grave, oppressed masses observing in silence …'

'Your own sister.'

'I would want to photograph it, but I wouldn't be able to sell it.'

'Why not?'

'Because, my dear Leo, I'm honest or cynical enough to know there is no market for a shot like that.'

'Why not?'

'Use your head, Leo. Koba, as symbol of the apartheid regime, as they say overseas, deserves a stone to the head.'

'Koba as silent witness? Like all of us? A scapegoat.'

'Exactly.'

'Poor Koba. So randomly selected. In lieu of all of us.'

They didn't talk much on the way back from the hospital. A young man who had come to visit Koba had remained seated at the bed when they left. Her boyfriend? How little she knew about Koba, thought Leo. How arrogant her attitude had been. She'd turned and walked back, not to Koba, but to him. Just stood next to him for a few moments. 'We keep believing that she'll recover,' she told him. 'We must keep believing.' He didn't impress her as a weak person. But the dejected attitude of the body and shoulders in the straight chair next to the bed stayed with her for days.

Fred was visiting her regularly. He took possession of the house. He hung his fisherman's jacket, with the multitude of pockets heavy with photographic equipment, over a chair, and made himself at home. The house began to absorb his smell, his personality. His aluminium case stood on her table, from the pigeonholes came lenses, filters, films. He was continually selecting, sorting, replacing. Sometimes he drank the coffee she brought him absently, sometimes he pushed everything aside to grab her in his arms. His physical presence overwhelmed her.

He brought her a bunch of yellow asters and shoved the stems in a vase of water, placed it in the dining room in the full sun.

'That's how I want to see you, always with flowers, yellow flowers and sunshine.' He swung her to him, pressed her head to his chest, kissed her till she was dizzy, then pushed her away, drew his fingers through her hair. 'Now remember. Yellow flowers and sun. Always.'

She laughed uncertainly. Still breathless, she asked, 'How can I guarantee sun? Why does it sound like fair-weather love, Fred, as though you're warning me?'

'Warning against all the soul-searching, girl. There's more to life than suffering. I want that frown on your face to disappear.'

'One gets so involved.'

She leaned against him. He pushed her away slightly again, looked her full in the face. 'Involved with me, that's what I want.'

She put her arms around his neck. 'I'm much too taken up by you, you very nearly make me forget.'

'Not nearly enough. Every weekend – for how many weeks? – you're away, busy.'

'I have no option, Fred. It's like you with your cameras.'

'My camera hungers for its pictures, my lambkin.'

'And I,' she said as if it surprised her, 'hunger for my people suffering on the Flats.'

He was an unpredictable lover.

Sometimes she felt disappointed that the tension that rose so rapidly in both their bodies at the merest touch was defused just as rapidly by him. Then she felt his attention was not on her, but elsewhere. At other times he could not get enough of the tiniest detail; of her face and her body; he was slow and calculating in his caresses, until the tension mounted unbearably in her. And the intensity of their coming together left her body exhausted.

The State of Emergency continued. Resistance at schools flared up and died down again. Leo was sometimes at home, aimless, for days. Mr Abrahams was adamant: 'You may not fear for your life, I do. The children lose their heads when they see a white face. Not all of them know you. Nor will you get through the police barricades. It's dreadful, the hatred and counter-hatred. They're burning people, Miss, they set people alight.'

Fred was excited beyond reason. He risked police barricades. He went out early and stayed away till late; came back tired and sweaty, begrimed with dust and soot. His eyes glowed with achievement.

'These are priceless images, my girl, if I go on like this, I will capture images for the whole world, for generations to come. It's history, Leo, history.'

She was swept away by his excitement. At the election the swing was so much to the right that the Conservative Party replaced the Progressive Federal Party as official opposition.

'It's catastrophic, Leo,' Fred said. 'Have people gone mad?'

From contacts in London he had news that the armed struggle was to intensify and that the local underground network of freedom fighters was to be increased. The State of Emergency was once again extended.

'PW Botha is cornered. Now just wait and see what he'll do: What was it your oom said: stronger cleaning agents until the hands themselves are corroded.'

But he had not expected it to be so extreme. In August he came home on a rainy afternoon. 'The final knock-out blow! From now on we're all dumb. All news and pictures will in future be provided to the media here and overseas by the government itself.'

He poured himself a glass of red wine. 'We drink to the resistance of the Fourth Estate! I'll not be dictated to so easily. My camera is my voice.'

Leo feared for his safety; he was spending every night in her house, his belongings in her cupboards. She passed anxiously until she saw his little pale blue car in front of her door again.

Early one Sunday morning there was a phone call from Fred's colleague, Cedric Kumalo. Leo grabbed the phone.

'Is Fred with you? Give ...' She passed the phone to him, she heard Cedric's breathless voice. 'All hell's loose, man, what you've been waiting for. Your chance, man. Get here quick.'

He gave him directions; a black child would wait for him next to the N2.

'Twenty quid, hey, he won't do it for less.'

With the pictures he took that morning, he made, as he had predicted, his own news.

His excitement mounted as he drove along the main road to the townships, saw the rows of Casspirs, at last picked up the child, swung the car across the central ridge through the oleanders, avoided the animals on the sandy road. The wheels spun in the sand, but he made it. In the distance in front he saw the red flames dancing over the shack roofs; how they licked, licked at the roofs, leaped up, fell back. A dance of flames against the hazy blue sky. Then he smelled the stench of burning rubber; deeper in the township where the great forbidden double highway ran, he saw the ominous spirals of thick black smoke that is caused by burning tyres.

When he stopped, partly behind a dune, the child who had sat in front next to him, was out of the car, beckoned him on. He grabbed his two cameras, felt automatically whether his spare equipment was in his pockets, slammed the car door, and hurried up the dune after the child. From afar he could hear the uproar and screaming, the thud-thud of shots, the senseless shouting through loudspeakers: Disperse! Disperse, or we'll shoot!

But they were already shooting, and the children streamed like lava between the houses in the direction of the row of Casspirs drawn up across the road; bare black legs and white vests and black arms throwing stones; nothing could stop them. Behind them houses burned, shops burned, a delivery van had been overturned and lay smouldering.

He had the camera with the zoom lens to his eye. He shot, held his finger on the button, the motor-drive whined as he fired off shot after shot. Then he lowered the camera, grabbed the second one with the close-up, wide-angle lens and began shooting, caught the expressions on faces; rage, fear, hatred. Then again the zoom lens, on the Casspirs, the faces of the policemen. God, what was it? Fear? Callousness? What made them do it? Their faces just as grim as those burning and throwing. But they fired accurately. The horde descending upon them began to retire. Then a new wave of violence erupted; the dry veld, where the police had rolled out razor wire, started to blaze. Women had appeared with buckets of water; cloths; helped those that had been shot to get away. He had gradually, as he took photos, walked nearer; he was out of the sand, on rocks.

His second spool was full, he was about to reload, when he felt the blow. A weight hit his shoulder and he lost his balance. His camera with the zoom lens swung away and as he fell, he heard it hit a rock. He couldn't regain his balance and tumbled forward, onto his second camera. He felt pain shoot through his chest, then he no longer felt it for rage had taken possession of him. As he pushed himself up and grabbed at the camera, he saw shards of the filter on the stone, and knew: the film was destroyed, for the side had torn open. He saw the boot of a policeman descend on the second camera. Power he had never known before surged through his body. He turned sideways and aimed a punch that sent the policeman reeling. Only to be pulled down by a police dog on a chain. Two men had to get the dog off him, he was pulled to his feet – to see the remains of his two cameras left behind on the rock, the torn aluminium alloy of the adaptor ring in pieces, like a wound. Handcuffs were put on his wrists and he had to stumble through the sand over the dunes to the police van.

Leo lay awake at night, counted the beams of light that passing cars threw against her bedroom wall. No news reached her. His colleague, Cedric, stayed away. She tortured herself with questions: Where is Fred? What had happened to him? She knew his fiery temper. He couldn't control it. Didn't he know she'd be worried sick? Didn't he love her? The yellow flowers were sere and faded in the vase before she heard of his detention. The news had reached his firm in a roundabout way.

Neville, her teaching colleague, came to Leo toward the end of the week. 'It's getting rough with us. Hundreds, thousands of people are being detained, they don't even know the reason. If they have a pamphlet in the hand, simply picked it up somewhere, they're carted off. With this new State of Emergency, for the umpteenth time, they mean business, pal.'

'Where can I look for Fred, where may I find him? How do I find out?' She had heard about the police dog. How badly was he injured? She, the strong one, the one with experience, felt helpless in her reaction. 'I must surely be able to reach him, take him money and food ... see him ...?'

She felt ashamed that she'd ever doubted his commitment.

'No ways. They say nothing. Don't give names, don't say where they're detained. True's God, they talk of 8 000 in detention. Where they're kept, goodness knows. Our bunch and I will be off one of these days. Our problem is the little printing press. They're watching us. We simply can't stop the work. We're printing innocuous stuff, God knows. Just to help the children a bit: How to cope with detention. How to prepare for detention. What to tell your folks; to know your ID number off by heart, find out how to reach an attorney, what your rights will be. We want to prepare the kids, pal, otherwise they can't take it. They do have rights. They must know what they are.'

They stood talking in the passage. He didn't want to sit down.

'It's too dangerous at our place, we need somewhere for the printing press.'

Leo knew he was hinting at the empty garage. Now and then street children came to the lean-to, not regularly.

She nodded. 'Fine.'

And so it happened that the little panel van was reversed to the door of the garage. The little iron printing press was manhandled down over a plank, and reams and reams of paper were unloaded. Then they began printing. An innocuous little pamphlet: *How to cope with detention*.

It could have been innocuous, the activity in the garage. Building, painting, renovation – coloured or black people were not conspicuous in back yards. Corrugated iron sheets were moved about to mask the thump-thump. Bricks were pushed over, tumbled; noises of building masked the printing sounds.

But Neville and his black friend from Khayelitsha who had a drink with Leo after the work was finished were not seen to be innocuous. The little panel van had left for the time being. The two men sank down on the long-pile carpet, exhausted but satisfied, drank a toast, placed their glasses on the music stool, temporarily relieved of the tension. A neighbour, suspicious that something untoward was going on in the yard next door to her, came to ring the front door bell with a plate of fresh scones. 'Just thought you might feel like some.' She had felt snubbed by the younger woman who was so aloof, never invited her in, and she crossed the threshold uninvited as Leo emptied the plate.

'Oh, I'm so sorry, didn't know you had visitors. Oh, and I don't see your friend, is he out of town again?'

She wasn't a telltale, wouldn't dream of being an informer, but among the people at her work there were ears, and she told her little item of news often and with gusto.

'The blacks are murdering each other up there in Natal, and look how the white boys have died on the border, but right next to you like that, my dear, in the house next door, it's frightening.'

It was three o'clock in the morning when they hammered at the door. About ten days after Fred's detention. Leo, half asleep, opened, was pushed aside. The house was searched, messed up as much as it had been by Ouma Agnes's murderer. Then out to the garage. The little printing press was inadequately hidden beneath old bags and plastic. Who the hell do they think we are, children, not to find that? said the police. But they didn't find the pamphlets. The packs of paper were burning, the entire lean-to and garage went up in flames, continued smouldering for days.

'Sufficient proof of what was going on here! But who the hell could have set it alight? Right under our noses?'

Leo was taken away.

When the steel door swung shut behind her, when she heard the key turn in the lock, the fear came. Not only for herself, also for Fred. Fear made her sweat; she was cold, but she perspired like someone who had run far and hard, she panted. Her body twitched, so that she crossed her arms and grasped her upper arms in an effort to control her panic.

9

The cell they had pushed her into was suffocatingly small. If she'd stretched out an arm from where she was sitting on the iron bed, she could have felt the wall opposite.

The arrival at Caledon Square police station had shocked her. There was suddenly a crowd of people around her – voices in protest, shrill voices, a high wailing. The sound rose above the sleeping city. White, black, coloured people; the white faces yellow in the sharp artificial light. A moving mass being pushed into the police station. She was taken by the arm and brought to the cell. After some time the door was yanked open and another woman was pushed in. Still later, a third. For the second she had made room on the bed with her: head at the foot end, feet at her head. At first the third woman had remained on her knees, then she collapsed on the cement floor.

Although she'd been warned against this, panic began to rise in Leo. The panic that she'd simply disappear, be pushed in somewhere and forgotten. She wanted to speak to the woman on the bed with her, but no matter how she nudged her feet, the woman didn't respond. She was sleeping the sleep of exhaustion. Had she been kept awake for nights on end in dark, or no, in too brightly lit cells? The one on the floor was also asleep. Or was everyone just too scared to speak? She wanted to tell someone her name, just to confirm her existence. The smell of the feet next to her was confirmation of her separate being.

After the initial silence there were more sounds. She was still awake, she heard the shuffling of feet as though people and still more people were being forced down the passages. She heard locks being opened and then clanked shut.

She strained to hear. An eerie sound came from somewhere – was it from the cells opposite the inner quadrangle? Or was she hearing it inside herself? She listened, every cell in her body focused on it. Gradually the self within her began to sway a little, first to the one side, then to the other side.

Recollection flooded through her.

It was women singing the slow, dragging lament for the dead. All along the stony road the women came, from all directions more joined them. Dressed in black, black scarves on their heads, their arms around one another, they swayed closer and closer to the row of open graves. Against the incline beyond the graves stood the hearses with the coffins, small, narrow coffins, and next to the hearses stood the Casspirs.

Akuhlanga lungehlanga,
Dade, nani bazalwana;
Lo mntu usishiyileyo,
Nguye ogodukileyo.

Akuhlanga lungehlanga,
Kunje kuzo zonk' iintlanga;
Kungumthetho ubaliwe,
Sisigqibo sigqityiwe.

She wept without realising it. She was held around the waist by the women with her, white women like her, in the graveyard illegally. There was no room between her body and the one next to her. They tried to join in the singing, the movement entered their bodies too. Never before had she felt so at one with others, her individuality merged in a greater whole. She would allow her feet to continue moving forward, she would let herself be taken right into the graves.

Akuhlanga lungehlanga,
Yonwabani lusatshana;
Nizilungisel' okwenu,
Xa nibizelwa kokwenu.

Akuhlanga lungehlanga,
Noko ngathi kubuhlungu;
Lo mmiselo wuqondeni,
Lo mmiselo wuqheleni.

They began humming in unison; from all the cells, from opposite the inner quad, from the square high in the wall now gradually growing lighter, she heard the singing.

The small, narrow coffins were carried along, the row of swaying women she was with, were slowly led – who led them? – to form a living wall between the black mothers and the Casspirs. How could the young soldiers shoot? How could they shoot through the living shield of white women? How would they disperse the funeral-goers with batons? What white hand would be the first to bring the baton down on the bent head of a white woman, the white neck exposed as if for the blow of an axe? She wasn't a mother, but she wept for the children who were to be lowered into the narrow open graves in the pale gravelly earth, she wept for the women who'd borne them. She felt purified by her grief, she felt fearless. Her spirit rose: she was nearer to God than she'd ever felt before.

Nizilungisel' okwenu,
Xa nibizelwa kokwenu.

Had she dozed off after all? The feet swung away from her face, the body at her feet straightened up.

'Good Lord, I nearly trod on your head. Sorry. You can call me Claude.'

The woman on the floor got up. 'Well, well, first night in Caledon Square. I'm Jo.'

'I'm Leo.'

She wondered whether the others were using false names. Whether they were informers, and whether they suspected her. One pleaded, 'I've been locked up for no reason, I don't even care about the struggle.'

The three of them, and others she knew as members of the Black Sash, were transferred to Pollsmoor prison the next morning where they were locked up in one cell for six months.

Sometimes the anxiety of the first night overwhelmed her again. During the day there was more normality and security among the women. But at night she thought: No one on God's earth knows where I am. It's the June school vacation. Mr Abrahams won't miss me. Neither will Fay. Cedric Kumalo has certainly been picked up. Put away. Neville too.

'I have an old aunt, over 80, she'll be mad with worry if I don't phone or get a message to her,' she told the wardress, a coloured woman.

'Bit late to think of that now,' said the woman.

She could distance herself from the crude treatment, the way they shoved her around, even removing her underwear in the booking-in room, which was little more than a thoroughfare, and the humiliating body search, in full view of men and other women. And in distancing herself even experience a kind of superiority.

For the moment it was also possible to subject herself to the routine, the blind obedience to get up now, wash now, eat from the tin plates now, now back to the cell. The clinking of the bunch of keys; the heavy doors locked behind her; even being cooped up with five other women in a cell with six beds and scarcely any room between them to move.

It was more difficult to isolate herself from the talking. The incessant talking of her five cell mates. The senseless, repetitive gnawing at and rehashing of the women's stories, until she could have screamed.

But eventually she grew accustomed to it.

But she continued to panic about the loss of self. She began to doubt if it was her body or her consciousness having these experiences.

1000 people detained without charge, denied access to lawyers and family, screamed the headline in the *Argus* the evening before they came to fetch her. It couldn't happen to her. Family members or a lawyer could make enquiries about a missing person, she knew that from her work. The organisation had warned people: make arrangements that someone, anyone, will make enquiries, should you disappear. Who would make enquiries about her? If only there was someone, the anonymity, lack of presence, lack of identity could be overcome.

She was detained in terms of section 28 of the *Internal Security Act*. That was all the man in civilian clothes had told her. It was engraved in her memory. Access to an attorney was not allowed. But the attorney could insist, at his instigation ... if he knew she was there. How long would it be before someone discovered she was there? And who? Fred had been detained. Was it then only Fred she could count on? Definitely not Tannie Leonora, she couldn't involve her. Someone would certainly have to bring her clean clothes, underwear, money, toiletries. Was there no one who could do that for her? Her schoolwork and extramural activities had taken up all her spare time. Did she have to wait until the schools reopened?

The other women couldn't help her. Enquiries were made about a few of them, their letters were censored, they couldn't give the names of other detainees. She demanded writing paper and a pen; she wrote to the Black Sash office to ask them to inform an attorney, and also to let Leonora know that there was no need to be concerned. She asked them to reply, so that she would know her letter had been received.

Her concern for Leonora was the focus of her thoughts, and probably also a lifeline.

Together with the five other women she was fed, let out in the small inner yard for exercise, given a turn to wash and shower, and at seven in the evening the door of their cell was locked for the night. They were given powder for the lice in the coir mattresses. They were given pills, sedatives, vitamin pills, handfuls of pills.

'They want to keep us drugged,' mocked Jo, also a single woman. She was freckled, and her pale complexion had a grey tinge in spite of the daily hour outdoors. The grey in her short red hair had become more noticeable.

'Keep the pills, hide them, we might be able to trade them.'

She didn't have any visitors either during the half an hour every second week. She sat cross-legged on her bed playing patience. They'd each been given a pack of cards and a Bible.

'One for the devil and one for God,' they'd joked.

Leo didn't enjoy card games, but she was thankful if they kept the other women quiet. They were an island of white women in the jail, locked away from the black women.

One night they heard singing again. They stood on the bed nearest the high barred window, tried to listen. The black women were singing, first in Xhosa, then a song in English. The sound rose and dropped, as if taken by the wind and wafted away.

'Know any Xhosa?' Claude was still standing on the bed, looked back at the others who had got tired and moved away.

'That's my bed, by the way,' Anne had protested. 'You're no lightweight, Claude.' But she kept on listening, and said: 'I think they're singing in English now to make contact with us. We should sing something in return.' The words of the funeral song were uppermost in Leo's memory, she repeated them:

Nizilungisel' okwenu,
Xa nibizelwa kokwenu.

The words of all the verses came flooding back to her, the words carried the others along. All six got on the bed again and half-sang, half-shouted the words up at the window, hoped they'd be carried by the wind, hoped the black women would hear them.

They sank back relieved when they heard the refrain in the distance and knew: the black women were answering. They know we're here, they told one another, they know they're not alone. Once again Leo sensed that she was part of something greater than herself.

When she lay on her bed again, she thought of Fred. May he also experience moments like these.

The only contact they were permitted was with the wardresses, white or black or coloured women who worked in shifts.

In the inner yard for exercise; in the passage where they sat at a table to eat. Porridge. Bread. Peanut butter, golden syrup. In the evening – could half past three, which was supper time, be called evening? – a stew of vegetables and something that was supposed to be meat, but was unrecognisable. The women who had visitors had money, and could nag the wardresses into buying fresh food for them. They shared it with the others. But Leo found it difficult to swallow. They weren't interrogated, they weren't physically abused, they'd simply been put aside. Out of the way.

God knows, thought Leo, if only I could have spoken to one of those self-satisfied white faces that came to fetch me. I would have told him a couple of things he doesn't know. Or does he know only too well? And does he choose not to know? It became an obsession: If only I could tell someone my standpoint. Even there in the cell she couldn't have an argument. One needed an Afrikaner to understand what had driven her so far. To realise the personal emotional implications.

'We're bugged, in any case, we can't talk,' said Jo.

She had a consuming longing to speak to Fred, to see him, to touch him, feel his hands on her body.

And then after how many days – three weeks? – the wardress came with her bunch of keys and unlocked and said, 'Come with me. You've got a visitor. Move your arse.'

The wardress plodded ahead of her, Leo couldn't take her eyes off the down-at-heel canvas shoes that were much too big for her. She stole a sideways glance at the other feet on the shiny polished black cement floor, rough black feet with a warder's black boots. There was only one other prisoner in the passage, but to her it seemed crowded. She didn't lift her head. After the confinement of the cell she seemed to have lost her ability to see any distance.

She signed a piece of paper that was shoved in front of her, she was in another room, in a circumscribed corner, she was pushed down on a hard plank bench, and at last, at the sound of her name, she looked up. Through the thick glass – had she always seen her through glass? – she saw the questioning eyes, the slightly frowning forehead, the half-open mouth as she pronounced her name, the so-familiar and so-beloved bearing.

'Leo, my dear,' she heard.

'Yes, Tannie Leonora,' she replied. Her eyes must have looked glazed, for she couldn't believe what she saw.

'Come now, Leo.' Again the slightly authoritarian sound to the voice that she remembered so well, that swept away the years, made her small again, Oumatan Leonora, the care-giver. 'Come now, Leo. I'm not a ghost. Look at me properly. It was difficult enough to manage to get here.'

The wardress stood next to them. Leo looked up at her. She nodded, indicated Leo should speak, pointed at her big man's watch on her wrist. Does she have some sympathy with me? Does she want to help me not to waste time?

'Tannie Leonora,' was all she could say. So softly, she didn't know if it could be heard through the glass.

But Leonora must have heard. 'It took walking about and driving around and asking and threatening, but I couldn't just let it be. You couldn't have been wiped from the face of the earth, all your friends have also gone.'

Her mouth was dry, but she managed to ask, 'Fred?'

'Fred? Still on holiday. All on holiday. You too.'

'Where to?'

'Well now, he's not far. He's fond of the False Bay coast. Not at all far.'

'You've seen him, Tannie?'

'Not yet, but I will. You first. Then I'll nag them until I'm allowed to visit him too. I nag, I cling like a burr, they can't get rid of me, eventually they give in.'

Leonora was different. Or had her perception of her changed? Leo had better control of her thoughts, she'd even have been able to look in the distance now, had she wanted to, she was gradually becoming herself again. But Leonora was sharper. More impatient. The vague Leonora who'd forgotten names at Frikkie's funeral – how many centuries ago? – was gone.

'I don't know what you got up to, but I'll help where I can. Who else is there to help?' She bent and lifted her handbag from the floor. 'We have to talk quickly, the time is flying. I've brought you money. Thirty rand is all you may get at a time. To buy yourself something to eat, or whatever. I've baked you biscuits, the ginger biscuits you like so much, and there's fruit – it was handed to the wardress. They'll let you have it. If they don't shove it down their own throats.'

'When did you discover I'd disappeared, Tannie?'

'You hadn't phoned or been to see me for three days, then I knew something was wrong.'

'Who's helping you with your shopping?'

'One manages if one has to. I take the bus to the city and shop at the O.K. Bazaar, and go back by bus. I only buy a little at a time so that I can carry it.'

'And at home?'

'Your home or mine? My house is fine. Your backyard was burnt a bit, but I'm sure you won't waste your tears on the lean-to where your ouma's body was found. The garage can probably be fixed up, but it looks pretty bad in there, blackened by smoke. What was burning I wouldn't know. One might almost imagine you'd set a match to it yourself before you were taken away, but they wouldn't have allowed that, I'm sure. Before they could search, it was burning. Just the yard and the dry grass and the stuff in the garage. And papers.'

'You must finish off now,' said the wardress.

'I'll tell you so that you know: I brought you underwear and soap and stuff, other clothes too, but I had to hand them all in with the money. Can you think of anything else for next time?'

Leo shook her head. 'Thanks Tannie. Actually I'm the one who should take care of you. And now this happens.'

'So far I haven't needed much care. One is buried too soon when one grows old. I'm doing fine.'

She also looked good, thought Leo. She looked proud – that old word again. Her thick grey hair was shiny and groomed. She was wearing new clothes, which Leo had persuaded her to buy, but she'd never worn before. Leo began to smile. It was good for her to have to make decisions again.

She asked, unnecessarily, really: 'How will you get home, Tannie?'

'That's a bit of a problem. The taxi is waiting outside. The meter must be ticking itself silly.' And when she noticed the smile fading from Leo's face – Leo knew how strictly she had to budget – she said in the old conspiratorial way. 'I'll get it back from Boeta Hendrik. I know just which button to press.'

She was getting up already, but Leo pressed her face forward, right against the glass. 'Tannie Leonora, you must visit Fred. Tell him I love him and I'm well. It's really not too bad here. White women are the privileged ones. Tell him: he always said we were just bleeding heart white liberals, we didn't really know what it was all about. Maybe he's right.'

Then the wardress took her arm and she was led away. She didn't object. Leonora was already walking away. She didn't want to create problems.

Only when she received the ginger biscuits, misshapen and askew, some a bit burnt and blackened, others nearly raw, not a single one quite as it should be, and she shared out the cookies; only then did the tears stream from her eyes. When had she told her great-aunt that she loved ginger biscuits? And had the solitary aunt never forgotten, and when her niece needed her, she valiantly baked some more? It seemed to her sadder than anything that had happened to her, and she couldn't stop the tears. She cried for the first time, uncontrollably, until Jo gave her an Ativan. 'We keep the pills for times like these,' she said, 'when you really need one.'

Bleeding heart white liberals. The thought plagued her. The night wardresses were coloured women. They rubbed their noses in it: You white women are the little pets in jail. Beds, sheets. Meals out in the passage. Walking around in the yard twice every day. D'you know how many blacks there are in a cell the size of yours? Twenty. Without beds. They sleep on the floor, packed in like sardines. And the black men. Eighty in a cell.

Some evenings they heard the black women's voices coming down the passage, like water beginning to flow. From other cells? How else? It happened regularly, in the evening before the lights went off at seven o'clock. Words, sentences. They discovered the women wanted to communicate something, news from the outside world. With so many more of them in a cell, so many more visitors and letters, they knew more than the white women. It became a news bulletin that was sung-spoken down the passage every evening. It was stopped. The white women tried to make contact. They were warned: Each time you lot open your mouths the black women will be punished. Better shut up.

Punishment meant that permission to buy something from the shop – cigarettes, sweets – was refused.

Leo deliberately suppressed the hope that Leonora would come again. But she came again. She brought money, food, she brought news of Fred. He sent greetings. She watched Leo closely. He sent love. He said he was sure children had caused the fire in her backyard. Children who'd been lying smoking there. Just as well, he said, one would almost think it had been planned. 'He's having a tough time finding an attorney. He'll be out one of these days. You too. You're looking better already. It does you no harm to lose a bit of weight.'

But the weeks became months.

The six women found being cooped up together difficult. Their nerves were in shreds. They were taking Ativans more and more frequently. Can't go on forever, Claude comforted Leo. Together they planned an exercise routine to make sense of the hours in the yard. They felt fitter, but continued to lose weight, they seemed pale to one another, even out in the sun. They kept on complaining and making demands until they were given permission to study. It wasn't easy on the beds. The food began to stick in their throats. Cold porridge, syrup and peanut butter. They vomited. Stopped eating. Ate again.

'The only decision you can make for yourself is whether to eat or not,' Leo complained to Leonora. 'Just whether you will swallow or not swallow.'

Then, one visiting day, Leonora didn't come. An uncomfortable, dejected Hendrik sat behind the thick glass. Leo, who'd got harder in her own way, felt like laughing. 'It isn't that bad, Oom. They don't torture or starve me, they've just put me away.' But Pappie looked ill at ease and unhappy. To have been searched, to have had his pockets turned out, to complete pages and pages of forms, to be distrusted in his own country, by his own people. It was more than he could stomach.

The previous few weeks had been a trial to him. All the doors he knocked at had been closed in his face. Old friends, in important positions he'd helped to place them in, suddenly had no time for him. Or tried to say: If we could, old friend, we would help, but we just can't. Only information, he had begged. Just what she has been accused of? And then, to his own discomfort, he had to add: and my second cousin, what is he accused of? Two family members? Surely not two! God in heaven, what had he done to deserve it? Had it not been for Mammie and her soft heart. For Leo, yes, Leo was like his own, but Fred, impertinent, insensitive, his own sister stoned to death.

Shortly after their detention Koba had slipped away in her coma. Although they'd never acknowledge it, it was a merciful release for Stoffel and Miemie. Tension like that could destroy one.

Understandably Leonora couldn't appeal to Stoffel and Miemie for help for Fred. Even before Koba's death, harsh words had been exchanged between them.

'Is Tannie Leonora ill?' Leo was asking.

'You're only allowed one visitor at a time. She'll come again next time. I've arranged for taxis. The poor woman was out of pocket: four times a month what with visiting you and Fred. I paid in the money. If only she'd let me know earlier.'

'Oh, Oom, we give you such a hard time.'

Suddenly his face crumpled, as if it was about to fall apart. It looked as if he was going to cry. Not that, just not that. She couldn't even put her hand out to him. But he pulled himself together, took out a handkerchief and blew his nose. 'If only I could understand why you do it. What is driving you. I believe in our cause. Have believed my whole life. And worked for it. And now this. Philip's son out of the country. Robbie's son in jail for a completely different reason. And the two of you here. And you are our descendants!'

He looked almost relieved when the wardress said visiting time was over. He got up from the little stool. 'Leo, my child.'

'Oom, we'll talk one day, we must. One day I'll be out of here, I promise you. Fred and I.' As she was led away she turned to catch a last glimpse of him, the large figure, with shoulders suddenly no longer so square. The slightly shuffling gait saddened her deeply.

How could she know of the self-control it had taken her great-uncle not to tell her: 'Fred wants out. He says himself that he must have been mad: he can't think what got into him.' The child looked so pale and miserable, how could he add to her hurt?

She was allowed to write a letter every fortnight. But not to Fred, and nor he to her. She wrote to her mother. And to Hendrik. Five hundred words. The words were false and sounded forced. The letters she received, too, meant little to her. She longed to communicate with someone. Even the police. If only they'd interrogate her. If only she could justify herself. To discuss matters truthfully with someone. She could perhaps make them understand, make them doubt. She formed no close friendships with the women in her cell. The women were all English-speaking, and two hadn't even been born in South Africa and she felt they didn't understand her at all. The cultural divide between them was too vast.

Three of them were released on the same day. Not at the same time. The wardress unlocked. Well now, one of you can pack. Yes, one is going out today. Now which one can it be? She paged through her papers provokingly slowly, eventually reading out a name.

Oh God! But they all cried and laughed at the cell mate's joy, helped pack, sent messages.

A second time. Once more the laughter and tears, the packing, the farewells.

The third time it was her name.

She followed the woman down the passage without any show of emotion, yet she was aware of deep fear, terror. The suitcase in her hand felt light, very light. Yet it anchored her to the cell, to the barred doors that slammed shut behind her one by one. It seemed that her hand with the suitcase remained behind invisibly, always would remain. She was afraid of looking ahead, down the length of the passage to the exit where Leonora was waiting.

10

'You're so thin, child. Let me see. And the hair so long and scraped back. I'll have to get you to a hairdresser.' But in the evening when Fred was with her, he said: No, I like your hair on the pillow like that, like a coronet; that's what hair should be; a woman's crowning glory. He played with her hair, twirled a small lock of it round and round his finger.

'I told the taxi driver to go directly to my house,' Leonora had said when they left the prison. 'Shade your eyes with your hand if the light worries you. They say looking in the distance, the brightness of the outside world, is difficult to get used to. I should have brought a pair of sunglasses.'

We have to become accustomed to so many things again, she said to Fred as they lay on her bed while the lights of cars in the street went past on the ceiling, and disappeared, went past and disappeared. She lay and watched them. Stared at them. She and Fred had to get used to each other again.

'I let your pa and ma and your Oom Hendrik know, but told them to wait until tomorrow to phone. You don't want everyone descending on you,' Leonora had said. It was only Fred at home with Leonora. Fred had been released the previous week, and Leonora had fetched him too. Oh, Tannie Leonora, what are we doing to you? Fred who rose from his chair in Leonora's small lounge and put his arms round her without a word. He, too, was thinner, his hair looked faded, there was more grey in the rusty red. But his eyes were fierce.

'The bastards,' he said. 'I'll never forgive them my cameras.'

'I've prepared a meal. There's no food in your house, Leo, and if you'd like to sleep here you'd be very welcome. But I thought you might prefer to go home. Fred can take you shopping tomorrow. There's nothing in his flat, a friend has moved in. The newspapers say a lot of people are to be released this week,' said Leonora.

Leo pecked at her food without much appetite.

'I understand,' said Leonora and moved the dishes away. 'I think you two should settle down now. Take her home in my car Fred – you know I don't drive any more.'

When they demurred, she said, 'I'm tired. Please just get on with it. I'll tidy up tomorrow.'

He came up behind her as she stood in front of the mirror above the basin in the bathroom. She looked at her face, and he looked at her face over her shoulder and then at his. He stroked her cheek with the back of his hand. She touched his cheek. There wasn't much to say. And no passion in her mouth that was pressed to his. Only her fingers digging into his shoulder. Shh, shh, he said to her, as to a child. He removed his lips from her mouth. His understanding touched her. Holding her head, he brought it to rest on his shoulder. Shh, shh, there's lots of time. She opened the cupboard above the basin. Their mirror images disappeared and the small remains of a previous existence lay on the little glass shelves. Shampoo, bath oil. His razor. His aftershave lotion. She looked at it all, the remains of a distant life.

'That's us in there,' said Fred. 'And it's going to be us again.'

He didn't insist on being present while she bathed, and washed her hair with shampoo, dried her body with a towel that seemed so big and so thick, so strange. Getting to know her body on her own, quiet, without sirens, without others walking in, was important. When she'd finished she felt less afraid to open the door and walk to the other room. She was wearing clean pyjamas. While he was bathing she went to the kitchen, but she didn't open the door to the backyard. She didn't want to look at the night sky yet, it was still too strange and too distant. She dried her hair. When he lay next to her she smelled the soap, the aftershave. She lay with her nose against his shoulder and sniffed him like an animal. He also smelled her hair. There was no desire or urgency in her for anything more. But he was eager, avid. He took possession of her repeatedly.

'They couldn't have killed everything in me, could they?' she asked later. 'They haven't left me with an empty shell for a body, have they?'

'I dreamed about being with you again so many nights,' he said. 'I wrestled with your image. It'll be all right, girl. Everything will be all right.'

'I fell asleep in your arms so many nights in my imagination,' she said. 'And now I disappoint you.'

'Shh, shh,' he said. 'There's plenty of time.'

'I feel as though I'm a shipwrecked castaway, washed ashore on some foreign beach. I feel distanced from everything, even from you.' She laughed, embarrassed. 'Did they warn you too? In the pamphlet we were printing, it said: don't expect an immediate interest in sex from a recently released detainee. Now I seem to be a textbook example …'

'Shh, shh,' he comforted her. 'Don't worry.'

'This afternoon I felt that I could only look at things that were close to me, near to me, everything at a distance hurt. Perhaps I've only seen what's nearby until now, perhaps I'll be able to look further and further from now on … As long as we're together.' She closed her eyes. 'Hold me Fred, so that I can feel you, so that I'm not so alone.'

He kissed her forehead, kissed each eye as it closed. She slept. He felt her breast rising and falling regularly. It touched him, the gentle movement of her breast.

Then he also slept.

'I must make a plan to visit my parents,' said Fred. 'I phoned them, but the conversation ended with Ma's tears and Pa's reproaches.'

He'd already found out that for humanitarian reasons they would be partially released from the banning order they'd both been placed under. They could go to Worcester, if they reported to a police station before leaving and in the afternoon after their return.

'Shall I go with you?' Leo asked. Then she added quickly, 'You must say whether it would be better or worse if I come with you.'

They were having breakfast in the room which had been Miss Marais's dining room, and then her grandmother's dining room, where the sun had streamed in and the red geraniums had done so well in the pots.

Fred reached out, took the knife from her hand, put it down. 'We do want to tell them about the two of us, after all. Maybe it'll comfort them if they know we're going to be joined …'

'… in holy …'

'… matrimony.'

'I think they believe I led you astray … On the other hand, my pa and ma think that you have …'

'In-doc-tri-na-ted me. They get the word from Oom Hendrik. When he came to see me in the clink that day, he solemnly assured me: I, as the older one, had in-doc-tri-na-ted you.'

'Shall I come along then?'

They'd had little contact with the outside world. Neville was in detention. Cedric still missing. Mr Abrahams had been detained, along with George September, another teacher. His wife, the social worker, had slipped through the net. No one knew what had become of Fay Mentoor. Colleagues from Fred's firm visited briefly. 'I must come and see you,' said Fred. 'There's my living to be earned … Any chance of insurance on my car? There's probably nothing left of it by now, out there on the dunes.'

'We can look into it. Come back to work when you feel ready.'

They went to the shops to buy food. And to Leonora's house. Leo had an odd feeling in her stomach when they took the N1 out of the city.

She put her hand on Fred's thigh, and as soon as the traffic eased up he took his left hand from the steering wheel and placed it over hers. It was the first time since his release that he'd driven out of the city. They were in her Golf.

'Ridiculous, hey? That I should be nervous in the traffic. Me, old daredevil Fred. But when the cars whip past me like that from behind … That confinement buggers one up.'

They stopped in Paarl and had tea in a café. The winter was not yet over: a light drizzle, green buds dripping on the oaks, branches dark with moisture. 'The weather's better this way, I wouldn't have been able to cope with bright sunshine.' From Du Toit's Kloof they looked down on the haze covering the valley. Only the hilltops showed above the mist like islands. Wellington, where her mother had grown up, was invisible.

The windscreen wipers kept going. Her nerves contracted and the tension in her stomach became unbearable. It felt as though it was rising in her throat. 'Stop,' she told Fred. He drew up in a lay-by. She opened the window. 'It's the windscreen wipers,' she said, 'I can't take the noise.'

'Then I'll switch them off. They're bothering me too, I must admit. We'll drive slowly. It won't be raining on the other side of the mountain.'

She began to cry when he stopped in the driveway of his parents' house on the outskirts of Worcester. He opened the door for her, Miemie came out. She put her arms around the crying girl. 'I don't hold it against you.' She pressed Leo's head against her shoulder. Fred put his arm around his mother's shoulders. 'Thanks, Ma,' he said to her softly. 'Ma, if I could bring Koba back.'

'I know, son.'

His father came home from school at lunch time. He shook Fred's hand, surprised to see Leo with him. 'I'm pleased you're free. Can't say I approve of what you did, against your own people, and against your own government and your sister …'

'I'm sorry about Koba, Pa. It was unnecessary and cruel. If I could have prevented it, I would have.'

'Unnecessary and cruel. That's what you call it, and your Ma's heart is broken, and the child completely innocent. Who had she ever harmed?'

Miemie was crying. 'It's not the children's fault, Stoffel.'

'I told you I was sorry, Pa. Bitterly sorry. What more can I say?'

They left it at that. 'I'll take you to her grave this afternoon,' said Miemie. 'We can take fresh flowers.'

Before Stoffel returned to school, Fred stood up. 'Pa, just listen here. You probably know about Leo and me. We are to be married next week, quietly, by a magistrate. We've already told Ma. Leo's parents also know. Everything just very quiet.'

His father didn't say much. Just: 'I suppose you know what you're doing. A big wedding would be inappropriate under the circumstances. Probably not possible either. Well, I suppose you have my blessing.'

He put down the case with his books and went back to Fred. 'God knows, I don't know what's going on anymore. Josias has been sent into the townships with the army, did your Ma tell you? He stands there and the black women come and spit on him. So that it runs down his cheek. And can he do anything? Just let the TV cameras catch him pushing or shoving a black woman, and the whole world screams blue murder. I'm telling you, Fred, God help me, I don't know anymore ... My daughter murdered, my son spat upon, and you put in jail by your own people. Where must we go? What must we think? Is right still right and wrong still wrong? Is betrayal still betrayal?'

He put his hat on, picked up the case again. 'I just hope you know what you're doing. You've always been clever, perhaps too clever.' He held out his hand. 'But you're still my child.' He kissed Leo on the forehead. She was crying yet again. 'Come, come child, you'll get over it. I've heard detention does things to the nerves. You couldn't help that Koba ...'

'Oom,' she spoke through her tears, 'it wasn't betrayal. You must keep believing that, Oom. Not betrayal of what is good in our people.'

'I don't feel like splitting hairs now, I'll be late for class. I'd better say goodbye.'

11

But the three uncles in the Transvaal were indeed busily splitting hairs. Robert was in Pretoria for a Broederbond meeting – he was still delegated despite the court reports about his son. Some of his friends might indulgently approve of Bennie's deed, perhaps they'd even been kaffir-fuckers themselves, he thought wryly. Hendrik drove across from Johannesburg. After the meeting they gathered in Philip's study for drinks and snacks.

With Barry overseas and the two daughters married, Philip and Maude lived together in ever more chilly politeness. In spite of his age – or was it in fact because of it? – Philip was becoming increasingly obsessed with carnal lust. For a woman like Nellie. It turned him on to think of the smell in her hairy armpit, the weight of her big hand on his buttocks as she pressed him against her. Unexpected stimuli, out of the blue, the mention of the word pastorie, or Worcester, or Hendrik's recalling Father, could cause the uncontrollable feeling to rise in him. He'd have to be careful: there had been other men of his age, respected leaders of the nation, with a fatal weakness ...

He pulled himself together, quickly mopped up the whisky he'd slopped, and gave the brothers their glasses.

Hendrik was speaking about Father. Old age had made him sentimental. Since Mammie's death there was nothing left for him but the past, and Belle. Yes, well, Belle.

'That little book Father found about the Boer War rebels who were hanged or shot ...' he remembered now. 'Way back in the early twenties I was old enough to understand. I remember him saying repeatedly: It was not a useless resistance, they were not losers. A nation needs its growth points, even be they painful ... so indispensable in the slow process of becoming a nation.'

Philip swallowed his whisky, thought of Barry. Slunk off with his tail between his legs. A flourishing practice here in the city not good enough for milord. Self-seeking.

Robert was beginning to worry him, his colour was high. He was hyper-sensitive these days. 'Father called the 1914 rebels,' he said, 'the invisible scaffolding – perhaps they used a different word in those days – of the nation. And with justification. But the so-called rebels of today? Fred and Leo – forgive me Philip, but Barry just as much – do the opposite, they undermine the nation. It isn't a growth point, it's betrayal.' And Bennie, his Benjamin. God, God, did You have to send that to try me?

'Careful with the word betrayal.' Hendrik wiped his forehead with his handkerchief. The memory of the visit to the prison was still a canker in his spirit. He kept thinking of the story of Braampie Nel. Perhaps really Leo's great-grandfather. 'That Leo child, she looked so awful – ashen, thin – but she persisted with fervour: Oom, we're rebelling for the sake of the nation. Against what's wrong. To exorcise the evil. In the interests of humanity. In the interests of a new nation.'

'New nation's cunt,' said Robert. 'Kaffir nation.'

Philip was disconcerted by Robert's crude word. 'Take it easy now, Boetie.' Almost against his will he said, 'We must concede: things can't go on like this. It's bitterly difficult to accept that the Afrikaners have become ...' He found the word hard to say, '... irrelevant, and to accept that we – as was stated in the meeting today – have to endure our status as a permanent minority.' He took another mouthful of whisky, a large one. 'But we must try again, but in a reasonable way ... Not by aggression. And, I say it against my own child, not by emigrating.'

Unwittingly he repeated Stoffel's words: 'Betrayal remains betrayal.'

And knew: in his own heart he had so often betrayed.

'Did anyone ever find out what had become of Nellie?' he asked abruptly, and his question caused the brothers to look at him in surprise. Dear God, the woman was incredibly ancient or dead and buried. Was their eldest brother wandering? The politics could mess one's mind up these days.

'Come, come and sit down,' they said. 'Loosen your tie. Get a bit of oxygen.'

Hendrik had assumed more authority since Miemie had put him at the head of the table at Frikkie's funeral, and before they left he said, 'Just a word about Leo and Fred. I spoke to them in … in … in the place where they were. I've thought about it a great deal. It seems to me that Fred was arrested because he arrogantly flouted the regulations, perhaps the whole thing was a blunder. But Leo.' He sighed. He thought of the little girl running up to him, her arms outstretched. He sighed again.

'I think that Father would not have been unproud of Leo.'

12

Agnes's wedding, SussieBelle's wedding, and then Leo's wedding. No need for a hat, Tannie Leonora, Leo had assured her. Just quick-sticks in the magistrate's office. Witness. That's all right, she'd sign in the book that it had taken place in accordance with the law, thought Leonora. She'd have to sign in her heart that it was also before God. So many marriages: Stuart's vow of fidelity before the pulpit hadn't been much use to Agnes. Still less Father's white hands spread over them. The thought of Father brought tears to her eyes. She dabbed them away with the little handkerchief dipped in cologne. Belle married on Hendrik's open stoep, with the wind threatening to blow the banana leaves all over the Bible. She'd rather not think about Belle.

The young people had been lent a friend's house at Kommetjie for a week or so. But they couldn't go off without any celebration. When they brought her home, they'd have a drink with her. Everything was ready. Along with the milktart her neighbour had been commissioned to bake.

The second witness was not allowed to sign, because he was black, a friend of Fred's. Oh dear. That too. She felt hurt on behalf of the young couple. It would never have happened in her day because they'd never have considered having a black witness. Now that the young people had been taught to be open-minded, they were pushed back again. Such an embarrassment. But the black colleague had pressed Fred's arm as if saying: Don't worry: what does it matter? The typist in the magistrate's office had signed in his place. The black friend had waited and come along to her house, she'd specially invited him. He even helped her wash the cups after Fred and Leo had left. If only the two of them could get some rest. Leo was so pale, almost transparent, with a sickly colour around the eyes; Fred's hair was much greyer than one would expect in a red-headed bridegroom. People were released regularly from prison these days, but they said it took a while. At least the two of them had each other. If only they could get some rest.

Even before the week was over, Fred was restless. If they climbed the sand dunes, he saw the fine circle of shadow drawn by the dune grass; if they went to the beach and looked at the fishing boats and heard the smack of the smooth fish bodies against the wet gumboots, he saw pictures. All around him. The curve of a boat, the glow of reflection when the sun set and the wind dropped. The birds coming in at sunset intrigued him.

'My hands are desolate,' he told Leo. 'I'm longing to take pictures.'

'We'll buy you the best, the latest. As soon as we get home,' said Leo. Out of breath she climbed the dunes next to him, her hand in his. She was alive again. The sea air fed her lungs deeply; the sun had banished the prison pallor from her skin. Her hair began to shine again.

'With what?' he asked. 'Car gone, cameras gone. They were my capital.'

Yet he made an appointment to see his former employer the day after their return. He wanted to buy from the firm, on credit.

'Come along,' he said to Leo. 'I want you to see where I work.'

She waited in his old office while he spoke to his boss. There was someone else in his place. A young blonde Englishman, Peter, with the same passion in his voice. An assortment of photos lay on the desk in front of him.

'We're busy with wonderful stuff,' he told Leo. 'Things are moving so fast we can hardly keep up.' He picked up two photos. 'Have a good look at these two: the printed photo is clearer than the original, which was slightly out of focus. We simply tell the machine "sharpen edges" or "unsharp mask" and it finds all the places where levels or colours meet, and heightens the contrast, and the contrasting edges around the objects enhance the sharpness of the image.'

'But how on earth?' said Leo.

The young man laughed. 'The computer is the key. Once the photo has been scanned you're working with digital data: millions of dots, or pixels, each with its own colour value. Do you like figures? Here they come. A resolution of 300 dots to the inch gives you 90 000 little dots per square inch. Enlarge the image sufficiently on the screen, and we can alter each one of those pixels individually.' He laughed again. 'Incredible!'

'It sounds so mechanical,' said Leo, thinking of Fred on the dunes, enchanted by the circles of shadow of the dune grass.

'But just think what we can do with it: we can duplicate elements in a photo, move them around, take out ... even combine parts of different photos, sky's the limit.'

Leo picked up some of the photos, put them down again.

The young man ran his fingers through his blonde hair. 'Photographers ask: Where will it all lead? It's all becoming so unreal that we'll end up where we started. But I find it enormously exciting, I'm standing on the threshold of it all. Have you heard of the digital camera? The still photo is recorded on disc, no film at all. Films require materials that have become scarce and expensive. Now we can copy the photo onto the computer and manipulate it, or make a print of it in the lab. The possibilities are unlimited; as soon as the images are digitised, I say again: sky's the limit. Send the photos by telephone line via satellite. Keep them on a CD. One CD can hold the entire contents of the Encyclopaedia Britannica! It makes your head spin, doesn't it?'

They heard footsteps in the passage. Fred and the boss.

'I'm moving in with you again,' he told Peter. 'Advertising work. And I got my two cameras. My mainstays, zoom and close-up lens, my Canon F-1. I can pick it up tomorrow on tick. Now I feel like a human being again.'

He was excited, the old glow back in his eyes. 'Come along, love, I want to go to the factory, just the floor below here. I want to show you. He made you dizzy with his talk, didn't he? One gets carried away.'

He took her arm, the young man put the photos away reluctantly. They went downstairs and reached a large hall-like room, not dark, just a soft dusky light. A couple of men worked silently behind machines that were totally strange to Leo. They nodded to Fred, one called out, 'Welcome back, old chap.' Then they were entirely focused on their work again.

'Everything happens at once,' said Fred. 'Photos are developed, fixed and washed simultaneously. Gone are the days of the old darkroom with the red light and the photos hanging on a line to dry!'

He let her walk ahead to a room where large machines with cylinders were continually turning a transparent film. Pictures, mostly colour transparencies, were mounted on the piece of film on the cylinder. Next to the box with the cylinder there was a computer terminal.

'That's the scanning process Peter told you about,' Fred said. 'As you can see, it's done automatically, without an operator. The laser beam analyses the transparency or photo in all its miniscule elements or pixels. And then proceeds silently.'

Then she had to walk ahead again to another room where a number of people sat, each in front of a computer, playing with the keys, calling up images on the screen.

'The photos are transformed into digital information now, ones and noughts, and they can do what they like with them,' said Fred.

The man at the computer moved away and Fred sat down. He called up an image of a sunset on the screen. 'D'you want more light on the horizon? Right.' He moved a handset with four buttons which was connected to the test board, selected the part of the photo he wanted to change. He pressed the buttons and replaced the dots with other shades of colour, took away or added. The colour grew more saturated or thinner as he worked.

'The photographer doesn't need to get up at the crack of dawn any more, he can get his colour effects in the factory, electronically. Some people say photography has lost its magic.'

'Has it, Fred?' she asked.

'No ways, sweetheart.'

They moved to the next machine.

'Now I'll show you how we duplicate an object. We call it pixel cloning.' He sat down again, began playing at the keys, called up the interior of a room. 'It's an advertising photo. What do you prefer? The red cushions on the bed or orange? A second reading lamp to the left against the wall? Or the reading lamp to the left of the bed?' As he spoke his fingers touched the keys lightly, his other hand moved the handset around. The tiny cross followed his hand on the screen, and new pictures appeared and disappeared.

'It's actually horrible,' said Leo, but softly, so that she wondered whether Fred could hear. 'It's the ultimate lie.' But was drawing not also lying, or painting? she thought. What had become of her great-grandfather's 'enscribing in light' the family was so fond of referring to? Was this the ultimate in creativity?

'So you can remove someone from a group photo, move the people together so that no one would know someone had been removed?'

Through her horror, Leo was aware of the small beginnings of excitement. 'There must surely be something real to start with? Can you program someone who wasn't in the photo into it? In news photos for instance?' Can news be fabricated? The big lie? No longer the traditional role of photography as the exact rendition of the truth – *the camera doesn't lie* – but now the lie in the guise of truth?

'In the States,' Fred said, 'videos are no longer accepted as evidence in court cases, because too much can be manipulated.'

'And you don't question whether it's creativity or lying? And what your Oupa Frikkie would have said of this?'

'Times they are a'changin', my lambkin. That's why I told you: always have yellow flowers in the sun. Don't look so aghast. They say the course of history determines one's actions. If you feel strongly enough about something, all boundaries disappear. It's also true for the photographer now.' He suddenly looked tired, brushed back the hair that had fallen over his forehead.

'Relax, Leo. The responsibility still rests with the person behind the camera. Today more than ever: individual morality. I wanted to show you the possibilities. The magnitude of it; that the camera which can photograph planets in space, right here on the table in front of us, as you rightly say, can make lies look like truth.'

She was sorry that she'd dampened his enthusiasm.

'Perhaps it's a monster we've created,' he said. 'Perhaps it'll devour us. Like the shadowy figures on the box devoured your ma's being. Who can tell? Everyone lies. They do, we do. And who are they? Who're we? I just take snaps to earn a living.'

They were on the iron stairway again, on the way down, out.

In a different way she was more upset by all this than by his dangerous riot photography. But she tried to hide it. 'I love you, Fred,' she said softly. 'I believe in you.'

13

Fred was pleased to start work again. Censorship was so strict and access to black residential areas so restricted that there was little call for political reporting. Overseas news agencies were given material by the government. The work in the advertising section was less exciting, but as his employer had said, 'You've probably had enough excitement for the time being.'

His first assignment was nature shots for conservation brochures. If only our people felt as deeply for our black and coloured population as they feel for shrubs, or the white rhino, or the eagles, or the penguins, was Leo's wry thought.

She found it more difficult to get a job. State schools, in white, coloured or black departments, were forbidden territory to Leo because no one who'd ever been detained was allowed to work in government institutions. She went to see the headmaster of an English private school she was referred to by one of her Black Sash friends, and got a part-time post there. The school was more accessible than those on the Flats. She was thankful that she didn't have to drive along the N2 any more. I'm a coward after all, she thought, I wriggle into the safe private school as into a cocoon.

It was a time of waiting. The land was divided into unrest areas. With so many people still in detention, so many handicapped by restrictions, black resistance was to a great extent without leaders. More and more young white conscripts were sent into black townships. White parents became concerned. Black parents lived in daily fear. The word 'necklace' acquired a new meaning.

One day she saw black, coloured and white English-speaking church leaders with linked arms, marching ahead of a crowd of demonstrators to the Parliament buildings. It proceeded peacefully. God, she thought, is there no end to it? And where are the leaders of my church?

At last, like a festering sore erupting, came FW de Klerk's announcement in Parliament on 2 February 1990.

In her English-medium private school the staff crowded around the TV. 'Incredible! At last! More than one ever could have hoped for!'

The banning order on the ANC was lifted, as well as those on the other resistance organisations: PAC, SACP, AZAPO. Political prisoners were released. The long-banned, almost mythical leader, Nelson Mandela, would soon be free. Apartheid legislation was scrapped from the statutes.

'The season of violence has ended. The time for reconstruction and reconciliation has come.'

Fred was sceptical. 'So now the Berlin Wall's come down, we can see that The Total Onslaught was a myth. With the red peril removed, the Party feels it can take on the black people.'

Gradually reality began to penetrate. Exiles started to return from overseas, legendary figures were to be seen on the streets of Cape Town, appeared on TV, sat at the negotiating table.

Leo tried to make Leonora aware of the new dispensation in politics. Leonora was 86, not always completely lucid.

'You were the crusader, Tannie, against the whole family, with your black sash at the Parliament building. You knew what it would lead to, Tannie. And now you can reap the reward.'

The enormous demands Leonora had made on herself when the

'children' had needed her had drained her strength. She was physically weak. Even shutting the outer security door that Fred had insisted on was too much for her in the evening. Often she neglected to lock it. At other times it remained locked all day. The thought that dominated Leonora's days was: I don't want to be a burden. She could no longer carry heavy bags, Leo did her shopping. She felt cornered, she found the security door offensive.

Leo told Fred: Our Ouma-tannie is weakening. We must visit her more often than ever.

But in Leonora's thoughts it kept recurring: I don't want to become a duty. I must find another way out. One afternoon she told Leo, 'A colleague from my college days has written that she is very happy in a retirement home in Stellenbosch. We both know other people there too. She has asked me to join them.'

When Leo began to argue, she said, 'It seems like a good idea to me. Not too far for you to visit. And not unnecessarily close.' She applied for admission.

One evening she stumbled and fell, and lay where she had fallen the whole night until Leo happened to open the security door with her own key the next morning. That convinced her that she needed to hasten her move. Luckily a room soon became available. During weekends Leo and Fred helped her to sort out things. She had to choose a few pieces of furniture and some books and pictures to take with her. It was a difficult task. Leonora had been the custodian of the family's diaries, letters and photos. Album upon album.

'I'll treasure them, Tannie,' said Leo. 'Just tell me who this one is, and that …'

Leonora couldn't always remember. 'My dear, I've forgotten their names, it was all so long ago …' Young girls in long white muslin dresses wearing big sun hats, standing under poplars on the banks of a farm dam, their reflection blurred and ripply in the shallow water, the reeds flattened by those who'd ventured closest – and a little to one side, her back against a tree trunk, head up, Leonora. Or on a riverboat, rowing along, her eyes far away – as if the ripples as the oar moved the water, carried her thoughts back to the past, or to the future, who could tell? Pictures taken on a swing in a garden, late afternoon, the tree shadows growing longer.

There was one photo Leonora put aside to take with her: of her and Robbie, a young boy of 12 or 14, in front of a palm tree. Her arm rested loosely around his neck, the other hand held his upper arm, just above his elbow. The sleeve had shifted up, exposing the bony young boy's arm, almost a man's. He looked embarrassed at being photographed, strained away from her body. 'See the blonde hair, the fringe? He was, I may surely say it, my favourite.' She didn't realise how tender her smile was, or the pride with which she held him. 'After Mother's death he was just a baby, he used to leave Nellie in the mornings and come to snuggle up with me. Sometimes had a little accident against my back.' Father and Mother's photos were to go with her, and one of the sister, Victoria, who had died so young.

Leo packed the rest in boxes. The faded photos of all the beautiful young people who had been dead for so long. Together with Father's war diary, the papers that had come to Leonora from Frikkie, Agnes's letters, other letters from the young SussieBelle, and a single one from an older Belle.

Leo looked up at Leonora. 'I feel I shouldn't read it, my ma had not intended I should read it. Do you know how estranged I have become from my ma, Tannie?'

'Keep it with the other things, child.'

The removal van came to fetch the few pieces of furniture. The second-hand shop would have the rest fetched. Only one divan was left for the last night, and a few things in the kitchen, and the bench on the back stoep. Her clothes had gone in the removal van. What was left would go to charity when she'd gone.

'Tannie, I'm so sorry Fred and I can't spend tonight, the last evening with you. I must address a group this evening, and Fred is working late. I must still go and prepare, it's an appointment I made long ago.'

'My dear child, it's a good thing for me to spend the last night on my own here in my house. There are so many memories …'

'Don't forget to lock up.'

'I won't forget.'

14

There are always memories. Leonora waited until Leo's car had disappeared. Carefully she took her hat and handbag, locked the door, plucked up courage and went down the steps. Down the street. For one last time. The alyssum smelled sweet, so sweet. For one last time the white frangipani flowers strewn beneath her feet. For one last time the great lush red hibiscus flowers pushing forward from the long row of shrubs, kissing her face. Now, now, she said, and wiped the pollen from her cheeks. Now, now, I'm just going away, I'm not dying yet.

The bus driver leaned right over to give her a hand. The walking-stick was over her arm, her other hand was on the rail. She gave him her little purse, he took the money out himself. In the city centre she got off at the OK Bazaars. She didn't like the OK, but she wouldn't manage to cross the street to Woolworths. Her head began to spin slightly. Step by little step she went to the basement where the food was, took a white loaf from the shelf. That was as much as she could carry. Shuffled into the queue, and paid. She had a little time to spare before the bus came again.

The flower-sellers. She shook her head at the hands pressing bunches at her – bunches of dahlias and carnations and violets and ericas and proteas and, oh, the delicate long-stemmed roses. But she looked and she smelled. She breathed in great gulps of it. Father's roses. The red ones, which he picked for Mother – every evening a long-stemmed red rose. The bus reached the stop for Kloofnek. She moved nearer slowly. That time the driver called to a friend on the pavement. 'Help the old lady, can't you see her?' She was taken by both arms, the bag with the bread hanging on her wrist, and lifted onto the bus. She paid and moved a little way down the aisle. She had a last look, as far as she could turn her head, up and down Adderley Street. It wasn't the same without the old familiar shops.

She had told herself: If the Lord wills it, that's fine, if He doesn't, that's also all right. But just go and buy the white bread in case He does will it. And overshot her stop. It's easier on the downhill, she told the conductor, but that wasn't the whole truth. It was cheating the Lord, but not much. Just below the bus stop at the corner sat her two old vagrant friends who camped out on the mountain. She often gave them food on her back stoep. Skottel and Maggie rested in the afternoon before taking the path up the mountainside. After they'd exchanged the empty bottles they'd scrounged for a full one at the bottle store.

She'd known they'd be there; the Lord had put them there. And they still had the bag of empties with them, they hadn't gone to exchange them yet. She stood next to them.

'Come, Skottel, wake up.' She pushed at him with her foot.

'Hey, missus, don' stan' 'n kick at me.'

Skottel was an albino, and his pinkish-white face was covered in freckles. His eyelids were pink and his eyes always looked sore.

'The missus isn' kicking,' said Maggie. Her headscarf was skew from lying against Skottel, she adjusted it. Her jersey was long, but unravelling at the elbows. It was brown now, and you couldn't tell what colour it had been before. She wore long pants under her dress, and the jersey over it.

Her feet were bare and rough. Skottel rose reluctantly, the bag with the bottles clinked.

'Don' break,' said Maggie.

'I'm not breakin' neve' breakin'.'

He saw the bread in the plastic bag hanging from Leonora's wrist. They were accustomed to getting food at her house, thought Leonora, they know the way there. Who would give them something warm to eat now?

'Bit o' bread, missus?' He rubbed his tummy. 'Empty like the dam in the dry time, missus.' He was a man from the Worcester district, worked on a farm there, had learned to drink there, because 'they give me my tot every day from when I was a li'l boy.'

'Bit o' bread?' Maggie also asked. She was from the Piketberg area, also from a farm, she and Skottel had been together for years.

'I have clothes for you,' said Leonora. 'A mattress and blankets too if you want them.'

'Come Skottel, we walk with her,' said Maggie, 'to her house.'

Skottel's lips were covered in blisters; he licked them, a blister broke and a little spit and blood dribbled down his chin. He dragged the bag, then straightened up and swung it over his shoulder. He staggered, but got going. Maggie helped Leonora up the slight incline.

Leonora unlocked the security gate. Skottel sat down on the step. 'I need Thee, how I need Thee, every hour I need Thee,' he began to sing. Maggie kicked his shoulder. 'Again they kick me, every hour I need Thee.'

Leonora put her handbag down on the floor of the empty lounge.

'Come to the back stoep,' she told Maggie, 'and tell Skottel to get up.'

She sat on the bench, with Maggie next to her and Skottel next to his bag of bottles on the cement floor.

'I'm going away,' said Leonora. It was only now that she realised fully what the emptiness of the house and leaving it meant. Her voice faded, she spoke more slowly. 'I'm going away, I won't see you again. I'm going to a place where they'll look after me. I'm old and it's better that others should take care of me. But they lock the doors of the place every night.'

'Cause why?'

'Because I'll not be allowed to go out in the night.'

Then she felt very tired. 'There's something I've been wanting to do my whole life. This is my last chance now, that's why I came to you.'

'Does missus wan' to come to the mountain wi' us?'

'Skottel, you stupid! She die there an' the police say it's us did it.'

Leonora laid her hand on Maggie's lap, found a thread of her ragged jersey and began winding it around her finger, round and round, Maggie pushed her hand away. 'Missus is unwinding my jersey.'

Skottel had settled down on the cement, the bottles clanked loudly in the bag. 'Empties, all empties ... Mus' I go all empty handed, mus' I then my Lord so meet? Not one precious soul to bring, nothin' to lie by His feet.'

'I can't go to the mountain with you,' said Leonora. 'I want to give you all the money in my handbag, look here, I'll take it out and give it to you now. And all the clothes in the suitcase, and everything in the kitchen, and the bed and mattress and blankets you can have if ...'

'If what, missus?'

'If you'll stay here with me tonight, here on the back stoep.' It suddenly became difficult for her to speak; her mouth, her lips were tired. 'Before I die, I want to see what the stars look like, the whole night long, and how the light starts to come, what it is that causes the light to come.'

'Hide me, oh my blessed Saviour, hide me ...' Skottel sang.

Maggie shut him up. She pulled her scarf low over her forehead, her black hair crinkled out from under the cloth. She wiped her nose with the hem of the jersey, her skin was dark, with little speckles, like scars from chickenpox. She sniffed. 'Don' get sad missus, it jus' come like that, you don' even know, then the stars' little lights is out an' then it's day.'

There was a loud rumble from Skottel's belly. Maggie's eyes were on the bread in the plastic bag lying on the bench next to Leonora. 'When his insides cry like that, he gotto get scoff, missus. Can I go break the bread?'

Leonora's head had dropped to her chest, she started up, suddenly lucid.

'Of course, Maggie, I bought it for you, and there's coffee and milk and sugar, I also hid away some jam for you.'

'A bit o' fish maybe?'

'No, but there's cold meat. Under the cloth in the kitchen. And there are mugs.'

She remained sitting on the bench on the back stoep, the bench that would go to the neighbour the next day. She heard Maggie switch on the kettle.

Dusk fell. Maggie brought her, just in her hand, a piece of bread with a slice of meat on it, but her throat was too dry, she couldn't swallow. When the mug of coffee was placed in her hand – with far too much sugar for her taste, but she swallowed it for the wetness – she managed to eat the bread. The other two ate inside.

'Doesn't missus want to come lie inside?' Maggie came to ask. She licked her fingers. She had no front teeth, she used her gums and lips to deal with the bread; she rolled the strips of meat into little snakes and sucked them up. 'I already work in a kitchen, I know 'bout it,' said Maggie. 'More tea, missus?' she asked primly, and to Skottel, coming in from the garden: 'You close up your pants, we not in the veld now.'

Gradually it grew darker. She heard Maggie open the suitcase that would go to charity, open it and strew things about, telling Skottel, 'Nothin' for you.'

'This li'l black coat thing is alri',' Skottel said and she heard Maggie, 'No, no, voetsak you pig.'

Leonora smiled. It was probably the little velvet evening jacket. She was afraid that they'd stay inside; she wanted them outside with her, so they could at last render the loneliness of the night sky comprehensible to her.

She called as loudly as she could, but that wasn't very loud, to Maggie.

'Bring the mattress out. Come and throw it in front of the bench. You sit here with me Maggie, then our feet are on the mattress, not on the cold cement. And Skottel …'

'Skottel won't sit nex' to the missus …'

'He can sit here in front of us. He can lean against us, it's surely better on the mattress than outside on the mountain.'

'We can't see the stars yet,' said Maggie. 'We mus' wait, it's still too light for the city lights.' She dragged the mattress out. Skottel lifted it from behind. They'd already forgotten about the clothes.

'We c'n sing,' said Skottel. He was sitting flat on the mattress, his back leaning against the bench. He scraped the bread from his teeth, and began to sing:

Away in a mange', no crib fo' His bed,
The li'l Lord Jesus lay down he's sweet head;

Maggie joined in:

The stars up in the sky look down where he lie,
The li'l Lord Jesus asleep on the hay.
The cattles ...

'I like that about God,' said Maggie. 'The hay an' the cattles, He's jus' like us in the mountain. D'you know, missus, long ago I got a baby in the mountain, but he die, didn' even breathe once.'

Skottel was still singing:

I love You Lord Jesus! Look at me from the sky,
And stay by me until the sun is up high.

'D'you know, missus, the pa he had problems with the li'l body. No, wasn't Skottel. Was a yellow Hotnot. He got a fright from the little body, so he run away.'

Skottel sat up straight. 'He didn' do right, jus' dump in the rubbish in a plastic bag. Me, I bury the li'l baby if it was my baby.'

'Then I never got a baby again,' Maggie said and she began to cry, but while she cried her head dropped forward and her eyes closed. Skottel in front of her started to snore softly. Leonora must have nodded off herself, she must have been dreaming when she suddenly started awake to hear Maggie, who was sitting upright, singing loudly and high: *Oh-ho, Star of wonder, star of night ...*

'Oh Lordy, Lordy it look like we bring the stars down on us when we sing.'

'Shut up now, Skottel, shut up, you mus' sing, that the whole lot come down on us so the missus can see.'

Leonora was enraptured. It must have been late, very late, the city lights had disappeared, the side of Signal Hill was a dark shoulder, but the firmament had descended upon them in a great swathe of stars as bright as jewels. Like diamonds catching the light, or was it her eyes full of tears causing the stars to grow bigger and bigger and to send out rays of light?

'There's no moon,' said Skottel. 'Always so bright if there no moon. We mus' sing for God too, not jus' for the Baby, isn't Christmas, what's wrong with us?'

He leaned back, his head sideways against Leonora's knee. Leonora felt a great joy come over her, blessedness.

Skottel took the lead with his deep voice, Maggie joined in. Leonora tried, but she was very short of breath.

Praise the Lord, praise the Lord ... the King of Heaven

Before the hymn was done Maggie was snoring. She drooped against Leonora, her head lay on Leonora's shoulder. Leonora felt her own head grow heavy too ...

Then someone tugged at her. It was Skottel's freckled, dirty pink hand tugging the front of her jersey. She looked up, startled. They were bathed in the light of early dawn. At first she didn't know where she was, then she realised.

'Missus want to see how it get light. Now see.'

His breath stank. Had there been a bottle of liquor in the bag along with the empties? Had they found a bottle in the kitchen cupboard? He pushed up her head, which had drooped in her sleep. She opened her eyes reluctantly, she was tired, half-asleep.

'Watch it, watch it now, missus. The', the', there 'tis.'

He shook Maggie too.

Let my old eyes just see what he wants me to see, what I've always wanted to see, before my chance is gone forever, before I enter the darkness myself.

Where is the start of the first bit of light that banishes night? She couldn't die before she knew that.

What he was pointing to was another star, not as bright, not as big as those in the dark of night, but she saw it, she saw it. In the east, far away on the green horizon beyond the bay where the low hills began, in the delicate oyster shade just before daybreak, low as if greeting the grey hills, hung the morning star. Evening star that had become morning star. Oh, dear Lord, was that the answer? The evening star that became the morning star. From afar she heard Father's words – she at his knee, he already near the end: The renewal that comes from the self. The rebirth. The resurrection. Fill your cup, for the water is around you.

The oyster-grey horizon began to glow pale rose. A thin gold line etched the hills.

'Why the missus crying now?' Maggie asked. 'Didn' we watch nice with you?'

She didn't speak. She nodded, and suddenly her head was just too heavy, it fell against Maggie, and she slept. Maggie slept too, and Skottel, exhausted by his vigil, curled up against the bag with empty bottles.

And that was how Leo and Fred found them when they anxiously pushed open the unlocked security gate and hurried in, saw the open suitcase.

'Tannie!' was all Leo said before she felt her throat contract. 'Tannie could …' but she didn't say the words: could have been murdered. Like Ouma Agnes. It suddenly seemed inappropriate. For the innocence in Leonora's eyes was like the innocence in Maggie's eyes, and the innocence in the pink-lidded eyes of the albino, Skottel.

'Weren't you afraid, outside like this, with everything open?' was all she said.

'We jus' open our eyes 'n we say: look after us, God. An' look after the ol' missus too. Then we sleep 'gain.'

'Where's my camera now?' said Fred. 'Hell, this would be a picture! The Nightwatch.'

Leo didn't say anything. She gathered the last of her great-aunt's belongings from the bathroom and bedroom and packed them in the overnight bag.

'We must lock up,' she said. She looked at the two ragged old vagrants who stood waiting uncertainly. 'You can have the bed and the mattress and the blankets and the clothes in that suitcase.'

But they didn't take much, just a few clothes.

'Take the blankets,' Leo encouraged. 'And the mattress.'

'Better we leave the mattress. On the mountain they murder us for the mattress.'

They each took a blanket, walked down the steps carefully and out the gate. Skottel bumped against Maggie, and she swore and gave him a hefty shove that sent the bag of empties flying.

'One would say they were drunk,' said Fred.

Leonora was still sitting on the bench on the back stoep. They thought she was sleeping, but she wasn't asleep. She rose heavily when they took her by the arms to help her up.

'She's stiff from sitting outside the whole night. God knows, if she wanted to do it, why didn't she take a blanket?'

'Why are we hanging around here?' said Fred. 'We might as well get going.'

He half carried, half supported Leonora down the steps of the front stoep. Locked the front door behind her for the last time. She wasn't aware of it, didn't look back either. It seemed as if she'd already set out on her journey.

Leo got in the back with her. 'Do you think we should still go around to pick up Cedric?'

'Why not?'

When Cedric got in, in Roeland Street, at the garage where his brother worked, Fred moved over to the passenger seat.

'You drive, I want to keep an eye on the back.'

He leaned back, tried to take Leonora's hand and hold it. 'Well, Tante, now we're on our way.' He could tell that Leo was upset, perhaps by what he had said about taking a picture. It looked as if there were tears in her eyes.

Leonora sat in silence for a long time. She looked at the low hills in the distance beyond the bay. They drove across De Waal Drive. She seemed gradually to become aware of the black man driving. 'Many, many years ago,' she began speaking, 'when dear little Robbie wandered away, he got lost, he wandered to the location, and a black man brought him back to us. Then Robbie said – fearful of a spanking, I suppose – "Aunt Issy, the black uncle was so kind to me."' She sighed deeply. 'Dear little Robbie. Little angel, I called him, my little angel.' Then she sat back in the corner again, Leo stroked her hands. 'You know, he never liked his name. He was named after Robert Moffat, the missionary, Aunt Issy wanted it so much. But how he hated it.'

Her head nodded. Leo let her rest against her shoulder.

When they reached the centre of town, Cedric said, 'Drop me at the second corner, and thanks for the lift, hey.' He drew up next to the kerbstone, started to get out, Fred had to move across.

'Goodbye, black uncle,' came the soft voice of Great-Aunt Leonora from the back seat. 'And thank you for driving us so well.'

'Wow!' Cedric said to Fred as he shut the door closed. 'How old is the granny?'

'Nearly 90.'

'Awesome!'

The retirement home wasn't far out of Stellenbosch. There was a beautiful garden where the residents could walk or sit in the sun. Fred pulled up in the parking area. But when he opened the door Leonora seemed unable to move.

'You're very stiff, aren't you, Tannie?' said Leo.

Leonora nodded.

When Fred brought the wheelchair to the car, the sister came with him.

'You didn't mention that she would be in a wheelchair.'

'It's only temporary, Sister. I think she's caught a chill.'

Leo and Fred supported her on either side, and helped her to sit. The sister began to push. Leo brought her odd pieces of luggage. To the first floor in the lift. The room in which she and Fred had come to hang the photos looked bare and unfriendly.

'The portraits?' Leo asked the sister.

'We had the room painted. The furniture has been put back, it's only the portraits missing … But now it's nice and clean.'

'May we hang them now?'

'Leave it for now, they're put away in the storeroom. We'll see to it tomorrow morning.'

'It looks so bare.'

But Leonora's head had already dropped forward again. They pushed the chair next to the bed, lifted her up and lay her on the bed, put a blanket over her legs.

The sister wasn't unsympathetic. She drew the curtain a little so that the sun wouldn't fall on the bed. 'We'll take good care of her. Think about it this way: she's no longer really with us. She's started to let go of the world already.'

'She's not so very old,' Leo argued. 'She didn't withdraw from us.'

The sister had arranged everything as she wished in the room.

'You can leave. Give her a few days, or a week or so, time to get used to us before you visit.'

They drove back to the city in silence.

'Did you find it difficult, Leo?'

'Very difficult, Fred. I've been closer to her than to my own mother. Not even my aunt, but my great-aunt. It's an entire era passing.'

'Past already, my love. Irrevocably past.'

'And in its place?'

He wanted to cheer her up. 'Well, things are probably no worse now. Chin up: it's what we wanted, remember? Why don't we go out for dinner tonight?'

'To celebrate?'

'Now you're being awkward, Leo. Let's go out in her honour. As a thanksgiving. If it must be a celebration, then a celebration of a new era. We're young, we'll have a better life.'

15

But the next few years didn't bring a better life, still less did they bring peace.

Leo applied for a post at a coloured school, but wasn't appointed. The unrest at schools continued. White staff members were not tolerated, white inspectors were chased away.

Leo wanted to make a contribution somewhere. She felt useless and dissatisfied at her job in the white English-medium private school. At last she found employment at an institution organising and initiating literacy programmes. She undertook a short training course and felt, with her teacher training as a basis, she'd be able to make a contribution. But the undertaking was privately financed, and the people who worked there were, to her mind, unmotivated; there were endless delays, inefficiency, unnecessary waste of time and money. One afternoon, after a frustrating effort to get something going, she caught the bus home, boarding at the stop near the Standard Bank in Adderley Street. She was early, the bus was empty, and she sat waiting while it filled up slowly. The passengers who came down the aisle included some flower sellers with armfuls of flowers wrapped in brown paper. It was getting late, they wanted to make a few last sales. She bought a bunch, pressed her face in the sweet elusive scent of the season's first sweet peas; the pale lilac and pastel pink was delightful. She became aware of a disturbance, she heard a restlessness amongst the passengers, the flower seller pushed her way out just as the driver hastily shut the double folding doors. The ignition was switched on, but the bus didn't move. A horde of protesting young black people came toyi-toying down Adderley Street towards them. They brandished sticks above their heads and raised their knees high in time with the rhythm of what they were singing. They swarmed around the bus. The sticks beat down on the vehicle and flat hands smacked against the metal panelling.

They shoved against the bus to the beat of the singing and jeering. It swayed from side to side, the driver sounded the hooter hard. Then the window behind the wire mesh was splintered by two, three hard blows from the ends of sticks. The driver stopped hooting and ducked. The passengers – white, Indian, coloured, black – clung to the seats in front of them as they were slung from side to side in the dangerously unstable bus.

'My God, what are they doing to us?' shouted a woman. Leo, who was clinging to her bunch of sweet peas, recognised her from her Black

Sash days. The tarred road came closer as they overbalanced, then the multitude of hands pushed the bus upright again and they saw shops and the sky. A child began to scream and the mother couldn't hush her.

'God help us, there comes the can of petrol,' screamed a coloured woman.

Then sirens howled and the yellow police vans rammed a passage through the black marchers. As fast as it had built up, the fervour left the young dancers. They slapped the bus a few last times and began wandering off singing down Darling Street.

'I was afraid, Fred,' said Leo, when he came home long after midnight. 'I was glad to hear the police sirens – can you believe it? I wouldn't have minded if they'd baton-charged the mob. What's happening to us all?' Her voice was bitter.

He sipped his coffee. 'Don't let it get you down. Remember the person you were – challenging the police, seeking confrontation every weekend at the funeral processions?'

'That was different. It was no big deal to challenge young white policemen. We knew they wouldn't do anything to us, just as you can safely dare to punch your father when you're a child. But this afternoon the black rage was directed at me and I was frightened.'

Fred was tired, he wanted to close the subject. 'Don't imagine the black and coloured women weren't just as frightened.'

But she persisted. 'We know nothing. We thought we were suffering together, but we were just fooling ourselves. Not only me, but you too. You said yourself you didn't have as tough a time in jail as the blacks. Six white women on beds against 80 of them on cement. Was the hypocrisy the reason why nothing seems to be solved? I told Oom Barry, so piously and omnisciently, about "protesting on behalf of other people" and about the "purest love". Did it take this afternoon to rub my nose in my own insincerity?'

The old anxiety and tension were back in her voice.

'You're working yourself up unnecessarily again,' said Fred. 'It's a period of transition, no one really knows what's happening in the country. Everyone's nerves are on edge.'

'But we must know what's going on. How do you think I feel about being glad to hear the police sirens! If we don't know, who does know what's going on?'

And a few weeks later, when he returned from a weekend photography assignment, she told him when he saw the TV was switched off, 'I can't watch the news anymore. The children don't go to school and the hospitals close down and the township murders go on. And they're singing *One settler, one bullet.*'

She kissed him half-heartedly. When she put supper on the table, he pushed his plate aside. 'Don't you think I've also had enough of photographing black corpses, children who have been burned to death by their own people with tyres around their necks? Do you think I don't know about the hatred the blacks have turned on our newsmen now? Stoning press cars?'

'And?'

'I just carry on.' He laughed. 'Photograph birds.'

She couldn't get rid of the thought that her protest as a white person hadn't been genuine, that she'd known only too well that nothing dreadful would happen to her. With her being a woman and white a double insurance policy. A female black skin was no protection, rather a challenge to the police, and if the police reacted to it, what remained? Torn flesh and blood, flesh and blood the same colour as hers, dead eyes staring heavenward …

'Jesus, Leo, it's their own people who are killing them too, not only the police.'

'The circle that was started has no end. And our part in the struggle was only a pseudo-struggle.'

'Get that thought out of your head, Leo. There's nothing pseudo about fighting against someone else's suffering. You can blame me, because I was just the hell in about my cameras, but you can't blame yourself. There's nothing pseudo about fighting for a principle. Think of Wilberforce. He fought against slavery, although there was no danger that he would be made a slave himself. No difference. Think of Neil Aggett, his white skin was no armour. Yes, think of Neil Aggett. That'll sort you out.'

He began to lose patience with her. 'Then just call it humanitarianism. Like with your street children.'

'My street children? Where are they now? Dead from exposure, hacked to death, starved to death, out cold from sniffing glue and thinners.'

'The world's a mess, isn't it?'

She hated the condescending tone of his voice. She pulled away from his arms.

'I was on the bus today, not you. I saw the hatred and it was directed at me.'

'It's a time of transition, Leo. No one knows what or where to. I also experience that. Where do you think I've come from now?

Photographing birds? No ways. The old stuff. Squatters' shacks burning, a child with a bullet through the head, women shrieking. And does my boss send me because of his humanitarian motives? Come again. He sends me because the pictures sell so well overseas.'

'Was it all in vain then? Has nothing changed?'

'Let's just hope these are just birth pangs,' he said. 'It's a tough birth. But what pisses me off even more, is that when the lid of the pressure cooker is lifted, corruption boils out. Our uncles in the Transvaal, I should imagine, were also knee-deep in it, and now they're crapping their pants with fear. The corruption of our so-called own people: I just can't take that.'

16

Leonora was over 90, and she was gradually declining. Her memory was failing fast. She recognised Leo, but sometimes asked of Fred, 'Who is that strange man sitting in my chair?'

It brought tears to the eyes. When she died quietly in her sleep one evening, neither Leo nor Fred could regret it. It was a quiet funeral. Belle wasn't well enough to travel, Hendrik suffered from dangerously high blood pressure, and Holtzhausen had to take care of both of them.

'One of the brothers could at least have come,' Leo complained to Fred. 'She was so fond of them. The big, expensive wreaths are not enough. I know Hendrik couldn't come, but Philip and Robert?'

In spite of his age, Robert was working feverishly with right-wing political groups. He looked more and more rat-like. He gnawed and gnawed, and wouldn't let go of the Verwoerdian concept: Afrikaners separate. Our own national entity, he pleaded at meetings.

It was impossible for the older generation to accept that power was to be relinquished without a fight after the election. The very idea was incredible. 'We fought for our country against the English, we can take on the black man too …' Were the two Republics to finally come to nought now?

And so it was that only she and Fred and his parents, Miemie and Stoffel, were in the little chapel to watch the coffin slowly glide behind the velvet curtain while the canned version of *Nearer my God to Thee* dragged on. It seemed discordant to Leo. She told her great-aunt: This isn't how it should have been, forgive me, Oumatan.

Young Josias had completed his Law degree and was articled to his uncle Philip's firm in Pretoria. Leo wondered whether he still thought of Emma. They seldom heard from Barry.

Leo took cardboard boxes full of photo albums, loose snaps, letters and diaries to her house in New Church Street. She sat looking at them for hours, until Fred said, 'That's enough now. You meant a lot to her, and she to you. Mourning her like this is unworthy of you and her.'

He suggested she visit her parents. She said: 'I'll wait until you can come too.' They went on a week-long visit. Hendrik's driver came to meet them at the airport. The old people – her parents also seemed old to her – were tense and distressed. They avoided national affairs and politics. The conversation didn't flow. Everyone was relieved when the driver dropped them at Jan Smuts airport again.

Only once had Leo felt that she was breaking through to her mother. It was in the bedroom the last evening. Belle was brushing her hair in front of the mirror, long grey hair that was thinning. Leo had taken the brush and turned it round and round. 'Ma, oh, Ma,' she said, and then she began to cry. For her mother, for Leonora, for herself. And to her surprise also for her grandmother Agnes, in whose house she lived. Belle stroked her forehead.

'Don't cry. Just don't cry. Nothing is as dark as it seems to you. The sun will shine again.'

She had looked at her mother in surprise. Those words from her mouth? Then she took in the faded eyes, the pale skin, the slight tremor of the hand. And she marvelled at the peaceful expression on her face. But at what cost, she thought, at what cost?

17

Fred's studies of west coast birds were so well received overseas that he was commissioned by a nature conservation magazine to cover the birds of the wetlands along the south-west coast near George and further north along the coast, to eventually make a complete photographic ecological record, as far north as Kosi Bay. The commission was undertaken in his private capacity, but, as agent, his employer would receive a small percentage of the fee.

Although he knew it would offend Leo, he said, 'No more dead children and weeping mothers, thank God.'

She took a few days' leave and went with him, at his invitation, to Velddrif, where he needed to take a few more shots along the Berg River.

'Our holiday at Kommetjie was a tense affair,' he said, 'this time you relax, hear. And just enjoy it.'

They stayed in a holiday cottage on the banks of the river, a few kilometres upstream from the village of Velddrif. Fred hired a rowing boat, and it was moored to a pole on the wooden jetty out on the river in front of their cottage. She had bought food and beer at Velddrif. She longed for the feeling between them to be restored, she resolved: no arguing, none of the pangs of conscience that so irritated him.

The first evening they relaxed. 'I feel like an ad for the good life, for beer, or something like that,' she joked as she sat on the edge of the jetty, beer in hand, feet dangling over the water. The sun had set, the sky around them was grey-blue, and a little line of golden light still lingered to the west. A light mist had started to rise from the sea. The birds had passed in great flocks to the island where they nested. She got up and walked to the braaivleis where he had made a fire, linked her arm in his. He kissed her lightly, then returned his attention to the meat.

'Have I ever told you? They're doing a book of Oupa Frikkie's work. Collector's works, art works. There's talk of using a picture of Leonora on the cover. Do you know the photo?'

She shook her head.

'I curse myself that I was too headstrong to learn from him as a young photographer. Wanted to do it my own way. Now I wish he was still here. But I'm not going to be left behind.' He tapped his finger against his head, the braaivleis fork swung on his little finger. 'This guy isn't going to be a runner-up.'

'Never, ever,' laughed Leo, and wished away the slight sharpness in her voice.

The next morning it was still misty when they got up. Fred was in a hurry, fussing over his equipment; she packed a picnic. He waited for her on the jetty, her footsteps in the gumboots sounded dull in the mistiness. He handed her into the boat. It rocked while she settled down; she felt excitement rise in her, tried to steady the boat so that Fred could hand her his cameras and tripod and spare equipment in watertight containers. He loosened the rope and pushed the boat into the water. Then he lifted the oars and began rowing the boat against the stream with slow, steady strokes.

She couldn't see anything around her. At times the mist engulfed him too; she only heard the dull slap of the oars, saw the rippling movement of the water next to her. After a while he rested the oars in the rowlocks and leant back. She helped him, they prepared the cameras. Two hung from his neck. He lifted the oars again and put them down in the water one by one, pushed the water back so that the boat rocked slightly and then moved forward.

Gradually the mist cleared. A fine line of light gleamed on the eastern horizon, a twin gleam in the west; the mist thinned, revealing a wide expanse of silvery blue water on which they floated. And then suddenly the silence was rent by the flapping of wings, the swoosh-swoosh of the flock of flamingos rising in a big noisy troop from the island near them, spreading out into a enormous, graceful, forward-pointing V.

Fred stood up in the boat. She hung onto the oars while he took countless photos. The camera clicked and the motor-drive whined. To her it seemed the clicking and the swoosh of the wings blended together, and she was flying with the birds, moving up through the cold air herself, going she knew not where. When it was over, he took the oars again, rowed noisily as if his tension had been defused, dragged the boat half out of the water onto one of the islands in the river, pounded a wooden spike into the wet ground and fastened the rope to it. He threw a tarpaulin open on the marshy ground. She carried the picnic basket, sat on the tarpaulin, struggled out of her gumboots.

'Sit down,' she said, and helped him pull off his boots. His feet were cold, she rubbed them warm, first one then the other.

He checked his cameras, reloaded them. 'Amazing! Just give me a morning in the lab, then you'll see wonders Oupa Frikkie could never have dreamed of.'

She forgot her resolve not to say anything that could offend. 'Why do you have to compare yourself with your oupa, Fred? It's different, the work you do, a different time, different equipment.'

'I'm not comparing, I just said it. You take me up on everything I say. Don't I do or say anything that pleases you any more?'

She didn't answer. They had coffee, ate sandwiches, walked about to stay warm, pushed the boat back into the water again and rowed on.

Wide peaceful landscapes stretched out on either side of the river. Here and there a wooden jetty, and a little cleared path to a wooden holiday cottage. Once they saw cattle and a farmhouse in the distance. It grew warmer. Fred pushed the boat against a protected bank with a small sandy beach, fastened it to a tree stump. She lay against him and tried to relax, tried to control the resistance increasing in her. He dozed. She closed her eyes, but thought: This silence and photographing the beauties of nature and birds is a cop out. It's closing one's eyes to reality.

The day drew on. There was suddenly a stir in the air again. Fred was awake.

'Come,' he said. 'We must hurry.' He loaded a camera, let her hold another, then decided: 'Keep it for now, see what you get, remember it's the close-up wide-angle lens.'

They began rowing slowly downstream. He's trying to involve me, she thought. The flight of the returning flamingos was a rushing storm over their heads. There was scarcely time to photograph the birds. The flight ebbed, the birds settled on the island, the beaks snapped and pushed against the twilight sky. Fred took countless photos, the motor-drive whirred.

'Get something?' he said as he sat back at last.

'Don't know, just clicked and clicked.'

'We'll have a look in the lab. Come, you also take an oar, then we'll get along faster. It'll soon be dark, and the mist will come up. One and two, and one and two, get the rhythm …'

The water was silver again as it had been that morning, the gold had moved to the western horizon, but the western horizon got dark first, then at last the after-glow faded from the eastern horizon.

'I'll just stay here,' said Leo the next morning early when Fred was preparing to go out on the boat again. 'I can't really take photos, I'm actually more of a burden. I'm tired today.'

She read, went for a walk, prepared a hot meal, and welcomed him home lovingly, but she knew she'd come to a watershed.

Before Fred left on a 14-day shift to the south-west coast for the next series of photos, he had a letter from an American ecological magazine: an offer of permanent employment and a work permit. No time limit. Implying that American citizenship might be arranged. Spelling out just one word: emigration. He moved the letter across the table for her to read. His face was expressionless. He watched her closely.

Leo's hands began to shake as she finished reading. Her body trembled. She was so cold that she crossed her arms and pressed her upper arms to her to retain body heat. She couldn't speak. She tried to smile at Fred, the smile was feeble.

'Point of no return?' she said.

He poured them each a brandy. 'Think carefully, girl. Be calm. Some people would say: If something like this is handed to you on a platter, it's impossible to refuse.'

'I can't, Fred.'

'I didn't say I could.'

'The possibilities for your work are unlimited …' Again she smiled wryly. 'You won't have to photograph hungry children or bloody little corpses any more.' Her smile was increasingly wry. 'You'll no longer have to be locally humanistic, but globally – can one say humanistic? – if you take photos of penguins or seals or pelicans? Or will a new word be created: "faunistic"? Globally faunistic.'

'Hold on a minute, Leo.'

She started to cry. 'I can't see a way ahead. There's no prospect of peace. Each time the negotiations break down. I feel like vomiting when I see nurses toyi-toying while babies die. There it is in the open. Racist? I no longer know what I think or what I want to think. It seems to me increasingly that all my concern with the traffic-light kids, even my going to jail, was nothing more than personal contrition, more of an ego thing than anything else. What's changed? Nothing. Fred, I don't know what to think; I think and think around in circles and get nowhere. Even before this letter, when my friends emigrated one after the other, I had already wondered, but when you never mentioned anything …'

'There's no rush. You needn't think now, let the thought percolate.'

'Percolate until it seems acceptable … how honest is the decision then? Have you decided already, Fred? Don't hide it from me. Have you decided?'

'I'm hiding nothing from you.'

But he was. After he'd gone, when she took up the letter lying on his table, and turned it over she saw the postscript, which read:

> *It might interest you. We know the quality of your action pictures. Our sister magazine runs regular articles on trouble spots round the globe. It might be 'birds' in Yugoslavia for all you know! Full range for your many talents.*

18

Leo was permanently weary.

The black adults for whom the literacy programme had been planned didn't turn up for classes. No one could blame them, using public transport was dangerous.

Negotiations between the parties had been going on interminably. An election was planned. Would some parties boycott the election?

Would it ever take place? The tension was tangible. Would illiterates be able to cope with the long list of participating parties?

Although Fred was reluctant to leave her on her own with the election so soon, she couldn't face packing up and going along to the Knysna and Plettenberg Bay coast and wetlands. But he couldn't postpone it, there was a time limit to the work. They had discussed 'post-prison depression' so often. Everyone had it, accepted it. But hers was going on too long – a year or four or five? Killing fields? Rolling mass action? Political assassinations. The killing continued. She was appalled that one could become accustomed to death. Twelve, fifteen, twenty people over a weekend. What did it matter?

At last: election day. She queued for hours in the drizzle to make her little crosses on the two ballot papers handed to her. The historic day everyone had waited for. And she just felt tired. Yet standing in the queue with the coloured messengers and gardeners and chars brought a certain sense of freedom and peace. But in their neighbourhood it was no novelty. We have taken buses together for a long time already, we crowd together in the little Ricci-taxis, shop together, we're friends, she thought.

On TV she saw the black people in cities and in rural areas and in the old homelands queueing up. It touched her; the hours of patient waiting, the obvious desire that all should proceed peacefully.

'It's because we prayed, madam,' a coloured woman in the queue had said to her.

'Not madam, Mrs.'

'Yes, madam.'

The country-wide mass meetings, across religious, colour and group borders, to pray for peace were something quite unique. Had it ever happened in another country? she wondered. Had the Catholic and Protestant Irish ever prayed for peace together? Or the Israelis and Palestinians, or the Muslims and Christians in Bosnia? In the Eastern Cape, she'd heard, there'd been a chain of prayer, for 24 hours round the clock for two weeks before the election, with people relieving each other every quarter of an hour, day and night ... Something like that must surely diffuse the hatred? She was filled with pride: *My country, my unique country ...*

She longed for Fred. It was a bad time to be alone, but she didn't contact friends. She was actually pleased that he was away, so that his old office couldn't call him in if violence should erupt. Then she thought of the message on the back of the letter: Did she misinterpret it? Did his camera still hunger for violence? How long would birds satisfy him?

The course of the election and the result were miracles. He returned, but had to leave again after a week, this time headed for the Natal coast.

She sat alone in front of the TV on 10 May to watch the inauguration of President Mandela. Once more she avoided her friends. She hadn't told anyone about Fred's offer from overseas. She doubted that his parents knew.

The inauguration seemed to be taking place far from her, in an European country, in Monaco, or South America, with the dignitaries, the Heads of State, the nobility moving past on the screen in a never-ending procession. Is it my old Union Building that has become so grand? The new president was dignified, charismatic, and commanded universal respect. The procedings reflected a new opening up of art and music, dance and drama. She felt a spark of pride. Had she had a share somewhere in this?

Yet there was a strange tension in her. She couldn't get rid of the tiredness and depression. Could this national euphoria continue? she wondered. And afterwards?

What decision should she and Fred take?

Away from this country and these people she would fade like a plant that is pulled from the ground. But wouldn't her spirit fade if she were to stay, if her thoughts could never escape the circle of violence?

She decided to consult her doctor. Perhaps he could prescribe a tonic or a shot of something so she'd be a bit livelier when Fred came home. And would be able to face the future with more courage.

'I feel tired and run-down, doctor.'

He was an old friend of Fred's, and before he examined her he asked, 'Where's my old buddy now? The world is too small for him. Has he got itchy feet again? Quite a special person!'

'He's taking nature photos along the Natal coast.'

He led her to the examination room. 'The times have taken their toll of you, eh? I don't like those rings under your eyes.'

When he told her she was pregnant, she realised: I knew it, deep inside. That was the reason for my depression, the tremor of fear, because another life is threatened. My child. A new thought. She tried it out.

'I'm giving you a letter to a colleague who'll take care of you. Everything's fine, Leo, you can relax. Nothing wrong, I predict a successful pregnancy. You're three months on. Had you not noticed anything yourself?'

They were back in his consulting room. He wrote a referral.

'I've always been a bit irregular, but I thought it was post-Struggle depression,' she smiled feebly.

'Vomiting?'

'Never.'

'Appetite?'

'Not much.'

'Nauseous?'

'Actually, yes.'

'Then what's the problem?'

His sympathetic words opened the floodgates. He was after all a friend of Fred's. 'Fred's had an offer of work overseas. My thoughts go this way and that. I want to stay here and work somewhere, but who wants my services? The coloured school didn't want me, they began to distrust me overnight. I don't know where to turn. I know he wants to go, but I can't get around to telling …'

'Take it easy now, Leo. You'll have to discuss it. The baby will also make a difference.'

She hadn't thought of that. It made her uneasy. She wasn't going to keep him here for the sake of the baby.

'I'll tell him myself, please don't say anything to him.'

'Right. But take your vitamins, get plenty of rest, drink milk. Everything will be fine, you'll see.'

She walked to the lift slowly, went in when the doors slid open. She looked at the staring, self-absorbed faces around her, she felt like telling them: Look at me, I'm pregnant. She wanted to shout it out. When the doors slid open so quietly again, she walked out through the entrance, into the street, into the sun. There had to be people she could tell. It would be two days before Fred returned, she couldn't reach him by phone.

She crossed the street, ridiculously carefully, so different from going to the doctor. Down the pavement past the entrance to the Tudor Hotel, to the little grey Methodist church. The iron gate was open, but the doors were closed. She'd have liked to go in. When last had she been in a church? But she wanted to tell about the baby, to the Lord who said *suffer little children and forbid them not to come unto Me, for of such is the kingdom of Heaven …*

Across the street were the people she was looking for – the street market on Greenmarket Square. She wandered through the stalls, touched a piece of copper work here, pushed back a row of dresses there so that the stand clanged. She saw tiny T-shirts, almost bought one, resisted. The life and people and colours on the square were a support, a prop, a foundation. She wasn't alone, there were women here who'd also been pregnant. The woman with the long Indian skirt, the big copper clip in her hair, already with streaks of grey, hair too long for a woman of her age, had also heard she was pregnant one day. And the granny sitting on the box behind the stall with T-shirts: life had taken its journey through her too. She felt like stretching out her arms and telling everyone: life is going forth through me too. To the young man with the earring in one ear and the unbuttoned shirt and the cross in the hair on his chest; to the old man with the white apron over his long corduroy pants; to the young women from Zambia and Zimbabwe, standing behind the long tables covered with semi-precious stones, mounted in brooches, earrings and necklaces, moving an article with graceful, long dark fingers, moving something so that the sun drew out the imprisoned light. I'm pregnant and I love you. All of you.

The day had been cloudy, but suddenly the sun was shining. Still a slight wetness on the paving, but the colours of the stalls were suddenly bright. She looked up. Dear God, the sky was so radiantly blue; the little white clouds like bursting cotton bolls, picked from pods in Africa; the sun beaming. She saw part of the incline of Devil's Peak – a dark green smudge between the buildings in Burg Street – and the soft green swell of Signal Hill behind the narrow gorge of shadow of Shortmarket Street. The voices around her sounded like the gentle droning of insects; a lorry drew up, a motorbike took off. My people, she thought. And then suddenly the tension again, causing her stomach muscles to contract. The doctor's words: the whole world is too small for Fred. And Barry's words: it's spiritual suicide to stay. Now she had to choose for herself. It hit her hard. Choose also for her child. No, she shook her head, no. Barry had been wrong and Fred was wrong.

And then suddenly from somewhere near her came the clear, transfixing sound of a saxophone.

She couldn't believe her ears.

The opening chords of the old, beloved, endangered anthem. Two guitars with it. It sang through her mind: *The call of South Africa ... Uit die blou van onse hemel ... ringing out from our blue heavens ...* and the melody went on, went on and on. She moved between the stalls, past the steps leading down to the lavatories, reached the more open part of Burg Street, and saw them: three street musicians, young black people. A cap for money on the ground in front of them.

The black youth with the saxophone played with total commitment, head thrown back, midriff heaving; the sounds rose to heaven, dropped in gentle minor key to *die diepte van ons see*, climbed again to the answering mountains.

Memories surged through her, all the guilty innocence: our mountains, our sea, our blue heaven ... in her days as a member of the Voortrekker guides, standing to attention as the flag was slowly hoisted, unfolded, and opened out in the wind.

The three played on. Another verse, the chorus again. By then she was standing right in front of them. The contraction in her stomach had vanished. Would this music have been possible a month before? Black youths from Crossroads, from Khayelitsha, from Nyanga coming to play *Die Stem* on Greenmarket Square. That was her absolution. That was her sign.

And when it ended, and the sad bass notes of *Nkosi Sikelel' iAfrika* streamed from the saxophone, it touched her just as much. Now came other memories: funerals, meetings, court cases, prison cells. She felt tears welling up in her eyes. The land of which they sang, the same country. And it hadn't all been in vain, her country for ever. And those three youths led her to the sound of the music of the symbol of her people, their people – no, our people – to the ideal, the unreal; past the borders of the past, and the reality of death and suffering, to a space beyond time.

She threw all her change into the cap. Precarious balance, said the doubt in her heart.

A voice spoke from behind her shoulder, she didn't recognise it at first, and turned: a tall lad, he'd shot up in the five, six years, Apools, the coloured street child.

'Just want to say, madam, it's me threw that match in the papers in your back shed. Made a nice fire, else you'd sit for long time in jail ...'

He spoke in passing; she wanted to stop him, grab his arm, but he was with friends, moved past, shoulders relaxed, hands in the pockets of his jeans.

Had she imagined it? Read the words into the murmur and low droning of the traders and buyers? Was it another sign?

She still felt a little light-headed. In Shortmarket Street there were a few places where she could sit down and have something to drink. She found her way there, she held on to the railing against the wall and went down to the basement of a restaurant she hadn't been to before. She saw bunches of dried leaves and flowers hanging from ropes fixed to the wall, and strange woven draperies in dark green and maroon and dark blue. A short, stout little woman in black was at the till.

She moved in at a table, moved in further along the seat, until she was nearly against the wall. When she looked up she saw the feet and legs of passersby through the high window. Like shadow figures through the thick dusty windows. The sound of their shoes on the pavement was muted, the chatter or shouting of their invisible mouths inaudible. Forward, forward, the continual walking forward of the feet.

A waiter in black trousers and waistcoat and red shirt stood questioningly at her table. 'Coffee, please,' she told him.

Caffeine ... the baby? She should have asked the doctor about that. Nonsense, she'd had some that morning. And if she hadn't known, she'd have drunk coffee the next day too. Yet it seemed to her that she was bearing in her body a sweet weight, a sweet responsibility. A responsibility to the generations past and the generations to come.

That she and her baby should, like the feet walking on the pavement above her, go forward, every step forward, in faith.

Something drew her attention. Between the dried grass and flowers and the strings of garlic against the wall she saw a slanted reflection – glass mounted on a dark wooden frame, oval, with a little gable and two wooden pegs on the right-hand side of the frame. Behind the glass were numerals and letters. It was one of the old-fashioned calendars she'd seen when she was young, where the date was adjusted by hand each day.

And as she looked at it, the little woman in the black dress climbed down from her high stool behind the till, and walked across to the calendar. She climbed on the seat, supported herself with one hand against the wall, and with her stubby fingers she began to turn the knob of the numerals. She stopped at 31. And began to turn the letter knob, quickly, and when she noticed that Leo was watching her, she smiled at her and said: 'I'm always tempted to stop turning at 31 February.'

Leo smiled back. Something stirred in her subconscious. 31 February. The possible beyond the impossible. And she thought: Whatever lies ahead, not precarious balance. Rather faith in the possible beyond the impossible.

Fred would go away, she knew that. She thought of his reply to her question the first time they met: Have you children? 'Luckily no.' She wondered about his first wife. Was she doing him an injustice by not telling him about the baby? She didn't think so, she didn't begrudge him his freedom.

And as she sat drinking her coffee in that unfamiliar cafe, she resolved: I'll raise the child here in our country.

And if it's a little girl, I'll call her Isobelle. In full: Isobelle. In full. In full.